IF I SHOULD NEVER WAKE

Jeanene Cooper

Published in the United States of America.

First edition: October 2008
Reissued: July 2009

ISBN: 0-615-34681-2
ISBN-13: 9780615346816
Library of Congress Control Number: 2008904836

Visit www.amazon.com, www.CreateSpace.com/3582977, or bookstores to order additional copies.

**To Kelly,
my best friend**

...where choice begins, Paradise ends,
Innocence ends, for what is Paradise but
the absence of any need to choose...

- Arthur Miller

*Foreword to **After the Fall** (1964)*

IN NEED OF MONEY

"WHAT CAN'T I LIVE WITHOUT?" Helena Moore pondered while studying her few meager belongings. She knew exactly how much time she had left to decide what few things to take with her, and she was determined to use each minute wisely.

Her motherly instincts drew her to a recent picture of her only child, Kiki. She picked up the framed photo and studied her six-year-old's chocolate eyes, ebony cheeks, toothless grin, and, of course, her beautiful braids of pitch-black hair. How Helena loved her daughter's hair – so satiny-soft, not wiry like her own.

Helena thought of bedtime, when her daughter would climb under her covers with those braids still tied in her hair and insist on hearing a story before untying them. So, Helena would tell her daughter about their life before coming to Windemere Island – about the warmth and sunshine they'd left behind in the Caribbean to move to the cool breezes of Northern Lake Huron. While she spoke, Helena would remove Kiki's ribbons and gently weave her fingers through her daughter's hair, untangling the braids until her hair fell softly once more. That was Helena's favorite time with Kiki, and she knew she would miss it terribly.

Helena set the portrait back on the shelf, knowing she would have to leave behind what she valued most.

Running through her mental list, she turned to her dresser, pulled open a drawer, and gazed at the few items of clothing she owned. Helena knew she could take very little with her or else someone would realize things were missing.

"If anyone suspects that you've packed, the deal is off," Helena had been told. She'd been reassured that everything she might need would be provided for her, but she still felt the need to bring some personal belongings.

Rummaging through her top dresser drawer, Helena pulled out a couple of panties and a sports bra. Other than the clothes on her back, this was all she dared to take. She placed the undergarments in the burlap book bag she'd been given to carry her things.

"Don't put too much in the bag," her contact had warned. "People might get suspicious if they see you hauling around a lot of stuff. If you want to get the money, then no one can suspect you planned to leave."

All this secrecy unnerved Helena, but she was willing to endure it for the promise of a very lucrative payday. With all that money, she would no longer have to work such long hours as a hotel maid, cleaning up after other people's messes – just as her mother had before her.

Helena's mother, Ms. Maya Moore, was a hard-working woman. After Mr. Moore passed away years ago, Ms. Maya started coming to Windemere every summer to earn a better wage than she ever could on St. Croix. Whenever possible, she would work extra hours and set aside the money in the hope that one day Helena would go to college. But then Ms. Maya had fallen down the steps of their apartment house, suffering a permanent injury to her back. There would be no workers' compensation, and their medical benefits were meager. Helena had to face reality: she would have to work to take care of her mother, and her dreams of a better life would just have to wait.

By instinct, Helena picked up Kiki's dirty socks and placed them in the corner hamper. She never minded tidying up after her own family, but resented cleaning hotel rooms for strangers. Helena wanted a better life for her daughter – never wanted her to be stuck cleaning up after others – so for Kiki's sake, she was willing to take this chance.

The hardest part for Helena was knowing she would cause both her mother and daughter great anguish when she left them wondering what had happened to her. It was all supposed to look so sudden, so unplanned, as if she had gone unwillingly. Ms. Maya would fret that Helena might be hurt or even dead, and Kiki would wonder whether she would ever see her mother again.

Helena grabbed a pen and looked for paper to write a brief note telling them that she was okay. She wondered how to reassure them without giving away too much. When she found paper, she considered writing, "Trust no one – Tell no one," but these words sounded so ominous that they might frighten them more than if she said nothing at all. Besides, it would be too difficult for Ms. Maya and Kiki to pretend that Helena had disappeared without a clue when they actually knew something more. Out of their concern, they would be torn over what to tell and what not to tell the authorities. No, it would be best to leave them in the dark.

She set down the pen and blank paper. Her mother and daughter would know the truth soon enough, and then all would be happy when the three of them were reunited back at their true home of warmth and sunshine.

Helena stepped to the bookshelf below her window and removed the novel she had recently signed out at the island library. At the start of chapter three, she found a worn photo she had been using for a bookmark. With her index finger, she caressed the picture's surface, lightly tracing the outline of Ms. Maya embracing Kiki. Helena took comfort in knowing they would have each other.

It seemed likely that no one would notice the book and picture were missing, and even if they did, no one would think much of it. Helena figured people would assume she'd been heading someplace to read, and this would further support the notion that she had not planned to disappear. Besides, she might be bored at this "mystery place" and the book might prove a pleasant distraction – plus this way she had an excuse to take the photo. With this justification, Helena tucked the picture back at chapter three and placed the book in her burlap bag.

With little time left before her escort would meet her at the dock, Helena knew she had to hurry. Besides, her daughter and mother would be returning soon from the movie she had sent them to see. She reached in the closet for a jacket to protect from the late spring chill blowing across the open Mackinac Straits. With a glance at the clock reading 8:30, she knew the time had come for her to go.

Under the glare of the building's security light, Helena took the rickety fire escape stairs off the backside of the house, hoping she would avoid feeling the need to say farewell to the other tenants. As she walked down the steps, Helena glanced for one last time at the unsightly view of the backyard dumpster. This was what she had seen and smelled out her window each day, an impression she was glad to leave behind.

As she crossed the street and walked into the darkness, Helena slowed to consider one last time the magnitude of the choice she was making. She felt so torn over leaving Kiki, but reminded herself that she was doing this for Kiki's sake. Resolute, she regained her determined stride.

Upon approaching the desolate dock, Helena noticed a caustic odor that seemed to be coming from the water. She pressed onward, noting that the smell was growing stronger as she stepped up a small ramp and onto the dock. Glancing down toward the water as it slapped the shore, Helena searched for some sign of what must have been a chemical floating on the surface. In the moonless night, she saw nothing.

Suddenly, a shoe scuffed directly behind her. She spun around to see a figure standing on the ramp.

"You scared me!" Helena released her breath.

"Time to go."

"You're not who I expected." She hugged her burlap bag tightly to her chest.

He lunged at her, his arms grabbing her about the waist. She gagged as he clamped a foul-smelling rag across her mouth. As Helena felt her body go limp, the stranger whispered in her ear.

"I never am."

Part I

AT INCEPTION

Chapter 1

ABANDONED

"HELP DESPERATELY NEEDED" struck me as a bit overzealous for a lead in a want ad, but it sure caught my attention. For a long time, I'd been feeling much the same way.

With care, I trimmed the help wanted ad from the classifieds, placing it with a couple of other clippings and my brief resume in a thin manila folder tagged *Carly Malloy — Starting Over*. I then slid the folder between the seat and gearshift of my rusted-out Chevette. The car was loaded to the ceiling with my few belongings, so I had to crawl into what little space remained for the driver's seat. I headed east on back roads lined with freshly budding maples, leaving behind the sun as it slowly dropped into Lake Michigan. Then taking highway 82 to the ramp at the 131 expressway, I turned and took new direction toward the north, heading away from what had once been home but could never be again.

After merging onto the sparsely populated expressway, I continued pushing the accelerator in hopes that my "Shove-it" could manage to rev up to sixty. But when I finally pushed the stick into fourth gear, the age-old problem of rattles and bangs returned.

"Just one more good reason to have left him," I muttered to myself, recalling how many times my ex-husband Rob had refused to let me take the car into the shop for repair.

"No, that's a waste of money when I can fix it," he'd say, then never would.

Now all I could do was pray the problem wouldn't get any worse, and that somehow this heap of rust would get me to the tip of the Michigan mitt.

Eventually I settled into the rhythm of the engine's odd noises, noting that I could count eleven "rattle-click" sounds between every tenth-of-a-mile marker. With no cruise control, I busied myself with an effort to maintain a steady speed by adjusting my foot each time I counted ten or twelve "rattle-clicks" between posts. But this preoccupation quickly grew old, especially when my foot started feeling numb from trying to hold such exact pressure.

I finally gave up my game when I reached the end of this stretch of expressway, then exiting onto a two-lane highway that took me eastward. Tapping and releasing the accelerator in an effort to wake my sleeping foot, I then had to brake for a slow moving eighteen-wheeler stuck behind a farm tractor. With too little power to accelerate past the log jam, I remained stuck behind the sluggish traffic until I finally reached the entrance ramp to I-75, the last stretch of expressway heading north.

Slouching down into a more relaxed posture, I turned on the car radio in search of a new distraction from the open road ahead. Unfortunately the antenna was broken, making it difficult to pick up any of the remote northern Michigan signals without loads of static. I clicked the receiver off and then found my mind wandering to where it so often lingered – at that devastating moment when I learned there were much worse things than divorce.

I could still remember where I was, what I was doing, when my life changed forever. I was watching *Cheers* while reclining in Rob's orange-tweed recliner, a 70's-kickback treasured by Rob that was left vacant when he decided to drive to the fitness center despite the lake-effect blizzard howling outside. Over the wind and the incessant tapping of sleet pelting the windows, I listened to Cliff Claven at the bar, dishing out "little known facts" to Norm, all while warnings of whiteout conditions and a note of a multiple car pile-up rolled across the bottom of the screen.

I was popping popcorn when the doorbell rang. Since I was home alone, I apprehensively pulled the door curtain aside to see who it was at such a late hour. It was a state trooper.

"Are you Carly Malloy?" The officer removed his hat from his graying hair and dusted snow off from himself.

"Yes, that's me."

"Could I step in for a moment?" Not waiting for a reply, he made his way in the door.

It was more than cold air that caused me to suddenly start shaking. "What is it?"

"I'm afraid there's been a bad accident."

"The pile-up on I-75." I felt my lips move as my voice echoed back at me inside my head. "I saw something about it on T.V. Is everything all right?"

But I knew it wasn't. My mind was racing as I tried to think of who might have been involved. It couldn't be my sister, Brianna. She was home from college, staying with my folks, and not due to be back until later in the week. And not Rob, since he'd just gone to the club, or at least that's what he'd said.

"I'm afraid not." The officer was no longer looking at me but rather staring at his hat in his hands. "There's never an easy way to tell someone this."

I couldn't let him finish, certain that I knew what he was about to say.

"My husband — how badly is he hurt?" I could barely hear myself speak over the thumping of my racing heart.

"Your husband?" the officer's gray eyebrows slanted with confusion.

"Yes, he's been gone a little while. You mean you're not here about him?"

"No, ma'am, I don't know anything about your husband. I'm here about your parents and sister. Their car was one of those involved in the accident."

"What?" I distantly heard myself reply while franticly trying to remember any recent conversations with family. Dad had said he wanted Brianna home for as long as she could stay, but then Mom had said something about visiting old friends in Bri's college town, maybe taking Bri to see their friend's son, some pre-med student. But they never would have left in this weather.

"I'm afraid I have bad news," I vaguely heard him say, his words sounding far off like those on the PA at Wal-Mart — always paging someone else, but never you.

"There must be a mix-up." Warm tears welled up in my eyes as I tried to deny what I knew must be true.

"Maybe you should sit down." The officer gently reached for me, taking me by the arms.

"This can't be!" I jerked away, refusing to sit. But when I caught sight of the pained look on the officer's face, I knew it could be.

"It was very sudden, Ms. Malloy. They didn't suffer. All three of them must have died instantly."

Instantly repeated in my mind as I drew myself back to the present, staring far up the road at a truck I was gaining on. Its taillights were a blur, and so I tilted my rearview mirror towards me long enough to wipe the mascara-stained tears from my bloodshot eyes.

With the expressway cutting along side a stagnant lake, I entered a cloud of what must have been a late-spring hatch of fish flies. Even over the engine's rattle, I still could hear the pattering sound much like that of a hailstorm as hundreds of bugs splattered on my windshield. I clicked on the wipers and pushed the washer button, but very little spray came out as the bug-guts smeared across my view.

"Another Rob-job," I muttered, recalling the time that my ex had tried to fix the wiper fluid dispenser but just managed to make the problem worse. That had always been his M.O. – fix it on the cheap, and get what you paid for.

My sadness always turned to anger whenever I thought of Rob's selfishness, of how insensitive it was for him to choose the day after my family's funeral to tell me he wanted a divorce.

"I just can't keep living a lie." The two-timer admitted he'd been having an affair with his trainer at the gym. "I tried to hold off telling you after the accident, but then I figured it'd be easier to accept the change since life's already up in the air."

"Easier for whom?"

"Hey, you're the one who's always telling me I've got to be more honest! I'm just taking your advice and being up front with you."

How considerate. There couldn't have been a worse time for him to implement his new honesty policy. I just wished he'd started sooner, back when the whole affair had begun, so I wouldn't have needed to add the humiliation of naiveté to my laundry list of anguish.

Returning my thoughts to my drive northward, I glanced from the highway long enough to see the tab of the manila folder peaking up between the seat and gearshift. I had written *Starting Over* on it as a reminder not to wallow in self-pity. I had to stop regretting that I'd dropped out of Michigan State to get married and work two jobs so I could support Rob through undergrad and business school. Instead of feeling sad that we'd never started the family he had promised, I needed to be grateful that there were no children who would suffer through our break up. With no ties between us, I could just walk away and begin anew — chalk up these years as a sort of internship that would give me real-world wisdom when I returned to finish my education.

Now back to square one, I would start over on my chem degree at State in the coming fall, but this time I'd have no financial backing from my parents. Dad's small life insurance policy had barely paid off his debts and the funeral expenses, and Rob had managed to blow what little remained on credit card debt before the divorce was finalized.

Rob's well-timed legal maneuver of declaring bankruptcy further complicated an already uphill battle for alimony, a fight my attorney was all too eager to take on but I was against. As much as I wanted to stick it to Rob, I didn't want to feel beholden to him for anything. I was bullheaded, determined to make it without him, but my current part-time job at the local Hallmark shop wouldn't provide enough hours or pay to make that possible. I needed a good paying job to help me achieve my pay-as-you-go education.

My only post-separation friend, Annahede Khali, had her own thoughts on how best to improve my financial situation. "You're never going to find decent pay in this hell-hole of a town. You need to find some place where the wealthy are all too eager to spend their money, and you can just help them out."

Annahede worked in her father's silver store next door to the Hallmark shop, and we would often have lunch together in the memorial park right across the street. As an immigrant from Saudi Arabia, her life experiences had given her a much different perspective from my own, and I found her thoughts to be provocative and fascinating. Although notably younger than me (she had just turned twenty and I was pushing thirty), she considered herself wise beyond her years and never hesitated to dish out her own brew of worldly advice.

"Carly, you've got too many memories lurking in the shadows of this town, and I can see how much it pains you when you keep bumping into that loser soon-to-be-ex-husband of yours and his shameless-hussy fiancé. You don't need that kind of grief."

"What hurts more is seeing people I know who just don't know what to say. When I bump into them, we have these awkward conversations as if we're strangers. I wish they'd just come out with it and say what they're really thinking."

"Well, you know I won't mince words. You need to get out of here, just like I do, and we're going to find some great place where we can start over and make it big."

I wasn't so interested in "making it big," but I certainly liked the idea of finding a good-paying job and a new place to call home. My hometown held too many memories, both good and bad, hidden in the corners of familiar homes and stores, parks and playgrounds, churches and the cemetery. The place had become merely an unpleasant reminder that everyone I loved had abandoned me, and so I finally decided to leave it for good.

I found myself squinting to see the road, but it was no longer due to tears. Dusk was turning to darkness as the sun set to my left. Even with the days growing longer with the approach of summer, this day was quickly coming to an end.

Grabbing the headlight switch, I turned the knob as far as I could but only the parking lights seemed to come on. I cursed my ex, assuming that the jammed switch must also be his fault, and I glanced down to see if I could fix the problem. Just as I glanced back up at the road, I saw it for a split-second out of the corner of my eye. From the budding shrubs in the median, its wide-eyed frightened face bore down on me as it charged my side window, giving me no time to react.

With a loud "thump," the white-tailed deer broadsided my Chevette, its face smacking against my left side window. I jerked the wheel to regain my spot in the lane, overcompensating and swerving too far to the left and toward the median. Pumping my brakes, I swerved back with my wheels screeching.

Suddenly a loud explosion sounded from the front right, followed by a flapping sound and a vibration that seemed to drag my car in that direction. Realizing I'd blown the front tire, I battled the car to the shoulder of the road, threw it into park, and turned on the flashers.

"Oh my God!" I exhaled, then brushed disheveled strands of dark brown hair from my face. Despite the uncontrollable shake in my body, it seemed that I was all right. However, my car wasn't.

"This is just great." I was supposed to rendezvous with Annahede at the Straits Ferry dock before 11:00 PM to catch the last ferry of the night to the island. Now I'd miss my friend and miss my boat – and would probably have to sleep in my overstuffed car for the night.

The headlights coming up behind me slowed and veered off the shoulder, pulling up behind me. Blinded by their glare in my rearview mirror, I was unable to see who stepped out of the truck-sized vehicle until he walked up toward me. I decided quickly to only roll my window down just a crack to speak, feeling safer until I found out the intentions of this stranger.

"Hey, we don't use-ly hunt our deers like that up here!" The gruff-looking man chuckled as he leaned in toward the small opening in my window. "Looks like that buck high-tailed it out a' here 'fore we could catch 'um, and yer car took a mighty beatin' for it. Need some help?"

In the glare of the truck's headlamps, I could clearly see the burly man's three-day-old scruff. His shaggy hair stuck out in all directions from under a baseball cap that read *Borwicz Towing*. Through the cracked window I caught a whiff of cigarette smoke intermingled with B.O.

I inched the window down a bit more. "Yeah, I don't know much about how to change a flat. Guess I haven't done it since driver's ed."

"Well, it's yer lucky day!" The stranger smiled at me with tobacco-stained teeth. "I'm in the tire business. Just got off work, matter-a-fact. I can get ya's fixed up in no time."

In a proud gesture, the man hiked his pants up under his wrinkled flannel shirt, but his beer gut still protruded in full view from my window.

"Oh, are you sure?" I still felt hesitant about trusting this fellow. "I hate to trouble you when you're off duty. Maybe we should just call someone?"

"Fergit that! Call my boss and he'll be headin' out here with the tow-truck I drive, haulin' yer car back to the shop, and chargin' your butt a heap 'a money fer what I'm offerin' fer free. Now, pop that hatch and let's get 'er done."

He did seem harmless enough and well intentioned, so I hopped out of the car and set about pulling my boxed belongings out of the back so we could get at the spare.

"Looks like ya got the '82 model here." The man hiked his pants again over this revelation.

"Yes, my parents gave it to me brand new as a wedding gift. I've had it for all ten years."

"These babies sure are tiny, but they've been known to hang in there. Yers looks to be in decent shape."

"If you only knew," I mumbled under my breath.

"Shouldn't go far on this here spare." The man removed the tiny doughnut wheel from the back and rolled it up beside the flat. "It's not for drivin' a long ways. How much farther you gotta go?"

"To the Mackinac Bridge."

"Shoo-wee! That's a haul. Bet they still got that dirty snow all piled up on the roadsides up there, but them highways should be plenty dry. That's a bit farther than I'd use-ly recommend drivin' on the spare, but yer probly okay if ya take her slow."

Taking it slow seemed the last thing I could afford to do since Annahede had been so adamant that I get to Windemere ASAP before the best jobs were taken for the summer. With half of the Lower Peninsula still to travel, I wasn't sure if I'd now be able to make it there on time. I could just imagine how furious she'd be if I didn't catch that last ferry.

"Can I help in any way?" I hoped there was some way we could speed up the process."

"Nope, I got her." The man stuck a couple of rubber blocks behind the tires. "No sense gettin' yerself dirty. I'll have her done in a jiffy."

"Can I get my jacket out of the car before you jack it up? It's getting pretty cold out here."

"Suppose so, but it don't seem that cold. Ya think this is bad, wait 'til ya get up north."

I reached in the car and quickly found my windbreaker jammed in between the seats right next to my prized folder. I grabbed both and got out of the car just in time.

"Best step aside so ya don't get hurt." The tire man had already positioned the jack, and so he started pumping.

Taking his advice, I moved to the freeway shoulder while slipping on my jacket. In the coat pocket I found a penlight that proved most useful as I tried to reread the folder's contents. The top newspaper clipping in the folder was the article that had started this venture – the one Annahede had given me entitled *Windemere Workforce Depleted*.

"This is our ticket out of here," Annahede had said.

The *Detroit Free Press* article stated that employers on Windemere Island customarily filled their seasonal positions with Caribbean natives that the locals referred to as "Saints" – called that because most originated from the islands of St. Croix, St. Lucia, St. Maarten, St. Vincent, and St. Thomas. Pairing up the Saints with Windemere seemed like the perfect arrangement since most of these hard working people faced rampant unemployment during the hot summer months and they were more than willing to travel north for the chance at the low wages paid on Windemere.

However, for some unexplainable reason, the employers were having trouble getting enough steady help from the Saints this summer. There were reports of complaints that some return employees had not shown up at all this year and that others had reported to work for a few days but then suddenly left without notice. All of this had left Windemere's business owners scrambling for last minute hires to fill these vacancies before the start of their busy season on Memorial Day weekend.

Now holding the penlight in my teeth to free my hands, I turned the article aside to reveal all of the want ads from island employers who were looking for waiters, cooks, busboys, maids, and even street cleaners. Annahede had clipped these from the paper as well, writing down information from those she had meticulously selected, then handed them off to me for my perusal.

"I'll head up to Windemere a couple of days ahead of you," Annahede had planned. "I'll scope out the housing and the best jobs. Then when you come, we'll go apply for our jobs together."

Totally engrossed in reading the want ads by penlight, I failed to notice the car and semi, traveling side-by-side, speeding toward us. With the car passing on the left, there was no room for the semi to move over and away from us. The two sped past, blowing a few of the want ads from my folder.

"Damn it!" The tire man's hat, caught by the gust that shook the Chevette, flew to the side of the road.

With penlight in hand, I set about searching the grass in hopes of finding each missing ad. "Guess he couldn't get into the other lane."

"Yeah, it wasn't the trucker's fault." The man paused just long enough to grab his hat and put it back on. "It's probly one of them out-a-state speed demons was tryin' to pass him. They're in such a great big hurry to get on up here to their cabin that they push them truckers or anyone else right on outta their way. Wish they'd slow down or just stay home."

"Are there really that many people who come from that far away to drive all the way up here?"

"Sure do." The man removed the last bolt and pulled the flat from the hub. "'Course lots come from Detroit, but you'd be surprised how many comes from further south. Indianers, now they ain't so bad, but them Ohians – Woo! They'd never drive that stupid in their state 'cause their troopers take 'um down a size. But when them buckeyes come on up here, they start drivin' like a bat outta hell."

"Well, I'll just have to watch out because at Chevette speed, I might get blown off the road."

The tire man's dark eyes squinted with puffy lower lids protruding as he chuckled at the thought. "So, what's ahead in Mackinaw City for ya?"

"Oh, I'm not staying in the city. I'm catching a ferry to Windemere Island."

"Windemere? Why that's right next ter that there Mackinac Island, ain't it?

"That's right." I continued picking up my clippings.

"I hear that Windemere's just another one of them places for rich folks. Are ya one of 'um?"

"Hardly." I laughed. "My friend told me Windemere isn't as affluent, that it's kind of the red-headed stepsister to Mackinac Island."

"Yeah, well I ain't never been there, so I don't know, but I once had a job to do on that there Mackinac Island." He paused from his work just long enough to scratch under his cap. "Them two islands are right next to each other, ain't they?"

"Yes, they are." I picked up another clipping.

"And I get all mixed up on the spellin' 'cause the city's different from that Mackinac Island. I says 'Mack-i-nack' to someone and they gets all high and mighty and starts tell me it's Swiss or French or somethin', and I don't care. They knows what I meant."

"It is confusing."

"And I know they're up in them Straits of Mackinac – up where Lake Michigan bumps into Lake... Lake... Lake..."

"Lake Huron."

"Yeah, Lake Huron. I knows my Michigan geography better than most – how them two lakes are split by the Mighty Mac. Haven't been to that there bridge, though – not since I was a kid."

Neither had I. My childhood memory of a trip to the Straits was a happy one, when my parents had driven all evening to bring me and my younger sister to Mackinaw City. We had arrived late at night and were dazzled by the image of the five-mile long suspension bridge illuminated by hundreds of colored lights running along the suspension lines to the top of its two lofty towers. Despite its imposing beauty, I was even more awestruck by the quaint island communities we visited the next day in the shadows of the Mighty Mac.

From the ferry docks located at the "Tip-of-the-Mitt" of Michigan's Lower Peninsula, our family had taken a steam-powered ship that once had been used to bring the affluent of Detroit and Chicago to their summer homes in the north. I had never forgotten the breathtaking beauty of the Straits, recalling the sight of various pleasure crafts crisscrossing their wakes as well as that of an eight-hundred-foot ore freighter whose many hands were out on deck. I remembered how everyone was having a great time out on the pristine aqua-green water. It was this happier time I longed to recapture.

"Almost done." The tire man cranked down on the tire iron. "Should have ya back on the road pretty quick."

"Thanks so much." I slipped off my jacket in preparation to get back in the car. "Maybe I'll still make it to meet my friend after all."

He continued tightening down the bolts. "So, what'll ya do with the car once ya get there? Can't take her to the islands, ya know. They won't let no cars over there."

"Yes, I know. My friend somehow arranged some cheap long term parking for me."

"All seems kinda snooty to me." He wrinkled up his nose with a smirk, his chubby red cheeks bulging. "With all them horses and bicycles putzin' around those islands, just give me a Harley over there and I'll show ya what's a real good ride."

"Well, I guess they're going for a quieter atmosphere. When you go there, you're supposed to feel like you've traveled back in time."

The man pumped the jack handle to lower the car. "Why the hell would I want to travel back in time? Can't think of a whole lot good in my past. I'd just a soon move on."

Since the car crash and divorce, there had been many times I had felt the same way. But thoughts of Windemere gave me hope that I could find happiness and a new sense of home. I had struggled to find this while remaining in my hometown, a place where everything seemed to be a constant reminder of what I had lost. I longed to find a new place to call my own.

"Well, she's all set for the road." He kindly went about packing my things back into the hatch. "Now promise not to drive her too hard and that tire should get ya there."

I reached into the car and pulled out my purse. "I can't thank you enough." I fished around in my purse for some money to offer him.

"No, now put that away. It's a favor I done, not lookin' for money. 'Sides, if yer headin' to that Windemere place, you might be needin' the cash more than me." And with that, he headed back into the bright lights of his truck.

"There must be something I can do to repay you," I yelled to him.

"Just pass it on." Through his lights, I could barely see him climbing back aboard his rig. "Oh, and don't hit no more deers. I'd like there to still be somethin' left in the woods to hunt come November."

As the truck pulled back on to the expressway and drove off into the distance, I paused for an instant to consider the kindness of a stranger whose name I never learned. How funny it seemed that I'd been afraid of someone who had been so kind when in the past I had trusted someone who had turned out to be a betrayer. I resolved at that moment to pass along the good deed by not being so quick to judge and getting to know someone before concluding who they were deep inside.

With no time to spare, I started the car and managed to force the light switch into the full on position, then pulled from the shoulder to continue my journey north. As I accelerated, I thought about the tire man's words – how he saw Windemere as a place for rich people – and I wondered if I could even afford to live there. Hopefully Annahede would have good news in the search for inexpensive housing and have some applications for good-paying work, but I wouldn't find out if I didn't get there on time. I'd have to push it a bit more than I'd promised.

With the thrust of the stick into fourth gear, the rattles and bangs returned. Surprisingly, I almost welcomed the sound. It was a reminder that I was heading in the right direction, away from a disastrous past and toward a fresh start.

"276," I announced as the mile marker passed by. Then I resumed my counting, this time checking to see if the steady banging from the engine coincided with the reflectors that frequently flashed along the side of the road.

Under the blanket of nighttime, there were few other signs of light on the horizon. At times I would pass a car or one would pass me, its red lights shrinking until they disappeared in the distance. Occasionally I'd spot the faint glow of a distant small town, its light growing brighter as I approached and then fading as I passed on by. The distance between towns was increasing as I drew closer to my destination.

"Exit 313," I read aloud. Then the next sign announced that there were only two more exits before reaching Mackinaw City. With this, I felt my worries about the tire, and the engine, and the past, all gently lifting from my consciousness as a new sense of optimism took their place. I was going to make it to Windemere where I would find a new job, and new friends, and a new future. Everything was going to be all right. Then a red light on the dash clicked on. It read, "Oil."

"Don't rain on my parade." I tapped on the signal with my fingernail. Amazingly, the light clicked back off.

Figuring it must be a sign, I continued onward with the determination – and the hope – that nothing would stop me now.

Chapter 2

BAGGAGE

"MY FOLKS ARE INSANE!" Annahede helped me with unloading my belongings from my car onto a large cart. "They've got some crazy notion that I'll want to spend the rest of my life working in their silly little jewelry business, and you know there's no way that's going to happen."

"Maybe they just need some time to accept your decision." Dropping another duffle bag onto the cart, I took in a deep breath of the cool, damp air rolling in from the Great Lake Huron. "I bet they'll be more understanding the next time you're in Rockford to pay them a visit."

"Go back to Rockford? Not a chance!" She laughed and rolled her copper eyes nearly to the back of her head. "I'm going to start a new life and stay so far from there that they can never make me work for them again."

It was then that I realized I wasn't so alone in my search for a new home.

Annahede continued to complain while helping me push my belongings through the graveled parking lot. "Ever since we moved to this country, Papa's made me work in that stupid Gold Diggers shop of his. He spends all of his time designing one-of-a-kind crap while my step-mother minds the till, pocketing bonuses for herself when Papa isn't looking."

Some time ago, I'd made the mistake of inquiring why Annahede chose to live with her father rather than her mother.

"You think I had a choice? When Papa made the decision to leave Saudi Arabia, he had to give up a few things, not the least of which was two of his wives."

Three wives were beyond my comprehension. "That must've been a bit confusing."

"Not really. We all knew where we stood – who belonged to which mother, who were the favorites and, of course, who was in charge. So when Papa decided he wanted a better life for himself, the selfish bastard never asked anyone else what they wanted."

"What did your mom do?"

Annahede had been surprisingly matter-of-fact in her response. "Nothing. In my home, women and children were to be seldom seen and never heard. All three dutiful wives silently accepted his wishes."

"So what happened to your mother?"

"Papa left her behind with one other wife and four of his children. He chose his favorite wife and three children to come with him and abandoned the rest. Guess I'm supposed to feel blessed that he found favor with me." She blinked her heavily outlined eyes, seductively running her fingers down a long strand of her satin-black hair.

I wondered what she might have meant by, "found favor," but never dared to ask.

"I remember the day we left. Mama kissed me good-bye, wished me well, and waved me off with a smile. It was as if she didn't care that I was leaving and that she'd probably never see me again." Annahede paused, and for a moment I thought she was going to cry. Then she gritted her teeth, adding, "I wrote her off, right then and there."

Annahede portrayed her mother as weak, but I saw her differently – as a mother overwhelmed with the grief of losing a daughter, but selflessly setting aside her own emotions to do what was best for her child. With few rights for the women of her family, her mother's complaining probably would have gotten her nowhere, and her weeping and wailing would have only disturbed her daughter. Instead, she likely had painted on a smile and sent her daughter off toward more opportunities and freedoms than she had ever known. I could think of no greater sacrifice than surrendering your child in hopes of giving her a better life.

The benefits of her mother's sacrifice were evident in Annahede's demeanor. Now away from her family, she was free to further display her headstrong determination.

"Step back." Annahede nearly pushed me aside. Then, with one massive heave, she single-handedly shoved the cart heaped with my belongings onto the dock. "I've done this a couple of times – finally getting the hang of it." She brushed dirt from her hands, then turned away, straightened herself, and headed for the ticket-taker.

Exuding the air of self-confidence she so easily could portray, Annahede strutted down the dock planks, her long, slender legs striding gracefully along the planks as she held her chin high, arching the soft curve of her neck to reach her full dominating stature. With an air of superiority, she boldly informed the ticket-taker, "We got it this far – It's your problem now."

As we boarded the ferry, I couldn't help but reflect on how much Annahede had evolved in the short time I had known her. At first, she had been so quiet, holding all of her opinions within her. But as I managed to earn her confidence, and she further Americanized, she started voicing her beliefs strongly – that is, just as long as her parents were not nearby.

They were odd ducks, to say the very least.

I first glimpsed Annahede's dysfunctional family the day I dropped in while they were moving into their store. Mr. Khali boldly displayed his work all over his person as his bulky hands weighed heavy with gaudy rings and fine golden chains made from unusual link patterns dangled from both his wrists and neck.

"How do you do?" He took my hand in his and kissed it with a slight bow.

"I'm fine, thanks."

"Such a beauty-ful woman to be gracing our boutique." He gave me an extended looking-over with his piercing black eyes. "We will have just the right bangles to set off your lovely olive complexion, won't we Mohani?"

Mrs. Khali simply nodded in reply. She too dripped with gold from head to foot, but her tawdry appearance seemed even more tasteless. She wore a fuchsia mini dress that fit too tightly to her ill-shaped figure, an outfit much the opposite of the black robe and veil I assumed she'd once been required to wear.

From my first encounter with the Khalis, I noticed that Mr. Khali did all of the talking. He bragged about his shop, gave me his business cards to pass out to the Hallmark customers, and expressed interest in designing something unique for me – that is, until he realized I had no money. Mrs. Khali nodded in agreement with each word Mr. Khali uttered, but if she dared to speak, he abruptly cut her off with his own words, or sometimes even with a clap of his hands.

"That's how he treats all the women in his family," Annahede later divulged. "He's an embarrassment to his people, and an even bigger embarrassment to me."

"You can't help it if he acts that way. You obviously can't tell him anything if he won't even let you speak."

"Well, he's going to hear one thing from me. I'm telling him that I'm leaving him and that sleaze-bag wife of his to their misery. I don't want his money, and I'm not working at his gaudy little shop. I'm through with him, and I'm moving to Windemere – and you're going with me!"

The idea sounded great when Annahede showed me the newspaper clippings and theorized that, with two of us living together, we could easily live cheaper and save money. But since the long drive north when I'd had a chance to think things through, I'd been wondering if rent would be too expensive even for two living together.

"Housing's not a problem," Annahede reassured me as we found our seats on the ferry. "There's cheaper housing more inland, away from the beach. That's where the local and seasonal workers usually live. And I found out they're leasing cheaper this season since a few of these Caribbean workers they call 'Saints' took off without paying – left their landlords high and dry."

"Yeah, I read about that in the *Free Press*. Guess they just packed up and left."

"And a couple of them never even packed! They just took off – left everything behind."

"Have they figured out yet why they've been leaving?"

"No, and I don't really care – just glad the rent's down."

"Well, I suppose." I put my purse down beside my seat. "So, now all we have to do is find out how much they're paying for these jobs – whether we're better off cooking or cleaning."

"You can just forget about that!" Annahede crossed her arms with a huff.

"But I thought –"

"You thought wrong! No slave labor for us – I've got bigger plans. I already went around and got applications for all the exclusive restaurants. We'll land ourselves a couple of waitressing spots, work our way in with the –"

"Hold on a minute!" This wasn't exactly what I had in mind.

"What's the problem?"

"I'm not so sure I'd be too good at waiting tables, and you… well, I can't imagine you wanting to wait on anybody."

"It's all just a part of the bigger picture." Annahede winked and flashed an almost diabolical grin. "It's all a part of making the right connections. I figure the tips from big spenders will get us the best pay while we're trying to get where we really want to be."

"And just exactly where is it that we really want to be?"

"At the top, of course."

"I don't know what 'top' you're aiming for, but I can't imagine getting there by waiting on people."

"Don't you get it, Carly? This way we can meet the island's wealthy business owners, schmooze with the important people. Once we get to know them personally, we can sell ourselves as candidates for more substantial positions with the bigwigs. And in the meantime, we'll make great money, which is exactly what you need right now. So, what do you say?"

As the ferry pulled from the dock, I sensed that I wasn't quite in sync with Annahede's ulterior motives. However, I did agree with the most important point: we both needed money, and big tips at a fancy restaurant were probably one of the best ways for two people with no post-secondary degrees to earn some. It seemed worth a try.

By the light of the waxing moon, the ferry's wake rose to a line of white foam that then dissipated into the peaks and swells of black waves tipped by glowing white light. It was a much different image of Lake Huron than the daylight one I'd recalled from childhood, but beautiful and mysterious in its own right.

Then a familiar vision came into view. To our port side, the magnificent Mackinac Bridge appeared. Powerful beacons of lights illuminated its two towers, and hundreds of colored lights twinkled from the suspension lines arching down between the towers and off to the sides toward land. It was an awesome sight to behold, and it brought back memories of happier times—ones that I savored and held so dear.

As our journey continued, the bridge grew distant and the glow of the islands' lights shown in the sky up ahead. The chill of the spring air was cutting, so I bundled myself up in my jacket. Spray rose up and misted my face as we struck the wake of another last ferry. This I also remembered from long ago, but it hadn't felt so cold.

"I know it's chilly, but you'll warm up quickly when we get to the little cottage I rented." Annahede tried to reassure me as she held back long strands of her satin-black hair that kept whipping in her face. "You're going to love the place. It's decked out with such high-end furniture and appliances. I can't believe what a steal we got on it from the old lady that used to live there."

"Just as long as it's heated." I pulled my jacket tighter around my shivering body.

When almost to Windemere, the boat turned to the port side and revealed a clearer view of the brightly-lit lighthouse of Beacon Point. I also recalled this place from the past because at the time it had looked almost haunted due to its terrible state of disrepair. But now it stood majestically as a welcome to the island, its restoration visible even in the darkness of night.

"What did they do to my haunted lighthouse?" I asked Annahede.

"Well, I guess they fixed it, and then they made it scarier than ever."

"What's that supposed to mean?"

"Well, I overheard a local saying that somebody bought the place, fixed it all up, and then they cordoned it off so nobody can go there. Now you can't even get anywhere near the place without the coast guard coming down on you. You know, it all sounds a little freaky to me."

As the ferry pulled into port, I looked back on the lighthouse. Its beacon kept rotating, the light vaguely revealing where black water met the distant shoreline, a view that was slightly obscured by a low, rising mist. But the light cut through the haze, scanning across the small clusters of lights that marked the small communities on the mainland, then whipping out across open water and coming full circle to cast its blinding beam on the island. My eyes followed the beacon as it headed back out to open water on its continual circular journey, the light broadening out from a majestic structure still shrouded in secrecy.

My curiosity aroused, I hoped that at some point amidst my new life on Windemere that the veil would be lifted, that outsiders would be allowed a closer look at this mysterious lighthouse. Then maybe I could put my childhood impression of its haunting to rest once and for all.

Chapter 3

SOUL SELLING

LANDING A DECENT WAITRESSING GIG proved considerably more difficult than I had anticipated. Annahede and I spent most of our first full day riding a rented tandem bike up and down the paved streets, avoiding other bicyclists and the fresh piles of horse droppings as we stopped at the finer restaurants to drop off completed applications. But at all the stops, I could see it in the managers' expressions and hear it in their voices when they asked, "And which of the islands did you say you come from?"

"We didn't!" Annahede snapped at a manager for one of the restaurants, snatching our applications back out of his hands. "We've obviously applied at the wrong place."

Following her as she stormed out, I climbed back on the bike seat behind hers. "Reacting to the boss like that isn't going to get us anywhere. We could have at least left our apps there, just in case something opened up."

Annahede pushed on the bike pedals and steered sharply away from the edge of the rustic boardwalk. "You *know* that's not going to happen. Those snobs only want to hire Saints." Turning us back toward town, she pumped hard on the pedals, taking us back past the many ornate gas lanterns that lined Main Street.

"Look out!" I yelled when I saw an old man step off the boardwalk and into the street dead ahead.

Annahede clanged her bike bell, weaving just in time to avoid hitting him. "Hey! Watch where you're going, old guy!" She never slowed down while continuing on with her tirade. "It's like these restaurants think the Saints are the only ones they can rely on to work hard and stay loyal to their place – and I bet they pay more money to get them to switch over and work for them. So they're not so loyal after all, are they?"

"But we wouldn't be, either," I pointed out while trying to keep my feet on the back pedals. "I mean, you said this was just a stepping stone for us, right?"

"But that doesn't make it okay for them to deny us a job. It's like reverse discrimination, and that's just not fair." Steering wide to the opposite side of the street, Annahede passed around a horse-drawn carriage just pulling out from the curbside. "And what's this guy doing?" she grumbled. "Does he need the whole road to drive that thing?"

"I don't know." I looked back to see the carriage driver shaking his head at us. In response, I held up my hands and shrugged to indicate that, as usual, I was not in control. He replied with a nod and tip of his hat while shaking the reins with his free hand, urging on his majestic Belgian cross horses to continue their clip-clop cadence as their heads nodded along with the rhythm.

As we approached the other end of Main Street, Annahede stopped the pedals and coasted. "We're running out of options."

"Then let's check out some of these shops along here." I pointed down one side street where hanging signs and sandwich boards littered the walkway, enticing visitors to stop by for a sure bargain. "Somebody along there's got to have a couple openings."

Annahede guided our tandem to the side of the boardwalk, dropping her foot to the ground to hold our balance. "All right, I'll try it. But... only under these conditions: that we only ask at the shops *I* think are worth it – you know, with more high-end appeal – *and*, you agree that this is *only* a temporary fix."

I had lowered my foot, too, holding us upright in front of a tiny diner that smelled of hamburgers and pizza. "Whatever you say – just as long as you finally let me get something to eat."

The streets' inadequate bike racks were overflowing with bikes rammed haphazardly into and around the few parking slots, so Annahede locked ours to a hitching post meant for horses and then led me into the pizza joint. There, I ordered two slices with pepperoni and a job application, but Annahede took the app from me and threw it in the trash on the way out the door.

"Not our style," she insisted, waving for me to follow her down the boardwalk.

Squeezing between dawdling tourists, I trailed along while studying the hodgepodge of tourist shops we passed by. They were selling all sorts of knick-knacks and toys and postcards – and then there was one shop specializing in T-shirts bearing slogans like, "My grandma went to Windemere Island, and all I got was this lousy shirt." These were *my* kinds of places, but Annahede would have no part with them.

"Come look at this place." She had stopped at the display window of a stylish boutique where she was studying the detail put into a gorgeous evening dress. "Not exactly what I had in mind, but I guess it's worth a try." With her head held high and her long neck extended to flaunt her fine yet simple gold jewelry, Annahede headed in – and I followed.

And so we continued on this way for quite some time, but unfortunately our efforts proved equally futile as the clerks at each shop told us they had no openings. Although they encouraged us to try the next place down, certain that their neighbor had been looking for help, we'd move along to the next store only to hear the same story again.

"I think they're feeding us a line." Annahede straightened her blouse. "That must be their way of getting rid of Michiganders when they only want to hire Saints."

"Well, we've got to keep trying." I continued walking but stopped suddenly when struck by a tantalizing smell coming from the next shop. "That's fudge." I turned and gazed in the window at large copper kettles filled with the chocolate concoction, a young man in a white shirt and apron stirring one pot with a long, wooden stick. Enormous overhead fans sucked up the aroma, forcing it through a duct system and blowing it out on the street to lure by-passers to stop in for free samples.

Annahede joined me, looking in the front window just as the young man removed boiling fudge from the kettle and smeared it on a marble slab. "They have these shops all over town," she told me. "They're a dime-a-dozen, sucking in visitors at every turn – guess that's why people around here call all the tourists 'Fudgies.'"

"Maybe we should get applications here." I stepped closer to peer in the shop window. "I know it's not high-end, but it does smell good, doesn't it?"

"Yeah, it does." Annahede opened the shop door. "And if asking for an app gets us free fudge, then I can't complain."

We indulged in the samples, departing the store with more than just two job applications. I splurged on the purchase of what they called the "fudge sampler" that we nibbled on as we walked along and checked at a few more shops for work. But by the time we had wound our way back around to where we'd left the rented tandem, we had finished with both the fudge and our searching, convinced that there were no jobs to be found downtown.

Annahede unlocked the tandem from the hitching post. "I overheard the fudge lady giving directions to a woman for some restaurant that's a bit off the main drag. I think we should check it out before we turn in the bike for the day."

I climbed onto the back seat, ready to ride again. "At this point, I'm ready to try just about anything."

A few turns and then a steep uphill climb brought us to the doorstep of a hidden little place called "Simple Pleasures," a fine dining establishment that we were pleasantly surprised to find bearing a sign for "Help Wanted." The manager, a Mr. Thomas Paigre, was short on waitresses due to the recent and sudden departure of three of his Saints.

"I'd prefer to hire more Saints." Mr. Paigre looked down his pointed nose studying our applications through his half-moon reading spectacles. "They're hard workers and don't usually quit without notice, but I guess things are different now. I'm forced to take a chance on local folks. So, are you ladies committed?"

"Most definitely." Annahede threw back her shoulders, further broadening the V in her blouse. "We've so admired your establishment and would love nothing more than to work here indefinitely."

"Really?" Mr. Paigre grinned, his squinty eyes seeming to study us in question of Annahede's sincerity. He removed his glasses. "Very well then. Since you're both experienced, I'll give you a try. You'll start tomorrow."

Mr. Paigre had already turned and left us before I could correct Annahede's assertion. "You told him we've waitressed before?"

"Oh, I just filled the blank lines with a couple fictitious restaurant names – nothing he'll ever bother to check out. You want a job, don't you?"

"Yeah, but not enough to lie about my experience. What will I do when he expects me to know things I don't know?"

"Fake it." Annahede put her arm over my shoulders and gave me a reassuring hug. "You know I'll be there to help you. We'll get through this together."

Annahede proved a natural at waitressing, performing her duties flawlessly while schmoozing away with Windemere's prominent business owners. It took only a few days for her to establish a rapport with some of the island's more prestigious visitors – including some of the politicians and lobbyists who frequently visited Windemere to cut deals and spin their doctrines. Although I tended to dislike these often arrogant patrons, Annahede gravitated toward them, impressed by their power, prestige, and of course, bottomless spending accounts.

These regulars were equally smitten by Annahede as they often requested her as a server whenever she was available. Mr. Paigre always obliged, seemingly pleased that Annahede had managed to enchant his patrons in just a matter of days.

Annahede's talent did not go unnoticed by Mr. Samuel Donahue, the less-than-reputable owner of Windemere's sole convention center. Like Mr. Paigre, he was also interested in keeping his customers content, and apparently he saw potential in Annahede.

After one long evening of indulging in fresh Walleye and one too many Manhattans, Mr. Donahue quite boisterously suggested that Annahede come see him regarding an opening he had for a convention coordinator at his facility.

"Don't misunderstand me, Annahede, because I really love your service." Donahue spun the ice in his drink, speaking with a slight slur. "I just think you're wasting your time and talents dishing up fish and booze."

"You think I have talents, sir?" Annahede placed his dinner plate before him, spinning it to offer just the right view of its presentation.

"Of course you do." He wiped remnants of salad from his furry mustache. "With your good looks and great rapport with the customers, I bet you'd book up conventions for me well into the next couple of years."

"You think so?"

"Oh, I know so! Just look around you," He took another belt from his drink, then waved his arms about the room. "These guys love you. They love what you're dishing out. And they'd love it if you could line them up with more to be dished out, if you know what I mean." With a wink, he stuffed a heaping bite of fish in his mouth and chewed, mouth open. "And I know they'll pay very well for what they want."

"Well then, for such excellent, good-paying customers, I think we could certainly find them what they're looking for." Annahede winked. "You know how much I believe in keeping the customers happy."

"Oh, yes, I do. So, you come see me at nine tomorrow morning and we'll finalize the deal." He slugged down the last of his Manhattan then stared at his empty glass. "Guess you better make it ten."

Annahede wasn't sure Donahue would remember this conversation at all come morning. Admittedly, I hoped that, for her sake, he had forgotten all he had said in his drunken stupor. But that was not to be the case.

Annahede burst in the cottage door. "I got the job! Donahue is going to pay me *so* much money, and just for, well, what he's calling 'public relations.'"

I just couldn't help but wonder – and worry about – what her true work-related duties would be.

I just kept folding our laundry. "Are you sure you want to take this job?"

"What? Are you crazy? Of course I do! This is why I've been kissing up to that sleaze Donahue for all these days. Now I've gotten in so quickly, and this is just the beginning."

"That's what I'm afraid of. The beginning of what?"

"Working at the convention center, of course! Yeah, and I've got some great opportunities to work my way up there, too. Do you have any idea how much money changes hands under the table at that place? Just do a few favors and there's cash in your wallet."

"Well, it's the favors I'm worried about." I continued folding, not looking up.

"What do you mean?" Annahede put her fists on her hips. "Are you still worried about all that 'dish it out' crap Donahue was going on about? He was just being drunk and stupid. You don't have to worry about me doing any of that sluttish stuff. I'm not going to sell my soul."

But I still worried that Annahede had already sealed the deal with the devil. Even if Annahede had no plans to act as an escort herself, I couldn't stand the thought of her possibly getting involved in some sort of escort service. Nevertheless, she pursued her dream, starting work immediately at the convention center – and resigning without notice from Simple Pleasures.

"I knew I shouldn't have hired you Michiganders in the first place!" Mr. Paigre tossed old job apps and his spectacles on the counter. "You can never count on them."

In the days that followed Annahede's departure, I became the target of Mr. Paigre's never-ending animosity. He constantly berated me for what he referred to as my inability to properly serve the clientele. I would have taken issue with his badgering, but I had to admit that I did struggle with some aspects of service, like the requirement that we remember people's orders without writing them down. Usually, if I made a mistake with this, it was easily remedied, but that was not the case one evening when I made a horrendous error.

"I'd like my fillet medium well, but not too medium." The elderly woman was heavy-set making it difficult for her to scoot up to the table. "I like that tiny hint of pink that adds a bit of moisture to the steak, but I can't stand to have it moo at me."

"The chef will need to butterfly cut it to prepare it that way." I pointed to her menu where this fact was spelled out.

"Well, of course he will, my dear." Her lips spread wide with her over-enunciation of each word, revealing that her harsh red lipstick had smeared on her two front teeth. "That's how they cook out that disgusting bloody-red middle. Anyway, I do want the béarnaise sauce, but leave off that bit of crab they like to sprinkle on it. I can't have crab – it doesn't set well with me. Oh, and I'd like extra of that béarnaise sauce. It's so yummy."

"And what potato would you like, ma'am?"

"Well, let's see. I guess I'd have Lyonnais potatoes."

"Ours are more of a hash brown, ma'am."

"Well then, have the chef add a little onion to mine. It gives them such a better flavor, don't you think? And ask him to slice the onion, not dice it. That gives it a much better texture."

"I'll see what he can do." I started to back away, hoping to find a moment to wait on my other tables.

"Oh, and don't forget to bring me a lemon for my drink, dear. This lime in my rum and tonic will never do. It totally ruins the taste. Here, I'll send this wedge back with you." She pulled the lime off the edge of her glass and placed it in my hand.

I was so sure that I told the cook to leave off the crab, but he claimed I didn't. And I didn't see it buried under that extra helping of béarnaise sauce, so I served it to the woman who it turned out was allergic to shellfish. After a few bites, she puffed up like a marshmallow in a microwave. That turned out to be my last night waitressing at Simple Pleasures.

Upon my firing, I headed back to our cottage with a surprising sense of relief. I had hated working at that place, feeling alone and abandoned there ever since Annahede had left. I found myself wondering if my subconscious had intervened, intentionally forcing myself to error so I could leave. Then I wondered why I hadn't just left days earlier when Annahede had quit. I suppose it was the need for money that had driven me to stay, and it was this same need that made me wonder what I would do now.

I arrived home expecting to find the place empty since Annahede now worked so many long, odd shifts of time. But to my surprise, I found Annahede at home, visiting in the kitchen with a couple of Saints I'd never met.

"You're home early." She seemed a bit surprised by my arrival.

"I'm home for good." I shut the door and went to the sink for a drink. "Paigre fired me."

"Oh, that's great!" Annahede threw her hands in the air with enthusiasm.

"Did you hear me? I said Paigre fired me. Tell me how that's great."

"Because now you can work for me."

"Work for you?" I took a quick drink from my water glass. "Since when are you an employer?"

"Since another local took notice of my 'people skills.' I've been contracted to do some, ah, soliciting I guess you could call it – to find some young women willing to commit to a few months of quiet, easy work, all for a major pile of money. Why, I was just talking to these two young ladies about the program."

I gazed at the two young Saint women, most likely somewhere in their mid to late twenties. They were still dressed in their maid uniforms, probably having just finished their long day at work. They both gazed back at me with timid grins but said nothing.

Annahede walked toward me. "Let me fill you in on the deal."

"No, I'd rather you not." I held up my hands in a motion to halt. "I think I've got a pretty good idea of what the deal is. It's just another scheme, another way of taking the money from under the table – to get rich quick and head for the top."

"Well, not exactly." She tilted her head and raised her dark eyebrows. "It's not a ticket to the top, but it sure is a ticket out. You see, it's so simple. You just have to –"

"I'm going to pass this time, Annahede. Why don't you go ahead and explain it to the girls here. They seem willing and interested. I've just got other plans in the works."

"What other plans?"

"You're too busy now – I'll fill you in later. Got to go." Quickly, I grabbed my jacket and dashed out the door before she could ask me another question.

When I left the cottage, I wasn't sure which way I should go but felt certain I needed to head in a new direction. I decided to walk a path I'd never taken before, along an overgrown brick sidewalk that led further inland.

As I hiked along the awkward path, I thought about Annahede, the stranger I'd thought I'd known so well. With her blatant hatred for her father's treatment of women, she seemed the least likely person to ever solicit girls for any unseemly purpose, and yet this was apparently what she was up to. I was rudely awakening to the fact that there were things Annahede valued more than the dignity of women – like money and the independence it could buy.

Stumbling across a misplaced brick, I tripped off the trail and fell to my knees on the cool clay earth. As I stood up and brushed the dirt from my hands, I noticed the glow of a neon sign barely visible through the overhang of weeping willows and low hanging maple branches. I continued along the path as it headed toward the sign, finally bringing me to the doorstep of a humble pub.

Although one florescent tube was burned out, I could still make out the name *Biminis* amid the remaining glowing light. Despite the chill in the air, the door was propped open, inviting passers by to just wander in. With little money in my pocket and no place better to go, I decided to give it a try.

To my pleasant surprise, I found it to be just the right place. The cozy timber and fieldstone room brimmed with an eclectic mix of Saints and locals, both young and old, who huddled together at rustic tables and the teakwood bar. They chattered and laughed over pints and pewter mugs as a fire roared in the corner fireplace. Even with the draft blowing through, Biminis felt warm and inviting.

"You're new!" A short, bleached-blonde barmaid greeted me while placing mugs on a nearby table. "Not a Fudgie, are you?"

"Trying not to be." I walked toward the bar.

"Well, then pull up a stool there and I'll bring you the first round on the house – Biminis' gift to newcomers, hoping you'll be sure to come back."

"How nice." I pulled back a stool and took a seat. From this vantage point, I could take in the camaraderie of the patrons. They seemed a tight-knit group, like everyone knew one another, strolling between tables and the bar to pick up new conversation with old friends.

"Hi there. I'm Pepper," the bleached-blonde introduced herself.

"I'm Carly."

"Glad you stopped in. So, what'll it be – what's on tap, or the door."

"Pepper!" A gentleman behind the bar yelled at her. "She's new – doesn't know your bent sense of humor yet, so just give her a break and give her whatever she wants."

"Sorry," Pepper said both to him and me. "Guess you can have whatever."

"Whatever's on tap is fine, thanks."

"Good girl." She grabbed a mug, stuck it under the spout, and pulled the lever to pour. "What else can I get you?"

"How about a job?"

"Oh, so you're a local then." Pepper handed me my beer.

"More of a local-wannabe."

"Hey, I like that one." Pepper grinned. "And I like you. Pretty funny, aren't you."

"Not usually. I'm just having a rough night – need to lighten things up."

"Well, I think you're pretty funny, and you didn't even have to tell me some short-people story or stupid-blonde joke to make me laugh, so you're all right with me. I'll see if we can get you an application."

As she stepped away, I took a sip from my beer then glanced around the place. The bar was filled with the working folks of Windemere Island who had likely come to Biminis at day's end to relax and unwind with those who had spent the day working every bit as hard. This was more my type of place – the kind of community, or family, that I had been looking for and very much wanted to be a part of.

Suddenly a gust of wind flared up, blowing the smell of springs' first cut of grass and the damp night air into the bar through the open doorway before catching the door and slamming it shut. At first, the startling noise brought a brief pause to all conversation, but then people began to laugh and pick up where they'd left off.

"Dot be de islond ghost blowon' de winds a change." A Saint across the room rose up from his seat. "Somedon's go-on' te be hoppenon' different 'round here – I con feel it."

The bartender leaned up to the bar. "Don't be expecting it to be a drop in beer prices." He chuckled, and the rest of the crowd laughed along with him.

But I could feel it, too. A change was coming, and I very much needed to get myself on the right track. I wasn't sure how everything would play out, but I knew the time had come for me to set my own course and see it through.

Chapter 4

KEEPING THE SECRET

THE HOURS QUICKLY CLICKED BY when I was on duty waitressing at my new job at Biminis. It was a surprisingly busy place but in a fun sort of way. I enjoyed waiting on the locals and Saints as they came and went after a quick snack or a coffee during the working hours, then piled into the place at quitting time for a cold one among friends.

Armed with a handy pencil stub and scratch pad, I had no problems keeping drink and appetizer orders straight. The tips weren't as good, but that was okay since I was given more hours to make up the difference. And I was much more comfortable working at Biminis where I was able to wait on those who considered me more of a friend than a servant.

I also loved my newly found neighborhood where I was working, a cozy little four-corner village called Me-Wanna-Go-Home. It was an area where most Saints lived and where Fudgies seldom set foot. With Biminis located just on the edge of the village, it seemed like a bit of a private club for the locals and Saints. The only thing the place lacked was a sign that read, "Fudgies Stay Out."

"It's not so much that we don't like the Fudgies." Pepper pulled clean beer mugs from the steaming dishwasher. "We love Fudgies – they're our life blood. It's just that after long days of listening to them ask stupid questions – like 'At what time does the five-mile-long Mackinac Bridge swing over to the island?' – I guess we just need a little break."

I wiped the damp mugs and placed them on a serving tray. "They don't really ask questions like that."

"Oh, yes they do! Just yesterday I was down at the dock when the Revolutionary War sloop 'Welcome' came into port. I heard a Fudgie down there telling the crowd how the sails were made out of skin taken from local sharks. Then he asked me about the Goodyear tires hanging off the side of the ship. He wanted to know if they were the originals or replicas."

Pepper was full of stories like these, always keeping things lively at Biminis. With her winning smile and contagious giggle, she made the patrons feel welcomed while still getting away with her quick-witted one-liners. At a height of only four-foot ten, she never let anyone push her around. For the occasional newcomers who tried, she'd quickly teach them that she could hold her own.

"Hey, little girl." A new, middle-aged patron unfolded his napkin and placed his silverware. "Are you old enough to be serving me a beer?"

"If you're not too young to drink it by yourself." Pepper grabbed his spoon and held it up to his mouth. "I'm too busy to be spoon-feeding the customers."

Amid her remarks Pepper seldom talked about herself or her own business, but she sure made it a point to know everyone else's. When it came to the happenings on the island, she knew all that was unfit to print, and then some, and she was willing to share her wealth of knowledge with me.

"You should know what's going on with that so-called friend of yours, Annahede," she told me while we were closing. "Since she started working at the convention center, she's become quite the little entrepreneur."

I scrubbed burned grease from the bottom of a pan. "Yeah, I know."

"No, I don't think you do. I hear she's lined up quite the harem, a nice blend of both locals and Saints for whatever suits the clientele."

Even though I tended to be very naïve, I still had an inkling that Pepper was right. Over recent days I had come home to the cottage to find Annahede meeting with one or two young Saint women and couldn't help but wonder what they were up to. But whenever Annahede would offer to bring me into the loop, I'd refuse and quickly exit.

Unfortunately, a time came when I didn't leave quickly enough. Late one night, I returned home after closing at Biminis and entered the cottage through the backdoor in hopes I wouldn't wake Annahede. As I entered the kitchen, I overheard Annahede sort of "interviewing a prospect" in the living room. I guess they didn't here me come in.

"I'm a bit narvous obout dis," I overheard a Saint girl tell Annahede. "Dares too moch secrot obout de people I'd be meeton'."

"Trust me, they're fine," Annahede replied. "They're very professional about this. You'll be very safe in their care."

"Ond you say I con't tell my Dod? I know he'll be vera worried obout me, ond I don't want to be frightenon' him."

"Don't worry about that. He sent you here to make money, didn't he? And he'll be so surprised when you return to St. Croix with more than he could've ever imagined. Besides, he's just been using you all along, sending you here all alone to make money for him. If you asked me, I'd say he's pretty selfish to be sending his sixteen-year-old off like that, so you shouldn't worry about what he thinks."

"You're only sixteen?" I interrupted, sticking my head around the corner to face the Saint.

"Who – who are you?" The Saint girl was startled by my sudden appearance.

"She's my housemate, Carly." Annahede turned to her guest. "Meet Lizbeth – and yes, she is sixteen."

"You're encouraging this sixteen-year-old girl to... to do whatever it is you're doing?" I walked closer to Annahede.

Annahede stood up from her seat, glaring at me with fierce eyes. "She's actually almost seventeen, and if she's old enough to be here alone, then she's old enough to make her own decisions."

"And you're telling her to not tell her father?"

"You were sayon' dot wos part of de deal." Lizbeth rose slightly from her seat. "Don't I hov to keep dis a secret?"

"Yes, you do." Annahede placed her hand on Lizbeth's shoulder, applying pressure that pushed her back into her seat. "Don't listen to Carly – she doesn't know what she's talking about."

"I know I'm talking about a sixteen-year-old – a minor! You shouldn't be getting a minor mixed up in your… your little brothel deal."

"Brothel!" Annahede indignantly sighed. "Is that what you think this is? You really are clueless, aren't you? You have no idea what's going on here, and I suppose if you're going to get up on your high-and-mighty ethical pedestal, it's best you stay in the dark."

"I'm not so sure dis is a good idea for me getton' into dis now." The Saint stood and pulled her sweater off the back of the chair. "I don't wanna be getton' messed up in some illegal do-on's dot might get me shipped bock to my dod in shame." She headed for the door.

"There's no shame about this." Annahede followed her. "I promise you, when your Dad finds out what you've done for others – and for your own family – he's going to be so proud of you."

"Yeah, bot he won't be hoppy obout my keepon' secrots from him. I best be waiton' on dis 'cause it's not right for me." The Saint quickly exited out the front door.

As the door slammed shut, Annahede immediately turned to me. "What the hell do you think you're doing, meddling in my business?" She stormed closer to me. "I had almost convinced her – almost. And then you had to come in here and start in with your self-righteous 'she's a minor' speech when you don't even know what you're talking about!"

"I just don't think it's right for you to encourage a child to do something that might be… questionable, and to lie to her parents."

"What you call 'questionable' isn't necessarily 'wrong.' And I didn't tell her to lie to her dad – I just told her not to tell him anything. Saying nothing isn't lying."

"And so, you see, that's how we're so different." I looked away from her. "I'm not willing to twist words to justify doing something I know I shouldn't be doing, and I'm –"

"It's not a bad thing we're doing! Frankly, I think it's a very good thing – for everybody."

"So, why's it such a secret?"

"It just has to be." She stepped around me, back into my view where she could look me in the eyes. "See, let me explain. It just starts out like this –"

"I don't want to know!" I covered my ears and stepped back. "Just leave me out of this. I'm so tired of coming home to all of your secret dealings and feeling like I have to leave. This doesn't feel like my place anymore."

"Nobody's making you stay."

I paused to consider this revelation. "You know what? You're right."

"Am I?"

"Yes. I don't have to stay. I can't really afford this place, and you can. I've been stressed out about my share of the cost of renting this place, but with your newfound wealth, it's no big deal for you to make the payments."

"Wait a minute – maybe I don't want to pay for this place by myself."

"But you put down the deposit money and signed the lease alone. Guess you've got the place all to yourself from now on."

Annahede tried to continue the argument, following me about the house as I haphazardly packed, but I ignored her. I was finished with the arguing, with the secrets, and with her. The time had come for us to part ways.

I quickly finished packing what little I owned and left with Annahede still yelling at me as I wheeled my suitcases down the road.

She stood on the porch, one hand on her hip and the other waving a finger at me. "You'll be back, and then you'll still have to pay your half of the rent once you realize there's no other decent place to live." Then she turned and went back inside, slamming the door behind her.

As I hiked along, dragging my few worldly possessions behind me, I did wonder where I would find a place to live. I feared that Annahede was probably right; that it would be hard, if not impossible, to find a reasonable place to live. It was a terrible dilemma that I knew I'd have to face tomorrow, but for the moment, I didn't really care.

I had the key to Biminis and figured this would provide me at least one night's rest with a roof over my head. It wouldn't be pleasant, but at least I'd be safe.

Letting myself in, I looked around for the best place to put my head down. The few booths in the place had bench seats with padding, but they were too short and narrow for me to lie down on. There was no way I was going to sleep on the dirty, beer-soaked floor, and short of pulling some chairs together, I was running out of options. Then I remembered that Mike had a worn out coach in his office. Since he was an open-door-policy kind of guy, he always left the room open to us for coming and going as we pleased, and so I decided to camp out there in hopes he wouldn't mind too much just this one time.

Pushing up on the cushioned, thread-bare armrest until it somewhat resembled a pillow, I rested my head on it and then pulled my old comforter up and over me. Rolling about a bit, I finally found a reasonably comfortable spot to rest. This would do for now, and so I closed my eyes in search of a little rest before sunrise, hoping that come morning I'd have the good sense to figure out where I should go from here.

Chapter 5

NO PLACE LIKE HOME

"THE DOOR WAS UNLOCKED when I came in this morning," a firm voice woke me. It was my boss, Mike Callahan, and he was standing over me with a baseball bat in his hands. "I thought somebody broke in, but guess it was just you – must have forgot to lock up."

Quickly, I climbed up from my night on his couch. "Oh, I am so sorry! I must have forgotten to lock up when I came in."

"No harm done." Callahan stepped away and put the bat back behind his desk. "Nothings broken, looks like nothings been stolen, and most importantly, you're okay. But you've got to be more careful, especially with all that's going on around here."

"Oh, I will be." I folded my comforter and placed it with my bags. "Sorry to even be here, and about all of my things. I just had a bit of a falling-out with –"

"Don't explain. I try to stay out of employees' business. It's no problem – just don't make it a habit."

"I won't."

I wanted to keep my promise, but wasn't sure how I would – that was, until I talked it over with Pepper when she showed up for work.

"My bunkmate got homesick and went back to St. Croix – left me holding the bill for my room at the boarding house."

"So there's room for me?"

"Well, I'm not sure I'd call it room, but there is a bunk you could sleep in. It's a really small space, but reasonably priced and that would sure help out both of us financially." Pepper punched her time card. "We'll just take your stuff there after work and you can stay 'til you decide. It beats another night on Mike's couch here."

When time permitted, we chatted on and off during our shift about Pepper's place, a third floor room in the island's largest boarding house located just north of Me-Wanna-Go-Home.

"What's with the crazy village name?" I asked when we met up at the cash register.

"Guess the Saints in the neighborhood didn't like the old name, Servitude – can't imagine why." Pepper started ringing up her table's bill. "About twenty-some years back, the Saints living there petitioned to change the name."

"But why 'Me-Wanna-Go-Home?'"

"That's pretty normal for them." Pepper continued punching the register keys. "A lot of Caribbean towns have names like that – like one in Jamaica called 'Me-No-Sen-You-No-Come.'" She punched the total key and reached for the receipt. "I always wondered if they got it from Harry Belafonte – you know, *The Banana Boat Song.*" She launched into her own rendition of *Day-O* but couldn't carry the tune.

I took over the register, punching the keys for my own table's bill. "Maybe they picked it because they'd rather be back at their homes in the Caribbean."

"That could be, because they sure as hell wouldn't call that boarding house home." Pepper placed her receipt on a change plate and started off for her table. "When you see it, you'll know what I mean – and I can guarantee you won't be singing about it."

We punched out at the same time, in the afternoon when others took over our shift. Then we hauled my belongings to the boarding house.

Upon arrival, I found Pepper's portrayal of the place to be disappointingly accurate – a giant step backward from what I'd grown accustomed to at the cottage. Annahede and I had enjoyed the luxury of a two-bedroom, one-bath home with a small kitchen and living area. In stark contrast, room 314 was an extremely cramped space within a four-story, poorly maintained structure. I was quite sure this single room dwelling wouldn't even qualify as a dorm room.

The living space was further restricted by its contents. The room was too small to accommodate twin beds, so bunk beds were pressed to one side. On the other side, Pepper had set up a makeshift kitchen just under the room's one window. It consisted of a small table cluttered with a crock-pot, toaster oven, and mini-microwave. Pepper had rented a miniature refrigerator that was stashed underneath. To the right of the window, two large lockers stood side-by-side and extended from floor to ceiling. There was hardly enough space left to turn around.

"There's storage space in the basement for stuff you don't regularly use." Pepper pushed one of my suitcases into the room. "But you have to be careful how you stack it. Things on the bottom might get wet if the place floods again."

"Floods! What are you talking about?"

"Not the main floors." She lifted my suitcase up onto the lower bunk. "This building's built on clay soil – doesn't drain well, I guess. When the snow melted late in the spring, we had a few inches of water in the basement."

"That's awful."

"Not much you can do about it. A few Saints left some of their things down there last winter and came back this season to find most of it ruined. Of course, our kind slumlord Frank Mansfield never bothered to move the stuff out of the water – just left it there to rot. And when the Saints asked for reimbursement, he told them to take a hike."

"Sounds like a great guy." I opened my suitcase and took out a few essentials.

"Yeah, he's a piece of work. The Saints here tell me that some of their bosses have complained for years about the awful conditions. Why, just last summer, six Saints went to the local first aid station for heat exhaustion." Pepper reached over to a mini-fan clipped to the foot of her bed and clicked in on low. "Now, I know the winds can be kind of chilly around here, but when it dies off and the sun beats down on this trap, it can get beastly hot in here."

Despite wondering what I was getting into, I continued unpacking. "Doesn't he get in trouble for that?"

"Who's going to fight him? You think these Saints or a few college students, or anyone else like you and me that lives in this place can afford attorney fees? No, we have to count on a good-hearted, philanthropic local with a thick wallet to do our bidding – and that guy is Vincent Hanika."

I had heard the name Hanika mentioned about town since my recent arrival. I had come to the conclusion that he was a bit of a recluse, often spoken of but never seen. He also sounded like a bit of a local legend, a self-made man who had done well by his community.

People had strong opinions about him; either they really liked him or deeply despised him. When working, I overheard some of my least favorite patrons uttering hateful remarks about him over cocktails, but those whom I most respected would often sing his praises. The same was true with the rest of my new neighbors inside the boarding house, and that was made most evident when I first met our proud, self-assured, robust next-door neighbor named Rosie DeSantaes.

"So, you're de one dot Pep-par's been tellon' us obout." Dressed in her customary muumuu, Rosie stayed seated on a crate in the corner of her tight room, a space that seemed too limited for someone of her stature.

"Well, hope it's all been good," I replied, remaining in her doorway with Pepper at my side.

"Ond I hope it's all been de truth, 'cause we don't need no more trouble oround here don we already got now." Rosie fanned herself with a magazine. "Whew! Should move bock to St. Maarten if it's go-on' te be dis hot in here! Dot bod mon's got to fix de air or I'll be next one ot de first aid station."

Pepper wiped at her forehead. "Yeah, I'm hoping that Mr. Hanika's threats will finally make Mansfield get it fixed right."

"Dot kind, rich mon, Mr. Honika – he's takon' on dot mean Monsfield for de sake of all of us!" She flailed her burly arms and shook her meaty fists as she ranted with passion. "He's de one who told dot Monsfield he'd be sue-on' him if he wosn't getton' us de air conditionon' we need."

Her room was too cramped to enter, so I spoke with her from her doorway. "I haven't met this Mr. Hanika, but I've heard about him – sounds like a really nice guy."

"Whot? You hovn't spotted de rich mon, Miss Carly? You need to be getton' out more. Why, he owns de biggest hotel on de island ond made mill-yons of dollors sellon' drugs – de honest way. Whot is it dey call dot?"

"Oh, you mean that he worked for, like, some kind of pharmaceutical company?"

"He didn't work for it – he wos de one ownon' it. Guess he sold it 'cause he didn't like how tings were go-on', and now de mon puts his money toward helpon' us folks."

Norma Paige, a neighboring Saint who garishly bleached her hair yellow, swayed her wide-hips up to the doorway and butted into our conversation. "Dot Honika hosn't done ennaton' bot a lot 'a big mon talkon'. He needs to do someton' obout dot Monsfield now before he –"

"Whot are you talkon' obout, littal garly?" Rosie stood, holding her head high as she marched to the doorway. "Dot Mr. Honika's been livon' here since before you wos born ond for all dot time he's been putton' his money into all sorts 'a tings for de less fortunot of us."

Norma scowled. "I hovn't seen none of it comon' my way. If he's soch de Mr. Rich Mon, why don't he jost come ovar here ond give me some of dot money dey say he's spreadon' oround?"

"Dares no reason to be givon' it to de ungrateful likes 'a you." Rosie crossed her arms tightly across her hefty chest.

"Beddar don waston' it oway on dot lawyar mon of his."

"Dot lawyar's de one who's gonna make Monsfield fix de air conditionon'. He's tellon' Monsfield dot if he don't get it fixed, Mr. Honika's go-on te sue him." Rosie jabbed her finger towards Norma. "Ond he's do-on' all dot on de Saints behof, includon' yours!"

"Well, de air's still not workon', ond if he's such de big mon, he should be do-on' a whole lot more obout it." And with that, Norma stormed off.

Once I moved in, I found there were many days when the air-conditioning malfunctioned and we were forced to revert back to the ineffective method of opening wide every screenless window in the place with fans blaring full force. Mansfield did come by to check on the system and he was livid to find what he called "a senseless waste of energy." We all knew his real concern was for the added expense on his electric bill.

"You idiots!" He wiped beads of perspiration off the bald patch atop of his head. "The system's trying to cool down the building, and you're up here letting all the cold air out by leaving your windows wide open. You're just making it worse!"

"We won't be closon' dese windows 'til it cools down oround here." Rosie stood firmly, feet apart and arms crossed, a stern look on her face. She had taken it upon herself to act as spokesperson for the building's tenants.

"Don't you people realize that you're just sucking in hot air with all these fans blowing full force? You're not thinking!" Mansfield gnawed an extinguished cigar butt, its potent stench still lingering on his mismatched madras shirt and shorts.

Rosie pounded her fist in her palm. "De fons will stay on 'til de air cools down." Then she turned away from Mansfield and marched into her room, slamming the door behind her.

Mansfield threw up his arms. "You people just can't be reasoned with! I'll be back to deal with this later!" Then he, too, turned on his heels and stormed off.

The following day, Pepper and I returned from shopping to find a pleasant surprise. Somehow the circulation system had been repaired and cool, comfortable air was pouring out of the vents into the building's corridors. We excitedly burst into our room to close the window and shut out the afternoon heat, but our exuberance turned to confusion when we found the window already closed.

Pepper stepped to the window. "Did you take the fan out of the window before you left?"

"No, I thought maybe you did."

Pepper set down her small bag of groceries on the lower bunk and stared at the unplugged fan sitting in front of the refrigerator.

I stepped inside and shut the door. "Did we forget to put it in the window before we left?"

"Not a chance. That thing's been running constantly for the past four days. It couldn't have..." She stopped mid thought to test the window latch. "It's locked – and we never lock it." She paused. "Somebody's been in here."

"Oh, that's crazy." I stepped to the window to look for myself. "Who would break in, then take the time to lock the window and door on the way out?"

The answer became obvious when Pepper unlocked the window and tried to open it. "What the hell!" Pepper jammed her fingers while jerking on the handle.

The window wouldn't open, not even a crack. Pepper checked the lock and yanked the window again. It didn't budge.

"Why won't this thing open?" She grunted through clenched teeth while attempting to jar the thing open.

Close examination of the windowsill revealed a couple of holes, one on each vertical side not more than an eighth-of-an-inch in diameter. Every hole contained fresh spackle.

"I need a pencil." Pepper grabbed one from the shelf and quickly whittled the putty from one hole, revealing the head of a nail.

She leaned back, staring at her work. "That jerk nailed the window shut!"

"What? You think Mansfield came in here and did this?"

"Actually, I doubt it. Bet he hired some jerk willing to do his dirty work for him."

I took the pencil from Pepper and whittled at another putty spot, wanting to see for myself. "So how did these people get in to do this?"

"Mansfield's got a master key to all these rooms. He probably had every window in the building nailed shut."

"I can't believe this! You mean to tell me he can come in and out of this room anytime he pleases?"

"Apparently."

"That's it! We're packing up and moving out of here."

Pepper glared at me. "And where do you think you'll be going this time? You know there aren't any reasonably priced places left to rent, and I can't afford to lose my deposit. Besides, you shouldn't keep running away from your problems."

Although Pepper's sharp words caught me a bit off guard, I knew she was right. I had to face Mr. Mansfield along with her and all the other tenants. Yes, he was in a great position to keep on victimizing his tenants simply because they couldn't afford to leave and had nowhere else to go. But with no other reasonable options, I'd just have to buck-up and make the best of things, at least for the time being.

I sat down on the edge of the lower bunk. "So, I admit it – we're stuck. Now what are we going to do?"

"For now, nothing." Pepper began unpacking groceries.

I stood up. "But what about all that 'standing up to your problems' business?"

She stopped unpacking. "Like I just said, for right now, there's no problem. The air-conditioning's working, and you know, it actually feels pretty darn good in here." She returned to unpacking, pulling the last two cans out of the grocery bag. "Yeah, I'm good with things, at the moment." She folded the sack and tucked it under her arm. "But I'll tell you what – the next time the air system shuts down, I'm busting that window wide open."

Admittedly, things were all right for the moment. We had food and shelter, and for the first time since the summer heat had set in, we had cool air circulating around us. I was comfortable and content for now, but deep inside me I knew I needed something more – and admittedly, I was looking forward to the next time the air conditioner would break.

Chapter 6

RUMOR HAS IT

"MISSING" WAS BOLDLY PRINTED across the top of posters I found tacked to bulletin boards on every floor of our building and stapled to telephone poles around the village. The posters included passport photos of two women, both Saints in their late twenties. At the bottom of their photos their names were listed: Missy Brown and Helena Moore.

"Dose two ladies hov been misson' for more don three weeks now." Rosie pointed to the women's pictures posted on our hallway bulletin board. "De islond police… dey know dares foul play here, but dey takon' dare own sweet time to do ennaton' obout it."

"Do you know them?" I asked her.

"Not Miss Moore. I've been told she's been livon' wid her momma ond her littal garl down closar to de row of hotals."

"I know obout her." Norma Paige stepped up, poking her ring-clad fingers at the photo of Helena. "I worked wid her. She's a real pain in de bott – got de boss mon te make me come in for her a couple 'a times 'cause dot daughtar of hars wos sick. Yoss, she's expecton' me te be workon' when she supposed te – dot garl's a real bitch."

Rosie glared at Norma. "You shouldn't be callon' dot kettol block when you're a big, fot pot yourself!"

Norma crossed her arms, huffed loudly, and stomped off.

"What about Missy?" I asked Rosie. "You know her?"

"Missy was livon' on de next floor obove us, ond I tink dot's hitton' too close to our home."

"I can't believe someone didn't hear something."

"Dot is, only if she went ogonst her will. Dey say dare wos no sign of a forced entray, ond all her belongon's were in ordar.

Nobody in de buildon' could remembar see-on' enna-one strange oround de place." Rosie turned from the bulletin board and walked toward our rooms. "But dot don't put mah mind te ease knowon' dares uddars misson' from our buildon'.

I tagged along. "There are others?"

"Not accordon' to de police, but we know dare are Saint womon who've left widout a word." Rosie stopped walking and looked me in the eyes. "So, no one really knows if dey are okay, now do dey?"

The disappearance of Saints who had been rooming in our complex raised more concerns regarding the safety of those who resided in the building. Although there had been no signs of any struggle or theft, some still wondered if the women of our building were being targeted for some reason.

Most of the locals who regulared Biminis had a different take on the situation. They had heard through their police connections that the girls were good friends who worked as housekeepers at the same local hotel and that they consistently walked to and from work together at the same set time each day. From these facts, people assumed the women had been abducted from somewhere between work and Helena's home.

"Stop fussin'. Them Saint girls are just fine," grumbled Bob Gould, a thin but rugged street cleaner who regularly took a seat at Biminis bar for his morning break. "Bet they just skipped town, probly went gamblin' at that Indian casino up in the U.P. – that's what we call the Upper Peninsula, in case ya didn't know, Carly."

"I know what the U.P. is, Bob." I noticed his first round was almost gone, so I started fixing another cup of coffee – with his usual half-shot of Jack Daniels again, of course.

Bob lifted his cup and took in the last of his drink, then set the empty mug on the bar. "Yeah, I bet they're havin' a good ole' time."

I took his empty cup, replacing it with a hot brew. "But they didn't pack anything, and they've been gone for a while. That doesn't make sense."

"Don't be stupid, Carly. It makes loads of sense." Bob tended to be cranky until he'd finished his second round. "I'm tellin' ya they didn't plan to go so long, but they probly hit it big on the slots or black jack, then headed out somewhere to blow their winnin's on clothes or jewelry or some other dumb thing women would buy."

"But that Helena girl wouldn't have left her daughter."

"Why not?" Bob lifted his steaming cup with his filthy, lean hands. "She knew her mom would watch her kid. She probably figured she'd ditch her excess baggage for a while — that is, until the money runs out. Then she'll be back."

There was no sense arguing with those who already had decided that these girls were off gallivanting. Even when it was reported that there had been no big winners at the casinos in recent days, their theories did not subside and their farfetched stories continued to fly.

I was astonished to discover that substantial number of Saints in my building devoutly believed in black magic and were convinced that evil spirits had whisked these two women away, probably as a punishment for their past evil deeds.

"Dose womon must 'a been do-on' bod tings to be takon' like dot," Rosie told a couple of girls in our hallway. "You best be livon' desont or de evil ones might be takon' you off right into de night!"

That same evening, the local voodoo priest known as the "obeah man" was summoned to help exorcise all of the evil spirits from the building. He went about the rooms and hallways burning a lot of candles and giving people gris-gris to wear about their necks. Then he squatted outside of Missy Brown's room with a dead chicken in his hands and quietly proceeded to remove its entrails.

I joined the spectators, absolutely appalled by what I was witnessing. "That's so disgusting! Why is he doing that?"

"Sh!" Rosie held her index finger to her lips.

"But he's making such a mess, and you know Mansfield will be so ticked!"

"Den let him be." Rosie moved her finger from her lips to mine, whispering, "Be quiet, garl. De obeah mon is reachon' out to de evil spirits who got Missy ond he's go-on te osk where dey hov takon her ond why she's gone."

After a lot of cutting, pulling, and blood-letting, the obeah man eventually gazed up. "Dese evil spirits are powarful. Dey'll only say dot it's secrot, ond dey will not tell us ennamore now."

I wasn't a gambler and had never practiced voodoo, so I couldn't speak from personal experience. But each theory struck me as too feeble a reason to abandon home and family. The only fact I believed the obeah man got right was that something evil was at work.

Chapter 7

DISPOSABLE

"GOT A MESSAGE IN THE TRASH today." Harvey Trudeau strutted into the bar for his morning cup of coffee. As one of the island's sanitation workers, Harvey enjoyed sharing with us all the titillating details of people's garbage.

"So, what's the message?" I poured him a hot cup of his usual decaf.

"This one was unique, a one-of-a-kind find." Harvey was known for trying to draw out the suspense on what usually proved to be insignificant.

"Let us all know when you're ready to share." I turned to wait on other customers.

"Okay. I'm ready." Harvey stood up from his seat to address the bar. "Everybody – I found something I'm supposed to keep it secret, but if you guess, I'll tell you you're right."

Callahan wiped spilled water off from the bar top. "It's too early for guessing games." He yawned.

"Then I guess you're not interested in what the police are checking out." He started to sit down.

"Okay. Okay. I give." Callahan tossed the damp towel over his shoulder. "Just tell us what you found, Harvey."

"All right then. Since I know you'll all keep it secret, I can tell ya." He rose to his feet again. "I found... a body."

"What are you talking about?" I abruptly turned back to Harvey as the bar's patrons and employees fell silent.

"I found a body. When I finished my first run, I went to unload, and there it was, face up in the dumpster... and let me tell ya, that's a creepy thing to find first thing in the morning."

"Whose body was it?" Callahan stepped out from behind the bar now that Harvey had everyone's attention.

"I don't know. Looked like some Saint woman. They seem to think it was one of them girls that's been missin', like a Morton or Morrow —"

"Helena Moore?" I guessed.

"Don't know her name. All's I know is it was definitely a Saint, dead as a door nail, staring me in the face."

"How awful." I returned to waiting on other patrons.

"You bet it was!" Harvey sat back down. "She's buck-naked, and looked like her wrists and ankles was all cut up and blood-crusted, like she'd been all tied up or somethin'."

I refilled a patron's cup. "You probably shouldn't be telling us all of this, Harvey."

He ripped open a sugar pack and poured it in his cup. "So, you don't want to hear about the note?"

"You didn't see no note, Harvey." Bob Gould interjected from a corner table, his coffee with whiskey gripped firmly in his fist. "Now yer just makin' stuff up."

"Swear on the good book, there was a note." Harvey ripped open another sugar pack. "There was a note stuck to the body with a great big mother-of-a-safety-pin." He poured more sugar into his coffee. "It was all crusted over with black blood, too, from where it got rammed through the meaty flesh on her —"

"That's just gross." I grimaced. "We don't need to hear all that." I returned to the bar to refill my coffee pot, noticing there that my hands were slightly shaking.

"It was just stuck in her hand!" Harvey opened sugar pack three. "And the note was like one of them ransom notes in the movies — you know, with letters cut out of magazines and stuff."

"So what'd it say, Mr. Know-It-All?" Bob slammed down the last of his Jack Daniels brew. "Bet ya don't know."

"Do so," Harvey added pack three to his cup and stirred. "Somethin' like how we need to 'dispose' of the Saints, or that they're 'trash' — or some kinda garbage-like words they used."

"See, ya don't know." Bob flagged me to bring him his second whiskey coffee. "You don't know nothin'."

"I do so. I just didn't want to stare or stick my face down too close, you know."

"And it's a good thing," boomed a voice from the doorway as the door swung shut behind him.

It was Windemere's Chief of Police, Beau Sinclaire, gracing us with his presence for the first time since I'd started working there. Pepper had told me a little about him – a native of the island who was respected by most despite being the son of the late Herbert Sinclaire, also a native who owned and operated Windemere's Ottawa Tavern until he drank himself to death.

"Little early for whiskey, ain't it, Chief?" Bob remarked.

"You know I never touch the hard stuff until afternoon, Gould – unlike some people I know." Sinclaire smiled at Bob, but then turned his attention to Harvey, walking directly toward him with a more serious expression. "I kind of figured I'd find you down here flapping your gums about this whole thing."

Harvey slouched a bit in his seat. "Well, ya gotta admit it ain't every day ya find a corpse in your dumpster, Chief."

"But I thought I asked you to keep it down about this, at least until word gets to the next-of-kin."

Harvey never looked up. "Sorry about that, Chief, but these guys at Biminis, ya know – they can just drag it right outta ya." He lifted his sweetened coffee and took a slurp.

Sinclaire stepped back from Harvey to address all the patrons and employees in general. "Well, I'd appreciate it if you'd keep this somewhat to yourselves until the mother's been told. She's been back in the Caribbean since her daughter went missing and we haven't reached her yet, but you know how fast bad news travels. And just remember, there's also a little girl to be thinking about in this mess."

"Understood," Callahan said. "Get you a coffee, Chief?"

"Sure, but I've got to get right back to the scene – told those troopers I'd just do some quick rumor control while they give the place one last look-over. You know, those state guys got their own way of doing things."

"Glad I'm not a cop today." Callahan poured the Chief's coffee into a tall Styrofoam cup. "That's got to be awful to see."

"It is." Sinclaire sighed. "It's bad enough for me, but for the troops? Let's just say I wouldn't want their job today."

While I cashed out a customer, I found myself wondering if Sinclaire was being honest. In my work I'd overheard more than one conversation about Sinclaire – how he'd wanted to become a trooper. The locals all said he'd been forced to settle for a job with the Windemere police when he failed to qualify for state training, probably due to that wrap of fat around his middle that forced him to buckle his belt down low, almost hidden under the bulge of his stomach. According to Pepper, he'd done well here, quickly making top rank and serving as Chief for fifteen years. But I had to wonder if, after all of these years, he was content with where he was and what he was doing.

"Coffee's on the house..." Callahan grabbed a plastic lid and pushed it onto the cup. "...with thanks for handling such a horrible situation." He handed the cup to Sinclaire.

"Well, thank you." Sinclaire took the gift. "Just doing the work I was meant to do." Then he turned to exit, making it a point to walk back past Harvey. "Speaking of plugging away at work, sure seems like you should be doing the same, Harvey."

"Naw, can't do mucha nothin' for a bit." Harvey nursed his coffee. "With all that yellow crime scene tape around them dumpsters, I been shut down. Guess I'll have to work late tonight, after you boys get finished with pickin' the place over."

"No, you'll be back at it shortly, Harvey. They're just about done."

Bob raised his mug of coffee with whiskey and tipped it in Sinclaire's general direction. "Good luck to ya, Chief. Bet ya got a bunch a gawkers to deal with, huh?"

"Not too bad," Sinclaire answered. "I pushed a couple away early on, and the troopers have kept the curious away since. With tourism down, there hasn't been much trouble, but it's best to keep the Fudgies away so they don't spread crazy rumors. We don't need them making things worse by scaring off the tourists – sending anymore packing for Mackinac Island."

"Well, at least it weren't no Fudgie that got killed." Bob snorted and took a swig. "Harvey here thought it was a Saint, weren't it, Chief?"

"Now, you know I can't confirm or deny anything like that, Bob, and I don't need you gossiping around when you don't know the facts."

After another swallow, Bob wiped his mouth and scruff with his free hand. "Then tell us the facts, Chief!"

"You'll know soon enough – probably too soon, in fact. The paper's already writing something, so get your scoop there. As for me, I best head back." Sinclaire headed toward the door, still speaking loudly enough to be heard by the entire bar. "Thanks folks for being quiet about this, especially for the family, but also for the sake of our island." And with that, he walked out the door.

Despite Sinclaire's plea, the whispers began the moment he stepped out of the door. At least no one spoke openly about events. They huddled in twos to quietly share their thoughts.

In the now subdued bar, Harvey no longer found an audience. He looked to me like he was about to burst when he quickly settled his bill, stiffed me on the tip, and took off. Something told me he wasn't in a hurry to get back to work.

It didn't take long for the rumors to spread like wild fire as newcomers to the bar brought with them more tales to tell of the day's events. As the day progressed, I listened as the stories became more farfetched and graphic, knowing full well that no one really knew anything. It seemed that this dead woman was to be victimized again – this time, by some horrible imaginations.

At least the release of a *Windemere Post* helped to squelch some rumors and bring us back to the facts.

The reporter confirmed that the victim was a Saint – a woman in her mid-twenties who was working as a maid at the French Landings. Her next-of-kin had been notified – a mother and daughter who had been forced to return to their homeland when the victim disappeared and they could no longer make ends meet. The victim had been identified as Helena Moore.

Those who were most intrigued, who wanted to hear the latest in titillating, gruesome details, were satisfied to learn the ultimate in disturbing facts: evidence suggested that she indeed had been bound, and there were suggestions that she may have been a victim of some kind of sexual assault. The coroner had not yet publicly released information regarding the cause of death, but it no longer mattered. For all who knew of this tragedy, everyone believed Helena had met with a terrible end.

Chapter 8

SPECULATION

WHEN TWO MORE SAINTS WENT MISSING, the rumor mill went into overdrive. It seemed like everyone had a theory about what terrible tortures awaited these women before their inevitable deaths, but no one had a guess about where to find them.

"This isn't right," I told Pepper as I climbed down from my top bunk and began dressing for the day. "It's like we're just waiting for more women to disappear or show up dead, and I don't see anyone trying to find these people."

"I'm sure somebody's working on it." Pepper stretched and slowly rolled out of her lower bunk. "But I'd guess they're not working too hard."

"Why is that?"

"Because they're just Saints." She yawned.

"How can you say that!"

"No, that's not how *I* feel. I'm just pointing out the attitude of the people in charge around here. You know there'd be a lot more effort put into finding them if they were locals or even some Fudgies. But that's just the general mind-set of the locals – unfortunate, but true."

Suddenly, there was a loud knocking on the door.

"Are you two ladies okay in dare?" bellowed Rosie from the other side of the door.

"Yes." I went to the door and opened it a crack. "We're just getting dressed."

"Just checkon' on de neighbors now dot we got a sign," Rosie explained. "Want to make sure evrabody's still here ond dey didn't take more of de womon."

I opened the door a bit further. "What are you talking about?"

"De sign. Come ond see it for yourself."

Pepper and I quickly dressed and headed out into the hallway where we found a group of people huddled around the bulletin board staring at something. Once we joined them, we jockeyed for position so we too could see what had captured their attention.

There was a sign, just as Rosie had said. It was made up of letters cut out from magazines and newspapers, then glued together on a piece of paper that was now tacked to our bulletin board. The message read: "SaINts arE tRaSH – gEt RId oF thEm oR elSe I WiLl gEt riD oFThEm fOr yoU."

"I con't stay here no more," one Saint woman whimpered and then dashed back to her room and slammed the door.

"We won't hov none of dot." Rosie lifted her hands in the air, gesturing to the remaining group. "We won't be drove oway by some littal mon tryon' to scare os. We need to stick togaddar. Don't be go-on' out olone, ond don't be ofraid. Dot's whot dey wont, ond we're not go-on' te give it to dem." She then stormed off in the direction of the whimpering woman.

With some looks of fear and others of defiance, the Saints gradually broke ranks and headed back to their rooms.

Pepper studied the message. "I've so had it with this. It's too sad around here. We need to get out – go do something."

I certainly felt the need to get away, too. "I'm game. What do you have in mind?"

"I'm not sure, but anything's got to be better than just hanging around here until we have to go work the late shift. Let's just go for a walk – see what we find."

We returned to our room only long enough to slip on good walking shoes. Then we headed out, away from the dismal air of the dorm and into the bright sunlight that offered hope for a better day.

We power-walked along the back streets, winding our way around the backside of a corral for work horses where a Saint was spreading out a bale of sweet hay with a pitch fork. As we came closer to Main Street, we encountered the morning street cleaners hosing dried horse droppings off to the sides of the road, the smell of damp pavement lingering in the air. Walking well off to the side on the grassy shoulder, we continued our stride as we made our way to the downtown boardwalks.

Pepper slowed the pace for a moment. "Hey, I know where we can go. There's this place I bet you've never seen before. I'm not even sure it's still open, but let's check it out."

"Today, I'll try anything. Just show me the way."

We walked briskly along Main Street, seldom troubled by a slow moving Fudgie as it was still early morning and the mass of tourists hadn't arrived yet. We passed by quiet ice cream parlors and cheap souvenir stores where an occasional owner was found sweeping the boardwalk or setting up a spinning display rack of postcards in preparation for the day.

The only hustle and bustle on the street was at the Pancake Chef where the smell of hotcakes and bacon drifted out to meet us. As we swiftly approached the place, a patron swung open the screened door and crossed the boardwalk in front of us. He held a styrofoam cup of coffee in his fist as he walked over to a hitching post and leaned against it, studying the horses tied to a carriage that stood idly at the curb waiting for customers, their ears twitching to swat away flies.

"I love this place in the morning," Pepper commented as we kept up the pace, quickly striding past the last of the stores to where the boardwalk met up with the island marina. There, cabin cruisers, sailboats, and yachts rocked to and fro in the wake of a Boston Whaler racing out of port. Loaded with fishing gear, the boat quickly motored past us and then turned out toward open water.

We then turned away from the marina and headed inland, crossing the street and walking uphill through Maritime Park.

"Where is this place, anyway?" I asked.

Pepper kept up her lead. "Not much further, but it is a bit of a hike."

Seagulls strutted across the park grounds in search of food, cawing at us as they reluctantly scattered from our swift feet. One followed us closely, gliding in the air just off to our side as we made our way to the back of the park. There we came to a flight of stairs made from railroad ties that ascended the side of a high bluff.

"It's up here." Pepper pointed up the staircase. "There's a bench halfway up. We can stop there for a break if you get too winded on the way up."

She took off, lightly tapping each step as she jogged her way upward. I followed as quickly as I could, ascending the stairs at a slightly slower rate. Up ahead, I could see that Pepper had reached the resting tier. She paused there, turning to face me. "Do you need to stop?"

"I don't think so," I panted, and so we both continued upward.

Near the top of the bluff, I found Pepper heading down a narrow side path that led into the trees, hugging the cliff's edge.

I stopped. "I thought we're going all the way to the top."

"Maybe later, but the place I wanted to show you is this way." She waved for me to follow her, leading the way along an unpaved path that weaved into some overgrown trees.

I finally caught up, walking right behind her as we followed the trail through a couple of tight curves winding inland. Around a corner, we came upon a dilapidated field stone structure perched precariously on the edge of a steep drop off on the side of the trail.

"Oh, my gosh, I can't believe it. The place is still here!" Pepper stepped closer to the ramshackle building.

I stayed back away from the place. "You brought me to see *this?*"

"Yeah. I wanted to see if this place was still standing."

And it was, but barely. The structure was approximately the size and shape of a large barn and it had numerous fractures in its grout. Its sagging roof was almost completely covered with moss. A weathered driftwood sign hanging on the side of the structure read, "*Perseverance* Maritime Memorial Museum."

"Bet this place's never been on the Fudgie tour." Pepper stepped to the sign, tracing the letters carved into the driftwood with her fingers. "I haven't been in here in years. We should check it out — see if it's open."

"I bet it's condemned." I kept my distance, convinced the place might collapse.

"Oh, it's not that bad, Carly." Pepper came back toward me. "Haven't you ever heard of the *Perseverance*?"

"I don't think so."

"Well, I have. It's a ship that sailed around here about a hundred years ago until it sank in a bad storm. There were a bunch of kids on board, and most of them died."

"Wow. Well, that's a real picker-upper. So this is where we came to get away from our troubles?"

Pepper shoulders dropped. "I'm sorry. I was just looking for something different. Guess I didn't think about it."

I felt badly for raining on her parade. "It's okay. It's still a good distraction. So tell me what you know about the ship – like, why were there so many kids on it?"

"If I remember right, it was used for some sort of reform program for bad kids, or something like that. But I don't know the whole story. Why don't we go in and find out?"

"Oh, I don't think so." I took a step back. "It doesn't sound like anything that's going to cheer me up."

"Yeah, but I can tell you're curious, and I am, too. Let's just take a quick look." Pepper grabbed my arm and pulled me toward the entrance. "It's a small place, so it won't take long."

Upon entering the building's quiet foyer, I first thought the place might be unoccupied. We then cautiously stepped into the next room where we found a hulking college-age boy sitting at a table, engrossed in a muscle-car magazine. He glanced up at us, seemingly startled, and fumbled up from his seat to greet us.

"Oh, customers!" He tossed his magazine into the table drawer. "I don't get many, but nice to see you. Can I help you?"

"I hope so," Pepper answered. "Is this place open to the public?"

"Oh, yeah." He cleared his throat. "This building was recently purchased by the Michigan State Park Commission for renovations. We're open during the park's standard hours: nine to five, Monday through Saturday, and eleven to five on Sunday."

"So, you're open now?" Pepper clarified.

"Oh, yeah."

"And what's the charge for admission?"

"While they're finishing renovations, there's no tours, but they don't charge you to just look around."

"My kind of deal!" Pepper headed for the next doorway. "So, do we start here?"

"Yeah, just go ahead." He returned to his seat and reached back in the drawer for his magazine.

Pepper backed up to his desk. "Maybe you could show us around – tell us things we wouldn't learn from just reading a bunch of signs."

He put his magazine back for a moment. "Oh, no, I can't do that. I'm not a tour guide – just a sort of junior curator. I just man the desk. But you two can easily find your way around. Just follow the corridors."

Pepper headed for the door to the corridor. "Well, since you're busy –"

"I'm sure we can find our own way." I pushed Pepper onward, hoping she wouldn't say more.

The curator stood up and followed us, taking just one step into the corridor. "Sorry that some displays are temporarily disassembled, but you'll see a few artifacts with explanations. When you're done, you'll wind up back around here at a small auditorium located just to our right."

"What's that for?" I turned back to ask.

"The people who owned it before made up a little slide show about the *Perseverance*. The state is making a more up-to-date presentation, but it's not done yet – so for now, this is all I've got. Do you want to see it when you're done?"

"Yeah, probably," I answered, pleased to see him growing a bit more accommodating.

"Okay. See you back here." He smiled then turned away.

We went our own way, meandering through a maze of hallways that were short and narrow with little to be seen. Each contained two to three glass-enclosed showcases that housed displays documenting construction of the ship and some of her voyages.

One corridor was noticeably longer and contained a number of smaller showcases, fourteen in all, each with a brass name-engraved placard mounted above it. Some displays were void of artifacts, not surprising considering the explanation given us earlier regarding the museum's current renovations. However, every glass window housed an enlarged portrait of an individual as well as a card noting the person's date of birth and death. Twelve of the portraits were of young boys and I noted their dates of birth to be in the years 1914 or 1915. Two of the portraits were of grown men, noted to be father and son, one born in the early 1880s and the other in 1900. All fourteen displays bore the same date of death: November 3, 1926.

I stared into the eyes of one of the young boys. "These kids weren't even teenagers yet. It's so sad."

"I know." Pepper was gazing at the pictures of the father and son. "It is pretty depressing. Guess I shouldn't have brought you here after all. Maybe we should go."

I glanced down the long hallway, considering the fourteen shrines erected to these lost souls. "But now you've piqued my curiosity. Let's quickly check out the slideshow, and then we'll get going."

We passed through the corridor and then entered a small room adjacent to the auditorium. There we saw only one assembled display case devoted to the survivors. It housed an enlarged photo of five boys and one adult huddled on a snow-covered dock. Each was wrapped in a heavy Mackinaw blanket, and each bore a grief-stricken look of horror and despair.

Pepper's eyes darted across the photo, taking in the faces of each survivor. "What possessed someone to take a picture of those poor people after all they'd been through?"

Admittedly, I was too taken with the picture to wonder about the photographer's motives. It was a moving portrait, with the true impact of this disaster captured in the faces of each of the six survivors.

The college kid poked his head into the room. "You got through there pretty quick. Now to see the show you just go on through that set of double doors and find a seat. I'll go turn on the projector."

The room was the poorest excuse for an auditorium I'd ever seen. With no other visitors present, no one blocked our view of the tattered screen as we took our places in the last of four rows of mangled theater seats. We struggled but managed to find two seats together that weren't bent sideways and didn't have rusted springs protruding through the seat covers.

The theater then went dark. An out-dated sound system emitted ominous chords of organ music as the sketched-image of a sinking ship flashed onto the screen. As the organ music faded, the taped voice of a soft-spoken woman announced, "The *Perseverance*: Fact, Myth, and Legend."

"I can see why this is free," Pepper whispered.

I tried to get comfortable in my slightly slanted seat, but couldn't. "It is pretty rough."

As images of both sketched and photographed events gradually flashed on the tattered screen, the woman's voice chronicled the history of the ship. She began with the inception of the teaching-vessel concept.

"The idea of constructing the *Perseverance* was conceived by Captain D'Arcy Kavanaugh II," the voice explained. "An experienced seaman, Kavanaugh had been sailing old schooner-type freighters on the Great Lakes since his childhood. With the onset of steam-powered and propeller driven ships, Kavanaugh had seen the schooner fleet diminish and the remaining schooners demoted to tow barges. In fear that the knowledge and understanding of sailing these great ships would soon become a lost art, Kavanaugh approached one of Windemere Island's most prominent summer residents, shipping tycoon William Talbott, with the idea of constructing a teaching schooner."

Pepper leaned in toward me, squirming a bit in her seat. "No surprise that some rich guy was behind this."

"Although Talbott Shipping had made the transition from sailing to steam powered vessels, Talbott shared Kavanaugh's concerns and wanted to invest in preserving the history of the shipping industry. Both men believed that people could be taught valuable life lessons by sailing such ships, and so they decided to share the wealth of these lessons with the most underprivileged – the street urchins that otherwise would never receive any sort of upbringing and education.

"The financial backing of Mr. Talbott made it possible to construct a 121-foot replica of the two-masted, gaff-rig schooner named *Perseverance*. The original *Perseverance* was built in 1855 and sailed the Great Lakes until it collided with the *Grey Eagle* in Lake Huron and sank off the coast of Cheboygan in 1864. Talbott and Kavanaugh chose this particular ship to replicate mostly because of the symbolic relevance of its name. They saw resurrecting *Perseverance* as representative of their goal: to instill the value of steadfast determination through the art of sailing."

Pepper squirmed some more. "So, that's why they named it that."

"Do you have to keep interrupting?"

"Sorry." She slid down in her seat.

The woman's voice continued. "The *Perseverance* was constructed and ready for test sailing by the fall of 1921. Kavanaugh and his two adult sons, D'Arcy III and Nolan, took aboard their first crew of seventeen boys, ages twelve through fifteen, in the summer of the following year and sailed the ship late into November.

"The Kavanaughs continued with this venture each year, taking on a full crew to learn the shipping trade by transporting wheat across the Straits. The program was such a success that many orphaned children had to be turned away. Although a lottery was utilized for choosing most crew members, an exception was made in the fall of 1926 when Talbott's twin grandsons, Albert and Phillip, were old enough to be considered. Talbott desperately wanted the boys to experience sailing this great ship, and so they were both given priority and joined the crew that sailed the *Perseverance* on her final voyage."

Pepper cupped her hand over her mouth, tilting it to direct the sound of her voice to my ear. "Now it's starting to sound scary." She couldn't contain herself.

The scratchy sound track returned to its more ominous music. "Kavanaugh was determined to deliver a significant load of wheat to a Canadian distributor. Ignoring the telltale signs of an impending nor'easter, the most savage of storms, he set sail fully loaded from Duncan City for De Tour Passage, the route to their final destination of Sault Ste. Marie.

"Kavanaugh had planned this to be the *Perseverance's* last voyage for the season, a mission intended to test the crew's newly developed skills and fine-tune its sailing instincts. Little did they know that they were about to be put to the greatest test the *Perseverance* had ever faced."

"Dah-dah-dum!" Pepper dramatically intoned.

"Stop it!"

"Okay, fine!" Pepper crossed her arms with a huff.

The woman's voice continued. "According to survivor accounts, Kavanaugh first viewed the inclement weather as an added challenge to test his students' skills. With their destination lying directly into the northeastern wind, the captain commanded his crew to tack back and forth, working the strong winds to their favor. But when the gusts suddenly increased to gale force, all aboard were caught off guard. The brutal nor'easter brought sleet and hail down upon the crew as they scrambled to batten down all hatches and shorten sail. But they unfortunately failed this unplanned portion of their test, for they were unable to secure everything before the lake swells reached heights of twenty-five feet or more."

I scooted forward to the edge of my uncomfortable seat. "Unbelievable."

Pepper glared at me. "Now it's you."

I gave her a nudge. "Hush up!"

"Even with each man and child suited with a life-preserver, all feared being tossed overboard. No one would survive for long in the raging, frigid waters of November. All held on for dear life as they prayed for the strength to ride out the storm.

"In such fierce weather, even an experienced crew could do little to navigate a schooner. With no engines aboard and winds powerful enough to rip the sails from the mast, the ship's rudder was the only tool for attempting to control their direction. As fierce winds and mountainous waves forced the ship backward, the crew could do little more than try to avoid capsizing."

As the music swelled, a series of sketches flashed more frequently on the screen, almost producing a sense of motion. They showed a ship rising and falling with the tremendous waves in what would turn out to be the *Perseverance's* final moments.

The narrator's voice became even more foreboding as she punctuated the dramatic conclusion. "The crew was holding its own when the schooner fell into further peril. Peering out through the dense sheets of freezing rain, Kavanaugh's son Nolan was the first to make out the silhouette of a large mass just off the starboard side of the stern. It was a whaleback – an oddly shaped, steam-driven freighter – and the *Perseverance* was rolling toward it.

"Try as they might, the crew was still unable to control the ship, and so it took only one more twenty-five-foot wave to slam the *Perseverance's* stern into the broadside of the whale-shaped ship. The schooner's wooden hull was no match for the 220-foot, steel-reinforced steamship. With another equally powerful swell, the *Perseverance* again smashed against the whaleback's hull, cracking the schooner's underside and splintering her larger lifeboat into kindling.

"Although the next series of waves actually drove the two ships apart, it was too late for the *Perseverance*. Her hull was fatally wounded and the schooner was taking on water. The captain and his sons knew she could not remain afloat through the storm.

"All accounts of the tale confirmed that Kavanaugh barked out the command for all of the crew to abandon ship. Apparently the captain did not initially realize what damage had been ravaged on the main lifeboat but once informed that the larger of the two dinghies was destroyed, he ordered the entire crew to prepare to board the intact dinghy nestled inside the remains of the larger boat.

"Both of Kavanaugh's sons knew the dinghy was too small to carry the entire crew. It might hold up to twelve children in decent weather but likely could handle only a maximum of nine or possibly ten and still remain afloat under such inclement conditions. Nonetheless, Kavanaugh repeated the order to ready the small vessel for all to board.

"Accounts differ on what happened next. Some hold that Kavanaugh's eldest son D'Arcy III remained the dutiful son, obediently guiding the crew in executing what would surely prove to be fatal orders, while Kavanaugh's younger son Nolan mutinously second-guessed his father's wisdom and disobeyed his command to save lives. Others believed that D'Arcy II and III were the heroes, maintaining the Musketeers' motto of 'All for one and one for all,' but the defiant Nolan and his faithless actions undermined their heroism. But whatever your viewpoint, one fact remained: Nolan and his father viciously disputed how the situation should be handled.

"According to the survivors, Nolan struggled with the others to prepare the dinghy to be lowered while he argued with his father over the manning of the lifeboat. Initially, his father overrode his challenge, sending the boys, one by one, to undertake the perilous process of crawling from the ship's swaying rail into the flailing dinghy. However, when eight boys were aboard, the ninth child fearfully began his descent but lost his balance on a rolling swell, plunging head first into the frigid waters. His screams could be heard vaguely over the raging storm as a swell washed him away from sight."

"Oh, how awful," I uttered.

"The captain urged the remaining boys to hurry aboard so they could lower the boat and search for their crewmate, but only two more scurried aboard. The eight boys still on deck were frozen in fear that they might meet the same fate with the relentless, icy waters, so young D'Arcy quickly boarded the dinghy and guided two more boys over to it.

"What happened next was disputed by the survivors. Some said that the lines gave way under the weight of the overcrowded lifeboat, while others believed Nolan cut the boat loose. Whatever the reason, the dinghy plunged into a rising wave and washed away from the ship with only D'Arcy III still aboard to navigate it.

"Then Nolan turned to his father, telling himmer-dod-lev-men-tor-rin-don…" the voice faded off, winding down in tone from alto to tenor to a low bass. Finally, it went silent.

"What the…" Pepper muttered as we both wondered what had happened.

We sat in silence, staring at an artist's rendition of the floundering lifeboat that stayed on the screen. After an extended pause, the image also shut down, leaving us in total blackness.

Immediately we heard footsteps make their way to the next room, followed by the muffled voice of the burly curator cursing the audio system.

"Sorry about that," he yelled to us, his voice echoing through the theater. "Come out to the lobby and I'll tell you what you missed." Then he returned to his cursing and what sounded like pounding on the projection equipment.

In his frustration he failed to turn on the auditorium lights, so we had to fumble our way across the row of seats and feel our way toward a crack of light emanating from between two swinging doors. We pushed them open, making our way back into the harsh light of the lobby.

The curator met up with us, holding a small mechanism that looked to be part of a tape player in one hand and poking at it with a screwdriver he held in the other. "So, do you have any questions?"

I was still caught in the suspense, barely able to contain myself. "Yeah, what happened?"

"Well, there's some loose wiring in the tape player we use for the program. Sometimes if you shake it, it comes back on, but I just —"

"I think she means what happened to the crew." Pepper sounded a bit edgy, as if she were about to lose her patience.

He stopped poking and looked up at us. "Oh yeah, let's see. You were at the point when Nolan cut the dinghy loose."

"So you know that's what happened?" I asked.

"Well, that's what everyone around here believes. They say Nolan cut the main line because he thought the dinghy would flip over if any more kids got in it. He knew his brother was on the dinghy and figured he could keep the boat upright."

"So, Nolan played God," I remarked. "He cut them loose and stayed with the other boys he chose to let die."

Pepper looked sternly at me. "You know, it's not like he killed them – and remember, he was planning to die with them."

I returned her stare. "Well, in a way, he did. If he did cut that rope, then he did it knowing that those kids on board would die as a result. At the very least, he was choosing to take a life – or lives – when they had no choice at all, and I think that's wrong."

Pepper crossed her arms. "So, I suppose you would've done nothing – just watched them all drown."

"No, I would've at least tried to get them all in the dinghy – give them a fighting chance. I mean, I couldn't imagine keeping them on board just to watch them die. It's bad enough that Nolan went down with the ship, but to watch those boys die, too –"

"No, Nolan didn't die," the curator interrupted. "He and one of the boys jumped ship just before it went down, taking Nolan's father and five other kids with it."

I turned to the curator in disbelief. "So how did Nolan survive being in the water?"

"Somehow he made it to the dinghy, climbed in, and kept it afloat until they were rescued." The college kid returned his eyes to studying the mechanism in his hands.

Pepper uncrossed her arms and stepped closer to the young curator. "That doesn't make sense. I thought there wasn't enough room in the dinghy."

"There wouldn't have been except D'Arcy fell overboard when he was trying to reach another boy who got knocked out of the boat. They say his body was never found."

I clearly recalled the last picture we had seen just before entering the auditorium. "So, that was Nolan in that survivors' photo we saw."

The curator never looked up from studying and prodding the gizmo in his hands. "That's right."

"But there were only five boys in that picture," I recalled. "What happened to the rest?"

"Once D'Arcy fell off the dinghy, the kids lost control and capsized." He blew on the workings, then poked at a tiny, levered attachment that clicked back and forth. "Some managed to right it and help others back in, but then some were washed away. It kind of went on like that, fighting the waves for a long time – must've took a while for that whaleback to stop and go back to help, especially in that kind of weather." He blew again, then kept clicking. "Others came to help, too, but it took so long that, when they finally got to them, there were only eight still on the dinghy – that would be Nolan and seven boys."

"Seven?" I wondered if he had that right.

"Yeah, one was already dead and another died just after they picked them up. The remaining six survivors are in that photo down the hall." He stopped poking at the machine and looked up at us. "And so, that's the end of it. The surviving kids went to an orphanage, and Nolan went on trial."

"What, was he court-martialed?" I asked.

Pepper scowled. "No, that can't be, because you can't court martial someone who isn't in the service."

The college kid looked at Pepper long enough to agree. "Yeah, that's right, and the state never filed criminal charges, but Talbott sued him for damages. He always blamed Nolan for his grandsons' deaths, since they were two of the boys left on board – said they could've survived if Nolan hadn't cut the dinghy loose."

"So, what was the verdict?" I asked.

He blew again on the mechanism. "They found him negligent,'" He prodded the gizmo and clicked the lever again. "The settlement was for only a couple hundred dollars – nothing that would break the Kavanaugh's. But Nolan was forever dubbed a killer. It seems like everyone around here blames him for the death of his father and brother, and all those boys – kind of like you did." He pointed at me.

"Well, I didn't say he was to blame."

Pepper raised her eyebrows. "Really?"

The college kid turned a tiny wheel by the lever. "So, rumor has it that he never sailed again. They say that's why he never comes out."

"Never comes out?" I questioned. "What do you mean?"

"Now that's just a bunch of gossip." Pepper took my arm and gently tugged in the direction of the door out. "Yeah, Nolan still lives here – with his whole family in a nice place along the island's highest bluff."

"I hear his son's family lives in the main house now." The curator poked a bit harder and the lever broke off the mechanism. "Dang it!" He looked back at us. "The family runs the island's biggest livery, called *The Gifted Horse* – and they put old man Kavanaugh up on the second floor of the servants' house to live. The poor guy never leaves the place."

"Yeah, I've also heard that one." Pepper tugged on me a little harder. "So, we'll just have to check that out sometime – see if Nolan is maybe standing in his window, just staring out at the water like some silly ghost story says he does."

The college kid picked up his broken piece off the floor. "Well, looks like you two don't have any more questions, so I'll just get back to my work." He looked back at his mechanism, trying to fit the broken piece back into its place. "Thanks for stopping by, and help yourself to a brochure on the way out." He then returned to his seat, ignoring his magazine and remaining focused on the repairs at hand.

We departed the museum and headed home with Pepper complaining most of the way.

"That kid was nothing more than a gossip-peddler telling a bunch of half-baked stories he's picked up from the local idiots who haven't got anything better to do than just make up stupid stuff. They're the same lot that keeps on making up things about those poor girls who are missing – just a part of the problem instead of being a part of the solution. And now we've got to go back to our place where we'll have to listen to more people just making up crap…"

While Pepper ranted on, I considered what I'd seen and heard. Yes, I had to return to the reality of concerns for my own safety and the safety of others, but I was also returning with a bit of a distraction – a fascination with a new mystery that seemed so much less threatening. I found myself captivated by the story of the *Perseverance*, and even more so by the tales told of the enigmatic Nolan Kavanaugh.

Of course, it was mostly gossip, something I'd grown to detest between tales of the Saints and Annahede. But despite the hypocrisy, I couldn't let this mystery go. I longed to know more, so much so that I knew it would'nt be long before I journeyed to see the home on the bluff where rumor had it that a hermit dwelled.

Chapter 9

A PRIVILEGED FEW

"HERE COMES TROUBLE," Pepper announced as a newcomer to Biminis took a seat at the bar.

It was Annahede. "Nice to see you, too, Pepper. It's been too long."

"No, it hasn't." Pepper pulled the tap lever and poured beer into three mugs she held in one fist. "Last time I saw you, you were still griping to Carly about the cost of living alone. So, is that why you're here – to nag her some more about moving back in with you?"

"Oh, no, not that." Annahede averted her eyes, looking beyond Pepper to where I stood behind her. "Just thought I'd drop by this quaint little establishment to see how you two were doing… and it seems you haven't changed a bit."

Pepper picked up a service tray filled with drinks. "No sense changing a good thing, I always say." She then headed for a table she was serving.

I stepped forward to the bar, dropping a cocktail napkin on the counter in front of Annahede. "So, can I get you some lunch?"

She looked at me. "Bar food? Oh, no, thank you. But I will have an iced tea, I guess, and I also need to see Collette Deroshia. She works in the kitchen here, right?"

Callahan poured tea in a glass with ice. "Yes, she does, but she's busy right now." His voice was even.

"Okay, then I guess I'll have to try again later."

"She'll be busy then, too." Callahan's eyes narrowed as he set the tea glass on Annahede's napkin.

Annahede lifted the glass and took a drink. "What, so you don't even give your employees a break?" She locked eyes with Callahan.

Callahan rested his fists on the bar in front of Annahede. "I give it to them, but they don't take it because I only hire hard workers here – not the kind that are looking to make an easy buck. They all like it here, including Collette, and so they're not looking to go anywhere else." With that, Callahan turned and headed for the kitchen.

"Isn't he touchy!" Annahede pressed the lemon slice in her tea with a spoon. "Well, that's okay. I'll talk to her later. But I'm glad to see you, Carly."

"Yeah, it's been a while." I politely smiled. "So, can I get you anything else?"

"No, but I think I might have something for you."

I hesitated.

"It's a job… much better than –"

"No thanks." I looked away from her, wiping down the bar with a dish rag.

Annahede took a drink and set down her glass. "Now don't get yourself all worked up. I'm not asking you to work for me, God forbid. No, I wouldn't make that mistake again."

"I'm happy here." I lifted an ashtray, wiping under it.

"Oh, yes, I can see how much you like cleaning up after people," she scoffed. "So, this would be right up your alley. It's just a –"

"Wait! I really don't want to know." I turned and headed for the register.

"Good God, you are so jumpy!"

I rang up her bill. "Well, I just don't want to get dragged into something."

"But I told you, it's not even for me! You'd be working for the Hamiltons up on the bluff – just housekeeping, and for that you'd also get free room and board in that beautiful cottage of theirs."

I walked back over to her from the register. "I told you, I'm happy here – not interested."

"Really?" She cocked her head, scowling in disbelief. "I can't believe you'd turn this down. These people are desperate –

been bugging me for a week to help them find somebody, so I'm sure they'd pay well. And have you seen their place? It's so —"

"I don't care." I set her bill on the bar.

"Oh, come on!" she unzipped her purse and rummaged through it. "Be a friend and help me out here."

I shook my head. "What's in it for you, anyway?"

"A finder's fee, of course!" Finding her wallet, she drew it out of her purse and opened it. "And there's something in it for you, too." She pulled out a fifty and tossed it on the bar top. "You keep the change there, just for looking at it – it's next to the last cottage on the bluff." With that, she quickly slid off her stool and hurried for the door.

"Hey, wait, Annahede! I don't want your money, and I didn't say I'd..."

But I was too late. She never turned back, and before I could say another word, she was gone.

Pepper returned to the bar, an empty serving tray in hand. "What a charming addition you brought to the island."

"No, *she* brought *me* here. I take no responsibility."

"Fine." Pepper wiped off her tray. "What trouble was she trying to stir up?"

"Oh, just trying to buy favors." I held up the fifty.

"Was she now?" Pepper winked at me.

"Now don't go making a big deal of it."

She placed her drink tray on the bar top. "And who was she buying these favors for?"

"Just stop it!" I opened the cash drawer, making change for Annahede's drink and pocketing my tip. "It was nothing, I'm telling you."

"Whatever." Pepper stepped to the tap and poured beer into a cold mug.

"Hey, would you know anything about a family on the island named Hamilton?"

"*The* Hamiltons? Where'd you get that one?" Pepper raised her eyebrows. "Is *that* who she's buying favors for?"

I slammed the cash drawer shut. "Just cut it out and tell me what you know."

She set down one beer and poured another. "I know they've got a lot of money, and they live with the exclusives up on the bluff, right next door to where the Kavanaughs live."

"The Kavanaughs?" I shook my head. "You mean the ones from the *Perseverance*? *Those* Kavanaughs?"

"Yeah, that's where the surviving son lives, along with *his* son and family." Pepper set the second beer on her tray. "So, what was Annahede telling you about the Hamiltons?"

"Oh, they just need a housekeeper." I threw the dish rag over my shoulder. "I told her I wasn't interested."

"Smart move. I wouldn't want to have to take care of that mansion."

"Mansion? Annahede said it was just a cottage?"

Pepper laughed. "Yeah, but not the kind of place you're thinking of – not like the one you lived in with Annahede. No, this place is mammoth."

"Really?" She'd piqued my interest. "I'd kind of like to see that."

Pepper picked up her tray of beers. "Oh, so still thinking about the offer – ready to ditch me, huh?"

"No, but I'm curious just to see these places. Besides, I'm getting paid almost fifty bucks just to look, remember?" Smiling, I picked up my pencil stub and headed for a table.

"Oh, was that the deal?" With her tray propped above her shoulder, Pepper followed me, heading over to wait on her own table. "Well then, when we punch out after dinner, we'll head up to the bluff and check out cottage row. Wouldn't want to let down Annahede now, would we?"

The rest of work went quickly as the dinner rush set in, keeping us rushing between tables with no idle time to think. By late evening we were quite tired, but I insisted that we still go see how the island's affluent lived before nightfall.

"They're not really the better half," Pepper pointed out. "More like the top ten percent with about ninety percent of the island's money in their pockets. Just wish they'd use it to build an easier way up there, but don't worry – I'm one of the few people who knows the short cut.

Our hike was not an easy one since Pepper's secret path was filled with large rocks and raised tree roots that tripped us up as we walked. We clumsily continued until we reached the end of the path where it intersected with a cobblestone road. At the crossroad, we found an antique gas light post with two ornately painted placards mounted one on each side. One sign pointed to our left and read "Me-Wanna-Go-Home." The other sign aimed right and was engraved "Windemere Bluff," pointing us in the direction we wanted to go.

I panted, trying to catch my breath. "At least I can find the way home."

"That'll be easy. Everything's downhill from here."

As we followed the cobblestone road in and out of a wooded area, it wrapped around to a breathtaking sight. Almost a dozen enormous, immaculate homes lined the high side of the road, each with its own spectacular view of the sparkling, white-capped waters of Lake Huron.

I stopped and stared. "You're right – they're mansions!"

Pepper extended her arm in the direction of the homes. "Those, Carly, are not mansions. They are what Windemere refers to as cottages."

"But they're too big to be cottages."

"Not around here… Just like our sister island Mackinac, they built these places here a long time ago to be summer homes for the rich and famous of Detroit and Chicago. Families would travel here on big ships the size of ocean liners just to get away from the hot summers downstate."

"I can't believe someone would build such a gigantic, gorgeous home only to live in it for maybe three months out of the year. If I owned one of these, I'd definitely be living in it all the time." I slowly started walking closer toward them.

Pepper strolled along by my side. "But way back then, it was tough to live on the island during the wicked winter. Now that things are more civilized, some of the owners do stay here permanently." She picked up the pace, as did I.

All of the cottages were Victorian in architecture and most sported three stories. Although varied in style and shape, each home flaunted a large veranda from which to savor the view. Surprisingly, though, not one person could be found on any of the porches. We only saw one person, an elderly gentleman hunched over a large flower urn on the steps of the first cottage. The sign hanging above it identified the home as that of the Addisons.

I could feel my jaw hanging open. "Could you imagine owning this place? I sure wouldn't want to have to deal with keeping it clean."

"So, you're still not interested in Annahede's offer?" Pepper kept walking, waving for me to follow. "Let's go down and check out the one she wanted you to clean."

As I walked on, I looked back to see the gardener occupied with plucking weeds from the pot, seemingly much too busy to stop and smell the roses. What a shame it seemed that the people who lived here were not out on their porches fully appreciating the awesome beauty that surrounded them.

Every home was so ornate, each having its own unique flair. However, despite their individuality, the houses did share one common characteristic – hanging over the doorway of every home was an engraved sign boasting the name of the proud residents. As I walked along, I noticed how these entrances read like a who's who of the elite of Windemere Island – Addison, Windsor, Radcliffe, Montgomery, DePalmer... and the names went on and on, each sounding more prestigious than its predecessor.

"There it is," Pepper announced, heading to the next home on the street.

Looking over at the enormous home bearing the name of Hamilton, I announced the obvious. "Okay, so I won't be taking *that* job."

Then following Pepper, I walked with her up to what appeared to be a historical landmark sign posted in front yard of the Hamiltons'. A seagull flew over, roosting on the plaque as we began to read its embossed synopsis of a property's history.

"You won't believe this one," Pepper said, obviously already familiar with the story.

The seagull cawed as I glanced over the tale of how this particularly unusual home came to have its unique architecture and gardens. The plaque told of how the home's original owner built the house as a birthday gift for his new bride. Since his wife's birth date was in April, he commissioned an architect to create a house adorned with the shape of her birthstone – the diamond. For this reason, all of the cutouts in the intricate trim work, as well as most of the windows, were all diamond shaped.

"Look at the roof tiles," Pepper pointed to the top of the house. "Even those are diamond shaped. Boy, that's a lot of detail to put into a roof just to have those white crows come and crap on it."

Sure enough, I glanced up to find a half-dozen seagulls perched on the rooftop amidst splotches of bird mess.

The rest of the story told of how the groom hired a local gardener to finish his labor of love by planting an abundance of sweet peas – the flower for April – all around the house. His bride was moved by his extravagant gift but also touched by a flair-up of her allergies. The pollen from the wildflowers caused her so much suffering that the newlyweds were forced to sell the place, moving on to an equally lavish cottage in the more rugged, less "flowery" terrain on the other side of the island.

I stepped away from the sign to continue walking the street. "All of that effort, and they barely ever even lived here."

"Yeah, must have sold it off to someone who didn't mind the gull crap. I bet those nasty birds were more of a problem than those sweet peas ever were."

"What's your issue with the seagulls, anyway? I mean, I've always thought they're kind of cute."

"That's what the Fudgies think. They come over here and throw them crackers and turn them into a nuisance. Now all I have to do is let them think you've got food and they'll attack you."

As if they had overheard and understood, two seagulls glided down from the roof and followed us, hovering like kites in the breeze at our backs as we stepped back to the cobblestone street.

"Now let me show you the Kavanaughs' place," Pepper said, leading the way to the next home with the seagulls in tow.

The massive cottage was the largest on the street, but simple in its structure and detail, not nearly as ornate as the others. Tacked to the far side of the porch railing was a small sign that read "Kavanaugh" in perfect script.

As we walked closer to the stately home, I noticed a smaller structure, similarly painted and trimmed, located toward the backside of the house. It looked somewhat like a carriage house except that it had many windows on both the first and second floors. There was something inviting about it, looking more like a real home to me than did the massive mansion that stood before us.

It wasn't until I was directly in front of the Kavanaugh cottage that I noticed him, a slight shadow of a man, barely visible in the upstairs window. He was leaning with his hands pressed against the frame of the window, staring out at the narrow view of Lake Huron. I watched him and his glance never parted from the lake – that is, until he noticed me.

Though embarrassed for invading his privacy, I thought it only polite to wave. I expected him to ignore me or just walk away, so I was quite surprised when he lifted his hand and waved back.

Pepper glared at me as I waved. "What are you doing?"

"Waving at the guy in the window."

"What guy in the window?"

"There's a man standing in the window right over there." I pointed to the second floor of the carriage house. "Just look for yourself."

Pepper pressed her fists firmly against her hips. "You're telling me that you see some stranger up there in that back window that just happens to be looking down here at you, and you two are just waving away at each other?"

Just as Pepper stepped back to glance, the figure turned and moved away from sight.

She stared at the window. "I don't see anyone."

"That's because he just moved away."

"Sure he did. You know, that sad slide show probably got you all worked up, and then that crazy college kid and all his stupid stories about how 'he never comes out' and all that crap – that's enough to make anybody start seeing things."

"I'm not seeing things! I know I saw some guy up there. He was looking out at the lake."

"I bet he was. And I suppose you're thinking it was the mysterious Captain Nolan Kavanaugh, or better yet, his never found, betrayed brother D'Arcy – bet it's his ghost come to curse this house because of the tragedy."

I shook my head. "Fine. Don't believe me, and babble all your nonsense. I know what I saw – and yeah, maybe it was the captain, but I suppose it doesn't really matter."

Pepper threw up her hands. "It sure doesn't. The only thing that matters to me right now is getting home so I can get some sleep. It's been a long day, and I'm beat." She then turned away and headed toward home.

I lingered behind just a moment to take one last glance at the window. There I found that the figure had returned to his post. Not wanting to interrupt his thoughts, I quickly turned away and jogged ahead to join Pepper.

All the way home and into the night, I couldn't help but keep thinking about the man I had seen. I wondered whether he was the infamous Nolan Kavanaugh, and if so, what he was looking for as he gazed out over Lake Huron. Maybe he was searching the horizon for some kind of reprieve from the memory of that agonizing moment when he had to choose – life for some, death for others. I imagined that he must be the haunted one, still searching those open waters for some sign of what he had lost – his ship, and then again, maybe something that ran much deeper – and I wondered if there ever would come a time when he would find it.

Chapter 10

COLLISION COURSE

THERE WAS SO MUCH MORE TO SEE on the island I realized after our evening hike. My curiosity had been piqued by our adventure to the bluff and so I wanted to explore Windemere much more thoroughly. But I was growing tired of having to walk everywhere I went.

The next morning as Pepper and I took a walk through town, I stopped in the bike yard of Pedals' Bike Rental Shop and took the handlebars of an old, single-speed Schwinn in hand. "Didn't you used to have one of these?"

Pepper stopped walking and turned back to me. "Yeah, until somebody lifted it right out of the backroom at Biminis. Pretty gutsy to steal a bike right out of a business in broad daylight – and it really pissed me off."

Pulling a bike from the rack, I pulled the handlebars right and left, turning the wheel as I imagined myself riding it. "I'm going to check and see if he'll sell me this one."

"What? Are you crazy? It'll just get stolen – probably end up right back here in this rack to be rented, and you'll be out the money."

"I'll just keep it locked up."

"And someone will cut the chain."

"I'll take my chances." I pulled the bike out from between the others and wheeled it toward the owner's kiosk. "Let's see if I can get a deal."

Pepper smirked as she followed me, looking more amused than angry with my resolve. "Hey, it's your money." She laughed. "But you know they'll try to overcharge you, and for what? That beat up old thing."

I wheeled the bike up behind three Fudgies waiting their turn to rent a bike. "Well, it's all I can afford — and besides, they can't overcharge me 'cause I don't have enough money to pay them anymore than it's worth."

Pepper felt certain I'd paid too much, but I was pleased with my deal — and with the sudden expansion of what had been my outer limits. I found my first day with my bicycle to be very liberating as I took what proved to be a quick, leisurely jaunt around the full circumference of the island before heading to work for my afternoon shift. The day of riding would have proven perfect had it not been for the onset of rain as I pedaled my way back to the boarding house.

"What are you do-on', ridon' dot bike in de night all alone? Dot is dangerous!" Rosie scolded me when I returned home.

"No need to worry, Rosie. I'm pretty fast on this thing." I chain locked my bicycle to the broken radiator in the hallway. "Besides, no more women have gone missing. Seems like it's pretty safe around here now."

"Don't test de demons. Dey just bide-on' dare time, waiton' for someone whose beon' foolush like you."

It wasn't Rosie that scared me off my bike, but rather it was the arrival of some summer thunderstorms that rained on my parade. For the next couple of days I patiently waited, and then the weather cleared and I ventured right back out into the sunshine for a ride.

That morning I made a trip to town, the late June sun beating down on my shoulders as the wind in my face kept me cool. Once on Main Street, I was forced to slow down by the crowd on the road and boardwalks. Numerous bicyclists weaved about horse-drawn carriages as Fudgies jaywalked about the street with shopping bags in hand. One Fudgie nearly sideswiped me with her baby stroller, then cursed at me as if it had been all my fault. By then I'd had enough, and so I headed away from the tourist trap and up into the wooded foothills in search of paths I'd not yet traveled.

As I traveled along, I happened upon one particular trail that took me out past what appeared to be an old military cemetery. Though the grave markers and tombstones were crumbling away, almost all of the plots were bedecked with floral arrangements and small American flags.

I slowed to watch an elderly Saint gentleman tend to the grounds. He knelt down to reach over a low headstone, pulling at a few blades of grass. The lawn was so meticulously groomed with the grass closely trimmed and all the leaves and twigs removed. This groundskeeper must have labored hard and long to keep the cemetery looking this way.

Catching my glance, the man pulled his foot up to stand as he waved at me. "Dis day's much beddar to be out ridon' ond takon' in all de sunshine."

"It's a better day for yard work, too." I coasted ever so slowly. "Bet you had a mess to clean up after the storms."

"Not too bod. Just enough to keep me in my job."

"Looks great." I continued on by.

Just past the cemetery, I came to an area where limbs of shrubs and pine trees had overgrown the path. If someone was responsible for maintaining this route, he was obviously less conscientious than the groundskeeper I'd passed. With branches snapping in my face and scratching along my legs, I pedaled harder, determined to get through the thicket quickly.

Suddenly out of nowhere, a tall, gangly man entangled in a hodgepodge of hiking paraphernalia backed out of the woods onto the path. With his eyes wide and unblinking like those of a deer in headlights, he scrambled but tripped as he tried to get out of my way. I swerved and managed to miss him, but my handlebar caught the strap of his water bottle, further jerking me from my path. The tug wrenched the handlebars, veering my bike to one side while my momentum continued forward. I was thrown more than ten feet, face first into the shrubs.

In shorts and a sleeveless top, my arms and legs were a scratched-up mess. Nevertheless, I pushed myself up and began to climb my way out of the bushes as the stranger came to my aid.

"Oh, my gosh! I am so sorry!" He reached over and got a firm grip on my arm, pulling me out as he kept asking, "Are you all right?"

"I think so. Are you?"

"Oh, I'm fine, but you look a little hurt." He reached up toward my forehead. "You're bleeding a bit up there."

I was getting over the initial shock and starting to come to my senses when I realized this stranger was reaching for me.

"I'm okay!" I jerked back from his reach, but apparently I wasn't all right. As I touched a moist, tender area just above my right eye, blood dripped down the side of my arm.

"Here. Sit down on the grass and let me help you."

Hesitantly, I knelt down on the ground and watched him as he yanked the blue and white paisley bandana from the top of his head to reveal his sweaty, buzz-cut blonde stubble.

"I'll just tie this on 'til we can get you back to town." His hands trembled as he fumbled with the fabric, trying to untie the knots already in it.

I was also shaking, my adrenaline pumping as my heart raced. Most of my symptoms were likely due to the accident, but my anxiety was rising with my suspicion. With all the tales of missing Saint girls floating in my head, I considered the fact that I had no idea who this guy was.

"What were you doing out here?" I was hoping to find out more about him.

"Oh, I was just out hiking and stopped to pick a few wild berries." The knots now loosened, he flattened the bandana and set about folding it. "Guess I just wasn't watching where I was going."

"Are you from around here?"

"Yeah, born and raised." His hands continued to shake as he tried to tie the bandana around my head. "My name's Abel — Abel Hanika."

The name sounded familiar and I felt less suspicious of a guy who at least claimed to be a long-time local, so I was a bit more willing to let him help me. "Well, it's nice to meet you."

"Not so nice under the circumstances." He fumbled with tying the knot, letting out a sigh of frustration. "And so who are you?"

"Carly Malloy." I took the bandana from him and tried tying it myself.

"I've never seen you around. Are you just a tourist?"

"No, a local – or sort of just becoming one." I finished tying the bandana firmly about my head. "There. That should do it."

"Well, Carly, I'm so sorry about this. It's all my fault."

"Don't worry about it. I'd just like to go home now."

"Oh, no, you can't do that."

I didn't like the sound of this. "Why not?"

"You need someone to take a look at that gash and make sure you're okay."

"No, that's not necessary," I responded, but it was a hard sell as I staggered to get up and then started limping my way back along the path. "Just get me to my bike and I'll head back."

"I'm really sorry, but that won't work either." With his still trembling hand, he pointed out my bike, now a heap of bent metal and wheels with the dislodged chain tangled around it.

I was stuck and I knew it. "Now how am I going to get back?"

"Don't worry. I'll help you." With trembling hands, he guided me a few steps over to a fallen tree. "Here's a better place to sit. Now, you just wait here and I'll be right back." Then he tumbled off down the path, clumsily stumbling over small rocks and branches along the way.

But I was worried, not just about my condition, but about this guy. I'd been programmed by Pepper to be paranoid about strangers, and I found myself wondering if I should get up and start running before he returned. But something told me to trust this guy. I hoped my instincts were right.

I began to feel weak, so I slid off from the fallen tree and leaned back against it. As I glanced at the sparkling rays of the morning sun filtering through the overgrown trees, I considered this stranger. His sweet, boyish face and slim, awkward stature were unfamiliar to me. Yet I felt like I'd heard of him somewhere before. Maybe it was from Biminis – but no, that wasn't it. I just couldn't remember, and with a splitting headache coming on, I had no desire to keep wondering.

In the distance, I could hear the noisy revving of some type of machinery. Whatever it was, the sound was getting closer and my anxiety returned.

Then I could see it, something large and yellow moving toward me. As it came more into view, it appeared to be some piece of construction equipment, something I'd never expected to see on an island where vehicles aren't allowed.

My guess was slightly off. It turned out to be a small tractor driven by the elderly groundskeeper I had passed earlier. Abel was perched on the back.

When the tractor came to a stop, Abel hopped off and jogged over to me. "We'll drive you down to town on the back. Do you think you're up to it?" he yelled over the roar of the tractor.

I still felt a bit weak, but wanted to get back to civilization. "Yeah, I'll be fine."

"Now don't worry about a thing. Mr. Raddison here promised he'd drive the tractor nice and slow." Abel nodded toward the driver. I glanced at the groundskeeper and he returned a smile. I wasn't overly concerned about this elderly gentleman. He didn't look like a speed demon.

With tremulous hands, Abel carefully helped me to my feet and over to the tractor. "We're going to get you out of here in one piece. I promise."

The trickiest part was actually getting up on the back. I tried to hop a couple of times, but I just couldn't get up alone.

"I'll lift you." He reached to grab me.

"Oh, no." I backed away. "I can do it."

"No, you can't. Just let me get you up there. I promise I won't hurt you."

Before I could resist further, Abel lifted me up in his arms, a hint of pine overpowered by Old Spice wafting from under his chin. Gently he set me on the dusty planks of the small bed attached to the back of the tractor, and then he hopped aboard and we were off.

We spoke very little during most of the trip to town. The tractor was loud and I really didn't feel up to yelling over the sound. Without a word, Abel removed an old towel from the side of the tractor and shook off the excess dirt. Then, with still quivering hands, he awkwardly bunched up the towel between us and motioned for me to lean against it. I was able to recline only slightly and made myself as comfortable as one possibly could on the back of a compact tractor.

Even though my head was throbbing, I wondered where I'd heard his name before. I was sure we'd never met, but I kept thinking that there was something familiar about his last name of Hanika… and then, it finally came to me.

I found the gumption to yell over the rattling tractor. "Is your dad Vincent Hanika?"

"Yeah. Do you know him?" he yelled back.

"Oh, no – just heard of his work."

"You must mean the hotel – the French Landings down by the bay."

"No, his philanthropy. Isn't he the one that got Mansfield to install air-conditioning at the Me-Wanna-Go-Home boarding house?"

"You might say so. How'd you hear about that?"

"I'm a grateful tenant."

Abel shot upright. "You actually live in that rat-trap?"

"Yeah, you can call it that, but we call it home," I loudly answered. "For some of us, that's all we can afford."

"I'm sorry – didn't mean anything against you. I know how hard it is to find cheap housing around here, and it's wrong how Mansfield takes advantage of nice people – like you."

"We don't let him push us around too much." My head was beginning to throb from yelling, so I left it at that.

We quickly made our way along the over grown pathway to a gravel road.

"Should be smoother now," Mr. Raddison yelled to me.

"Thanks." I just hoped we'd get there soon.

I knew we were getting close to town as we started passing by more Fudgies, all of them stopping to gawk as we noisily made our way toward Main Street.

Abel didn't seem to notice the tourists. He looked to be deep in thought until he turned to me with a stern, serious expression. "My dad's not the only one worried about the safety of that building. You know, Mansfield's been cited twice for code violations, and he still doesn't fix the problems."

"But they'd shut the place down if it wasn't safe," I yelled to him.

"Not necessarily. The town's wondering what happens if they displace those people. Where would they all go?"

"So, you're telling me that place stays open, even if it's not safe, just because there's no place else to put the people?"

"Possibly," Abel yelled back. "That's why my dad's thinking about building his own housing complex."

"Really?"

"What do you think motivated Old Mansfield to install climate control?"

"I thought it was your dad's lawsuit."

"He didn't care about that – figured his liability insurance would cover it. No harm, except maybe a higher premium. But when dad offered to help pay for air-conditioning and threatened him with competition, then he started moving."

"So, is your dad going to build?"

"Not yet. He's giving Mansfield a chance to clean up his act. But I doubt that'll happen."

I doubted it, too. I'd seen Mansfield's type before, in my own ex-husband – the type that's so exceedingly selfish and greedy that it's hard to believe they could ever change enough to make a difference. However, I did at least now feel some sense of hope for the future, especially for those people who more permanently reside in the building. It seemed that the living conditions would have to get better, because if they didn't improve in Mansfield's building, then they certainly would be better in a new boarding house.

Although such a revolution would not come until some time down the road, I still found comfort in knowing that a change was indeed coming. The present had it challenges, but I felt optimistic when considering the future.

As we rolled along passed the growing throngs of staring Fudgies, I closed my eyes to the warm glow of the sunshine and rested my aching head against the towel, resting my weight on

Abel's side. Despite the rattle and shake of the tractor, the bounce of rolling through an occasional pothole, and the ache of the bump to my head, I was still able to push the bad aside and daydream about what was yet to come. For a few moments, I rose above it all, thinking only of pleasant thoughts as we made the trek to our final destination.

Chapter 11

ANOTHER STRANGER

CALM MOMENTARILY TURNED TO CHAOS when Abel clumsily threw the door of the first aid facility open wide and shouted, "Hey! We need some help here!"

The attending male aide appeared immediately, paused only for a second to glance at my bloodied bandana, then quickly reached for my arm and gently guided me toward the hallway.

"For crying out loud, Abel. You could've called for the ambulance." The aide continued to reprimand Abel as the two of them guided me down a short hall toward an examining room.

"There's an ambulance on the island?" I wondered if there were more vehicles here than I'd realized.

"Just for really bad accidents." Abel shoved open the exam room door, slamming it against the interior wall. "But you're not hurt that badly."

"Let me be the judge of that." The aide gently supported my arm, helping me over to the exam table. "Now be careful as you step up." He continued to support me as I climbed up and took a seat on the end of the table.

"I got her here as quickly as I could!" Abel leaned against the open door. "You better take a look at that cut on her head first, Deke."

"I know what I'm doing here, Abel." Deke didn't look back, instead stepping closer to study my face. He looked closely at the bandage on my forehead, his dark eyebrows bent down in a scowl. "Why don't you wait outside?"

"But I'm the one that racked her up like this! I just want to make sure she's okay."

I looked around Deke at Abel. "I'm just fine – no need to wait around for me, but thanks for the lift."

"Hey, Carly, it's the least I could do." Abel took a couple of steps from the door towards me.

Quickly, Deke turned and cut him off, reaching up and grabbing Abel by his slouching shoulders and turning him completely around.

"And now what you can do is wait outside." He pushed Abel out the door and toward the waiting area. "This shouldn't take long, so just sit down and read a magazine."

"Let me know if you need me," I heard Abel yell from the lobby.

Then Deke returned, swiftly shutting the door behind him. "Okay, where were we? Oh, yeah. I was just about to look at that cut." He reached for the knot in the grimy bandana and gently tried to untie it. "Nice sanitary bandage we've got here."

"There's not much else to use in the woods." I reached up and helped loosen the knot. "I was out riding my bike and we had a bit of collision."

"That's no surprise with Abel involved. He's an accident waiting to happen." With the knot now untied, he removed the bandana. "So, I heard Abel call you Carly, right?"

"Yes. And you must be Deke."

"That's right." He turned from me and studied his supplies on a small countertop, scratching at the golden brown curls behind his ears and the dark stubble on his face. "So, are you just visiting the island for the day?"

"Oh, no. I live here."

"Really?" He then turned on the faucet in a small basin and scrubbed his hands. "Can't say I've ever seen you around."

I watched him wash, his broad shoulders snugly filling out his white lab coat. "Well, I don't think I've ever seen you around either, Deke."

Drying his hands, Deke slipped on rubber gloves and then grabbed some gauze and a bottle of hydrogen peroxide. "This stuff won't hurt. I promise." He stepped back to me and leaned in close, staring again at my head with his emerald eyes. Reaching up with the gauze, he dabbed at my wound, the strong scent of Polo cologne evident over the hint of bleach that lingered in the air.

I blinked with each touch, anxiously anticipating any possible pain. "Actually, I probably shouldn't be calling you just Deke. It's Dr. Deke, right?"

"Oh, no. It isn't." He smirked a boyish grin, one corner of his mouth upturned. "At least it isn't yet." He then gave me a wink.

"Why? Are you still in medical school?"

"Well, not exactly – at least, not for humans." He smiled again, and then lightly pressed a few pieces of gauze against my wound.

"If not for humans, then for what? Monsters? You've got to know that's not terribly reassuring when you're about to fix my face!"

He laughed. "No, for animals."

"Oh, so you're in vet school. That's encouraging."

"Hey, I know my stuff here." His scowl returned.

"Oh, I'm sure you do – I was only kidding." The last thing I'd wanted to do was offend this handsome gentleman, especially while he was working on my face. "So soon-to-be-doctor, am I going to make it?"

Deke lifted the gauze from my head and pulled over a floor lamp. He then clicked on the light and turned it toward the gouge in my head. Placing his finger and thumb around the wound, he leaned in – his closest look yet – and I found myself comforted by his gentle touch.

In the glare of the bright lamp, he turned his gaze to my eyes. "I think you're going to need stitches."

"No, it's not that bad."

"Yeah, it is." He grabbed a roll of medical tape, then pressed more gauze to my head and taped it in place. "It's an awfully deep cut, and I wouldn't want to see a bad scar left on such a pretty face."

I was flattered, but also concerned. "Great. So how long will it take you to stitch me up?"

"Oh, I'm not going to do it." He took a seat on a rolling stool, the wheels squeaking as he rolled it up to a tiny desk, and then he started scribbling on a prescription pad. "I can't do that procedure – I'm not a people doctor. Remember?"

"Oh, yeah. So, then what am I supposed to do?"

"We'll ship you over to a hospital on the mainland. I know Dr. Pasquenelli there who's great with a needle and thread. She'll have you stitched up and out of there by dinner time."

"But I've got to get to Biminis – I have a job there, and I don't want to get fired."

"No work today." He stood up and opened the door to the hallway. "You'll probably be up to working in about twenty-four hours."

I stepped down from the exam table. "My boss is going to be so ticked."

"Nonsense – Mike will understand."

I stepped toward the doorway. "You know him?"

"I've lived here long enough to know most of the locals. I can give him a call and explain, if you want me to. Knowing Callahan like I do, I'm sure he'll understand."

He was right about Callahan. In the brief time I'd worked there, I'd already witnessed a couple of late call-ins and no-shows. No one was fired for it, and somehow we managed to get by even when we were short-handed for the night. I was lucky to work with such hard-working, understanding people.

Deke stopped me at the doorway and spoke in a low voice. "So, can we trust Abel to see you to the hospital after he did this to you?"

"Oh, it's not his fault – just an honest mistake. I was riding my bike on some rough back trails when I ran into him – literally. He said he was picking berries for his sister."

"Sounds like him." Deke smirked. "He's a bit eccentric, but a decent guy who means well. I'll have him get you over to the hospital, then I'll get over after closing to check on how you're doing." Before I had a chance to argue, Deke paged his friend back to the room. "Hey, Abel. You can come back now."

"Gee, I hate to trouble you," I said to be polite. But in all honesty, I was hoping this good-looking vet would pay me a visit.

"No trouble. Things are slow here, as usual, so I should be able to close at five and then come over to make sure they're treating you right. And then maybe I can help you get back over to the island. Is that okay?"

There would be no argument from me. Abel seemed harmless enough, as long as he wasn't picking berries, and I'd look forward to a ride home with Deke – a chance to get to know him better.

With the plan set, Deke made a couple of calls, fetched a wheelchair from the hallway closet, and sent me off with Abel to catch the next departing ferry.

Chapter 12

LACK OF DISCRETION

"SOME WOUNDS LEAVE PERMANENT SCARS if they're not taken care of properly and in a timely fashion." With steady, latex-gloved hands, Dr. Pasquenelli used a long Q-Tip to dab iodine on my forehead. "But I'm sure we got to this in time." She kept her bottom lip clenched tightly between her coffee-stained teeth as she carefully negotiated my wound.

"Yeah, this guy named Abel got me on a ferry and over here in no time." I grimaced while clutching the side of the examining table, anticipating the possibility of sudden pain. "He seemed to know just the right people to get me here in a hurry."

"So, he's still going to be here to get you home when we're done?" Her puffy, bloodshot eyes squinted as she stared at her work.

"Oh, yes, and I'm hoping Dr. Deke might make it over here by then, too."

"*Doctor* Deke, huh?" Dr. Pasquenelli smiled. "You must mean Deke Kavanaugh."

"Kavanaugh?" I pulled away and looked upon her with surprise. "You mean he's a Kavanaugh."

"Well, yes, that's his name. He's been a big help to us, keeping that island first-aid station open." She then popped the trash can lid with her foot and tossed away the Q-Tip along with her gloves. "Well, I'm just sorry you had to wait so long once you got in the hospital." She tucked a loose, curly lock of her graying blonde hair back into her hair band. "You just caught us at an unusually busy time."

"It's okay. Your receptionist explained all about the car accident – sounded like those people were hurt pretty badly. And I know you can't anticipate when something like that's going to happen, so I just needed to wait my turn."

"Well, thanks for being so understanding." She slipped on clean gloves, then grabbed a syringe from a steel tray and removed the cap. "Okay, this shouldn't take long." The doctor approached my forehead, the needle pointed right at me. "You'll feel a small prick, then a slight burning sensation."

Small? Slight? I wondered if physicians were taught this less-than-accurate terminology in medical school, or if they made it up on their own. At least the "numbing sensation" description was accurate. I could no longer feel anything on my forehead and scalp.

Dr. Pasquenelli pressed a fresh square of gauze against my forehead. "If you could, I'll have you keep this pressed against your head."

"Sure." I took hold of the gauze, feeling its softness against my fingertips but sensing only pressure against my head.

"Thanks. Now, let's get ready to stitch this up." She turned back to the steel tray, then paused as if uncertain about what to do next. She looked about the spattering of medical paraphernalia before her, then turned to scan the countertop. "Now where did she put the suture?" She began lifting scattered boxes and plastic wraps, glancing under each one. "Sally?" she yelled, paused, and then repeated, "Sally?" No one responded.

"What about there by the sink?" I pointed out what appeared to be a needle and piece of string lying behind the faucet. "Is that what you're looking for?"

"Oh, my gosh!" The doctor sprang to her feet, grabbing the leftover suture and tossing it with her gloves into the nearby medical-waste container. "We've been so overwhelmed – the nurses are still transferring patients to ICU and downstate, but that's no excuse for this mess."

Despite the scattering of open boxes and wrappers, I felt confident this doctor was taking every precaution to keep her work safe and sanitary, and so I wasn't that concerned. "It's okay. Don't worry about it."

"But I am worried about it." She scrubbed the sink area with antiseptic, then turned to me and shrugged. "We need restocking but I've got no staff to do it. I guess I'll just have to ask you to wait a little longer. Are you okay to hold that gauze on while I run down to O.R. for some sutures?"

"Oh, sure." I crossed my free arm across my chest, using my fist as a rest for my elbow so my arm would not grow tired.

"You are way too understanding, and I so appreciate it." She smiled. "I'll be right back."

And with that, I was left alone.

Stark white walls were of little comfort as I sought a distraction from this imminent medical procedure. The rack attached to the side of the medical supply cabinet contained only two magazines: *Ducks Unlimited* and a worn copy of *Field and Stream*. I speculated both were likely the tell-tale remnants of an earlier ER visit paid by either an avid fisherman who hooked himself with his own lure or a hunter who shot himself in the foot. I hopped off the examining table and walked over to the two publications, looking over the cover on each one long enough to confirm what I'd already suspected – that tying flies and pricing firearms was of no interest to me.

I returned to the examining table, still holding the gauze to my head as I wiggled my way back onto the long, white sheet of paper that rattled as it bunched up underneath me. Once situated, silence fell over the room but for the dull, distance commotion of people in neighboring rooms.

Then I overheard what sounded like a woman giggling. At first I wasn't sure where it was coming from, so I leaned a bit forward to listen into the hallway but only heard the sound of squeaky shoes and rubbing polyester as a heavy-set nurse waddled past my door. I sat back, still listening, and then heard it again – an irritating kind of snigger that sounded so close, it made me feel like the woman laughing was right in my own room.

Then a slight motion caught the corner of my eye. I turned to the countertop and noticed someone moving behind a small specimen door that had been left cracked about halfway open. The giggling continued, seeming to come from the box.

Next I heard a voice, but it was different from the giggler – masculine and almost at a whisper, but clearly audible. "Yeah, I put another stiff from that accident in the morgue fridge. You shoulda gone with me."

"Now what on earth would make me want to do that?" the giggling woman asked.

"Well, if not curiosity, then maybe you could just keep me company so I don't get SCARED!"

"Shh!" the woman hissed then giggled. "You're going to get us in trouble."

"Oh, come on! They've been so busy, this is your big chance to see what it's really like. You should see it! They've got this crazy machine down there that kind of looks like a meat slicer from the deli. Bet they use it to shave brains."

"Oh, that is so gross!" More giggling.

"And there's these jars on the shelf that got blood and eye balls and fingers and –"

"Will you cut it out?" It sounded like she gave him a soft pat, less convincing and more flirtatious.

"Nope. I'm not giving up 'til you go with me!"

"Well, I'm not going. It'll give me the creeps and I don't want to get in trouble."

"But you're just a volunteer – can't get in much trouble if you don't even work here."

The woman sighed. "Yeah, but *you* could get in trouble, even lose your job."

"What are you talking about? I've got official business down there."

"Sure. The groundskeeper has official business in the morgue? I don't think so."

"Hey, the nurses asked me to help out, so I helped out. And if that means I cart bodies, I cart bodies."

"Just doing a good deed."

"That's right. And, well, I can't help it if they've been so sloppy down there that they've been leaving out files for people to see."

"Oh, my God!" Over the sound of shuffling papers, the woman sounded genuinely shocked. "You're not supposed to have these!"

"Keep it down!" he insisted. "They were just thrown there on the desk, out in the open for everybody to see. If they wanted to keep them private, they should've put 'um away."

"But that doesn't mean you take them!"

"Shh! No one's going to notice they're gone. Besides, everyone's so busy right now they haven't got time to look at this stuff. So let me show you my favorite snapshot."

The shuffle of papers continued as the woman urged him to stop. "This is no joke – you've gone too far."

But the man would not spare either of us the gory details of his discovery. "Look. It's that Moore girl from Windemere– you know, the one they found in that dumpster."

I knew without seeing that they were looking at photos of Helena Moore.

"Not a real flattering shot, wouldn't you say?" He laughed. "And here's her profile. Gee, it must've been a bad hair day."

The sudden scurry of footsteps in the hall must have startled the couple as they shuffled the papers and moved away from my visual vantage through the specimen door. A pair of nurses darted through the hallway. Trying to sound official, the man muttered, "So, I brought this information back for the doctor to look over." After the footsteps passed, they resumed their whispered conversation.

"You've got to go down there and put those back right now," the woman pleaded.

"Okay, but not before I show you this." More papers shuffled. "Look here. It says how she died – from drowning."

"What?" The woman sounded as surprised as I was. "But how can that be? You can't drown in a dumpster."

"I know," the man agreed. "So somebody must've put her there after she died."

"And why would somebody do that?"

"Well, I suppose I… I guess, I'm not sure," the man mumbled, sounding a bit distracted.

"And what's that part say?" The woman now sounded more intrigued, insisting on an answer as the papers rattled once more. "What are you reading now?"

"Well, that's weird."

"What?"

"Sh!" the man reminded her to keep her voice down. "Well, a bit further down here it says they don't think she was sexually assaulted, but it also says that she was pregnant."

"Now you've done it – dug up a bunch of dirt on this poor woman. Let me see that." Papers crinkled and shuffled, the woman sounding quite determined to see the dirt for herself.

"Wait a minute, wait a minute!" The man held his ground. "It says it right here, see..." Papers rattled. "...it says she was pregnant with more than one child."

The woman paused. "Yeah, but it's not all that strange to be expecting twins."

The papers crinkled some more before the man added, "Try triplets, times five."

"What!"

I thought I must have misunderstood their whispers, so I turned my head and leaned in to listen more closely.

"That's what it says, right here," he continued. "Says she had at least fifteen buns in the oven – maybe more."

"That's not possible."

Those were my thoughts exactly. Surely there'd been an error in the autopsy. No one could be pregnant with that many babies, and certainly no woman could survive such a pregnancy – or maybe that was the point...

More papers rattled, the two of them not speaking as they must have been looking over the rest of the report.

"Wow." The man cleared his throat, finally breaking the silence. "Yeah, that's what it says, all right. Man, the guy who did this... that's one fertile son-of-a-bitch."

"You're such a jerk!"

I heard what sounded like another half-hearted slap along with a bit of laughter from both of them.

"Andy, did you get those receptacles emptied yet?" another female voice suddenly interjected into the conversation.

"I was just explaining to Sherri here how to do that so she could help me." His voice had quickly converted to strong and serious. "Figured two hands were better than one."

The new female sounded impatient. "And one set would be better than none. We've got so much waste lying haphazardly around here — you need to get it cleaned up, stat."

"We'll get on it right now."

"No, *you'll* get on it now," the extra voice countered. "No offense, Sherri, but I don't want to risk getting a volunteer contaminated with syringes and such. I don't want you or others exposed, and Andy knows how to handle it safely."

"That's fine with me," Sherri replied.

"With me, too," Andy agreed. "But before these slave drivers put poor Sherri to another task, she needs to take these back down to the morgue. Dr. Reed wanted them delivered there immediately."

"Oh, and I can see you were following his orders *so* promptly," the woman flatly remarked. "Okay, Sherri, take these down, then check with Madelyn for what else needs to be done. And as for you, you're coming with me. We're going to get this garbage out of here before I have to get angry."

"Hey, I've seen you get mad before, and it wasn't pretty." I could hear Andy joke with the older nurse as his voice trailed out of the neighboring room and into the hallway.

"Just great!" Sherri muttered regarding her imminent date with the morgue, then shuffled her way out of the adjoining room.

With my arm growing tired from pressing the gauze to my head, I rested my elbow on my thigh. Then staring at the barren walls, I considered this revelation about Helena Moore's remains. Could I have heard correctly? Did that man actually say that the dead woman had conceived more than fifteen children at once? How could that be?

"This should do the trick," Dr. Pasquenelli's voice startled me as she entered the room. Her eyes never looked up, instead focusing on the armful of supplies she was carrying. "Sorry it took so long, but things are even more disorganized down there — as if that's possible." She set the supplies on the edge of the counter, then picked up just one small, flat package. "So, are you still numbed up?"

"I think so. Can I put my arm down now?"

"Just a second."The doctor ripped open the small package with an already threaded needle inside it, then reached toward the area just above my eye and took hold of the gauze. "You can let go now — I've got it."

I lowered my arm, extremely relieved to no longer need to hold it to my head.

With her free hand, Dr. Pasquenelli picked up the threaded needle and brought it up to my forehead. "Did you feel that?"

"No. Not a thing."

"Okay, then let's see what we can finally do with this. First, let's have you lie down," Setting down the needle and thread, she lowered the back of the examining table "There. Now let's lean you back." She took hold of my arms and helped me lower myself until I was lying flat. "How's that?" she asked.

"Fine, I guess."

"Good then," she replied as she removed the gauze from my head.

Glancing up at that moment, I happened to see the white, cottony fabric saturated with blackish red blood. My stomach turned so I averted my eyes, trying to avoid watching the doctor's work as her hands pushed the needle into my head. I felt no pain — just pressure and some tugging as she worked. I knew I could get queasy just cleaning raw chicken for dinner, so there was no doubt that I didn't have the stomach for watching medical procedures.

"Well, it seems that, despite the long wait before we got to this, I think it's going to stitch up all right," Dr. Pasquenelli tried to reassure me. "Sorry you had to wait so long, but that was a wicked car accident we've been cleaning up."

The mention of a car wreck brought instant flashbacks of my family's accident, and my stomach turned again. I could feel the cold rush running through me, a tingling sensation that came along with the sudden vision of small dots of white light swirling before my eyes.

The doctor stopped a moment and stared at me. "Are you okay? You look a little white all of a sudden."

"Oh, I'm fine — maybe just a little woozy."

With her free hand, the doctor reached over and pulled a clean, white towel from the shelf. "I'll tuck this under your head and try to get you a little bit more comfortable," she said as she pushed the rolled towel under my neck. "Is that better?"

"I'm fine, really," I answered.

"Okay, but we'll stop a moment – just give you a quick break."

I was still feeling sick, but didn't want her to stop; I just wanted to get this over with. In the idle moments, I stared at the ceiling, my mind drifting back to thoughts of my family as I wished they were here with me.

The doctor reached to the bottom of the examining table. "Here. Let me get these out of your way, too, so you can move your legs around." She grabbed one of the stirrups at the base of the table, twisting and lowering it until it was out of sight. "It's not like we'll be needing these today."

The stirrups proved a distraction from my own personal tragedy, reminding me of the unexplained fate of Helena Moore. I still wondered how so many pregnancies could be possible, but didn't really want to reveal to the doctor what I had learned.

Dr. Pasquenelli lowered the other stirrup. "Well, you're starting to get your color back – looking a lot better. So, do you think we can go ahead and try to finish you up?"

"Sure. I'm fine." I adjusted myself on the table, making myself comfortable. "So, you must sometimes have to examine pregnant ladies in here, huh?"

"Oh, yes, we do." The doctor changed into a clean pair of surgical gloves. "We get our fair share of women who aren't sure if they're in labor.

"Do you ever deliver babies?"

"Seldom." She picked up the needle and returned to stitching. "Most ladies who are in labor usually make it from here to obstetrics before they deliver, but occasionally we get to catch one who just can't wait." She tugged on the suture as she continued her work. "Why do you ask? Know someone who's expecting?"

"No, not directly. But I overheard someone talking about a lady who was pregnant with – well, multiple babies."

"Twins and triplets are more common than you think."

"What about more than that?"

"Now quads and quints are the flukes. I know of one woman who gave birth to sextuplets, but they were born quite premature and faced a myriad of abnormalities. Unfortunately, some of them didn't survive."

"What if someone was expecting more than that? Would the babies likely die?"

She paused before answering. "There's not enough room in a woman's womb to get more than five or six close enough to term to survive outside the mother. Their lungs and other vital organs just aren't well enough developed. Modern medical technology can do a lot of things, and maybe someday it can do more, but for now there's still no better incubator than mom."

"So, what do you think would happen if someone was expecting – oh, let's say, maybe ten or so babies?"

"Ten?" The doctor paused, looking me right in the eyes for just a moment, then shaking her head. "Wow!" She laughed as she knotted another stitch. "Now that would be one for the Guinness Book. I could guess what would happen, but there's no need to because that just isn't possible. Humans never naturally conceive that many children at once, so the only way you could ever have such a circumstance would be by in-vitro – and there's no reason why anyone would do that."

"You mean test-tube babies?"

The doctor pushed at my forehead, taking another stitch. "Yes. They've been doing in-vitro for quite a few years now, having more and more success with it. It's been a controversial process, and *very* expensive. So, to help contain costs, they've been fertilizing more eggs at once – as many as thirty – and then freezing most of them for later attempts." She tugged at my head, tying another knot. "Then they implant just some of the embryos – maybe up to four or five at once, hoping one or two will take. But ten or more? No, they'd never do that. Nothing good could come of it."

"Why? What would happen?"

Dr. Pasquenelli stopped stitching and stared at the stark wall for a moment, then turned to me with her sullen answer. "Well, of course, they'd all die – and there's a good chance the mother would, too."

I wondered if her morose response was an indication that she knew of Helena's circumstances, but I didn't ask, trying not to reveal my own knowledge of the situation. Instead I remained silent, waiting to see if Dr. Pasquenelli offered anything more.

She continued stitching. "With that many fetuses in one woman, it wouldn't take long before they would start choking off one another. Even if they managed to make it through the early stages of pregnancy when the cells divide and multiply, eventually they would run out of room. Then they'd spontaneously abort, and that's when the mother would be in danger – when she started hemorrhaging. No ethical doctor's going to do that, even for the most desperate of women, and certainly no sane doctor would allow such a situation to continue."

Dr. Pasquenelli's response left me still wondering if she knew I was inquiring about the Moore case. Despite her detailed conjecture, she never implied that she knew about the situation. Quite the contrary, she held to her belief that such a scenario never would, and never should, happen.

"Well, this should do it." She tied off my final stitch.

With our time together coming to an end, I questioned whether or not I should come clean with what I had overheard. I felt a bit embarrassed that I'd heard this through eavesdropping, but figured that wasn't my fault. What was most important was for her and others on the hospital staff to know about this breech of confidentiality before it likely turned into raging gossip on the streets.

Just as I opened my mouth to confess, Dr. Pasquenelli spoke first. "I'll go find a nurse to bring in some instructions on how to care for this. Then she'll bandage you up and you'll be all set to go. Thanks again for your patience, and you're all set. Take care, now."

Before I had a chance to say a word, she hustled out the door and off to her next case.

This time there was no waiting for service as the nurse entered my room while I was still changing out of the examining robe. As

I slipped back into my shirt, I noticed for the first time that it was spotted with quite a bit of blood.

The nurse also noticed. "Head wounds can make such a mess, honey. Let's get you something else to wear home."

"I'd appreciate that."

She stepped out of the room long enough to retrieve a scrubs top that she handed to me. "You might want to wear this home. It's not so fashionable, honey, but it beats the bloody shirt. You'll want to wash that out with some peroxide when you get yourself home."

"Thanks."

"No problem." With her efficiency, she launched into an expedited explanation of how to care for my wound. She also gave me a card identifying the date and time for having my stitches removed and a plastic bag for my bloody shirt. Finally, she gave me another bag filled with so many samples of bandages and ointments that I'd be set not only for this injury but for any other I might have for the rest of my life. This lady was giving away the store.

She handed me a pen. "Just sign this discharge form and you're good to go. Any questions?"

"Yes. How do I get out of here?"

"Now some people can find that challenging, honey, but you've just got to remember that this hospital's a lot like Oz. You just got to follow the yellow squares to the elevators, then look for the directions there that'll take you anywhere you need to go."

"Thank you." I signed the paper. "Guess I'm all set."

"Oh, yes you are, honey. And you got two sweet, smiling gentlemen out there in the lobby waiting to help you get on home, so you're definitely all set. Have fun."

So, Deke had arrived and Abel had waited. With the two of them to escort me, I was sure I'd have an interesting boat ride back to Windemere. For that reason, I was all the more grateful for the kind nurse's insightful offer of a decent shirt. It certainly wasn't chic, but it undoubtedly would make me more presentable for rejoining my new acquaintances.

Sporting an aqua green medical top and an ugly bandage across my head, I set out for the lobby to meet up with my new companions and find my way back along the yellow brick road.

Chapter 13

THE MUFFIN MAN

SURVEYING THE DAMAGE in the mirror of the ferry restroom, I pulled back the bandage and counted at least eight stitches running perpendicular to my eyebrow. With the bandage on, it didn't seem too bad, but I felt like Frankenstein's bride with the bandage off. I only hoped there would be no permanent scarring once the stitches were removed.

One might have thought I had eight hundred stitches for all the attention I was given by my two escorts as we made the voyage back across the Straits to Windemere. While Deke wrapped me in his jacket to ward off the evening chill of the Straits, Abel pestered me with his requests to also somehow be of service.

"Can I get you something?" he sweetly asked, but it was a senseless question. Ferry rides were short and the ship had only the bare essentials. Unless I wanted a life jacket or a roll of toilet paper, there was nothing else to get.

When we arrived at the docks, Deke was first to insist that he walk me home.

He took me by the arm to help me off the boat. "Nothing like a ferry ride to make you lose your footing. You might feel a bit woozy, so I better make sure you get home all right."

"But it was my fault you got hurt." With still shaking hands, Abel took hold of my other arm. "The least I can do is walk you home."

Deke surprised me when he also took hold of my other arm, almost pulling me away from Abel. "Now, you know it's not your fault, Abel. It was just an accident, and you've got to be tired after such a long day. Just go home to your family and I'll make sure Carly gets home all right."

"I'm not that tired." Abel's voice escalated, becoming more argumentative. "I can walk her home. We've bothered you long enough."

"No bother, Abel, but it's a problem for you. Your dad's got to be wondering where you are. You should head home and help him out with your sister." Deke's voice sounded parent-like, quite odd for a conversation between two grown men who looked to be in their late twenties.

Abel scowled as his trembling hands tugged at my arm. "Dad's not going to be worried, and he can handle things himself. I've got time, but you're the one that doesn't. I know you've got work to do at your dad's place."

Deke had now lost his temper, his eyebrows lowered and nostrils flaring. "It can wait!"

"Then so can mine. You're always doing this – butting in when I meet people, and you've got to one-up –"

"Me? What about you? You don't let me –"

"How about I get some say in this." I jerked my arms from both of them, shocked at this sudden turn in the both of them. "I'm just fine to walk home by myself."

"Are you kidding?" Abel flailed his arm with animation. "You really got banged up. What if you get faint?"

"And it's not safe." Deke's voice was as soft and gentle as before, an amazing transformation from just a moment before. "I just want to make sure nothing happens to you."

"I can do that," Abel started in again. "I've got enough time to –"

"Okay, no more bickering," I scolded the two. "We'll all go. Might as well waste more time for both of you."

Reluctantly, they both agreed.

Over the next few days that brought an end to June, I witnessed an amazing outpouring of affection from these two men. It started out innocently enough, with each sending me cards and flowers to wish me well, but it became increasingly uncomfortable when each started asking whether I was seeing the other.

"Of course I am," I would answer. "He's my friend, just like you."

And neither was satisfied with this response, hurling insults about the other – a supposed friend – that were obviously intended to make me dislike or mistrust someone I was just beginning to befriend. This made me deeply question the nature of their apparent rivalry. How could they ever make friends, and how could they ever *be* friends with one another, if all they seemed to endlessly care about was "winning"?

Deke struck me as the more competitive of the two, always striving to one-up Abel's kind gestures or demeaning his behavior as that of a star-struck schoolboy.

"That poor Abel." Deke stood in my doorway holding a small paper sack tied with ribbon. "Heard he dropped off some sparklers for you to light on the fourth."

"Yes, he did." I stepped aside and let Deke slip in to my tiny room. "I thought that was nice of him."

"Well, he tries. It's just that, well, without his mother these last years, he hasn't had much guidance in what kinds of gifts women usually like to receive." He handed me the bag. "Of course, I've learned from my mother that most ladies prefer *sparkle* over *sparklers*."

I opened the bag and removed a tissue-wrapped item, a delicate cut-glass charm on a fine, silver chain. "You shouldn't have, Deke. I can't keep accepting these gifts."

"It's no big deal." He took the chain from my hands and stepped to my window, draping it gently over the deadbolt so the charm dangled below it, refracting the rising sunlight. "You don't even have to wear it. Just enjoy it here."

"Well, it's very pretty." I smiled.

"Yeah, I thought you'd like it." He took the wrappings from me and tossed them in the waste can. "Just be careful on the fourth that you don't get burned by that silly little gift from Abel, the poor guy. Just wish he could try to grow up a little."

I didn't know what to say – seemed like I never did. If I defended Abel, then Deke's belittling would just continue. I didn't think there was much I could do about it, so I just ignored it.

For the next few days, the occasional gift-giving continued – along with the criticism – until I realized that I couldn't keep ignoring, or rather accepting, all of these gifts. I finally knew the situation was way out of control the morning a knock woke us up at the crack of dawn.

"I am not answering that!" Pepper threw her covers over her head. "Tell those boys it's too early for today's drop-off."

"Just be quiet." I turned the lock and opened the door.

"Good morning." Abel stood there, his characteristically shaky hands holding out a brown paper sack. "Breakfast."

I pulled my pajama top closed around my neck. "What's in the bag, Abel?" I yawned.

"It's something I picked just for you." He grinned, then thrust the brown paper sack toward my face.

I took hold of the bag and peeked inside. "Muffins. How thoughtful of you." I yawned again.

"They're huckleberry muffins — enough for both you and Pepper to have some."

"Thanks a lot for thinking of me, Abel." The comforter over Pepper's face muffled her deadpan voice.

"No problem, Pepper." He took the bag from my hands, reached in and removed one muffin to display. "I made these from berries I picked in the woods just yesterday. You can't beat fresh huckleberries."

"Well, they look good, Abel." I leaned against the door. "I promise I'll eat one once I wake up a little bit more."

"Okay. I bake a lot for my sister, Gretchen, and she really likes them, so I thought you two might like to try them. I swear I didn't hurt anyone when I was picking them." He laughed a bit awkwardly.

Despite my exhaustion, I found myself smiling at Abel's poke at himself. "Well, I appreciate it and hope you didn't go to too much trouble."

"No trouble. I've kind of been the happy homemaker for my family ever since Mom passed away — doing a lot of the household chores and caring for my big sister. I'd do just about anything for her."

"And what is it you said she has again? Was it Hunter's disease?"

"Huntington's," he corrected me.

"That's right. So, she needs a lot of help, does she?"

"Enough." Just like when I had asked before, he didn't elaborate.

I struggled to envision Abel as anyone's "little brother," with his towering physique that slouched over to meet me at eye level. But at the same time, I could understand that sense of brotherly love his sister must have felt toward him. I felt it, too, as did most anyone who knew Abel. He had a kind, gentle demeanor that, despite his quirky ways, gave him an endearing quality that made you want to reach up and give him a big hug.

"Oh, and I've got something else." He stepped just out of sight in the hallway, then returned to the doorway pushing a bicycle he balanced with his tremulous hands. "This is for you, too."

"Oh, Abel! I can't accept that!"

"Can't accept what?" Pepper threw back her covers.

"A bike. I can't accept a bike."

"Yes you can." Abel tipped the bike to give me a better view of the beautiful twelve-speed Raleigh. "I'm replacing the one I mangled."

"But mine's repairable, and it certainly wasn't this nice."

"It was nice enough, and I ruined it. Besides, I figured you needed one with a bit more maneuverability so you wouldn't wipe out when avoiding any sort of undesirable obstacles." His face flushed a bit.

"Oh, Abel. You're far from an undesirable obstacle, and you're so sweet to offer me this gift, but I just —"

He put down the kickstand and tipped the bike onto it, then stepped closer to me. "Don't think of it as a gift. It's just payback for the bike I mangled — and just a little thank you for being a good friend. Okay?"

Though it seemed an extravagant gift, I figured this was Abel's peace offering meant to put the past behind us and to repay what he considered to be a debt. But I worried that my accepting it might lead him on in some way.

He reached in his pocket and took out a small key. "Use this for the chain I put on it and keep it locked up somewhere inside the building so nobody steals it." By a tiny, attached key ring, he passed the key toward me.

I crossed my arms across my chest and just looked at the key, afraid that accepting it might jeopardize our friendship. The last thing I'd ever want to do was hurt Abel.

He drew back the key. "What? You don't like it?"

"Oh, no. It's very nice."

"Wrong color?"

"No. No. Red's very nice."

"I would have preferred blue," Pepper interjected. "So please remember that when you get me one, Abel." She threw the covers back over her head, then mumbled from underneath, "Would you please just take it so I can get back to sleep."

"Yes, take it." He grabbed my hand and, with trembling fingers, pushed the key into my palm. "Gosh. I was afraid you wouldn't like it – that I picked the wrong one or something."

"Oh, no, Abel. It's an awesome bike. Thanks. It's just –"

"Yours. Good enough then." He grinned.

"Yes." I kept the key. "Good enough."

"Great."

There was an awkward pause. Abel made a fist and rubbed it in his palm, still grinning and looking at me.

I pointed at the bike. "Well, guess I better bring that thing in here until I can get dressed and go find some place to keep it."

"Oh, yeah." Abel took the bike by the handlebars and clumsily wheeled it into the tight quarters. "So, now that you've got wheels again, I thought maybe you might go trail blazing with me tonight. There's some early fourth-of-July fireworks they're going to shoot off and I thought we'd go check them out."

I paused and looked at the bike. "You said this was just a gift between friends, right?"

"It's not a date, Carly. It would just be two friends out having a good time together. What do you say?"

It seemed a harmless enough invitation, and Abel seemed to be clear about our relationship. Besides, I was scheduled to work the night of the fourth and hadn't known about these other fireworks. I was sure they'd be a spectacular sight out over the Lake Huron and I was eager to see them.

I pulled the bike the rest of the way into the room. "Okay. Meet me at Biminis – we'll leave from there."

"Okay!" Abel exclaimed as he beamed with his endearing smile. He turned on his heels and took a step to leave but caught his foot on the bike spokes and tripped. A bit pink in the face but still smiling, he awkwardly picked himself up and strutted out of the room and down the hall, out of sight.

Chapter 14

THE EFFECTS OF ALCOHOL

PUNCTUALITY WASN'T HIS STRONG POINT, and so it was no surprise when Abel failed to show up on time. Since he'd seemed so eager to go gallivanting about the island, I had wondered if he might possibly show up by the end of my shift at Biminis. But when my work was nearly finished, he was still nowhere to be found.

His tardiness led to an unexpected visit from someone I'd never seen at Biminis. Since I seldom worked the night shift, I was only just beginning to develop a familiarity with the evening regulars, but this clean-shaven gentleman with curly locks and emerald eyes was not one of them, although I was getting to know him well.

"Good evening, miss barmaid." Deke took a seat on a barstool by the register.

I was just cashing out, counting up my meager tips for the night. "Why, Deke. What brings you to Biminis?"

"Well, guess I'm here for the usual – something to drink, a little socializing."

"No doubt, you'll find both here." I gave him a smile and a wink. "I haven't punched out yet, so how about I get you something to drink?"

"Ah, yes. How about a Tanq'n tonic?"

I hadn't heard that request since working at Simple Pleasures. "What?"

"Doesn't Mike have Tanqueray here? That seems like it would be pretty standard."

"Oh, I'm so sorry, sir." Tilting my head down with eyes lowered, I dramatically curtsied. "I thought you said you wanted a 'Tankin'

Tonic' – figured it might be some fancy new drink for those who descend down to us from the bluff on high."

"The bluff on high, is it?" He grinned, his eyes twinkling. "That's a good one."

"Well, I'm so sorry, kind sir, but we simpletons down here don't have Tanqueray – just the house gin."

"Hey, well that's actually just what I 'descended' down here for. The house gin sounds great, or I could even just have whatever you've got on tap."

"Coming right up," I obliged as I grabbed a large mug, placed it under the nearest beer tap, and pulled. I decided to give him a true taste of our cozy tavern by treating him to our patrons' favored brew, a cold mug of Strohs. With the head overflowing, I placed it on the bar before him. "Here you go – the Tanqueray of beers."

As the head settled, Deke raised the mug and took a hearty swig. He puckered his lips and his face grimaced at the unfamiliar flavor. "Wow! And so what do I owe you for this fine beverage?"

"If you're brave enough to drink it, then this one's on me. Guess I feel guilty for serving you what non-connoisseurs consider Detroit River water."

"Is that what they call it?"

"Yeah, so if you can finish that one and you're foolish enough to want more, then I'll catch you on the next one."

"Fair enough, but at least let me tip the service." He dug into the pocket of his tight jeans, pulled out a dollar, and tossed it onto the bar.

"No need." I tried to push the dollar back to him, but he stopped me by placing his hand over mine.

"Please, at least let me do this." He squeezed my hand over the dollar.

"Okay," I answered, slowly retracting my hand from his warm touch, the dollar still in my fist. I dropped it in with the rest of my tips then pushed all the bills and change off the edge of the bar and into my hand, tucking the fistful of money into my shorts pocket. I'd have plenty of time to count it up later.

"I was hoping you might get off work soon. Maybe we could take a walk, stop downtown for a drink or dessert."

Simultaneously, I felt both delight and disappointment. "That's such a nice offer, Deke, and I'd love to go, but I can't. Wish you'd asked sooner."

"What, you've already got plans?"

"Yeah, Abel's stopping by."

He raised his mug and took another bitter swig. "You know, I do understand how you probably don't want to hurt his feelings and all, but for what it's worth, I think it's probably best for him if you cut things off – not lead him on any longer."

I rested my fist on my hip. "I'm not leading him on. He knows we're just friends. I've made that perfectly clear."

"Really?" Deke took a couple of swallows and grimaced again. "Well, maybe at one point he thought that, but I'm not so sure that's the case anymore – now that you accepted that nice bike he gave you."

I drew back and raised my eyebrows. "You already know about that?"

"Of course I do. Abel tells me everything, and he was so excited about giving you that bike – figured that would be a step in the right direction."

"The right direction?"

"Yeah. Toward a relationship." Deke took another swig, then pushed the mug away. "Wow! I just can't drink that crap. Anyway, now that you're going out with him tonight, I bet he thinks that's another step, and –"

"We're not 'going out' – at least not in the way you're suggesting." I grabbed the mug and threw its contents in the bar sink with a splash.

"Well, you may think you're not, but he thinks you are."

Before I had a chance to argue further, a voice boomed from a group of partying sailors. It was Rafae Battiste, a year-round Saint and Biminis' regular who piloted tourist boats for the Straits Ferry Line. He was yelling something I couldn't quite understand, but it was enough to evoke a cringe from Deke who slouched down on the bar.

Rafae yelled a second time, this time his voice much clearer. "D'Arcy?" As he climbed up from his seat and slowly sauntered towards us, I wondered what he was up to.

Rafae and his fraternity of mariners were known for their occasional outbursts, so his behavior came as no surprise. They were all considered just a bunch of boisterous attention-seekers who frequently disrupted bar chatter with shouts from the corner round table, a spot they liked to consider their own. From that vantage point, these deckhands would sometimes single out a patron or employee to harass. I was afraid that this time it was going to be me.

"Don't worry," I tried to reassure Deke. "Rafae's all bark – only preys on the timid – kind of like a vulture after a wounded animal. I'll take care of this."

Only days earlier, Callahan had been forced to deal with the unruly table when the group started conducting their own impromptu Miss Biminis contest. Every female who walked through the door had been verbally evaluated then rated on a scale of one to ten. Each reluctant entrant's score was then flashed on cards and announced aloud for the few who were amused to hear. When our hardest working dishwasher Collette came through the doorway with her long dreadlocks swaying along the back of her petite frame, she met with jeers and a score of negative two, sending Callahan off the deep end. He took away their cards, confiscated their drinks, and kicked the lot of them out for the night. When they returned the next day, he wouldn't let them have their table back until they apologized to Collette. It seemed a hollow apology, one followed with laughter from most of the gang.

I never understood why Callahan didn't permanently ban the clan from the bar since most patrons disdained the crew for their offensive behavior. Surely their bar tab did not outweigh the number of potential customers driven away in disgust over the clan's distasteful conduct. Nevertheless, the gang of ruthless interrogators remained as gatekeepers of Biminis, leaving us all to wonder when we'd next fall victim.

"D'Arcy?" Rafae pushed a chair aside, clearing his way to the bar.

I looked down at Deke. "Is he talking to you?"

"Afraid so."

"Is that your name? D'Arcy?"

"Afraid so."

I knew he was a Kavanaugh, but hadn't figured on him being so closely related to those from the tales I'd heard.

I stared at him as if seeing him for the first time. "So, you're one of *the* D'Arcy Kavanaughs?"

"Yeah. Yeah. That's me. Afraid so."

"D'Arcy!" Rafae bumped into a table, slopping a bit of his beer out on the floor. In his inebriated state, he swayed slightly as he pressed his Docksider over the spill and ground it into the floorboard before continuing his way toward us. "I see you there, D'Arcy!" He grinned.

"This guy can get pretty obnoxious," I warned Deke.

"So I've noticed." Deke further lowered his head.

Once at the bar, Rafae pulled up a stool. "Why Du-Arcy-Ka-Va-Naw!" he slurred as he tried to enunciate each syllable but seemed to miss the mark. Deke was practically lying on the bar as Rafae slapped him on the back then reached his arm across his shoulders and hugged him. "How the hell are you?"

Deke raised his head to answer. "Just great, Rafae."

"So, what brought you down off the mountain top, ole' boy? Don't most of the high and mighty on the bluff stay away from such lowly places like Biminis?"

"You know me better than that, Rafae."

"That I do, Du-Arcy. Don't tell me you're here to hit on our pretty little Carly?"

I felt my cheeks go flush. "Deke's just here for a little something to drink, something to –"

"Deke?" Rafae paused, staring at Deke. "Are you still letting people call you Deke like your mommy used to? I thought I told you never to use a nickname that rhymes with geek. Besides, what's wrong with Du-Arcy? It's got all of that tradition, all that heritage, all that – prestige."

Deke sat up, pressing his palms against the bar. "I just prefer Deke, thanks."

Rafae leaned in toward me, lowering his voice slightly. "Well, let me explain this to you, Carly." His pungent breath reeked of beer. "Mommy named him after Daddy, but Daddy wasn't keen on the name – must get confusing with all those Du-Arcy's in the house. So, they start calling him by his initials, DK, and I guess it stuck. It's just that some shortened it to one syllable, so instead of DeeKay, it's Deke. I still think it sounds too much like geek."

Deke clapped his hands together. "Yeah, it's that simple. Well, glad we got that taken care of –"

"Oh, but it's not that simple, is it DeeKay?" Rafae turned toward Deke. "Because it's not just Daddy you're named after."

"Yeah, but Carly doesn't want to hear all this, and I –"

"Sure she does."

I shook my head at Rafae. "So, how do you know all this, anyway?"

Rafae laughed. "What, DeeKay didn't tell you? Why, me and this boy here, we grew up together! My daddy is his daddy's "monservont" – lived with him since my mommy died, rest her soul, when I was just four."

I lowered my eyes. "I'm sorry."

"No, it's okay, because I got to grow up with this guy!" He punched Deke in the arm. "Yeah, his mommy made me her own personal charity case, telling all the locals how she'd let me hang around the place just so I could learn to talk right and stop jabbering like a Saint kid." He elbowed Deke. "You've got a kind family there, kid." Rafae took a swig of his beer. "Yeah, those Kavanaughs, they're just seeped in the tradition of caring for others – been doing so through five generations, way back to the great Captain D'Arcy Kavanaugh, and his father before him." Rafae smiled, winking at me. "And that makes DeeKay here 'Mr. D'Arcy Kavanaugh the fifth.' Pretty fancy, huh?"

I looked at Deke. "I've heard about your family, Deke – about the *Perseverance*."

Deke's nails were nearly digging into the surface of the bar top. "Yeah, that's great." He ground his teeth while glaring at Rafae.

Rafae leaned against the bar for support. "The poor guy — name comes with a lot of baggage, don't you know." He leaned toward Deke. "Hey, too bad you're not the fourth like your daddy. Then you could drop the whole Deke-geek thing and just call yourself 'Four.' Now *that* would be a great nickname, especially for golf!"

"Yeah, too bad that won't work for me, Rafae." Deke stood up from his stool, turning his back to Rafae and leaning in toward me. "Since we can't get together right now, how about on the fourth? I could take you horseback riding, and then we could see the fireworks."

Rafae overheard him. "Smooth, DeeKay, real smooth,"

I glared at Rafae as I leaned in toward Deke. "I've got to work late on the fourth, but I'm off that morning."

"Morning's no good, DeeKay." Rafae leaned toward the both of us. "It's hard to hit on a girl in daylight. Kills the mood."

Deke smiled at me. "I'll bring the horses by your place about nine." Then he turned to Rafae, throwing his arm around his shoulders. "It's always great to get unsolicited advice from someone who has such a suave way with women, Rafae."

Rafae returned the embrace. "Well, it's my pleasure old buddy. You know I've always looked out for you, like the time I helped you out with Marla. Man, that babe was ticked off! But I fixed things — made it so you two could still go down by the lake and —"

"I'm sure Carly's had enough reminiscing for one night." Deke's face looked flushed. "How about I join your table. I'll buy you another round while we hash over old times."

Rafae released his embrace. "Excellent!" With a stagger, he led the way back to the table.

Stepping from the bar, Deke looked back at me with a grin. "If you can't beat 'em, join 'em'. You go have a nice time with Abel, but remember, you're just friends." With a wink, he turned and followed Rafae to where he joined up with the throng of drunken sailors, leaving me to continue with signing out for the night.

With Deke deep in the clutches of the boisterous sailors, there would be no opportunity for further conversation. Besides, I knew Abel would be arriving sooner or later and I didn't want to subject him to the humiliation of likely remarks from the frat boys. I quickly pocketed my evening's profits and sneaked out the back door.

Chapter 15

FIREWORKS

After waiting for about ten minutes in the chilly island air, I decided Abel could find me just as easily at the boarding house. I stuck my head back into the bar area just long enough to tell Pepper where I'd be, then headed back out the kitchen door, unlocked my new bike, and headed home.

I wasn't more than a hundred yards downhill from Biminis when I met up with Abel. I stopped to find him winded from feverishly peddling up the steep embankment that led to the bar. As he tried to catch his breath, he struggled to speak.

"Thought – I'd – missed – you." He was gasping for air.

"You almost did." I wheeled my bike over closer to him. "I thought maybe you got tied up somewhere, and I wasn't sure you were coming."

Abel was finally catching his breath, his forehead dripping with sweat. "I left awhile ago, but I had a problem." He wiped his sweating, shaking hands on his loose shirttail. Somebody left a broken beer bottle in the road and I ran over it. Must have punctured my tire – I had a blow-out."

I looked more closely at him. "Are you hurt?" I knew all too well the potential for injuries brought on by such mishaps.

"No, but I had to go back home to change."

"Why? Did you rip your clothes?"

"Not exactly." He paused. Even in the dim light from the street lamps, it was obvious he was blushing. "I ran into a street cleaner's wheelbarrow."

I tried so hard not to laugh, but I had to giggle at the thought of Abel covered in the day's less-than-fresh horse manure. He must have been so humiliated when it happened, and even more so now.

Yet he was such a good sport about it as he joined me in a hearty laugh.

Abel lifted his feet and began to pedal. "Hope I'm not as ripe as I was half-an-hour ago. I showered and slapped on some of Dad's aftershave, but I probably still smell like 'Ode to Horse Dung.'"

I took off after him, still laughing as we rode our bikes down the hilly terrain to Main Street. We were finally regaining our composure as we passed by blocks of shops and continued on in the direction of Windemere Bluff. As the sun was now setting, I followed Abel's lead, taking a couple of unfamiliar turns then heading up a steep embankment.

Abel came to a stop, hopping off his bike and flagging me to a stand-still, as well. "Let's walk up this part – it's too tough to bike it."

In total agreement, I climbed off my bike and hiked at his side. As I pushed my bike along, we came upon a hut about the size of a one-car garage. It had been made from tree limbs, grass, and mud, and it looked almost like an igloo.

I paused to take a better look. "What is that?"

"You've never seen the chapel?"

"I've never even been on this road. You're saying that's some kind of church?"

"Native Americans built it here when French fur traders came to the region. Missionaries also came here to convert the locals. Must have had some luck since they built this."

"Seems like I learn something new about this island everyday." I began pushing my bike again, hiking on past the hut chapel.

Abel continued to lead the way. "Well, there's a lot to learn here – a lot of history, and new things being unearthed all the time. Why, just last week, some archeologists on the backside of the island found the remnants of what they think might be the foundation for an old British ammunitions bunker. Must be more recent than from the French period – from a time later on when the British took control of the settlements here and over on Mackinac Island."

As we hiked to the hilltop and remounted our bikes, Abel continued to detail the island's history and how it fit into the larger scheme of the King of England's desire for colonies throughout the world. I rode along, listening intently as we made our way up to and past the cottages on the bluff. Then we turned onto a narrow path headed back into a wooded area I had not yet explored. As dusk was falling, it was hard to see where we were headed.

I pedaled hard to keep up. "Where are we going?"

"You'll see." Abel continued blazing the trail, undaunted by the falling darkness.

Temporarily the ground graded slightly downward, so I coasted along, the faint clicking sound of my bike wheels almost obscured by the growing chirp of the evening's crickets. My bike then slowed as we approached another point of ascent, so I downshifted and began pumping away in preparation for the laborious climb. With the momentum I'd started and a few tough cranks of the pedals near the peak, we finally arrived at what turned out to be a secluded ledge overlooking the main harbor of Windemere.

"This is my favorite spot." Abel pushed down on his kickstand and climbed off his bike. "You can see so far out over the lake from here."

Swinging my leg over my back wheel, I also dismounted. "The water is so beautiful from here, with the moon's reflection... oh, and look! I can see the lights on the Mackinac Bridge from here."

Abel pointed toward the northern end of the bridge. "All those lights glowing over there are on Mackinac Island." He then pointed to the opposite side of our vista. "And I'm sure you recognize that light turning off Beacon Point."

"The lighthouse." I smiled. "You picked a perfect place to watch the fireworks."

"And, I brought the best treats, too." In the fading light, he pulled out what appeared to be a blanket. "Figured we could snack while we're waiting for the show to begin."

In the nighttime shadows under a cluster of maple trees, Abel located a flat patch of grass where he awkwardly tried to spread out the blanket. Offering to help, I pulled at the other side of the blanket, smoothing it out as I heard Deke's voice echoing in the back of my head. To my dismay, this was beginning to feel too much like a date, but at this point, there wasn't much I could do about it.

"Why don't you have a seat – get comfortable." Abel said as it appeared in the shadows that he was doing the same.

I sat down and crossed my legs, noticing the soft breeze that was lightly rustling the leaves above us. With no streetlights, I could only make out Abel's silhouette as he appeared to remove what looked like a bottle from his backpack. It was now too dark to see what was in it.

"Hope you like cherry wine." He took out plastic glasses and placed one in my hand.

The wine was thoughtful but made me feel more uneasy. "So, ah... When do the fireworks start, anyway?"

"Soon enough."

In the blackness, I still could make out the silhouette of Abel's ever quivering hands trying to pour some liquid from a bottle into my cup. Once filled, I took a swig.

"Wow." I puckered up from the sour taste, hoping he couldn't see me grimace. "That's different." I didn't have the heart to tell him that it must have gone bad, but I knew I couldn't drink it all. So, in the shadows of the maples, I quietly reached behind my back and poured most of the contents of my cup onto the grass.

Abel poured himself a glass and took a drink. "Ooo! Not one of their better bottles."

"Oh, so it's not supposed to taste that bitter?"

"No, not at all." He took my glass from me. "Sorry about that."

I gazed out over the water. "Shouldn't the fireworks have started by now?"

"They will. Meanwhile, try some of these." He struggled to steady his hand as he held out a small container for me to blindly dip into.

I fished around in the sticky contents. "Feels like raisins."

"Dried cherries." He took some, as well, then spoke with his mouth full. "Mm. Now *these* are good."

He passed the container back to me and I reached in for a few more, but then I froze. I heard something, like the sound of leaves and twigs crunching under foot.

"What was that?" I whispered, certain that something was out there.

Abel paused for a moment and listened. "I didn't hear anything."

As I sat perfectly still and carefully listened, all I heard was a few leaves lightly rustling in the trees overhead, the crickets still chirping, and the distant clip-clop of horses still running on the streets below. "Must have been the wind or something."

"Or maybe a squirrel." Abel took the container back, grabbed a fistful, and pushed them in his mouth.

"Yeah, he's probably after our cherries, and I'm not going to share them with any flea-bitten critter that —" I froze as a stick snapped behind me.

Abel was still chewing. "What's wrong now?"

"Didn't you hear that?" I whispered.

"Hear what?"

"I know I heard something, and it's getting closer,"

"What did it sound like?" Abel softly questioned, but I never got the chance to answer for myself as the woods answered for me. This time a tree branch rustled within a few yards of where we were sitting. Something was definitely lurking nearby.

I stood up and stepped to my bike. "Let's go, Abel."

Abel stood, too, grabbing his blanket from the ground and spilling the cherries. "I'm not sure running's such a good idea."

"Why not?"

Before Abel could answer, a glaring flashlight lunged from the trees and blinded us as it quickly approached.

"Hullo, folks! How ya doin', eh?" came a blaring voice from behind the flashlight. "Ya havin' a little party up here, eh?"

I cowered, too scared to answer the dark figure behind the glaring light. But Abel stood tall, undaunted by this stranger.

"We were waiting for the fireworks to start, that is, until you showed up." Abel actually took a step toward the stranger. "What are you doing, coming up here and scaring us like that?"

"I'm doin' my job, by golly." The stranger stepped closer, focusing his light on me. "And are ya up here of your own choosin', ma'am?"

His voice was laced with a heavy "Yooper" accent – a dialect found to be prevalent among the natives of Michigan's U.P.

Abel never gave me a chance to answer. "Of course she's here of her own choosing! Do you really think that I'd bring a woman up here to take advantage of her? You know me better than that, Macke."

It was Officer Eino Macke of Windemere's police force. I'd seen him on Main Street a couple of times before, riding a bike with upright handlebars and a large wire basket I figured he used to carry his equipment. His bike peddling ways earned him the nickname Officer Schwinn at Biminis, a name I thought I'd best be careful not to call him at this moment.

Macke glared his flashlight in Abel's face. "Sorry 'bout dat, Abel, but I gotta ask, ya know." Then Macke turned the light back on me. "Ya need to answer da question all fer yer-self, Ma'am. Do ya want ta be here, eh?"

"Yes, I chose to come here." I was feeling less frightened about speaking to a police officer than the bogeyman I'd thought had been lurking in the bushes.

"Could ya show me some kinda identification, say a license or someting with a picture?" Macke finally tilted his flashlight downward. "Ya know, I'm gonna need ta see some I.D. from dah both of yous, Abel."

"Oh my gosh!" I realized I didn't have my I.D. with me. "Mine's back in my room. I'm sorry, but I don't normally carry my driver's license on the island."

"Dat should be okay, ya know, 'cause dah drinkin' age, it's only twenty-one and, ah, I figure ya look plenty beyond dat, by golly!" He laughed.

"Well, thanks, I think." I swallowed his insolence.

"So, if ya can just answer a couple a' questions." Officer Macke continued his interrogation.

"Sure I can." My eyes had readjusted so I could finally make out the short, slight frame of my inquisitor – someone who seemed hardly worth fearing.

"Okay, let's get down dah basics, yah know, like your name is?"

"Carly Malloy."

"Nice to know ya, Miss Malloy." He tucked his flashlight under his left arm and reached with his right hand to shake. "And can ya tell me if ya live here on dah island?"

I shook his hand. "Yes I do."

"And so ya must know dah island ordinance number 467-167.2a – dah one strictly prohibitin' any alcohol consumption on public land."

"But I wasn't drinking." I hoped he wouldn't detect that single swig of sour wine on my breath.

Abel crossed his arms and stepped even closer to Macke. "We're well aware of the law, Officer, and I'm sure you're well aware that this is my dad's property."

"Ya betcha by golly I knows it, but I also knows dat yer papa donated dah land to dah island fer all ta enjoy. Dat makes it a public place, don't it, eh?"

Abel's hands went to his hips as he lifted his chin in a stern posture I'd never seen from him before. "Haven't you got anything better to do than going around bothering people with this nonsense?"

Macke straightened his belt. "Now, ya looky here, young whipper-snapper! Dis here isn't no nonsense. We gots arselves a hellava mess goin' on with a predator on dah loose, don't ya know."

"And you know I'm not him, so why don't you move along and do something useful!"

"I am, by golly!" Macke gripped his flashlight and shook it at us. "I'm cleanin' up dah misbehavior around here – glad I got to ya before dah situation got outta control!"

Suddenly, a bright glow exploded over the lake, followed in seconds by a loud bang.

"Great." Abel slapped his hands to his side. "And now we're missing the fireworks." Abel stuffed the blanket into his bag as he stepped to his bike. "So now that you've ruined our plans for the evening, I guess we'll just be moving on."

"Not so fast, Abel." Macke sidled over to us. "Now ya gone and gotten all disrespectful on me, don't ya know, and so I guesses dah best ting ta do now is ta turn dis matter over to yer papa, eh."

"Oh, for Pete's sake, Eino!" Abel maliciously kicked the stand up on his bike and climbed on. "You don't need to go and wake up my dad. He's got enough on his mind – doesn't need to be bothered."

"Eh, he does got troubles, but I've got dah responsibility ta do my job, don't ya know. It's not like I'm gonna take ya in and makes ya take dah breathalyzer, but it's my duty ta tell yer Papa where ya been." He took his flashlight and searched through the trees. "Now, where'd I go and put down my bike, eh?"

Abel turned to me. "Let's get going so I can get there first and tell my dad what Officer Crazy's been up to."

Macke wandered deeper into the wooded area, scanning the ground with his flashlight. "I must a dropped dah darn ting down heres somewheres."

We were just taking off when Officer Macke finally found his bicycle. He must have hopped on and pedaled quickly as he managed to catch up to us once the path turned to pavement. He then blew his whistle and flagged for us to move over so he could pass. Once in front of us, he looked back at us and waved his hand in a motion to indicate that we should follow him. Then he turned forward and straightened his back to pedal proudly down the bluff, leading his captives on to Windemere's finest hotel – and to certain humiliation.

Chapter 16

THE POWERFUL AND POWERLESS

THE JOLT OF A BLARING BUZZER sounding in the middle of the night would likely alarm most people, but Mr. Hanika appeared surprisingly composed as he responded to the late interruption at the front door to the residential suite in the hotel.

"Oh, it's just you, Abel, and I see you have your friend with you." Mr. Hanika ignored the officer, running his fingers through his thick mop of silver hair. "She's lovely, just as you said, my boy. Oh, and I'm afraid I'm quite a wreck, dear, but it's very nice to meet you." He extended his hand and flashed a charming smile.

I shook hands with him. "My pleasure, sir."

"Sorry to be troublin' yas, Vincent, especially at dis late hour, don't ya knows." Macke looked at his watch. "Shoo-we! It's half-ways to midnight, by golly!"

Vincent turned to Macke. "Yes, Officer. Has there been some sort of problem I need to know about?"

"He's just making a problem, Dad." Abel scowled at Macke. "I told him not to sound the buzzer, but he was all hell-bent on waking you up."

"Now, ya sees how dare is a bit of a problem, and a lot of it has to do with dah attitude I'm gettin' heres."

Abel heaved a sigh.

"Abel." Vincent's voice was short and firm. "I apologize for my son's impatience, Eino. So, what started all of this?"

Now that he had his desired audience, Officer Macke launched into a somewhat embellished detailing of the evening's events. Abel did try to insert a couple of correction along the way, but his father immediately stopped him, telling him he'd have plenty of time later to explain his side of the story.

Once Macke finished weaving his tale, Mr. Hanika extended ample apologies for our misbehavior as well as for any inconvenience we may have caused.

"Well, thank you, Officer Macke, for all your concern for these young people. I guarantee you I'll do whatever I can to see to there's no more problems like this."

"Dad, I'm a grown man. You don't —"

Vincent held up his hand and motioned Abel to stop.

"Yeah, well looks to me like yer gonna have yer hands full reignin' in dat one." Eino turned on his heels and headed for the door. "Best be gettin' back at it now dat my shifts almost gonna be done. Gotta keep after dah undesirables, don't ya know — Can't have a buncha hooligans scarin' off dah Fudgies." He waved in the air as he headed out the door. "Well, guess we got dis all done heres, so goodnight to all of yas."

I watched out a side window as Eino mounted his trusty Schwinn, flipped a switch that turned on his handlebar light, and headed out to finish his night of overseeing the island's street sweepers and stray dogs.

Meanwhile, Abel launched into his defense. "I'm telling you, we weren't doing anything wrong, Dad. He made a big deal out of nothing, just to make himself look important. You know how he's always trying to impress you and —"

"Okay, Abel. I get your point. And yes, I do know how he is and what his motives are — Trust me when I tell you I know him better than you could ever imagine."

"I'm sorry for your trouble, Mr. Hanika," I interjected.

"Please call me Vince. Mr. Hanika makes me feel like the old man that I am."

Admittedly, I had noticed that Mr. Hanika looked surprisingly elderly to be Abel's father. He had a curvature in his back that caused him to hunch over, and years of sun exposure had leathered his sun-spotted skin. With his receding hairline and wire-rimmed spectacles, he could have easily passed for Abel's grandfather.

"Okay, it's Vince then." I took a couple of steps toward the door, preparing to leave. "Well, again I'm sorry to have bothered you at such a late hour, and I really should get going so you can get back to sleep."

"No, don't you give it another thought, Carly. I've been in the hotel business just long enough now that I've adjusted to late night awakenings, and I won't hear of your leaving on such a sour note." He turned to Abel and motioned him forward. "Come on, son. Bring your friend out back and we'll whip up some popcorn. I could go for a midnight snack."

Abel placed his shaky hand on my back and gently guided me away from the front door. "Yeah, come on in. Since we missed the fireworks, you can at least stay for a bit."

I nodded in agreement, and then followed Abel back to the kitchen where we each took a seat on a barstool at the central island counter. Vince reached into the massive pantry and took out a pan of Jiffy Pop popcorn. He then cranked the knob on the stove until the blue gas flame leapt from the burner, and then he grabbed the Jiffy Pop by the handle and placed it on the stovetop. The room quickly filled with the aroma of hot oil.

"I just love these things." Despite his elderly appearance, Vince's face glowed with a child-like smile as he jiggled the wire-handled tin over the flame. "I figure, why use the microwave kind when you can have all this fun popping it?"

As Vince held the pan over the fire, Abel sat quietly for a time, almost sulking. His eyebrows were turned downward and he stared at his hands clasped tightly together, his fingers grinding to and fro as he leaned on the countertop.

He finally looked up and spoke. "Dad, why wouldn't you let me argue my side while Eino was here? I mean, he was being so ridiculous."

A couple of kernels popped.

Vince shook the pan. "I already knew your side, son, because I trust you and I know you weren't doing anything wrong."

"But you let him stand there and say all that stuff about me — about us. He made it sound like I was some threat to Carly, and it was so embarrassing."

More kernels popped.

"I'm sure it was embarrassing for both of you." Vince smirked at me, and then continued shaking the pan. "Try not to be too upset with Eino, though. He tries to do the best he can, even if he sometimes is a little overly-enthusiastic."

"A little!" Abel protested.

The popping grew louder and steady as the foil on top of the pan began to rise.

Vince lifted the pan, shaking it vigorously. "I do think he's really trying to look out for you, and everyone – what with all the concern over those missing girls, Eino has to keep his eyes open for any trouble, and he can't be making exceptions for you. He certainly wouldn't want to put you in any questionable situations."

"But we weren't doing anything questionable!"

I felt my cheeks warm, blushing at the direction this conversation was taking.

Vincent didn't respond right away, turning his total focus for the moment to shaking and tossing the hot pan. The foil atop quickly unfurled into a large silver ball, and so Vince removed it from the stovetop and placed it on a hot pad, a couple of stray kernels still crackling inside.

"Stay clear or you might get burned," he warned us, then stepped to the utensil drawer, slid it open, and pulled out a knife. "I know you didn't do anything wrong, and you two know that, but others don't." He stuck the knife into the top of the foil dome, releasing the steam that swirled toward the ceiling.

Abel went to the cupboard and pulled out the salt. "Well, I don't really care what others think."

"But you should, especially right now." Vince used the knife to carefully push back the foil sides, further releasing the tempting aroma of hot corn into the air. "What, with those girls that are missing, people are really suspicious right now." Vince pushed the pan toward me. "Help yourself, Carly."

I reached for some, but Abel flagged me away.

"Needs salt first," he suggested, shaking some on and then taking the first bite. "Yeah, that's better. Now have some."

I grabbed a fistful of hot kernels and popped a couple in my mouth, letting them briefly melt in my mouth as I savored the delicious mix of butter and salt. I then crunched up the remains. "Well worth the wait." I smiled, happy to talk about the corn rather than the embarrassing appearances of our encounter with Macke.

"Glad you like it." Abel took a handful for himself, then turned back to his father. "So, you think Eino actually might try to peg me for killing that girl, and maybe for taking the others?" He shoved popcorn in his mouth.

"Heavens, no." Vince sat on the barstool next to mine and snatched a couple of hot kernels for himself. "But, God forbid, if any more girls go missing, then people may be coming around asking a lot of questions about where you've been, what you've been doing. I just think it's best to stay above reproach – don't give anybody a reason to even wonder about you in the first place.

Abel was still chewing a mouthful of popcorn. "Listen. I'm not about to let a bunch of gossiping locals decide what I am and I'm not going to do. Life's too short for that, and you of all people ought to know that, Dad. So, I'm going to live my life the way I choose."

Vince folded his hands in front of him, a slight grin on his face as he looked upon Abel. "Understood. But please just be careful when making your choices. That's all I ask."

"You know I will be, Dad." Abel reached over to his father and gave him an affectionate pat on the shoulder. "Now, if I could just train Eino to not be so —"

Suddenly, a loud thud came from behind me, followed by the clatter of something falling to the floor in a nearby room.

"What was that?" I jumped and spun around in my seat.

"I thought she was asleep," Abel said to his father as he rose from the table.

Vince stood up, as well. "I thought she was, too. Bet she heard us talking."

"Who was that?" I started to get up from my seat.

With relative calm, Abel gently pushed me back into my seat. "Oh, you don't need to get up." He then headed in the direction of the crash, reassuring me as he left. "It's just my sister, Gretchen. No big deal. I'll get it, Dad."

"Thanks, Abel." Vince sat back down with me. "She was probably wondering what's going on out here – curious girl doesn't like to be left out of the loop." He popped a couple more kernels in his mouth. "She tends to break things, what with her – well, has Abel told you about Gretchen?"

"Just that she has some illness, and she likes muffins."

"That she does." Vince nodded and smiled, then crossed his arms and assumed a more somber expression. "Gretchen has a... um... well, a rare medical condition that limits her ability to move. She has a lot of trouble holding on to things, and she makes some kind of strange – oh, or involuntary motions. She – she sometimes knocks things over."

Despite his openness, Vince sounded hesitant to reveal all the symptoms of his daughter's condition. I didn't want to seem nosy, but wanted to express my concern. "I'm sorry," was the best I could muster.

"Oh, there's no need for sympathy." Vince clapped a hold of his hands. "There's all sorts of treatments coming along now to help us conquer even hereditary conditions. We're going to kick this thing – I'm sure of it."

"You sound pretty optimistic." I took a few more kernels of corn, then pushed the pan away from my reach.

"Well, I am optimistic, and hopeful. I think things will turn around soon." Releasing his hands, Vincent pressed his palms against the table. "But enough about our family quirks. Let's talk about you. Abel mentioned that you just moved here this summer."

"Yes, in May."

"And that you lived in a cottage with Annahede Khali for a short time."

"Yes, but I don't anymore." I was surprised he knew this much about me.

"I know of her, from an acquaintance of mine." Vince bit his lower lip. "She can be a bit of a troublemaker."

"Don't I know!" I laughed.

"Well, just thought I'd mention it – with you seeming like such a nice young lady and all, I just thought you might like to know that she's probably one person worth steering clear of."

I smiled. "I try to."

Vincent leaned back in his chair. "And, no doubt, you've probably heard the worst of the rumors about why some of these missing women have disappeared."

"I work at Biminis, so I hear it all."

"Do you?" His eyes narrowed, studying me. "Yes, I'm sure you hear everything you'd ever want to know by working there."

"And plenty I'd rather not know."

"Yes, it's a rather challenging business, isn't it?" Vincent straightened up in his seat and pushed the popcorn from his reach, as well. "You know, you've been a wonderful friend to Abel. He talks a lot about you, thinks you're pretty special, and so that makes you special to me, too." He smiled, then leaned in closer toward me and spoke a bit more softly, almost as if letting me in on a little secret. "And as someone who's so important to us, I'd like to ask you to be extra careful around the island right now. I mean, it's not my intention to scare you, but I think there's a lot more to these disappearances than meets the eye, and…well, we sure wouldn't want you to fall prey to whatever's going on around here."

It had been a long time since I'd felt like someone was looking out for me – like I was part of an extended family that truly cared about me – and I had to admit, it felt good.

"Thanks for your concern, Vince. I have been trying to be careful, and I've got to say that I feel a whole lot safer now that I have a bike again."

Vincent stood up and cleared what was left of the popcorn. "Well, glad to hear that bike gives you some sense of security, but please still be careful about where you go and, maybe more importantly, who you go with. I have some real concerns about this Annahede girl, and think it best that you keep your distance from her."

I could feel my eyes widen and my jaw drop. "You don't think Annahede's got something to do with this, do you?"

"Maybe, but I can't be sure." He popped the garbage lid with his foot and dropped the leftover Jiffy Pop in the canister. "Word has it she's doing private work for some powerful person who wishes to remain anonymous. You wouldn't happen to know anything about what she's been up to, would –"

"What *who's* been up to, Dad?" Abel returned to the room, taking up his seat beside me. "Hey, where'd the popcorn go?"

Vince lifted his foot from the pedal and let the lid drop. "I have no idea." He smiled.

"Gosh, I leave the room just for a moment, and all the corn's gone."

"Gretchen's okay?" Vince asked, returning to the table.

"All tucked in, and just a broken glass to pick up. She was just trying to get up and come meet this Carly-girl she's been hearing about." Abel winked at me. "But I convinced her to wait 'til another time – said I needed to get you home since it's so late, and that we didn't want to wake Libby."

"Libby?" I asked.

"Gretchen's daughter," Vince replied. "She lives here, too, so Abel and I can help take care of her.

I stood up from my seat and pushed my stool under the countertop. "Wow. So, you've got three generations here."

Vince held up four fingers, then raised his thumb and some fingers on the other hand as he added more. "Yes, there's the four of us, and the front desk help, and the bellhops, and of course the cleaning staff, and...well, I guess we're just one, big, happy family."

"Well, it's been so nice to meet you, Vince." I extended a hand.

"The pleasure's been mine." He took my hand between both of his and gently squeezed it with a slight shake. "Come back sometime soon to meet the girls, will you?"

"I'd be happy to."

With a final swap of smiles, I turned and followed Abel as he guided me back to the front door and out onto the chilly street. A brisk breeze was blowing in off Lake Huron, and so Abel wrapped me in his Mackinac jacket to keep me warm as we rode our bikes back to the village.

Upon arriving at the boarding house, we dismounted bikes and Abel saw me to the building door. There he reached to retrieve his coat, but as he did, he leaned in closely as if looking for a kiss. So, I gave him one, right on the cheek – just like the ones I use to give my mom or dad or sister whenever we parted ways. It was a kiss of family affection, and I knew it wasn't what he was looking for. But it was all I had to give him, at least for now.

I went up the stairs and into my room where I found Pepper already sound asleep. Quickly I changed into pajamas and climbed under my covers. It was chilly in the room now, a stark change from the heat we had experienced during the day. I had learned that such broad changes in temperature were pretty typical for summertime on the islands of the Straits.

I curled up tightly under my comforter as the sheets felt cool against my skin. But I warmed them up quickly, the layers of blankets and sheets insulating me against the elements.

Yes, I was finding comfort in this place, at this moment, here on this little speck of land in the middle of a mighty lake. And for the first time in quite a long time, I thought – just maybe – I'd finally found where I belonged.

Chapter 17

FRATERNITY

THE VILLAIN INTENT ON SNATCHING SAINTS struck again on the very night Abel escorted me home. It was the same night that Officer Macke had obsessed over denying us any opportunity to peaceably drink cherry wine on a secluded bluff, rather than focusing on his real job – to protect the island's women from being taken against their will. I couldn't help but wonder what might have happened that night if Macke had left us alone. He had foolishly neglected his most sacred obligation – to protect and defend – and just thinking of it made me feel like I wanted to scream.

When I overheard at the boarding house the name of the latest victim, I just couldn't believe it. I quickly dashed over to Biminis to see if Callahan had heard the same.

The door was open and I heard noise in the kitchen, so I headed back there where I found Callahan unloading glasses from the dishwasher. "Thought Collette did this last night, but she just left it, then didn't show up for work this morning." He shook his head. "That's not like her."

In shock, I raised my hands to my mouth. "Oh, my God, Mike! She's really gone."

"Gone? What do you mean, gone?"

"I mean, she's been taken, I think." I reached into the dishwasher and pulled out a couple of hot plates, stacking them on top of the others on the countertop. "I overheard people talking about it at the boarding house. They said she never came home after work last night."

Callahan stopped removing the dishes and stared at me. "You're just covering for her, right?"

I shook my head.

"Well, what the hell?" He scowled as he leaned against the counter. "And she didn't call somebody, or leave anyone a message?"

"Not that I know of."

Callahan grabbed a towel from the countertop and wiped his hands before walking over to the phone.

I pulled two glasses from the dishwasher. "You don't need to call the police. Rosie already did, and she got the run around about how she hasn't been gone long enough to —"

Callahan picked up the phone receiver. "I'm not calling the cops." He poked the phone's buttons.

"Oh. Well, if you're calling someone in to work, don't worry about that. I can punch in until maybe Collette comes back, or we hear something."

"Thanks. That would help." He still continued his call, putting the receiver to his ear. "And I think Marla's scheduled to come in to open, so we should be fine."

"So, then who are you calling?"

He held up his hand to me, now speaking into the phone. "Yeah, is someone named Annahede working there today?" He paused. "She's not? Well, then put me through to her boss, Sam Donahue." He scowled. "Well, then give me that number." He grabbed a pen and scribbled on a scrap of paper, then hanging up without another word and punching in the new number. "If I can get a hold of Donahue, maybe he can help me find that little snake Annahede," he said to me, once again holding the receiver to his ear. "If she was so hell-bent on talking to Collette the other day, then I want to find out if she knows something about all this."

It proved tough enough to track down Mr. Donahue, but finding Annahede turned out to be nearly impossible. She was off work while Donahue was gone, and she was nowhere to be found.

Later that day, I did overhear Callahan's end of a phone conversation with Chief Sinclaire. Callahan told him a bit about Annahede's recent visit to the bar and how she'd asked to chat with Collette. It was a brief conversation, and by the way Callahan slammed the receiver down at the end of the call, I got the clear impression that his concerns had fallen on deaf ears.

The impact of Collette's disappearance on the community of Saints quickly became clear as almost all the female boarders in my building no longer went anywhere alone, arranging now to travel about in groups of three or four. I noticed our neighbors had invested in deadbolts like the one Pepper and I had already installed on our door. One Saint even enlisted the help of the obeah man who painted a rancid concoction of herbs and dead animal remains around her doorway. She was determined to do whatever it took to ward off what she believed was an evil spirit that had descended upon the island.

As if people weren't already on edge, the gossip that hit just before the fourth of July proved even more disturbing. Someone had somehow managed to find out a few crude and tantalizing details regarding Helena Moore's autopsy, a leak that came as no surprise to me after my recent visit at the hospital. Nonetheless, it was troubling to spend my overtime shift at Biminis listening to people coming and going with the same crass hearsay.

The morning gossipers started the day off with tales that sounded reasonable enough to believe.

"Some guy assaulted her – ya know, sexual-like," Harvey contributed over his hot cup of sugar coffee. "I heard two ladies say so when I was pickin' up their cans. They was talkin' about some 'topsy report thing that one gal's sister heard about from her nurse friend."

I wiped down a nearby tabletop. "Boy, that's kind of the long way about to get your info, Harvey. Not sure you can rely on that one."

"Oh, it's solid." He slurped from his steaming cup. "They also said she'd got pregnant from the whole thing."

Now that seemed an understatement from what I'd heard before.

"Just provin' again that ya don't know nothin', Harvey." Bob Gould was his usual provocative self, just getting started on his first whiskey coffee as he sat at the bar. "You gotta know girls don't get pregnant that fast, 'specially if they're dead!"

Harvey put his cup down hard, slopping coffee onto the table. "I know what I heard, Gould, and I gots it right. That girl was knocked up, I'm tellin' ya. There's no doubt about it."

There certainly wasn't any doubt, and that rumor spread quickly. Periodically I overheard conversations between more sensitive folks, those who sounded sincerely grief-stricken to realize that not just one, but at least two lives had been taken. I couldn't help but think about how little they knew – about how many lives really had been taken through that one act of killing.

By afternoon, word of her pregnancy had become old news. Gossipmongers took it as fodder for spinning their many speculations as to why this unfortunate woman had fallen victim to her killer, and all of their talk was giving me a headache.

"Must've been an unwanted pregnancy." Old Mrs. Greir had come in for a Coke after she'd finished cleaning rooms at the Grand. She dragged on her third cigarette, the long butt hanging from her leathered hands. "I hear she already had one unwanted child – probably couldn't deal with another."

Lou Jeeter was at the table next to her, sitting with his chair backwards so his spindly legs straddled the chair back. "Maybe it was de foddar, found out obout his garlfrond beon' pregnont ond didn't want te hov no more kids draggon' on his wallot." Lou tipped his glass to his lips, the ice clinking as he slugged back the last of his Jim Beam. "I know dot my wife, she cont hov no more kids or I'll be in de poorhouse. Ond my ex, she's been garnoshon' money from my checks so I gotta be workon' two jobs now. I con see dot – how it might 'a been drivon' a lessar mon te kill."

"Or maybe she was holdin' it over him – trappin' him into a marriage he didn't want no part of." With a cough, Mrs. Greir blew smoke, the haze drifting up over her sagging, bloodshot eyes.

I choked as I waited on her, the smoke adding to what had already been an awful cough that I'd been coming down with for the past couple of days.

"Yeah, entrappin' – that's gotta be the deal." Bob Gould grumbled from the bar, his words a bit slurred from his third Jack Daniels.

"Dink you so smart, Mr. Gould?" Lou scratched at two-day's scruff on his chin. "Well den, why don't you be tellin' us what dah heck killed dah womon."

Bob set down his mug, folded his hands, and smirked haughtily. "Simple. Botched abortion."

The three continued this debate, going around and around as more patrons came and went. And when the three eventually departed, they left more storytellers in their wake – only these were the most vicious of gossipers, all trying to out do one another with their outrageous tales.

It had been a tough day and I was dragging, my body feeling unusually achy from being on my feet for so long and fighting with that cough. I felt exhausted, so tired of all the nasty talk about Helena Moore – but unfortunately, the worst was yet to come.

It was no surprise to all the employees that the notorious fraternity of ferry captains and their dock hands turned out to be the worst of the storytellers, all embellishing their tales with gory details that suggested a prolonged, torturous death.

"Bet Helena's man decided to teach that slut a lesson for forgetting her birth control." Gunner rubbed his beer gut then pushed his belt lower below it. "He probably tied her up to his Sea Ray and took her for a little body surfing, full throttle."

The circle of drunken sailors pounded the table, roaring in support of Gunner's abusive remark until a young redheaded dockhand with a crew cut yelled at them, trying to turn their attention to him. He held up his beer mug toward the group, his smooth cheeks that lacked any signs of hair growth, making him look too young to be drinking.

"No way." The kid sipped his beer. "That would be too kind." Foolishly, he was trying to out-do Gunner's attempts at slander and unfortunately didn't seem to know better.

"Oh really!" Gunner leaned forward, resting his elbows on his knees as he stared at the newcomer. "So, how do you see it, punk?"

"Well, I figure the girl probably pushed for the 'C' word – you know, a commitment?"

"Yeah, we know the 'C' word, kid." Rafae Battiste was seated with the group, but he wasn't hyped up like the rest of them. He remained calm and composed, slowly turning his mug back and forth in his hands. "But just because we know the word, that doesn't mean we'd ever be stupid enough to use it."

"Ooooo!" The rest at the table exchanged high-fives.

The kid continued. "Yeah, well, no doubt this guy wasn't interested in getting hitched, either, and the little tramp could see this. So, what does she do? She blackmails him — threatens to tell his other woman."

Many hooted, spinning their fists in the air with approval. I was so offended by what he was saying, and even more so by the sort of groupthink support he was getting. I was disgusted, turning my back to them as I waited my tables with apologies extended to each.

The kid sat down, coming in closer to his audience to finish his tale. "Of course the guy didn't take that entrapment crap very well, so he ties her up in some dark, dripping-wet crawl space with rodents gnawing at her wrists and ankles."

"All right." Callahan had finally heard enough, thank goodness. "We don't need to hear anymore crap."

But the kid ignored him. "And she's screaming and she's carrying on, so the guy slaps her around and shoots her up with drugs and —"

"Feeds her dog food!" Gunner slammed the tabletop, retrieving his lost audience. "Stuck that bowl right in the bitch's face and made her gnaw it out — lick the platter clean!"

"Hey!" Callahan threw a towel over his shoulder and put his fists to his hips. "I said that's enough!"

But the crew didn't respond to him as they roared with pleasure, banging their beer mugs on the tabletops. All the noise was aggravating my already splitting headache.

"More! More! More! More!" Their chant was not only for continuing the brutal stories but also for refilling their mugs, and they desired both so they could quench their voracious thirst.

Pepper was steamed, already putting in motion her act of vengeance. "I'll teach those macho morons they can't degrade women like that, whether they're living or dead."

She had gone to the mudroom behind the kitchen and snatched the water and food bowls from Scout, Mr. Callahan's Jack Russell Terrier. After emptying the dog food into the garbage can and the water into the janitorial basin, she took both and, without washing or wiping either dish, rammed each bowl under the beer tap. Then she yanked down the handle, filling both bowls to the brim. With a bowl clenched in each fist, she then stomped over to the sailors' table and threw both down in front of Gunner and Rafae.

"Stick that in your face, you stupid bastards!" And with that, Pepper marched away.

"Well, I guess Pepper won't be waiting on us anymore tonight." Rafae smiled, and then he winked at me.

I never quite knew how to take Rafae. There had been moments in recent days when I'd seen his softer side, like when I spotted him helping Mr. Raddison fix his lawn tractor when it had broken down, or when Harvey had hurt his back and so he went around with him to help finish his garbage run. And there was the time I saw him drop off groceries for an old Saint in my building who was recovering from a twisted ankle. Yes, I felt sure he had a kind heart, but it was seldom seen when he was keeping company with such a lousy bunch.

"Maybe we can get Carly to bring us drinks." He batted his eyes with exaggeration. "Please?"

"Oh, I think you've all had quite enough for one night." I coughed, then passed by their table.

"Hey, that's okay, Raf. I'm all set here." Gunner plunged his face into the bowl before him, lapping up some beer before resurfacing. "Hey, this isn't bad, but we're gonna need more, and I'm sure that pretty little thing over there will keep us in the brew. Won't ya, Carly?"

Callahan intervened. "She can only serve you if you cut it out with all the rude talk."

Rafae nodded in agreement with a grin.

I stepped back to their table. "Yeah, your stories were starting to make me feel sick."

Gunner looked up from his bowl and leaned toward me, speaking softly. "Aw, we were just having a little, harmless fun, Carly. What, don't you want to hear a different tidbit, about Old Doc Renaulte and her little gyno-clinic back behind Me-Wanna-Go-Home?"

I cleared my throat. "I think I'll pass."

"Yeah, well, I understand Helena spent quite a bit of time there getting that special kind of medicine only Mamma Renaulte can dish out. You know, they say that Saint spent so much time up in the stirrups that —"

"Stop it, Gunner!" Rafae scowled at him.

"What the hell's up with you, Raf-A-E?" Gunner stuck his thumbs in his front belt loops, tightening up his arms.

Rafae moved slightly forward, straightening his back and pushing out his chest. "The lady said she's heard enough."

Gunner stared back but said nothing. After a long pause, he tilted his head slightly and smiled. "Yeah, boys, I think poor Raf-the-girly-boy's had enough, too. Wouldn't want to upset him, would we.

The group chuckled a bit, but not much.

"Right." Rafae nodded. "I don't want anybody giving me any bad dreams when I'm trying to get my beauty sleep."

The group laughed outright now, as if they sensed that peace had been made. I then walked away, heading to the bar to fill up some pitchers, and Rafae followed behind me.

I stuck a pitcher under the tap and pulled down. "Did somebody leave the door open? It feels kind of cold in here."

"What, are you kidding?" Rafae leaned across the bar and took my first filled pitcher, then set it on a platter. "With all these sweaty guys in here, the place is a hothouse."

With the second pitcher filled, I set it on the counter and rubbed my hands together, blowing on them.

Rafae took the pitcher but never took his pitch black eyes from me. "Hey, are you okay? You're shaking."

I gazed at my hands. They were slightly quivering. "I guess I don't feel so well." Pushing my hair from my face, I leaned against a bar.

"You look awful, Carly."

"Gee, thanks for the flattery."

"No, I mean it. You look white as a sheet."

"It's those awful stories they keep telling over and over again. They're making me sick."

"Are you sure that's all it is?" Rafae reached across the bar and pushed his palm against my forehead.

The fraternity must have been watching us since Rafae's gesture was met with catcalls and whistles from a couple of dock hands still at the table. In response, Rafae used his free hand to gesture a thumbs-up. They cheered, then went about their own business.

I knew the gesture gave merit to their implications, but at the moment I couldn't have cared less. I really did feel lousy.

Rafae removed his hand from my head. "I think you've got a fever."

"I do?" I coughed with an awful hack I could no longer hold back.

"Yes, you do, and I think you should go home." Rafae stepped around to the back of the bar and gently took me by the arm, guiding me away from the beer taps.

Pepper approached the bar. "Hey! Where you going?"

I stopped moving. "Yeah, I've got to finish my shift."

Rafae spoke firmly. "No you don't. Pepper and the others can cover this crowd."

"No." Pepper crossed her arms, scowling. "I will not wait on those idiot friends of yours."

Rafae turned to her. "Fine. Then don't. Cut them off, send them home – I don't care. But she's leaving." He was now pulling me away from the bar and toward the coat rack.

Pepper gazed at me leaving. "Hey, you look like crap."

"So I hear." I tried to smile but it wasn't in me.

Rafae waved his arm in the air. "Hey, Callahan! I'm taking this one out of here. You don't want her making all the employees and patrons sick, do you?"

Callahan waved back. "Get her home. We'll be fine."

"Settled." Rafae grabbed my windbreaker and tossed it on my shoulders. "Let's go."

The frat boys were still attentive, hooting at us as we stepped out into the chilly night.

I slipped my arms into my jacket and started heading toward the back of the building. "You don't need to walk me. I've got my bike back there."

"Leave it." He ran his hand through his wiry black hair. "It's locked up. I'll get it back to you tomorrow."

"I'm not that sick." I stopped and hacked. "I can just ride home."

"You shouldn't go alone. There's at least one crazy guy out there preying on women and —"

I feigned a stunned look. "Really, Oh, I thought you said it was just some trapped boyfriend getting even with his girl." I coughed hard. "He'd have no reason to hurt me, would he?"

"You know I don't buy all their bull, Carly. Now come on. Let's get you home before you hack up a fur ball."

I started walking. "So, why do you put up with it when they carry on like that?"

Rafae stuck his fists in his pockets as he walked at my side. "I know they can be real jerks, but they're the people I hang with at work everyday. I just take the good with the bad and the ugly — and I do suppose there's a lot of ugly, but I figure it's just a guy thing."

"If that's a guy thing, than I'm glad I'm a girl."

"Well, so am I!" Rafae winked.

The clear, crisp night air seemed cooler than usual, probably because I was spiking a fever. It was futile trying to snuggle up for warmth inside my lightweight windbreaker.

I cleared my throat. "I hate to ask but, I'm so cold and, well, you said you were actually kind of hot back there, so "

"Say no more." He slipped off his lightweight jacket and held it up.

I slid my arms in. "Thanks. Sure you won't be too cold."

"I'll be fine."

Once stripped of his jacket, I noticed that Rafae was still in uniform. In the bright glow of the waning moon, light reflected brightly off the bleached white of his heavily starched, short-sleeved shirt that was trimmed in gold braid. It starkly contrasted against the deep ebony of his Caribbean complexion.

When we reached a steep incline along the way, Rafae extended his arm to me with a bit of an exaggerated bow.

I coughed away from him, then took hold. "Thank you."

I did lean on him, glad for the support as we both puffed a bit with each step. His breath was a mix of spearmint gum and alcohol, a scent evident over a hint of English Leather.

At the hilltop, I pulled him to the left. "I live this way."

"In Me-Wanna-Go-Home?"

"Yeah, in the boarding house."

"I've got a couple of friends who live there. Do you know Guion Leveque?"

"Can't say I do."

"In the summer he loads luggage and drives carriage for the Stone's Throw Inn, and in the winter months we do odd jobs together – ferry maintenance and delivery services – you know, stuff like that."

"So, he lives here year 'round?"

"One of the few Saints who does." He continued helping me along as he spoke. "He's a funny guy. One time he bought some cheap coins stamped Mackinac & Windemere at the Fur Traders' Shop and passed them off to cheap tippers who expected change for a dollar. He told them they were Island currency – a must to get into some of the more elite attractions on both the islands."

"Bet they didn't appreciate that."

"Yeah, and I bet they spent a lot of time looking around for the elite places they were suppose to get them into. Anyway, he didn't do it for long – got in trouble, as you can imagine."

I sniffled, my nose about to drip in the chilly air. Rafae took a tissue from his pocket and handed it to me.

"Guess I came prepared." He smiled.

Rafae's camaraderie proved surprisingly hospitable but difficult to enjoy when I felt so lousy. I was most pleased when he finally got me to the comfort of my room.

"You slip off your shoes and I'll get this off." Rafae pulled a heavy Mackinac blanket from the foot of my top bunk. "Now, give me those jackets."

I pulled my aching arms out of both. "I'm cold."

"I'm sure you are." He took his jacket from me and then draped mine on Pepper's bed. "But don't you go bundling up in blankets or you'll spike your fever. Do you have any Tylenol?"

I pointed to the bottle and he grabbed it, taking out two pills and handing them to me. He then found a Styrofoam cup and went out into the hall just long enough to retrieve a glass of water.

"Now, drink plenty of fluids, and get out of those clothes when I'm gone. They'll just keep your fever up." He stepped to the open door. "I'll get with Pepper about getting your bike back to you tomorrow. Get some rest." And with that, he left.

The frat would be disappointed if they heard that Rafae saw himself out without making a single pass. Even with my illness, they would have expected more. But the facts seldom mattered as the truth was not the type of story told by patrons of Biminis.

Chapter 18

TOO KIND TO BE CRUEL

A FEW CHILDHOOD ILLNESSES had affected me in my early years, but I could not recall ever being this sick. I was convinced it was due to the lack of fresh air circulating in our building – that the new air system was likely harboring infectious illnesses. With the windows nailed shut, there was no way to get fresh air, and I felt trapped in a breeding ground of disease.

Over the course of a week, I'd gone from a simple cough and sneezing that was typical with allergies to a deep cough and congestion that seemed to have settled in my chest. By the middle of the month, my cough turned unproductive and my voice went hoarse.

"You have *got* to go see a doctor," Pepper insisted as she headed out for a double-shift at Biminis. "You get yourself some medicine for that cough before everybody gets sick."

Deke was supposed to come by to take me for another horseback ride, but there was no way I was going anywhere today. When he stopped in to get me, I was surprised when he seemed more putout than concerned.

"Just wished you'd called to let me know." He stood in the doorway, wary of coming in.

"I'm sorry." I choked, still resting under the sheets in my loft. "I overslept – figured you were already on your way before I could have called, so I thought maybe you could save me a trip to the first aid place."

"But I told you before, Carly – I'm not a doctor, and nobody there can write for meds. You're going to have to see a real doctor on the mainland at their clinic."

"Oh." I blew my nose. "Well, I still hate to trouble you, but do you think you could ride over there with me?"

"Sorry, but I can't. I just had time for an hour's ride before I had to get back to help my Dad."

"Oh, okay."

"So, I've got to get the horses back – guess we'll just have to reschedule. Hey, let me know how you come out over there." And with that he took off, not even shutting the door as he left.

I was both surprised and disappointed that Deke didn't seem interested in helping me get to the doctor. Since Biminis was short on help, Pepper couldn't get away to take me either. I thought about trying Abel but didn't want to trouble him. Finally I decided I could handle going by myself.

From the three available ferry lines, I chose to ride the one that Rafae worked for, admittedly in hopes that I'd run into him. But it turned out that he wasn't on board either the boat I took over or the one I just happened to catch on the way back home.

In the short time at the clinic, I was diagnosed as having a severe sinus infection. With a bag containing drug samples of an antibiotic, a decongestant, and a cough suppressant, I was sentenced to bed rest for the next seventy-two hours with a threat that recovery could easily take even longer. Although I hated the idea of being cooped up in my tiny room for so long, I resigned myself to stay put so I could get over this evil bug.

Despite my good intentions to not trouble anyone, I did prove to be quite a nuisance to Pepper. She ran errands for me, bringing me comfort foods and keeping the room tidy, all on top of her many hours of work. She was a big help to me in my time of need, but I could tell it was wearing on her.

For that reason, I was almost glad when Abel soon found out I was sick. It was late in the evening when he arrived at my door bearing freshly picked wildflowers and homemade chicken-noodle soup. The broth was warm and satisfying, the perfect medicine for my ailing condition, but the flowers were another matter. They were in full bloom and loaded with pollen, the last thing my sinuses needed in this enclosed environment. I hated to disappoint Abel, so I chose to say nothing, figuring I'd get rid of the bouquet after he left.

The only problem was that he wouldn't leave. After arranging the flowers and watching me eat soup, he pulled up a chair bedside and planted himself as if he had plans to stay for some time.

I intentionally coughed, much deeper than necessary. "Gee, Abel, I hope you don't catch this."

"I'm not worried. I've got good resistance to bugs."

"But this is pretty awful." I coughed out of necessity, my words tickling my throat.

His hand shook as he handed me a glass of water. "And that's why I should stay here, so I can take care of you – get you things when you need them."

I took a drink. "But I'm not good company. I'm too hoarse to speak – just need to rest."

He didn't take the hint. "Well, then don't talk. Just lie back and relax." He retrieved the glass from me and went to set it down but dropped it. "Dang it. Can't seem to keep a grip on things these days." He picked up the unbroken glass and set it aside.

I did try to relax as instructed, but it was uncomfortable to lie there in silence with Abel sitting there just below my bunk. It was awkwardly quiet for a moment, and then Abel shifted in his seat, maybe seeking a more comfortable position on the hard desk chair.

I cleared my throat. "I feel kind of stupid with you just sitting there and –" I coughed. " – not talking."

"But I just wanted you to rest. Tell you what – you just close your eyes and I'll do all the talking."

Not exactly what I had in mind, but rather than hurt his feelings by telling him outright to leave, I decided I'd try it. "Okay."

"Nope, no talking. Just listen. Now, let's see, what could I tell you… Oh, yeah. Dad talked to Chief Sinclaire about what a GREAT job he's doing, and I guess Sinclaire told him a bit more about how the Moore girl –"

"Don't want to hear it." I covered my ears.

"Oh. Okay. Well, Dad also said he's got an idea for a new project. He's thinking about investing in a better medical facility to be built here on the island. That way, when people get sick – you know, like you are right now – then they don't have to go all the way to the mainland to get treated – you know, like you did. He figured

it would help people, especially like the Saints, who can't afford
to be running back and forth across the Straits, and it'll make it
better so that -blah-blah- you know, because when you're feeling
sick -blah-blah- the last thing you want to be doing -blah-blah-
blah- is all of that going back and forth and back and forth and
-blah-blah-blah-blah-…"

I had dropped my hands from my ears and must have dozed
off briefly, but not for long. It proved hard to stay asleep with
Abel rambling on. I faded in and out of his one-way conversation,
hearing bits and pieces of what he had to say.

"…but a lot of people don't know -blah- Dad came from
meager beginnings -blah- became a field rep in pharmaceuticals
and invested in products -blah-blah- put his money where his
mouth was…"

I briefly wondered how much money it would take to silence
Abel's, but figured I'd caused the problem in the first place. So I
drifted back into dimly listening.

"…bought a fertility research clinic -blah- a sort of test-tube
baby business -blah- the gamble paid off millions and millions and
millions…"

I saw thousands of dollars whirling in the air, and then thousands
more washing up on the shore as the waves of the big lake broke
on the sand. Bills floating in, and some washing back out… and
then I realized I was dreaming, fading back into listening to Abel.

"…people always trying to take advantage of Dad -blah-
researchers refused work on new concepts -blah-blah- betrayed him
-blah-blah-blah- unethical -blah-blah-blah- deceitful -blah-blah-"
Abel then hit the wall with his fist.

"What!" Startled, I sat straight up.

"Sorry! Sorry!" He stood up and shakily took hold of my sheets.
"Climb back under and I'll quiet down. I'm sorry. I just get so
carried away when I talk about how they treated my dad at that
company when all he was doing was just trying to help people."

"I'm sure he was." I lightly coughed, trying to suppress it, and
snuggled back down under my covers. "So, what was it that this
company did to him?"

"Well, Dad was upset with all the shareholders because they
weren't willing to pursue this new breakthrough — it's very

promising research in organ and tissue donation. But these business-types, they were under a lot of pressure from politicians and lobbyists who kept on threatening to use their influence to undermine profits if they went ahead with this research – just a bunch of dirty politics."

Now wide awake, I was listening intently. "So, what did your dad do?"

Abel sat back down. "He cashed in his stock and used the money to start his own research foundation. He calls it the Willington Abel Institute of Medical Research. Kind of catchy, isn't it?"

I started to answer, but choked and coughed.

"Don't answer, sorry." Using both hands, he handed me my drink glass still a third full of water. "This should help."

I finished off the water and carefully handed back the glass, nodding my head with thanks rather than speaking.

Abel set the glass on the window ledge. "Anyway, Dad named the institute after his two kids: Gretchen Willington Hanika, and, of course, me. Tah-daaaah." He bowed and sat down. "And despite all the threats and controversy, his new enterprise did really well, mostly because of the great staff he was able to get to come along. Why, he persuaded some of the most prominent researchers in donor research to join him."

"And so how –" I coughed. " – did you end up here?"

"Here on Windemere? Oh, that's because Dad used to visit here when he was a kid, and he always dreamed of coming back. Since Gretchen was toying with the idea of a career in hotel management, well, he saw this hotel for sale and decided to use some of his profits to purchase the French Landings. He thought he'd run it until Gretchen took over, and then figured he'd finally retire and enjoy his newest investment as more of a pastime – kind of a family thing."

"How nice." I smiled, pleased that I hadn't coughed.

"Yeah, he also bought the lighthouse at Beacon Point. It's a kind of historical landmark. You can see it on a clear day, a bit of a distance out there off shore." He waved in the direction beyond my window. "Maybe you've seen it?"

I nodded, recollecting the spooky old lighthouse that was now posted off limits.

"Sure, you probably saw it when you took the ferry to the doctors. It's hard to reach, though, out on a really hazardous point. I thought Dad should put in some kind of extended dock out there, but I guess he doesn't want to encourage sightseers to try and come around. Yeah, at first he was going to restore the old lighthouse and turn it into some kind of maritime museum. But then Gretchen started getting worse, and so he put that plan aside – turned the place into a sort of private annex for the institute, instead, where some work could be done right here by the island."

"Really?" I was fascinated by this, wondering what kind of work it might be possible to do out there. But I figured all of my questions would involve too much talking, so I decided to wait and ask them later when I was feeling better.

Abel crossed his legs in his chair. "So, Dad closed off Beacon Annex from the public. I suppose he figured out that he just couldn't let –"

The door abruptly flung open, and there stood Pepper. "And what are you doing here?" With hands on her hips, she stared down Abel.

Startled, Abel fumbled up from his seat. "I was just trying to help out Carly while you were gone."

"Well, I'm back." She marched into the room and looked up at me. "And you're still awake! You should've been asleep by now."

With my raspy voice I tried to reply, "Well, Abel was just telling me about his family and I –" I choked, my cough having returned.

"You stop talking and get some sleep." She then turned on Abel. "And you – you get out of here this minute. She needs her rest."

"Okay, now that somebody's here, I'll get going." Abel headed for the doorway. "Hope you're feeling better, Carly. I'll stop back in the morning to see how you're doing."

"Not before ten o'clock!" Pepper shoved Abel through the doorway. "Now just go home!" Then she slammed the door shut.

I leaned over from my bunk and looked down on her. "Wow."

Pepper glared back. "You should learn from my example. You need to be more forceful with him."

I cleared my throat. "I'm not exactly up to reaming him out."

"You don't have to ream him out, but you shouldn't keep leading him on like that."

"What? I'm not leading him on!"

"Oh, really? Well then, what do you call it when you regularly stay up late to converse with a man that you know has a crush on you? And what do you call it when you accept gifts – some quite expensive, mind you – from this man?"

I cleared my throat. "Oh, he's just a nice person."

"If you *really* believe that, then you are so naïve, Carly. That guy has fallen for you, and you are killing him with your kindness."

"Really. So what am I supposed to do?" I coughed. "Just tell him to get lost?"

"Yeah, you just may have to do that. You've got to be more assertive, Carly. Tell him you can't accept his gifts, you can't go biking, and you can't let him spend his whole day here watching over you."

I hated to admit it, but I knew she was right. It seemed so harmless to be friendly to such a kind person, but I wasn't being fair. I considered Pepper's advice carefully and resolved myself to a new code of conduct in regards to Abel. From then on, no more passive agreeability. I had to say "no," and mean it.

Pepper leaned on the side of my mattress. "You know he's going to show up here by ten o'clock, if not before. So, what are you going to do?"

"Well, I guess I'll tell him I'm just too sick to visit and to come back later."

"No. You're too sick to have visitors, you've got to sleep, and maybe you'll call him later. And then you don't call."

"But isn't that –"

"Rude? Exactly. Just remember that it's cruel to be kind. You're doing him a favor."

I cleared my throat. "Okay, I'll just –"

"Quit talking. You need to rest your voice so you can get rid of that awful cough before I catch it." She slipped on a light jacket. " Now, do you need anything before I take off?"

"No, but where are you going?"

"Well, it's drunken sailors night, remember? Most of the sailboats from the Chicago to Mackinac Yacht Race are in, and a lot of yachtsmen have made it over to Windemere – don't want to miss out on the fun. A bunch of us are heading down to the docks to see how many make fools of themselves."

"Well, just be careful." I swallowed to avoid a cough. "Don't want you down there leading on any poor, unsuspecting sailor."

"Oh, that's a good one. Yeah, that would be me, with all this charm..." She smiled as she flicked off the light, and then went out the door, locking the deadbolt behind her.

As I snuggled up under a couple of blankets, I faintly heard the less than sober voices of some gentlemen attempting to harmonize as they wandered by our building. Their boisterous rendition of "The Sweetheart of Sigma Chi" was miserable, but they nonetheless sounded quite pleased with their efforts as they applauded themselves at the conclusion of their pathetic performance. Even with the sealed window muffling the sound, I could tell it was a rowdy night on the island. Officer Schwinn would have his hands full tonight, I thought, as I drifted off to sleep.

Chapter 19

FINDING MY FAULT

I FELT AS IF THE WORLD WAS CLOSING IN on me as I gasped for breathable air but couldn't find any. I coughed and choked each time I tried to inhale, and my lungs ached from the effort. This was no longer the mere symptoms of an illness. It was as if I were somehow drowning.

Although my eyes were wide open, I saw nothing but darkness, my eyes burning from the filth surrounding them. A heaviness settled upon my chest, a weight that made it increasingly difficult to breathe. I tossed and thrashed in an effort to break free but felt I couldn't get away. I was trapped.

Faint voices calling out to me sounded muffled and very distant. I tried to call back to them but my raspy voice was inaudible. They were too far out of my reach.

For a brief moment, my thoughts drifted to Collette. I envisioned her much the same as Helena had been found – her wrists and ankles bearing deep cuts encrusted with dark blood, eyes closed forever, buried deep in a pile of filth and waste. And I was there, buried beside her.

Was this real? Had I actually been abducted and buried alive?

The crash of shattering glass startled me from my nightmare. Though my room was too black for me to see, I could tell something had broken my window. Now I could hear the voices outside much more clearly. They were pleading, "Get out of there!" and "Jump!" I could even hear a familiar voice. It was Deke yelling "Carly!" My nightmare continued, but now it was real.

Even with the window smashed open, I continued to choke as I gasped for fresh air. My eyes burned as I strained to adjust to the darkness, but I still couldn't see a thing from my upper bunk.

I managed to free myself from the entanglement of sheets and rolled sideways out of my bunk.

Sharp pains shot through my body as I landed in shards of glass scattered about the floor. My attempts to scream out in agony were thwarted by my inability to breathe, and so I reserved what little strength I had remaining to drag myself to the window. As I pulled myself up to the window ledge, I could barely make out the gray silhouettes of objects around the room. Then I noticed the pitch black cloud hovering over my head. It was smoke.

As panic overcame pain, I crawled to the door. Clasping the deadbolt, I unlocked the door and grasped the doorknob. It burned in my hand as I felt heat radiate through the door and against my body. With black smoke pouring in under the door, I realized there was no escaping this way.

Crawling back to the window, I made out the glistening image of glass splinters still remaining in the window frame. The rock that had crashed through the window had left too small of a hole for my escape. Instincts kicked in as I lunged toward the image of the largest object on the table. I grasped the microwave and frantically heaved it through the window. Then I grabbed the chair and used its legs to chip away the few remaining glass splinters. When the sill was cleared, I plunged my head out the window and gasped a refreshing breath of clean air.

I was met with cheers of encouragement from the people below. "Come on! Get out!" The crowd was yelling not only to me but also to others precariously hanging out of their windows.

Below me, Deke plunged forward from the crowd and ran to a spot just under my window. "I can catch you, Carly! Just jump!"

I had a lot of faith in Deke, but the three-story drop before me looked terribly daunting. Though I was desperate to get out, I wasn't that desperate yet. I had one more idea.

Surrounded by the roar and crackle of the fire outside my door, I reached back into my smoke-filled room just long enough to grab sheets from the beds. I hastily tied two together, bound one end to a chair and wedged it against the frame of the window. With a silent prayer that it would be sturdy enough to bear my weight,

I took the makeshift line in hand and climbed up onto the sill, and then attempted to wriggle through the opening.

Deke was still standing below, yelling at the top of his lungs. "You have got to get out of there now! I swear I'll catch you!"

As I climbed outward, again I met with pain. This time it was a warm, burning sensation just below the knee brought on when I caught my leg on a shard of glass. But the heat from the fire was intensifying and I knew I was running out of time. I worked through the pain as I strained to clear the window and lower myself closer to Deke's reach.

Scaling my way down the exterior wall, I reached a second floor window before I ran out of sheet, and out of strength. With Deke's arms outstretched below, his steady voice encouraged me to let go, and so I released my grip and plummeted toward the ground. Deke faithfully attempted to catch me, but two stories proved to be too steep a descent as my landing knocked him to the ground. Fortunately, he broke my fall and neither of us was seriously injured.

Still coughing and bleeding from numerous cuts, I managed to get up on my hands and knees before Deke lifted me up into his arms and carried me a safe distance from the building. He gripped me with a powerful embrace, trying to reassure me with a panicked whisper in my ear. "You're okay. You're okay. You're okay." He kept repeating it as if saying it enough times would make it be true.

I finally caught my breath well enough to speak. "Yes, I am okay. What happened?"

Now a safe distance from the building, Deke set me on the ground. "The whole place is going up!"

I turned and looked up for my first glimpse of the whole building. As smoke billowed from most windows, fierce flames burned at both ends of the structure. It looked as if the fire were burning from the outside inward.

Deke was panting. "The end stairwells are completely engulfed. You took the only way out."

I was dazed and confused. "How did it start?"

"I don't know, but let's not worry about that right now. We better check to make sure you're okay." Deke surveyed my cuts and scrapes.

"I got cut by the glass on my floor. Somebody must have thrown a rock through my window."

"That was me." Deke lifted the hem of my long nightshirt to examine a deep gash on the side of my calf. "I was yelling for you, but you didn't answer." He lifted his T-shirt and pulled it over his head. "I figured you couldn't hear me, so I better do something to get your attention." Methodically, he began tearing his T-shirt into broad strips for bandages. "I'm sorry if I hurt you." He carefully tied one over my deepest wound. "Sorry to say I think you're going to need stitches on this one."

I coughed and half-smirked. "Hey, I think I've heard that line before."

With utter chaos growing around us, I couldn't help but feel fortunate to be safely out of the fire. Others mingled about us, some crying out to those still attempting to escape the building while others sobbed and wailed, totally gripped with the thought of losing a loved one. The tide of emotions was overwhelming as we all gazed at the fiery inferno.

A glaring red and white light swung around atop the island's only fire truck while its hoses drew water from a horse-drawn water wagon. With the heat intensifying, the crowd was driven further back from the building, the flames now lapping at the sides of the structure as the blaze raged furiously out of control. In the distance out over Lake Huron, I could hear the faint sound of one slowly approaching siren. It would be at least another fifteen to twenty minutes before fire trucks ferried in from the mainland would arrive at the scene.

Deke helped me up so we could move farther away from the building. That's when we ran into Pepper.

She grasped me by the shoulders, tears in her eyes. "I thought you were dead! How did you get out?"

"I knocked out the window." I choked a bit on a cough. "Isn't that something you've always wanted to do?"

"You're such an idiot!" She hugged me. "So, how'd you two get out?"

"Deke was already out. I just tied sheets together and got lower so I could jump to him."

Pepper looked puzzled. "So you both jumped?"

"No, I told you, Deke tried to catch me." I coughed.

"Not Deke – Abel. Did he jump, too? Where is he?"

Deke grabbed Pepper by the arm. "What are you talking about?"

Pepper's eyes widened. "You mean, Abel didn't find you in there? He was sure you were still in there and... and I tried to stop him."

I thought back to earlier. "Yeah, you told him to leave, not to come back before ten tomorrow. Don't you remember?" I knew she had to be mixed up by all the commotion.

"But I ran into him in town, and when we heard about the fire –"

Deke took hold of Pepper's other arm and shook her. "Where did he go?"

"We were on the other side of the building looking for Carly, and he asked if she was still in there – and I didn't know. And when we couldn't find her, he figured she was still inside. So, he went charging into the smoke – might have headed for the fire escape, but I'm not –"

"You both stay here." Deke took off running through the crowd.

A cold shudder coursed through my body. "Oh my God, Abel! I've got to get him out of there!" Coughing again, I started to follow Deke, but my knees buckled and I stumbled.

Pepper caught me. "No, you can't go!"

"But he's in there because of me. – They both are, and I'm responsible. I've got to go." I pulled away from Pepper's hold and tried to move toward the structure.

"Get a grip!" Pepper grabbed my shoulders and wheeled me around. "You're in no shape to go in there, and you don't want them to have to go looking for you again, so give Deke a chance."

I reluctantly followed orders, but time passed ever so slowly as Pepper and I huddled together and watched the blaze intensify, the flames crackling and roaring like the sound of a stiff wind. Then we heard the wail of the sirens finally growing closer as the minutes dragged on. It seemed an eternity before more help arrived, but they eventually made their way up to the building.

The lawn around the burning structure resembled a war zone with some paramedics but mostly average citizens tending to the needs of the many wounded. Some were afflicted with burns and scrapes, but the worst victims were suffering from smoke inhalation. As more victims were pulled from the structure, it seemed their symptoms grew worse by the moment. Those who could delay treatment did so voluntarily so those in more desperate need could receive immediate treatment. As one paramedic offered to examine my wounds, I shooed her away to help someone in greater need than myself.

I gazed into the raging flames as they continued to burn out of control, wondering if both Deke and Abel had lost their lives on account of me. As I stared at the structure and the chaos about it, I heard the voices of the firemen at one end of the structure calling out a repetitive warning.

"It's going to go!"

And just as they predicted, the far end of the structure heaved and began to give way. I watched in horror as the fourth floor collapsed into the third, then into the second, and finally crashed to the ground spewing flames and debris out into the scattering crowd. The rest of the structure was still standing but likely wouldn't for long as the flames quickly consumed what remained of the building. Deke and Abel had to be out by now if they were to survive.

I couldn't stand by and wait any longer, so I took advantage of the distraction created by the collapse to free myself of Pepper's embrace and charge toward the structure.

Pepper was immediately on my heels. "Come back here!"

But I continued onward, plowing through the crowds of onlookers and wounded. "Abel? Deke?" I choked a bit, but remained determined to find them "Abel! Where are you guys!"

No one answered.

Still coughing and choking, I managed to scream out both of their names in one final desperate plea.

An elderly gentleman came forward from the crowd and placed his hand tenderly on my shoulder. "Deke Kovonaugh?"

I gasped. "Yes! Do you know where he is?"

"Follow me." He plowed through the crowd and closer to the smoldering building, and I gimped along behind him.

Pepper finally caught up. "Deke told us to wait back there! Now he won't be able to find us!"

"This guy knows where he is." I waved for her to follow.

We both anxiously tagged along, weaving in and around rescuers frantically working to save and comfort the wounded. We stayed right behind the stranger, a man who seemed vaguely familiar though I couldn't recall where I'd seen him before.

"Jost a little furddar." The man motioned for us to keep moving forward. "Wish I hod my troctor to get os dare a bit fostar."

Then I remembered. It was Mr. Raddison, the graveyard grounds keeper.

I was limping a bit, but determined to follow. "Are Deke and Abel okay?"

Mr. Raddison didn't answer, continuing on his trek at what seemed like a snail's pace. At least we had finally made our way around to the other side of the building.

Suddenly, an ever so slight and frail Saint still dressed in her maid's uniform grasped my arm. "No one's helpin' me save my baby! My garl's in dare ond you gotta help me get her out!"

Stunned by her heart-wrenching plea, I paused for just a moment. But what could I do? I was sure anyone still in the building at this point couldn't make it out alive, and I needed to get to my own friends. I grew frightened as she continued to grab at my wrists and pull me, so I forcefully tried to break free of her grip.

She clasped tighter and sobbed. "You got to be helpin' her now!"

A local minister stepped forward. "I'll help you, miss. Just come with me." He gingerly took hold of the mother's arms.

She wept heavily as she released her grip. "Oh, tank you. You such a kind mon. Come ond quick help me find my garl."

The minister began guiding her away from the building. "We should go check over this way first."

Suddenly, she was opposed to the minister's guidance. "No! No! I won't look in dat morgue!" She collapsed in the minister's arms. "You just gotta be helpin' me get her outta dare!" Deeply saddened by this woman's grief, I nonetheless turned away from her plight and plunged forward, trying to ignore her calls as they faded into those of the mass. Then the building further creaked and snapped, another portion collapsing and forcing us to make a broader loop to circle the building at a safe distance from the fire and those battling it.

Although it seemed to take forever, we finally made it to a central area where paramedics were hovering over the injured, furiously racing to save their lives. I noticed one man feverishly performing CPR on a body burned beyond recognition, and I wondered if I was prepared to see what had become of Deke and Abel.

Mr. Raddison lifted his hand and pointed to a clearing straight ahead. "Dare are your fronds."

In front of me, I saw the back of a shirtless man who was kneeling on the ground, intensely working at something before him. There was a paramedic to his right and a woman I didn't recognize to his left, both also knelt down and equally fervent in pursuing the task before them. Without even thanking Mr. Raddison, I gulped, fighting the sobs that were welling up and about to spill out. Slowly, I approached the figures with Pepper at my side, clasping my hand.

When the shirtless man turned to grab an oxygen tank and mask, I could see it was Deke. Tears fell from my eyes as I silently offered a prayer of thanks for sparing his life. But as I moved closer, my elation turned to grief as I saw the soot-blackened figure lying at their knees. It was Abel.

"Oh my God!" I cried and coughed as I fell to my knees beside Deke.

"Keep her back!" the paramedic shouted to Pepper, and for once she willingly accepted a command as she grabbed a hold of me and held me back.

I turned to Deke. "What happened? Is he going to be all right?"

"Just stay back and let us work, Carly!" Deke grabbed an oxygen tank and efficiently attached a long plastic tube to it.

"He doesn't seem to be burned, but the smoke inhalation's severe. I've got him intubated." The paramedic reached for the other end of the tube and began attaching it to a balloon-like apparatus protruding from Abel's mouth and to the side of his face. "Let's bag him."

With this instruction, Deke grasped the oxygen tank and cranked the handle as the paramedic rhythmically squeezed the balloon. I could see Abel's soot-covered chest rise and fall with each compression.

"Take over!" the paramedic barked. Deke grabbed the bag and continued to pump oxygen into Abel's failing lungs. With Deke in control, the paramedic was free to radio for transportation.

"We have a male – twenty-seven – in respiratory distress. He's arrested once, but we got him back. He's intubated and ready to move. Request immediate air transport. Over."

The voice on the radio came back. "We're backing up here, but bring him in to transport, stat. Over."

Deke began piling the necessary equipment at the foot of the gurney. "Is he stable enough to move?"

The paramedic was also packing up. "He has to be. We have to get him on a vent, now."

"I'll lead the way." The assisting woman snatched up the paramedic's bag and charged ahead into the crowd.

I grabbed Deke's arm. "I'm going with him."

Deke glared at me, jerking his arm away. "No! You're staying here!"

I cleared my throat. "But I want to stay with –"

His brow was furrowed and his voice curt. "This isn't about what you want! Just be helpful – go and tell his dad what happened. At the very least, you owe him that!"

His words cut deeply, insinuating I was to blame for Abel's condition – a responsibility I was painfully all too willing to accept.

Deke nabbed the last case of the life support equipment. "First get my dad and have him arrange to get Vince over to the mainland. Tell them we'll be at Mercy." And with that, they lifted the gurney bearing Abel's failing body into the mob and disappeared from our sight.

"We need to get you to a doctor, too." Pepper tried to remind me of my own cuts, but her suggestion fell on deaf ears.

"Not until we find Mr. Hanika." I stared at the collapsed structure smoldering before me. "I at least owe Abel that."

Pepper brushed my disheveled hair from my cheek. "Don't go blaming yourself for this, Carly. It isn't your fault."

But I knew otherwise as I finally turned from the fire and wandered off into a darkness much blacker than the night.

Chapter 20

HAUNTED

SINCE HIJACKING BICYCLES WAS A CUSTOM deemed acceptable on Windemere Island, Pepper never flinched as she helped herself to an unlocked tandem "two-seater." I vaguely recall her wheeling it around in the direction of Windemere Bluff, then commanding me to get on the back seat. I must have still been dazed from the events unfolding before us as I initially didn't respond.

"Get on!" Pepper yelled.

Then I checked back into reality. Grasping the rear seat handlebars, I gently guided my thigh over the seat as my leg throbbed from my wounds.

"Be careful not to bump your leg against the bar." Pepper hopped onto the front seat. "I'll do the peddling. You just come along for the ride."

This was easier said than done as the rear pedals coincided with Peppers and had to rotate with each push. I tried removing my feet from the pedals and holding my legs out, but that proved even more painful than just letting them rotate. I finally resigned myself to leaving them on the pedals and just riding out each rub and bump.

"We're almost to Kavanaughs'," Pepper alerted me.

I sighed, knowing relief from the physical pain was at hand while the emotional agony was just beginning.

Still on an incline, Pepper heartily pumped at the pedals. "Are you doing okay?"

I cleared my throat. "I'm fine." Looking down at the shirt Deke had tied to my leg, I noticed it was encrusted with blood. The wound seemed to be holding for now, so I figured the stitches could wait.

As we passed each of the immense cottages on the bluff, I noticed they were all dark except for their massive, ornate porch lights that attracted fish flies by the dozens. Despite the distant sounds of anguish and calamity, the island's elite remained oblivious to the events in the nearby village. Either they didn't know, or didn't care.

Unlike the situation at other cottages, the downstairs living area of the Kavanaugh's house was well lit, and so we were not surprised to be greeted efficiently at the door. However, we were somewhat surprised by *who* answered the door.

"Oh my, ladies!" The Saint Hailey Battiste looked equally surprised to see us as he opened the door dressed in a cotton bathrobe and rubber-soled slippers. "It's so late for de two of you to be stopon' by, ond wid all de co-motion wit de fire down dare – Ond Carly!" He glared and pointed at me. "Dot's pojomos dot you're wearon' dare! Whot are you tinkon'?"

Pepper hadn't met Mr. Battiste, and she was abrupt in her response to him. "And who are you?"

"I'm Hailey." He patted his wiry, disheveled gray hair, trying to smooth it down." I keep de house for de Kovonaughs."

"That's right." Pepper made the connection. "Rafae's dad – he told me you worked here, but right now I –"

"Did he now?" Hailey interrupted, scowling with a look of concern as his dark eyes studied us. "Don't tell me my boy's been octin' up ogain, causon' mischof – Oh! Ond he's got no hond in dot fire, does he?"

"Oh, no," Pepper answered. "We came here because Deke told us to –"

"Oh, tonk goodness!" Hailey glanced down, wiping his brow. "I wos ofraid dot my boy got in trouble. Well, os for Mr. Deke, he's out for de evenon', but please step in de house ond – My!" His eyes popped wide open as he looked more closely at us. "You two look like you been in de dirt, ond all sweaty! Whot's wrong?"

"It's the fire!" Pepper shook her hands with urgency. "We have *got* to see Mr. Kavanaugh right now. Sorry about the late hour, but it's an emergency. So, could you just go and wake him please?"

"Oh, he's not sleepon', miss." Hailey pulled the door open a bit more and motioned again for us to enter. "Poor Mr. D'Arcy, with Mr. Deke gone he's hod to be out bock wid de sick colt for de longest time. Ond den when he finally got ta bed, de old huskey starts de howlon'. Most hov been all de strange noises come from de fire dot stirred up de dog. So, Miss Constance, she told him to eedar shut up de dog before de neighbors started complainon' or else she'd divorce de mon ond send him pockon' off to live in de kennel with de pack ond —"

Pepper wasted no time heading back out the door, pushing me along with her. "Sorry, but we've got to see him right now. He's still out there, isn't he?"

"Well, de barkon' stopped, but I'd bet he's still out dare in de bock of de house." Hailey followed us out onto the porch and pointed around the side of the house. "Follow de stone pavars down dot way ond you should find him." Then he backed up to the doorway, mumbling as he reached to shut the door. "He'd be much better off if he moved out dare anyway."

As I coughed and tried to clear my throat, Pepper helped me quickly gimp off the porch and we headed down the poorly lit path that led along the side of the house. As we awkwardly pawed our way through the darkness, I could see the distant glow of the fire lighting up the night sky. I could also hear the commotion of the mob and the wail of sirens echoing from fire trucks finally arriving by ferry to the island. It was likely these unfamiliar sounds that originally alerted the dog, but the pack remained surprisingly silent as we approached the small barn.

By the light of a Coleman lantern, we could see D'Arcy Kavanaugh, his salt and pepper hair so similar in color to that of the wild eyed husky he was petting that one might have thought him just another member of the pack. But then he turned and stood up, his sturdy stature and weathered, tanned skin revealing him to be the master of the pack. With his leathery hands, he gave his husky one last, hearty scratch on the neck before stepping out of the kennel, latching the gate shut as he finally noticed us. "Girls? Well, you're out late to be looking for Deke, but I bet you're still awake because of all the commotion with —"

"The fire." Pepper finished.

"Yeah, looks like a doozy! I wanted to get over there to help out, but first I had to settle down my lead dog before he got the whole pack going – and got the neighbors ticked off."

I stepped into the glow from the lantern, still choking a bit. "We came – to get your help."

D'Arcy looked at me, seeming to notice the soot on my face. "Hey, it looks like you've been into it." He then stepped to the side and started heading toward the dark path. "Yeah, I bet they could use all the help they can muster up. That old sawdust pile's been sitting there for almost a century, left over from the logging days. I told city council they should get rid of it before it lit up. Just a hazard waiting –"

I followed behind, still coughing as I limped toward the path. "It's not the sawdust pile, sir."

He stopped in his tracks. "It's not?"

"No, sir."

He turned to face me. "The boarding house." He paused, then looked down. "It was just a matter of time."

It was as if he could read my mind. I coughed, not needing to answer.

D'Arcy extended his lantern toward me, now looking at me with a more intense gaze. "You're hurt." His eyes lowered and he knelt down by my leg, further studying my injury as well as the unusual logo imprinted across the fabric dangling from my calf. Amidst the twist of the knot and the blood stains, its slogan was barely legible. "Mush the Canyon." He could still decipher it. "That shirt's from the Agawa Canyon sled race. I got it for Deke."

Pepper knelt beside him. "Deke's okay. He sent us here to get you to help –"

D'Arcy turned his gaze to Pepper. "That's your place on fire, isn't it?" He quickly stood up and held his lantern close to me. "And it's yours, too, isn't it Carly?"

"Yes, and it's –"

"Is anyone hurt?" His questions came more quickly now.

I stuttered and choked, trying my best to answer, but no words would come.

"I'm afraid so, sir." Pepper stood again. "And we've come to get your help in letting someone know – notifying next-of-kin."

"And who's that?"

"Well, it's Vincent Hanika."

"Oh, no. Abel." D'Arcy's dark eyes fell as he took a deep breath and exhaled. "How bad?"

Pepper also glanced downward. "I'm not sure, but he was having trouble breathing and it looked pretty bad to me."

D'Arcy paused, then looked up. "Well, let's go. Fill me in as we walk." He then turned and quickly headed back along the path adjacent to the house, lighting the way as we followed.

Walking briskly back to the porch, Pepper gave a quick recap of how events had unfolded. As she recollected my escape from the building and Deke's daring rescue of Abel, D'Arcy was noticeably relieved that both his son and I were all right but he was devastated to hear of Abel and other casualties. With the full scope of the situation in perspective, D'Arcy took charge and proposed a plan of action.

"I'm sure the ferry lines will call in their captains and crews to run all night, but they may be transporting a number of people to the hospital and could be backed up for hours." D'Arcy looked out at the whitecaps cresting on the moonlit water. "It's a bit choppy on the big lake, but we can still take my boat to the mainland. Pepper, you ride Carly down to the old coal dock by Fischer's Launch. I'll get Vince and bring the boat around to meet you there."

"No, we should go with you." I tilted my head away for a quick cough. "I've got to be there when Vincent finds out – to admit that it's all my fault."

Pepper had lost her patience with me. "Why, you couldn't even tell D'Arcy! What do you think you're going to do there?"

"Well, I'll just have to buck up and tell him I'm the one that caused this to happen."

His expression kind but firm, D'Arcy looked at me as he took hold of both of my shoulders. "You look at me and listen, Carly. This was not your fault. You didn't start that fire, and you didn't tell Abel to walk into it. He's a grown man who made his own decision to go in there. You're not responsible for that."

I appreciated the words of wisdom, but still found it difficult to convince myself to agree.

D'Arcy let loose and lowered his hands. "Besides, Vince is an old friend, and it's best that he hear this from me. Now, let's get going so we can get to Mercy and find out how Abel's doing." He then turned to Hailey who was back at his post in the doorway. "Hailey, go tell Ms. Connie you're coming with me."

"She'll be fighton' mod dat I'm leavon', Mr. D'Arcy."

"Well, then wake my mom and leave just long enough to take her over there to stay with the girls for now. Connie probably won't even notice you've left if you aren't gone too long, but do hurry up and get Ms. Maeve over there, pronto. I'll go on ahead."

"Okay, Mr. D'Arcy."

With that, D'Arcy handed off his lantern to Hailey, then descended the porch steps and dashed off into the darkness. I heard what sounded like a chain rattling, and then he quickly reappeared aboard his Raleigh three-speed as he headed into the light cast by the street lamps. He pedaled hard as he headed full tilt to the roadside, then turned and headed toward the French Landings.

Pepper was equally speedy in commandeering our hot tandem, but I was still a bit slow on the mount. With a little help from her, I again managed to swing my tender leg over the back of the bike and settle into the rear seat, ready for what would be a short ride to Fischer's Launch.

While Pepper was climbing aboard the front seat, I turned my head to cough and found, at that angle, I could see the glow of a lantern flickering from the window on the second floor of the Kavanaugh's carriage house. The light danced upon the pains of glass and illuminated an elderly man poised in the frame of the window, gazing out at us. Then just as suddenly as I had noticed him, the man leaned to one side, blew out the lantern, and the window disappeared into the darkness of the night.

As Pepper pulled from the curb, I wondered about the figure and recalled him from our past visit to the Bluff. The ghost had come again, and I was haunted not only by him, but also by what was yet to come.

Chapter 21

THE DANCE OF DEATH

IMPATIENT PATIENTS CROWDED TOGETHER in the compact waiting room, some sitting on table tops, others sprawled out on the floor. We were considered the lesser of the injured, with those among us suffering from many scrapes and bruises, a few broken bones, but nothing that was life threatening. Everyone understood the delay as many overwhelmed doctors and nurses worked feverishly on patients with much more serious injuries. But the cumbersome quarters, coupled with the sighs and tears of those awaiting word of their loved ones, made the small waiting area nearly unbearable.

An elderly Saint with a swollen ankle hopped on his good foot to the single picture window and pulled the cord to raise the blind and reveal dawn's first light. "The hope of a new day," he announced to the masses as he negotiated the crowded floor to return to his seat.

The fiery glow of the rising sun illuminated the horizon and silhouetted a distant stand of towering white pines. Under usual circumstances, I would have taken pause to savor such an awesome view. But these were not normal circumstances, and the beauty of daybreak stood in stark contrast to the barren white walls and the antiseptic aroma of this medical environment. I had plenty of time to spare, but could take no delight in the gorgeous vista. In fact, I felt guilty for noticing it at all.

One of the island's more vocal Saints, a slight woman by the name of Regina Goullea, gathered herself up from her post on the floor and left her vigil at the side of her injured daughter to sternly approach the glass windows closed on the main desk.

Regina tapped her long, painted nails against the glass. "My daughter over dare, she's got a lot a bod pain! Ot least get her some pain pills 'til someone con see her!"

The receptionist slid the glass window open. "I'm so sorry, ma'am, but I can't do that. I'm not authorized to dispense meds."

"Well, den get someone who con!"

"I'll see what I can do." She then slid the window shut.

An equally anxious older woman with weary eyes and disheveled white hair spoke from the crowd. "You can't bother the doctors while they're tending to the serious patients."

Regina bristled at the woman's implication. "You high ond mighty locals, you dink you somehow love your children more don us – dink your kids deserve better treatment don ours. Well, I tell ya what, lady! My daughter's just os deservon' of ottention os yours, ond I'm go-on' get it – right now!"

The feud had captured the undivided attention of everyone in the crowded waiting area, and we watched in amazement as Regina bolted for the ER entrance. The receptionist lunged for the door and attempted to lock it down as the livid mother rattled the doorknob, demanding access. Meanwhile, the older woman rose deliberately from her seat and walked with a steady gate to Regina. We all watched the woman transform as she approached, her expression changing from determined to one of rage.

With glaring eyes and a set jaw, the woman jabbed her index finger at Regina. "My daughter's back there, and she's no better or worse than your daughter, but she's my child, and…" She choked, her voice quivering as she shed a tear. "And she may not make it." Her set jaw quivered for a moment, then clenched tighter. "You are *not* going to go back there, and you are going to wait your turn, so just sit down!"

Silence hovered as the spectators awaited a response. After a long pause, Regina surprised anyone taking bets by backing down. She made no apologies but held her chin high as she returned to her spot next to her daughter on the floor. The mouthy little Saint had met her match.

Regina's adversary had taken no pleasure in her victory. She leaned against the ER door, lowered her head, and quietly wept.

I watched as a burly Saint man rose from his spot and went to the woman, gave her a gentle pat, and then helped her back to her seat. The image flashed me back to that moment when I had lost those I loved most, and how the kindness of strangers had helped me make it through that horrible time.

Since I wasn't a mother, I could only imagine how awful it must be to fear for your own child's survival. My thoughts then drifted to Vincent who was somewhere nearby consulting with the doctors, enduring the same anxiety as this mother, wondering whether his son would live or die.

My own speculations regarding Abel were intolerable. As a survivor, he'd likely face an excruciating recovery process, the likes of which seemed unimaginable. His agony would be immense, ongoing, inescapable, and he'd probably never be the same. Maybe he'd be better off –

"No!" I blurted.

Two Saints seated to my right turned their heads and stared at me, their scowling faces indicating their confusion over why I had blurted such an outburst.

I coughed and cleared my throat while waving at the two of them. "Sorry. I'm just getting over a bug."

They grimaced, turning their backs toward me.

My mind returned to contemplating the unthinkable. What if Abel didn't make it?

My eyes darted about the waiting area, hoping to catch a glimpse of Pepper returning with news, but she was still nowhere to be found. She had left me alone just before sunrise, promising she would not return until she found out at least some information regarding Abel. The deal was made with the condition that I stay put and wait my turn to see the doctor. I reluctantly agreed at the time, but now I was contemplating rescinding my promise.

Many times I was tempted to check at the glass windows to see if the receptionist knew about Abel's condition, but I had watched others attempt and fail to solicit information regarding other patients' status. The staff was too busy to keep the front desk totally updated, and only next-of-kin were being notified. Besides, like the devastated mother still weeping, I too did not want to keep doctors and nurses from attending to those in dire need.

"Decaf?" inquired a cheery woman dressed in hospital pastels and cloaked with an apron. She tried to pass a steaming Styrofoam cup to me, but I declined. Others around me accepted the peace offering.

"You're still waiting for a doctor?" D'Arcy asked over my shoulder.

A bit startled, I turned around and looked up to find him holding two cups of coffee, one extended toward me.

I cleared my throat. "I think they assigned me a number." Taking the hot cup from him, I lightly pressed it between both of my hands, warming my palms. "They said they'll call me when they can see me."

"That coffee still has the lead in it – it should clear your sinuses and help keep you awake 'til they get to you."

I blew the steam from the coffee's surface. "Is Abel still in the ER?"

"No, he was transferred to ICU a little while ago."

I coughed. "How is he?"

D'Arcy paused long enough to take a seat on the floor. "I'm sorry, but the news isn't good."

I lowered my eyes and tried to convince myself that the worst could not be possible. "He can't be dead."

"Oh, no. He's hanging in there." Despite these positive words, D'Arcy's somber demeanor and wavering voice best articulated the truth about the situation. "The doctor told Vince that he's in critical but stable condition. They've got him on life support, and he's holding his own."

"So, what does that mean?"

"Well, I guess it means he's got machines keeping him going for now, until he can breathe on his own."

"And how long will that be?"

"You know, the doctors were pretty well occupied with other patients, Carly, so they didn't really get around to answering all of the questions we had. I'm sure as soon as you get stitched up, we can see what more they know."

I cleared my throat, then set my untouched coffee on a side table and started to get up from the floor. "So, can I see him?"

D'Arcy gently took hold of my wrist and kept me from getting up. "You really need to stay here and get stitched up first, Carly. We were all up there waiting for quite awhile. Abel's dad's the only one who's gone in to see him, and he's only been in there a short time. I just left Deke up there in the waiting area, just in case Vince comes out while I'm down here talking to you."

I looked out the window at the sun as it continued to rise, warming the room. "Deke is so angry with me."

"No. He's just worried about Abel, just like the rest of us, and he probably took it out on you. But we've got to keep positive about this – keep on praying for the best."

A nurse slid the glass window open and yelled into the waiting area. "Seventeen? Is seventeen still here?"

"Finally!" Regina took her daughter by the shoulders and guided her to the ER door. "I con't believe how long it takes you people to help us. No soprise dot da Saint women are disappearon' and dyon'!"

For a moment, a stunned silence hung over the room. Then gradually, people returned to quiet chit-chat.

"What number are you?" D'Arcy asked.

"Nineteen." I put my fist to my mouth and coughed.

"Oh, good. You won't have long now." He took a sip of his coffee. "And you should have them check your lungs for smoke while you're back there."

"Oh, I'm just getting over a bad bug." I tried to clear my throat. "I'm actually getting better."

"Really?" He took another drink. "Well, as I was saying before, about Abel – I just know that we've got to remain hopeful and supportive because… well, because I know Abel, and he has always been a very determined guy. So we have to be equally determined. He's got what it takes to make it out of this, Carly. We've just got to hang in there with him."

There was something reassuring about recalling Abel's tenacity, an essential characteristic for one determined to survive. His persistence was evident when he talked me into accepting that bike, and when he convinced me to go for a ride up past the bluff for a few swigs of cheap wine. He doggedly pursued my attention, offering me his unreserved companionship despite my taking it for granted. And he had the will to plunge into a burning building, to sacrifice his own life in an attempt to save mine . . .

I buried my hands in my face. "This is all my fault."

"What are you talking about?"

I looked up, tears rolling down my face. "He went in to save me!" I sniffed and coughed. "And I know he wouldn't have done that if I hadn't —"

D'Arcy brushed the tears from my cheek. "Now, wait a minute." He then handed me the napkin from under his coffee cup. "Are you going to sit here and blame yourself for the actions of others?"

I wiped my tears with the napkin.

"Why, if you're looking to lay blame, there's plenty to go around," D'Arcy insisted. "Like, how about blaming whoever started the fire, or maybe Mansfield for nailing the windows shut and making the place such a fire trap to begin with?"

"Or maybe you should blame me!" Pepper suddenly appeared, taking a place on the floor to my side and sternly staring at me. "It's my fault for talking you into living with me in that dump to begin with. Yeah, that's right. It's all my fault. Take me to court. If you're going to arrest someone, then take me in!"

I glared back while clearing my throat. "Now, that's just ridiculous."

"Oh, really? Is it?"

I realized her point.

D'Arcy took a drink of his coffee. "So, if we've got all of this blaming business out of the way, then maybe we can focus on what's more important here — like how we can help the Hanikas get through this."

"Good idea." Pepper put her index finger to her lips and pondered. "Hm. Now, I wonder what we could do..."

D'Arcy set his cup aside. "Well, I have a proposition that would help out the Hanikas, and I think it would help out you two young ladies at the same time."

Pepper lowered her hand and cocked her head to the side. "And what would that be?"

"Well, earlier on when Vince, Deke, and I were waiting to hear how Abel was doing, we started talking over some long-range plans – you know, in case Vincent ends up needing to spend a lot of time here at the hospital with Abel."

I shook my head. "Oh, I hope that won't happen – that he'll get better pretty quickly."

"Of course, we all do, but just in case we've got to think a little bit ahead." D'Arcy whirled his Styrofoam cup, watching the remainder of his coffee spin around in the bottom. "So, if Vince wants to be here, then he can't work the front desk at the Landings – and unfortunately, he's short handed there right now. He said he had a couple of young ladies working there for awhile, but they recently left, probably because of this missing Saints thing. So, we were wondering if you two might be up to handling the desk duties for the time being – maybe move into the hotel and oversee the place."

Pepper's eyes widened. "You bet we can!"

I, on the other hand, was very reluctant. "Wait a minute. You want us, just a couple of inexperienced girls…" I paused to swallow, avoiding a cough. "You want us to run an entire hotel, all by ourselves?"

"Well, not exactly. You'd just need to cancel out as many of the current reservations as you can. Vincent wants to close the place to visitors. I'm sure the Fudgies will be ticked off, but they'll just have to get over it."

Pepper looked perplexed. "So, we'd just be there to close the place down?"

"That, and then check out the vacant rooms to any Saints who lost their place in the fire and need a place to live. Vincent's decided that if he's already got to shut the place down, he might as well help out the Saints that need a roof over their heads. So, your job would be to lease out the available rooms for some reasonable monthly rate – say, whatever Old Man Mansfield was getting. I'm sure you two could handle renting out a few rooms, and keeping the place tidy."

Pepper's jaw hung open until she reached up and pushed it shut. "You mean to tell me that Mr. Hanika's going to let the two of us, and a whole bunch of Saints, stay in that beautiful hotel – all for the same price as Mansfield was charging us to live in that tinderbox?"

"Or less, if that's what you two decide to charge."

I was stunned. "I can't believe this. That would be such an amazing offer even under normal circumstances. But now?" I swallowed. "While his son's fighting for his life? How could he even think to do such a thing under these circumstances?"

"He's just a good-hearted, well-intentioned man," D'Arcy explained. "I've noticed this about Vince before – that when things seem darkest for him, that's when he tends to give the most. Maybe it somehow helps him through the tough times. I don't know for sure, but that's just who he is and what he does."

Pepper raised her hand. "Hey, whatever his reasons, I'm in, and so is Carly since we —"

"Wait a minute," I stopped Pepper. "Don't forget that we have another job obligation, and I can't imagine Callahan being too happy with us both quitting on him at the same time."

D'Arcy smirked, his weathered skin wrinkling about his green eyes. "Hope I didn't overstep my boundaries, but I already talked to Callahan. Under the circumstances, I got him to agree to let you two take a leave for now, and then he even guaranteed you both your jobs back when you're finished. Guess he thinks a lot of you two."

Pepper raised her chin, looking proud. "Yeah, well, we are his hardest workers, of course." She then looked more serious. "But we are currently homeless and, quite frankly, we could really use the help ourselves, so tell Mr. Hanika that he can count on us. Right, Carly?" She pressed her elbow into my side.

I could think of no other objections. "Well, yes. Tell him thank you and that we really appreciate his offer."

"I will." D'Arcy nodded. "And thank you."

"Eighteen," the nurse announced through the window, and an older man stood up and headed for the door.

"Shouldn't be long, now," D'Arcy assured me. "But while you're waiting, there's something more I need to ask, and it's specifically a request of you, Carly."

"Of me?" I coughed.

"Yes. You're probably aware that Abel's sister and niece also live back at the Landings."

"Yeah, Gretchen and her daughter Libby. I think Abel said that Libby's about seven-years-old, going into second grade, if I remember right. He talked – well, *talks* a lot about them."

D'Arcy folded his leathery hands. "I'm sure he does. Gretchen and Libby have been living at the hotel ever since Gretchen got sick. Her husband didn't want to deal with it, so he abandoned them – left them on the Landings' doorstep, and has never been seen or heard from since."

"How awful!" I thought back to the night Eino had taken me and Abel to the hotel and recalled the startling noise when Gretchen had fallen. "I remember when Vincent said something about Gretchen's illness making it hard for her to move."

"Yes, that's right. She has a degenerative disease that's left her unable to care for herself, let alone for her daughter, so Vince and Abel have been taking care of them."

I cleared my throat. "But now they can't." I lowered my eyes, searching the floor for something I knew wasn't there.

"Yeah, if Vincent wants to be here with Abel, then he can't be at the Landings to care of Gretchen and Libby. Now, my mother's there right now to help – she does that every now and then – and I know she can handle things for today, and maybe tomorrow. But she's elderly and, although she'd never admit it, I know it would be too much for her to handle for any long period of time."

Pepper looked surprised. "You know, Vince has got a lot of money, and everyone knows it, so I don't get it. If she's that sick, why doesn't he just hire some doctor to be there all the time?"

D'Arcy folded his arms across his broad chest. "He does have a doctor, Doc Arlington, who's in and out to see her quite a bit. But Gretchen's not very fond of doctors, and that's probably pretty understandable given her situation. So Doc doesn't live there, and he's been busy doing some research work that will hopefully help Gretchen in the long run."

I thought again about the night I'd been at the Landings. "Vincent talked about his daughter beating this disease thing that they call Hunting's or something like… well, Abel told me the name of it but I just can't remember."

"She has Huntington's chorea."

"Hey, I've heard of that!" Pepper surprised us both with her knowledge of such an obscure condition. "I read about that in *People* magazine, or maybe a newspaper somewhere. They were doing these experimental brain surgeries to help these people who had Huntington's and Parkinson's."

D'Arcy rubbed the thick patch of dark gray stubble on his face. "Huntington's is similar to Parkinson's. It's a condition that sort of short circuits a person's nervous system – makes you have abrupt, kind of twitching movements that can't be controlled. It makes it harder to walk or talk, to eat, to get up and get dressed, and sometimes even to sit. Then the chorea part is like these large, jerky, dance-like gestures." He twisted his arms slightly as if attempting to vaguely mimic the motion he was describing. "It keeps the body moving awkwardly like this, in a kind of wave of never-ending motion."

Pepper waved her finger at us. "Yeah, I read all about that. It's called Saint Vitus' Dance, but others call it the Dance of Death."

I sat up straight. "But people don't actually die from it – do they?"

D'Arcy bit his lip. "In its late stages, Huntington's will bring on loss of memory, hallucinations, dementia. It's a totally incapacitating disease – and yes, it eventually kills its victims."

I covered my mouth with my hands. "Oh, my God." I paused, and then lowered my hands. "And I did hear somebody say this disease is hereditary?"

D'Arcy nodded. "Unfortunately, yes. And the devastating fact is that it's a dominant trait. If one parent has it, then each offspring has a fifty-fifty chance of developing it. In this case, it apparently came down through Mrs. Hanika's side of the family. Her father died from it, her sister died from it – and she eventually died from it. So, now Gretchen has it, and she may have passed it on to Libby."

I had to ask. "And what about Abel?"

"Hopefully it's passed him over."

I was learning quickly that D'Arcy was an eternal optimist but I, as I'd always suspected, was quite the opposite. I felt it well up inside me, this growing certainty that all the times I'd seen Abel stumble and fall were no longer attributable to mere acts of clumsiness. There had to be more to it than that, and what made me most certain was the recollection of his trembling hands . . .

D'Arcy placed his hand on my shoulder and looked at me with wide eyes and his reassuring smile. "One thing at a time, Carly – Just take it one step at a time. Now, we were hoping that maybe you'd consider leaving Biminis to be a fill-in caregiver – with free room and board and a decent salary, of course."

I choked, avoiding a cough, and then brushed away a tear I felt welling up in my eye before it could drop. "Well, I'd really like to be of some help, and I'm pretty sure I could take care of a little seven-year-old girl, but do you really think I could handle taking care of Gretchen?"

"There's not a doubt in my mind. It won't be nearly as difficult as it might sound. Gretchen can still do quite a bit for herself, and she quite prefers it that way. You'll find she's quite determined, a lot like her brother."

"Well, if you think I can handle it –"

"I think you can handle much more than you give yourself credit for."

"Oh, for Pete's sake, Carly!" Pepper flailed her arms in the air, calling the attention of others in the room. "Just take the job, or I will!"

D'Arcy held up his hand. "No, I'm sorry, Pepper. Nothing personal, but this job is only Carly's to accept or decline."

Pepper's forehead tightened and her eyebrows tilted inward, her facial expression turning sour. "Well, that's fine. I didn't want it, anyway. I'll be too busy running the place."

D'Arcy turned back to me. "Carly, I think you should know that Vincent specifically asked for you to do this."

I sniffed and cleared my throat. "Why me?"

"Because he's a good judge of character, and because he sees in you what his son sees in you – a decent and caring young woman. He believes in you, Carly. He thinks you're someone he can trust with this responsibility. So, can he count on you?"

I gazed out the window at the sun continuing its rise over the pines, marking the start of a new day. "Yes, I'd be happy to help take care of them."

D'Arcy grinned. "Vince will be pleased, and relieved."

"Nineteen." The nurse announced, then looked around. "Is nineteen still waiting?"

I coughed. "I'm right here." I waved and began to get up.

"The nurse looked at me. "Hey, we don't have time for a cold right now."

Now standing, I pointed at the shirt tied to my leg.

"Oh. Come on back."The nurse slid the window shut.

D'Arcy stood up and helped me toward the door. "Now you get stitched up while I go back to see how Abel's doing – and to give Vince the good news."

Looking up at us, Pepper remained seated on the floor. "Oh, and in case you're wondering, I'll be waiting right here when you're done so I can help you gimp up to intensive care. Deal?"

"Deal." I turned on my one good leg and negotiated my way around those still on the floor, quickly making my way through the ER door. I picked up my stride as I headed toward the familiar examining area, driven by a fervent desire to see Abel just as soon as possible. I wanted so badly to see him, to see Vince, to see Deke. I wanted to know if they would forgive me for any way I had contributed to this, and to find some sort of reassurance that they were going to be all right.

I hopped up on the gurney before the nurse had the chance to tell me to do so. She looked a bit surprised, but I didn't bother explaining my eagerness. I just did whatever I could, hoping to speed up my impending engagement with a needle and thread.

Chapter 22

UNCOVERING THE CHARADE

LIKE A VOYEUR SNEAKING A PEEK, I looked between the half-turned blinds that draped across the observation window into Abel's room. I could see his long, frail body lying motionless, except for the ever-so-slight rise of his chest with each compression of the ventilator pump.

Tubes and wires snaked about him, with each leading to some contraption monitoring his vitals or administering some life-sustaining element. Neon green lines bleeped across a screen in rhythm with his struggling heart, and a vacuum-style hose ran to a plastic tube wedged in his mouth and secured in place with surgical tape. Although he was obviously unconscious, I couldn't help but wonder if he was in any kind of pain.

Vincent was holding vigil at Abel's bedside. The elder gently stroked his son's forearm and gazed upon his somber face, calmly uttering some soft-spoken private words of love and encouragement to the sedated and unresponsive body before him. I watched in awe of Vincent's animated, smiling expression as he spoke to his son as though the lifeless figure would, at any moment, rise up and enthusiastically join the conversation.

But he didn't. He remained still as ever, and it broke my heart as his father ceased his dialogue, kissed Abel on the forehead, and then bowed his head in solemn reflection.

"I got you a sandwich." Pepper had returned from the cafeteria and was holding two sandwiches wrapped in cellophane. "How's your leg doing? Still numbed up?"

"Yeah, I can't feel anything." I looked at the sandwiches. "One must be tuna. I can smell it from here."

"Beats the smell of Clorox and puke." She handed one sandwich to me. "This one's ham and cheese, if you prefer."

"No, thanks. I'm feeling a little sick to my stomach."

"That's because you haven't eaten."

"No. It's because Dr. Pasquenelli gave me a couple doses of that cough syrup with codeine – said I needed it so I don't get worse."

"Oh. So that's why you're looking glassy-eyed." Pepper withdrew the sandwich and put both of them in one hand. "Well, I'm going to make sure you eat one of these soon. You need to get something in your stomach before you –"

"I will. I promise." I swallowed, no longer feeling such an urge to cough, and then I looked back at Abel. "Did you happen to hear anything about how he's doing?"

"I overheard a nurse talking to D'Arcy. She said he's got a fighting chance."

"What else did she say?"

"Same as D'Arcy told us – that he's stable, the machine's doing the breathing, and only time will tell."

I bit my lip. "I don't know. He looks so weak."

"That guy's got more guts than you give him credit for. If it's possible to get off that vent, then he's going to do it."

"I wish I had your confidence."

"I wish you did, too!" Pepper smiled. "Come on. Let's go down to the waiting room and eat these sandwiches."

I cleared my throat. "Not right now."

"But you haven't eaten anything, and you're still not over that sinus infection."

"I know, but I just got up here." I looked at Pepper while trying to hold back my tears. "I'm just going to stand here a little bit longer, just to see if there's any change or if the doctor comes by and says anything."

"Okay, but I'm timing you." She pointed at her watch. "Five minutes, and then you're going to eat. I'll get us something to drink, too. Anything sound good?"

"I don't care."

Pepper's hands went to her hips. "Yes, you do. Coke or Pepsi? I recommend that you stay clear of the Vernors, but the Dr. *Pepper* will cure whatever ails you." She smirked.

"Whatever."

"Well, okay, then I'll just get lost, but mark my words." She wagged her finger at me. "I *will* be back to get you in exactly five minutes if you don't come of your own free will." With that, she walked off.

My gaze returned to Abel and his father who seemed frozen in time. I kept watch over them for only another minute before I had to admit that I was feeling the effects of a lost night of sleep. Still weak from my illness and injury, as well as from the medicine, I decided to go catch up with Pepper and head for the waiting room to await any news.

"Well, this certainly throws a wrench in your little scheme." Deke had stepped up behind me, his voice startling me.

"Oh! I'm sorry." I coughed to clear my throat. "What did you just say?"

Deke glared at me, his forehead furrowed and his green eyes looking more angry than sad. "I suppose a rich, hopeless romantic like Abel makes for perfect prey when a woman is looking to advance herself, and her pocket book."

I was confused. "What is that supposed to mean?"

"You know exactly what it means. I wasn't stupid to your little game of faking all that affection for poor, clumsy Abel."

Stunned, I felt my mouth gaping open. "You mean, you actually think I was pretending to —"

"Of course, you were!" His coffee-tainted breath bellowed across me. Then he pointed at Abel through the glass partition to his room as he lowered his voice. "I've seen that guy heartbroken before, and you were dragging him down that same road. I tried to warn him, but he wouldn't listen — and now, just look at him."

Blinking back tears, I turned to look through the blinds at Abel, tenuously clinging to life. It was there that I momentarily lost all need or desire to even attempt to defend myself against such an outrageous allegation.

Deke sighed heavily. "So, I hear you've initiated a new plan: can't court the son when he's unconscious, so care for the daughter, live at the house, weasel your way into the family by a different route."

I stared at Deke in such total disbelief, even wondering for a moment if this was really Deke that I was talking to. I stared deeply into his tired, blood-shot eyes, wondering if I'd find him there. "Is that really what you – think? I mean, your dad was the one that –"

"Oh, yes. You've got them all snowed over right now." He stepped closer to me as his scowl deepened, his voice growing more threatening. "You know, though, that sooner or later they'll figure out what you're really up to. So, if you had even the very slightest shred of decency, you'd give up this charade and turn down Vincent's crazy offer to have you move into the Landings."

My eyes filling with tears, I just continued to stare as I felt too dumbfounded to speak.

"But I suppose you won't be turning it down, will you." He smirked. "Of course, I understand. I mean, what reason would you have to turn down another opportunity to continue in the good graces of such a forgiving, charitable, and very wealthy family?"

Wiping at my eyes, I finally managed to speak. "I'm only doing this because they want me to, and I want to do whatever's best for them."

"Really! And I suppose you feel qualified to be the judge of what that is. You know, you don't know squat about this family. You're clueless about the tragedies they've already had to suffer through, and you know nothing about the challenges they face every single day. This trauma is going to take such a toll on Vincent. I don't think you can begin to imagine."

"I've lost loved ones." Tears were now streaming down my face. "Trust me. I can imagine."

He paused, seeming a bit taken back by my remark, looking as if he were mulling it over. Then he drew in his breath and began pacing, staring at the floor rather than me. "I've known these people all of my life. Abel and I grew up together and we've shared everything. I was with him when his mother died, and I was with him through the funeral. And after the funeral, when everyone else had gone home, I was still there, taking him to lunch when he didn't want to eat, talking to him, and listening to him, when he just couldn't sleep." Deke stopped pacing, looking up at me with tears now forming in his sad eyes. "I've done the same for him since he found out about his sister, while he waits around for her to die. And I was there for him after the doctors told him that he has Huntington's, too."

My eyes widened. "But that can't be. Your dad said –"

"He doesn't know, and see how little you know. Of course Abel has it. His mother passed it on to both of her kids, and Gretchen might have passed it on to Libby." He shook his head. "But I've watched these people face their tragedies with such dignity – and I will not stand by and let you take that away from them."

"I'm not trying to take anything away from them!" I insisted, shaking my head in utter disbelief. "All I'm trying to do is help."

Deke rolled his eyes. "Oh, I can see that! All that kindness and concern toward Abel, and look where that's gotten him!"

Again I gazed between the blinds at Abel's unresponsive state. Vincent had resumed his attempts to converse with his son, seemingly confident that his voice was being heard.

Deke peered through the blinds, too. "I just can't help but wonder if you feel even the slightest bit sorry."

"What, for being nice?" My indignation was escalating, but I kept my voice down so as not to disturb Vincent. "You know, I happen to care a lot about Abel, and about his family, but if you find that so hard to believe, then maybe you're the one with the problem."

Deke stepped in so closely that our noses almost touched, and there in his emerald eyes I saw all the sadness and exhaustion and resentment he harbored. But as he spoke in almost a whisper, I could only find malice in his voice. "The only problem I've had... is you."

I blinked hard, clearing my eyes as I absorbed his words. "You can't mean that."

He clenched his jaw as he looked away from me. "Oh, yeah, I do. I've been watching you string him along like some love-sick puppy, and trust me, it's not the first time. I've seen other women hurt him, too, so I wasn't about to stand by and let you be the next one."

"So – I suppose that's the only reason why you've been giving me the time of day." I swallowed hard. "So, it's really you who's been putting on the charade."

He snapped back, scowling at me as he took in a deep breath, held it, and exhaled. "I do *not* have to explain myself to you." He then turned away and headed toward the waiting room.

"Don't bother," I called after him. "I'm sure I wouldn't understand if you tried."

"Sh!" A passing nurse stopped to scold me. "You'll just have to leave if you can't keep it down – for their sake." She gestured toward Abel's room.

"I'm so sorry," I replied, but the nurse was already past me, heading into the next room to assist some other person. Nonetheless, she had already helped me, snapping me back from the shock at Deke's bewildering transformation to the reality of this moment.

Gazing back through the blinds, I watched as Vincent stroked Abel's arm, seemingly oblivious to the astonishing argument that had just concluded. As I looked upon father and son, I remembered what was really at stake here – that Abel's life still hung in the balance, and not only because of the fire, but also because of Huntington's.

And then I wondered, who would there be to blame for that?

Part II
AMID DECEPTION

Chapter 23

FINDING HOME

LIKE THE CALLER FOR BINGO NIGHT, Pepper drew numbers from a basket to determine which Saints would be given a room at the hotel. The lucky ones were given a key as their pass to move in, and the rest were sent packing, forced to move on. They would have a difficult struggle, taking up temporary shelter at the school gym until they either found more permanent housing or were forced to return home to the Caribbean.

"Dare are odder choices, you know." Norma Paige held her double chin high, throwing her wide hips to one side as she made an announcement at the conclusion of the lottery. "Dose Saint garls who didn't get a room, you con see me obout renton' ot onoddar place."

A middle-aged Saint scratched the graying stubble on his chin. "Only de womon? Dot doesn't sound fair."

"Well, dot's too bod for you." Norma ran her ring-clad fingers through her bleached hair, smirking with a snide expression. "Maybe you con get some womon to give you her room here ot de London's ond den she con move ovar to de nice place I got. It's a moch beddar deal don dis one, enna-way, so I'm shore she'd make de trade."

"A better deal than this one?" Pepper raised her eyebrows in disbelief. "I don't think that's possible."

Norma cocked her head, smiling. "Trust me – dare is."

"Ond where would dot be?" Rosie DeSantaes pushed her clenched fists into her broad hips.

"Well, it's ot de convention center, where all of de rich mon come to spend dare money. A womon named Onnohede, she told me she'd give us de best deal if –"

I was not one bit surprised. "Let me guess — All you have to do is a little 'favor,' but you don't know yet what it is, because it's all so secret."

Norma inhaled, holding her breath as she stared me down. "You're tinkon' you so smart!" Exhaling, she crossed her arms firmly. "We'll see who's de smart one when all de garls move dare for de beddar deal."

Despite Norma's threat, every person who was offered a room moved in within a couple of days. In order to accommodate as many people as possible, we placed the maximum number of people allowed by fire code in every room. Those whose numbers had been drawn last had to be assigned hideaways or rollaways to sleep on, but not a one of them complained. They all seemed most grateful to have a place to rest their heads, especially at such a nice place at a very nominal price.

Since most everyone lost all of their belongings in the fire, it wasn't difficult for people to move into their rooms. Fortunately, a few volunteers gathered together donations of some clothing and supplies, and a couple of self-appointed leaders from our group of tenants managed to fairly disperse it all in a way that met most everyone's essential needs. To my surprise, these leaders also put together a work schedule assigning all the tenants to a regular job so that all of the daily cleaning and maintenance of the building would be taken care of at no charge.

All of these volunteer efforts helped us out tremendously, freeing up our time to deal with the difficult task of calling all of those people who had booked rooms and informing them that their reservations had been canceled. Fortunately for me, Pepper proved quite adept at handling this undesirable task, putting together her own explanation that, to my astonishment, left the patrons almost grateful for the cancellation.

"Yes, I'm really sorry about this inconvenience," she told a patron on the phone. "But believe it or not, you're really getting the better deal here. Trust me. You really wouldn't want to come here right now, anyway, because the fire caused a bunch of the restaurants and attractions to close down."

I leaned in on the front desk. "No, it didn't."

She covered the phone mouth piece. "Sh!" Then she took her hand back off. "No, they didn't catch on fire, but because the main building for housing all of the employees burned down, a lot of workers had to leave the island, and with no workers, there's no food and no fun for you."

"That's not true. They're living here."

She covered the phone again. "Just shut up!" Her hand dropped. "Oh, yeah. The other hotels are open, and you could try to get a room with them, but hey, I'm telling you, you're the lucky ones. Those people don't get a chance like this to cancel their reservations, and so they're stuck coming here at a really bad time. So, do you want to try them, or do you want me to book you a room with us for something next year when things will be much better?" she paused. "Well, I think that's a really smart decision, if you don't mind my saying so. Now let's see what we have open for you next July…"

With Pepper so skillfully abating any potential problems from disgruntled customers, my time was freed up to tend to my most important obligation – caring for Libby and Gretchen. First, I needed to just get to know them, and for them to get to know me so that, hopefully, they'd be comfortable with having me around.

I was so glad that Vincent left the hospital long enough to be with me the first time I met Gretchen. I wanted him there so he could help me better understand her condition and how best to care for her. I also hoped that Vincent's presence would help make the transition from him to me as her main caregiver a bit easier for Gretchen to accept. Unfortunately, though, that was not to be the case.

"Sorry I've been gone the last couple of days, sweetheart." The elder Vincent leaned down to Gretchen in her wheelchair and placed his veiny hands against her pallid, gaunt cheeks, steadying her head until he managed to give her a kiss. "But I knew you'd understand how important it would be for me to be with Abel right now. So, has Ms. Maeve been spoiling you?"

With her arms twisting about, Gretchen slid down a bit and then slouched forward, the straps on her wheelchair still holding her upright in her seat. "Is – Abe-l – dead?" she mumbled, struggling to be understood.

"Oh, of course not, sweetheart!" Vincent brushed aside her mop of disheveled brunette hair. "I think he's looking a little bit better this morning. Mr. D'Arcy's with him, and I'll be heading back to see him soon. I just wanted to come see how you were doing, and I wanted to introduce you to Abel's friend, Carly."

"Friend?" She threw her head back, her face remaining expressionless but for a few uncontrollable contortions.

I stepped a bit closer, thinking she might be able to see me better. "Hi Gretchen. Nice to meet you."

"If – he – nev-er – met – you," she slowly stammered through clenched teeth, then refused to finish her thought. She didn't have to.

"Now, Gretchen." Vincent gently rubbed her shoulders. "I know you remember Abel telling you about Carly, about how nice she is – and so, until Abel gets better, I've asked Carly to come stay with us and help take care of –"

"No!" Gretchen's motions quickly intensified, her whole body thrashing about as she occasionally launched an obscenity my way.

I watched as Vincent firmly pressed against her arms to her sides while he steadily insisted that she try to calm down. Within a minute or two, she seemed to grow weary and began to slow down, her arms and legs still moving about but not with the same ferocity.

"That's it." Vincent rubbed her arms, then looked up to me. "You've got to realize, Carly, that Gretchen can't always control her body the way you and I can. I'm sure she wants you to know that her actions are nothing personal. They're just a trait of her illness, and something we all just have to deal with. Right Gretchen?"

I continued to watch Gretchen, her fluid motions extended into to her feet and hands. Her fingers twisted and bent, gradually attempting to grasp a plastic plate that had somehow managed to remain in her lap. With a quick jerk, she tossed it like a Frisbee, flinging it with surprising accuracy right at my head.

I ducked and it hit the wall. "Wow! Nice shot!"

I wasn't sure, but I thought she was trying to grin.

"That's unacceptable, Gretchen!" Vincent admonished his daughter as if she were a child. He then knelt down at the side of her wheelchair, gently stroking her head. "You know I understand your frustration, honey, but you can't take it out on Carly. She's here to help us – but if you won't let her, then I guess I'll just have to hire back that live-in nurse we used to have."

Gretchen's head drooped forward like a floppy doll's, but her limbs continued to flinch and contort. "Not – yet – Dad." Her plea, spoken slowly but with a noticeably curt tone, was slurred as she struggled to enunciate each word.

Still at his daughter's side, Vincent briskly rubbed her arm to console her. "Well, I don't think you're that sick, honey. Why, I think you're doing really well right now. But you know we've got to have someone here when I'm gone, and if it's not Carly or the nurse, well then –"

"Not – Doc!"

"No, and not Doc Arlington. He's too busy with all the research he's doing and has to stay out at Beacon Lighthouse. So, he'll keep on stopping by here to tend to your meds and therapy, but I've got to have Carly around the rest of the time – you know, to help you take care of Libby."

Gretchen's bony legs continued to vibrate while her frail, ashen hands reached out, one at a time, as if seeking to pluck some invisible object from thin air. But without grasping what her hands sought, they twisted and retracted, her fingers continually searching the void of space for something that wasn't there. This senseless dance continued with uniform motion, only varying in severity when she was aggravated by some external stimuli, and so I wondered if I was the one prompting her motions to grow worse.

"So, Carly's going to keep on running the place." Vincent seemed to ignore Gretchen's increased agitation. "She and Pepper are going to tend to the rooms, and when I'm over with Abel, Carly will be around to help with our chores. Right, Carly?

"That's right." I smiled.

Gretchen's face contorted. "It's – Abe-l's – job!"

Vincent took hold of Gretchen's hand, patting it gently. "Of course, it is, honey. And she's just going to do all the chores that Abel use to do just to help us get by."

Gretchen's motions quickly accelerated, notably agitated by Vincent's reply.

"It's just temporary, Gretchen!" Recognizing her anxiety, Vincent massaged her neck and shoulders. "It's just until he gets better – until he can come home. You know, we've got to have someone we can trust to do Abel's work while he's recovering, and we can't very well expect him to be whipping up a batch of brownies for us if we want him to get better, now can we?"

Although Gretchen continued her involuntary contortions, her gestures did diminish in intensity with her father's reassurance that he had not given up hope for Abel to recover. Her head again drooped as a moment of calm returned, but her limbs continued in fluid motion, her hands twisting outward and then withdrawing much like a cat does when kneading the arm of a chair. As her movements continued, steady and fluent, she seemed momentarily assured that life would eventually return to some sense of normalcy, whatever that might be for someone whose world seemed tedious, trying, and unequivocally hopeless.

"I'm going to go say 'bye' to Libby now." Vincent kissed his daughter's forehead. "I bet she's out front with that box of dog treats trying to get Asa to sit up and beg."

"He – won't – fetch."

"Well, we'll just have to see if we can teach a new dog old tricks!" He winked at her. "I'll be home soon. Come on, Carly."

I followed Vincent as he led me through the family room to the large deck overlooking a gorgeous view of the Straits and the Mackinac Bridge. Sure enough, there on the beach stood Libby, a sweet little girl with disheveled blonde hair that had turned bleached white in the sun. Her fluorescent flowered one-piece suit twisted about her, one shoulder strap turned inside-out and the other hanging off her shoulder. A dusting of wet sand clung to her shins and forearms as she clenched a box of Milk Bones in one hand and dangled a soggy dog biscuit with the other, all while a darling black and white husky pup sat up on his back legs begging for the treat.

"No, Asa! Don't eat it! Bring it back to me!" Then she raised the treat high in the air and tossed the biscuit toward the shoreline. "Go fetch!"

The playful pup rambled after the morsel, wading his paws into the gentle waves lapping at the beach. He fumbled momentarily as the biscuit washed to and fro with the water's motion, but then managed to grasp the treat in his teeth, walk it to drier land, and burrow down into the warm sand to savor each crunchy bite.

"No, Asa!" Libby scolded as she chased down the confused puppy. "You're supposed to bring it back to me!"

"Try a stick, Libby," Vincent yelled to his granddaughter. "It'll work better."

"Bumpa!" Libby dropped everything, abandoning her pet to charge up the beach toward us.

"Tried to tell her that, Vince." A robust, blue-haired lady perched in a lawn chair just off the deck was shading her fashionably bespectacled eyes as she gazed up at Vincent. "But she's one bull-headed little thing – won't listen to a word I say."

Vince folded his wiry hands. "Sorry about that, Maeve."

I recognized the name. Maeve was Deke's grandmother, the matriarch of the Kavanaugh clan.

She slapped shut the magazine she'd been looking at and slowly lifted herself from her perch, smoothing out her bright floral dress as she stood. "I tried to tell that little girl that the mutt would just keep gobbling those things up – told her that, with all those dogs living around my place, you'd think I'd know a thing or two about dogs. But she thinks she knows it all. Reminds me of her grandpa, I'd say."

"She is a bit strong-willed, Maeve."

"Hard-headed is what you call it!" Now standing, Ms. Maeve revealed herself to be short but spry as she quickly folded up the chair that was more than half her height and placed it firmly under her arm. "It shouldn't take but a couple of tries and a little common sense to figure out that the dog isn't going to bring the biscuit back. But no – she won't listen. I can't tell who's got more rocks for brains – the girl or the dog."

By then, Libby had climbed the deck stairs and lunged into her grandfather's arms, oblivious of the insults.

Vincent scooped up Libby and then turned to respond to Ms. Maeve. "Well, this is Carly, the gal I said was coming by and would be taking over now."

I smiled and waved, yelling to her. "It's nice to meet you, Mrs. Kavanaugh."

She waved back with her free hand, nodding with a half-smile. "It's Maeve. Pleasures mine, and you don't have to yell – I can hear you just fine." She lowered her head, her smile seeming to broaden with amusement.

"Okay." I nodded.

"So, she's all yours now." With her free hand, Ms. Maeve pulled her walking cane from the sand pile next to her but didn't use it as she gradually waddled up the path leading away from the beach. The puppy, having finished his treat, chased after her, jumping up at her side. Despite her commands to "Shoo!" and the few swats she took at him with her cane, the pup refused to give up his pursuit.

Vincent whistled sharply. "Come on, Asa. That's enough."

To my surprise, the pup spun around and scurried back toward us. Then Vincent motioned for Libby to extend a farewell wave.

She dutifully complied, yelling at the woman, "Thank you, Mrs. Kavanaugh."

"And thank you, little miss know-it-all." She never turned back, continuing to waddle onward.

"Old Mrs. Kavanaugh sure is a silly fuddy-duddy." Libby snuggled further into her grandfather's arms.

Vincent quickly loosened his firm hold on the little girl whose cheeks and nose were pink from the sun. He stared into her gentle brown eyes. "Now, who taught you to say such a thing?"

"Why, Uncle Abel did." Libby sounded convinced that her uncle would have never lead her astray. "He said Mrs. Kavanaugh was always strict with him, too, when he'd go to play at Deke's house. Guess they got in a lot of trouble with her, too, just like I do sometimes."

"I can imagine so." Vincent grinned. "But that's because you don't like to listen to advice, just like your uncle, and that can be a problem sometimes."

"I listen, Bumpa. I just don't always do what they say – got to think it through for myself, don't you know, and decide what's right.

"Oh, really?" Vincent tickled Libby's ribs. "Well, I have a hard time arguing that point, especially with such a pretty little girl who knows her own mind." He poked her ribs again.

"Stop it, Bumpa!" she giggled, feigning resistance.

He did stop, grasping her by the chin and pressing her freckled nose up to his. "Well, we just have to figure this out – when's the right time to just do what we're told, even if we disagree, and when's the right time to stick to our guns." He pointed at her, his thumb up, and then lowered his thumb as if shooting her. "Pow!" His eyes popped wide as he poked and tickled her again.

Libby giggled until the tickles subsided. Then she wrapped her arms around Vincent's neck, gazing over his shoulder to take notice of me. She raised her finger and pointed squarely between my eyes. "Who is she?"

"Why, that's Miss Malloy. She's a good friend of Uncle Abel's."

"Call me Carly." I smiled at her.

"Carly." She smiled back, her tongue bulging through at the hole where her front tooth was missing. "I heard Uncle Abel talk about you. Are you his girlfriend?"

I felt my cheeks flush.

Vincent set Libby down and brushed her nose with his finger. "Well, she's a girl, and she's his friend, so I suppose that makes her so." Vincent winked at me. "She's going to stay here to watch over you and Momma when I'm at the hospital."

Libby stayed close to her grandfather's side. "Is she the one that got Uncle Abel hurt?"

I wondered how a seven-year-old could reason her way to such a question, and quickly concluded that she wouldn't. It had to be someone else's question she was repeating, one spoken in her presence by a person she trusted.

Vincent knelt down beside her. "No, Libby. It's not her fault. I'm not so sure it's anyone's fault. Sometimes bad things just happen, and there's no one we can blame."

Libby's smile was melting away, replaced by a much more somber look. "Is Uncle Abel going to be okay?" She stuck out her lower lip.

"He's getting the best of care, honey, and they're doing everything they can to make him better." Vincent bit his own lower lip. "I'm just hoping he can get back here soon so he can help you out with that darn dog."

"Oh, yeah. He is a naughty one." Her smile returned. "I should try to teach him a trick that I can show Uncle Abel when he comes home."

"Now there's a good idea." Vincent stood and patted her head. "You better get to work on it."

"Okay." Libby then turned to me. "Hey, can you teach Asa to fetch, Miss Carly? He just won't listen to me."

"Well, I've never had a dog," I admitted. "But I suppose I could give it a try."

"Great!" Libby eagerly turned and went tearing down the porch steps yelling for her pup to tag along.

"I think you've made a friend." Vincent grinned at me.

"Well, it's a start, but I'll be in some big trouble if I can't find something Asa will bring back."

"I'm sure you will – and I'm sure things will improve with Gretchen, too."

I wished at that moment I could share in his confidence. "I don't know, Vincent. I want to be of help, but it seems like I only upset her."

"Please try to be patient with her. I know how she is, and I'm sure she'll come around if you'll just give it a little time."

In as much as I was willing to give it all the time necessary, I still couldn't figure out why it seemed so important to Vincent that I be the one to take on this job. Surely with all of his affluence and influence he could hire someone less personally involved and more medically qualified to tackle this position. But for whatever reason, he was determined to have me take the post.

"I think Gretchen's concern for Abel has just magnified all the frustration she normally has just with her own condition," He explained. "It's obvious that she needs someone to help her out around here, but even more than that, I think that what she really needs right now – is a friend."

I wondered if this was the reason why Vincent was so eager to hire me over anyone else. For whatever reason, somehow he must have perceived me to be the best candidate for befriending his daughter. Based upon her reaction to me thus far, he seemed to be mistaken, and I remained concerned that I wouldn't be able to bridge an already difficult gap between us. Nonetheless, I felt obliged to at least give it a try.

"Come on, Carly!" Libby beckoned me from my thoughts to come join her on the beach. Asa was at her feet, sniffing and pushing the now empty box of Milk Bones along the sandy shore. The pup had not yet noticed that both of Libby's fists were overflowing with dog treats.

"So, do you think you can consider this home for a little while?" Vincent raised his eyebrows, looking for a commitment.

"Oh, I think so. Besides, I've always been a sap for cute kids covered in sand, especially when they come with a puppy."

"And Gretch?"

"Well… I'm willing to give it a try – if you think she is."

Vincent's expression relaxed and he grinned. "Thank you, Carly. You won't regret . . ."

"Car-ly!" Libby was growing impatient, now under siege at the paws of a very hungry, feisty pup. "Come help me!"

"Guess I better get to work – if you call it that." I grinned as I walked toward the steps to tackle my first official duty.

"Oh, it can be work with that one. She can be a real task-master sometimes."

"There's worse things I could be asked to do," I assured Vincent while unearthing a half-buried piece of driftwood for fetching lessons.

The slap of the waves against the shore made it somewhat difficult to hear Vincent's final comment when he left the porch. I wasn't absolutely sure, but I thought I heard him say, "Yes, there are worse things."

Chapter 24

INSECURE

THE POLICE RELEASED THE BODY COUNT shortly after the fire. Three people had died en route to the hospital, and five women, all of them Saints, were unaccounted for. No bodies were found during the initial examination of the rubble, raising hopes that most, if not all of these women would eventually be found elsewhere.

Then on the last day of July, the *Windemere Post* reported that one of the missing Saint women had recently shown up at her estranged husband's home on St. Maarten Island.

"It says here that she managed to escape the fire with most of her belongings," Pepper told me over the top of the newspaper as we each nursed a cup of coffee at the Landings front desk. "Says she tried to move on to Mackinac Island and get a job there, but she couldn't find work."

"Yeah, at this late date, good luck." I smirked at Pepper before taking a sip from my mug.

"I never met this girl." Pepper scowled as she continued glancing over the article. "It says she roomed alone and didn't really know anyone to tell where she was going, and then her job on Mackinac didn't work out." Glancing up, Pepper raised her eyebrows. "No surprise there, huh. Anyway, says she was running out of money, so she headed back to the only family she still had – her ex-hubby, who then let the authorities who'd come looking for her know that she'd been found."

"So, see – there *are* people looking for the missing women then, aren't there?"

"I suppose." Pepper turned the page. "But you can't say they're looking too hard if the only one they've found practically showed up on their doorstep."

It took weeks from the time of the fire for authorities to sift through portions of the building that were thoroughly incinerated. There they found the remains of three more of the Saints whom they were eventually able to identify by dental records. But by mid August, all of the remaining rubble had been meticulously scrutinized and removed with no trace of the three other women. Now all that remained in the community of Me-Wanna-Go-Home was a huge hole in the ground and a growing fear that more Saints had been kidnapped… or worse.

While business owners who depended on a strong summer season promoted the belief that those missing would eventually show up alive, others were not so optimistic. Amid the gossip of locals and Saints alike, depraved tales of these women's horrible demise resurfaced. Pepper and I found these stories to be particularly prevalent among the tenants of the Landings, leaving many frightened enough to worry about security measures for the building.

"We're gonna hov our own night-watch progrom." Rosie handed me a chart of names and times. "You post dot list of de people donaton' dare time over dare on de wall so de volunteers remembar when it's dare night to keep a watch over de buildon'."

"Well, make sure they check with Pepper." I stuck the list on the bulletin board. "She usually works the night shift, and she tends to have her own way of doing things."

"Don't I know dot!" Rosie rolled her eyes. "Hey, ond you need to be removon' dose extra room keys dare." She pointed at a peg board of keys hanging behind the desk.

"But we use those sometimes, you know, for cleaning and repair work."

"I know – I know." Rosie stepped behind the desk and removed the peg board, the keys jingling on their hooks. "But it's no good hovon' dem where enna-body con get ot dem. Dey need to be locked up for safekeepon'." She handed the board to me.

"Well, I'll talk to Pepper – see what we can do."

Since Pepper had been willing to take on almost all of the responsibilities for managing the building, I deferred to her on the majority of decisions that needed to be made. Although she ran a fairly tight ship, I found her to be surprisingly accommodating to most every request made by the tenants. However, when increased fear about Saints disappearing brought the obeah man to the hotel one afternoon bearing his special brand of protection, Pepper drew the line.

"Oh, no you don't!" She stopped the doctor at the front desk. "You are not bringing any of that putrid concoction in here."

"But de womon called me to come here." He held out his bucket for her to see.

I looked at Pepper. "Don't you think you should at least check it out before you say no?"

Pepper held her nose and squinted, taking a quick glance in the bucket and then quickly turning away. "Okay! No way!" She glared at me. "Next time, you look!"

I laughed.

She turned back to the man and pointed into the bucket. "Looks like you took the time to put some special herbs on that rancid road kill you got there. But here's the bad news, mister – you are *not* going to be painting *any* of that anywhere in this building. Is that understood?"

"But we hov to ward off de evil one who's snotchon' up our womon." The obeah man dipped a primitive-looking brush into the bucket and stirred its contents. "Dis will fight off de evil spirits who hov been takon' our womon away to de empty place."

"That stuff will send women *running* for the empty place!" Pepper grabbed the bucket and tried to yank it away from the witch doctor.

By this point, a crowd of residents had gathered, watching to see who would win the war of wills. In as much as many Saints steadfastly believed in the power of the obeah man, no one was stepping forward to defend him. I was convinced that they would be equally relieved if he were to leave without having dispersed his bucket of decaying animal remains.

Just then, D'Arcy happened to stop by, stepping through the gathering group of Saints. "I just wanted to see how things were at Mr. Hanika's, and what's this?" He looked over at the obeah man who was tugging his bucket from Pepper's clutches. "Why, Good Doctor Raoul, is it!"

Seemingly surprised by D'Arcy's greeting, both Pepper and the doctor stopped pulling. Pepper released her grasp, stepping back as Raoul lowered his bucket to his side.

"So good to see you again." D'Arcy stepped in closer to Raoul, his hands folded and held to his chest. "What would be your business here at Mr. Hanika's home today?"

Raoul looked from D'Arcy to Pepper, pointing at her with his brush. "Dis foolish womon keeps me from doin' de businoss of freeon' dis place of spirits, Mr. D'Arcy." He stuck his brush back into the bucket and stirred. "Please explain to her dot I donate my time to do dis for her own good, ond for de good of dem all."

"Of course." D'Arcy closed his bright eyes and nodded his head at Raoul with reverence. Then he slowly turned to Pepper, his eyes now open wide and his mouth curling into a reassuring smile. "It is for the good of all that we let Raoul shield us with his wisdom and his magic."

Pepper looked stunned. "You're kidding, right?"

"Oh, no." D'Arcy shook his head, still smiling with the bright white of his teeth and wide eyes starkly contrasting against the deep tan of his face. "Surely the good doctor knows how best to defend these Saints from the man or beast who seeks to steal them away in the silence of the night."

Pepper was now wide-eyed, as well. "What the hell are you talking —"

"You dink it's a beast!" Doctor Raoul had stopped stirring.

"Oh, I defer to your judgment, Wise Raoul."

"It is possoble." Raoul rubbed his chin while pondering the likelihood.

"If you believe it so." D'Arcy crossed his strong arms across his chest, patiently awaiting the obeah man's response.

Raoul held his finger up as if testing the wind. "Certonly it's possoble, ond so we'll need someton' strongar." He dropped his brush into the bucket and held his arms up to the people. "I'll be bock wid de protection from all dot trettons us. Keep a vigillont watch for de beast 'til I um able to come bock." He then turned away and walked out the front door.

Pepper threw up her arms. "Oh, just great! Now he'll be back with something even more disgusting, I suppose."

"I doubt that. He'll probably just bring some ashes to dust on the door frames." D'Arcy sounded knowledgeable of the voodoo ways. "He might burn a little incense, too, but it's nothing like that sheep dung he hauls around."

My eyes widened. "Is that what that was?"

He laughed. "Oh, that's the least of it. Trust me, you don't want to know the rest." He then headed for the door.

"I hope you're right." Pepper reclaimed her post behind the front desk. "Because if he comes back here with the same –"

"I know him all too well, Pepper, and he won't. He's very predictable – just got to see things from his way of thinking and send him off in the right direction." D'Arcy grabbed the doorknob. "As long as he thinks it may be some kind of creature stalking these women, he'll use the same brew he's always dusted around my kennels and barn." Pulling open the door, he added, "Helps keep all the monsters away," and with a smile, he left.

And just as D'Arcy predicted, the obeah man returned early that evening with a jar filled with odorless ashes, obviously a major improvement over his previous concoction. But Pepper was unimpressed as he walked right past the front desk, once again refusing to stop and ask for any kind of permission to conduct his business.

Pepper was hot on his tail as he passed by. "Hey! You're not supposed to –"

"Wait!" I grabbed her before she could leave the desk. "Just let it go, Pepper."

Removing my hand, she scowled, thrusting out her lower jaw as her fists went to her hips. "That's some kind of security system we've got going here, when some certifiable nut can just march in here without a question asked and do whatever the hell he wants to."

I raised my hands up in a gesture of surrender. "Hey, it's your desk – your decision. I've got to get back to the girls and don't have time to deal with this, so take over, and I'm sorry for butting in."

"Yeah, well… I know you're just trying to help me calm down, and, well, I appreciate that – I suppose."

"Thanks for understanding." I patted her shoulder. "So, you got it under control here if I go back to check on the girls?"

Pepper took a deep breath. "Yeah, I'm good –"

Just then, the front door opened and in walked Annahede.

" – or maybe I'm not." Pepper added.

"Well, look at this!" Annahede greeted us with a smirk. "I didn't expect to find the two of you right here, tending the desk. I figured you'd have hired others to do all the work for you."

Pepper's eyes narrowed. "No, we don't delegate our dirty work, like other people we know."

"Good for you." Annahede removed a thin red scarf from her neck, smiling at Pepper. "Well then, you won't mind staying at the desk while I have a little chat with Carly here, will you?"

"Oh, not at all!" Pepper crossed her arms firmly across her chest. "Let's see, so the first thing I have to do as a part of my job here at the desk is ask you a bunch of questions, like – What the hell do you want?"

"Sorry, Pepper. You shouldn't take this too personally." Annahede turned to me. "This is just between me and Carly."

"Is it?" Pepper snapped.

"Now don't go having an inferiority complex on me. You can handle it."

Pepper inhaled, preparing to cut loose.

"That's just fine, isn't it, Pepper?" I held up my hand to her, hoping to stay off another battle. "You and I were just talking about all the things we needed to do to improve security, and you were busy with that anyway, weren't you?"

"Oh, yes! I'm deep into it." She surprisingly went along. "I need to get going on all the ideas we have to keep the riffraff out of the place, because you just never know when an unsavory character might come along, do you?"

"And, while you're getting started, I'll talk to Annahede quickly in the storage room." I turned to Annahede. "I'm sure we won't be long."

Annahede ran her scarf through her hand. "Not at all."

At my direction, Annahede followed me across the foyer and over to a small side room. With my master key, I unlocked the door and let her in first, both of us stepping around boxes of office and cleaning supplies to make our way in.

I clicked on the ceiling light and shut the door. "So, what is it you need?"

"Well, I just wanted to talk to you, one boss to another. So, I see you've landed yourself quite the management spot after all, and at such a posh hotel!" She looked around her, bags of Styrofoam cups and napkins stacked to her side. "It's almost like we're in competition with each other." She laughed.

"Nothing's posh about running an apartment building."

"For now, maybe, but I bet you could win your way into staying on here permanently. All's it would take for you is just a little more schmoozing with Hanika. I hear he's quite fond of you."

"I'm not into schmoozing – just glad to help out," I said, wondering where she was going with all this. "So, what was it you wanted?"

"Oh, just a quick favor." Her eyes widened. "I just need to chat with a couple of Saints staying here, but last time I came by, that fat watchdog Rosie said I had to clear it with you first. I told her that I knew you and that we go way back – that I was sure you wouldn't mind – but she wouldn't have any part of it. Sorry I had to trouble you when you've got more important business to tend to."

"Well, that shouldn't be a problem." I reached for the doorknob, considering our business concluded. "I'll just have Pepper sign you into the guestbook, and if you need a room number, she can look it up on the chart so we'll know who you're here to see."

"Just a minute." Annahede held her hand out motioning me to stop before I turned the knob. "Actually I've got quite a few people I need to see."

"Well, okay. Just give Pepper all of the names and she'll help you out."

"But you see, I don't exactly have any names. I'm here to just pass along a little business proposition."

Feeling my temper rising, I took a deep breath and then exhaled. "I'm sure you can imagine how concerned these people are about their security, so you can understand why I can't let just anyone go wandering around the place, knocking on doors."

"But I'm not just anyone! You can vouch for me. You know I'm okay."

I looked down at the doorknob, turning it. "I'm sure you can drum up names. Come back then and I'll let you see them."

Just as I pushed against the door to open it, Annahede grabbed my hand and pulled it shut.

She leaned in closely, a hint of spearmint on her breath. "What I have to offer these people is so simple, and it's so very lucrative, I know they'll want in." She glared at me, her features tight and forehead furrowed. "But we have to act quickly or the opportunity will pass us by."

"You know, this really isn't a good time for me."

"It's not for me, either." She laughed. "Trust me."

"Trust you?" I laughed, too. "I'll have to think about that. Come back tomorrow after lunchtime. I'll be around here then, so check back —"

"It's got to be now!" Annahede grabbed the door and now pushed it wide open, stepping out into the foyer. Then she headed in the direction of the hall leading to hotel rooms. "Just let me check the first three or four doors, and if I don't find a couple of interested people, then I'll leave."

"Annahede, no!"

To my surprise she halted, frozen in place as if contemplating her next move. She then turned and marched straight up to me until our noses were nearly touching, her eyes dark and scowling.

"This is *so* important to *so* many people." She jabbed her forefinger at me to emphasize each *so*. "You cannot begin to imagine the impact this could have."

"Listen, I've got to go. The girls are waiting. Pepper, can you see Annahede out?"

"Can I!" Pepper perked up at the desk.

"Hold it! Hold it!" Annahede spoke with desperation, a tone I'd never heard in her voice before. "Okay, I see you want to play hardball."

"I don't want to play anything! I need to go clean up from dinner and I —"

Annahede held her mouth open, shaking her head with a look of astonishment. "You are so shrewd! I never saw this in you! All right, then. So, do you just want a finder's fee or are you looking for a position?"

"I have no idea what you're talking about."

"Oh, enough with the naive act!" She threw her arms up in the air and then wrapped one tightly around my shoulders, pulling me in close so she could whisper. "All the locals know about the politician's pool, and it does turn an excellent profit, but this deal is so much more phenomenal. They'll set you up in permanent retirement for just a few weeks' work, if you can even call it that."

Certainly this was the end of my naïveté, at least in regards to Annahede. Here she was, blatantly confessing to her involvement in this call-girl operation, and no less trying to solicit me as well as others into the business. Inasmuch as I was offended, admittedly I was just the tiniest bit curious about what kind of service landed someone permanent retirement.

"And what, pray tell, is this new deal?"

"Oh, no, no, no," Annahede wagged her finger in my face. "You know that secrecy has always been a part of the package. You agree to partake, then we unfold the details at our discretion. So, are you game?"

I removed Annahede's arm from my shoulders. "Too risky for me."

"Well, that's fine for you, but why don't you let the Saints decide for themselves. I bet there are women here who would love to jump blindly into this deal so they and their families won't ever have to scrub tubs and toilets ever again."

"You might be surprised how many people would rather clean dirty toilets than turn tricks for dirty politicians."

To my surprise, Annahede laughed. "They don't pay this kind of money for tricks. This is a much more worthy cause than you could ever imagine. But I guess you'll never know." She turned away from me, boldly heading again for the guestrooms. "I promise you a stipend for anyone I'm able to convince today."

Annahede's stride was quick, but Pepper was quicker as she jumped from her seat and dashed over to grab Annahede by the arm. I wasn't quite as fast, but it didn't take me much longer to get a hold of Annahede's other arm.

"You two let go of me!"

"Not 'til you're out of here." Pepper wouldn't release her grip, tugging her toward the door.

"You let me go this instant, or I'll call Vincent!"

I released my grip. "Let her go!" I yelled at Pepper, my only concern being that Annahede would trouble Vincent with this whole episode.

Still holding her firmly, Pepper stopped dragging her but looked her straight in the eyes. "You get out of here, and don't ever come back." Then she released her.

"You idiots!" Annahede brushed herself off, straightening her disheveled blouse. "You really have no clue, do you?" She stared at me, rubbing her arms. "Why, you're so busy pretending to be so self-righteous, helping that poor girl back there by feeding her and dressing her – just grooming her to die –"

Before I knew what I was doing, I slapped her. "Get – out – now."

Annahede put her hand to the side of her face. "You know, they call that assault." Rubbing her cheek, she walked toward the door. "Well, I guess there'll be no talking any sense into anyone around here. Don't trouble yourselves, girls. I can see myself out." She pulled the front door open, stepped out, and with a brisk yank, slammed the door behind her.

Pepper's grin was ear to ear. "Wow! Way to go, Carly!" She took up her seat behind the desk, leaning back in her chair. "So, it looks like I can make a full time job of just keeping all the evil out of the place."

"Yeah, well, thanks for your help."

"Hey, it's a tough job, but someone's got to do it." Pepper rested her elbows on the desk.

"Okay, so now maybe I can finally get back to the girls, clean up the dinner dishes and get them ready for bed." I headed toward the Hanika's living quarters.

Pepper flagged me down. "Hey, if she comes back, can *I* slap her?"

I smiled. "Just call Macke and let him take care of it."

"Have her arrested? Oh, I'd like that!"

"Well, I doubt we'd have grounds for it, but I'm sure our Officer Schwinn would jump at the chance to grill Annahede."

"Yeah, and that would really irritate her – about as much as she's irritated me. That's a great idea. Now I can't wait until she comes back."

"No doubt, she will." I swung open the door to the Hanika's living quarters. "And who knows? Maybe Macke will be lucky enough to figure out what the heck that girl is up to, because quite frankly, I haven't got a clue."

Chapter 25

RUNNING OUT OF TIME

THE RIGORS OF SAINT VITUS' DANCE were taking their toll on Gretchen. She had not yet been totally incapacitated by this disease, but the advancement of her chorea-like motions made it awkward for her to tackle many of the simple tasks of daily living.

Early on in our new relationship, I did everything for her, waiting on her hand and foot. I figured she'd appreciate all of my efforts and that my hard work would help us to become friends. But to my surprise, quite the opposite happened. It seemed that the more I did for her, the more she resented me as she continued to take potshots at me whenever she was in range.

"I'm just trying to help you," I explained as I picked up the broken pieces of a bowl she had shattered on the floor.

"Don't." She rolled her head. "Let – me."

"You want to take care of your own dishes?"

She threw her head back. "Yes."

"Well, okay. You can do that."

"Of – course –" She paused, her face contorting, and then she finished, " – I – can."

And so I learned through trial and error how best to help Gretchen, and how to avoid rocking her boat. Over the first weeks I spent with her, I watched her agitation lessen to the point that she only managed to slug me once or twice a week. I was hopeful that it wasn't just a sign that I was getting better at ducking and that instead, this was evidence that our relationship was improving.

Of course, the most important lesson I learned over time was not what *to* do for Gretchen, but rather what *not* to do for her. Despite the great frustration she experienced in attempting fine and gross motor tasks, Gretchen longed to be a productive participant in life. So, I looked for simple yet meaningful projects for her to work toward, always attempting to avoid demeaning her efforts with some unnecessary task.

After much experimenting, I discovered that Gretchen found satisfaction and reward in the mundane task of sorting. If given a pile of objects that she was physically able to manage, she was content to sift through them, categorizing them as needed.

With this discovery, I wheeled her into Libby's room to give her a shot at organizing all the toys that were so often left in total disarray. I gave her ownership of the project, letting her decide what part of the mess we would work on first. And most importantly, I involved Libby, teaching her the importance of responding immediately and without question to her mother's short commands. Of course, it was an ongoing job, a work in progress, and that was the beauty of it. The task became a wonderful connection between mother and daughter, giving both a newfound appreciation for one another.

"Clean – up – time," Gretchen called to her daughter.

Within seconds, Libby showed up in the doorway to her room. "Again? But we just finished sorting out all of those Lite-Brite pegs."

"And that wasn't so bad, was it?" I crossed my arms as I looked down at her.

Libby lowered her gaze. "I guess not."

"Bar – bie – shoe – Is." Gretchen's hands contorted and jerked, striking the cafeteria-style tray on tabletop in front of her and sending its contents of tiny doll shoes spilling to the floor.

"Oops, Mom." Libby dropped to her knees, picking up the loose shoes.

I dropped to my knees, too. "Let me help."

Libby put a handful of shoes on the tray. "I just really don't want to do this right now. Can't I do it later?"

Spotting a Barbie glass slipper under the back wheel of Gretchen's chair, I picked it up and placed it on the tray. "But you've got a friend coming over, and you're running out of time."

"I promise I'll do it before she gets here." Placing the refilled tray back in front of her mother, Libby looked at her mom. "I just started watching a show. Can we do this when it's over?"

Gretchen's arms continued to twist about, barely missing the tray. "Yes."

"Thanks, Mom." Libby took a hold of her mother's head, holding it steady so she could kiss her cheek. "Love you. Be right back." And she dashed off.

"Anything else?" I asked Gretchen.

Her head dropped, her body swaying and weaving in continual motion. "Socks."

"Socks it is."

I wheeled Gretchen to the kitchen and up to the breakfast table, facing her toward the back window that looked out over Lake Huron. Grabbing the laundry basket, I spread the family's clean, warm laundry across the tabletop. The fresh smell of hot cotton greeted my nose as I removed all the socks I could find and piled them loosely in front of her. Gretchen put her arms up, trying her best to control them as she kneaded the pile with her palms and wrists. Just like with the toys, she struggled to grasp most anything and so she pushed the socks around the smooth surface of the table until one managed to meet with its pair.

I picked up the matches, folding them together. "I have to admit that I don't like matching socks. My ex-husband would always misplace one, and I'd get so frustrated when I couldn't find a match."

"That's – why – he's – ex." She contorted a half-smile.

I laughed. "Yes, one of many good reasons."

"Other – family?"

"Yeah, at one time." I put the folded pairs in the basket. "I had a mom and dad, and a sister. But they're gone now."

"Died?"

"Yes. A car accident."

Gretchen swayed about, knocking a couple socks to the floor. "Sorry."

I picked up the socks and put them back on the table. "It's been hard, but you get through it I suppose."

"My – mom –" She swayed while pushing another pair together. " – gone – too."

"I know. I'm so sorry." I wondered, just for one moment, what it would be like if I knew I was going to die the same way my mother had – and soon.

"Dad – worr – ies."

"Yeah, he's got a lot on his mind right now."

"A – bel's – strong."

"Yes, he is, and you are, too."

"Hm." She twisted her head upward as her body bobbed frontwards and backwards, almost willing herself to nod. "Ven – ti – late – ?"

"Ventilator? How's the ventilator going?" I finished her thought for her. "Your dad says okay. It's doing its job."

"Get – off?"

I placed another pair of socks in the basket, pressing them flat with my hands. "They're still trying to get him off. Your dad said they lowered it yesterday, but I guess Abel wasn't ready yet."

"The – doc – tors?" She was swaying more, seeming to get agitated.

I went to her side, firmly massaging her shoulders as I tried to sooth her restless body. "Oh, they're still working on it. I'm sure they'll figure a way to get him off that machine," I told her, hoping she wouldn't recognize the uncertainty in my voice. "Now let's get this job done before Libby finishes her show."

I tried to keep both girls busy, hopefully distracted from thinking the worst. I wanted to keep their hopes up, but it seemed like every time Vincent came home, there was no good news to give. Anything I would tell them truthfully would be news they wouldn't – and I wouldn't – want to hear.

Vincent had been so kind to keep me informed of what the doctors were telling him, no matter how distressing the latest news might be. In return, I tried to maintain a hopeful front whenever in his presence, but by the end of the summer, my attempts to keep a positive outlook were wearing thin.

"Well, I do think things are going along pretty well here with the girls," I told Vincent when he came home one evening. "I think they're getting use to me, and Gretchen hasn't tried to throw anything at me lately." I smiled.

Vincent smiled back. "Yes, and Libby seems to have taken quite a liking to you." He picked up a small pile of letters I'd set aside for him and thumbed through them. "Whenever I come by, she seems to have some story to tell about what you've been playing with her that day. Thanks for all the special attention you're giving her right now. She really needs it."

"Well, she's a sweet kid. That makes it easy."

"So, summer's coming to an end here, Carly, and I need to know what you've decided." He tossed the letters on the front desk top. "Are you going to be able to hold off your return to Michigan State, maybe stay here a bit longer?"

"Well, I decided that since things seem to be going along pretty well here that I probably shouldn't rock the boat by up and leaving."

Vincent took my hand and shook it. "I am so glad, Carly. This will really help us out, and we're glad to have you here. I just hope it doesn't mess up your plans too much."

"Oh, no. I've waited this long, it's not a problem to wait a little bit longer. Besides, I feel like I've learned a lot here, and I've got to admit, I really like the work. I just wish it hadn't happened because of…" I looked down, scratching at a hangnail. "Well, you know. I wish Abel was getting better."

"I understand, Carly." He put his arm over my shoulders and gave me a reassuring squeeze. "I wish he was, too."

I wiped at my eyes before any tears had a chance to fall. "So, when's the next time they're going to try to wean him from the respirator?"

Vincent bit his lower lip. "I'm not sure, Carly, if they're even going to try to do that anymore."

"What do you mean? Why not?"

Vincent took my hand in his and patted it, then looking back up to meet my eyes. "That just doesn't seem to be working, Carly. They think maybe there's too much damage to his lungs."

"Well, they have to keep trying – don't they?"

He smiled, releasing my hand. "Oh, we haven't given up yet, and you shouldn't either. The doctors are talking about one other approach they want to try soon, and we'll just have to see how that goes."

"Well, that's good." I smiled back and hopped up into the tall chair on wheels behind the desk.

"But Carly, we do have to face the possibility that this might not work. The fact is I'm going to have to be making some tough decisions here pretty soon."

My smile left me. "Like what?"

Vincent walked to the back window and gazed out at the breaking waves of Lake Huron, his arms crossed behind his back. "We're running out of options, and I don't want to continue to see my son suffer." He glanced down. "If he can never breathe again without that machine, then the time may come when we have to let him go."

I pressed my palms against the desk top. "But you said the doctors want to try something, so they must still think it's possible that –"

He turned and looked over at me. "Carly, they're the ones that think it's over. I'm the one making them try this one last shot."

I bit my nail, pausing to grasp what Vincent was saying.

With his arms still behind his back, Vincent slowly walked back to the desk, looking down as he watched one foot step in front of another. "I'm sorry to tell you this, but it's important for you to know what's going on – so nothing comes as too much of a shock to you, and you can help the girls get through this."

Leaning on the desk, I rested my chin on my fingers. "I understand, and I appreciate that."

"So, you also need to know about some arrangements I'm making, just in case." He stepped to the desk, rubbing his finger along its edge. "I've contacted some people I know in the organ donor business and asked them to start the process of lining up some potential recipients." He bit his lip and looked up at me.

"So, you're thinking about donating... some organs." I couldn't bring myself to say Abel's name in that sentence.

"Yes, if Abel dies, that's what will happen." He paused, rubbing his hands together. "And I guess it's just a perk with my business that I can make a couple calls and make sure this is handled in the best way possible."

I sighed. "So, they're looking at people who need some kind of transplant?"

"Specific transplants that match Abel's circumstances. Of course, he can't be a lung donor." Vincent looked down for a moment, pausing with a sigh, and then clearing his throat. "But he could be a donor for a heart, corneas, kidneys... There's a lot of possibilities, so I've got to start narrowing this down if I want to make sure everything's in order when — or, of course, if — the time comes."

"But that time hasn't come, right?"

"No, we're not giving up, and you shouldn't either, Carly. This is just a precaution, because I'm determined to avoid having any regrets that we could have done something better — including trying to save my boy's life."

"Well, I have no doubt you're doing everything you can, Vincent. Thanks for keeping me informed, and tell Abel I'll be over to see him soon."

"I'll do that." He headed for the door but stopped just short. "I hope you understand, Carly. I've spent a lot of my life trying to convince other people to make something good come out of their tragedies." Then he opened the door. "I guess I'm just afraid it might be my turn to finally practice what I preach."

Chapter 26

WORKING GIRLS

THE COLORS OF AUTUMN OFTEN COME EARLY in Northern Michigan, and so it was no surprise to see the maples and poplars already flecked with tones of brass and crimson at the start of September. As expected, Windemere's Fudgie population began to diminish after Labor Day, but with many weddings scheduled for the color season, there was still plenty of work to keep the Saints on the island well into the fall.

Most of the tenants stayed on at the Landings. What few rooms became available, Pepper quickly filled with people who had been staying at the high school shelter and were so grateful to finally have a place with more privacy.

The new tenants gladly took on shifts for the night watch, and the program was finally starting to work out quite well for us. From seven at night to seven in the morning, anywhere from one to three tenants would keep a watch over who was coming and going. Visitors signed in, wore name tags, and whenever possible, they were escorted to the room they were visiting. Of course, most nights were very quiet, and so Pepper and I came to a point where we found tenants we could trust to run the front alone, giving us the occasional moment for some much needed free time.

We were always glad when every now and then we could get away long enough to visit Biminis. Not surprisingly, it felt a bit different to be there as a paying patron, but it quickly became familiar once we inhaled the stench of spilled, stale beer. Callahan kindly allowed us free reign behind the bar, and so the place still had the fit of the worn out, broken in shoe it had always been.

Of course, the place had always come with dirt – the same old stories we'd had to endure back when we had worked there. So, it was no surprise when Pepper and I entered the place to find that, although summer had come to an end, the depraved speculations of the round table had not.

Captain Nick, a blue-blooded member of this fraternal order of mariners, was slouched down in his chair resting a mug on his beer-gut with one fist while waving the day's newspaper in the air with the other. "I don't care what that rag prints." He tossed the *Windemere Post* across the large table toward Gunner. "All them cops are sayin' those girls aren't missing – probably just went back home to the Caribbean or somewheres else, and it's just too hard for 'um to track all of them down." He laughed, his belly shaking. "Yeah, I bet them working girls did go home – home to their sugar daddy, that is!" He gurgled and spit, trying to drink his beer while still laughing.

"What a deal for those broads!" Gunner slammed down his mug and then used the newspaper to sop up the beer that had slopped out in front of him. "Yeah, and we're not talking about your average street walkers, here. I bet these call girls got their own elite operation going on – helping out all those poor little political VIP's, with both their business, and their pleasure." He laughed, seeming quite proud of himself.

Captain Nick wiped his mouth with the back of his fist. "Bet those pretty little Saints got greedy with all that cash changing hands. They probably tried to pocket some and that'll tick off your pimp every time."

"Pimp, my ass!" Gunner smacked the table. "That little Poli-Sci guru Alex Prescott ain't no pimp. He's what you call a smart business man. He's got the connections with the high-ups while making a sweet profit, and I bet he's sampling a bit of the goods on the side – if you know what I mean!"

The mariners roared, elbowing each other with approval while pounding their beer glasses on the table. Belinda, the newest barmaid hired in place of Pepper and myself, warily approached the fraternity to see if their banging was a request for more brew. Her timid demeanor made her live bait for the throng, and they chewed her up with lewd propositions before she had the chance to retreat back to the bar.

"Hey, no more trouble for Belinda, guys," Callahan yelled at them from behind the bar. "Otherwise I'll have to put Pepper back to work."

Pepper raised her glass, toasting the round table, but they were not intimidated.

Captain Nick lifted his nearly empty glass, too, proposing a toast. "So, here's to Prescott – a man who knows how to keep his women in check."

From my more secluded spot perched atop a barstool by the cash register, I watched as the boys cheered on one another, clanking their glasses together in a show of unity and support. Then I noticed that one of them wasn't cheering. Rafae Battiste remained quiet in his seat, notably abstaining from the uproar. His mug remained on the tabletop, his fist clenched to its handle. He appeared to be oblivious to what his comrades were doing, his deep mahogany eyes gazing outward into nothingness.

Gunner also took notice of his pal's disregard. "Hey, Rafae – What's gotten into you?"

Rafae released his mug handle and crossed his arms across his chest. "Let's see. If you include the one in the dumpster along with the seven from the fire, that's eight women dead. Then there's anywhere from four to a dozen or more Saints missing from before the fire, and three more still missing since the fire." He grabbed his chin as if coming to a realization. "Oh yeah, and there's one man who's near death in the hospital even as we speak. So..." He glared at Gunner. "I guess I'm struggling here, but I don't get what you're celebrating."

It took one of their own, and one for whom they all had tremendous respect, to bring this fraternity to such an immediate, stunned silence. Even Gunner's jaw was hanging open for just a moment, but he quickly recovered.

"Hey, you know, I never said Prescott killed any of those ladies!" Gunner leaned back in his seat.

Rafae shook his head. "Oh, of course you didn't!"

Gunner held up his hands, palms open. "And all those missing ones, why, the cops don't even think they're missing. They're just off doing... other things." He laughed.

Rafae's eyes narrowed as he leaned in close to Gunner's face. "But some people *do* think they're missing, Gunner, and they're kind of upset about it. So, I'm thinking that maybe you should be just a little more careful when you're shooting off your mouth."

Captain Nick scowled. "Hey, since when are you such a softy?"

Rafae turned to Captain Nick only to find all of his cohorts staring at him, waiting for some kind of explanation. He paused, then answered. "Well, ever since you simpletons started worshiping a loser like Prescott! That guy's nothing more than a wuss in a designer suit. He couldn't run a whorehouse if his girls were Penthouse pin-ups!"

Nick flipped his captain's cap off his head and scratched his bald spot. "Okay, Mr. Authority-on-the-Subject, so who are you guessing is the mastermind?"

"I'm not guessing. I know. It's Annahede."

"What!" Gunner jumped up from his seat. "That shapely little Arabian spit-fire? You think she's got the smarts to run a racket like that?"

"Oh, yeah." He nodded. "She's smart, clever as a fox." Rafae turned in his seat to look at me. "Wouldn't you agree, Carly?"

I did agree that Annahede was smart, and cunning, and deceitful – and after her visit to the Landings, I was left with little doubt that she had some kind of major call girl business going on. But was she the reason why these women were disappearing? That seemed a lot harder to believe.

Rafae stood up and walked toward me. "Come on, Carly. Can you help me out here?"

"No comment." I sipped on my Diet Coke.

He took up a stool beside me. "You lived with the woman. You know how she's been working the system, making all the connections. She's driven by a want for money and power, and this scam gives her both."

I held up my hands in a gesture of surrender. "Hey, I stay as far away from her business as I possibly can. I have no idea what she's up to."

"Well, I do." Rafae stood back up. "I know girls she's approached, and they're not the type to do business with us scum-of-the-earth locals – not when they can turn tricks for rich guys."

"What's the matter, Rafae? Couldn't get any?" Captain Nick snickered.

Rafae stared at him. "Well, some of us don't have to pay for it, Nick."

Nick frowned as the other seamen hooted.

Rafae approached the group. "I bet you anything those girls are on Annahede's payroll, lined up with some special gig."

"Oh, yeah." Gunner nodded. "She probably hooks them up with the wrong kind of guys – the kind that –"

"Or maybe the right kind," Rafae interjected.

Gunner scowled. "And you don't think *that's* a bent way of looking at things?"

"No, I meant maybe they're kept women." Rafae grabbed his chin, considering the possibilities. "They might be sitting pretty somewhere, set up in some fancy penthouse."

Gunner looked at the crew. "Those horny politicians have all the luck." He high-fived everyone within reach.

That was enough for me. I told Belinda to keep the change as I handed her a five to cover my tab and headed out the door into the night. Just when I was adjusting to the chill of the brisk wind blowing in from Lake Huron, I was surprised to be joined by Rafae who jogged up to catch me.

"Sorry about all that guy talk." He walked at my side. "I know you don't really appreciate our perspective on these things."

I stared ahead, increasing my stride. "Well, I actually did like what you said about those poor people who've been injured and killed, but why couldn't you just stick to that?" I looked over at him. "Why'd you have to add all that stuff about some kind of prostitution ring craziness?"

He smiled at me. "Don't be naïve, Carly. You know that's what's going on."

"And you really think Annahede has something to do with these girls disappearing?"

"There's no doubt in my mind."

I stopped. "But we weren't even living here yet when the first two girls went missing."

He also stopped walking. "She may not have started all of this, but she's sure enough seeing it through. I have no doubt she's neck deep into all of this."

"So, why don't you think the police have done anything about it?" I started walking again.

Rafae stayed close to my side. "Do you really think that Chief Doughnut Hole's going to shake things up with all the high and mighty politicians he's been hobnobbing with?

"Well, it's his job, isn't it?"

"*You* may think so, but that's not the way *he* sees it. Beau Sinclaire has always seen to it that those in high places are happy, and to hell with the rest of us – especially the Saints."

"So, what's he got against Saints, anyway?"

"A couple of things." Rafae held up two fingers, then lowered one. "For one, he blames them for getting him stuck in this dead end job of his."

"Why's that?"

"Well, a few years back, there was a kind of Saint uprising. They were making all kinds of demands for better working conditions, living conditions, and for higher pay. Imagine the nerve!" Rafae laughed.

"Well, obviously nothing came of it."

"Oh, but they were dead serious. They even tried to start a union, right here on Windemere."

I waved my hand at him. "No way."

"Yes, way!" Still walking, Rafae raised his shoulders and pushed his hands deep into his front pockets. "But then tough ole' Beau Sinclaire came along and ran roughshod over the big-wigs. He told them that if they didn't clear out, he'd do a Jimmy Hoffa on them."

"He did not say that!" I hit Rafae's arm.

He held up his arms. "No, he did, really, and everybody around here knows he did. You can take that one to the bank." Rafae smiled. "So, he did such a great job of controlling the union guys and the Saints that the locals decided they wanted Sinclaire to be their Sherriff for good."

Still walking, I looked over at Rafae. "And Sinclaire found that to be some kind of problem?"

"Well, it is if you have higher aspirations, and Sinclaire did." Rafae smiled. "He decided he wanted to run for mayor, but the locals made sure he never won."

"How?"

"Well, they kept him off the ballot for a while, and then when he finally made it on, they just cranked up the rumor mill – told business owners that Sinclaire had a hidden agenda to ban the employment of any non-U.S. citizens on the island."

"And they believed it?"

"Oh, they found that very easy to believe, especially since everyone knew he'd had that affair years ago."

I must have looked stunned. "What affair?"

"Yeah, that one's pretty scary to think about, isn't it?" Rafae snickered. "I know it may be hard to believe, but when Sinclaire was younger and newly married, he had an affair with – get this – Rosie DeSantaes."

I stopped dead in my tracks.

Rafae also stopped, crossing his arms. "And remember, she was also younger, and not quite so – robust."

I stared at him. "You have *got* to be kidding."

"I swear, it's true." Rafae crossed his chest and held up two fingers together in Boy Scout fashion. "His wife divorced him over it. Then Rosie got all pissed off when he became such a hard ass over the whole union thing – as I'm sure you can well imagine."

"Yes, I can."

"So, she finally dumped him, too, and he's been hating all of the Saints ever since."

"Wow." I began to walk again, but now much slower. "And so, this is why you think that the chief isn't doing much about the missing – and the dead."

Rafae followed along, looking at the pavement as he spoke. "I think he has every reason to just leave it alone."

"And you still think the women who are missing just up and left voluntarily?"

"Most of them, for the right price... Yeah, you bet."

I thought about Collette from Biminis. "But I just can't believe that about Collette. She was happy at work and —"

"And you've said you didn't know her that well." Rafae added. "You know, a lot of times we assume people won't do something because we'd never dream of doing it ourselves. But people do a lot of foolish things, especially when there's money involved."

I continued walking slowly, deliberately, thinking this all over with each step. "What about the fire? How's it related to all of this?"

Rafae kicked a pebble in the road. "Maybe it's not."

"What, you think it was just a coincidence? But there's women from the building that went missing the very night of the fire. That can't be just a coincidence."

"True, but remember the fire left them with no home or possessions. Seems like a good enough reason to sign up for Annahede's program, or maybe just to leave and go somewhere else to start life over."

As we strolled along, I thought about Annahede, recalling all the times I'd overheard her making some vague offer to a Saint woman. And I remembered her recent visit to the Landings, her insistence that she be allowed to approach random Saints about some lucrative scheme. With this, I wondered if it could be true that these women, although involved in something unseemly, were actually safe. But then, I remembered Helena.

A gust of cool air blew through, and I rubbed my hands together. "So, what do you think happened to the Moore girl?"

He looked at his deck shoes as he took each slow steady step forward. "Ah, it's a rough, ugly business, this prostitution stuff, and if Helena ended up pregnant, as I've heard she did, then you know..."

"So, you think some politician killed her?"

"Oh, no — at least, not directly." He glanced over at me. "I wouldn't be a bit surprised to find out that she died at the hands of a hitman. These politicians play in the big leagues, and I'm sure they'd pay a lot of money to quietly undo the damage, especially before a spouse or some constituent back home found out about some little – indiscretion."

"Well, I wouldn't call it a *little* indiscretion." I shook my head, remembering what I'd overheard at the hospital.

Rafae glanced at me inquisitively. "And why's that?"

I bit my lip, questioning whether I should reveal what I'd heard. I'd never even told Pepper, probably because I was a bit embarrassed about the eavesdropping, but also out of respect to the Moore girl.

Rafae's eyes widened. "Hey, you know something, don't you?"

"It's nothing," I tried to convince him, but somehow my expression betrayed me and he was great at reading it.

"Come on, tell me," he insisted.

"Well, I overheard people talking at the hospital, and they said something kind of crazy?"

"What?"

"That Helena was pregnant with what looked like it could have been more than a dozen babies."

Rafae suddenly stopped. "What are you talking about?"

I stopped with him. "I heard these two people talking about the Moore girl and they said she was carrying at least fifteen babies."

He stared at me. "Well, that's just crazy."

"I know it seems nuts, but I did hear both of them talking about it. They sounded pretty surprised but they did seem to believe it – and you know, I believe it, too."

"That's got to be just more sick gossip." Rafae shook his head and looked down as he began walking in longer strides. "There's no way anyone could be expecting that many babies at once."

Jogging to catch up, I came up beside him and kept pace. "I know it sounds crazy, Rafae. I thought the same thing when I heard it, but I am absolutely sure that's what they said."

He tilted his head, glaring at me as he quickly walked along. "Well, then, they must have got it wrong."

"No." I shook my head. "Those people I heard — they were reading it right out of the official autopsy report."

Rafae slowed and then stopped, placing his hands on his hips as he stared up at the waning moon that was barely visible through the lightly overcast sky. He looked to be intense in thought, as if this new revelation had thrown off his original theory and he must formulate a new one. He used his thumb and index finger to scratch the corners of his mouth and then rub his chin.

I stepped over closer to him, crossing and rubbing my arms to warm myself. Ahead of us the dim street looked wider than usual, probably because it was so deserted. This late in the season, most shops closed early and the few Fudgies still on the island would head inside by nightfall to avoid the chilly air. As I stood on this desolate street, feeling a sense of vulnerability, I was especially glad to have Rafae at my side.

"It's just a sliver," Rafae muttered.

"What?" I looked at him, finding him pointing up at the only light visible in the night sky.

Following his arm to his hand and onward up to the sky, I gazed with him at the faint hint of the moon. "Oh, yes, it is a sliver." I paused, then added, "I suppose you think I'm crazy, maybe hearing things. I mean, how could any woman naturally conceive that many children, all at once?"

"It's simple." Rafae lowered his arm and turned from the moon, staring at me with his dark eyes. "You can't."

I sighed. "So, you don't believe me."

"No, I do believe you, Carly." He gently took hold of my arm and tucked it under his, turning then to guide me along as he escorted me toward the Landings. "And you're right that she couldn't conceive all those babies naturally, but that's not to say that it couldn't be done. There's lots of test tube babies that prove that fact."

Under the circumstances, I hadn't considered this to be a possibility. "So, you think she might have been somehow surgically impregnated, and with that many eggs?"

"I don't know, but there's one thing I do know."

"And what's that?"

"That I'm going to find out." He smiled and winked at me. "And when I get some answers about this, Carly, I promise you'll be the first to know."

Chapter 27

CLOUDS OF SUSPICION

STOPPING EACH STRANGER WHO ENTERED the Landings made the place feel a bit like some maximum-security facility that required high level clearance to pass by the desk. Pepper tried to lessen this impression, greeting each person who came through the front door with the same polite inquisition about how she could be of help, but some of the Saints posted for guard duty were much less tactful.

Rosie proved to be one of the more intimidating security guards, demanding immediate, satisfactory responses to a flurry of questions she hurled at each newcomer. One cool autumn evening, I witnessed her ferocity as she stalked her next victim, a thirty-something man who came through our front door.

"Boy! It's a bit chilly out there tonight." The man shut the front door behind him, but not before letting a few of the yellow maple leaves that danced in the wind on the doorstep blow in with him. "Oh, sorry about that."

"Not a problem," I reassured him. "It's not like that's the first time the leaves have blown in here."

"So, tell me, whot's de nature of your business here?" Rosie aggressively approached the man, a clip-board held tightly to her side with an air of superiority.

The clean-cut man seemed a bit taken back as he turned to answer her abrupt question. "Well, I was – uh – just interested in a room, I guess."

"You *guess*? Ond ot dis late hour?"

"What are you doing, Rosie?" I held up my hands. "It's only eight o'clock."

The man ran his fingers through his short whitish-blonde hair. "Well, we were just heading back to our hotel room, and I thought I'd stop to see about staying here when —"

"You already hov a room, ond you're lookon' for onodar one? Boy, con't you see de no vaconcy sign blinkon' out dare?" She pointed out toward the front of the hotel.

I reached for her clipboard. "Rosie, give the man a chance to tell us —"

"No-no-no!" Rosie shook her head, holding her forefinger to her mouth in a command for silence.

The man rubbed his hands together. "Yes, well we saw the sign, but we wanted a room for next year. We thought that —"

"Ond who is we? Do you hov odder men wid you out dare?" Rosie headed toward the front window, bobbing her head about to try to catch a glimpse of someone who might be there.

"Rosie!" I tried to intervene, but she was commanding the young man's attention.

"They're my wife and kids." The man motioned outside toward a slight woman with two elementary-aged boys, all smiling and waving back at their dad through the window. "We just finished dinner and were walking back to our hotel."

"Ond so why don't you wont to stay ot dot hotel next year, I'm wonderon'?"

"Because we thought we might like this one."

"Cut it out, Rosie!" I finally managed to get the attention of both of them. "I am so sorry, sir. I'd be happy to help you set something up." I motioned toward the desk. "I apologize for the misunderstanding, but we've had unusual circumstances here —"

"Yes, I can see that." He did not step toward the desk, but instead, headed for the door. "I think I better discuss this a little more with my wife, and maybe we'll stop back at a better time." He looked over at Rosie. " — sometime when it's not so late." Then he walked out the door.

I waited for the man to leave before turning to Rosie. "Thanks a lot!"

"Don't menchon it." She smiled. "Just do-on' de job dot I volunteered to do."

I thought it was bad enough to have Rosie watching the front door, conducting an inquisition whenever an unfamiliar face entered. But the worst of them all turned out to be our newest resident, an audacious Saint by the name of Leila Pence who had just recently moved over to our place from the shelter. Leila proved to be ruthless in her inspections, questioning even those she knew to be residents of the building. As far as she was concerned, no one was without reproach, and that included me.

"Hi Leila," I greeted her as I came in through the front door the next night at a little past midnight. "Everything still quiet around here?"

"Mostly." She sat up straight behind the desk. "So, where hos Miss Malloy been off a-gallivonton' dis evenon'?" She lowered her chin and arched her eyebrows, preparing to interrogate me.

"Biminis, as if that's any of your business." I walked past her, heading toward the Hanika's living quarters with intentions of checking on the girls.

"Awfull' late te be out strutton' oround, 'specially wid de likes of dot Rafae Battiste."

"Rafae is harmless." I stopped at the desk long enough to sort through some late mail deliveries.

"I know all obout dot mon ond dose sailor boys he hos been hangon' oround wid. Dey been mouthon' off ond tellon' some nosty stories obout whot's happenon' to de womon. Be no surprise if dare de ones takon' all de Saint ladies."

I smirked. "I'm sure they'd be flattered to hear that you think so, but I'm afraid they're all talk and no action, Leila."

"Not true, not true." Leila straightened her petite frame and dropped her hands in her lap. "Dose boys, dey been havon' dare way wid some of dem womon, ond not of dare chooson', mind you."

"I don't recall Chief Sinclaire arresting any of them on rape charges, Leila." I didn't bother to look up at her.

"If your dinkon' dot Chief Sinclaire would evar take a Saint garl's word for it, den you got onoddar ding comon'."

"Yeah, well, those sea boys like to tell all sorts of stories, sounding all tough, but none of us take them seriously, anyway." I ripped up a couple of sweepstakes mailers.

"Just you be carful oround dose boys. I'd be stayon' clear of dot gang before people start wonderon' if you're in de cahoots wid dem." Leila crossed her arms tightly. "Or maybe you already know a bit more don you let on."

"Think I'm part of the conspiracy, Leila?" I baited her. "Maybe this whole deal where I've opened the hotel to a bunch of Saints, maybe it's all just a front for those guys to prey on more women!" I raised my eyebrows, staring her down.

Leila paused, seeming to consider my sarcasm. "Well, maybe!" She squinted and nodded, looking as if she was taking my suggestion seriously.

I laughed. "Okay. You let me know when you've got this whole scam pieced together."

As I quickly finished ripping up the day's junk mail, I watched Leila out of the corner of my eye. She continued to study me with suspicion, never saying a word as she got up from behind the desk and walked over to the reception area. She took up a seat on a cushioned ottoman from where she could see both the front door and the seven-inch television, its silent image projecting a late night weatherman's predictions about tomorrow's weather.

Just as I was about to toss out the mail remnants and head for Libby's room, someone familiar to me entered through the front door.

Leila was to her feet. "Ond whot's your business so late ot night?"

"My business is with Hanika, as if it's any of yours!" Max Arlington, Gretchen's doctor, gave no time to Leila. The funny little man clad in an oversized peacoat marched quickly past our unarmed guard and straight up to the desk.

Leila was right on his tail. "Hey, wait a mi-not!"

Doc was not intimidated by Leila as he strode right up to me. "I know it's late, but I've got to see Hanika." He stroked his little waft of stringy brown hair sideways across the bald spot atop his head. "Wake him if you have to."

"Hey, I osked you a question!" Leila followed him up to the desk. "Whot are you do-on' here?"

Doc Arlington leaned with one hand on the desktop as he used the other to press his horn-rimmed glasses back onto the bridge of his nose, now staring at Leila. "Who the hell are you?"

I tried to defuse the situation. "She's a night watch guard, Doc. Just never mind."

"Never mind!" Leila was livid.

"It's okay for him to be here, Leila." I tried to reassure her, hoping she wouldn't launch into another inquisition. "Since you're new here, you just haven't met Doc yet."

Leila pointed at Doc. "Ond you know dis mon?"

Doc had lost his patience with the prying Saint. "Yes she does! Now, just get lost!"

I looked over at Leila. "This is Dr. Arlington. He's the family's doctor – lives out at the lighthouse. He's a good friend of Mr. Hanika's, Leila, so trust me, he's got clearance."

Leila appeared reluctant to accept my explanation and was gathering wind to speak.

Doc cut her off. "You should also know that Mr. Hanika doesn't take kindly to snooping, and he just might be inclined to evict someone who's sticking her nose into his business!"

With a scowl, Leila huffed. "Well, dot's just fine!" She turned from the desk and returned to her post along side the black and white TV.

I now spoke to Doc in a low voice. "Vincent spent all day at the hospital and just got home a couple of hours ago, so I really hate to wake him. You sure it can't wait, Doc?"

"Wouldn't be here if it could." Doc also lowered his voice to a whisper. "It's urgent business, and he's become a very hard guy to get a hold of. I've got to do this now."

I knew Vincent would be rising early tomorrow morning to return again to Abel's side at the hospital, so I remained quite reluctant to wake him. However, Doc was adamant, and since he had proven to be a devoted family friend, I felt certain the issue must be urgent.

"All right, but be very quiet so you don't wake the girls."

I escorted Doc into the family living quarters, then had him
wait there as I went down a side hallway and gently rapped on
Vincent's door.

"Who is it?" His voice sounded groggy, noticeably deep.

"It's Carly. I'm sorry to wake you, but Doc Arlington needs to
see you."

There was a pause. "Tell him I'll be right out."

Through the closed door, I could hear him rising from bed, so
I quietly walked back down the hallway to the living area. There I
found Doc slouched down in a chair with his feet up on the coffee
table.

I sat down in a chair next to him. "Vincent said he'd be right out
in a moment, so can I get you some coffee while you're waiting?"

He scowled at me. "Decaf?"

"Yes."

"Then no."

"Oh... Okay."

Just then, I heard the soft voice of the youngest in the family
call out from the hallway. "Carly? Is that you?"

I looked over at Doc.

He held up his hands and shook his head. "Hey, I didn't wake
her."

"I suppose you didn't, but I need to check on her." I got up from
my seat and left him waiting as I went back to the hallway, walking
quietly to Libby's door in an effort to avoid waking up Gretchen,
too.

I opened the door a crack so I could whisper in. "It's me, Libby.
What do you need?"

"Is Bumpa leaving again?"

"No, he's just getting up to see someone, then he's going right
back to bed."

"Are you sure he's not leaving? Is Abel okay?" Her voice wavered,
her anxiety evident even in the darkness.

"He's not leaving, Libby, and everything's all right." I stepped
into the room dimly lit by a nightlight. I straightened her covers
and tucked them in around her. "There. Now, you need to go back
to sleep."

"Will you lie down with me, just until Bumpa goes back to bed?"

I gently pushed Libby to one side of the bed and took up the space beside her. From my position, I saw Vincent pass by in the hallway. I then turned my chin upward, tilting my head back so I was now staring silently at the ceiling. Libby snuggled up next to me and I rubbed her back, trying to soothe away her apprehension as the men's voices droned just down the hall.

"What is it?" Vincent sounded less than patient with this late night visit from Doc.

Doc snapped right back. "You've been so busy with the hospital I haven't been able to reach you!"

"Well, I'm sure you can appreciate why I'm spending so much time there. I don't think Abel's going to make it, Max, so I've got some tough decisions to make."

Libby shifted in the bed, twisting the sheets around her.

I tried to divert her attention. "Let's hear your prayers."

"I already said them," she whispered.

Doc's voice rose again. "Well, you've got important decisions to make here, too, don't forget." His voice was harsh. "We have to keep this moving forward or you stand to lose a lot more."

I stroked Libby's head. "Well, I didn't hear your prayers, so say them for me."

In a barely audible voice, Libby began to whisper, "Now I lay me down to sleep and pray the Lord my soul to keep. If I should die before I wake, I pray the…" Her whisper faded further into a soft, muddled murmur.

Vincent's voice filled the void. "…and you have no idea what it's like. It's beyond words to see your own son like that, wondering if he'll —"

"I couldn't hear the last part," I whispered to Libby, hoping she hadn't heard her grandfather.

"I finished," she insisted.

I let it go. Humming softly to her, I rubbed her back in circular patterns as I listened to her breathing grow steady.

"I'm sure it's bad," Doc told Vincent, his voice rising again. "So, what've you decided to do?"

"If the time comes..." He paused. "...when the time comes, I'll do what's right."

"Carly?" Libby whispered all of a sudden. "If somebody doesn't wake up – because he just can't wake up, and God knows he can't – then does God take that person's soul right then, or does He have to wait to take it?"

I held Libby tightly, gently patting her on the back. "I'm sure He waits until it's a person's time, Libby. But you don't have to worry about that right now. Let's just get some sleep." I then got up from the bed just long enough to push the door almost closed before climbing back in next to Libby. Although it was only open a crack, the men's voices still carried.

Vincent's tone had turned business-like. "So, what's the problem that just couldn't wait?"

"Well, I thought you should know the frozen stock we'd been waiting for finally arrived."

"Well, that's good."

"No it's not!" Doc insisted. "Some of it's too far gone – I can't use it."

"What!" There was a tone of alarm in Vincent's voice I'd never heard before. "So we can't move forward?"

Libby's breath was steady and her arm around me felt heavy. I hoped she was drifting off finally, and so I kept as still as possible.

"Now I've got your attention, don't I?" Doc snickered. "Well, don't get your tail in a knot, Vince. There's still plenty of stock to work with – that is, for now."

"Then what's the problem worth waking me up for?"

"Well, even though I now have the stock, I still *don't* have enough help to move it along. I've been saying that I need more assistants to make this thing work and –"

"No you haven't," Vincent disagreed. "I thought you had more than enough help."

"No, they can't handle as much at a time as I'd hoped they could," Doc explained. "And we've got to move more quickly. I mean, you of all people should know that even though some stock made it here okay, it's got to be on its last legs. So we've got to make hay while the sun shines – and of course, while your girl's still alive."

I gasped, the words taking the wind right out of me. But then I felt Libby shifting again, so I tried to relax.

"Well, you've already set up your own contacts for more help," Vincent went on. "I don't even know who your people are so I —"

"And I still think that's best." Doc insisted. "But my security guy says no one else wants to volunteer."

"Well, then up the benefits — make it more worthwhile."

"Money's not the problem, Vince. Both my people say the ones they've asked are a bit…" He paused. "They're afraid, and that makes them reluctant to make the commitment — you know, with all that's been going on around here."

"Well, I don't blame them." Vincent paused then asked, "And you're sure your people don't know anything about how that poor woman ended up in the dumpster, or God forbid, how that fire started?"

"I've already told you they swear they had nothing to do with any of that."

My heart pounded loudly in my ears as I wondered who Doc's *people* might be and what they were up to.

"Yes, I know you told me that," Vincent remarked. "But I find myself still wondering… and you *know* that if I find out they had anything to do with starting —"

"You can wonder away, Vince." Doc interrupted. "But in the meantime, I need more help."

I looked at the door where a thin crack of light shone through as my mind accumulated more questions. What had these *people* done, how were they helping — or maybe *hurting* — and what was it that they needed more help to do?

"All right, then, maybe you can send your people down to the Caribbean to recruit," Vincent suggested. "We'll try to get some Saints down there to come back up here for the winter. I bet if we ask around down there, we can find a few more people willing to commit."

"I've told you, Vince, we cannot go beyond the reaches of Windemere because we'll lose our protection, and besides, we're already taking a big risk with word getting out as it is!"

"You really think that would be a problem?"

"Most definitely! If this gets around, especially down there, and we're not there to contain it… well, then word *will* get to the wrong people, and we *will* be shut down. No, we have to stay here, on this island, and recruit only from within."

"Okay, okay. Then I'm all out of ideas, Doc." Vincent sounded tired. The visits to the hospital and the worry that came with it were surely taking their toll. "So, what do you suggest?"

"Actually, I was thinking that maybe we could bring on some locals."

"You know my feelings about that." Vincent sighed, and then it was quiet for a minute or so.

I wondered if there was some connection here to the missing Saints. Were they not really missing at all, and not involved in some escort ring, but rather, had they become involved in whatever Doc and Vincent were up to?

"I guess if you think it's absolutely necessary," Vincent sounded tired. "I suppose we may have to check with the locals, but don't forget our criteria when you're picking who to talk to."

"Oh, of course." Doc agreed. "And I thought I might start here, at the Landings. There's a couple here that fit the mold, and I think they'd be willing to —"

"Absolutely not!" Vincent's voice echoed through the hallway.

"But they're very loyal. I bet we could trust them to —"

"I know we could trust them, but I don't want them to be mixed up in this. If this goes south, I don't want them in trouble for being involved. This stays out of my home."

I couldn't help but wonder whether I was one of the *them* Vincent was referring to.

"Oh, so you're worried for them, but it's okay if *I* get in trouble." Doc snapped.

"You've been in from the beginning, Max. It's your idea — your baby. But they haven't been involved — they don't know anything about this."

"And you're sure of that?"

"Absolutely. And it's going to stay that way. I need them here, so you'd best get help elsewhere — and soon!"

Doc sighed. "All right. I'll do what I can. Just hope it's in time to make a difference for your family."

"It has to be, so you find more volunteers no matter what I have to pay them," Vincent demanded. "And I expect you to do it totally on the up-and-up. You follow the rules we set up so this is done ethically."

"Ethically?" Doc laughed. "Your colleagues already say the whole business is unethical."

"Well, they're wrong, and what they're letting happen on their watch is also wrong. So we're going to get it right – and with decency and dignity. You just keep it that way, Max, because I won't be a party to it if it isn't."

"No matter what?"

Vincent never hesitated. "No matter what – and you best remember that."

I stared at the ceiling, my mind racing to understand their conversation.

"Okay. It's your money, so it's your deal." Doc's voice grew more distant as he headed for the door.

"Yes, I guess I do have the money, but I sure don't have time. We have *got* to press ahead and find a break through *soon*." Vincent sounded desperate. "You have your people spread some more money around with the ones who were on the fence. For the right amount, I think you can ease their suspicions enough to convince them that their time and any inconvenience would be well worth any risks."

"We'll see what we can do." Doc paused just a moment. "Well, Carly must have gone to bed. Just tell her I'll be back to check on Gretch sometime next week, whenever I can manage to get away."

I heard the door close as Doc left the living quarters.

In the darkness, I went over what I'd just heard. It sounded like Doc could use some help from me and others, but Vincent's adamant opposition would be enough to keep me from getting involved, at least for the time being. Whatever they were involved in, it sounded like things weren't going very well.

Libby's hand had gone limp in mine, so I released it and carefully slid off the side of the bed, then pulled the covers up across her shoulders and placed her favorite doll where I'd been.

Gazing at Libby's sweet face in the dim light, I thought about the scheming I'd just overheard. Although the effort behind the scenes sounded more directed at finding a way to save Gretchen, I remained certain that the intent was broader than that. It also was intended to save Libby – to spare her from the terrible agony of losing her mother and, God forbid, from possibly losing her own life someday. And it was supposed to help save Abel… that is, if he ever miraculously recovered from his current, perilous condition.

Gently kissing Libby's head goodnight, I said my own prayer aloud. "Please save her. Please save them all."

Chapter 28

LETTING GO

THE GALES OF NOVEMBER CAME EARLY to the Straits, stripping the trees of their beautiful golden foliage, and us of our hope that Abel would ever recover.

It was mid-afternoon when Vincent walked in the front door of the Landings, surprising me by appearing much earlier than he normally returned from the hospital. "I had a heart-to-heart with the doctors today." He removed his gloves and hat, placing them on top of the front desk before looking up at me, his face weary and drawn. "They've tried and tried, but Abel's just not responding."

I held back tears, maintaining a somber but stoic facade while my heart ached inside. I knew that, inasmuch as it hurt me to hear this, surely Vincent was hurting more. So I wanted to comfort him, to say something that would somehow ease the pain of this decision, but the words just wouldn't come.

"I'm going to head back to the hospital shortly, to finalize all the arrangements..." He paused, gathering himself. He stared at the floor, his eyes red and puffy, but he seemed determined to shed no more tears. "I just needed to come over – to tell the girls."

Still speechless, I gazed at Vincent, realizing for the first time how he appeared to have aged years in a matter of a few all-too-short months.

"I'm thinking I should give Gretchen the chance to say good-bye to her brother in person." His voice was sullen but remained steady as he looked me in the eyes. "Do you think you could handle getting her over to the hospital tonight?"

I'd never taken Gretchen past the grounds of the hotel, but figured I could somehow manage it. "Of course."

"Good. I've already called Maeve and she said she'd be over around seven-thirty to stay with Libby so you two can catch the eight o'clock ferry. Sorry to have you travel so late, but I'd like to give Gretchen the privacy of the last boat before midnight, and I set it up with a ferry captain I know that can help you."

"It's not a problem. The eight o'clock will be fine."

"Okay, then – I'll plan on that." Vincent sighed, averting his eyes by staring once more at the floor. "I guess I didn't think this would happen today, but I was sitting there at Abel's bedside, and the look on his face…" His voice wavered slightly. "I could just tell, it was time."

Again, I was speechless, tears welling up in my eyes.

Vincent stepped from the desk and headed toward the living quarters. "Well, I need to break it to Gretchen first before Libby gets home from school. I'd like to have you come with me, if you would, in case I need your help with her."

Surprised by his request, I nonetheless obliged, leaving the desk unmanned for the moment and heading to the back with him. There we found Gretchen right where I'd last left her, pushed up to the table so she could fiddle with the laundry as she waited for Libby to walk home from school.

"Hey, there's my girl." Vincent began with a cheerful disposition, kissing his daughter on the cheek.

Gretchen's head jerked as she twisted sideways in her wheelchair, trying to see her father. "Why – are – you –"

"Here?" he finished for her. "Well, I came back to set up a chance for you to come over to the hospital, honey – thought you might like to come see your brother."

"He – bed – er?" Gretchen struggled to ask since she was showing signs of increased difficulty in enunciation.

"Well, no. I'm afraid not. You see, honey, he's –"

"Why – go?" Gretchen's expression was unclear, as usual, but her sudden increase in volume told me she was agitated, and suspicious.

Vincent took a deep breath and exhaled. "Well, I wanted you to see your brother because… well, since he's not getting better and he seems to be suffering, the doctors and I decided –"

"No!" was the only warning Gretchen uttered before thrashing her arms across the table, sending all the laundry and the basket to the floor. "Don' – pull – plug!"

Vincent quickly threw his arms around her, trying to hug her into submission. I stepped to her side and tried massaging her shoulder and neck in an attempt to calm her down. Neither of our efforts seemed to do much good.

"Libby's due home anytime, and it will really upset her if she sees you like this." I tried to appeal to her responsibility as a mother.

This point seemed to slightly ease her agitation, but she remained terribly upset. "Why – 'im?" Her body still seized and contorted as her eyes streamed tears.

Still hugging his daughter, Vincent's eyes also filled with tears. "I just don't know, honey. Sometimes bad things happen to good people, and there's just no reason – no one to blame."

We could find no words to comfort her. The heartbroken woman nearly convulsed out of her wheelchair as she intensely wept and moaned. Try as we did, neither of us could find a way to console her – that was, until the presence of a seven-year-old girl brought her back to moderate control.

"Are you okay, Momma?" Libby grabbed a hold of her mother's flailing arm, a deep sense of concern evident in her high-pitched voice. "Why are you crying like that?"

"I – ver – ee – sad." She shook.

"What happened?"

Gretchen choked up, her body shuddering.

Vincent let go of Gretchen so he could turn to embrace his granddaughter. "You're mom might have trouble explaining it all, so I'll give it a try." Kneeling down, he took Libby by the shoulders, holding her back just far enough so he could look her in the eyes. "Your mom's upset about your Uncle Abel. He's still having a lot of trouble breathing."

Libby stared back at Vincent. "Aren't the doctors going to fix him?"

"Oh, they've been trying very hard, Libby. But his lungs are very, very, very hurt. So hurt that they just won't heal."

Libby paused, thinking it over. "Is it time for him to die?"

"Yes, honey. Uncle Abel's going to die."

Libby frowned as her eyes formed large tears that plopped on her cheeks. She tried to maintain a stiff upper lip as she hugged her grandfather and then climbed into her mother's lap to give her a hug, as well. But the large tears were dropping steadily to her cheeks as she came towards me.

She threw her arms around my neck, then loosened her grip to look me in the eyes. "Are they going to use Abel's body to help other sick people?"

I gazed back at her, quite surprised that she was even knowledgeable of such an option. "Well, I'm not sure, Libby."

"Yes, they are," Vincent answered. "I've made all of the arrangements for some organ donations, so your Uncle Abel's going to be a hero. He's going to save some other people's lives."

"That's good." Libby half smiled as she wiped her nose on her shirtsleeve. "Uncle Abel liked to help everybody. That would make him happy."

"Yes, it would," I agreed, recalling that this was his true character. I could still recall the broad, childlike smile stretched across his face each time he brought me a gift. And he had given me so much, not just in tangible items but also in his sweet demeanor, his kind heartedness, his selfless giving... the kind that brought him to run into a burning building just to save me. Then the guilt rushed through me again and I turned my eyes downward, unable to look upon this grieving family. I couldn't help but feel at least partly to blame for their pain.

Vincent stayed a bit longer, making sure we all were accepting the inevitable no matter how difficult it was to face. He finally left shortly before dinner time, leaving us to a somber meal of lasagna.

I poked at Gretchen's plate and took up a forkful for her to eat. Normally she would be willing to accept my help in feeding her, but on this night she refused my offers, only willing to gum the side of a small slice of garlic toast. Libby also seemed to have lost her appetite, poking at her food until the pasta separated from a layer of meat and cheese.

"I want to go with you to the hospital so I can see Uncle Abel, too." Libby set down her fork.

Gretchen tossed her head. "You – don' – wan – to."

"Yes I do, Momma."

"Re – mem – ber – 'im…" Gretchen struggled with her articulation. "…how – he – wa – zz."

I stood up and picked up my plate, starting to clear the table. "Your mother's right. I bet you have happy memories of your uncle."

"But shouldn't I go say good-bye?" Libby picked up her plate, chipping in to help me.

I picked up Gretchen's plate. "Uncle Abel is so sick, it's almost like he's in a deep, deep sleep. I'm not sure he'd even be able to hear you, but I bet he already knows what's in your heart."

"You think so?" Libby asked, carrying her plate to the kitchen counter.

"I know so. Just like I know how you feel about him in your heart. So, that's where you need to say good-bye to him, Libby – in your heart, because that's where it matters most."

Thankfully, she seemed satisfied with this idea, and so she surrendered her need to go to the hospital with us, opting instead to play in her bedroom once she had helped me stack all of the dishes in the dishwasher. There she remained, still quietly dressing up her dolls when Ms. Maeve arrived to watch over her.

"Thanks for occupying the little busy-body," Ms. Maeve said to me as she adjusted her black cashmere cardigan. After patting a couple of her tightly permed curls into place, she took up her post in the rocker by the fireplace.

"Not a problem." I slipped on my heavy coat, preparing for a cold ferry ride.

"And that puppy's tied up, I take it."

"Oh, yes. He's out back in his doghouse."

"Then all's in order." Ms. Maeve pulled her crocheting from her oversized purse. "Now just to do something to keep my hands busy, and my mind off that poor boy."

"Gretchen's all bundled up at the front door, so I better get going before she cooks." I pulled my mittens out of my pockets. "I turned a bed down for you in the guest room, in case we run late."

"Oh, you'll be plenty late, my dear." Ms. Maeve pushed and pulled with her hook and thread. "My clans over there, too, thinking they'll be of some sort of comfort to Vince, so they'll be wanting to say their good-byes, too."

I slid my hand into a mitten. "Mr. Kavanaugh's at the hospital?"

"And Mrs., God help you," she muttered. "And Deke's over there, too."

Deke. That was certainly not an encounter I had counted on, but it came as no surprise. We'd seen each other in passing from time to time since our falling out, and our simple, short greetings had at least grown cordial over the past few months. But to meet up with him again at the hospital, and under these circumstances... I hadn't thought it possible for the situation to be worse, but now it was.

Ms. Maeve continued stitching. "I told them not to be butting in, that it was a family matter, but my daughter-in-law's got her own ideas – thinks she's so important that she's got to be there. She'll probably just end up causing a scene, carrying on like it's her own son." She stopped stitching, her forehead furrowed and lips tightened as she shook her finger at me. "But don't you let her bother you, or Vince or Gretchen, for that matter." She returned to her stitching. "The whole bunch of them needs to learn to keep to their own business and stay out of others'."

Heeding her warning, we headed out into the brisk winds of an overcast night. I wheeled Gretchen down to the docks where we met up with the three-decked ferry named "The Victor." A couple of deckhands helped me get Gretchen across the ramp and onto the back of the ship where we were then greeted by, to my surprise, Rafae.

"Good evening, ladies." Crossing one arm across his chest and bowing slightly, he grinned. "I'll be your captain for this evening's ride across the Straits." He stepped beside me, taking the handles of Gretchen's wheelchair from me. "Now let's get you below deck, Gretch, before you freeze out here."

I followed behind Rafae as he pushed Gretchen from the stern platform into the enclosed main deck of the boat. He parked and locked Gretchen's wheelchair in the back row of seats, then offered me a place on the bench beside her.

"You should be fine here," Rafae patted Gretchen's shoulder. "It's kind of rough out there tonight, but once we get her up and running, I'll try to give you a smooth ride." And with that, he dashed out onto the stern platform and climbed the steep steps to the next deck.

Within moments, the engine revved as the deckhands scrambled to untie the boat. They pushed off, leaving Rafae to maneuver a one-eighty turn and then take off from the calm waters of the protected harbor out into the rough swells of Lake Huron.

I tucked Gretchen's blanket a bit more snuggly about her. "Are you warm enough?"

She squirmed and rocked uncontrollably in her seat. "Yes," she answered, her movements once again loosening the blanket I had wrapped around her.

I looked about the lower cabin and noticed we were almost all alone, joined only by a young couple toting their sleeping toddler in a stroller. At one point, I noticed the man gawking at Gretchen, naturally curious about her never-ending contortions. But with a sharp nudge from his wife, the man turned around and the couple ignored us for the remainder of the trip. We then were left alone to quietly contemplate our own private pain over the events of the evening that lay before us.

Gretchen and I remained mute as the ship's bow cut through the swells en route to the mainland. Despite our silence, it was far from a quiet ride as the roaring engines propelled us through the crashing of waves breaking on the bow, and the stiff winds rushed past the vibrating pains of transparent Plexiglas. Then, as we approached the shore, the engines groaned in reverse and the entire boat swayed with the churning waters as Rafae carefully maneuvered the ship up against the dock. Once docked, the boat continued to rock as the crafts mighty wakes reverberated back off the shore.

The three other passengers quickly disembarked for land, leaving me to fumble with the wheelchair brake and to try to move Gretchen along the rocking floor. Fortunately, a deckhand quickly stepped in to help me wheel Gretchen back to the stern platform.

"Thank you." I tried to offer him a tip.

"Oh, no need." He waved me off. "We're supposed to be helping you tonight — would have gotten down here sooner but we were tying off the ship."

I pushed Gretchen closer to the ramp. "So, could you help me get her on to the deck? Our ride is supposed to be here to pick us up."

"Your rides up top." The deckhand pointed toward the upper deck.

Just then, Rafae came to the back railing, looking down at us. "You should have waited so I could've helped you off. Just hold on a minute and I'll get things shut down, then be right there."

We waited there for a moment, the bitter wind making our wait seem much longer than it was. But Rafae did get the boat closed up fairly quickly and then came down to wheel Gretchen across the ramp, down the dock, and then over to the parking lot as I walked along at their side.

I held my scarf up to my face, talking through it. "Do you think you can lift Gretchen into your car?"

"Not a problem," he answered as he wheeled Gretchen around the lot and over to a rusted out, baby blue, Ford Tempo. "It's nothing snazzy, but it gets you where you're going."

I wasn't sure what Rafae's plans were from here. "Are you going to just drop us off or are you staying with us at the hospital?"

"I'm all in," he replied as he set the brake on Gretchen's chair. "All right, young lady. Your chariot awaits."

"Are you sure you can get her in there?"

"Of course I can." Rafae pushed Gretchen's thrashing arms up against her, then scooped his free arm under her and carefully lifted her from her seat. With surprising ease, Rafae placed Gretchen into the car, strapped on her safety belt, then again carefully pressed her outreaching hands toward her to make sure they were out of the way before closing the door.

I headed around to the passenger side door. "Wow, you're good."

Rafae opened the driver's door and hopped in. "I've had a little experience." As he strapped on his own safety belt, he turned to grin at Gretchen. "Gretch and I go way back, don't we?"

I also looked back at her, noticing the hint of a happy expression amidst her contortions.

"You know Rafae?" I asked her.

"We – dance." She threw her head back.

Rafae turned the key and dropped the stick into reverse, backing out of his parking spot. "Prettiest girl on Windemere, and she wouldn't go to the Lilac Festival dance with me." He dropped the gearshift into drive and started weaving his way out of the lot.

"Too – young."

Rafae flicked on his blinker then made a left and headed south. "Okay, so I was a little bit younger than you."

"Still – high – sc – hool."

"Details, details." Rafae snickered. "Well, at least you were still willing to dance with me while your girlfriend danced with Abel."

The mention of Abel brought a long silence to the car.

Rafae finally broke the silence as he glanced back at Gretchen in his rearview mirror. "I just saw your brother yesterday, Gretch. He was still doing about the same as the last time I saw him."

A bit surprised, I looked over at Rafae. "You've visited Abel?"

He glanced back. "Maybe three or four times. We go back, too. Right, Gretch?"

I heard Gretchen sniffle and turned around to find her nose dripping, eyes watering, unable to wipe her face with hands that seemed to have minds of their own. I rummaged through the glove compartment, pulling out an old McDonald's napkin and reaching back to wipe Gretchen's face.

Rafae kept his eyes on the road. "I'm sorry. I didn't mean to upset things."

I grabbed Gretchen's hand and squeezed it, "It's okay," I reassured them both. "It's a tough night, but we'll get through it together."

Gretchen dropped her head and then rolled it back up, softly moaning as she swayed to and fro. My eyes filling with tears, I flashed a quick smile to her and then turned back around before she could notice. Looking over at Rafae, I saw him glance in his rear-view mirror before turning his eyes back to the road, his hand rubbing the bridge of his nose to wipe away his own tears.

Rafae sniffled. "You know, I hate to lose him, but you don't want him to suffer, either. And when you see him there, stuck on those machines, you'll see that it's the right thing to do."

I'd been trying to maintain, but I finally lost it, almost coughing out my tears. "I just don't know where –" I caught my breath. "– you get the strength to let go." I continued to sob.

"You get it from him." Rafae reached over, gently rubbing my back. "When you look at him, you'll see that he's just trapped between life and death. It's kind of like he's stuck in this sort of medical purgatory, and I'm sure he doesn't want that."

I caught my breath. "But how can you know?"

Rafae glanced at me, then back to the road. "Trust me. You'll see it in his face. Vince sees it – he's seen it everyday. And now we've just got to have the strength to go along with that – say enough is enough."

"Let – mmm – go." Gretchen sniffled from behind us.

I turned around to find her still swaying, staring up at the ceiling with tears again streaming down her face.

I took out another napkin and reached back to wipe her face again. "I'm sorry, Gretchen, but I didn't quite hear what you were saying. Did you say, 'Let him go'?"

Her swaying slowed but the chorea-like impulses continued. As her hands and fingers twisted, her arms stretched outward from her sides and I watched her uncontrollable yet fluid motion as a silhouette in the headlights of a car coming up behind us. With arms twisting, I could make out the whites of her eyes as she seemed to focus on me in a way she had never done. With total determination, she clearly proclaimed her wishes:

"When – it's – time –" She paused. "Let – me – go."

Chapter 29

GRIEVING RIGHT

A SELECT GROUP OF MOURNERS HUDDLED in the waiting room as Rafae escorted Gretchen and me in to join them. I recognized some of them, such as the minister of Windemere's Lutheran church, Pastor Fritz Goebel, who greeted us solemnly at the door.

"Glad you were able to make it, Gretchen." Pastor Goebel squeezed her shoulder. "You seem to be doing well."

Gretchen slid in her seat, her hands kneading the air as one arm jerked backward, striking the pastor in the hip. "Saw – ry," she struggled to utter.

"Quite all right, my dear." Pastor Goebel released his grip, massaging his side as he stepped back from her. And this is Father Frank, the hospital chaplain." He motioned toward an unfamiliar, gangly fellow wearing the collar of the clergy who flanked his side.

"Pleased to meet you." Father Frank extended his hand to each of us.

We made our way further into the room, passing by the couple of blue-haired women I knew to be the Zender sisters, the proprietors of Windemere's bookstore. The two of them would sometimes drop by the Landings, always bearing a plate full of freshly baked cookies for Vincent, their favorite widower.

"Good evening, Carly." The elder Zender spoke almost in a whisper. "So sorry to see you under these circumstances."

"Yes, so am I." I shook her hand, and then her sister's.

Then of course, I recognized the Kavanaughs, father and son, their heads tight together as they quietly shared conversation.

"Carly." Deke nodded at me, acknowledging my presence.

"Deke." I nodded, returning the courtesy.

To the other side of Deke sat an unfamiliar, middle-aged lady. Tall and slender, the woman was splendidly dressed in all black from head to toe. She held her black-gloved hand up to her face, covering her mouth as she whispered to Deke. Then she held up her other gloved hand in which she held a hanky, all but pointing at me and Gretchen with it as she obviously spoke of us.

"Yes, she's the one," Deke quietly answered his mother, whatever her question was.

The woman lowered her hand from her mouth and then abruptly turned her head away, pointedly ignoring us as she dabbed at her tearful eyes. "Such a benevolent boy, that Abel. So like him to be mindless of his own well-being when trying to save the Saints and others among the lowliest of the island."

Deke wrapped his arm around the woman's shoulders, trying to console her. She responded with a pat of Deke's hand that was pressed against her shoulder.

D'Arcy leaned forward, resting his elbows on his knees as he rubbed at his tired eyes. "I'm not sure the Saints would appreciate your referring to them as 'the lowliest.'"

"You know perfectly well I meant nothing derogatory!" the woman snapped back, the crow's feet broadening as her gray eyes narrowed and she pursed her lips. "It's simply common knowledge that they're needy, and as citizens of Windemere, we try to do all we can to help them out."

"I'm sure Dad knows what you mean, Mom." Deke patted his mother's shoulder before removing his arm from about her.

"Of course, he does." Mrs. Kavanaugh straightened her back, folding her hands and dropping them in her lap. "It's very obvious that Vincent has done much for those people over the years, fighting for better housing and even leasing his hotel to them at a meager pittance. But then to lose his son on account of them, why, it's an absolute tragedy!" She sniffled, blotting at her nose.

D'Arcy stood up, arching his back and rolling his broad shoulders as he spoke softly but firmly to his wife. "Constance, please stop it with the blaming. It's not going to do anyone any good, especially Vincent, so just let it go, at least for tonight."

A nurse entered the room, seeming a bit uncertain about interrupting what was obviously becoming a bit of an argument. "I'm sorry, but I'm looking for Gretchen. Is she here yet."

"She's right here." I rubbed Gretchen's arm.

The nurse looked at me. "Okay, good. Could you please bring her this way? Mr. Hanika wants her to join him in Abel's room."

"Sure."As I pushed at Gretchen's chair to turn it around, I noticed that the gathering of people had all turned their focus to us. Rafae reached in to help me negotiate the cramped space, pulling the chair slowly back and forth to maneuver around all the people.

I relinquished control to Rafae, turning my attention for only a moment to glimpse at Deke, finding his sullen green eyes fixed upon me. He remained a mystery, so very devoted and yet so very spiteful. His pained expression was hard to read, looking both sad and angry, and I wondered if I could have ever distinguished his loving loyalty from his loathing distrust.

"I can take her down, Rafae." Deke reached out to Gretchen's chair, trying to take control.

"No need," Rafae firmly grasped Deke's arm before he could reach the handle grip. "Carly got her this far, so I'm sure she can push her down the hall."

"Yeah, but you don't need to go down there, too." Deke stood tall, staring Rafae in the eyes. "It's really a private matter, and they don't need everyone to go busting in there for a gawk."

"A gawk!" Rafae inhaled, crossing his arms tightly across his chest. "You know, we *all* feel real badly about this. You don't hold the patent on emotions here tonight, so don't you think the rest of us have a right to grieve?

"Of course. I didn't say you couldn't —"

"Then you need to back off." Rafae jabbed his finger at Deke.

"That's enough guys." I took hold of Gretchen's chair myself, pushing her toward the door.

"Wait, Carly," Deke insisted. "I still think it'd be better if I took Gretchen down."

Rafae glared at Deke. "*I'm* not going to go down there, Deke, because you're right — it *is* a private matter — and that's why you're going to stay out of it, too."

Pastor Fritz held out his hands. "Now I'm sure we can all reasonably —"

"Let Deke take Gretchen to her brother." Mrs. Kavanaugh rose to her feet. "He's like family to them, and it'll make it easier for them."

Rafae threw his arms up in the air, now glaring at Mrs. Kavanaugh. "And you don't think Carly's like family? After living with them all this time?"

"Yes, but she's just a stark reminder — you know, of what caused all this —"

"Stop it, Constance!" D'Arcy scowled at his wife, then shook his head as he ran his fingers through his disheveled salt and pepper hair. "I thought I told you to cut it out with the blaming, but you just have to keep at it. Now, for God's sake, you need to just stay out of this."

Deke turned to the nurse. "But Vincent didn't ask for Carly, did he?"

"I don't remember." The nurse stared at the ceiling, biting her lip.

D'Arcy scratched his head and turned his gaze to the floor. "Oh, son." He sighed. "You need to stay out of this, too."

"I — wan — Car — ly." Gretchen squirmed in her seat, struggling to speak. "Car — ly, — take — me."

"You heard the girl!" Rafae squeezed Gretchen's arm and then smiled at me. "She's all yours."

The group stood silent and sullen as I walked the gauntlet, pushing Gretchen passed them all, following the nurse out into the hallway and down toward Abel's room. As we approached, I saw the back of Vincent who was standing in the doorway, facing his son as he waited for us.

Vincent heard us approaching. "Ah, there's my girl." He lowered his head toward Gretchen, his eyes conspicuously bloodshot. "I hope the ride here went all right."

"Rafae was a big help." I pushed Gretchen up to her father.

"Ye — s." Her head twisted sideways and her arms reached forward, circling the air before her.

"Well, let's see your brother." Vincent acted remarkably calm as he took the handles of the chair and pushed Gretchen into the room.

"I'll just wait out here," I told them, but they didn't turn to answer.

Vincent continued into the room and I heard him speak to Abel as if he was awake and alert, his voice as normal as it could be. "Hey, your sister's here to see you, son. Let's push her over here and we'll sit and talk to you for a few minutes…"

Not wanting to return to the aggravated mob, I leaned against the white wall outside of Abel's room. From there, I was able to hear some of the soft-spoken conversation Vincent was inferring between the siblings.

"Gretchen's going to miss you, and I will too." Vincent's voice rose and shook as he struggled to finish. "But we understand why you wouldn't want to go on like this."

I heard Gretchen let out a moan as her father sniffled, and then, as if in unison, they both wept fiercely. Alone in the hallway, I started crying, too, but I didn't want them to hear me. So I went further down the hallway, past the nurses' station and through a set of double doors where I found the chapel. There I took a seat in a pew where I wept and prayed and wept some more.

In my solitude, it felt like time was passing slowly. Then I'd think of Abel, of his impending death, and then it suddenly seemed that time was too short and flying by fast. I leaned back in the pew, staring at the shadows on the stark white ceiling, then closed my eyes to rest them before weeping again.

Someone tapped me.

"Oh, my God!" I shot upright. "Vincent. I didn't hear you come in."

"It's okay." He jumped back from the side of my pew, then offering a brief, brave smile. "Gretchen's done, so I took her back out to the lobby to be with the others."

"All right." I stood up "Then I guess I better get her back home now."

"Before you go, I thought you might want to see Abel —" he paused, lowering his head. " – one last time."

I felt my lips tighten in a frown and my chin jitter as I fought not to cry. Then I wrapped my arms around Vincent, hugging him tightly as I whispered in his ear, "Thank you."

He hugged me back, then released me. "You go on ahead. I'm going to stay here for a few minutes – got a few things I want to say."

I switched places with Vincent, leaving him in the pew as I walked out of the chapel and back toward Abel's room. The hall was very quiet, filled only with the sounds of machines pumping and beeping as nurses' rubber-soled shoes scuffed the floor. I slowly approached Abel's room, very anxious about how I would react when seeing him this time.

I had visited Abel quite a few times since the accident, but this was definitely altogether different. With other visits, I had always entered with the determination to sound encouraging. I'd make it a point to sit at his side and talk to him, saying how much we missed him and how we couldn't wait until he was better.

This time though, I entered totally defeated, determined only to manage to say good-bye without losing it. And so I went into his room and took up a seat at his side, holding back the tears.

I gazed upon Abel's emaciated body as if realizing for the first time that he was nothing but a shell of his original self. And I looked at the unceasing machinery around him that held him like a prisoner, continuing to sustain life but unable to sustain living. They had him trapped in a kind of medical limbo or purgatory, a place between life and death where they had chosen to keep him – and from which we must now choose to set him free.

Inasmuch as it pained me to lose someone who had once been so full of life, I realized by looking upon him that he was in essence already gone. As this father had rightfully decided, it was time to let him go.

Vincent returned, stepping in the doorway. "I was thinking it might help you to know about the people Abel's going to help through his organ donation." He stepped closer, looking down at his son. "There's a grandfather with nine grandchildren in Beaver

Dam, Wisconsin, who will receive Abel's liver. His corneas will go to a woman in Minneapolis longing to see her only grandchild for the first time. And his kidneys will save two people: one, a mother of three small children in Syracuse, and the other, a young Canadian woman who's traveling a long distance tonight for her operation."

I managed a slight smile. "That's good to know."

"Of course, we couldn't donate his damaged lungs, but there still is his heart." His voice broke only for a moment, a tear rolling down the side of his face as he held his head up, taking in a deep breath and regaining his composure. "Such a strong yet tender heart has to go to someone special. So, tonight it will be given to a teenaged boy who will surely die without it, and Abel will then spare a loving family from losing someone very dear to them." His voice rose, choking back the emotions as he reached down and squeezed his son's arm. "I'm so proud of you, son," he wept. "I'm so proud of you."

"I'm so sorry, Vincent." I didn't know what else to say.

Vincent raised his head, gathering himself well enough to look at me. "You should say your good-bye now, Carly. They'll be taking him to surgery shortly, so it's really your last chance."

It's difficult to describe the mass of emotions that swelled within me as I stood before the two Hanikas. I was so grateful to Vincent for the kindness he had shown me, and grateful to Abel for the same, as well as for the efforts he'd made to try to save me on that terrible night not too long ago. And now I was here, feeling all the guilt, and sorrow, and despair, and pity, and anger, and regret... Oh, all the regret, for having stumbled into the life of this family, for having in any way encouraged Abel's overtures... and for not having loved him as he wanted to be loved. All of the "what ifs" flooded in as I leaned closer to Abel.

For a moment, I flashed back to the memory of losing my parents and sister, all gone in one sudden moment without ever a chance to say goodbye. I had so regretted never having that opportunity to speak to them that one last time, knowing I'd never be able to again. But at the same time, I had been relieved to know that they hadn't lingered, hadn't suffered – and I felt so badly for all the time Abel had lifelessly remained with us, never giving him any choice about when he could finally let go.

I wiped away the blur of tears so I could clearly study the shallows of his gaunt face. He looked as though death had already visited, but he had not yet departed. This pitiful cadaver still entrapped the soul of an angel longing to be released.

With his head gently clasped in the palms of my hands, I bent over and tenderly kissed him on the bridge of his nose.

I could have sworn the corners of Abel's mouth slightly raised in a smile, and I held my breath waiting to see if he would awaken. But in an instant, the expression I thought I'd seen had disappeared. It was then that I finally came to realize that Abel was already gone.

Chapter 30

A CHANGE IN SCENERY

THE BITTER COLD BESIEGED US at Thanksgiving as the howling gales blew in the first snow of the season. By this time, most of the Saints had departed for the Caribbean, and so the Landings stood vacant and lifeless with only me, Pepper, Rosie, and Leila still in the guestrooms.

Life was equally sullen in the living quarters as Vincent set about sorting through Abel's belongings. He compiled a few tokens to be kept as treasured remembrances, then boxed the rest of the items to be donated to the Saints upon their return next spring. Even in the deepest recesses of his grief, he found comfort in giving what was no longer needed for the benefit of others.

There was no open casket vigil for Abel. After his organs had been removed and all life support shut down, and when the doctors finally pronounced what we came to realize had in essence been true for some time, then the rest of Abel's remains were donated to science.

At the time of the loss of my own family, I had opted for the traditional practice of embalming and burial. I felt at the time the need for a final resting spot where I could go and pay respects when I pleased. But I had to admit that I hadn't visited my family plot for many months now. It had seemed at that time to be the right decision, to do what I considered "normal." But as the months passed, I came to realize that my decision had been mostly about my own need to sense that, although they were gone, I still knew where they were.

I had expected the same "normal" procedure for Abel, but the family had chosen otherwise. Their life, and death, experiences had brought them to their own sense of what was the right choice to be made at the time of death. So, despite my desire for a "resting place" for Abel and my aversion to the image of him as someone's anonymous cadaver, I did come to accept their decision as right for this family so afflicted with such deadly misfortune.

Vincent arranged a private memorial service in honor of Abel's life, setting its date in mid-December to accommodate the needs of some people he wished to have attend. Pepper and I went together to the simple ceremony, the island church adorned with beautiful bouquets of white roses and a display of photographs chronicling Abel's all too brief life.

"Look at him there." I pointed for Pepper to see the photo of a young toe-head in a sandbox.

Pepper bent over to study the photo more closely. "Wow! Libby looks a lot like her uncle."

"She sure does." Rafae sauntered up beside us as he, too, looked over the photos. "There's a big family resemblance."

"I guess I hadn't noticed it until now," I admitted, looking over at Libby standing by her grandfather.

The service was quite informal. Pastor Fritz asked us to gather briefly in the pews so he could share words of faith and comfort with us. Pepper and I took our seats with Rafae, the three of us sitting directly behind Vincent and Libby and with Gretchen in her wheelchair positioned in the aisle to our side.

At the end of Pastor Fritz's comments, he concluded with an invitation for members of the audience to stand and share their own personal remembrances of Abel. At first no one stood, the room silent as people pondered what they might say and then tried to build up the confidence to say it. After a prolonged pause, someone stirred across the aisle from us.

"Here's something." Deke came to his feet, first talking just to the Pastor, then turning to the rest of us. "As a kid, Abel was obsessed with Dad's sled dogs. I remember when we were about twelve this one husky had a litter of pups and the runt was born with a bum leg. Dad said the best thing to do was to put the poor pup out of its misery, but Abel wasn't about to let that happen."

I pulled a tissue from my pocket and dabbed at my eyes. Then as I lowered my hand, Rafae took hold of it and gave it a squeeze. I looked to his face and found there a reassuring smile.

"For the longest time, we thought that pup had been eaten by a bobcat or wandered off to die somewhere," Deke continued. "Come to find out, Abel had hidden the thing over in the old barn by Admiral Wheaton's tomb. In such a short time, it had grown into a no-manners mutt we named Rollo, the biggest scoundrel of the pack, and worthless to the sled team because of his gimpy leg. But Abel didn't care. He figured every life was worth saving. That was just like him to rescue the mangiest pup of them all."

As Deke took his seat, I bit my lip, sensing the deeper meaning in his story. Rafae seemed to sense it too as he gave my hand a firmer squeeze before letting go to rise to his feet.

"A couple of years back, Abel helped me pull a prank on old Deke over there." Rafae cleared his throat. "I rigged the railing on my ferry so that if you leaned against one small part of it, it'd give way. I talked Abel into making sure nobody else leaned against it and to try to get Deke to lean on it."

Deke stayed seated, turning to Rafae with a confused look on his face. "No, he wasn't in on it – he helped pull me out of the water."

"But that's the beauty of it, Deke," Rafae replied, continuing his story. "Abel never told you, but he *was* in on it – and the thing was, that would be just like him to rescue somebody that he'd just tricked. He could never find pleasure in someone else's pain, and so he had to rescue you – the mangiest pup of them all." Rafae then sat down, flashing me another grin.

There were a few smiles and chuckles around the church as people imagined the playful yet kind side of Abel. Others began to get into the spirit of the testimonials, rising to tell similar stories of their experiences with Abel. But the most poignant presentation came from a surprise guest among us.

"None of you know me." An older man with pallid skin was helped to his feet by the woman beside him. "I'm not from around these parts. But Mr. Hanika kindly saw fit to invite me to participate in this ceremony, and I figured it was the least I could do for all he's done for me."

With a cough, the man cleared his raspy throat and seemed to waver unsteadily as if about to lose his balance. The woman to his side righted him and encouraged him to continue.

"My wife here and I are forever grateful for the gift of life given to me by this dear boy, Abel. His liver is now my liver, and it has given me the hope that I will have the chance to see my grandchildren grow up, maybe even get to see some of my great-grandchildren someday. So, I'm just here to tell you that without Abel's sacrifice, that couldn't have happened."

Surprisingly, no one wept or even sniffled. All were silent, seemingly mesmerized by this miracle of a man who continued to speak before us.

"Now, I'm a simple man, and I was kind of baffled by the notion of a liver transplant. But I've since been told that it's not just the blessing of this poor boy's liver that made all this possible, but it's also the grit of his father for continuing research on these kinds of organ donations. Now I'm just the modest owner of a hardware store, but I got to tell you – without these people, I'd be the dead owner of a hardware store. I'm a lucky man, blessed by two selfless gentlemen, and I owe them a debt of gratitude."

As the woman helped her frail husband back to his seat, the room erupted in applause. But the man did not stand for a bow for he knew, like everyone else in the room, that we were clapping for Vincent and Abel – for the example of their lives.

Once the applause died off, the church returned to silence as no one was willing to tell any more stories after such a moving tribute. So, Pastor Fritz quickly drew the brief gathering to a close, concluding with an invitation for everyone in attendance to join the family at the home of the Kavanaughs for a reception.

"I'd rather pass on the reception," I told Rafae and Pepper as I put on my coat to leave.

"What, and miss out on all that bantering with Deke?" Pepper wrapped her scarf tightly around her neck. "Oh, come on. I want to see this." Throwing on her coat, she headed out into the snow to commandeer one of the many waiting horse drawn taxis.

I slipped on my mittens, looking over at Rafae. "Well, Vincent did ask me to come to help him deal with Gretchen and Libby, so I guess I should go."

"Well, I can't go. I've got to get back to work." Rafae pulled the collar of his peacoat up around his neck and opened the door, holding it for me as the snow blew in. "But you should go – to help out Vincent, and in memory of Abel."

I paused, then nodded. "I suppose you're right." Buttoning up my coat, I went out the door and headed for the taxi Pepper was holding, waving good-bye to Rafae as he headed the other way.

A short ride up the bluff brought us to the front door of the Kavanaughs where we were greeted once again by Hailey Battiste. "I con take de coats ond gloves." He extended his arm to take in all of our winter gear before waving us on through the foyer. "Just keep go-on' straight ohead ond make yoursevs ot home. Dares coffee ond tea ond snocks for your likon' – just help yoursevs."

Following Hailey's directions, we walked ahead into an extravagant Victorian living room with high ceilings and ornate crowned molding. From floor to ceiling, lace and fine fabrics were perfectly draped about an abundance of antique furniture. The place reminded me of an expensive gift shop where people feared accidentally breaking something very valuable. It was more of a show place than a home, a room where I could never imagine getting comfortable. I wondered if the whole house was like this, whether there were any casual spaces in the house – and I was curious if the house had always been this way. Had this been the environment in which Deke had grown up?

Some guests mingled about the living area nibbling from platefuls of fine hors d'oeuvres they held in their hands while being careful not to touch or bump into their grandiose surroundings. Others gathered in the adjoining dining room around a splendid spread of appetizers and desserts.

Pepper tapped me on the shoulder, whispering in my ear. "I've got to find the ladies' room."

"Fine. You do that."

"I think I'll look upstairs – maybe do a bit of snooping to see what the rest of the place's like."

I cocked my head, squinting at her. "Now don't cause any trouble, okay?"

Pepper held her hands up, shrugging. "Who me? Wouldn't dream of it." She smiled then headed back toward the stairs in the foyer.

Looking back toward the dining room, I spotted Vincent, Libby, and D'Arcy, the three gathered by the elegantly arranged dining table. Libby stood closest to the table, her shirt sleeve just missing a fine crystal water goblet as she reached across all of the silver and china to pick through an overflowing assortment of the most extravagant of appetizers.

"Watch out, Libby!" I headed quickly toward her.

D'Arcy was right next to her and reached down quickly to avert any accident. "Let me help you there, little princess." He gently took hold of her arm, lifting it out of harm's way before snatching a fistful of something off the table and putting it behind his back. "Now, I've got just the thing for you." He knelt down beside her.

Libby grinned with excitement. "What is it?"

"Pick a hand." With his hands closed, he thrust his two fists out in front of her.

Libby pointed to his left hand. "This one!"

D'Arcy opened his left and revealed four brightly speckled jellybeans.

Libby squealed with delight as she nabbed the booty and shoved it quickly into her mouth. Chewing with her mouth open, she asked, "So, what's in the other hand?"

Mr. Kavanaugh opened the other hand to reveal five more candies. "I could never fool you." Handing them over, he further muddled her already windblown hair, sending her dashing off as he stood and looked over at Vincent. "That was a befitting memorial – simple, yet reverent."

"I thought so," Vincent agreed. "But this spread you've put out is anything but simple. Constance has outdone herself once again."

D'Arcy sighed. "Well, my wife has never mastered the fine art of simplicity." He smirked then popped a jellybean in his own mouth. "She tells me she doesn't believe you can ever do too much, and this is the result."

"Well, it was really nice of her to offer to do this." Vincent took a small slice of cheese, placing it on a cracker.

"Yeah, she tries." D'Arcy grabbed a couple of small china plates, handing one toward Vincent. "Here. Please fill it up."

"I'm fine." Vincent waved him off. "I'm going to go see about Gretchen." He turned and stepped into the living room.

D'Arcy turned to me, offering the plate my way. "Carly, you take one and fill it up, then."

I held up my hands. "Thanks, but I'm not that hungry."

"I won't take 'no' for an answer from you, young lady." D'Arcy took both plates himself and set about filling one with a number of finger foods from the elaborate buffet. "You've got to help me by eating this stuff up or else my wife will be feeding it to me for the next month."

"Well, I suppose I could have a little something."

"Now that's more like it." He continued piling food on the plate, beginning what looked to be a second layer.

"Oh, I don't need much." I tried to stop him from piling on more, but it was no use.

"Nonsense." He put two finger sandwiches precariously on top. "You need some nourishment, and what you don't eat, you can share with the girls."

"Well, I suppose I could."

"Of course you can. Now take this over by Gretchen and give her a few bites, too." He carefully handed the plateful toward me. "She's probably hungry, and what you two don't eat I bet that little nymph Libby will polish off with her jelly beans."

"I don't think I've had the pleasure of meeting this young lady." Constance Kavanaugh held her pointy chin erect, gracefully interrupting us as she grasped her husband's arm and gazed over at me. Adjusting the strand of large, black pearls about her neck, she looked pointedly at the heaping plate in my hands and then smiled graciously – a rather tight smile. "You must be the new help Vincent hired on for the Landings."

D'Arcy grimaced, commencing introductions. "Carly, you haven't been formally introduced to my wife, Constance Kavanaugh."

"Nice to meet you." I quickly set my plate to the side of the table, feeling my cheeks beginning to flush, and I extended my hand to hers.

"Oh, yes, I've seen you before." She extended her thin arm and took my hand with a flimsy grasp, daintily jostling my grip. "You were at hospital that terrible night when we all came to say our farewells."

"Yes, that's right."

D'Arcy picked up the heaping plate, trying to hand it off to me again. "Yeah, you know, Carly helps out with Gretchen, and she was just heading over to give her something to eat. Why don't you take this on over there and –"

Her eyes remained locked on mine. "That's right. Deke told me all about how you were one of those welcomed into the good graces of the Hanika home." She folded her hands daintily in front of her. "How nice it is that you were able to find residence there after that ghastly fire."

"I've been pretty fortunate." I again took the plate from D'Arcy, at his insistence.

"And such a lovely place for you to have been able to stay. But I would assume now, since Abel has passed – the poor dear – that you'll be moving on, too. Weren't you preparing to return to some waitressing job in your hometown, or something like that?"

"Carly's still very much needed here, Constance. Vince still has a lot going on, and Carly's been a big help with the girls. I'm hoping she'll stay on, at least until the Hanikas can get back on their feet."

Constance's eyes narrowed on her husband. "Surely it's no longer necessary for her to stay on, and if she does, it will just prolong returning the Landings to its rightful state. It needs to go back to being an inn, not some shoddy dormitory like it is right now."

"Actually, I think the place is in pretty good condition, but Carly could be pretty helpful in getting the old girl back in order for next season. Couldn't you, Carly?"

"Well, I could try." I timidly grinned.

D'Arcy returned a smile. "She's been great with the girls, and that's given Nana Maeve a much needed break from all the times she's had to watch them."

"Nonsense." Constance smoothed out the tablecloth. "It's done Maeve wonders to get her out of the house and away from that hermit of a father of yours – gives her something worth living for."

"Speak for yourself!" The cross voice of Ms. Maeve came from behind us. I turned to see her waddling up to join the quarrel, her lips pursed and white eyebrows turned inward as her stern expression tightened the deep wrinkles across her face.

Anticipating a gathering storm, I once again set my heaping plate of food on the table behind me.

Constance widened her eyes and smiled tightly at her mother-in-law. "Why, Nana, I was just suggesting it's good for you to get out once in awhile, get some fresh air and enjoy such a vivacious child as Libby."

"Fresh air, my foot!" the Kavanaugh matriarch snapped. "You just want to get me out of my own house so you can go and gaudy it all up with some more of that highfalutin, garage sale knickknack crap you call antiques. I've had just about enough of all this junk in my house!"

With that, Nana Maeve used her walking stick to tap at an ornately carved plant stand. The delicately painted vase perched on top of it wobbled slightly.

Constance quickly reached over to settle the vase and its stand, her voice remaining carefully controlled. "No need to make your usual scene, Nana – especially when we're hosting such a solemn occasion."

"I'll make a scene in my house if I choose to." Nana Maeve raised her voice, causing a couple of heads to turns. "I'll have a damn conniption if I please!"

D'Arcy gently put his arm around his mother. "For Vince, Mama," he softly said to her.

Nana Maeve's chin tightened as she raised her head. "For Vince, then." She lowered her voice, turning once again to her daughter-in-law. "Speaking of Vince, I'd say that Carly here's doing a fine job taking care of him and those girls, and that she ought to stay on." She glared at Constance. "That would keep me freed up so I can spend more time with that hermit, as you feel at liberty to call him – and maybe I can get him out for a walk, take in some of that island air you're all so hell-bent on us breathing."

Constance suddenly lost the color in her face, her eyes widening. "Now, there's no need to be rash. You shouldn't be pushing Captain Kavanaugh when you know how much that dear man favors his solitude."

"Maybe, maybe not, but I know how much *you* favor his solitude." Nana Maeve shook her head. "I know you're just fretting about how the crazy Captain might get out on the streets and somehow embarrass you in front of your high society circle."

D'Arcy held up a hand. "Okay, I think we've had enough of this little mother-daughter love-fest. Why don't we go mingle with some of our other guests?" He wrapped his arm around his wife's shoulder and gingerly guided her away.

I watched as Constance stepped away, her shunned, sour expression immediately transforming into geniality upon the sight of some all-important guests.

"She can turn it on and off like a spigot," Nana Maeve remarked to me. "Guess she had it cranked on full force when she met my son. Then the drought came and the well went dry."

"Have I offended her in some way?" I asked her.

"No, my dear. It's just that, according to her book, you haven't 'arrived' yet, and for some reason she doesn't want you to. Must be you threaten her in some way, and as you can see, she doesn't take kindly to strong women."

"But I'm no strong woman."

"Oh, yes you are – in your own way. But don't go worrying about her. Quite frankly, I'm hoping you won't arrive, either, because I like you just the way you are, Carly, and I wouldn't want to have to start hating you just because you turned into a snob like her."

"Well, I doubt I'll be 'arriving' anytime soon, Ma'am." I picked up the carefully balanced plate again from the table.

She scowled at me. "Well, you will if you keep up that polite 'Ma'am' crap! You call me Maeve, or Nana Maeve, just like the kids call me."

"Okay, Nana Maeve."

Maeve grinned, her eyes twinkling. "That's better. Now tell me how you got mixed up with these crazy families." She took one of the finger sandwiches from the top of my plate and began munching away at it.

"Well, that's a bit of a long story, and I was just bringing this food to Gretchen and Libby when —"

"I'm not dead yet, and not planning on going anytime soon, so I've got lots of time to spare. I'll just come along while you tell me how you met up with my grandson."

"Oh, okay then." I walked along slowly at Maeve's side, making our way to a corner of the living room where Gretchen's chair was parked. There we found Libby sitting on the floor at her mother's feet, quietly playing with her plastic horses.

"Well, I met Deke when I had an accident on my bike and needed stitches," I told Maeve. "Abel took me to see him at the first aid station."

Maeve laughed. "Oh, so I bet they were fighting over you, weren't they?"

I was surprised by her comment. "Well, not really, but... well, I guess they were, sort of." I set the food on an end table near Gretchen, just far enough away to avoid her flailing arms. "I brought you some more food," I announced to Libby and she jumped up, helping herself to a couple of phyllo triangles.

Maeve nodded. "Of course, they were fighting over you. Those two spent their lives competing with each other, and poor Abel usually came up on the short end. Must have been vying for your favor, and then that's why Deke's all torn up, blaming himself for what happened."

"No, Deke blames *me* for what happened."

Maeve scowled. "Is that what he told you? Well, guess that's his way of trying to rid himself of the guilt. I don't know why he's doing this. He's all broken up over something neither of you could have helped, and it's so obvious he's taken a fancy to you."

I let out a short laugh. "Oh, I don't think so."

"Trust me on this, Carly. I've had years of experience, especially with that boy, and I know what it is when something's eating him up. A lot of it's Abel, but it's also what to do about you." She motioned with her walking stick toward a nearby group of visitors who were talking with Deke and then reached for another finger sandwich. As I followed her gesture, my eyes met his. I glanced briefly at his seemingly belligerent expression, then turned away.

"I think you might be mistaken, Nana Maeve."

"Rubbish!" She caught sight of Deke looking our way and raised her voice as she called over to her grandson. "Deke! Get over here. Your Nana wants a word with you."

I felt the urge to run and hide as Deke approached, but I knew there would be no escaping the clutches of Nana Maeve. In desperation, I reached for the plateful of appetizers on the table and shoved a cream puff in my mouth, figuring I couldn't be expected to speak with my mouth full.

"What do you need, Nan?" Deke respectfully inquired, his captivating green eyes glinting even in the room's dim light.

"Clear something up for me, would you?" Maeve pointed her cane at me. "This young lady here has been asked to stay on with the Hanikas until next Fudgie season. What do you think about that?"

Deke turned from his grandmother to gaze at me and I realized I must look an attractive sight – both of my cheeks ballooning with cream puffs, my fingers holding another ready to be crammed in with the rest.

"If Vince needs her help, then I suppose she should stay." Deke tactfully answered.

"But how do you feel about it?" Nana Maeve pressed.

"I'm sure Carly knows that's her choice."

"I see." Maeve squinted at her grandson, considering her next move. "Well, your father tells me you're going to be staying on a few months so you can do your vet school rotation with that heard of animals he keeps."

"That's the plan, Nan. The horses should keep me busy for a while, and of course there's plenty to do with the dogs, too."

Nana Maeve mischievously smiled. "You know we love having you around, Deke, but your grandfather and I are getting on in our years. It gets to be a lot of commotion with you coming in late on some nights, and then trompsing around so early with your dad to get out in the morning. I'm afraid we're not up to it any more."

Deke looked confused. "Well, I'm sorry if I've disturbed you, Nan, but I'm not sure what you want me to do. I can try to get in earlier and be a bit more quiet when I —"

"Oh, no – no – no. A young, virile fellow like you needs to get out and socialize. Can't have you cooped up with the horses all day, or God knows what you might take to doing. No, we need to get you a place of your own."

Suddenly I saw where she was going, and it unnerved me. I shoved two cheese cubes in my mouth and just kept on chewing.

"Say then, I've got an idea!" With her finger in the air, she raised her eyebrows. "Carly, I bet there're plenty of rooms open at the Landings since the Saints left."

I nodded, pointing at my mouth to indicate I still needed to chew and swallow before speaking. Maeve must have taken my nod as agreement, quickly turning back to Deke. "Why don't we set you up with a room at the Landings?"

"Oh, that'd be a pretty big imposition on Vince, I think." Deke shook his head. "Besides, I'm just a poor college student so I don't have the funds to —"

"My treat!" Maeve eagerly interrupted. "If I'm the one putting you out, then I'm the one who pays. And as for Vincent, I know he'll be glad to have a man around the place to help out, as sort of a protector." She clapped her hands together around the handle of her cane. "Oh, why didn't I think of this before? I need to go tell Vince, so you two work out the details." And with that, she waddled away, leaving Deke and I to gawk at one another's stunned faces.

"What did you do to bring that on?" Deke asked as if I were somehow responsible.

I gulped as I swallowed my last bit of cheese. "It wasn't my idea!"

"You must've said something."

"Why do you feel the need to blame me for everything?" I blurted out, surprising myself.

He paused briefly, looking down at the floor then back up at me. "Well, I guess I shouldn't assume it's your fault. My nan manages to get some pretty crazy ideas all on her own, so maybe I shouldn't jump too quickly to that conclusion."

I was very surprised to hear this. "It's okay. We all make mistakes — and she's kind of a determined lady."

"That she is." He smiled. "Ah, well, I guess I might be in the market for a place to stay. Do you think Vince would lease me a room?"

I was about to answer him when I was interrupted by a tug on my sleeve.

"Bumpa sent me over." Libby looked up at me, smiling. "He wants me to stay with you while he takes Mom somewhere."

"Okay, good — you can have another snack if you want." I pointed to the plate of food.

Libby searched through the plate on the table and snatched a cookie from it, looking over at Deke as she took a bite. "Are you coming to live with us, Deke?"

Deke smirked at Libby as he knelt to her level. "Have you been listening to other people's conversations again, Libby?"

"I wasn't trying, but your Nana talks real loud so I heard what she said. So, are you going to move in or what?"

"Well, sounds like Nan wants me to, and usually she gets what she wants."

"Yipee!" Libby leaped for joy, hugged Deke about the neck, and then turned to me. "It'll be so much fun, Carly, like a giant sleepover party that goes on and on. We can play Go Fish and Aggravation, and Bumpa will make us Jiffy Pop." Then she planted a big kiss on Deke's cheek. "I'm so glad you're coming. It'll help us all start to feel better."

"I suppose it will." Deke laughed, then turned to me with a smile still on his face.

I had to smile, too, not only happy to see Libby so giddy for the first time in a while, but also pleased to see Deke smiling — something I hadn't seen in a long time.

Chapter 31

PICKING A FIGHT

HOLIDAYS WOULD NEVER BE THE SAME with no family to share them with, and so I dreaded the thought of my first Christmas alone. Of course, I wasn't missing my ex as much as I thought I would – he seemed to belong to a life and a world I'd left behind. But I found that the loss of my sister and parents weighed even more heavily on my heart as Christmas quickly approached.

Visits to the Windemere General Store proved my most frequent reminder of what I had lost over the past year. Each time I entered the store, my eyes were drawn to the flashing tree lights and garland decorating a central display table filled with gift ideas. It was there that I would always spot the perfect gift for Mom or Dad or... and then I'd remember that I couldn't give them a gift this year, or any year – that I would never give them anything ever again.

Resigned to the fact that Christmas would arrive soon, I decided to be proactive by making plans. I briefly considered Pepper's kind invitation for me to travel downstate with her to her folks' home in Marshall, but soon I decided against it. It would be a long trip now that the ice was forming on the Straits, halting all ferry traffic and making airplanes the only means to get off the island. Despite my close friendship with Pepper, I just didn't feel up to taking two flights and then a long drive just to go spend the holidays with people I didn't even know.

But I was pleased when Vincent asked me to join his family for Christmas day. Although Abel could no longer be with us, these people had become like family to me. I could think of no one I'd rather share both the joy and sadness of this holiday with, no people that I felt more at home with than the Hanikas.

I also was glad to finally have a room all to myself, space that I didn't have to share. I moved into the first room on the right just off the lobby, near the rooms where all remaining tenants were staying now that the heat had been turned down in the remainder of the empty hotel. I found it comforting to have Rosie and Leila right across the hall from me, and it was nice having Deke move into the room next door, as well.

Deke's location made it practically impossible for us to avoid running into each other, and so it offered us the chance to mend our ways. Although our first couple of encounters felt somewhat tenuous, in a short time we both seemed able to put our bad feelings behind us and I felt like we were gradually working towards becoming friends once more.

All too soon, though, we came back to the realization that we couldn't put everything from the past behind us. Rumors spread non stop when another woman was reported missing, reawakening fears that we thought had finally begun to fade. And then, when the police disclosed the fact that this latest possible abductee was not a Saint but rather considered a local, it was all too noticeable that a much greater sense of anxiety suddenly engulfed the entire Windemere community.

"I got de scoop on de misson' white garl de people all so worryon' obout," Leila announced at my doorway. "She's obout twenty-someton', ond dey say she hod drinks ot Biminis de night before she disoppeared."

Deke crowded up to my doorway. "So, maybe your good ole' boating friends had a little something to do with this after all, eh Carly?"

"And keep their mouths shut about it for all of this time?" I laughed, coming to the doorway. "Not a chance. That's so unlikely, there's got to be something else…"

"Dare is." Rosie's voice echoed over the heavy sound of her winter boots as she stomped down the hallway, joining our conversation. "I know who de misson' garl is."

Leila turned away to face Rosie, hands on her hips. "Ya do? Who is she den?"

Rosie's stopped where we were gathered, crossing her arms in front of her heavy chest. "She's on de payroll ot dot Windemere Convention Centar, ond Carly knows all obout her. It's dot Onnohede Khali womon."

I gasped. "Annahede? That can't be right."

"Oh, yes it con. I know for de foct dot de garl is gone, olong wid all de odder womon we've lost."

It was so hard for me to believe that Annahede could have fallen victim to whoever was behind this – that she could ever fall victim to anyone, for that matter. She had always been so strong willed, as tough as nails, and I had thought no one could ever get the better of her. It seemed more likely to me that she just found some bigger and better opportunity and moved on without a word to anyone. That would sound more like her, but then again, I could be wrong.

In the few frigid December days that followed, two more women from the area who had been working at the Convention Center failed to show up for work. Sam Donahue, Annahede's so-called boss, was up in arms since this left him short on help for the holidays.

"I lined up these yuppy lobbyists to come here between Christmas and New Years, and I promised I'd set up a whole lot of partying," Donahue told Vincent, dropping by the Landings. "Now I've got all these important people coming here and these girls take off, leaving me with nobody to get this whole party put together!" Donahue turned to me, looking me up and down with his beady eyes. "So, maybe you could loan me Carly for a short time. What do you say, Carly?"

"Sorry, but no," Vincent answered for me. He looked tired these days yet still managed to flash me a reassuring smile. "I need her here to help me take care of things."

"Suit yourself." Donahue looked me over once more and then tossed me his business card. "But if you change your mind, sweetheart, that's my direct number. You can talk right to me." He winked at me, making my skin crawl as Vincent quickly saw him out the door.

Because of the circumstances surrounding these disappearances, the locals now seemed to be split in their opinions about what had happened and who was responsible. Some blamed Donahue for their departure, believing his seedy behavior would be enough to drive anyone away. Others thought more sinister powers were at play as they turned their suspicions inward, thinking for the first time that one of their own might be behind all of this.

In an effort to keep residents calm, Chief Sinclaire and Officer Macke split up and made rounds, trying to reassure residents that they were on top of the situation and that they could ensure the safety of everyone. Sinclaire was the one who showed up at the Landings, knocking on all of our room doors to summon us out for a group announcement. I stepped into the hallway just in time to find him rapping on Rosie's door.

"You've got to come out here, too," Sinclaire yelled through her door as he shook off his hat and stomped his boots, trying to knock off the freshly fallen snow. "You need to hear this."

Knowing the past between these two, I wondered how bad the scene would be when she finally opened that door. But when it eventually swung open, I was surprised when she didn't say a word – not one. She just glared at him and swaggered slowly into the hallway, her body language speaking volumes about who she believed to be really in charge.

Sinclaire glared back at her for a moment, watching her take her place among us before he turned to address our assembled group. "I just wanted you to know that it won't be long now. We've got a good idea who's responsible for all this, so it's only a matter of time before we've gathered together all the necessary evidence to make an arrest."

"You know someone's behind this?" Deke blurted out before adding, "Well, I suppose that's good news."

"So, who's de bod mon?" Rosie demanded to know.

"You know I can't tell you that, Rose. Got to hold those cards close to the vest until I can play 'em."

Rosie scowled, squinting as she studied him. "I know you, Beauregard, ond you're not tellon' us 'cause you just don't know."

"You don't know everything, Rose." He stared back at her. "I'm not telling you yet because I don't want to let the perp know we're on to him."

"Him,' huh?" Leila noted the reference.

"Yes," Sinclaire confirmed. "It seems pretty obvious that the perp is a guy."

Rosie huffed. "So, you know who de bod guy is, ond you won't tell us so we con steer clear of him? Dot doesn't seem right to be handlon' it dis way."

"No surprise you disapprove." Sinclaire folded and bent back his hands, cracking his knuckles inside his gloves. "Well, so sorry to disappoint you, Rose, but that's just how it's going to be."

Ignoring their interchange, I interrupted. "Can't you just tell us what we should do to keep safe until you've taken care of this? Maybe you could tell us at least where we should or shouldn't go."

Sinclaire raised an eyebrow. "Well, the element of surprise may be helpful, so I can't tell you too much. But I guess I could suggest that you try to avoid being alone with some of the more criminal elements that like to hang around all the time over at Biminis."

"Criminals at Biminis?" I retorted. "I'd be the first to say that some of the characters there can be quite rude at times, but criminal? I can't think of anybody criminal around there, and I'm quite sure the regulars wouldn't take too kindly to your suggesting that they are."

"I'm not directly accusing anybody yet, Carly, but you did ask me for advice, and I'm just trying to give you a little."

"And we appreciate your keeping us posted." Deke jumped in, patting him on the back.

Sinclaire raised his chin and pushed back his shoulders. "Well, I'm just trying to be helpful in protecting these young ladies here."

Rosie rolled her eyes, turning with a huff to head back to her room.

Sinclaire looked to Deke. "I'm glad you're here to keep a watch over these gals. I'll try to stop by and let you know if anything changes. Meanwhile, keep this place locked down, and keep your other eye on Vincent and his two girls, too, if you would."

"I think we're good here, Chief." Deke saw him into the foyer and I followed them.

Sinclaire opened the door. "With an extra guy around the place, I'm sure you'll all be plenty safe if you just hunker down here for now." Then he headed out into the blustery snow squall, his large form fading as he hiked out toward the silhouette of his snowmobile. We heard the engine start and rev as he disappeared into the whiteout.

"Well, dot wasn't too helpful." Leila shook her head. "He's got worped ideas obout how to keep all de people oround here safe from de bod mon."

I had to agree. "Yeah, he says he's trying to keep us safe, but he lets whoever he thinks is a kidnapper just run around the island and then won't tell us who the guy is!"

Deke pushed the door shut and walked toward the rooms. "Let's just give him a break." He waved us off. "He's got to build his case so the guy won't walk, and he said he's close to an arrest, so give him a chance." He continued past us, heading to his room.

Leila looked at me, her hands on her hips. "Well, I con only hope dot Officer Sinclaire's a bit more eager to get de bod mon now dot he's taken de white womon. He ond de oddars didn't worry too moch before."

"Unfortunately, I have to agree," I admitted. "But at least we can now look forward to it all being over with soon."

"Ya, dose locals, dey will be putton' de pressure on de chief 'til he gets de whole problem solved – be it one way or onoddar."

From that point on, we did try to be more cautious about our coming to and going from the Landings. Whenever we had some place we needed to go, Leila and I would go together or get Deke to escort us. Sometimes Rosie would accompany us, too, but she refused the need to be escorted herself.

"No kidnoppar's go-on' te try ond nob all 'a me!" she insisted. "He's not lookon' for some big ole' womon, ond even if he wos, I'd beat some sense into his fot head if he tried layon' a finger on me." I would have tried to convince her to use our help, but something told me she was right – that no one in their right mind would ever try to mess with Rosie.

Chapter 32

THE OFFENSE

THE ONE WARNING WE RECEIVED from the chief that we chose to ignore was the one about Biminis. With Vincent now around most of the time, I wasn't working nearly so many hours helping out the girls or running the hotel. And ever since winter had set in Leila's regular job had been cut back substantially. So the both of us suddenly found we had a lot of free time to spend.

"Hey, how about we go over to Biminis and find out what's going on around the island," I suggested to Leila.

"Whot, ond listen to dose loud mouth mon tell dare bod stories obout de misson' womon?"

"Trust me, we can ignore them." I tried to reassure her even though I knew it was very difficult to do. "There'll be lots of people there with better things to talk about than that."

"Well, just os long os I don't hov to talk to dot Rafae mon. I hear he's a bod one."

"That's not true – just another false rumor." I felt much more certain about this statement. "If he's there, I'm sure you'll find out he's really all talk but a teddy bear inside."

After bundling up, we hiked the snowmobile trails all the way over to Biminis. Once there, we took up seats in a cozy corner booth, a spot we chose mostly because it was the farthest distance from the round table. Unfortunately, though, we had very little money to spend once we were there.

"Resorting to coffee so the refills are free, Carly?" Mike teased us as he poured me a cup of decaf.

"Well, it's cold out, so the coffee's good." I poured cream into my cup.

"You hate coffee." Callahan remembered.

"I been teachon' her dot it's beddar for her don de beer." Leila took a drink from her own cup.

"Tell you what," Callahan said. "Belinda just quit, so I'm short on help. I'll give you girls time and a half to work some hours for me, but only if you train her right, Carly, and you both have to be willing to work every one of these last few days until I close up for my holiday break on Christmas Eve."

I smiled. "That would be great!"

"Is dis a good idea?" Leila looked uncertain. "I hovn't waited de tables in owhile."

Callahan's expression changed, looking a bit sullen. "Well, maybe I shouldn't –"

"It'll be fine," I reassured both of them. "It'll all come back to you quickly, Leila. And remember, with people wanting to ease their winter blues along with celebrating the holidays, just about everyone on the island will be coming in here to have drinks – and for us, that means a whole lot of tips!"

With visions of a significant pay day, Leila agreed, and so we started training immediately, able to work that very first night and every one there after. Callahan was able to put us on the same shift, making it safe for us to travel to and from work as we could always go together.

On the twenty-third of the month, I spent the morning with Gretchen and Libby, helping them wrap their gifts and put them under the tree. Of course, I had to do almost all of the wrapping for Gretchen, her chorea-like motions having increased in the past month to the point where she was losing all control. She was also having more difficulty communicating, and what little she said was no longer as coherent. She was continuing to slip away from us, both in mind and body, and I tried to avoid wondering if this would be her last Christmas.

Eventually Vincent returned from running all his errands. "Thanks for holding down the fort. I can take it from here, so you just hurry along and get dressed for the night."

Tonight was a special celebration at Biminis when people would dress to the hilt to honor what had come to be known as

"Christmas Eve-Eve." Callahan had promised to dress in his Irish green sport coat if we committed to dressing up in our best. He even paid for a carriage to pick us up and get us there, so we were more than happy to oblige.

Both Leila and I wore festive cocktail dresses adorned by sparkling costume jewelry. Callahan gave a quick round of applause to us for cleaning up so nicely, then he hurried us off to our assigned tasks. By mid-afternoon, we had set up a large table of hors d'oeuvres, all free for the taking in hopes of enticing patrons to order more of the spiked punch and eggnog.

The customers poured in, all dressed elegantly in suits and dresses. But the frat boys, not to be out done, showed up in tuxedos they'd rented and shipped in from the mainland. Most were in simple black tie, a couple opting for tails, but the stand outs were Rafae and Captain Nick, dressed in flashback pastel tuxedos with matching ruffled shirts.

"Nice mint green!" Rafae complimented Captain Nick as he strolled in.

Nick took a bow, then modeled for the crowd. "And you look mighty fine in that powder blue, Rafae. Guess you'll have to be fighting off the ladies with that getup!"

Leila grumbled, "Dey're just all obout demselves, tryon' te out dress de oddars. Whot a couple of showoffs."

"Hey, look at Leila!" Captain Nick sidled over her way. "Well, you're lookin' mighty fine this evening, aren't ya?"

Leila took a step back and glared.

Nick stepped closer to her. "Guess I didn't know you Saints could clean up so nice. Yes, you look —"

"— like you'd bring us a beer!" Rafae threw his arm over Nick's shoulder and dragged him away from Leila, giving her a wink of reassurance before pushing Nick into a chair. "You know, you don't even have to be drunk to be an idiot."

Captain Nick laughed along, adjusting his mint green jacket. "Oh, just give me a break, will ya Rafae?"

"Just leave the new help alone or there won't be anyone left who's foolish enough to wait on you. Okay?"

Nick bobbed his head in mock earnest agreement as the two headed back over to the gang.

There was quite a big turnout of regulars, some coming by early and most staying until late, so the party was in full swing by a little past eleven. The punch and eggnog were all gone by then, so Callahan suggested the patrons switch over to their favorite drinks. But some drunken newcomer named Charlie was not satisfied with this.

"We got-to have some-thing spe-cial to drink," Charlie insisted, over-enunciating his words. "How a-bout we get some champagne!"

Those within earshot cheered.

"I don't think so." Callahan threw his dishrag over his shoulder. "I've only got the really expensive stuff downstairs, storing it for a wedding at a friend's hotel this spring. We can't get into that."

"But I'll pay for it, re-place it." Charlie staggered to the bar, holding out his credit card for Callahan to take from him. "Two rounds for the house, on me."

A louder cheer went up from the crowd, word spreading that free drinks would be coming. Although hesitant, Callahan reluctantly rang up the charge and headed for the basement.

"It's on me!" Charlie yelled, the most popular man for a brief moment most likely to be forgotten by morning.

Leila and I searched for champagne glasses, realizing quickly that we didn't have enough.

I reached into the upright freezer, pulling out an iced glass mug. "Think this'll work?"

"Dey'll like dot." Leila smiled. "Dot way, dey'll get more to drink!"

Callahan hauled three cases up from the basement while Leila and I popped the corks and filled all the glasses. The crowd policed themselves, ratting out anyone who had the nerve to try and take their second round before everyone had a chance at their first. They all gave Charlie a pat, gladly accepting a glass or mug as they prepared to ring in the day of Christmas Eve.

Deke's expression looked less than festive when he burst in, dusting the snow from his head and shoulders as he approached me at the bar. "Where have you two been?"

"Right here." I poured champagne into a cold glass mug. "We couldn't leave at eleven with this big party going on."

"When I got back from my folks and you weren't at the hotel, I tried calling here but the wind knocked the phones out." He pulled off his gloves while climbing up on a barstool. "So, you can imagine, I got a little worried."

"Thanks for checking up, Mom!" Captain Nick crooned, much to the amusement of those at the round table. Another sailor chimed in with some feeble ridicule but he was too drunk to make any sense. The table turned to making fun of his slurred speech, quickly forgetting about Deke.

"I'm sorry, Deke." I put a mug full of champagne down in front of him. "Why don't you at least join in with everyone until we close? Then we'll all walk back to the hotel together. Okay?"

Deke smiled, unwrapping his scarf from his neck and then lifting his mug to take a drink. "Oh, my! That's great stuff – not Callahan's usual."

"And even better, it's on the house." I smiled back.

But the revelry of the entire room was stifled when the front door swung open and Officer Macke moseyed in. He sauntered toward the bar like a marshal would in Dodge, eyeing the customers as he made his way past their tables.

Unzipping his oversized parka, Macke revealed that he was still in uniform. "Evenin', Mike," he greeted Callahan.

Callahan walked over to meet Macke, placing an empty glass in front of him. "Sorry, but you missed the eggnog, Eino. Good news is, though, that Charlie's bought champagne for the house. Can I get you a glass?"

"Nope. I'm still on duty, don't ya know."

Callahan reached for the soda nozzle. "Then how about your usual Vernors?"

"Gotta pass. I got official business to tend to here – can't be participatin' in all da hullabaloo ya gots goin' on, fer sure."

"Then what can I get you?"

"Well, ya can get me one a' yer patrons, by golly. I'm gonna need ta have words with Mr. Bah-ttist-ee."

All eyes turned to Rafae, still sitting with the frat boys in his powdered blue tux.

Rafae raised one brow, looking bewildered as he gazed back at the onlookers. "Champagne was legal the last time I checked, Eino." Rafae raised his glass, motioning for a toast.

Macke didn't crack a smile. "How 'bouts we talk dis over outside, Rafae – ya know, man to man like." He stood, approaching Rafae's table.

Rafae shook his head. "Not until I've finished my drink. Why don't you just grab a glass, pull up a chair, and join the fun. The party's just getting started."

Macke walked over to Rafae and stood right behind him. "Ya got some business ta discuss over with me, don't ya know, so we bests deal with it outside a' here."

Rafae stood up, turning to glare at Macke. "My business is right here."

Everyone stopped talking, stopped drinking, stopped doing whatever they were doing. The bar went silent.

Macke's face tightened, turning red. "So we gotta do it yer way, eh?" He reached to his belt and took out his handcuffs. "Den I suppose my business is gotta be done here, too, by golly." He grabbed one of Rafae's wrists, hitting it with a cuff that spun around and locked. "You got de right to remain silent. Anything you says can and *will* be held against yas –"

"Hey! What are you doing?" Rafae's eyes were wide.

"I'm arrestin' ya, don't ya know, and yer interruptin'. Now, what was I sayin'? Oh, yeah – anything ya says can and will be held against ya in dah court a' law. Ya gotta right ta –"

"I have the right to know what I'm charged with!"

"Well, now, we'll starts ya off with dah kidnappin', fer sure, and den I might toss in murder, dependin' on dah mood I'm in when I get ya to dah station." Macke swiftly took Rafae's other arm and twisted it back before Rafae could react, then slapped the loose cuff closed on Rafae's other wrist.

His arms now securely bound behind him, Rafae glared at the officer. "Are you crazy!"

"Ya best not be talkin' back to me like dat, eh!" Macke's face was now beet red. "Now, don't ya go interruptin' me again, ya hear? You got dah right to a lawyer, and if ya can'ts afford one, den will getcha one appointed by dah courts a' law."

All patrons collectively turned their attention to the confrontation in the center of the room. I couldn't believe this was happening, and obviously neither could anyone else.

"I've heard all that rights crap before!" Rafae yelled, spit flying. "You're just putting on this whole arrest charade in front of all these people just to make it look like you're doing something about those missing girls."

"It's no char-rade, Rafae, and I got me a whole slew a' questions fer ya ta answer – like, where ya was at on dah night before dat girl up and disappeared?"

Rafae shot back, "Which girl?"

"Which girl?" a dockhand from the round table repeated under his breath. Then snickering, he added, "Why, you sly dog, I'm not worthy!"

Rafae shot him a glare. "Shut up, you moron!"

The dockhand fell silent, his smirk instantaneously transforming into a sullen expression.

Macke jerked Rafae by the cuffs. "Ya betcha ya knows which one I'm talkin' about here."

"Oh, I thought you might finally be concerned about one of the Saint ladies, but you're just talking about that one who's on Donahue's payroll, aren't you."

Macke yanked up his pants as he stared Rafae in the eyes. "But ya *was* here with dat one A-rab lady dah night before she up and went missin', weren't ya, eh? So, I'm bettin' ya probly just didn't like her bein' such a teaser and such when she said she wasn't sellin' herself ta dah likes a' yous, did ya, huh?"

"No, that's not what she told me." Rafae smirked. "She said she'd take just about anybody's money – except yours!"

"Ya thinks yer so smart, don't yas!" Macke shoved Rafae toward the door. "Well, we'll sees how smart ya are when yas done talkin' it over with dah chief, by golly."

"Hey, should one of us come with you?" a younger member of the round table offered.

"No need," Rafae yelled back from the doorway. "I'll just tell ol' Beauregard and his lap dog Schwinn here what they want to hear. Then we'll share a few doughnuts, a few laughs, and I'll be back on the streets in no time."

"Oh, I wouldn't be all so cocksure of yerself if I was yous, don't ya know." Macke gave Rafae another push. "Betcha won't be all so full a' yerself once we gets done showin' ya all dah evidence I got from dat shameful place yer callin' home."

"What?" Rafae's smug expression quickly changed to a scowl. "Did you go and break into my apartment?"

"Well, I got probable cause, fer sure. Even found some of dat A-rab's stuff laying lollygag around dah place. Yeah, ya got some explainin' to do about dat fact, eh."

Rafae surprised me when he laughed in the face of such a revelation. "Nice one, Eino. Planting evidence now, are you? Wow! You *are* desperate to make it look like you're doing your job – when we all know you couldn't catch a crook to save your life."

"Well, I gotta big crook in my custody now, don't I, ya smart-aleck!" Macke gave Rafae a final push through the door and out into the flurry of snow before he turned back to face the gawking crowd. "Show's over, folks! Go on back to all yer carousin' and carryin' on now, ya hear, and have yerselves a merry Christmas, eh!" And with that, Macke zipped up his parka and marched out of the bar, disappearing in the swirling snow that whisked its way across the pitch-black night.

"What the hell?" one deckhand broke the silence, and then the entire fraternity launched into a round of Twenty Questions. Everyone in the bar followed suit, asking questions of one another in a search for how Rafae could be involved in the disappearances.

"I hov olways known dose boys wos no good." Leila picked up Rafae's mug along with some others. "Just still wish dot Offeesar Mocke hod arrested dot Nick-mon instead. He's de really bod one."

"But that's what's strange." I said as I picked up empties and took them back to the bar. "Out of that whole gang, Rafae's the last one I'd expect to have anything to do with this."

"I connot believe you defendon' dot deviont mon!" Leila slapped her serving tray on the bar top. "Why, de offeesar said dey found some of dot Onnohede's tings ot his place, so he's gotta hov someton' ta do wid dis."

"But Rafae would have nothing to do with Annahede – he knows she's trouble."

"So, maybe dot's *why* he's hod someton' te do wid her, cause dot boy is no Saint, ot least not in de Bible sense, I mean." Leila argued. "But you… you still try ta defend de mon when he's olways bon hangon' oround wid dose racist, sexost pigs!"

"But he doesn't always partake in their carrying on, you know, and I've even seen him try to rein in the tribe when they've gotten too far out of line – just like he did for you, Leila."

"And he doesn't walk away from them either, now does he?" Deke set his glass down. "For all the times he's just stood by and let those others just keep at it, I think he's just as guilty when he doesn't stand up to them, or at least just walk away."

"You know those guys are the people he has to work with, just like I work with you." I glanced at Leila. "And good or bad, he probably sometimes has to just put up with them."

A large belch rose up from the round table, followed by boisterous laughter.

"Okay, and maybe it's mostly the bad," I added. "But that doesn't mean he agrees with them – and it sure doesn't mean he's guilty of kidnapping." Keeping busy, I began to sort the dirty glasses from the mugs. "Maybe you guys don't agree, but I think Macke's got the wrong man."

Callahan stepped over by us. "No doubt," he agreed with me, pulling down the tap to pour a mug of Stroh's. "And it sure seems like Macke *knows* he's got the wrong man."

"And just what is it that makes you think that, Mike?" Deke asked. "Macke sure looked like he meant business to me."

"Yeah, but he can't just go snooping through someone's house without a warrant, and he never mentioned having one." Callahan released the tap, allowing the beer head to roll over the side of the mug. "And besides that, he knows he can't make an arrest stick if he's been sloppy with somebody's rights."

"What are you talking about?" I was confused. "I heard him read Rafae his rights — when Rafae kept interrupting him, remember?"

Callahan pulled the tap again, starting to pour a second beer. "Yeah, but didn't you notice? Macke didn't even tell him what he was arresting him for — that is, until Rafae called him on it. Rafae knows he was out of order, and I'm sure he'll tell his attorney, who will in turn have Rafae out of jail in no time."

"Are you sayon' dot Macke orrested Rafae even dough he knew dot he didn't take de womon?" Leila cocked her head at Callahan. "Now whot would possess him to do dot?"

"Pressure." Callahan rolled the second head off the top. "The kind you're under to get these two beers over to the corner table before I fire you." He pointed over Leila's head, smiling.

"Oh!" She jumped to it, grabbing the beers and dashing off toward the back of the room.

Callahan looked back at me and Deke. "Yeah, those cops are under a lot of pressure now that the missing girls aren't just Saints, I'm sorry to have to admit. So, maybe he just made an arrest to quiet the locals — get off the defense and onto offense, making it at least *look* like this is all nearly solved."

"Or maybe he thinks Rafae can somehow lead him to the kidnapper, or maybe even the missing women." Deke picked up his mug and put down the last bit remaining of his champagne.

Wiping the counter, Callahan brushed some crumbs to the floor. "But doesn't it seem odd to make an arrest for kidnapping when you don't even have any evidence that a kidnapping ever occurred to begin with?"

"Hey, Carly!" Captain Nick stood up at his seat, yelling at me from the round table. "It's almost midnight, and we could use a little more cheer over here to ring in Christmas Eve, so light a fire under it, will ya?"

"Your last round for the night, so enjoy it." Callahan commanded, then walked away to wait on someone further down the bar.

"Come on, Callahan! Don't let that old party-pooper Macke ruin a good time for us." Captain Nick was too inebriated to keep his balance while standing, and so he sat down. "The night is still young, Mr. Bartender."

"Oh, no," Callahan yelled at him. "I will not have your mommy mad at me because you're too hung over for Christmas Eve mass."

The frat roared, mocking and slapping at Captain Nick.

"Whot a lousy bunch of bogus friends!" Leila pointed out, returning to the bar to grab her tray and set up glasses on top of it. "Dare buddy gets hauled off on de charges dot he's de kidnoppar, ond dey're just worried obout where dare next drink is comon' from." She sneered, filling the glasses and then heading back toward the self-absorbed table.

Deke fiddled with his cocktail napkin. "Yeah, they don't seem too worried about Rafae. They're probably no more convinced that those charges will stick than we are."

"Well, I hope we're right." I started filling up a pitcher with beer. "I've spent enough time around Rafae to know he's just not capable of this. Why, he's even walked me home a few times, and I'm still here, aren't I?"

"Oh, has he?" Deke leaned back, studying me.

I shut off the tap. "Don't you look at me like that." Taking a firm grip, I pulled the pitcher away and started walking around the bar. "You know perfectly well he's all talk. He's been a total gentleman."

"Really?" Deke laughed at the thought. "Now *that* is hard to believe."

I could feel Deke's eyes on me as I took the pitcher over and handed it to Captain Nick. As the table cheered my delivery, I looked back at Deke, gleaning from his green eyes just a hint of curiosity, or interest, or attraction, or... I wasn't sure exactly, but it was something I'd seen there before, back before that terrible night when we lost Abel.

Leila brushed past me on her way back to the bar. "So, whoevar's de one do-on' dis, he's still out dare on de prowl?"

"I suppose so." I also walked back.

Deke looked at us both. "Well, until we're convinced that the kidnapper's been caught, you two need to be careful. And I think I'll keep staying in my room, even for Christmas night. Then I can just head to my folks for meals and church, and our little gift exchange. But I'm not on dog or horse duty for the holidays, so I should be able to spend most of the time with you girls."

Leila gave him an exaggerated hug, and then batted her eyelashes at him. "You're de sweetest mon, do-on' us de favor by givon' up de fun ot Momma's te stay wid de likes of us."

Deke turned a bit red. "I didn't mean to suggest that it was any kind of problem, Leila. I mean, I like it there."

"Don't worry, Deke. We understand." I pinched his cheek and then went behind the bar to open one more bottle of champagne.

Leila gave an overstated curtsy to Deke. "Ond we, de lowly, humble servonts to de rich ond powerful of de island are so very grateful."

"Twenty seconds to midnight," Callahan announced to the entire bar.

I set up three glasses, quickly filling them with champagne.

Deke shot Leila a scowl. "Are you saying I'm a snob?"

She laughed. "No, I'm just baiton' ya, Deke boy, 'cause you're de easiest fish te cotch!"

"Ten, nine, eight…" Callahan began the countdown, and everyone in the bar quickly joined in.

"Very funny." Deke smirked at Leila. "Keep on teasing me and see if I stick around."

"…six, five…"

"Con't take de joke?" Leila smiled at him.

I set three glasses filled with champagne in front of us.

Deke took two, handing one to Leila. "Yes, I can."

"…three, two, one…"

Picking up my glass, we clinked them together and then each took a drink.

"Happy Christmas Eve." Deke grinned, giving me a wink... and for the moment, it was just that.

Deke did hang around as the bar eventually cleared out, and he kept us company as we went about our work. He even helped Leila put away the leftovers while Callahan emptied another load of clean glasses and I swept up the floor.

While swinging the broom to the sounds of *I'll be Home for Christmas*, my thoughts drifted to past holidays with my parents and sister, and even the happier times with my ex. And of course I thought of Abel, and how tough this Christmas would be without him. I wondered, too, about Gretchen, if there was any hope for her, or for at least one more Christmas beyond this one.

"Hey, why so glum?" Deke walked over to me.

I looked down at the floor, focusing on my sweeping. "Oh, all of this mess, it's just a little overwhelming sometimes."

"Can I help?" Deke picked up the dust pan from the corner where I'd last left it.

"Sure, thanks." I swept together a pile of food and dirt. "You know, I don't think you're on the clock."

"Not looking to get paid." He held the pan down on the floor while looking up at me with sad eyes. "You know, I've been missing him, too."

I looked back at him, my chin quivering. "I just think... it just won't be the same without him."

He let the pan drop as he stood up to hug me. "No, it won't, but you can't help that. You've just got to try to not think about that, and make it as happy as you can for Vince and the girls."

"I'll try." I hugged him back, tears welling up in my eyes.

Deke took hold of my arms, holding me back away from him where he could look me in the eyes. "Now, let's get this done so we can get out of here and head home."

"Okay." I nodded.

Deke released his hold and knelt back down to the dust pan, holding it as I swept all the dust and debris into it. Then he carried it over to the garbage as I finished the last bit of sweeping.

Starting to brush together one last pile, I yelled across the room to Deke. "So, do you think Rafae's been able to break out yet, or will we not see anything of him until morning?"

"He's a pretty smooth operator," Deke replied, walking over to me. "I think he'll talk his way out of there yet tonight."

"I still don't get it, though." I swept a pile together.

"Well, don't worry yourself over it." He knelt down and put the pan to the floor, taking in the last pile. "These things have a way of working themselves out."

"It's just that, of all the people at that table he could have accused, you'd think he'd have gone after someone else."

Deke walked back across the room, dumping the last of the debris in the trash can. "And who knows? Maybe he'll be back to arrest some others from the table, because God knows – there's plenty of dirt in this place that's in need of cleaning up."

Chapter 33

DEEP IN THE SHADOWS

LOOKING A BIT UNDER THE WEATHER, two clean-shaven sailors sat in the back pew of Windemere's largest church, St. Francis of Assisi, as we entered for the interdenominational Christmas Eve service. Deke and I walked up the aisle together and then separated once we found our respective families. Deke took a seat next to his dad, further separating his mother from Nana Maeve – probably a good idea unless Nana gave him an earful during the service. And I had the pleasure of sitting between Libby and Vincent with Gretchen parked in her chair in the side aisle right next to her father.

Just four blocks from the Landings, this gorgeous church of St. Francis seemed the perfect place to ring in Christmas. Its ornate altar was beset with red and white poinsettias and the side rails wrapped with strings of colorful Christmas lights and fresh greens, their fresh pine scent filling the church. We were all invited to sing along to the tunes of the most familiar of Christmas hymns, but the massive pipe organ was played with such thunderous passion, it nearly stifled the voices of even the small choir.

Unfortunately, the music seemed to agitate Gretchen, her contortions increasing with each new verse until we thought she might slide out of her chair. As we sang the last verse before the readings, I took charge of Gretchen, quietly telling Vincent that I'd just wheel her out to the lobby where I could hike her back up in her chair and let her calm down a bit during the sermon.

Once situated in the lobby, Gretchen's frenzy quickly subsided. I knelt at her side, straightening her disheveled hair as Pastor Fritz delivered a stirring message about how a bright, distant star brought so many to one small, isolated, simple location where hope was born. His sermon was brief, concluding with his suggestion that we all remain ever watchful for God's guiding light in our lives. And with that final thought, the organ roared to life once more.

To avoid further agitation, I quickly wheeled Gretchen out a side door where an extension of the roof line sheltered us from the lightly falling snow. After pulling up Gretchen's lap blanket to cover her chest, I then looked up to see a number of carriages lining the street, their horses harnessed with bells that jingled as they twitched their ears and snorted steam. They waited along the row of glowing street lamps, hitched to posts wrapped in garland and white tree lights that glistened against the dusting of snow.

"It's cold, but very beautiful, isn't it?" I told Gretchen.

"Aww," she answered, her mouth gaping and eyes wide.

I huddled at Gretchen's side as the final chord of "Hark! The Herald Angels Sing" echoed out into the brisk, night air. As the church bell chimed the service's end, I felt truly immersed in the spirit of Christmas.

"Let's wait back inside," I suggested, wheeling Gretchen back into the warmth of the lobby.

The overindulgent sailors from the back pew were the first to exit, followed by Bob Gould grumbling something about the pastor being too long-winded. Then the Kavanaughs exited, Nana Maeve smiling and waving at us before turning back on her daughter-in-law.

"You're supposed to put your offering in the plate, not hand it to the pastor on the way out!" Maeve protested.

"Well, it was cash and I didn't have an envelope to mark it for my account." Constance tucked her wallet back in her bag. "Besides, I didn't want someone spotting it loose there in the plate and taking it for himself."

"So, you don't trust the ushers?" Maeve waved her hand and rolled her eyes, then waddled toward us. "She thinks she's the only Christian in the house." She laughed as she passed by us, adding, "Merry Christmas, girls – have a better one than I'm going to have!"

"It'll be a good one, Mom," D'Arcy Kavanaugh insisted. Then he wished us both a happy holiday before following his mother out the side door.

Constance stopped long enough to take Gretchen's hand and lean down toward her. "No matter how bad things might seem, I still hope you manage a good Christmas, my dear." She released her hand and, without ever looking at me, she headed out the door.

Deke brought up the rear. "I'll see you ladies later." And with a smile, he too departed.

After more people passed by us, I finally caught sight of Vincent and Libby approaching. But before they made their way to us, I was surprised to see another familiar sailor step from the crowd.

"Merry Christmas, girls!" Rafae greeted us, first giving Gretchen a gentle hug before giving me one, too.

"Well, look who managed to escape." I smiled, both surprised and relieved to see him.

"Nope. No need to break out." He tucked his hands deep into his pockets, smirking. "Chief just let me go."

"You're kidding!" I was shocked.

Finally coming up beside us, Vincent extended his hand. "Merry Christmas, Rafae. Glad to see you could join the congregation tonight."

"Yeah, Macke wanted me to spend the holiday with him, but I said I had a previous engagement." Rafae laughed.

"Hi, Rafae!" Libby jumped at his side.

"Well, and a happy ho-ho to you, too, little girl!" Rafae gave her a squeeze.

Vincent stepped to one side, making room for others in the lobby to get past us. "So, the chief dropped the charges, did he?"

"He never even filed any." Rafae cocked his head. "I don't suppose you had anything to do with springing me out of there, did you?"

"Me?" Vincent pointed at himself, his eyebrows arched. Then he laughed. "I could only wish I had that much pull."

"Well, I'm just glad at least Sinclaire's got a little sense, because that Macke's a whack job!" Rafae shook his head. "He must have been just blowing smoke – trying to scare me into telling him something I didn't even know. Guess he was barking up the wrong tree."

With the church finally cleared out, Pastor Fritz walked over to Gretchen and took her hand in his. "Merry Christmas to you, dear… and to you, too," he added, taking my hand and giving it a friendly squeeze.

"Hey, nice sermon, padre," Rafae interjected.

"Why, thank you, Rafae." Pastor Fritz smiled. "May you all have a blessed Christmas now." He then folded his hands and headed back into the church.

Vincent took a hold of the handles on Gretchen's wheelchair. "Well, I think he's trying to close up, so we best head out." He gave Gretchen a push, heading her back to the side door where he then wheeled her down the handicap ramp.

"Yeah, let's go!" Libby took Rafae's hand and tugged him along as I followed.

"Oh, I know what you're in such a hurry about," Rafae replied as he walked at her side. "You just want to see if you have any presents yet, don't you?"

"No, that's silly. Santa won't come until I'm sleeping."

"So, she's just in a hurry to get to sleep," I added as we all caught up to Vincent and Gretchen at the foot of the ramp.

"And where are you headed to spend what's left of Christmas Eve?" Vincent asked Rafae as he pulled on his gloves.

Rafae wrapped on his scarf. "Back to my place, headed for a good night's sleep."

"Well, we can't have that!" Vincent insisted. "Go to bed too early and you might wake up when ole' Santa Clause comes tiptoeing around your place, scaring him off."

Libby tugged on Rafae's scarf, looking up at him with a most somber expression. "And then he might leave you coal!"

Rafae returned a look of concern. "Oh, but I'm afraid I might be getting coal anyway. I'm just about at the top of Santa's naughty list right now."

Vincent waved for Rafae to come along. "Then you'd better come with us – maybe you can get in a few good deeds before midnight."

"Well, I'll see what I can do." Rafae grinned, turning with us as we headed toward the Landings. He took hold of Gretchen's wheelchair handles from Vincent, wheeling her on ahead of us along the freshly shoveled boardwalk. "Let me start by giving the prettiest girl on Windemere a ride home."

We followed along, Vincent and I each grabbing one of Libby's hands as she skipped between us. With her hops getting higher and higher, we pulled her up when she jumped, swinging her between us as we followed her mother on the brief journey back home.

As we walked in the front door, we were greeted in unison by Rosie and Leila cheering, "Mar-ee Christmose Eve!"

Vincent removed his hat. "And the same to you, ladies."

"Oh, ond look who's sprung from de jail now," Rosie noticed, pointing at Rafae. "How'd you monoge dot?"

"Just sweet-talked Sinclaire, and you know how well that works." Rafae grinned.

Rosie scowled in return. "I know no soch ting."

Vincent intervened. "Thank you both for keeping an eye on the place."

Rosie cautiously slid off her stool. "Wosn't a problum, Mr. Vinsont. We olready hod our celebration earlier, so we're go-on' te call it a night. Come on, Leila!" She waddled off, heading for her room.

"Comon'," Leila yelled back as she hopped off her seat, then followed Rosie while waving at us. "Hov a nice evenon'."

"You, too," Rafae answered. He then gathered up coats from everyone. "Hey, where'd Deke the Geek go after church?"

"He's spending time with his family before he comes back tonight." Pulling Gretchen's wrap off, I handed it to Rafae.

"Ah, Christmas Eve with Constance and Nana Maeve." Rafae considered it as he hung our winter gear on a coat rack behind the front desk. "Just thinking about the two of them, brought together for Christmas Eve, probably going for each other's throats…"

Gretchen let out a laugh, squirming and rolling until she almost slid out of her chair.

"Oh, you think that's funny?" Rafae leaned over her, helping to slide her back up and securing her in her seat. "Yeah, that'd be my idea of entertainment, too."

"Perhaps you'd prefer to join them, and your father, too, since I'm sure that's where he is," Vincent suggested as he took hold of the handles on Gretchen's chair and pushed her toward the Hanika's living room.

Rafae smirked. "No thanks, I'll pass."

"Then come over here and help us put together a snack for Santa." Vince waved for all of us to follow.

"Yippee!" Libby shouted, dashing toward the kitchen.

"Ladies first." Rafae motioned for me to go, then followed up behind me. "Being a gentleman, and making snacks for Santa – If this doesn't get me in good with the big guy, then I don't know what will."

Vincent parked Gretchen where she could watch and then helped Libby get out a plate. "Let's make sure we leave carrots. The reindeer really like those."

"Okay!" Libby's face gleamed. "We'll leave nine, in case Rudolph comes along."

Rafae pulled out a glass from a cupboard. "Is there milk in the fridge?"

"Yes," I answered, pulling out a Tupperware box full of sugar cookies. "Help yourself."

He opened the refrigerator and pulled out a quarter-full carton. "Have you got enough?"

I looked. "Go sparingly."

"No, you can't!" Libby dashed over, taking the carton and glass from Rafae. "We've got to be nice to him – and we have to warm it up."

"Okay." Rafae lifted Libby up to sit on the countertop. "I can help you with that."

As he leaned over to assist, we were all suddenly jolted by a horrific scream from Gretchen.

"Aaahhhhhhh!" She launched into a fitful tirade, her arms swinging, nearly throwing her to the floor. "I – elp!"

Vincent dropped the carrots to the floor, hurrying over to embrace his daughter. "It's all right, honey. We're all right here."

Gretchen still thrashed about, wailing uncontrollably as she knocked Vincent over.

I reached for him. "Are you all right."

"I'm fine!" His answer was curt, his voice determined as he grabbed hold of Gretchen again, smoothing down her hair in an effort to console her.

Rafae stayed beside Libby, gently hugging her as she sobbed into his shoulder. "She's okay," I heard him whisper to her, but she knew better.

Gretchen continued to scream with sounds I hadn't heard from her before. Most of it was unintelligible, but at one point I thought I made out something she was yelling.

I moved over toward Vincent. "She just wants to help us."

Vincent quickly glanced at me, then grabbed Gretchen's head, holding it as steady as he could while trying to look her in the eyes. "You can help us, Gretch. I know you want to help."

Once released, Gretchen's head dropped, her hair falling haphazardly in her face as she moaned and wept. Then I thought I heard something else from her, some decipherable words amid her more guttural sounds. The sounds were "Ss – ma – gr – le."

I had it. "She's saying, 'She's my girl'!"

"Yes." Vincent hugged her. "She is you're girl, just like you're mine. We can do this, Gretch. We can do it all together."

Rafae lifted Libby's chin, tilting her head in the direction of her mother. "See? Your mom's doing a lot better now."

Gretchen was calming a bit, but she looked far from better.

"I don't think so." Libby's lower lip quivered.

"Then let's cheer her up by counting the carrots with her," Rafae suggested, lifting her off the counter and taking her over to where Vincent had dropped the carrots. He then scooped some up off the floor and handed them to Libby. "Here you go."

Libby held the carrots tightly in her fist. "I don't think she wants to do it now."

"Sure she does!" Rafae insisted, taking them from Libby and placing them on the table beside Gretchen.

I turned Gretchen toward the carrots, hoping she could still push them around like socks. "Come on, give it a try, Gretchen. Do it for Libby."

Gretchen's arms flailed about the table, sending most of the carrots scattering to the floor. She continued with her moans and grunts, her head swinging sideways then dropping forwards, her disheveled hair covering her face.

Vincent rubbed her arm. "She's just so frustrated."

Rafae dropped to his knees, picking up the carrots. "I think Libby and I should take these and the plate full of cookies out to the front desk to leave them where Santa will see them."

"Oh, that's a great idea." I followed Rafae's lead, trying to coax Libby into following him out of the room so Vincent and I could try to calm down Gretchen.

"But Mom wanted to help us do it." Libby sniffled, wiping her face on her shirtsleeve.

"And she can." Rafae stood and took her by the hand, guiding her away. "We'll go count out the carrots and get the plate all set up, and then we'll bring your mom out to check everything over and make sure we've got it right." He quickly grabbed all of the necessary elements and scooted her out of the room.

As Libby left, Gretchen's tantrum escalated again. Try as we might, she remained inconsolable, and so we had no choice but to let her anger run its course until she eventually calmed down on her own.

Vincent gently stroked her head, moving her hair back out of her face. "It's the dementia – makes her lose her temper and fly out of control. She gets these misconceptions about what's going on around her – about how she's being treated."

"I wish I could think of some way to calm her down when this happens." I studied Gretchen's expressionless face. "Nothing seems to work anymore."

Vincent rubbed his daughter's shoulders, looking down at her. "And you're having these uncontrollable fits more and more often, aren't you, honey?"

She stared off into space, a bit of drool dripping from the corner of her mouth.

I grabbed a tissue, dabbing her lips. "Is there anything else we should do?"

Vincent rolled Gretchen back from the table. "Just try to shelter Libby from it, and avoid agitating Gretch as much as possible – but I know how tough that can be."

Turning Gretchen toward the back window, Vincent positioned her chair so she faced the snow covered lake – a view her vacant eyes never seemed to notice. Vincent and I each took a chair from the table and, placing them to each side of Gretchen, we sat down beside her. We sat there for a short time, mostly in silence except for the sounds made by Gretchen's never-ending motion. Vincent occasionally patted Gretchen's thigh or rubbed the back of her neck.

"I'm afraid we can't wait any longer." Vincent broke the silence. "I need to take Gretchen to the Caribbean soon to start her experimental treatment."

"That far?" I was surprised. "You can't get her help any closer, like someplace in this country?"

He shook his head. "Wish we could, but they tend to frown on this cutting edge experimentation we've been trying. There're too many hoops and no government funding for this kind of trial in the U.S."

"Sounds kind of risky."

"I suppose in some ways it is, but when you start to get desperate, you start to take more chances."

Gretchen choked then moaned, her arms jerking up and then pushing at the emptiness before her.

"You okay, honey?" Vincent pushed back her shoulders, massaging as he looked back to me. "Yes, I'd hoped to wait until after that trip I'd planned for the first of the year – you know, to go to the hearings in DC to try and drum up some government funding for another new, experimental procedure."

"I remember."

"The researchers think this one shows real promise, that it may stop or even reverse the progression of Huntington's. But it's controversial – always controversial, and so we've got to get the congress, and their money, behind it."

"I understand," I nodded. "And I said I'd watch the girls while you were gone."

"Yes, I know, and I appreciate that, but now I'm thinking I may need to leave sooner, and take Gretchen with me." He held his daughter's hand in his. "I think we've got to get this new trial started now, before she's too far gone."

"So, when will you go?"

"As soon as I can make arrangements. Maybe as early as Sunday."

"That's only three days away."

"Yes, it is." Vincent folded his hands, leaning his chin on them as he put his elbows to his knees and stared at the floor. "I was hoping I could leave Libby here with you. We'll be gone for a while, and I'd like to get her right back to school after the break – not disturb her schedule."

"Of course. I'd like to do whatever I can to help."

Vincent turned to me and smiled. "I'm sure you will."

Although I was relieved that Gretchen didn't throw another fit over her father's announcement, I was also troubled – afraid that she was quickly losing what little sense she still had of her environment. As sad as it was, I found myself conflicted: Should I wish for her coherence so she can both know and agonize over her situation, or do I pray her into oblivion?

We sat there, silent, and I considered the future as well as the past.

"Thank you, Vincent…" I told him. "…for bringing me into your home and your family, and for believing in me."

Vincent studied his palms then rubbed his hands. "You know, one thing I always admired about my son was that he was a good judge of people's character." Lowering his hands, he looked at me. "Abel had such a grand opinion of you, spoke of you with such high regard, that I knew you were someone I could trust."

My face burned, flushed with embarrassment as I fought back tears. "Well, I'm not sure why he thought so highly of me when I'm such a simple, average person."

Vincent looked upon his daughter as he rubbed her cheek. "I've seen the care you've given my daughter, and I know that takes more than an average person." He looked to me. "Yes, you are simple, but in such a decent way, Carly. You're honest and principled – always stay simple like that, and don't ever let others corrupt your standard of decency."

I gazed at Gretchen, petting her disheveled hair. It broke my heart to see her helplessness. "It's been my pleasure, sir. Just wish I could do more for her – could've done more for Abel."

"And don't go carrying around regret, Carly. We all have ours, but life's too short to be dwelling on it." Then turning from me, he gazed out the back window into the darkness. "If you've made mistakes, as we sometimes do, then accept the consequences and just move on, doing the best you can to do what you think is right."

I didn't respond. Instead I turned my gaze to the view before Gretchen, looking outside at the beautiful cool blue highlights created by the moon's reflection against the snow. In the yard, the blue color was satiny smooth, dotted with the tiniest of sparkles that seemed to twinkle with the wind. Further out, though, the terrain turned rugged where snow had fallen on the peaks formed by the collision of wind-driven ice flows. The tones of blue were much darker there, filled with shadows that continued outward until the deepest blue went black, finally disappearing into the distance.

I could hear the wind howling, picking up speed as it blew in from the big lake. And I could hear the chatter between Libby and Rafae, growing louder and happier, drowning out the steadily decreasing whimpers coming from Gretchen as time marched on.

Then the foyer door opened and Libby walked in, carrying a plate full of cookies. "Okay, Mommy. We're ready for you to look at what we picked out."

Rafae came in behind her, a fistful of carrots in one hand and grabbing the glass of milk from the counter with the other. "Come on, pretty lady." He came up behind Gretchen's chair, speaking gently as he tried to coax her to peaceably respond. "We want to know if these cookies will get us the biggest, bestest gifts. Right, Libby?"

"Right, Rafae!" Libby eagerly shouted, holding the plate in front of her mother for her to see.

Gretchen's arms lunged uncontrollably forward, knocking the plate from Libby's hands as her mother convulsed into another frenzy of spasms. Libby jumped back, cowering from her mother's gurgles and shrieks as the rest of us reached for Gretchen, trying to steady her. But it was too late. She thrashed so wildly that she quickly slid out of her seat, continuing her rabid tantrum on the floor. Again there was no consoling her, so we waited for her seizing to subside before trying to upright her again.

"There you go, beautiful." Rafae cautiously cradled her as he struggled to tuck her back into the wheelchair. "Let's try to get you back in your driver's seat."

Vincent took hold of the chair handles, backing up his daughter and heading for the bedrooms. "Guess you've had all the commotion you can take for one night. Let's get you to bed."

When I looked for Libby, I found her huddled beside the couch, tears quietly streaming down her cheeks. I went to her, crouching down and cuddling her.

She wiped her tears on her sleeve. "Mommy's going to get coal in her stocking, isn't she?" More tears fell as she began to sob.

"Oh, no, no, no." I rocked her back and forth in my arms, stroking her head. "That won't happen, Libby. Santa understands that your mom is sick and that she can't help it when she gets like that."

Libby looked up at me, sniffling. "Then, I'll get coal."

"What makes you think that?"

"Because it's my fault. I'm the one that keeps on making Mommy mad," she whimpered.

"No you're not, sweetheart," I whispered to her, snuggling her closer. "I know it's hard for you to understand, but she's not acting like this because of you. She's just frustrated because her body can't do what she wants it to. So, there's no one to blame for your mom getting mad, or for her getting sick. Sometimes it's nobody's fault when these things happen, and I'm sure Santa will understand."

She rubbed her eyes with her fists. "So... nobody's getting coal?"

I tapped her nose with my forefinger. "Absolutely no one."

Rafae found us and knelt at our side. "Not even me?"

"Not even you!" I smiled at Rafae, so grateful for all of his help with the girls and his efforts to try and keep us in good spirits. I snuggled with Libby, my chin on the top of her head as I gazed at Rafae. In the deep recesses of his charming face, I could find no shadow of a bigot, or a kidnapper, or a killer. I found only a sensitive soul who was determined to help this woeful family make it through a most heart-wrenching holiday.

Now certain that he couldn't be guilty of any crime, I repeated myself with total confidence: "Not even you."

Chapter 34

A BREAKTHROUGH

"NO VACANCY" GLOWED IN NEON barely visible under the dusting of new snow that blanketed the Landings' marquee. The sign seemed misleading as it implied we were full to capacity, but quite the contrary, the place stood nearly vacant but for the seven of us remaining – and that number was about to drop by two.

Leila pointed at the sign through the front window. "I don't understand why you're botheron' wid turnon' on dot light, ennaway. It's not like we're go-on' te hov a bunch 'a de Fudgies lookon' for rooms now dot de storm socked us in. Nobody'll be tryon' te get to dis islond right now."

I picked up the magazines scattered on the foyer coffee table, straightening them before putting them back down as I tidied up the place. "But it's supposed to clear up a bit today, so some fools will fly in here and get stuck when bad weather comes rolling back in tonight. Then they'll need a room, and you know there are other places they can stay, Leila. I just don't want to deal with telling people where else they can go, how to get there, and why they can't stay here. No, not today."

"Bot Rosie ond I'll be here. We con tell dem to leave."

"I said I just don't want to deal with it!"

I'd been moody the past few days, maybe suffering from the after-Christmas blues, or just the winter blues, or maybe even the plain old I-feel-so-badly-for-this-family blues. Christmas day had been miraculously wonderful – just what the Hanika's had deserved. But since then, things had been tense. Vincent became impatient with the uncooperative weather, growing more and more desperate to get Gretchen on a flight out with each passing day. Gretchen continued her outbursts and seizing; it was a sight that pained us all to see, but it was likely taking its greatest toll on Libby.

Vincent had arranged a medical flight that was on stand-by, explaining that it was well equipped and manned by two medical technicians who would be best able to get Gretchen as comfortably as possible to their destination. Now all they needed was a break in this weather.

"I think today's finally our day." He pulled his suitcases into the foyer. "Maybe you can help me move Gretchen's bags out here, too."

"Glad to," I answered, heading back toward her room.

Vincent followed me. "I'd like to get everything ready to go out the door. When this begins to let up, I want to be able to just call those cab guys with their snowmobiles to come and load up, then get us over to the airport as quick as possible."

Sub-zero temperatures had blown into the area earlier than usual, causing sheets of ice to form and shift in the Straits until the protected harbors of Lake Huron were firmly iced over. Only the freighters could now brave the treacherous winter water, and soon even some of them would find themselves locked in the ice, unable to break free without the help of the nearby Coast Guard Ice Breaker Mackinaw. For now, commerce was the only business of the Upper Great Lakes. The rest of the ships were docked for the long winter season.

With all of the ferries shut down, aircraft became the only means of transportation off the island. Once the ice was thick enough, a snow bridge would be marked with leftover Christmas trees augered into the ice, plotting a trail where the snowmobilers could safely travel between the island and the mainland. But for the time being, it remained too risky.

Everyone had been stuck on the island for four days since Christmas. This relentless winter storm kept all the planes grounded, so it verged on miraculous when the weather finally cleared well enough for Vincent and Gretchen to depart. Some roads still weren't plowed and were blocked to carriages, so Vincent had opted to travel to the airport by snowmobile.

The cab guys brought a special sled attachment on the back of one snowmobile that they used to transport Gretchen. Then another sled was used to haul luggage while a third towed Libby behind me as I rode piggy-back with one of the cab guys. It was a quick but frigid ride, making our way over snow banks and around fallen limbs as I thought about how glad I was that we hadn't tried a carriage. Once at the airport, the men placed Gretchen on a gurney so they could get her into the turbo prop Saab on the runway.

Vincent lifted a piece of his luggage off from a sled. "I left those numbers and addresses by the phone, Carly, so you can get a hold of me anytime you need me. I also left an envelope marked for Doc right next to the numbers."

I picked up the next suitcase, handing it over toward him. "I saw where you put them."

"Make sure Doc remembers to take that envelope when he stops by. He may not come right away since Gretchen's gone, but it's important that you get it to him when he comes the next time."

"I'll take care of it," I promised.

Vincent handed the last of the bags to a crewman, helping him finish with loading everything into the cargo hold. Then he went over to Libby who was bundled up and tucked into one of the attached sleds. He yelled to her so she could hear him over the loud revving of the plane's engine. "I promise I'll take good care of your mom while we're gone – just like I always do – and we'll get back just as soon as we can."

Libby said nothing. She just looked at her grandfather, her eyes squinting and her nose red from the cold.

He leaned over, embracing Libby in a big bear hug. "Now you take good care of Carly, and I'm sure she'll watch over you, too. I love you." Kissing her pink cheeks, he then turned and boarded the plane.

As the plane prepped for departure, the two cabbies that had transported Vincent, Gretchen, and their luggage to the airport left for their next destination, leaving one cabby behind to take us home. With Libby already in his pull-behind sled, the cabby helped me onto the back of his snowmobile and then drove us a safe distance from the plane. He stopped and parked sideways, allowing us to watch the plane taxi and then take off. As it climbed with ease toward a break in the clouds, I turned back to see Libby as she kissed her mitten and threw her hand toward the sky, a final farewell as the plane disappeared from our view.

I hopped off the back of the snowmobile and walked back to Libby, double-checking to make sure she was wrapped up warmly and secured for the journey home. "We'll head back, now. Are you all set?"

Libby nodded. "I miss them already."

"I do, too." I tightened her scarf. "But they wouldn't want us moping, so when we get back, I've got a bunch of ideas for fun things to do. Just hold on tight 'til we get back!"

I had to do some quick thinking on the short ride back, compiling a mental list of activities to keep us busy. When we made it back home, we stayed outside to build a snow fort and then launched snow balls at the occasional unsuspecting passers by. With our hands growing cold, we headed in to warm up with mugs of hot chocolate dotted with mini-marshmallows while playing a few rounds of Pop-O-Matic Trouble.

"I'm home!" I cheered as I finally struck the right roll to get my last game piece into my home base. "Wow. So I finally beat you."

I don't know if it was just because she had lost or because we had just finished our fourth round, but Libby had had enough. "Okay, what's next?"

"Sorry, young lady, but I'm all gamed out." I felt I'd done enough distracting and now it was time to get into the new routine that would be our life until Gretchen and Vincent returned. "Guess it's time to get to the real life stuff."

"Aw. Do we have to?"

"Yes, we have to, but it won't be so bad. Besides, we can try and make a bit of a game of the work, too, I suppose."

The plan to make chores into a game worked fairly well at first as Libby saw cooking and laundry as tasks that weren't so unpleasant. However, when I suggested that we play "clean the bathroom," her interest in games suddenly lost its appeal and she retreated to her room to read and play alone with her dolls.

And so went the hours as they rolled into days of the mundane, the lousy weather taking its toll on our mood. We were pretty much housebound through New Years Day, and all of us longed for enough sunshine to save us from an interminable bout of cabin fever.

Hope of a cure arrived on Sunday, the last day of vacation before Libby was to return to her small island school. On that morning, we awoke to the awesome sight of Jack Frost's finest art – matchless symmetrical etchings of glistening ice sketched on our window panes, further illuminated by the warm, refreshing light of the brilliant sunrise. The snow had stopped, the skies had cleared, and the dawn was beckoning us to come and play.

Libby was up early, bounding toward the back door with newfound enthusiasm. "Let's make more snow angels! It's perfect outside." She grabbed her mittens.

"Not quite perfect." I pointed out through a clear patch on the glass to the thermometer mounted on the window frame. "It's six below zero."

"But the sun will keep us warm."

"Not warm enough, I'm afraid. But if we give it a little time, the sun should bring up the temperature, and then we can go out."

"Oh, come on, Carly." Libby frowned.

"Tell you what. Let's fix breakfast, then we can check the thermometer again after we eat and clean up."

Although the proposition of more housework didn't please her, she reluctantly agreed to the plan. However, her definition of breakfast was a quick Pop Tart on a paper plate, and then she'd be out the door. Most mornings, I would have welcomed the request for such a simple meal, but it wouldn't do today when I was trying to buy time for it to warm up outside. I insisted we fix pancakes for us as well as the tenants, and so she moped about the kitchen gathering up the necessary ingredients for me and then setting the table while I mixed up the batter.

When all was prepared, I turned on the griddle then brushed off my hands. "Okay, you can go invite the others to come now."

Libby smiled. "Okay!" She dashed off, the bounce now back in her step.

I had enough time to make a half-dozen pancakes before Libby returned with Leila and Rosie in tow.

Rosie wore her usual moo-moo and had her hair wrapped up in a turban. "Whot a nice sarprise for us, you hovon' such a lovely meal te start dis sunny day!" She smiled, her eyes looking a bit puffy.

Libby tugged on my shirt. "Deke said he'd be a few minutes getting around." She grinned up at me, displaying her missing teeth. "He brought Mocha over here last night!"

Leila plopped herself down at the table, elbows up as she cradled her chin in her palms. "Oh, yes'm. Dot dog con make a whole lotta whine-on' noisos."

"No, that was Asa." Libby walked to the table and pulled up in a seat beside her. "He tied Mocha up to Asa's dog house and brought Asa in to sleep with him."

Rosie pulled her chair out far enough to make room for her to maneuver herself into it. "Now, why would dot boy wanna do someton' like dot?"

Libby was still grinning as she reached for the plateful of pancakes. "He said that Mocha was sick." She used her fingers to take two pancakes from the stack on the table.

"Wait." Rosie scowled. "Dot dos *not* make sense."

"Yes it does." Libby plopped the pancakes on her plate. "You wouldn't want Mocha barfing in the hotel, would you?"

Rosie's eyes bulged as she pinched her nose. "Oh! Tonk you for sharon' dot foct wid us."

I added six more hot pancakes to the top of the stack. "Well, I hope Mocha's okay."

"She's fine." Deke strolled in with Asa at his heels, the dog dashing up to the table to beg for scraps as Deke took the last seat at the table. "Thanks for the breakfast invite, Carly."

"No problem." I poured more batter on the griddle. "So, what's the deal with Mocha?"

"She broke into Dad's feed barn and ate a bunch of pigs' ears — too dumb to know when to stop."

Leila lifted her head and picked up the serving plate. "Ond too dumb to know when to stop all 'a dot whine-on'." Taking two pancakes for herself, she passed them on to Deke.

Deke took the plate. "Oh, that wasn't Mocha. That —"

"It was Asa." Her mouth full of pancakes, Libby didn't wait to swallow before interrupting. "I already told you that."

As if on queue, Asa looked up at Leila, licking his chops before reverting back to panting.

Deke took three pancakes from the serving plate before setting it down by Rosie. "Could you ladies hear him carrying on?"

"All dot whimperon', you bet we heard it!" Rosie stabbed the next four pancakes with her fork and dragged them to her own plate. The bottom pancake slid off her fork, falling to the table and then to the floor where Asa quickly dashed over and devoured it.

"Well, I'm sorry about that." Deke reached for the butter. "I thought I was the only one he was keeping up."

Leila glared at Deke as she poured maple syrup on her pancakes. "Whot wos dot dog's problum, ennaway?"

"Syrup, please," Deke politely requested, and Leila somewhat grudgingly turned it over to him. He poured a small pool to the side of his pancakes before closing the small jug and setting it down. "Well, Asa was whining because he wanted to go back to his dog house and play with his old buddy, Mocha, but I couldn't leave him out there. They were barking and carrying on, and I needed to let poor Mocha sleep off her pig's ear hangover outside — you know, because I couldn't let her do that in here."

"And why's that?" I asked, piling the last six pancakes on the serving plate before pulling a chair from the side of the room up next to Libby and squeezing in to take a seat.

"Well, because she needed to get rid of all that rawhide somehow." Deke dipped a forkful of pancake in syrup and stuck it in his mouth, chewing it well before continuing. "She kept up-chucking half the night. Tossed most of it up, but I figured she'd have other duty to do as she digested what's left. So, I left her outside to do that. I figure I'll just clean up after her later."

"Well, my belly says donk you for sharon' dot one ovar my breakfost." Leila pushed away her plate of half-eaten pancakes.

Libby immediately seized the plate and cleared it from the table, eager to move along the clean up so she could get outside. As she picked up the syrup jug and went to put it away, she was interrupted from her task by a knock at the door.

"I'll get it." She banged the syrup jug hard against the countertop and dashed into the lobby to answer the door, Asa barking along at her heels. I followed behind to see who would be paying us a visit this early in the morning.

By the time I'd made it to the door, Libby had already pulled it wide open to reveal Rafae standing on the porch. He was warmly outfitted in snow pants and a bulky down-filled jacket accessorized by a matching set of green knit mittens, hat, and scarf. With two sets of ice skates draped over his shoulders, he looked like a Hans Brinker wannabe.

"Good morning, girls! How about joining me in a skate?"

I shook my head "I think it's still too cold out for that."

"Not at all." He smiled, stepping in through the doorway as Asa jumped on him with a greeting. "This is perfect Northern Michigan weather. You've just got to dress for the occasion."

"Yippee!" Libby threw her arms in the air. "Finally, we get to go outside!"

"Not so fast Libby." I tried to hold her off, but she was already out of earshot, back in the kitchen announcing that she was going skating with Rafae.

I looked back at Rafae. "So, where can you even skate around here?"

"What, are you kidding! The island's surrounded by solid ice, and you don't know where to skate?"

"Well, I wasn't sure it's safe."

"Of course, it is! There are spots around the island where it's solid, so they're starting to mark the snow bridge. And over in the harbor there's that break wall that calmed the water enough for it to freeze smooth. With all this cold weather we've had, I bet it's got to be more than a half-foot thick there."

"But it's still too cold for Libby to go out."

Libby returned just in time to hear me, and she scowled. "Oh, come on, Carly!"

Rafae took her side. "Just put on her snow pants, wrap a scarf around her face, and she'll be good to go. Come on – the day's marching on!"

"Well…" I could think of no other objections. "I suppose if you know it's safe, then we can give it a try."

"All right!" Libby cheered. "Come on, Asa." The dog followed as Libby dashed off again to get her winter gear.

Rafae smiled, seeming equally pleased. "Great. Here's a pair I borrowed for you." He grabbed hold of the ties of one pair of skates that were draped across his shoulder and handed them over to me. "Thought you might not have your own skates, so I brought these for you. Hope they're close enough in size. They're eight-and-a-halves."

"I wear nines."

"Perfect."

"How do you figure?" I hesitantly took hold of the skates. "They'll be too tight."

"With ice skates, too tight's a good thing."

"And did you bring a pair for me?" Deke stepped into the lobby, wiping his hands on a napkin.

"Ah, nooo." Rafae cocked his head. "I wasn't aware that I needed to."

Deke crossed his arms across his chest. "That's okay. We can all skate on the lake at the base of the bluff. It's close to my folks' place, and I can quick run and get my skates, and then catch up to you."

Rafae's eyes narrowed. "Don't you have some important vet work you're supposed to do this morning, D-K?"

"Nope. Did more than my fair share all last night." He stretched. "Time to enjoy a day of R&R."

Libby scurried back into the lobby. "I can't find my skates. Bumpa keeps them in my closet, but they're not there."

Rafae stepped forward, taking her by the shoulder and guiding her back into the living quarters. "I'll help you find them, and then we'll get you bundled up. That'll give Carly time to get ready so we can get going." He winked back at me.

"I'm just going to clean up after Mocha and get him back to Dad's kennel before I come out. I'll meet up with you on the ice, then." Deke hustled off in the opposite direction, returning to his room to get ready.

I walked back into the living area where I found Rosie and Leila cleaning up from breakfast.

Rosie stacked the plates. "It's lookon' like you gonna hov your honds full, whot, dealon' wid dose two boys today." She smiled. "You just head on outta here, hov a good time wid Miss Libby."

"Didn't mean to leave you with a mess." I reached for a dirty plate.

"Leave dot! Leila ond I got dis under control. You just go make sure dot garls havon' some fun – keep her mind off her momma, now."

I took her up on her offer and bundled up in my warmest winter gear. Once dressed, I returned to the lobby where I found that Rafae had more than satisfactorily covered Libby from head to foot. There was only one thing missing.

I looked down at the boots on her feet. "Where are your skates?"

"We couldn't find them." Libby smiled. "But it's okay."

"Really?" I couldn't understand why she looked happy about this.

Deke was grinning, too, holding his chin up high as if quite proud of himself. "Right outside this door is the solution, the best thing on blades – a Flexible Flyer.

Libby tapped Rafae's arm. "Could Asa pull me?"

"If it makes you happy, I don't see why not."

With a couple of long leashes and a fitted dog harness, we managed to connect Asa to the sled's steering handle. We used a shorter leash to keep the spunky pup under control as we made our way from the Landings along the boardwalks and paths until we finally came to the water's edge.

Rafae and I dusted the snow off a thick piece of driftwood, taking a seat so we could tie on our skates. Then we set out on our blades, skimming along the snow-dusted ice while Rafae kept Asa on the leash with Libby in tow.

We wound our way along the shoreline until we came to the base of the bluff where flights of snow-covered planked steps weaved their way up the side of the cliff. As we waited for Deke to join us, we skated on the rugged surface of the harbor where most of the snow had been windswept away to the shore.

"It's a little bumpy here." I struggled a bit to maintain my balance.

Rafae laughed. "That's what you get when nature makes the ice. It's not like we can bring a Zamboni out on the lake." He leaned to his left, skating a circle around me while guiding Asa along with Libby squealing in delight.

"Show off." I stopped, watching them circle around me. "I didn't expect any Zamboni, but these bumps are slowing me down."

Rafae cut in, scraping ice with the sides of his blade to make a quick stop. "Trust me. This is smooth in comparison to how it can get out here."

"I believe you." I carefully pushed off, gliding slowly.

Rafae pushed off with more force, skating fluidly as he guided Asa along. He formed broad curves that he tightened as Libby's squeals escalated. Then with a swifter, tighter turn, Rafae brought Asa about and sent the sled skidding sideways at a speed fast enough to toss Libby from the sled and send her somersaulting across the ice.

"Whoa!" Rafae dug in his skate to abruptly stop.

"What are you doing!" I reprimanded him as I klutzily skated over to retrieve Libby.

Rafae got to her first. "Are you okay?"

Rolling her over, I pushed her snow-covered scarf off her face to reveal that she was half crying and half giggling from the reckless tumble.

Rafae pulled off his gloves and brushed the snow from her cheeks. "Want to try that one again?"

She smiled but shook her head.

"I think she's had enough of that," I told him.

"Oh, come on!" He pulled her upright, placing her back on the sled. "You were having fun going fast."

She laughed.

I pulled the scarf back up over her face. "She's had enough speed, Rafae. Just take it easy so she doesn't get hurt."

"She won't get hurt," Rafae assured me. Reaching under his coat, he unbuckled the leather belt from his jeans and then slid it out of his pant loops. He held it by the buckle, dangling it in front of Libby. "Look, I can keep you strapped on with this."

I laughed. "You're going to lose your pants over this?"

He handed me the leash to restrain Asa, ignoring me as he ran his belt through the runners under the Flexible Flyer.

Libby's anxious eyes peeked out over the top of the scarf tied over her nose and mouth. "I don't want to fall off again. If I get hurt, then I can't hang on the monkey bars when I go back to school tomorrow."

"So, you're not going to fall off, I promise." He finished threading the strap through the belt buckle and brought the ends up and over her. "There's no way you can, now that I've got you strapped in here."

"Are you sure?" Libby gave a nervous laugh.

Rafae tightened the strap over Libby's lap and buckled it. "Now I'm sure." With his index finger he tapped at her scarf right where it covered her nose and then gave her a smile.

I wasn't sure about this. "I still think you should keep it slow so the sled doesn't tip. You know, it's possible that —"

"Everything's possible, Carly." Rafae began to put on his gloves. "Relax. It's going to be fine."

Suddenly I saw something out of the corner of my eye — a distant white blur on the horizon, followed by a somewhat larger black blur dashing after it. Before I could turn to figure out what it was, Asa let out two brisk barks and took off in a mad dash toward the faint honking and barking coming from the blurs.

I had no chance to react before Asa dragged me into motion behind him. Unable to maintain my balance on my skates, I tumbled to the ice and lost my grip on Asa's leash. He went dashing after what I now realized was a loose dog who in turn was chasing a low-flying swan. Both followed the bird away from the shore out toward the open water — and Libby was still strapped to the sled in tow.

I quickly fumbled to my feet, frantically attempting to skate after them as fast as I could. Rafae was already well ahead of me, skating madly after them while yelling for Asa to come back. But the dog was caught up in the frenzy of the chase and the sled sped along behind him as Libby's hysterical screams for help moved further away.

When the swan eventually took higher flight, the two dogs abandoned the chase of the bird for the amusement of playing with one another. Their gates slowed a bit, buying us time to gain on them, but then the burly black dog charged away from us again and Asa resumed his pursuit despite our frantic pleas.

Far ahead of me, Rafae came within range of the dogs once they paused again to frolic. The black dog dodged backwards in a zigzag pattern as Asa was easily taunted into further play. When close enough, Rafae madly lunged for Libby, throwing his arms tightly around her from the back of the sled. This sent the black dog scurrying further out toward the thinning ice with Asa now dragging both Libby and Rafae behind him.

"Push off! Push off!" I could hear Rafae yell frantically at Libby as they struggled to free her from the belt that held her to the sled. Rafae was banging and dragging the toes of his skates in an effort to grip the ice with the jagged edges on the fronts of the blades. The sled did seem to be slowing as Asa tired from lugging a heavier load. But then it happened...

"Oh my God!" Still skating, I watched in horror as the black dog broke through the ice and splashed into the frigid water. When the black figure bobbed back to the surface, he frantically clawed at the edges of the ice surrounding him. Try as he might to climb out, his efforts proved futile. His claws could not grip the slick surface and his pawing only cracked and chiseled more ice away from the edge. He whimpered as he paddled to stay afloat.

Although seconds can seem like an eternity at such a moment, it seemed immediate that Asa slowed and backed off, bringing Libby and Rafae almost to a stop behind him. I gained on them, Asa pacing in a small back and forth motion while Libby and Rafae remained seemingly motionless in their place.

As I clumsily skated closer, I could see Rafae grab the limp reins to the dog harness and slip it off the end of the sled's steering handle. With the reins still looped through the dog's harness,

Asa was able to further tug on the sled causing Libby to let out a frightful scream each time the dog yanked to break free.

"Stay Asa!" I futilely yelled at him. Still some fifty yards or more away from them, I tried to skate faster but just ended up falling to the ice. Rolling up on my knees, I struggled back up on my blades and then continued my clumsy pursuit.

After three or four jerks, Asa managed to pull loose from the sled, whimpering somewhat at the plight of his desperate playmate before turning to dash away from the open water.

With Asa no longer tied to the sled, Rafae went about freeing Libby from the belt. He squatted as he cautiously wiggled her backwards off the sled and then shoved the sled away.

"Lie down," he commanded Libby while he slid his legs out from under himself and flattened his stomach to the ice. Then he grabbed Libby's coat sleeve and began dragging her backwards across the ice just as I hurried to reach them.

I was just a few yards from Rafae when he must have heard my skate blades. He quickly turned his head just long enough to yell at me. "Stay back!" Then he turned back to Libby, continuing to cautiously pull her backwards.

I dug in the toes of my skates, the cutting sound echoing across the open lake. Glancing down at my footing, I could see why Rafae spoke with such alarm. The windswept ice below me was devoid of snow, revealing what some call "blue ice" – ice frozen so clear you can see through it. Staring through its transparent surface, I could see an intricate pattern of cracks. Had the cracks been thick, it would have been a good sign that the ice ran deep. But these cracks were thin and were severing the fragile surface that was the only barrier between us and the icy waters below.

"Lie down!" Rafae yelled at me. "But do it carefully!"

I started to turn. "No, I'll back up." I figured we should all make a mad dash for the shore.

"Trust me!" he pleaded. "It'll distribute your weight."

I tried to gingerly lower my knee to the ice, but I was so unnerved with fear that I slipped on my skates and banged both knees into the ice, breaking slightly through the surface. As the frigid water pooled and soaked into my snow pants, I remained in a doggie position, the palms of my gloves pressed to the damp ice, waiting for Rafae to tell me what to do next. In the stillness, I could hear both the dog and Libby whimpering.

"I've got you, Libby." Rafae continued to slide her along with him as he backed up toward the shore. "Carly, slowly slide your arms forward."

I cautiously thrust my arms ahead of me and reached out as far as I could. As I slid, I heard the faint crackling of the ice snapping and stiffened at the thought of plunging through the surface at any moment. But I managed to flatten myself out without further breaking the hole under my knees, and so I pressed onward.

"Roll over," Rafae yelled directions. "Get your knees out of the hole. Then use those jagged toes on your blades to push away."

I rolled first on to my back and then kept on rolling as I returned to my stomach before attempting my first push off. The process seemed too slow for such a perilous situation, but I placed my trust in Rafae.

Libby's whimpers were growing louder. "It's cracking!" she yelled. "I can hear it!"

"You're doing great!" Rafae's voice remained confident and steady. "Just try to lie still and let me do the work."

But Libby's anxiety was getting the better of her as she continued to pull her knees toward her chest and then push off with her blades. Finally I heard that dreaded sound, an almost simultaneous crack and then splash, further accentuated by Libby's scream. I cocked my head and caught a glimpse of Libby, the lower half of her body dropping into the water.

Her high-pitched shriek echoed outward toward the shore as well as the open water.

Rafae maintained his hold on her. "Hold on! Hold on! Don't squirm or you'll break more ice."

"It's cold!" she shrieked, continuing to thrash in a frenzy.

I watched helplessly as Rafae tugged at Libby's arms, trying to free her from the waters. But with each pull, the ice did in fact further break away, and now Rafae was in danger of going in, as well.

Then from out of nowhere, a miracle arrived in the form of a bright orange extension cord tossed out to the two struggling at the water's edge.

"Grab it, Libby!" came Deke's voice. I turned back to find him and an elderly man standing back on more solid ice, the other end of the lifeline gripped firmly in Deke's hands. "Hold on and we'll pull you out."

Rafae handed the cord to Libby. "You can do this, Libby. Just don't let go!" he coaxed her.

With wet mittens, she grasped hold of the cord, and with just a couple yanks, they managed to pull her free of the water. Deke and the older man continued to pull, dragging Libby to them. The elderly man took Libby into his arms, keeping her close to him as he stripped her of her wet clothes.

Deke had looped the cord in his hands, holding it like a lasso. "Rafae, heads up." He started swinging the cord, preparing to throw it back out to Rafae.

Rafae slid back slightly away from the hole in the ice. "I'm fine here. Toss it to Carly first and get her off."

Before I could object, Deke turned the spinning motion of the cord toward me and tossed the line in my direction.

The cord slapped against the ice a couple of feet from my side. As I reached for it, I heard a cracking sound from Rafae's direction. I glanced at him, frozen in place.

Grabbing the cord, I turned to yell back at Deke. "You should get Rafae first. He's on the edge. He's going to go in."

"No time to argue." Deke jerked on the cord, pulling me toward him. "Just hold on and we'll get him next."

I heard another cracking sound behind me and looked back to see Rafae still lying flat to the ice, still as could be. "I'm okay." He tried to assure me, but I wasn't convinced.

Once on firmer ice, I released my grasp on the cord. Deke had already wound it back into a lasso, looping it as he had pulled me in, and now rocked it back and forth as he prepared for his final toss.

"It's coming at you, Raf." With a heavy heave, Deke threw the line at Rafae. Much of it landed with a splash in the hole Libby had left behind, but Rafae managed to fish the line over from the edge as Deke began to reel it back in.

With a snap, Rafae's upper body tilted downward; the ice below him began to give way. "Let's make this happen, DK!" He wrapped the cord tightly about his wrist, gripping it with both hands as he waited for Deke to save him.

Deke gave a tug and pulled him partially from his reclined position, but Rafae's weight and the new angle of his body was making him now harder to pull from the hole. I still had on my skates but figured I could help, so I grabbed the excess cord and dug in with my blades, helping Deke to pull again.

It took only a couple of heaves to get him up from the decline and back on to flat ice. I helped with one more pull but managed only to slip and fall to the ice.

Deke leaned backward, tugging the cord toward himself while taking a few steps backward to finally pull Rafae to more solid ice.

Rafae pulled himself upright. "Thanks, man," he panted, steam billowing from his open mouth. "Libby's okay?"

Seeing that Rafae was safe, I turned towards Libby who was wrapped in the elderly man's coat and snuggled in his arms. Quickly I climbed up from my seat on the ice and skated over to her.

Her face was so pale, tinged with blue, and her lips were purple. "Where's Asa?" she asked through chattering teeth.

I placed my palm against her ice-cold cheek. "He high-tailed it for shore – probably home by now, honey."

"What about that other dog?" she chattered.

The elderly man hugged her reassuringly. "He ran home, too. Bet he knows he's in a boatload of trouble." His words were believable enough to console Libby, but I could see his expression and knew this was not the case.

I brushed back Libby's bangs so I could look into her eyes. "We've got to get you warmed up."

Bundling up Libby more tightly in his coat, the elderly man managed to lift her. "You're wet and still on skates, so Deke can get her." He rubbed Libby's back through the coat. "She's doing better now that we got her wet things off, but she needs something to cover her legs."

"Here's my coat." Deke offered, slipping off his down parka and wrapping it around her legs. He also took off his gloves and set about slipping one loosely over her tiny foot.

Rafae joined us, slipping off his gloves and scarf. "I've got nothing to give you, Libby. Sorry, but my stuff's soaking wet." He squeezed the water out of them.

Deke placed his remaining glove over Libby's other foot. "We've got her covered, Raf."

The elderly man passed off Libby. "Deke, you run her right back to the house, get out the blankets and warm her quick as you can."

With Rafae and I still on skates, Deke carrying Libby, and the elderly man walking at a steady gate, we all made it to the foot of the bluff within a couple of minutes. But as Deke mounted the stairs and climbed upward with Libby in his arms, I realized Rafae and I couldn't make the quick ascent with ice skates strapped to our feet. We no longer had our boots as we'd left them off in the distance by the driftwood log where we'd put on our skates, and now was not the time to go retrieve them. So, we'd either have to clumsily climb the steps while balancing on our blades or pause to unlace and remove our skates before making a mad dash in stocking feet through the ice and snow still remaining on the steps. I was reaching for my laces to go for the latter when the elderly man gently took hold of my arm to stop me.

"She's going to be all right." His green eyes twinkled, his slight grin reassuring. "Deke will get her up there quick enough, so don't get yourself hurt racing up there." He released my arm and began his own ascent, still talking back to me. "Keep your skates on, but be careful. She needs you to be okay, too."

Following the man's suggestion, I grabbed the right-hand rail and began the upward climb. Wrapping my left arm snuggly around my chest, I tried in vain to warm my cold, wet body. My teeth chattered as I dug my skate blades deep into the snow with each step.

Half way up the first flight, I glanced back at Rafae. "You're coming along?"

He was also holding firmly to the rail, steadying himself as he gradually made his way up the stairs. "I'm right behind you." His voice quivered and his teeth chattered.

I stopped. "Go ahead of me so I can make sure you make it up there all right."

"I'm fine." He lifted his eyes, taking five or six quick steps to come up right behind me. "Just keep moving and I'll make sure *you* get up there okay." Then he wacked my behind.

I turned my focus back to the stairs ahead, noticing that the elderly man was a couple of flights ahead and that Deke had already made it to the top. Although aware that Libby was now a short distance from the warmth of the Kavanaugh house, I'd find no relief for my concern until I finally saw the pink return to Libby's cheeks. So, I dug in deep and stepped quickly, urging Rafae to keep up the pace. With my whole body freezing and my legs aching from each stilted stride, adrenaline pushed me forward and I refused to pause until I reached the summit.

Chapter 35

BETTER JUDGMENT

"I CAN'T IMAGINE WHAT POSSESSED YOU to go out there so far!" Deke held the door for Rafae, reprimanding him as he entered the Kavanaugh's home. "Didn't you see how thin that ice was? How could you do something so stupid? You all could have drowned!"

"Hey, yeah, thanks for pointing out the obvious, Geek!" Rafae slapped Deke on the shoulder and then crossed his arms tightly across his chest, still chattering. "I might not have known we were in danger if you hadn't pointed it out."

Still holding the door, Deke turned to me. "You need to get in here and warm up."

I stepped in through the doorway, still in my skates, and clumsily trudged a few steps down the long hallway.

Deke came up behind me. "What kept you from getting Libby off that sled?"

"That was my doing," Rafae answered as he took a seat on the staircase, stripping off some of his wet clothing before starting to untie his skates.

I turned back to Deke. "I let him strap her on the sled with his belt so she wouldn't keep falling off."

Deke shook his head. "I can't believe you'd let him do something so dumb."

Rafae glared at him as he pulled off one skate. "Gee, well, I'm sorry I'm not as wise as you!"

Deke took a step toward Rafae as he threw his arms up in the air. "Hey, it doesn't take a lot of smarts to see that was an accident just waiting to happen."

"Well, I guess I'm not all-knowing and all-seeing like you apparently are!" Rafae pulled off the other skate and stood up. "What, now you can predict accidents before they happen?"

"Just cut it out you two!" I snapped. "It was just an honest mistake."

Deke turned back to me. "And is that what you're going to tell her mother, and her grandfather?"

"We'll tell them the truth." Rafae stepped over to the hallway closet, pulling it open and helping himself to one of Deke's jackets. "And I'm sure they'll be more understanding than you ever could be."

"Well, I just don't want to see Vincent feel that he's got to come back here." Deke looked at me as he headed for the living area. "He's already got enough to worry about without also worrying about whether Carly can take care of Libby and keep her safe."

I felt heat returning to my face, my voice rising. "That family trusts me to take care of her, and that's exactly what I intend to do!" I turned away from Deke, plodding the rest of the way down the runner and into the living room. There I found Libby bundled up on a couch, flanked by members of the Kavanaugh household.

Traipsing up to the couch, I tilted my skates on their sides and managed to sit on the floor beside her. "How're you doing?"

"I'm okay now." She no longer chattered but her lips were still purple.

Nana Maeve, who was sitting on the couch at her feet, adjusted the blankets that were swaddled around Libby. "I think she's warming up nicely."

The younger Mrs. Kavanaugh sat upright directly across from us. Alone at one end of a loveseat, she wore a simple brown dress, her legs in taupe stockings and crossed properly at her ankles. Her hands were clasped and pressed firmly to one side of her lap. "Could you please slip off those skates, Carly?" She nodded her head toward my feet. "They're cutting up the rugs, and I'm sure you already gouged the wood floors."

"Oh, of course." I quickly pulled at the laces.

Maeve scowled at her daughter-in-law. "Could you give it a rest, Connie! We have better things to be concerned with than the floor."

Mrs. Kavanaugh smoothed out the fabric of her dress. "Well, the urgency of this dreadful event seems to have passed – Libby seems all right now, and so I just thought she might have the common courtesy to remove those blades before walking in here on my good rugs."

"I'm very sorry," I apologized, sliding my feet out of the skates.

Maeve slid forward in her seat, her eyes narrowing. "But Connie, you forget once again that they're not *your* rugs – they're *my* rugs. And if she wants to cut them up she can go ahead, because I don't really give a damn!"

Hailey the housekeeper entered the room just in time to break up the feud. "I hov de hot cidar for you, little miss." He handed a steaming mug toward Libby. "Dot's pretty hot, so blow on it ond just sip."

I helped Libby sit up so she could take hold of the mug. As directed, she blew on it then attempted a swig. She winced. "It's still too hot, Hailey."

Rafae stood in the archway from the hall. "Well, Libby! I thought you'd *never* say something was too hot after the dunk you took in that freezing water." He smiled at her, then turned to his father. "Thanks for getting her that, Dad."

Hailey looked sternly at his son, giving him no reply or gesture in response. He just took a couple of steps back from the couch, moving nearer to the kitchen where he took up post, appearing to be waiting for his next directive.

Constance Kavanaugh shook her finger at Libby. "Your Bumpa will be very upset to hear you were on that ice. I'm sure he taught you better than that." She then turned to look at Rafae. "And I thought we taught you better than that, too."

Rafae held out his hands and shrugged. "What? We just went skating and the ice was fine where we started!"

Maeve rolled her eyes. "Oh, for Pete's sake, Connie! You know perfectly well that the ice inland was just as safe as can be, and they had no way of knowing what was going to happen. Why, your own son was on his way out there to skate, too. Weren't you, Deke-my-boy?"

Deke took a seat in a side chair, nodding toward his grandmother. "I suppose so, Nana."

"See? There you have it." Maeve nodded back at her grandson. "You're a smart boy, Deke, and you could have just as easily been out there when this happened. We just need to be glad that everyone's all right."

Constance stood up, her chin held high. "Well, just the same, I think we should inform Vincent and let him be the judge of whether the right decisions are being made for Libby."

I looked up at her. "Oh, yes, I plan to call him. I hate to worry him, but he and Gretchen should know what happened."

"You should use our phone." Constance flagged her hand toward Hailey, a gesture intended to direct him to see me to the kitchen.

Hailey must have comprehended the gesture as he stepped over and leaned toward me. "If you'd come olong wid me, Miss Carly, I'd be hoppy to show you de phone."

I smiled at Hailey. "Thanks, but I don't have the number with me. It's back at the Landings by the phone there."

He then backed away, returning to his post.

Constance sighed. "Well, we don't have his current arrangements here, so you'll just have to run back there and call. But you best do it right away, Carly. I think Libby's family deserves to know immediately what's happened so they can decide what else should be done in her best interest."

"I think I can go with you." Libby threw back one side of her blanket and started to crawl out of her bundling. "I'm much better now, so I want to go home."

"Oh, no you don't!" Maeve pushed her right back in place and tightened the blanket back around her. "We'll get you home in a little while, but not yet."

Constance stepped over to Libby, reaching down with two fingers to push loose strands of hair to the sides of her face. "But maybe she shouldn't go back for now, at least not until Vincent returns. I think it might be best for her to stay here in Nana Maeve's care."

"Of course, you would think that!" Maeve scowled at her daughter-in-law. "And I suppose you'd also think it best for Deke to move back here, too."

Constance smiled at her son. "Well, yes, he could. You know, Carly's a big girl and she can take care of the place with those Saints she's keeping company with."

Deke cocked his head and squinted with an expression of uncertainty. "But I just settled in over there, mother, and now you want me to turn around and move back here?"

"Oh, yes she does, and I'll tell you why." Nana Maeve leaned back, crossing her arms. "Your mom wants to be back in control, have you back here under her watchful eye so she can tell you how to live your life."

"What utter nonsense!" Constance scoffed.

"Really?" Maeve replied. "Well, I'll have you know that I'm not some feeble-minded fool that can't see what you're up to."

"Don't get yourself upset, Nana." Deke stood up and stepped behind his grandmother, reaching over to gently rub her shoulder. "I know it's best for me to stay put at the Landings – at least for now."

"But you're needed here," Constance insisted. "Your father needs you, I need you, and God knows those dogs need you, too."

For the first time, I noticed the distant howling of dogs, probably coming from the kennel out back.

Deke backed up toward the entryway. "Asa's probably wandered back and gotten the pack all worked up. I'll go see about it, Mother – get them settled down before Dad gets back." He turned and left.

"Good boy!" Nana Maeve yelled after him, then turned on her daughter-in-law. "But I've got news for you, Constance. When this little girl's warmed up, she's also going back to the Landings, right where she and Deke belong. So, you stop your meddling and keep your nose out of other people's business."

"Wow!" Rafae smiled, his dark eyes popped wide open. "You still call 'um like you see 'um, don't you Nana! Well, tell you what…" He stepped toward her. "How about *I* run back to the Landings and get the number so Carly can stay here with Libby. Why, I can even just give Vincent a call right from there and tell him what's happened."

"No." I shook my head. "I'm the one who's responsible for Libby, so I should be the one to call."

"Please don't leave, Carly." Libby frowned, grabbing my arm and anxiously holding it. "I want you to stay here."

"See, you're needed here." Rafae nodded toward Libby. "I'll just borrow some boots to go get ours by the driftwood, and then I'll run over to the Landings, get the number, and run it back here for you to call. How's that sound?"

"Fine!" Maeve scooted forward, struggling a bit to stand up from her seat. "You go get the damn number, Rafae, and get it back here before Constance has another conniption fit!"

"I'll do no such thing!" Constance huffed.

Loosening Libby's grip, I pulled the Landings' master key from my damp pants' pocket and tossed it toward Rafae.

Missing his catch, he retrieved the key from the floor and then turned to Maeve. "Yes, ma'am!" He feigned a brisk salute before departing the room.

"Don't you 'yes ma'am' me, Rafae!" Maeve took hold of the walking stick leaning at her side and pushed herself up from her seat. Then she waddled after Rafae as she wheeled the stick like a weapon, swatting in his general direction. "You come back here, you smart aleck! Never let you talk that way to me before, and I'm sure as hell not going to let you start now."

"Guess I better go save Rafae before she clocks him with that lethal weapon," the elderly man who'd helped us off the ice said quietly. He stepped forward from a shadowed corner near the kitchen doorway, a place where he had stood unnoticed by me until now. With a confident gait, he walked out of the room in pursuit of the two.

Constance motioned her hand toward the departing man as she spoke to Hailey in a barely audible voice. "Why is *he* still down here?"

Hailey cocked his head at her, replying in a level voice. "Why, he wos makon' sure de little garl wos go-on' te be all right, o'course."

"Well, she's obviously fine," she snapped back. "So you need to go make sure he gets back where he belongs."

"Yoss, mom." He dipped his head in an ever-so-slight bow. As he turned from her, though, I caught a glimpse of him rolling his eyes.

I looked at Libby, "Do you know that older man?"

"Don't be concerned with him," Constance interjected. He's just an old ninny, that's who he is."

"No, he's not," Libby giggled. "Bumpa says he's a great man – calls him Captain even though Bumpa says he's not a real one."

Constance scowled at Libby. "He certainly is *not* a real captain, and there is nothing great about him." She plucked the cocoa mug out of Libby's hand. "You shouldn't drink this in here. You might spill it on the new upholstery." With the mug in her hand, Constance stormed out of the room.

I waited for her to leave before whispering to Libby. "Is he Nolan Kavanaugh?"

"I can't remember his whole name, but I think it was something like that," she answered. "Bumpa says he saved some boys from a ship that was sinking."

"The *Perseverance*." I recalled the story of the ill-fated voyage that had taken the lives of this man's father and brother, and a number of young boys who were left behind. But Libby was right – this man hadn't taken lives, but rather, he had saved some. And today, he had helped to save our lives, as well.

"I almost never see him," Libby added. "Nana Maeve says he gets kind of sad sometimes, probably because he's real old and doesn't go out on the water anymore. She told me he pretty much just stays home most of the time."

"Well, I can see that," I replied, remembering the day when I thought I saw him peering out from the upper window of the carriage house and looking out over the water.

"But I think he should go out more." Libby sat upright, pushing her blanket to the side. I was pleased to see the color returning to her cheeks, the pink coming back to her lips.

I rubbed her back. "Well, he came out today, even in the cold."

"Yeah, he did!" Libby smiled. "All the kids at school say he's a hermit, but when I go back I'm going to tell them he's not a hermit at all – that he's really a nice man."

Libby was right and the rumors were wrong. This man wasn't evil or scary, at least not today. No, today he'd been kind and considerate, looking to help others. I didn't know if he was a *great* man, but for us he had been a real lifesaver, and to me it seemed that he deserved to be treated with much more dignity than the island had afforded him.

"Yes, you tell your friends that they shouldn't make up stories about people," I encouraged Libby as I tried to straighten her twisted covers. "It's just not right."

I thought about the stories – the differing tales of what had supposedly happened on the *Perseverance* – and I realized that the only ones who would ever really know what happened on that ship were the ones who were there. In addition, I began to realize that the *Perseverance* had claimed its victims in ways beyond death. It had also taken the reputation of this seemingly decent man and left him branded as wicked. It had robbed him of the lakes he so loved along with his own integrity. And it had sent him into a self-imposed exile, one that he apparently would only leave for cases where he was called to help rescue someone again.

"Can I just get up now?" Libby asked, interrupting my distant thoughts.

"Oh, no, let's get you lying back down again," I told her. "You should rest a little longer."

Surprisingly, she didn't argue as she curled up under the blanket. "Okay…" She yawned. "…maybe a little bit, but then get me up so I'll still have time to play."

"I will," I promised. "But for now, I'll stay here beside you, get just a short rest myself."

I snuggled up next to her in silence, my mind then drifting back to thoughts about the eldest Kavanaugh. I realized then that

I hadn't even thanked him, or Deke, for saving our lives today. Of course, I'd get the chance to thank Deke soon enough, but as for the great Captain, I wasn't so sure. I hoped he'd come out again sometime soon so I'd have the chance to thank him. Then maybe I could visit with him, find out more about him and his family, and even maybe hear him say what it was that *really* happened on that ship so many years ago.

Chapter 36

WHO NOT TO TRUST

THE CALL CAME WITHIN AN HOUR of Rafae's departure from the Kavanaughs' house. Hailey answered it, taking me to the study where I could talk privately.

"De calls from Mr. Honika." He spoke softly in my ear, keeping his words from being overheard by those still in the house as well as Vincent on the phone. "He sounds ogitated, ond he's oskon' obout Libby's occidont."

"What?" I wondered how he could already know.

"He told me dot Rafae called him ond told him whot hoppened." Hailey looked down, shaking his head. "I'm sorry obout my boy, Miss Carly. I know dot you told him not to, but he musta ennaway."

I took the receiver. "It's okay, Hailey. Thanks."

"He osked to talk to Libby, too. I'll go ond fotch her." He was still shaking his head as he left the room.

I put the receiver to my ear. "Hello, Vincent?"

"Carly. Rafae called about the accident and said Libby's okay, but I just wanted to hear from you. She's all right then?"

"She's doing great. Her body temp's normal and she's sitting up, raring to go – right back where she started." I bit my lip, awaiting a reprimand.

"But she must be pretty upset," he said. "I'm thinking we should come home until she gets over this."

"Oh, I really don't think you need to, at least not for her sake. She's fine with it – seems like she's already over it. But if you'd feel better about it by seeing her, I'd understand. It's just that I hate to take you away from there when Gretchen needs you, and I don't see any need since Libby's doing fine."

Vince paused a moment to consider this. "Well, if you don't think it's necessary, it's probably best that we stay. We're really starting to make some headway here."

"I'm so glad to hear that."

"Yes, and I hate to leave with things going so well."

"Really, I would tell you if I thought you should come, and I can keep you updated on how she's doing – let you know if anything changes."

"I'm sure you will," he replied. "I have no doubt Libby's in good hands, and I know you'll keep us posted."

"For sure."

"Yes, I trust you explicitly, Carly. It's just that... well, I guess there are others I'm not so sure I can trust anymore."

I was taken back by his curious comment. "What do you mean?"

"Well, I need you to be a little more careful about the people you're choosing to trust, and in particular, I'm concerned about Rafae."

Immediately I assumed that Rafae had taken the blame for the accident when he had called Vincent, and so I wanted to set the record straight. "You know, I've got to take the blame for what happened today, Vincent. I mean, I was standing right there when Rafae started belting Libby to that sled, and I actually thought it was a good idea. I just didn't –"

"An honest mistake," he interrupted. "You both tried to do a good thing and neither of you meant any harm. No, that's not what I'm talking about."

Now I was confused. "Oh... well, then what?"

"It just concerns me that Rafae had the master key to the place – free reign to go over there and rifle through all of my papers and personal belongings just to find this phone number."

"Oh, I'm so sorry, Vincent. I guess I was just in a hurry to get the number and I didn't want to leave Libby – I wasn't even thinking about what he'd have to go through to find that."

"I realize it was a bit of an emergency." He sounded very understanding, his kindness only making me feel worse.

"But I know how much you guard your family's privacy, so I should have —"

"I understand," Vincent cut in. "But I'm thinking that since a cloud of suspicion's still hanging over Rafae's head, you probably shouldn't let him in our place without supervision."

"Rafae?" I questioned as this seemed an abrupt change in Vincent's opinions about the man.

Vincent sighed into the phone. "Well, yes, under these circumstances, I just think it's best for now."

I was confused but didn't want to concern Vincent more than I already had, so I figured it best to just oblige. "Okay. I'll try to be more careful with my choices."

"That's all I'm asking," Vincent replied. "And I know I can trust you to do just that."

Just then, Libby entered the room, still wrapped in a bulky blanket. She was followed by D'Arcy who was clad in a hat and parka as he guided Libby to a love seat off to one side of the room. He waved his hand and slightly tilted his head at me, motioning for me to continue my conversation without interruption.

On the phone, Vincent continued. "So, must be that Max hasn't picked up that envelope yet, right?"

"No, he hasn't. And I was wondering if he'll even be able to. I don't know how he can get over from Beacon Point since the ice on the channel is still open in spots."

D'Arcy drew his head back and scowled, wrapping a scarf about his neck while looking somewhat taken back by what I'd just said.

"Oh, don't worry about that," Vincent reassured me. "He has his ways — you can count on that. He'll be by soon enough, so when you get back to the Landings later on, I'd like you to check and make sure that package is all right."

"All right?"

"Well, just that it's right where it was before, still sealed shut and waiting to be picked up. I'd just feel better about it if you'd let me know whether there's been any problem. Okay?"

"Okay." I couldn't help but wonder what it was about the envelope that had him so concerned. "Do you want me to let you know when Doc finally does come by for it?"

D'Arcy cocked his head, his eyes widening.

"Sure, that would be helpful," Vincent replied. "And you know I'll be calling frequently to see how Libby's doing, so you can tell me what you find out then. Do you think she'll be up to school tomorrow?"

"Knowing her, she'll want to go no matter what. But don't worry – I won't let her go if she doesn't get a good night's sleep or shows any other signs of needing time to get over this."

"Good plan." He finally sounded more upbeat – more like himself. "I'd best get back to business here. You can reach me at the first number on the itinerary if there's a problem."

"I will."

"Can you put Libby on the line?"

"Sure. Just a minute." I set the receiver down and turned to Libby. "Your Bumpa wants to speak with you."

D'Arcy helped Libby back up and pulled the blanket snuggly about her shoulders as he walked her to the phone.

Libby's bottom lip quivered. "He's going to be really mad at me."

"Oh, no, he's not mad at you, Libby," I told her. "He's just glad you're okay." I put the receiver to her ear. "Here he is."

She took hold of the phone, a hesitant grin on her face. "Hi, Bumpa." She paused. "Yeah, I'm okay now." She paused again, then nodded her head. "Yes, it was scary, but I'm okay."

Standing off to Libby's side, D'Arcy zipped up his parka as he whispered to me. "Was Vincent just talking about Doc Arlington?"

"Yes," I whispered back.

Libby's grin was growing more reassured with whatever words she was hearing through the phone. "Rafae," she said, then added, "and Deke and the great captain, too." She paused to listen intently before finally raising her own question. "So, do I have to stay here or can I go back home with Carly?"

D'Arcy stepped closer to me, continuing to keep his voice near a whisper. "And did you say something about Doc still being out at Beacon Point?"

I turned to D'Arcy. "Yes. I guess he's working on some kind of research project that —"

"Still?" D'Arcy no longer whispered as he pulled me to the side, away from Libby's pleasant chat with her grandfather.

"Well, yeah, I think so. He's been working on it for quite a while I guess."

"I know, but I just thought that… well, with everything that's been going on, I thought Vince had agreed to…" D'Arcy scowled as he rubbed his chin, deep in thought.

D'Arcy raised his eyebrows. "Well, maybe I'll just have to find out what he's up to now." He pulled on a pair of heavy work gloves.

"Where are you going?" I asked. "Is there something wrong?"

"Oh, I don't think so. No, I'm just heading out to work on the snow bridge – hauling all the leftover Christmas trees out on the ice and lining them up to start marking the trail."

"You're doing that?"

"Some of it," he answered. "They'll still need to auger some holes to hold those trees so they don't get blown off course." D'Arcy pushed his down-filled collar up around his scarf and snapped it over his chin. "Yeah, it's a big job – takes a while, and it's darn cold out there."

"So, are you going to go to the lighthouse to see Doc?" I asked D'Arcy.

"Not now." He turned toward to door. "This project's keeping me pretty busy for the time being, so it'll have to wait."

I couldn't help but think back to what I'd overheard Doc discussing with Vincent. "Do you think Doc's doing something he's not supposed to?"

D'Arcy glanced back at me, seeming a bit agitated. "Well, I don't think so. It's probably just… a misunderstanding. That's all." Then he headed toward the door.

Suddenly I felt the need to tell him what I knew. "Doc's trying to recruit locals."

Coming to a dead stop, D'Arcy turned his head slowly to look back at me. "What did you say?"

I took in his reaction. "I overheard Doc talking to Vince, saying something about recruiting some locals to help him."

"He did, did he? And did he say what for?"

I shook my head.

D'Arcy looked down, his eyes searching the floor for answers that weren't there. Then he shook his head as if shaking something off. "No, no. It's probably just fine. I'll catch up with him next time he's over here, and I'll just make sure..." He looked at Libby, still on the phone, and then looked at me. "But when he comes by next time, I just want you to make sure somebody's there with you. Okay?" His voice was low but steady.

"Okay." Now he had me worried. "But what if he —"

"It'll be fine." He turned for the doorway. "You all just stay together, keep an eye on each other — just like you have been — and you'll be okay." With that, he left the room.

"I love you, too, Bumpa," Libby sweetly sang into the phone. "And tell Mommy I love her, too." Libby's smile was wide as she set the phone receiver back in its cradle. "Bumpa said to tell you what he said — that maybe you're kind of like a big sister to me. And I said yeah, that I thought you were, too."

I caught her in a big hug and then guided her back to the love seat. "Well, I suppose I am kind of like an older sister — but maybe one that sometimes bosses you around too much, huh?"

"No, not *too* much." Libby took a seat, pulling her feet under her and bunching up like a ball under her blanket. "But since you do tell me what to do, and you do try to teach me stuff and make me dress warm, and you feed me and sometimes take me places... I guess I was starting to think that sometimes you're more like a mom."

I searched for the right thing to say. "Well, but I guess I can't be that, because you already have a great mom who loves you very much — so I suppose I like the idea of being more like a sister."

I had to admit it *was* a nice thought. There were times when I really missed my real sister, and although I could never replace her, it was comforting to find Libby there, filling that void in my life that had left me feeling empty.

Libby nodded. "Yeah, it might hurt my mom's feelings if she heard me say that, so guess I better stick with sister."

"Good enough," I agreed, giving her another hug.

"I always wanted a sister, too," she continued. "Like someone I could play with, tell secrets to, but it's better I don't have one 'cause there's all that getting sick junk that's in my family." She scratched her ear. "I wouldn't want a sister who's just gonna catch that sick stuff like Grandma and Momma did, 'cause then I'd always be worrying that I was going to lose her or something."

I stroked Libby's bangs from her eyes, studying her as I was struck by the magnitude of the burden this child faced. At one time, I'd thought I understood her situation since I knew how it felt to lose my entire family. But as awful as my losses had been, they hadn't been like this. Mine had been without warning, without the agony of seeing its gradual, painful approach. It had been simultaneous, one massive loss all at once that I could grieve all at once – not a prolonged grieving process that played itself out over and over again. And it had struck me well into my adulthood, certainly not as a seven-year-old forced to confront such a bleak reality at such a tender age.

"So, thanks for being like a sister to me." Libby smiled. "You make a great one 'cause we're not really related, so I don't have to worry about losing you, too," she added before leaning back and shutting her eyes to rest.

Chapter 37

SCATTERED PIECES

I GREW IMPATIENT, THEN CONCERNED as even more time lapsed from when Rafae had first departed for the Landings and yet still hadn't returned. Wondering what had happened, I finally decided to borrow a pair of boots and dry mittens from Hailey so I could make the trek home to see what was taking him so long.

"I'm sure he'll be back any minute," Deke tried to convince me. "If you wait a little longer, Libby's clothes will be dry, and then we can just take her back with us."

"No, I want to see what's keeping him," I insisted as I tugged on Hailey's bulky Sorel boots and tied them up tightly. "Besides, it'll give me a chance to put an extra blanket on Libby's bed, and then I can bring back a pair of dry, warm pajamas for her to wear on the way home."

"Then I'm going with you." He pulled a pair of boots out of the front closet and sat on the stairs to put them on.

"That's up to you – whether you want to go back now, or later, or whenever."

"I'd just as soon go now – to make sure everything's all okay around there."

I slipped my arms into my coat sleeves, pleased to find them now dry. "What do you mean by all okay? Why are you so concerned?"

He finished tying up his boots. "Well, before Dad left, he told me to keep an eye on you – well, and the other ladies, too."

I wondered if Deke knew why his dad was acting so concerned. "Yeah, for some reason he seems a bit worried about Doc coming around the place."

Deke nodded. "Dad says that Doc's the perfect example of how genius doesn't fall far from the edge of insanity."

"Really?" I wrapped Hailey's scarf around my neck. "I wonder why your dad thinks that," I replied as I replayed Doc's last visit to the Landings, a scene that quickly brought me to the same conclusion.

"Haven't you noticed?" Deke questioned me in reply. "The guy's certifiable."

Hailey stepped into the foyer and walked to the front door. "I om so sorry my boy is takon' so long to get bock, ond dot you got to go out oftar him."

"It's no problem, Hailey." I walked to the door as Hailey opened it for us, my breath already steaming in the brisk air. "Just make sure Libby minds you and Nana Maeve, and we'll be right back." And with that, I headed out.

Deke exited right behind me, quickly catching up to walk at my side. Together we hustled along, making our way down the bluff in record time, especially considering our big boots and the snow-covered pathways we had to trudge along. Puffing from our brisk pace, we wound our way closer to the Landings where, about a block's distance away, we noticed what appeared to be a couple of police snowmobiles parked out by the glowing No Vacancy sign.

I paused. "What the...?"

Under his parka hood, Deke shook his head. "What has Rafae done now?"

We strode ahead even more briskly, climbing up the front steps and stepping up to the open front door, looking in on a scene we could never have imagined.

My jaw hung open. "What happened?"

In the front lobby, all of the furniture had been overturned. Papers were scattered all across the floor, intermixed with books, pens and pencils, and various knickknacks as well as some broken glass. The entire place had been torn apart.

"Who did this!" I took one step into the lobby.

Officer Macke was there to stop me at the doorway. "Hey! Ya can't be contaminatin' da crime scene, eh!"

Deke tried to step in, too. "But we live here!"

Eino Macke held both ends of his police baton, pushing it toward Deke's chest to stop him from entering. "Caught da criminal in da commissionin' of da crime, don't ya know."

Deke scowled. "You caught whoever did this?"

Eino smiled. "Ya betcha, by golly! Only he wasn't here just ta tear up da place. He was kidnappin', and maybe he'd a killed again, too, if I hadn't stopped –"

"The kidnapper was here!" I sidestepped them both before Macke had a chance to stop me.

Chief Sinclaire was in the foyer behind the desk, donning protective gloves as he cautiously sifted through the rubble.

I was worried about Rosie and Leila as well as Rafae. "Is anyone hurt?"

"'Fraid so, I'm here to tell yas." Eino took in his breath as if he was about to tell us who.

Sinclaire held up his hand, motioning Eino to stop. "No need to trouble these folks with the details. They just can't come in here right now." He waved his hand, gesturing for me to move back.

There was no way I was leaving. "But I'm supposed to be responsible for –"

"Gotta move ya back, Miss." Eino had me by the arm, pulling me back toward Deke with a surprisingly strong grip.

"Okay! Okay!" I reluctantly moved back to Deke's side by the door. Now out of Sinclaire's earshot, I persisted. "You tell me right now, Eino – who's hurt and what happened? I'm running this place, and I have a right to know."

Eino puffed up his chest, sticking his thumbs into his belt loops. "Well, it's lucky for all of ya's dat I came by here just in da nick of time, smack-dab in da middle of da commissionin' of a kidnappin', dat's what it was." He rocked onto his toes then to his heels, then back to his toes, lifting himself upward to look as tall as possible. "Yeah, I apprehended da perpetrator, den locked him up in da station 'til da chief can process him."

I held my hands up in frustration. "And who is he?"

Eino tilted his head. "Why, it's your good pal, Rafae, for goodness sakes!"

"Rafae!" I shook my head. "No, he had permission to be in here. I sent him to get something, and I bet he just got caught up in whatever was going on here."

Eino smiled. "You betcha he got caught in somethin', and it was my handcuffs, don't ya know!" His barking laugh sounded more like coughing.

Deke turned to Sinclaire, speaking loudly enough for him to hear. "So, do *you* think Rafae did this?" He motioned toward the overturned furniture.

"Aw, Eino." Sinclaire shook his head at his assistant. "What are you telling these people?"

"Well, Miss Malloy here – she was sayin' how she's got the right –"

Sinclaire didn't wait for Eino's explanation, stepping away from the back side of the desk to approach us. "Yeah, Eino here says Rafae was trying to make off with Miss Pence."

"The letch!" Eino interjected, furrowing his eyebrows.

"Leila?" My eyes darted between the two officers. "Is she all right? What happened to her?"

"She'll be just hunky-dory," Eino offered. "Just gettin' her checked out with the doc, all righty."

Sinclaire came closer, crossing his arms across his chest. "It's a good thing Eino noticed the door ajar and came in to check, apparently just when Rafae was making his move."

Deke scowled as he crossed his arms, too. "What was he doing?"

As Macke opened his mouth, Sinclaire cut him off. "I'd rather not discuss the details, but let's just say he was trying to remove her from the premises against her will."

I was dumbfounded. "This just doesn't make any sense. I sent Rafae here for a phone number."

Sinclaire removed a notepad and pen from his pocket. "So, you gave him the key?"

I nodded. "Well, yeah."

"That must be how he got in." He made a note. "Now, when Eino got here, he says he found the place torn up like this. Looks like more than the ruckus to nab Leila was going on here – appears more like he was maybe looking for something, don't you think so, Carly?"

I shook my head. "I did send him here to find Vincent's phone number, but he wouldn't have done *this* to look for it." I motioned toward the overturned furniture.

"So, maybe he was digging around for something else." Sinclaire scowled at me. "Maybe he was looking for some kind of information…"

I thought about the checks but said nothing.

"…could've been looking for a note or something of the sort you might've told him you had at one time or another."

"I have no idea what you're talking about."

He stepped close to me, studying my eyes as he spoke. "Well, like something that might tie him to this Annahede's disappearance – I mean, according to Donahue, you knew the girl pretty well, and she was –"

"That dirtbag Donahue doesn't know squat," I snapped.

"Maybe he is a dirtbag, but as Annahede's boss, he seemed to think maybe you knew something – that Annahede might have passed a message along to you so that if Rafae ever did anything bad to her –"

"Wait a minute!" I shook my head in disbelief. "When it comes to Annahede, I have always made it a point to stay out of her dealings. And as for Rafae, even if somehow he *was* the island kidnapper and he *was* hell-bent on snatching another woman – which I still find hard to believe – then I can't imagine he'd be stupid enough to try to kidnap someone from a place where he knew we could tie him to the scene with a key and a phone call."

Sinclaire stepped aside and picked up a floor lamp that was lying on its side, righting it. "You know, I've dealt with criminal minds for a long time, Miss Malloy, and I can tell you that they often do far from logical things. Their deviant minds work on a wave length that's a lot different from ours, so you've got to try to think like them." He sighed. "So, if I'm thinking like Rafae, then I suppose I see an alibi in this little errand he was running for you – that I can say, 'Oh, I was just there because Carly sent me, and that's why my fingerprints are all over the place, and this whole thing must have happened after I left because it didn't look like this when I was there.' Why, he might even claim that he forgot to lock the door, so that must be how the *real* perp got in here."

I looked down, taking this all in. "I still just can't believe Rafae's behind this."

Sinclaire smirked. "Oh, and I'm sure he'll have plenty of excuses — He always does," he snickered. "And I bet he's counting on you to vouch for him — you know, since you're the one who sent him here in the first place, and because he's got you believing he'd never be capable of doing this to these women."

"Of doing what?" Deke held up his hands and shrugged. "I still don't get it. I mean, what reason would he have for taking any of those people in the first place?"

Macke looked annoyed. "Da thing is, we haven't had da time to ascertain da motive yet, eh! Ya know, dis is an ongoin' investigation, and were just gettin' started 'round here." He hiked his pants. "But we got it under control for now, ya know. And ya can betcha I'll be doin' some interrogatin' when I get back to da station, and den we'll find out all da reasons pretty lickety-split."

"You just leave that to me," Sinclaire instructed Macke. "I want first crack at that smart-ass, so don't be talking to him when you go back there. I've just got to check the last couple of things here. He turned his gaze to me. "Maybe I can get this place back opened up for you people in a short bit — just want to make sure I didn't miss anything, like maybe some note left for Carly that she was somehow unaware of." He shot me a final angry glare and then went back to the desk, giving the area a final look-over.

I turned to Macke. "So, where's Leila? And where are these other women?" Don't you think you need to be finding out where they're —"

"Now don't be gettin' your tail in a knot, Missy!" Macke held up his hand like a crossing guard would to stop traffic. "Da culprit didn't divulge dat info yet, but don't you worry, eh. We'll get to the rock bottom of dis mess and get dose ladies back safe and sound, pronto!"

"And Leila?" I asked again. "I was hoping I could see her — make sure she's okay."

"Sorry, but ya can't do dat." Macke shook his head firmly. "Da poor girl, she was so frightened, don't ya know, dat she said she didn't want to be 'round here – said she wanted as far away as she could be – which ya can understand given what she's been through and all. So I sent her to a real nice facility that's kinda a bit farther from here."

"I don't understand?" Deke tucked his hands deep in his pockets. "Isn't she just over at the mainland?"

"Oh, ya might say that's so," Macke rocked to and fro on his feet. "Then again, it's nowhere you knows about. She's sorta been isolated – ya know, ta help her feel safe again, and for her own protection."

"Isolated?" I questioned. "So, her friends can't see her? How's that supposed to make her feel safe?"

"Ya know, miss, ya ask too many questions." Macke's hands went to his hips. "I told ya dis is all an ongoin' investigation dat's just gettin' fired up here, and dare's a whole lotta stuff we still gotta sort out, by golly, and so... yeah." He rubbed his chin, smirking at the invisible light bulb glowing over his head. "As a matter-fact, I should take da two of ya's over to da station for some questionin'."

Deke scowled, his eyes darkening. "Questioning? What sort of questions would you need to ask us?"

"Maybe just da background info, like what ya was doin' before da perp left for da scene of da violation – ya know, all da important stuff like dat." Macke moved toward his boss, stepping around an overturned chair. "Hey, Chief. I'm gonna take dese two witnesses back over to da station ta get dare statements, eh?"

Sinclaire was staring at the pieces of paper scattered about the floor and he never looked up. "Knock yourself out, Eino."

"Come on now." Macke tried to herd us out the door.

"Wait a minute!" I held my ground. "If we've got to go, first I need to get Vincent's phone number so I can call him and let him know what's happened here."

Macke kept pushing me back. "No, ya got all sortsa time for dat kinda business later. I gotta talk to ya now while events are still all fresh in your minds, ya know, by golly!"

Back stepping, I remained insistent. "But if I could just get the number, at least I could —"

"Not now!" Macke gave me a firm shove that seemed to surprise him almost as much as it did me.

"Hey, watch it!" Deke demanded.

Macke stuck his baton under one arm and swatted his hands at us. "Den ya best getta move-on. Da place is still a wreck anyways, so ya'd have a tough time of it tryin' ta find da number in dis mess, don't ya know — just a needle in da haystack."

Finally surrendering to Macke's command, we tightened up our scarves and headed back out into the cold. Stepping toward the boardwalk, I briefly thought about turning and going back to the Kavanaugh's, at least just long enough to let Libby know why we might be longer than originally planned. But once I considered that we'd have Macke in tow, I realized that such a stop would do more harm than good.

"Libby's going to be worried," I told Deke.

"She'll be more worried if you tell her what happened," he pointed out as he walked at my side.

"Well, I've got to tell her something."

"We can make something up, like that the stray dog came by and we let it in, and it knocked over some things and broke some stuff." As Deke weaved his tale, puffs of steam rose from his lips. "We can call her from the station and tell her we've got to clean up the mess and take the dog back to its owner before we go get her. That should hold her off, at least for a while."

"Dat's a real good story, ya know," Macke approved as he trudged along behind us. "And ya can make dat call just as soon as we got your statements down."

Obviously my words were being overheard by the big ears behind us, so I chose not to say anything else the rest of the way to the police station. With little said by either Deke or Eino, as well, we continued along the boardwalk mostly in silence except for the crunching of snow under our boots.

As we walked, I thought about Rafae — how I couldn't ever imagine him attacking these or any other women, and how much

I wanted to hear his side of the story. That was the one good thing I saw coming from our forced detour to the police station – that we just might get a chance to see Rafae and to hear what he had to say for himself.

With all that had happened, I found myself wondering if there might be some dark, sinister side to Rafae that fortunately I'd never encountered before – a bit like the side that creeps out when he's drinking with the boys at Biminis but even more deviant and hateful. I tried to envision this but could only picture his gentle side – the side that always treated Libby and Gretchen, and me, with respect and compassion – and that continued to make me believe that these charges simply could not be true.

However, there were also the eyewitnesses – people that I trusted, like Leila and the police, as well. They all had pointed their fingers at Rafae, so what was I to believe? And with what I had seen with my *own* eyes – that Leila was gone, the hotel was in shambles... and even the warning I'd heard from Vincent, telling me that I shouldn't trust Rafae. It was now nagging at me from the back of my mind.

All of these ideas and bits of information kept swimming around in my head, still not coming together in any way that made sense. All they could tell me was that some piece of the puzzle was missing, and that there just had to be something else.

Chapter 38

WHAT'S HIDDEN BENEATH

"IT'S ALL A SET-UP TO FRAME ME!" Rafae yelled from behind bars at a flat-nosed muscle man dressed in a pitted-out, light blue button-down.

Deke and I had just finished up our useless interviews with Officer Macke and had finally managed to get permission to spend a few minutes with Rafae.

Deke walked into the cell room first, stepping over close to the bars. "What have you gotten yourself into now?"

"Oh, nice to see you, too, Geek." Rafae flashed Deke a smug grin and then immediately reverted back to the harsh glare he'd been giving his visitor. "I'm telling you there's some kind of conspiracy going on here! I must've come close to something important at that hotel – got to be why they knocked me out." He lifted up the zip lock bag of ice that was melting as he held it to the top left side of his head.

"Oh!" I could see the egg-shaped bump protruding just above his left ear. "That must hurt." I reached with my fingers toward the lump, wanting to feel for myself how bad it was.

"Ouch!" Rafae ducked from my touch, again pressing the icy compress against his wound.

The visitor tucked papers into his briefcase. "But you said you didn't see this Leila girl there at all –"

"What did you do to Leila?" I impatiently interjected. "– and the whole place, it's a mess! What were you doing?"

Rafae held up his free hand, a motion of surrender. "Hey, *I* didn't do anything – to Leila or the place!"

The visitor closed his briefcase. "And you said you saw a bunch of bills and letters, kind of like anybody'd see in any ol' hotel, right?" He shook his head, loosening his tie. "Rafae, you've got to give me more than some crazy conspiracy story to hang our hat on, buddy, because I can't go to the judge for a dismissal just on this."

Rafae lowered and shook his head. "Fine. Whatever."

The man pulled a business card from his shirt pocket and handed it to his client. "Well, I'll go see when they think I might be able to talk to this Leila girl and maybe she can clear this up. In the meantime, if you can think of anything else, don't say a word about it in front of those officers. Just give me a call and I'll come over to walk you through it. Okay?"

"Okay..." With his free hand, he took the card and read it. "...Elliot."

Elliot headed for the door that led out of the two-cell holding area. "I'll see about bail – can't make any promises, but I can probably at least talk the judge into letting you stay here rather than hassle with flying you over to the mainland."

"Great!" Rafae laughed. "You know, I think I'd actually rather hang out on the mainland with a bunch of criminals than have to stay here with that dink Sinclaire and the little Yooper."

"Oh, I doubt that." Elliot opened the room door. "Hang in there and I'll get back with you if there's any action." With that, he walked out, leaving the door ajar.

"Elliott Smythe, Public Defender," Rafae read from the business card, then tossed it along with his bag of ice out between the bars of his cell. "With defenders like that, who needs enemies? Hey, Deke, think you or your dad could line me up with a better attorney? You know, like someone who gives a rat's ass about whether I get out of here?"

Deke clasped a bar, leaning toward it. "I'll look into it. In the meantime, fill us in."

I leaned in closer, too. "Yeah, what do you know about Leila, and what's all this about thinking there's some kind of conspiracy?"

Rafae leaned in to whisper. "Well, I can't say much with Officer Schwinn out there listening." He tipped his head toward the door.

Stepping back from the cell, I reached for the door to push it shut just as an arm reached in. I must have jumped a foot.

"What's with all da whisperin' in here, eh?" Eino held the door open, entering into the cramped cell room with us. "Is Rafae here tryin' ta tell yas all dose wild tales he's been makin' up about all-a-what happened?"

Rafae crossed his arms and narrowed his eyes. "Eino, my man! You know, I was just thinking you should probably get Ol' Chief Beau a big box of doughnuts down at the coffee house. That way maybe he won't be quite so mad at you when he gets back from figuring out that I'm not the one who did this!"

Eino swaggered up to the bars, his head held high. "Now ya know I can't just leave yas here. I'd miss out on it when ya finally gets around to confessin' to da whole kit'n'kaboodle, eh?"

"So, all you're waiting around for is my confession?"

"You betcha!"

"Well, then why don't you just pick up that card there and give my defender a ring." Rafae pointed at Elliot's business card on the floor where he'd thrown it. "I guess I've decided to tell you something, but I'm not about to say anything without my lawyer."

Eino's mouth hung open, his eyes popping wide after a long blink. "Well, okey-dokey den!" Smiling, he leaned over and picked up the card, "I'll call his office an' have him come right back when he gets dare, eh?" He straightened his hat as his expression quickly changed from shock to elation. "Hey, if I hurry her up, I might just catch da guy before he gets over to his snow machine!" And with that, Eino eagerly darted out of the room.

Rafae leaned in again, whispering. "That should buy me a minute without that idiot listening. Look, I'm telling you both, I think I'm in here because somebody thinks I got too close to the truth about these women..." He paused, his eyes darting to the door then back to us. "...and I think it's got something to do with that envelope for Doc Arlington I found at the Landings." His face was serious, his eyes intent on us.

"What are you talking about?" I kept my voice to a whisper despite my outrage at learning that Rafae *had*, in fact, snooped through Vincent's things. "What were you doing rifling through the Hanika's private papers?"

"I wasn't rifling!" His voice rose. "I had to look around a little to find that number, and when I saw that envelope right there, I flipped it over thinking the number might be on the back."

"But it wasn't, was it?" I scolded him. "It just had Doc's name on it – and not yours!"

"Yeah, but when I flipped it, the desk lamp was on and the light sort of shined through it and... well, it looked like there might be some checks inside." His eyes wandered away from mine.

"So, you just ripped into it?" Deke sighed. "I can't believe you! What were you thinking – that they might be for you?"

Rafae scowled. "Of course they weren't for me, okay? But I guess my curiosity got the better of me, especially when I held them up closer to the light and saw at least one check with a few more zeroes than I'm use to seeing."

"So, you decided to open it, didn't you?" I was outraged. "Just because it looks like a lot of money doesn't make it okay to just open somebody else's mail!"

"Sh!" Rafae held his finger to his mouth, craning to watch for Macke to return. "Yeah, I suppose it doesn't make it okay, but then I saw what looked to be the name 'Collette Deroshia' on one of the checks, so I got more curious."

"Collette?" Deke cocked his head at Rafae. "Who's that."

"She worked with me at Biminis," I answered him. "That is, until she suddenly didn't show up."

Rafae looked down as he kicked his heel against the bars, absently knocking some dirt from his boots. "And when I saw what looked like the name 'Annahede Khali' on another check, then I thought it might be worth it to open the envelope and take a closer look."

"Annahede?" I lurched back with surprise. "Why would Vincent make out a check for Annahede – and Collette – and then leave them for Max to pick up?"

"I was wondering the same thing." Rafae crossed his arms. "I'm also wondering why he's paying them thirty thousand dollars – each."

"Thirty thousand!" Deke's eyes bulged.

My stomach dropped. "Why on earth would he owe them that kind of money!"

"Yeah, I was curious about that one, too." Rafae leaned closer toward the bars with an air of confidence. "So, that's why I called Vincent."

"You called Vincent to ask him about personal checks that were none of your business to begin with!" Deke shook his head in disbelief.

"Well, not exactly," Rafae answered. "I didn't want to play all my cards up front, so I just hinted around a little about it. But he didn't bite – suppose I wouldn't either if I were him."

I remembered Vincent's admonishment earlier, of how he had warned me not to trust Rafae. Now I understood why Vincent had said this – but I was growing increasingly unsure about whom I could trust. I studied the floor while I mulled this all over. "There's got to be an explanation here – like some kind of coincidence that I'm just not –"

"Carly," Rafae spoke softly.

I looked up at him, gazing into his dark, honest eyes.

Holding a bar in each hand, Rafae pressed his face between them. "I found more checks in that envelope." He paused, letting it sink in. "They were all made out for the same amount – but they had other women's names on them."

Deke leaned in closer to us. "I think I see where this is going. Okay, so we all know Vincent's a nice guy who's got a lot of money, and that he can be very influential – and since he's always trying to help other people out, maybe he knows some high and mighties that got caught up with Annahede and some of her call girls and –"

"Collette's no call girl!" I couldn't stand by and let him say otherwise.

"–Well, escort, or whatever – anyway, he's probably just trying to help some people cover up some sort of indiscretion, and in the process, give some ladies in need a better life – some cash in their pockets and a reason to leave behind their lives of servitude. Yeah, so maybe it's a little dicey, but I'm sure it's with the best of intentions."

"What are you talking about?" I glared at Deke, still in disbelief over both Vincent's potential involvement and Deke's skewed perspective.

"No, I don't think that's it, Deke." Rafae shook his head. "You know, what's really got me worried is the list of names I found on those checks." He reached back to the leather Levi's patch stitched between the belt loops on his jeans and pulled out a tiny, folded scrap of paper.

"Is that the list?" Deke pointed at the scrap.

"Yeah, Sinclaire could've searched me all day and never found this." He smiled, holding it up. "I wrote all the names down and tucked them away, and then I stuck the envelope in a less obvious spot – someplace where the bastard that pistol-whipped me wasn't ever going to find it!" He laughed as he reached up and carefully touched at his goose egg. "Ouch!" He grimaced.

Suddenly, I heard a creaking sound followed by the sound of wind coming from the neighboring room. "What was that?"

Both guys looked at me with curiosity as I turned away from them and walked over to the doorway. There I was met with a blast of frigid air coming from the front door that was ajar, swinging slightly open with the winter breeze. I stepped over to the door, took a peek outside and, seeing no one, closed it tightly.

"Let's see what it says here," Rafae was saying when I returned. He held up an old cash register receipt and flipped it over, revealing a list he'd scrawled on the back. "Yeah, you'll see some other familiar names on here, too." He handed the scrap to me.

I quickly scanned the names, noting that Collette and Annahede were listed along with well over a dozen others.

"They're all women." I studied the list more closely, taking in each familiar name with astonishment. "And all the women that people thought might be missing... they're all listed on here."

"Not quite all," Rafae whispered. "You'll notice there's no check for Helena Moore – must mean you don't get paid if you end up dying."

I shuddered at the thought.

"Well, if someone's dead, then I guess you don't have to worry about her talking," Deke muttered. "Sounds like hush money to me."

"But from Vincent?" I still refused to believe this.

"Well, it's definitely from his account," Rafae confirmed. "But I'm not telling Sinclaire about this yet – not until I can put a few more pieces of this together. So that leaves me stuck in here, because those checks are what proves I didn't do anything."

"Didn't do anything?" Deke was appalled. "You open up private mail, trash the house, put Leila in the hospital and –"

"Hey, I didn't do anything to her!" Rafae's fists tightened around the bars. "I didn't even see her there! I was just looking around at some other papers, seeing if anything there explained the checks, then somebody wacked me on the head."

Deke shook his head. "Yeah, but Eino tells us he caught you red handed trying to take off with Leila. Now how do you explain that?"

"What? You expect me to explain why Schwinn and his boss, Chief Doughnut Hole, are framing me? Hell, I don't know!" Rafae scoffed. "But you have to admit their story makes no sense. I mean, why would I try to take Leila by force, with her kicking and screaming the whole way, when all I'd have to do was say, 'Hey, Leila, could you help me with such'n'such over at Kavanaughs?' – or Biminis, or wherever. I know she'd come with me, and that'd work a whole lot better than fighting her."

"That's a good point," I told Deke. "That whole story just doesn't make sense."

Deke crossed his arms across his chest. "Okay, but I still don't understand why they'd make this up, and it doesn't explain what happened to the place, or to Leila."

Rafae released the bars, running his hands through his dark, curly locks. "Well, for all we know, Leila's probably just fine, and maybe even she or Rosie know something about how the place got trashed." He rubbed his fingers firmly at his temples, grimacing as he accidentally touched his goose egg. "I'd like to track them down and talk to them – see what they know. But I can't do that while I'm stuck in here." He kicked at the bars.

"And from the looks of it, you may be stuck in there for a while," Chief Sinclaire announced as he strolled into the cell area, his hands firmly pressed against the sides of his spare tire.

Rafae tilted his chin upward, his face tightening. "Nice to see you back, Chief. Done so soon with looking for all of that evidence that's going to get me out of here, are you?"

"Oh, not so fast, Rafae." Sinclaire walked right up to the bars so he could get in Rafae's face. "No, I saw Officer Macke chasing down the public defender who was already headed back to his office on his big ol' snow machine, but that's going to prove to be a big waste of time."

Rafae snickered. "Well, that's what I was going for."

Sinclaire's eyes narrowed. "Yes, I'm sure you were. But I can tell you now that guy won't be back here anytime soon – I've already got him tied up with some other Island business that can't wait and should keep him busy for the rest of the evening, so you might as well hunker down here for the night." He smirked.

"Well, gosh darn it all, Chief!" Rafae slapped his thigh and then backed away from the bars toward the cot along the back wall. "I suppose that's okay with me, though, because I didn't really want to have to cook tonight anyway, and so I'm just kind of looking forward to seeing what you're going to whip up for me tonight." He took a seat on the cot. "Bet it'll be something real special!" He smirked broadly, turning as he tilted his head back and brought his legs up to lie down.

Sinclaire glared at him. "Yeah, it'll be something special, for sure." Turning to walk away, he muttered, "Might even spit in – I mean, throw in some special sauce, if you're lucky." Laughing, he went to slam the door but then thought better, leaving it wide open as he departed.

With Sinclaire gone, Rafae jumped up from the cot and came back to the bars leaning toward us to whisper. "Get me another attorney, like maybe the guy I had last time – but first, find Rosie and Leila."

"I'm sure we'll be able get a hold of them and then find out what they know," I promised him.

"And you've *got* to get a hold of those checks – but when you do, don't bring them back here," Rafae quietly added. "Take them to Deke's, and then all of you should stay there until I can get out of here and we can all figure this out together."

"Dad's got that safe, you know," Deke reminded Rafae. "We'll keep the checks in there until Dad's lawyer gets you out."

"Thanks, Deke-my-man." Rafae's tone was sincere as he reached through the bars and gave Deke a friendly punch in the arm. "I owe you one, pal – and you, too, Carly."

"You best save your thanks 'til we've earned it," I quietly pointed out. "We've still got to find the girls, and the checks, so tell me – Where did you put them?"

Rafae motioned for me to lean in closer, so I pressed the side of my face against the bars. He held up his hand, one side of it to his mouth and the other side almost touching the edge of my ear so only I could hear him as he whispered. "Look behind the photo of the Hanikas."

I turned to him, closely looking him in the eyes. "Which one?"

"It's the four of them, together," he softly answered. "With Abel... and Gretchen before she got sick. And Libby's just a baby in it. I think it's a 5×7, with a wooden frame and –"

"I know the one." I knew it all too well – the picture I would examine every time I had a private moment at the desk. It was a portrait of three generations; the proud father standing with hands on the shoulders of his two children seated before him, and with the newest addition to the family embraced in her mother's arms. The photo displayed what appeared to be the idyllic family, a perfect facade to veil the real tragedy of their lives.

"We've got to get going." Deke took me by the shoulders and guided me toward the door. "Just hold on until we get back."

Rafae stepped away from the bars and toward the back of his cell. "Hey, you know where to find me – don't think I'll be going anywhere soon."

As I moved toward the doorway, I glanced back. "We'll be back as soon as we can."

Rafae went back to his cot, cocking his head as he sat down. "Oh, promises, promises." He grinned.

I left the room with that parting image of Rafae; another façade, I thought, for the real concerns he was hiding behind it. I figured, though, that at that moment, we were all hiding a lot of our real concerns, and that the time was coming soon when we'd need to finally resolve them – one way or another.

Chapter 39

FADING TO DARK

SPECKS OF WHITE FILLED THE DESOLATE SKY, a light snow falling as we headed back to the Landings. The light of day was already waning, typical for this far north in the middle of winter. Darkness would fall within the next couple of hours.

"We missed lunch." Deke's breath puffed out from under his parka hood as he spoke. He pulled up his coat sleeve with his gloved hand, looking at his gold-banded Seiko. "It's getting close to four, and I'm pretty hungry."

"I've lost my appetite." Steam rolled out in front of me, as well, puffing upward with each exhale while I hiked along as quickly as Hailey's Sorrels would carry me. "All I want right now is to find out what's going on here – and to make sure Leila and Rosie are okay."

We were only a block from home when we happened upon Eino. He quickly strode up to us, acting like he was on an urgent mission, as well. "Well, by golly, lookey who finally made it back home!" He smirked, stopping right in front of us.

I just kept on walking, sidestepping my way around him. "Yeah, I need to look the place over, get things picked up so —"

Eino turned and quickly caught up to me, grabbing me firmly by the arm. "Hey, where da ya think yer goin' now?"

I turned back at him. "Home! Now let me go!" I tried to jerk my arm from his grasp, but he had a good hold on my jacket and just wouldn't let go.

"I can't let yous in dare, ya know! It's da crime scene, an' we still got it roped off so ya don't mess with da —"

"We just saw Sinclaire, and he said you're done!" I jerked again but couldn't get free.

Deke met up with us, placing his gloved hand gently on Eino's arm. "Hey, how about you let her go and we work this out, okay?"

Eino glared at Deke, then released his grip, holding his open hands up high as an indication of surrender. I pulled back, taking a couple of steps away before turning back to stare at him.

"What do you think you're doing?" I rubbed my arm. "I have a right to go back to my home, and I don't need you –"

"Of course, ya do." Eino lowered his hands. "But I'm just tryin' to preserve da scene, ya know, so we can make sures we got all da evidence – maybe checks one last time to make sure da boss didn't miss out on somethin' small or whatever."

Deke stepped back, looking surprised by Eino's comment. "Are you saying you don't think Sinclaire went through the place thoroughly enough?"

"Well…" Eino lowered his head to one side, curling up one corner of his mouth until his eye above it was almost shut. "I guess I'd just tell yas dat da chief has some real strengths, but investigatin' crime scenes has never been one a' dem."

"So, you want to go back in there and start looking around again?" I shook my head under my hood. "Just when I thought we were done with this…" I paused, brushing a bit of snow off from my coat sleeve. "Well, come on along, then, and knock yourself out." I turned to continue my hike home, motioning for both men to follow me.

Deke hesitated but Eino hustled up to my side, talking at me as we walked. "Just wait a minute now. You two shouldn't be goin' back in da place yet. Ya might contaminate any stuff I might find, don't ya know."

I kept walking and avoided looking at him, continuing to stare straight ahead. "We'll stay out of your way – just got to grab a couple of things and then we'll be gone, and you can have run of the place."

"Ah, dang it!" Eino flailed his arms while keeping pace with me. "I just finished a big hullabaloo with Rosie – finally got her outta da place, and now yous guys are gonna give me the same aggravation?"

I stopped dead in my tracks. "You saw Rosie?"

Eino also stopped just ahead of me. "Yeah. After I seen da defender, I swang on back by da scene to dig a bit more, an' dat's when Rosie came on by. But I told her what I'm tellin' you — dat yous guys gotta clear out while I do da final thorough checkin'."

Deke had caught up to us. "So, she's left? Well, where did she go?"

"Oh, she just headed on down to da Cup-a-Joe Café — only diner dat's open today, don't ya know. She said she'd sit dare an' wait it out 'til I'm all done with da investigatin'." Eino took a couple of steps backwards, away from us and toward the Landings. "So, why don't yous guys head on over to da pub an' sit awhile with her, eh? Then I promise to come tell ya when I finish up — get yous back in da place lickety-split."

I turned to Deke. "You go on to Cup-a-Joe and find out what she knows, if anything. See if she's got some idea where we might find Leila, too."

"Now I told yas ta leave Leila alone, don't ya know," Eino argued. "She needs time ta get over da whole awful business."

Ignoring Eino's directive, Deke asked me, "What are you going to do?"

"I'll go in here and get those things we came for." With my back to Eino, I winked at Deke. "Libby will want her pajamas to sleep in, and I'll just grab a couple other things and then meet you back at your folks' house. Okay?"

"I don't know." Deke furrowed his brow, his emerald eyes gazing at me with concern. "Dad told me to keep an eye on you and not let you —"

I took hold of his arm and leaned so closely that the fur trim on his hood brushed against my cheek. "Your dad didn't know all of this was going to happen. Now we've got to split up to cover our bases. I'll be fine." I let go of him, backing away toward Eino as I finished. "Get some lunch while you're talking with Rosie. I'll get our stuff and be up to the bluff before sundown. Bye." I waved and turned away as I heard him protesting from behind me, but I never looked back. I just kept going, hiking past Eino who was uttering more complaints of his own.

"No! I told ya I gotta do da better search, ya know!" He remained glued to my side as we walked the last block. "If ya go an' mess up da scene, dares no tellin' if we'll ever put away da culprit. Or worse off, maybe we'll lock up your pal Rafae when he wasn't da bad guy after all, eh? Yeah, ya might cost me findin' da bitta evidence dat would exonerate your buddy dare!"

"But that can't happen if you're so sure he's done all this, now can it?" I snapped back as we stepped together onto the front porch.

Eino's lips tightened as he took a deep breath and puffed up his chest. "Ya know, I saw what I saw, an' dares no changin' dat fact." He reached for the door handle. "Rafae was wrastlin' 'round with Leila, even pushed her to da floor, an' I don't know how ya explain dat!" He turned the doorknob and pushed the door open, never using a key.

I couldn't believe my eyes. "You left the place unlocked!"

"Yeah, but I been right here on da street wid ya! Never let de place outta my sight!"

"I cannot believe this!" Thoroughly disgusted with all the police action I'd witnessed this day, I entered the place to find it still totally trashed. "Well, looks like tidying up isn't a part of your job description – suppose that'll fall to me." I reached down to pick up an end table that had been tipped upside down.

Eino grabbed my arm to stop me, pulling firmly at first but then quickly lightening up his grip. "Sorry," he did apologize. "I just need ya to try and leave da stuff alone 'til I'm done here, if ya would, ya know."

"Okay." Leaving the table where it was, I headed for the front desk, carefully negotiating my way around the many items scattered across the floor.

Eino followed on my heels. "But I thought ya just needed stuff from da livin' quarters. What ya need over at da desk?"

"Just Vincent's phone number and a couple other papers here." I started sorting through the scattered papers, looking under them for signs of any of the photos.

Eino pulled his leather gloves from his pocket and pulled them on before touching anything. "Oh, my good Lordy! I wish ya wouldn't mess with da papers yet. If ya'd just let me do it, ya couldn't do –"

"Here it is." I had uncovered a frame that was face-down on the desk top.

"A picture?" Eino snatched it, tipping it over to reveal that it was Libby's class photo from this year. "Of da little girl?"

"Oh, no. that's not what I thought it was." I kept digging.

Eino started searching through the papers, as well. "Guess I don't quite understand what ya might be searchin' for den. Why would ya be lookin' for da pictures when ya just got to clear out for da night, eh? Ya know, we're not gonna keep ya outta here for good or somethin'."

I quickly tried to think of some excuse to satisfy Eino's insatiable curiosity. "It's just that, well, tomorrow's the first day back to school, and Libby's supposed to bring a family picture with her." I kept pushing around the papers, hoping I'd find that other frame. "I'd hate to have her be the only kid without one, you know – she'd be really embarrassed."

"Well, why didn't ya say so, eh?" Eino backed away from the desk and carefully negotiated his way around an overturned couch. Reaching down beside it, he picked up a frame from the floor. "Yep, by golly, it's still over here. Saw dis earlier when we sorted out da mess." He brushed at the face of it with his gloved hand, sweeping away a few small shards of glass. "Afraid da glass is broke, though."

I carefully walked over and took the frame from his grasp. "Yes, this is the one I was looking for." I flashed a smile for him. "Thanks for helping me."

"Ya betcha. Now, ya just needs ta clear out."

"I can do that." I turned from Eino, leaving him to do his searching while I cautiously headed toward the living quarters. On my way, though, I stopped at a small bookshelf that was cluttered but still upright and placed the picture face down on the cleared top shelf where I could disassemble the frame. Sliding aside the tabs that held the backing in place, I pulled the backing upward and, popping it off, revealed an envelope with "Dr. Max Arlington" still scrawled across the front of it in Vincent's handwriting.

Suddenly, I noticed some kind of caustic smell. It was as if opening the frame had released some foul odor that had been trapped inside. I quickly emptied the contents out of the frame and onto the shelf, searching for the source of the smell while being careful not to cut myself on the broken glass. Grabbing the picture of the Hanika's, I gave it a sniff but found nothing. Then I picked up the envelope, noticing where the top had been slit open. I figured Rafae must have used some sharp-edged object like a knife or a pair of scissors since the opened edge looked like it had been cut rather than ripped. I pushed the corners of the envelope together, opening it wide to reveal the checks inside. I took a sniff. The smell was stronger, but it wasn't coming from the envelope.

"What the – !" were the only words I managed to exclaim as powerful arms reached around me and jerked me backward, squeezing both of my arms to my sides. As I struggled and tried to regain my balance, a damp rag was firmly pressed over my nose and mouth. I fought harder, but the inescapable stench quickly overwhelmed my senses.

My body went numb, my legs collapsing from under me, and the last thing I could remember was the sensation of falling – just as everything suddenly went black.

Part III
THROUGH CONCEPTION

Chapter 40

GONE BUT NOT FORGOTTEN

MY HEAD AND LIMBS FELT LIKE DEAD WEIGHT as I struggled to awaken from what must have been a long, deep sleep. Barely cracking my eyes open, I squinted in the blur of fluorescent light that glared down on me from the ceiling. As I tilted my heavy head, I could find no refuge from the intensity of the light that reflected against the stark white of the ceiling and down the bare walls. Closing my eyes, warmth washed over me, relaxing my whole body as all went still and I... I...

...I tried to open my eyes again, but the light was still so bright. I blinked, trying to adjust my vision so I could see where I was, but just the effort of thinking about it felt too burdensome when all I really wanted to do was rest. My stomach ached and my head whirled as a queasy feeling came over me.

Trying to get comfortable, I turned my head to the right where I saw bright blue dancing with gray and white. With a few blinks, the contrast of color and shade took the form of sky filled with billowing clouds. On my face I could feel the coolness radiating from the window, its glass frames cornered with ice and speckled with frost. Although I couldn't see the sun, I felt its presence as it reflected brilliant dots of sparkling white within the symmetry of snowflake-like formations fading in and out as my eyelids grew heavy and I...

...I woke with a start, a deep, blaring noise shocking me from my sleep before it went silent. Still squinting, I gradually opened my eyes to find that the room was now dim, the florescent light off and the sunlight fading. Dazed and confused, I tried to recollect if I'd just overslept or maybe had too much to drink. My mouth was so dry that I longed for a cold drink but I had no gumption to get up and get one. Shutting my eyes, I turned a bit as I tried to get comfortable, but that loud blaring sound startled me again. My eyes shot open and darted about the gray shadows of the room, unable to find any sign of whatever was making such an alarming sound. Still exhausted, I closed my eyes once more and tried to rollover into a more snuggled up position, but I found that no matter how hard I tried, for some reason, I just couldn't turn over.

"What's – on – my –" I mumbled through parched lips. The mattress and pillow felt unfamiliar, a bit firmer than my own bedding, and something was holding me to the bed. I tried to roll again but felt a firm tug at my arms that kept me from turning. Too achy and tired to keep struggling, I rolled back to stare at the cold gray of the rectangular ceiling fixture, its faint pattern of aligned dots growing fainter as the gray grew darker and the shadows deeper and room closed in as I descended into black…

In a blink of an eye, the room was light again. The glow from the ceiling light above was no longer so blinding, and so I opened my eyes a bit wider, taking in my surroundings. To my right, the sky outside the window was now overcast, making it also easier to look at. Trying to get my bearings, I pulled to the right in hopes of sneaking a look at my surroundings, but I was halted at the wrist once again.

"I – can't – get –" I panted through a bad case of cotton-mouth as I yanked against something that refused to give.

Dropping back, I rolled my head to the left and looked downward, slowly closing and then opening my eyes to clear my vision. Staring at my wrist, I blinked in disbelief when I found it bound to the bedside with a brown leather strap. Quickly turning to look at my right wrist, I found it, too, was secured to the bedside.

"What the…!" There was something else; a long, clear piece of plastic tubing was attached with large strips of surgical bandage to the underside of my right arm just above the wrist. The tubing ran from my arm along the side of the bed and up to a glass bottle of fluid hanging above and behind my right side.

Panic set in with a rush of adrenalin. I thrashed about, throwing all of my weight into loosening the straps. As I tugged at my bindings, I suddenly realized my ankles were bound, too. I looked down toward my feet, unable to see what was holding them in place. I was covered with a crisp linen sheet along with the thick wool of a Mackinac blanket, making it impossible for me to see my legs. But my struggling had pushed the bedding off my upper torso, revealing that I was now dressed in a cotton hospital gown.

"How'd I get in this?" My racing heartbeat throbbed in my ears. "Hey! Who did this to me!"

No one answered.

"Hey!" I yelled again, my voice echoing against the stark white walls.

It felt like the room was spinning as my eyes darted about my surroundings, searching for some sense of familiarity that was nowhere to be found. All I could see were three blank walls and a window filled with blank sky, all stark white until my panic brought back the darkness…

When I came to, the room was dark but for the deep, moonless blue of overcast night. With a start, I gasped and then returned to panting, catching myself as I felt the room begin to spin again.

"Calm down. Calm down," I panted, willing myself into enough self-control to keep myself conscious.

As my breathing grew steady, I looked about once more but still found nothing. Then a strange flash of light whirled past the window, lighting up the sky and room for a moment just a bit longer than a bolt of lightning would, but then disappearing just as quickly as it came. Left again in the darkness and now frightened beyond words, I closed my eyes and looked inward for some idea of what had happened.

Thinking back, it was all so foggy. I could remember that I'd gone skating and that… Libby, she had gone through the ice! And she was… okay. Yes, she was safe at the Kavanaugh's, and I sent Rafae to get Vincent… No, Vincent was gone, so I'd gone to get Rafae at the… the jail? But why would I see him there? I must have been dreaming.

Then I opened my eyes. The night sky flashed again, a glimmer of light that disappeared in an instant, leaving me in darkness once again. I realized then that this wasn't a dream — it was a nightmare.

"Oh, my God!" With a rush of anxiety, I squeezed my eyes tightly shut and prayed it would all go away. My chest heaved with each gasp for breath, rising up under the blanket and hospital gown that could scarcely protect me, leaving me vulnerable to whatever — and whoever — was out there.

"Who would. . .?" I whimpered, unable to complete my thought aloud even though my mind kept racing onward. I just couldn't remember where I was, how I got here, or who might have brought me here. What was worse was I couldn't figure out why I was strapped down, and how I ended up in this flimsy cotton thing, or who put me in it, or how they put me in it, or why they put me. . .

It was still dark but dawn appeared to be breaking when I finally roused from another blackout. Figuring I must have hyperventilated, I resolved myself to not let that happen again. I took in a deep breath and then gradually exhaled, trying to steady my nerves and clear my head. But my temples were throbbing, the pain beating in my ears and making it so hard to think straight. I reached up and rubbed the sides of my head with my fingertips.

Suddenly, I stopped, jerking upright in bed. "I'm loose!" Pulling my bare feet out from under the covers and turning my legs to one side, I climbed off from the bed with a momentary, exhilarating sense of relief.

"Yoss, a' course, ya are," a voice startled me.

I abruptly turned to the space behind the head of my bead, finding there a petite Saint with long dreadlocks seated on a chair between two closed doors.

The Saint cocked her head. "Your lookon' ot me like I'm a ghost or someton'. Whot, ya don't remembar me, Carly?"

Of course, I did. I had never forgotten that day when Collette had failed to show up for work at Biminis, the day she'd simply disappeared. I had figured I'd never see her again — until now.

Chapter 41

NEVER TO RETURN

"BUT HOW DID... WHERE'D YOU COME FROM?" I asked, staring at Collette in utter confusion. "I thought no one was in here. I called out, but you must've —"

"Oh, I jost got here," she explained. "I didn't hear ya callon' enna-one, so ya most a' yelled before I wos in here."

"Here?" I stammered, gazing at the door frames and the white cupboards with counters to the outside of them. "But this room isn't... I don't remember. Did *you* bring me in here?"

"Oh, no." She chuckled, casually crossing her legs. "Ya hov dis all wrong. *I* didn't bring ya here."

Suddenly, that deep, bellowing sound blared again, but Collette never flinched, seeming not to even notice it.

"What was that, and how'd I end up in...?" I unsteadily stepped toward her.

"Whoa!" Collette jumped from her seat, quickly coming to my aid. "Take it easy dare." She took my arm, steadying my balance before I had the chance to fall. "Ya need te sit bock down while you're still snoppon' out a' dis."

"Out of what?" I staggered back to the bed, taking a seat on the edge.

"De medication. Ya most still be a little sedatod — takes a while te get out a' your systom."

"Sedated?" I squinted at her in my confusion. "Why? Where am I?"

"You're ot de Beacon Lighthouse."

"The lighthouse?" But how'd I get —"

The loud, deep blare interrupted me, the foghorn's tone echoing outward as it reverberated against the panes of glass.

I turned to gaze out the window. "We're in the tower?"

"No, in de house ottoched to it," Collette replied. "Dis is where dey bring ya, once ya volunteer."

"Volunteer?"

"Yoss." Collette sat beside me. "When ya volunteer te help wid de research, dey bring ya here te stay."

"Research?" I rubbed my head. "But I don't remember anything about that."

"Dot's not surprison'. I wos pretty confused when I farst got here, too. It takes o'while te get use to de medison dey inject in os — it con sometimes make ya woozy." Collette pointed at the coil of tubing taped to her arm.

"Medicine? Is that why I'm...? I don't get this." I shook my head. "Who are *they*?"

The foghorn blared again.

"Well, it's mostly Doc Arlington. He's de one do-on' de experimonts dot are go-on' te help —"

"Doc!" I shot up. "I know Doc! He'll help me."

"Well, a' course he will. He wos olready in te check on ya while ya were still sleepon', ond den he brought me op here te be wid ya when ya came oround. I'm shor he'll be bock op te see ya in a bit."

"He was in here with you, and he saw me... so he knows I'm here?"

"Certonly he does. He knows all a' de womon dot are livon' here, ond he's takon' good care a' all of us."

"All of us? How many are there?"

"Oh, dare's a bunch of us garls." Collette smiled. "More don a dozon or so, I dink. It's hard to keep trock wid so mony, ond we don't see each oddar dot moch. Doc says it's beddar dot way, bot it's not so bod."

"So, all the missing women..." I remembered as I tried to piece this together. "They're all here?"

"A' course. We're all here, jost finishon' de job ond den waiton' te be paid all dot money so we con go home."

"And you're all... he's doing experiments on you? On us? Is that what you said?"

"Yoss, Doc's been teston' out some experimental stoff. Dot's why we hov dese." She cautiously rubbed around the tape holding the tube to her arm. "Dot's de port he uses for injecton' de trials."

"He does what!" I looked back at my arm where a piece of tubing hung loosely with a cap on the end, the connection to the hanging bottle having since been removed. "He put drugs in this? Is that what…?" With a sudden rush of nausea, I felt the cold swell of anxiety pulsing through my whole body.

Collette scooted closer to my side, pressing her hand reassuringly against my shoulder. "No, ya don't hov te worry obout dis." She patted my back. "I've hod dis done a bonch a' times olready, ond I'm fine. See?" She held out her arms.

Stunned, I stared at her. "That's crazy!" Taking in a deep breath, I stood up.

Collette reached toward me. "Ya probobly shouldn't get op yet. You're still a little groggy."

Ignoring her, I managed to walk without stumbling over to the window. "I just can't believe I said I'd do this! I don't remember…" Pressing my hands against the cold glass panes, I looked out to where the vast, frozen lake met the golden glow of the horizon just before sunrise "Why'd I get involved in… in whatever this is?"

"Well, for de money, a' course – I mean, dot's de reason why all a' us came in de farst place."

I shook my head. "But I don't need money. I've already got a job and –"

"Whot, sarvon' people drinks for tips? Dot's a lousy job, waiton' on slobs like dose sailor boys olways pickon' on us. No, I don't want te be somebody's slave, hovon' te clean op dare dishos – not when I con make a ton a' money here ond nevar hov te work ogain."

"But I'm not… not…" I stuttered. "…I work for Hanikas now, and… and I like it there."

"Really?" She cocked her head at me, looking somewhat confused. "I didn't know obout dot." She paused, rubbing her chin. "Bot it's still de best deal te do dis job for jost a short time ond get so moch money, ond den ya con do enna-ton' ya want, evon go bock te workon' for de Honikos, if dot's whot ya like."

"But it's just that…" I picked at the tape holding the IV port in my arm. "I don't know about this. Am I some kind of guinea pig or something?"

"Oh, I wouldn't pick ot dot." She gently pushed my hand aside. "No, it's not like dot ot all, bot I do undarstond how you're feelon'. I kinda felt de same way when I farst got here, bot my farst roommate, Missy, she told me de same ting: Don't worry, cuz I've hod it done ond it's okay. Bock den, I tought *she* wos crazy, bot it turned out dot she wos right. It's no big deal."

I rubbed my churning stomach. "I don't know. It seems like —" I stopped suddenly when I heard the slide of the deadbolt.

Collette quickly stepped toward the left door. "Oh, dot most be Doc."

The door opened slowly, quietly, and only far enough for Doc to stick his head through the opening. "And so, how's it coming along in here?" he asked Collette before turning to see me. "Oh! You're already up and around now, are you?" With a look of amazement, he stepped the rest of the way into the room and closed the door behind him. "You should probably take it easy, though. Let's help you sit down so I can take a look at you and see how you're doing." Walking toward me, he pushed his horn-rimmed glasses back onto the bridge of his nose before extending his hand to me.

Collette followed up behind him. "Yoss, I wos tryon' te get her te relox, bot she wos oskon' all sorts a' questions ond —"

"I don't know why I'm here, Doc!" I told him. "I can't remember what happened, or how I got here. It's all a blur."

"Well, that's pretty typical." He took me by the arm and guided me back to the bed. "You just sit down."

Following his lead, I stepped back to the bed and sat on the side. "I'm still so tired, and I'm aching all over — my head, my stomach…"

Doc placed one hand on my shoulder and used his other to guide my legs back up onto the bed. "That's normal, really. Just lie down while I check your vitals."

"Normal?" I asked as I turned and leaned back. "Normal for what?"

"Normal for a first treatment." Reaching into the pocket of his lab coat, he drew out his stethoscope and, placing them in his ears, pressed its disc to my chest. "Now, just breathe like you usually do."

"A first treatment of what? I don't get —"

"Sh-sh." He scowled behind his glasses, staring at the disc as he listened intently from one spot to the next. "Sounds good." Lowering the disc, he removed the stethoscope from his ears and draped it around his neck.

Still feeling a bit crampy, I asked, "So, I'm okay then?"

"It's going well," he replied without looking up, instead grasping my wrist to check my pulse.

"What's going well? What are you doing here, and why am *I* here?"

"Because you wanted to be here," he calmly replied as he stared at his watch. "I always figured that once you knew what we were trying to do here, you'd want to help out. Now hold on..." he added, counting to himself as he calculated my pulse.

"But I don't *know* what you're trying to do here," I said. "I heard something about some experiments and research. Is that what you're doing?"

"Something like that." He released my wrist and turned to Collette. "Get me that cuff over there."

Collette stepped behind the head of my bed, asking as she moved away, "De one on de countar?"

"Yes," Doc answered before turning back to press his fingers under my chin and around my neck. "I'll give you something for that achy feeling," he said as he reached for the tube hanging from the IV bottle.

Quickly sitting up, I felt the room begin to spin. "No, I don't think I want you to do that."

Doc dropped the tubing. "I'm not going to hurt you," he tried to reassure me as he placed his hands firmly on my shoulders and pushed me back toward the mattress.

Despite my misgivings, I felt too sick and too weak to fight back. With tears welling up in my eyes, I leaned back against the bed. "You're scaring me, Doc."

"There's no reason to be scared," he replied matter-of-factly, as he took hold of the IV tubing once again and inserted the end of it into my port. "Now, this is just saline right now, so that won't affect you. Then once I'm done checking you, I'll give you something to help you feel better."

"Ond den you'll be bock te normal, like me." Collette smiled, handing a blood-pressure cuff to Doc.

"But I don't want you putting anything in me." I wiped away my tears. "What did you put in me to begin with, and what is it supposed to be doing to me? Why do I... I feel so awful?"

"Oh, that's just from the sedative," he answered as he wrapped the blood-pressure cuff around my left arm. "That'll wear off eventually, and then you'll feel as good as new." He pumped on the rubber bulb, inflating the cuff around my arm.

"But didn't you put something else in me, too?" I rubbed my cramping stomach, certain there had to be something more.

He put his stethoscope back in his ears and pressed the disc to my arm. "No, just a sedative," he replied, releasing the bulb and watching the dial as the cuff deflated.

"So, then... why did you knock me out?"

"I didn't," he said, then turned to Collette. "She's 124 over 97 – higher than I'd like her to be."

"You didn't?" I asked him.

He ignored me, still talking to Collette. "I'd like to see if we can get that down, so she needs to take it easy, try to keep her calm and –"

"How am I supposed to keep calm when I don't know what's going on!" I shouted with all the energy I could muster.

He cocked his head, looking at me over the top of his horn-rimmed glasses. "Now, that's counter-productive, getting yourself all worked up like that. You know, you asked if you could help, and you can, but you have got to trust us and start cooperating."

"I asked?" I searched through the haze of my memories, trying to recollect.

"Of course, you did," Doc insisted. "And it's so like you to want to do this, Carly – not for the money, but just because you wanted to help those you care so much about."

"Bot de money's on extra bonos, too," Collette added.

"Yes, it is," Doc nodded then pushed his glasses back in place. "So, you have every good reason to stick this out."

I still couldn't remember. "And who am I helping?"

"Boy, you still don't remember anything, do you?" Doc swiped his stringy hair off his broad, shiny forehead. "Well, it'll come back to you soon enough, because I know how much you wanted to help out the Hanikas, and even though I know Vince had reservations, I'm sure –"

"The Hanikas," I repeated from what he'd told me. "I *was* helping the Hanikas, and I'm supposed to be taking care of – Libby!" I shot up. "I left Libby! Where is she!"

"Now stop dot!" Collette grabbed me by the arms, trying to force me back down.

"Libby's fine," Doc quickly added. "She's still with the Kavanaughs. I'm sure Maeve'll take good care of her, and you'll see her soon enough."

"So, jost lie bock down!" Collette insisted as she finally got the better of me and pushed me to the mattress. "Ond let's put dese covars bock op on ya," she added as she pulled the sheets and the Mackinac blanket back over me. "Wid jost dot hospitol gown on, ya might cotch a chill ond get sick, on den it'll jost take dot moch longar ond put off are pay day – ond we wouldn't want dot, would we?" She tucked the blanket in over me. "Dare. Is dot beddar?"

"No, it's not," I grumbled. "I don't want to be here. I just want to go back and this all to go away." I rolled to my side, away from Collette, and closing my eyes, pressed against my throbbing temples. "I didn't volunteer for… for whatever this is. You just put me out and brought me here, didn't you, Doc?" I opened my eyes just enough to glean a look at him. "Or if you didn't, somebody did."

"You asked to help, Carly, even if you don't remember, which is pretty typical for all the girls who've come here." Doc looked away from me, taking a hold of my IV tube and studying it. "I need to get this drip right."

I strained to recollect what had happened, remembering only a really bad smell like rotten eggs. Just the thought gagged me, and so I closed my eyes, now trying to forget.

Collette tried to set my mind at rest. "It wosn't 'til I jost reloxed ond stopped tryon' dot my doughts came bock te me."

I opened my eyes and looked at Doc. "You didn't knock me out, did you?"

"I already told you I didn't," he answered as he pulled something from his pocket and then fiddled with an attachment on the side of my IV tubing.

"So, if you didn't..." I thought more about Doc, about the times he'd come to see Gretchen and managed so many of her symptoms in such a thorough way. For all the times I'd observed Doc's obstinate behavior, I'd reached the conclusion that what he lacked in bedside manner he more than made up for in his passion for healing.

"After this, you'll feel much better," Doc assured me as he dropped the attachment and the tubing fell back at my side.

"It wasn't you," I mumbled as I recalled that horrible stench, and then the rag over my face and... and then it went black and I woke up here.

"There's no sense in you staying in here," I heard Doc tell Collette. "She'll sleep for a while, so I'll get you back to your room."

"But who?" I asked, closing my heavy eyes as I thought back to the Landings and the terrible mess. My mind drifted to Deke – he'd been with me, but then we went to see Rafae and... and we parted ways when he went to meet Rosie. Then I went back, and Eino was there, and he... well, he was being Eino. I remembered that we were talking and I found the photo...

"Bot shouldn't we keep answeron' her while she's tryon' te fall asleep?" Collette sounded so faint when she asked.

"No, go on back to your room," Doc answered as I heard the distant clicking of the door. "It wouldn't matter if you did," he added, and he was right.

As my mind, along with all of my aches and pains, began to fade into nothingness, I came to my final realization. "Eino," I mumbled, without a care in the world.

Before finally fading out, I heard Doc's reply: "And now that you know, he'll never let you return."

Chapter 42

SECOND ONE DOWN

LIGHT BLURRED INTO SHADES OF NIGHT as long lapses of unconsciousness distorted any sense I'd had of time. Many days – maybe even weeks – had to have passed, but when I finally came out my drug-induced state, it was impossible to know how many. As I began to gain my strength back, I came to realize that I was stranded not only in place but also in time.

"What day is it?" I asked Collette one morning during one of her many extended visits to my room.

"I don't know," she answered tersely as she opened one of the lower cupboards and scrounged through a box underneath the countertop. "Whot diffarance does it make, ennaway?"

"None, I guess." I walked to our window where what seemed a never-ending downfall of heavy snow had finally ceased, revealing a dull, overcast day. "But I'd just like to know. That's all."

"Well, it's one day closar te os finoshon' de resarch, ond den getton' all dot money ond go-on' home – dot's whot really moddars." She pushed the box back in the cupboard and shut the door. "Remind me te osk for some more toilot papar. We're down te de lost roll in here."

"Scrounging for the next roll of toilet paper – so, that's what our lives have come to," I sulked as I stared out of the window, studying where the rugged shoreline that surrounded the lighthouse met with the ice leveled out amid more placid drifts of a light, windswept snow as I had on other days gone past – although I couldn't say which ones.

"Ah, if ya start complainon' ogain like ya olways do, den I'm go-on' te hov te leave." With her book of crossword puzzles in hand,

Collette went back to her usual chair and sat down. "Now, help me wid dis one: sevon leddars total, second ond thard leddars are *A-L*, ond it ends wid *N-T*. De word means *ottentive te womon*."

"Hmm. Guess *Arlington* doesn't fit, does it?"

"Nope, bot a good guess, I soppose, since Doc does pay os a lot a' ottention."

"Yeah, but I've learned not to complain so much about my aches and pains, or else he'll put me back into one of those drug-induced stupors."

"*Gollont* hos two *L*'s, doesn't it?" Collette asked, staring at her crossword puzzle.

"Gallant? Yes, it does." I sighed as I scanned the vast expanse of snow-covered ice that, in the distance, dissipated into the open waters of Lake Huron. I figured that's what it would take – someone gallant – to make such a daring journey out to the lighthouse… to find me, and take me home.

"Ond dot fits." Collette penciled in the word.

"Who do you think that is way out there today?" I asked as I watched someone on a distant snowmobile haul more pine trees out on the ice to mark the snow bridge.

"I told ya before, it could be enna-one," she answered, her nose still in her book.

"Maybe it's D'Arcy today," I hopefully suggested. "And maybe he'll come over here. I keep thinking about how he told me he was going to talk with Doc and –"

"How mony times do I hov te tell ya? Evon if D'Arcy, or enna-body else for dot moddar, comes snoopon' oround out here, it's not like Doc's go-on' te invite dem in for tea!" she scoffed. "Besides, Doc says de work is go-on' well ond we're olmost done, so we'll be getton' paid ond go-on' home soon!"

I wasn't so optimistic. "When I can't even remember what day it is, it's hard to comprehend the word *soon*."

"Well, don't ya worry – soon'll be soon enough." She smiled. "Now help me wid dis next one: starts wid de L from de lost one, eight leddars wid de sixth one de leddar I, ond it means *to become weak or discouraged.*

"Me," I answered.

"Dot's not evon a good joke – too short ond not de right leddars." She shook her head, her dreadlocks flopping from side to side. "You con do beddar den dot – you're not evon tryon'."

"I guess that's the point," I replied, never looking over at Collette. Instead, I kept watching the distant figure as he stopped to pull some of the dark foliage off the back of his sled and then climbed back on his snowmobile, continuing on his way. "I wonder how much longer it'll be before they finish the snow bridge. I know there's still open water, but if you look over there, it looks solid for as far as I can see." I pointed to an area of the lake where there appeared to be no sign of open water.

Collette never looked up from her book. "Who knows? Dot depends on de temprachar, I suppose." She paused. "Whot obout *loggon'*? Ya know, like when you're loggon' behind? No, dot doesn't work."

"Well, there are a lot of trees out there now, all lined up heading out that way, waiting to be stuck in the ice." I watched the distant person drop another tree to the ice and then head onward. "The path kind of arches, wouldn't you say?"

"Con't tell from here," she replied while counting boxes in her puzzle. "Yoss, it's got eight leddars, domn it all." Then she looked up. "It's probably jost crooked – most be hard te try ond keep it straight for soch a long distonce."

"Yeah, I suppose so," I continued watching the trail take form, glad for the chance to finally see a bit of what was going on beyond the confines of my room.

Although I still couldn't account for the days, I was sure that many had passed while the heavy downpour of wind-driven snow had obstructed my view. But now I could see well beyond the enormous cement platform below my second-story window, noticing for the first time how the lighthouse's foundation was protected by a mass of rugged, ice-covered, limestone boulders. This enormous rock pile extended outward from the platform, declining for twenty or more yards to where treacherous peaks of ice had formed.

"Tundra," Collette blurted.

"What?" I cocked my head to look at her. "Yeah, I guess it's a tundra farther out there," I agreed as I looked beyond the frozen peaks to where the ice seemed to level out beneath the cover of swirling snow.

"No, *tundra*." She repeated, now pointing into her book and then scribbling down an answer.

"But *tundra*, that doesn't mean *weak or discouraged*," I corrected her.

"No, but it means *treeloss, arctoc plain*, ond dot's five ocross." she replied. "Dot gives me *N* os de tard leddar down."

"Oh. Well, good for you." I looked back out the window, down at the heavy black chain draped between steel post lining to outer edge of the cement foundation. "That's not much of a railing out there, is it."

"Ya don't need moch," Collette replied. "Nobody would try te go enna-where out dare – ot least, not in dis weaddar."

I wondered about that. "But if that's the case, then how did I get here?" I remembered again that Eino had been the last one I'd seen. "I wonder if Eino brought me here somehow, maybe on a snowmobile – but in early January, maybe the ice was still too thin." I paused. "Maybe he used a boat – but I don't know where he could've launched from with the ice so thick along the shoreline."

"Ya wondar too moch, garl. Jost relox ond dink obout someton' hoppy, like counton' op all your money, or solvon' dis crossward wid me." Collette looked in her book. "*On oddiction* endon' wid *T* – Oh, dot's easy: *Hobit*." She wrote in the answer, adding, "Ond dot gives me de lost leddar *H*, so help me get dis *discouroged* one: *L* – blank – *N* – blank-blank – *I* – blank – *H*."

I did appreciate Collette's efforts to keep things upbeat, to help me whittle away the dull hours of waiting and waiting – and for what, I didn't know. But it was hard for me to keep from wondering and worrying about where all of this was going. My curiosity had increased since the return of my faculties, leading me down a path of inquiry into what was happening around me – and to me. But I remained uncertain as to whether or not I really wanted to know all there was to find at the end of that road.

"Try *Languish*," I suggested.

"*Languish*." She counted the squares. "Yoss, dot's it!"

"Good." I pressed my forehead against the cold window pane, trying to glimpse a view of the floor below us. "Is your room downstairs?"

"No, I sleep in a room jost a coupol a' doors down." She waved her hand off to her right.

"Hmm." Pressing my cheek to the glass, I tried to catch a glimpse of her window but couldn't. So, flipping the deadbolt, I slid open the lower sash."

Collette jumped from her chair. "Whot are ya do-on'!"

"Just looking."

"Bot we're go-on' te freeze te death!"

"Only a minute," I told her as I stuck my head through the screenless frame and looked off to the side. Blinking in the arctic air, I looked to both sides and found that my window was the middle one of seven in a row, all appearing to be the same shape and size as mine. Then looking upward, I spotted the roofline right above, indicating that we were on the top floor of the large, box-shaped structure. However, farther off to my right I could also see a white brick edifice attached to ours, its outer walls seeming to angle off one another at about forty-five degrees to form what appeared to be an octagon-shaped tower. The structure extended high into the air, well beyond our roofline, and was topped by an ornate glass structure encircled with a wrought iron railing.

"The lighthouse," I uttered into the faint, frigid breeze.

"A'course it is!" Collette yelled as she yanked me back into the room and slammed the window shut. "Are ya crazy!"

"No. I just wanted to –"

"If ya get sick, den ya con't do your part ond it'll take dot moch longar te get done wid de work!"

I'd never seen Collette like this. "I'm sorry. I won't do it again."

"Well, ya beddar not, cuz we con't offord te hov ya get sick like dot Leila womon did. Den we'd be down one more garl ond it'll take dot moch longar te –"

"Did you say Leila?" I interjected.

"Yoss, de one dot came jost before you."

My heart raced. "Leila's here?"

Collette flipped her dreadlocks to the side. "Yoss, she's here, bot she's not helpon' out now dot —"

"How do you know she's here?"

"Cuz she was stayon' in my room, for goodnoss sakes… dot is, until she came down wid de fevar. Den Doc moved her to her own room so we wouldn't catch whotevar she hos."

"What's wrong with her?"

"I don't know." Collette turned away, going back to her chair and sitting down.

I followed her. "Well, how's she doing? Is she going to be okay?"

"I'm sure she's fine," she answered with assurance while retrieving her book and flipping through its pages. "She's jost got some viross I bet."

"Are you sure?" I asked. "Because maybe it's not a virus — maybe it has something to do with… with whatever it is Doc's doing to us."

"No, dot wouldn't be it." Finding her place, she studied the page. "Doc wouldn't do enna-ton' te hart os."

Looking down, I stared at the plastic tubing still attached to my arm. "How can you be so sure?"

"Well… cuz he nevar hos," she reasoned. "Now, let's see… I still con't figure out dis second one down…"

"But there's no way you could even know that," I argued, growing increasingly frustrated with her inane logic. "I mean, you said yourself that you're pretty much separated from the others, so how can you know that they're all okay?"

"I jost know…" she impassively replied. "Dis one hos five leddars ond de second one's on E —"

"No, you don't!" Determined to keep her undivided attention, I grabbed her by the arm. "You don't know what he's doing to us, and you have no idea what's happened to anyone else, do you!"

Startled, Collette dropped her book and jerked away, breaking free of my grip. "He's jost tryon' te help people, so he wouldn't —"

"Maybe he's not *meaning* to hurt anyone, but that still doesn't mean that he hasn't... and you have no way of knowing if he has!"

"No, ya don't ondarstond..." Collette stood and backed away from me.

"I understand enough. I know that a lot of women are missing, and that one ended up dead, so we better make sure that doesn't happen to another —"

"Doc didn't do dot," she insisted. "I don't dink Helena wos evar evon here, ond if she wos, he wouldn't a' hart her cuz he's tryon' te help people. We're all helpon' dem, ond getton' paid for it, too, so we jost hov te cooperate, keep on —"

"Keep on letting him inject drugs into us?" I pointed at my arm. "Is that what we have to do?"

She stepped back toward the door. "Whotevar it is, it's not harton' os. Look — I'm fine, ond you're fine, so it most be warkon'."

"But Leila's not fine," I argued. "She might end up the second one to die if this goes on, and who knows who else is here, maybe sick or dying, too."

"No, Doc's takon' good care a' os."

"Really? So, is that why he drugs us? And is that why he keeps us separated? So we don't have any idea who's living and who's —?"

"I told ya before, ya osk too mony questions!" She yelled at me, then turned and pounded on the door. "Doc! Hey, Doc! I wont te go bock te my room — now!"

I kept at her. "Tell me who else you've seen here — any of the other missing girls?"

"No, I hovn't seen enna of dem in awhile," she answered me and then yelled again. "Doc! Put me bock in my room now!"

"Please, Collette — tell me, who did you see?" I pleaded. "I just want to know who else is here, and then I can ask Doc how they're doing — what's going on with them."

"Doc! Come get me!" she yelled at the door and then turned back, glaring at me as she lowered her voice. "Ya need te jost leave it alone, be glod dot whotevar he's do-on' wid os is workon' okay.

Den it'll all be ovar wid soon ond we con jost take our money ond get out a' here."

"Just tell me, who else did you see?" I asked, refusing to relent. "What about that first girl I heard about – that Missy girl that disappeared with the St. Amour girl. Is she here?"

"She's done," she told me. "She went home, ond we will soon, too, if ya jost stop dis!"

"She's okay? You saw her?"

"Jost stop!" she yelled. "Doc! Get me out a' here! I've hod it wid dis crazy garl ya got me in here wid!"

The deadbolt turned and Collette stepped back, waiting for Doc to enter.

I didn't wait, though, as I launched into my tirade. "Doc why are we locked up like this? Can't we see the others? I want to know if they're okay."

The door slowly opened just a crack, a feminine voice coming from behind it. "Stop that pounding, Collette. You're going to upset the others."

"Oh, it's you." Collette took a step back from the door. "Obout time someone came. Dis one's all in a' fronzy – beddar get her someton' te calm her down."

Then the door opened the rest of the way, revealing the woman behind it. Her long, satin-black hair draped to one side, contrasting sharply against the stark white of her lab coat.

I gasped. "Annahede."

Chapter 43

PLAYING ALONG

"YOU'VE CAUSED ENOUGH TROUBLE already, so what is it now?" Annahede asked angrily, rolling her dark eyes.

"I... I..." Too stunned for words, I stepped back.

"Yeah, always about you, isn't it?" Annahede snapped, then turned to Collette. "So, what's the problem?"

"She jost won't shot op!" Collette pointed at me. "She's oskon' too mony questions obout whot we're do-on' ond who's here ond —"

"But I thought you didn't want to know?" Annahede interrupted, directing her questions to me. "I thought you didn't want to hear any secrets?"

"What are you doing here?" I finally managed to ask her.

"Helping, which is what you should be doing, too."

"So, they took you, too – that's why you disappeared? Because I thought maybe you..." I paused, looking at the jacket that covered her arms. "But where's you're IV port?"

"See, I told ya she osks too moch," Collette contended.

"I'll take care of this," Annahede assured Collette, crossing her arms as she cocked her head toward me. "I'm here helping in a different way – sort of like a coordinator, you might say."

I felt my jaw drop. "You mean, you're in on this, too?" I shook my head. "I can't believe you'd do something so... and now you've brought me into this, too?"

"No, that's where you're wrong, Carly. I had nothing to do with bringing you here," she insisted. "You said you wanted no part of this, so I left you out of it."

"Then how did I —"

"Well, obviously you changed your mind – must've told Eino differently," she speculated, arching her brow. "He's the one who brought you here... when you volunteered."

"But I don't remember volunteering."

"Nobody evar does," Collette replied. "All dot medison makes it hard te remembar – I told ya dot before."

I wasn't so sure. "I do remember Eino – he was at the Landings when I went back to find the checks, and when I –"

"The checks!" Annahede stepped closer to me. "You found the checks?"

"De money!" Collette came closer, too. "See, I told ya de money would be comon' soon! Dot hos te mean dot we're olmost done, once ond for all!" Smiling, she clapped her hands.

I thought about it a moment, trying to remember. "Yeah, there were some checks inside of a picture frame, and when I found them, I pulled them out and..." I recalled the smell I'd tried so hard to forget. "Rotten eggs."

"What?" Annahede scowled, looking perplexed.

"I remembar dot, too," Collette told us. "Jost before it all went block, dare wos dot smell like rotton eggs."

"Chloroform," Annahede acknowledged, then looked at the floor, muttering to herself. "So, that's where all the checks went."

"Chloroform?" I repeated back to her. "Is that how I got here?"

"Oh, that stuff is harmless." Annahede looked back at me, shrugging. "It's just what Eino likes to use to get all the volunteers here – only a precaution, so there's no problem."

"No problem!" I snapped. "You mean, so we don't put up a fight when he kidnaps us!"

"Oh, stop it!" Annahede glared at me. "He didn't kidnap anybody! You volunteered!"

"And why on earth would I do that!"

Collette smirked. "For de money, a' course! So, where are de checks?"

Annahede ignored her, leaning toward me. "And in your case, Carly, I'm sure you volunteered because you wanted to help out your buddies, the Hanikas."

I remembered sometime ago, when I'd first come to the lighthouse, that Doc had said the same thing. "But I don't get it. How is being here helping the Hanikas?"

Annahede laughed. "Oh, if you don't understand that, then you've missed the whole point."

I looked down, pondering all that I knew. "So, all of this research is... Doc's trying to cure Huntington's, isn't he?"

"Dot, ond some oddar diseasos, too," Collette answered.

"So, you see?" Annahede brought up her chin, staring down her nose at me. "This research is all for a very important cause. It could save hundreds – no, maybe thousands of lives, and that includes the lives of some people you *claim* to care so much about. So, you better start cooperating and –"

"You *know* I care about the Hanikas, but I don't want –"

"Shut up!" she shouted in my face. "If you can't get with the program here, then you have no idea what it is to care. Why, there are women here who don't even know the Hanikas, but they want to help – women who are committed to doing what has to be done here, just like Collette has already."

Collette looked a bit taken back by Annahede's outburst, but still agreed. "Well, yoss, I want te help, ond it's helpon' me, too, cuz I'll get the money and –"

"So, if you don't remember volunteering," Annahede continued, "then you need to just get over it, because you *should* have volunteered. Now, you have to stop making trouble around here and go along with the program."

"The program? What, letting Doc test these drugs on us and –"

"He's not testing drugs on you! Don't be ridiculous – It's not like that."

"Well, then tell me what it is!"

"I'll tell you what it is!" She shook her finger in my face. "It's the only way you can really make a difference – instead of just sitting around all the time feeling sorry for the Hanikas and never doing anything to really help them."

"What are you talking about!" I yelled back. "I've been with the Hanikas every day, helping them in every way possible. You have no idea what I've been doing."

"Oh, yes I do!" Annahede crossed her arms, shifting her weight as she glared at me. "You cook and fold clothes, get Libby to school, and then you push Gretchen around in that wheelchair all day while you feel sorry for her. Yeah, you've been wrapped up tight in all your pity and self-righteousness, so busy trying to make things comfortable for them when you know it's a losing battle."

"No. I'm fighting for quality of life, making every day –"

"Quality of life!" Annahede scoffed. "You'd rather try to do all that feel-good stuff instead of doing the *tough* work by coming here and making a *real* sacrifice. No, you've been too busy playing 'nice' for everyone to see – sucking up to people with all that gushy kindness like you did with that poor Abel kid... and look what ended up happening to him because of all your good intentions."

Without a word, I slapped her hard across the face.

"Why you little..." Annahede sputtered before slapping me back.

Collette had seen enough, running from the room as she yelled for help. "Doc! Doc! Dare fighton'!"

Brushing my disheveled hair from my eyes, I seethed with absolute hatred, staring down Annahede. "What happened to Abel was *not* my fault. I didn't start that fire."

"But you were the reason why he went into the fire!" she fiercely argued as she gently touched the flushed patch of finger marks appearing on her cheek. "If it weren't for you, he never would have gone in there, and he'd still be –"

"No. No." I shook my hands at her, waving her off. "I am *not* listening to this – I *don't* have to put up with this." Stepping away from her, I headed for the open door. "This is absolute nonsense, and I'm not listening to anymore of it."

Annahede was right behind me. "And where do you think you're going?"

"I'm going to find Doc, and tell him I'm done here – that he's sending me home right now. I have had it with –"

"What's going on in here!" Doc suddenly appeared in the doorway. "Are you all right?" He looked me over.

"I was just coming to see you," I replied, stepping back from the doorway to let him come in. "I've had enough of this, Doc, and whether I volunteered or not, it's time for me to go home."

"Whoa-whoa-whoa!" He held his hands up toward me, motioning me to stop. Then sighing, he turned back toward Collette who'd come along behind him. "Why don't you head back to your room now, and I'll be along shortly," he told her.

"Glodly!" she replied, dashing off.

Doc closed the room door and then turned back to me, taking me by the arm and guiding me back into the room toward my bed. "Collette said you two got into a fight. Are you okay?" He was still studying me from head to toe.

"Yeah, I'm fine, but I need to go now."

"And I'm fine, too." Annahede scowled as she came up behind us, rubbing her cheek. "Thanks for asking."

Rather than giving her any sympathy, Doc turned on her, instead "What're you doing, coming in here to stir up trouble!"

"Hey, it wasn't me!" she argued. "I heard some noise – Collette was pounding on the door, and you were still doing that procedure so I had to come in and try to get things under control before the –"

"And you did such a fine job of that!" he snapped back. "You could have hurt one of them, and then we'd be down –"

"What's wrong with Leila?" I interrupted, demanding to know. "Was that the 'procedure' you were doing – taking care of Leila?"

"Leila!" Doc repeated, glaring at Annahede.

"Hey, I didn't say anything about that," she told him. "Collette must've let that one slip."

"Yeah, I know about Leila," I told Doc. "What are you doing to her – to all these women? Is she going to be okay?"

"She's fine, and you need to just calm down now," Doc insisted, walking toward me with his arms outward as if trying to herd me back to my bed. "This isn't helping things."

"But I don't want to help! I want no part of this – any of it! I just want to go home... now!"

Doc's voice remained steady as he folded back the sheet on my bed. "You're just feeling anxious, and that's normal, so why don't you just sit down here and I'll –"

"No." I stayed standing. "I don't know what you're up to here, but I'm done. Now take me home!"

"I told you she'd be unreasonable," Annahede muttered.

Doc ignored her. "It's okay, Carly. Just sit down here and we'll talk about it." He reached for my arm. "And I'll give you a little something to help you calm —"

"No!" I jerked my arm away, pressing the IV port to my chest. "You are *not* doping me up anymore! Now you just tell me where my clothes are and I'll get dressed while you get ready to take me back… however it is that you'd do that."

Doc pressed his hand to his broad forehead, drawing it back along the top of his head to pull his stringy hair away from his face. "That's just not possible, Carly."

"What do you mean?" I asked. "There's got to be some way — you have to have some means of transportation that —"

"You can't leave." He stared at me over the tops of his glasses.

I studied him for a moment. "You mean it's not possible, or that you *won't* let me leave?"

"I can't allow it, because we really need your help here and now that you know what —"

"I don't know anything!" I insisted.

"Oh, yes, you do!" Annahede shot back. "You know that Eino and I are helping, and that's enough!"

"Yeah, but I don't have a clue what you're doing!" I told them both. "I am *so* in the dark here, and I really don't want to know anymore about what you're up to, if that's what it takes to get me out of here."

Doc stepped to the window, looking out over the frozen lake. "You know where we're doing our research, and you also know about the girls staying here, so you see… we can't just let you go now."

"Yes, you can," I argued. "You have to!"

"No, we don't," Annahede quarreled with me. "That was the deal we made with all the volunteers: no one leaves until we're through with this."

I walked to Doc's side, pleading with him. "If all of this isn't hurting anyone and you're doing it to help Gretchen, then you can trust me to keep quiet about this. You know that I'd do anything to help the –"

He turned on me. "No, I *don't* know that! With the way you've been carrying on around here, I don't know what you'll do!"

"I... Well, I... I just don't..." I was at a loss for words, stunned by Doc's abrupt burst of anger.

"There's too much at stake here," Doc continued as he looked away from me, toward the ceiling. "No. You made the commitment, and now you're going to have to stay."

I reached out to him, taking a hold of his forearm. "But Doc, you know it's wrong to keep me here against my will. That would be like kid –"

"No, it's not!" He shook off my grasp, still looking away from me. "You volunteered to do this, and I'm just holding you to your word. So you need to stop all this complaining and just buck up to your commitment."

"Everyone else here is," Annahede added. "So, you have to, too."

I refused to relent. "But I didn't ask to do this! Eino just took me and –"

"Nobody took you! You volunteered!" He glared right at me, scowling with his angry eyes that were magnified by his glasses. "Now, you're going to stop talking up all of this kidnapping nonsense and bide your time until we're finished, because what we're doing here is much more important than your sudden whim to go back home!"

"But I need to go back to the Hanikas," I argued. "Libby needs me, and they'll wonder where I am. I know Vincent's supporting you here, and I know he didn't want me involved, so just take me back."

Annahede shook her head. "I'm telling you, Doc, her ties to Vincent will cause us more harm than good."

Doc ignored Annahede, stepping to my bed as he waved his arm toward it. "Now, you're going to get back up here and lie down for a while until you have a chance to calm down!"

I stepped back, panic pulsing through me. "No. You're not going to knock me out with some sedative again."

"You get up here now or I *will* put you out!" Doc yelled.

I froze in place, crying out to him, "What are you going to do to me?"

Annahede grabbed me by the arm and pulled me toward the bed. "He's not going to do *anything* to you right now, *if* you cooperate!"

Going along, I followed her and climbed up on the bed, my heart racing as I shook from head to toe. "Now what?"

"I told you, you've just got to lie there and settle down!" Doc demanded, firmly pushing against my shoulders.

Trembling, I pushed back. "No, I don't want any more drugs. Tell me what you're going to do to me."

Still pushing, Doc grumbled, "I'm just going to have you lie down! That's it!" Unable to force me down, he turned to Annahede. "I'm going to need your help."

Annahede moved toward the cupboards. "I'll get the restraints."

"No!" Frightened at the prospect of being tied down to my bed, I succumbed to Doc's demands and slowly lowered myself to the mattress. "But *please* don't sedate me again, Doc. I'll try to calm down, I promise."

Doc sighed. "That's all I'm asking of you."

Annahede opened a cupboard door. "I think you better still restrain her, Doc. You don't know what she might do to herself if she's like this, and we can't have her —"

"I told you, I'm fine," I insisted, trying to play along for the moment. "If you don't try to put that IV thing in me, I'll be okay."

Avoiding my eyes, Doc looked me over from head to toe. "Well, that'll work for now. Of course, eventually we will have to sedate you again when we need your help with our work here, but we'll save that for another day — cross that bridge when we come to it." He stepped back from me, turning to Annahede. "I think we're good here now. Why don't you head down to Collette's room and get her settled in — make sure she's all right after this, okay?"

"Are you sure?" Annahede asked him, the restraints now in her hands.

"Yes, I think Carly's going to come around on this."

"I'm just fine, really." I breathed deeply, trying to calm myself to their satisfaction.

"Suit yourself." Annahede returned the restraints to the cabinet and then turned back to wave her finger at me. "Behave yourself, Carly, so I won't have to come back in here and set you straight." With that final threat, she turned on her heels and stormed from the room.

"Let's keep you warm so you don't end up sick." Doc pulled the blanket and sheets over me, smoothing them out on the side. "No sense taking your vitals right now – not after that little episode. They'd just be all out of whack anyway." Crossing his arms and smiling gently, he looked down my legs and then back to my chest. "I'll come back in a while to check your blood pressure and everything else. So, do you think you'll be okay if you're in here alone for a little while?"

"Sure." I managed to flash him a reassuring smile. "Give me a little time to gather myself."

"Of course." He stepped away from me, taking a few steps toward the door before stopping to add, "I do appreciate what you're doing here, Carly. I appreciate all the volunteers, and I don't take their service lightly. I realize that this is a huge commitment, and so you should know that I'll take good care of you just like the others." He paused. "And I do understand your curiosity about all this, but I remain convinced that the less you know, the better our chances to see this through. However, I can tell you this: what I'm doing here will not harm you, and it will help so many people." His voice grew stronger as he warmed to his speech. "We're really going to make a difference here, Carly. We'll finally make the breakthrough that I've been working towards for so long, and then the scientific community will *have* to admit I was right – that the solution is right here in front of us. Then we can put all the politics behind us and…" He paused again. "Well, I suppose you don't want to hear all of that now, do you?"

"It's fine," I replied, biting my lip.

"Well, I just wanted you to know that you're in good hands, and that everything's going to be fine. So, I'll be back to check on you in a little while." His footsteps headed toward the door. "Get some rest," he added, and then I heard the door open and close, followed by the sound of the deadbolt locking.

I sprung from the bed, quickly stepping to the window. Pressing my head against the glass, I searched the lower side of the building for a door but found only a row of windows.

"I wonder…" I mumbled to myself, certain that there had to be some way out of the building but unable to figure out where. Of course, at the moment, it didn't really matter since I had no means of escape from the island even if somehow I was able to break out of the building. But that fact didn't stop my mind from racing.

I figured that Doc had to have a means of transportation stashed somewhere around the place, but without free reign to search, there was no way of knowing. I'd just have to keep my ears and eyes open, hoping to come across some hint about how he connects with civilization. Then, with the right information, maybe I could make a move.

I backed away from the window and sat on the edge of the bed, thinking for a moment about what might be ahead of me if I didn't somehow escape. I looked up at the IV bottle hanging from the post at the head of my bed, wondering when I would feel the cool saline flowing again in my veins, and then the warmth washing over me as I faded back into oblivion.

"No!" I closed my eyes, pushing the fear of the unknown away from me. Dwelling on the worst-case-scenario would not help me. I needed to remain focused on what I could do to avoid letting anything bad happen – keep thinking about ways to get out of this.

I stepped back to the window, looking out through the lightly falling snow at all the work already accomplished on the snow bridge. Many more trees had been put in place forming a long arch that headed far into the distance before finally coming to an end, leaving only a small patch that still needed to be completed. I figured that if the temperatures stayed down amid overcast skies, the ice would thicken enough in the thin area, making it possible to finally connect the bridge to the mainland. Then once finished, there would be frequent snowmobile traffic, bringing more people into close proximity to Beacon Point.

Turning back to my bed, I tossed around my sheets and blanket, wondering if I could tie them together to form some sort of signal to hang out my window.

"That won't work," I muttered. Tossing the covers back in place, I figured such an attempt would be stopped too quickly by Doc and those loyal to him. They'd have my covers back in the window so fast that I'd never have a chance to get anyone's attention. And what's worse is that I'd be in so much trouble that Doc would definitely agree to keep me in restraints, making any future attempts at escape absolutely impossible.

I plopped back down on the bed, frustrated but not ready to surrender. So, maybe that plan wouldn't work, but there had to be another one – a better one – somewhere out there. All I had to do was think of it, and I knew I had idle time ahead for doing just that. But that time would not be infinite, for the clock was ticking down to when Doc would come again to inject me with a sedative and do God-only-knows-what to me. So, I knew I had to quickly develop a foolproof plan to save myself, and maybe others, as well, for there could easily be others stuck here against their will.

My plan for the moment was simple: play along for now, acting as cooperative as possible while quietly maintaining my own integrity and plans for escape. It seemed a safe and smart plan – a way of keeping my wits about me while avoiding any development of some crazed case of Stockholm syndrome. I'd just ignore Doc's talk of helping others, including the Hanikas, and remain focused on my most important mission: to find some way out here, and soon.

I reclined back on my bed, taking in a deep breath and exhaling as I tried to clear my mind. I pulled up my blanket and rolled to my side, staring out the window for inspiration. Before further plotting my escape though, I came to one simple yet significant revelation. I was lying down, *not* because Doc had made me do so, but simply because I had chosen to.

Chapter 44

A BEACON OF HOPE

THE FOGHORN BECAME MY ENEMY, blaring at regular intervals to remind me that time was moving forward and yet I still had not discerned a doable plan for escape. Like an insomniac, I couldn't sleep for the next few nights. Instead, I'd lie in bed, wide awake, devising one clever escape plot after another. But each time I'd reach the same conclusion – that all of my ideas lacked the same significant element: how to unlock my door so I could gain access to other parts of the building.

As days went past and exhaustion set in, I'd find myself dosing off and on during the day for very short, restless periods of time. Then I'd wake with a start, fearful that Doc would try to sneak up on me and start up a sedative. With this ongoing fear, I once considered yanking that awful IV port right out of my arm, but then figured better. I had no doubt that if I did this, Doc would just install another and, in addition, sedate me or tie me up or worse – maybe start one of his so-called 'procedures.' Knowing this, I resorted to the only other tactic I could think of: napping on my stomach with my tube-injected arm tucked snuggly underneath me.

After one unusually long nap, I woke up to find my arm tingling from sleeping on it for so long. Pulling it out from under me, I rolled to my side and gazed out the window, finding that night had descended while I'd slept. Streaks of wind-driven snow hurdled horizontally past the window, each dashing white line starkly contrasting against the deep blue, moonless sky. I watched as the flying bands of white suddenly turned brighter, lighting up with the night sky for one brief moment before, just as quickly, fading back into darkness. I waited a few moments, knowing that the lighthouse beacon would steadily sweep across the other side of the lake shedding light along its journey while making its way back to brighten my point of view once more.

It didn't take long to get a feel for the beacon's rhythm, its steady flashes serving as another reminder that time was passing by and I no longer had any control over it. I was losing faith, resigning myself to accept that whatever Doc had planned for me was going to happen, and soon. Try as I might, I couldn't stop the inevitable, just as I couldn't stop the light from flashing or the foghorn from blaring, or time from marching onward.

Of course, I wouldn't go down without a fight, but now was not the time. For now, I needed to rest, saving up my energy for whatever was yet to come. So, I rolled back onto my stomach, tucking my arm under me and closing my eyes in hopes of warding off my insomnia and getting some more rest.

Then I heard the deadbolt slide, turning slowly until it clicked into place. My heart racing, I shot upright, wondering what Doc would be coming in for at such a late hour.

The door barely made a sound as it slowly swung open, the beam of a flashlight becoming more visible as its source came out from behind the door. Then the light turned to me, glaring into my eyes.

I held up my hand, sheltering my eyes from the blinding light. "What are you up to now, Doc?" I asked, trying to sound resolute despite the tremble in my voice.

"Carly! Is that you?" a female voice whispered.

I climbed out of bed as the light came closer, staring at it in disbelief. "Pepper? That can't be you!"

"Hey, wish it wasn't!" Pepper lowered her flashlight as she walked quickly to me, her face now illuminated by the glow from the light. "I had no idea you were stuck here!" She threw her arms around me.

I hugged her, whispering back, "I thought you were at your folks!"

Lowering her arms, she released her hold on me. "I was, but when I got back to the island, Eino was there at the airport and offered me a ride – in hindsight, something he must've had planned because that's the last thing I remember before I ended up here. Was he the one who got you here, too?"

"I think so," I answered in a low voice, stepping back to sit down on the edge of my bed. "How did you get in here?" I pointed at the open door.

"Oh, yeah – better shut that!" she whispered, quickly tip-toeing over to quietly shut the door. "I don't want them to find out I've got this!" In the dim light emanating from the outer edges of the flashlight that she held down at her side, her other hand drew a key from her hospital robe pocket and held it out for me to see. "I got this from Doc when he wasn't looking." Releasing it into her palm, she wrapped her fingers around it, squeezing it tightly in her fist. "Gets me out of my room so I can look around at night – check out the other rooms."

I pointed at her fist. "So, that's a master key? We could use that to –"

"No, I think it's just for the rooms… although I haven't had the chance to try much else."

"Well, we need to try!" I insisted, still keeping my voice down. "We'll look around – see if we can find a snowmobile or something that –"

"Whoa-whoa-whoa!" Pepper pocketed the key, walking back over and taking a seat on the edge of the bed beside me. "If we get caught sneaking out of our rooms, we'll be bound up for sure – trust me, I know!" She rubbed her wrist. "But try to escape? No way! That could be so much worse – it's deadly business out there!"

"But we have to get out of here!"

"You don't think I know that?" she quietly replied. "But it's no good if we get killed trying, just like that Helena Moore girl did."

"So, Helena *was* here, too – and that must mean it was Doc or Eino that put her body in that dumpster then!" I felt myself beginning to shake uncontrollably.

"And how do you think that happened?" Pepper cocked her head at me. "She drowned trying to get away from here!"

"You're kidding, right?" I asked, even though I knew she wasn't. "But how can you know that?"

"I found Missy, the girl that went missing with her."

"What, here?"

Pepper nodded, setting her flashlight on top of the bed. "Yeah, I stumbled onto her when I went sneaking around the place, and she told me about how she tried to escape with Helena during last summer. They broke out and tried to swim for it, but when she realized she couldn't make it, she swam back here."

"But what, Helena couldn't make it back?" I speculated.

"She never tried to. Missy said she didn't give up — kept swimming for the island until she was out of sight."

"And she never made it." I looked down, contemplating Helena's horrific fate. "But the note, and the dumpster where —"

"All Eino's doing," Pepper interjected. "Missy heard it from another girl here, how Doc was so pissed off at Eino for setting all of that up, using her to make it look like some nut-job was behind all this."

For a moment, I wondered about Eino's roll in this, and how much more he might be responsible for.

"Yeah, and then poor Missy," Pepper quietly continued. "She assumed Helena made it, so she was expecting someone to come rescue her at any time. Bet you can imagine how she felt when some new volunteer showed up here and told her that her friend was dead... and no less that help wasn't coming after all."

I sighed, thinking this over. "That's horrible, but it's no reason for us to give up trying. I mean, we're not going to swim for it. We're trying to find transportation and —"

Pepper leaned toward me, whispering as she pointed to the window. "Do you have any idea how wicked the weather is out there? You'd die in no time in those conditions, especially dressed like that!" She pointed at my gown.

"Well, we'll look for clothes and bundle up!" I argued in a soft tone. "With that key, maybe we can get into —"

"What, a few extra layers? And then what?" Even in the dim light, Pepper's eyes looked wild. "We don't even have the key for a snowmobile or a boat or whatever, and I don't know how to hot-wire stuff, though I wish I did!" She paused. "So, what are you thinking – that we'll walk home? Not a chance!"

I turned to look out the window as the wind furiously whipped the snow through the darkness, realizing she was right. Despite all of my plotting, I had to admit that, at least for the time being, it was too dangerous to attempt an escape.

I bit my bottom lip, gazing helplessly at my good friend. "What's going to happen to us?"

Pepper sighed, looking down. "I'm afraid I know a bit of that, too." She looked back up at me. "He's already gotten me."

I grabbed her arm, whispering, "What do you mean?"

"Well, Doc was trying to sedate me again –"

"He's done that to me, a couple of times."

"No doubt." She quietly conceded, nodding. "Yeah, he's knocked me out a few times while I've been here. So, one time when he slid the saline needle into my arm, I reached over when he wasn't looking and slid it back out."

"Did he catch you?"

"No, not right away – I kind of tucked the tube under my arm so it looked like it was going into me, and so when he shot some sedative into my IV, it didn't go into me... but I acted like I went out."

I was amazed by her gall. "So, what happened?"

"Well, I didn't see anything because, remember, I had my eyes shut, trying to act like I was unconscious. But I did hear him doing a lot of tinkering around, before he..." She paused.

"He what?"

She scowled. "He pulled the blanket off the foot of my bed and grabbed my legs – dragged me down until my butt was almost to the end, my legs just hanging there..." She shook her head. "Then he pulled out some kind of stirrup-like things – they must've been attached under the bed somewhere, because the next thing I know, he's got my feet in them and has me propped up like they do at a gynecologist's office."

"Oh, my God!" I clasped my hand over my mouth, my heart racing. "He didn't... what did he do to you!"

"Nothing at first, because he was still fiddling around with stuff – sounded like instruments clanking together. And of course, I'm getting so upset at this point, but I hung in there and kept quiet because I still wanted to see what the hell he was up to! So, I've still got my eyes shut, and he must've brought over a lamp because I could feel the heat from it. But then when he pushed on my legs, that's when I'd had enough."

"So, what did you do!" I whispered, feeling nauseous as I imagined what she'd been through.

"Well, first thing, I jumped up and scared the crap out of him, that's what I did!" She whispered, throwing her shoulders back with a smirk of self-confidence. "Then I yelled at him and, yeah, I asked what the hell he was doing. Well, he was all upset and started telling me that it wasn't how it looked – that he's doing all this for science and that I needed to cooperate. But *I* told *him* that I wasn't going to cooperate with *that* kind of business, whatever his sorry excuse was. Then I hopped off the bed and headed for the door, and that's when he yelled for help from that little bitch friend of yours, Annahede. I didn't know *she* was here – bet you didn't, either!"

"Actually, I did," I nodded. "So, did she come?"

"Oh, yeah, and then I get into this big fist fight with her and Doc, and I was actually holding them off – that is, until Doc stuck me with a shot full of some drug to knock me out. That's the last thing I remember." She looked at me. "And then I was coming around, feeling like I had some terrible hangover, and hurting all over – probably because I put up one hell of a good fight, but I guess not good enough. So, that Doc, he must've still managed to..." She scowled. "...implant me."

I felt my jaw drop. "What did you say?"

"You know – that's *got* to be what he's doing," Pepper replied in a soft but firm voice. "Think about it – Helena was pregnant when she died, and you told me about how many she was expecting. That sort of thing doesn't just happen."

"That can't be!" Trembling with fear, I leapt off the bed and went to the window, searching the night sky for answers. "How are we going to get out of here!" My voice was rising. "I can't let him do this to me! And you...!"

Pepper walked up to me. "Sh! Keep your voice down!"

I paced, continuing my rant at a whisper. "We've got to get you some help – fix what...whatever it is he did! Oh, my God! Do you think you're pregnant?"

"Of course, I do," she answered. "And I do want to save you from having this happen to you, too, but not at the risk of us dying! We have to come up with a better plan."

Still keeping my voice down, I looked her in the eyes. "I've been trying to think of ways to escape, but I kept getting stuck up on the locked doors. So, now that we've got a key, we have to look around for some way out of here."

"No," Pepper insisted. "I told you, it's too dangerous."

"Well, it's too dangerous to stay here!" I shouted.

"Sh!" she snapped. "If you wake someone, we're done!" She grabbed me by the shoulders, shaking me. "Now, get it through your head: we can't just walk out of here, so we've got to think of a way to get the help to come to us! Think about it that way. How can we get someone to come and find us?"

I took a deep breath, trying to calm down and regain my wits. "I thought about using my sheets for a signal."

"Yeah! We could tie them together and –"

"No, it won't work." I stepped to my bed, lifting my sheets and blanket. "They're so light colored, no one'll see them in this weather, especially against this house."

"But you're forgetting about the key," she whispered. "What if we draped it from the lighthouse tower?"

"Could we even get up there?" Stepping to the window, I pressed my face against the ice-cold glass, looking at the tower in the darkness.

"I don't know. I haven't been down there yet, and I don't even know if there are doors or if they're locked and whether or not this key would work on them." She scratched her head. "I also don't know yet where Doc's room is – if he stays down there, we'd probably run into him."

"Well, that's a chance we'll have to take." I studied the tower, the glaring beacon twirling about the top. "But it's not going to work up there, either," I whispered to Pepper.

"What do you mean?" She stepped over to look for herself. "If we tie two or three together and hang them up there, they'll blow in the wind and –"

"And Doc'll see them long before anyone else will. I'm telling you, they're too light. They won't be seen against a white overcast sky or in the snow... and even if the sun's shining on a clear blue day, I don't think anybody would even think much of it anyway. No, I've already thought this one through, and it'll just get us in trouble."

Pepper wouldn't give up. "What about at night? It would show up against the dark sky, and with that beacon flashing, it'll light up the white. Plus that way, Doc'll be asleep so he won't –"

"No one's going to be out here at night, and it's too far away from land for anybody to see," I quietly argued.

She pointed outward, into the darkness. "But when that snow bridge is finished, you know there'll be people just stupid enough to ride across it at night. They'll see it – I'm sure!"

"I wish you were right, but have you looked at this?" I pointed out the window at the tower.

Following my finger, she looked up toward the swirling beacon as it came around, lighting up the night. "Yeah, I looked. So what?"

"That beacon is so bright – if you look toward the tower from anywhere out there, that's all you're going to see. I don't care what's hanging off from there, if somebody looks this way, the only thing they'll notice is..." I stopped mid-sentence, suddenly realizing what else I was saying.

Pepper sighed. "Well, maybe it's still worth a try. So we might get in trouble, but if we don't take a chance –"

"Wait! Wait!" I interrupted her, speaking a bit louder in my excitement.

"Sh!" she scolded me. Then she quietly asked, "What?"

"The light – that *is* what people see!"

"Yeah?"

"So, if somebody looked out here and didn't see it, they might think that something was wrong!"

Pepper smiled. "Yes! They would!" She threw her arms around me. "You're a genius!"

Patting her on the back, I cautioned, "Yeah, but we still don't know if we can get to it, and if so, whether we can knock the thing out."

"Of course, we can! Where there's a will, there's a way." Pepper released me, a new sense of confidence in her voice.

"I hope so," I whispered back. "So, when do you want to scout out the plan?"

"Scout it out?" She picked up her flashlight. "There's no sense in that! If the coast is clear, we go!"

"What? Now?"

"Yes, now! We can't afford to wait!" She headed for the door.

Walking behind her, I could feel myself trembling as adrenalin coursed through my body. But for the first time since I'd arrived at the lighthouse, the racing of my heart did not immobilize me; rather, it empowered me, making me feel wide-eyed and full of energy, ready to take on the world.

Pulling the door open, Pepper waved the flashlight in my direction, motioning for me to follow her. "Come on, let's go!" she whispered, the light dimming as it went with her out the door.

Looking back one last time at the flash of the beacon, I grabbed my robe, pulled it on, and turned to follow her. Taking a deep breath, I readied myself for the unknown ahead, grateful for finally getting the chance to, once again, shape my own destiny.

Chapter 45

STOPPING THE CLOCK

THE LIGHT WAS ALREADY FADING AWAY from me when I stepped through the doorway into another room. In a flash from the beacon through a side window, I saw boxes stacked around the room, likely some of the supplies we used here at the lighthouse. With no time to explore, I continued through the room in the shadows, following the fading hint of light to the room's other door and stepping through it into the hallway.

Quietly shutting this door behind me, I turned and looked down the hallway, finding that Pepper had made her way to one end. There she'd encountered a door, and after testing its handle, found it to be locked.

As I tip-toed closer in my cotton socks, Pepper held her finger to her mouth, motioning for me to keep silent. Then she brought the flashlight upward, holding it very tightly to the door as she directed its beam toward the lock. Drawing the key from her pocket, she carefully pushed it in and tried to turn it. With a faint scratching sound, the lock gave way, turning until it clicked into the unlocked position.

"Yes!" Pepper's exclamation was barely audible as she removed the key from the lock and placed it back in her pocket. Then ever so cautiously, she gradually turned the doorknob and pulled, but the door would not give. Tugging a little harder, it finally budged just a bit, screeching as the door sweep dragged against the threshold.

"Shoot!" Pepper mouthed without uttering a sound, her face contorted in a grimace.

I held my breath as Pepper tugged again, the door giving another screech in return. Then she gave it one last yank, the door screeching one loud, last time before popping open. Pepper looked at me, taking in a deep breath and exhaling as I released mine, both of us blowing out through pursed lips.

She pulled the door wide open, waving for me to enter as she whispered, "You first."

I stepped past her and through the doorway into the cold, dark space ahead of me. "I can't see," I whispered to her.

Coming in behind me, Pepper swept the flashlight once quickly around the area to reveal the octagon shaped room with a spiraling staircase winding upwards around us, attached to the outer walls of the room.

"It's freezing in here," I whispered to her.

"Not as bad as outside, but cold enough," she agreed as she shut the door.

I shivered. "Must've skipped the insulation in here."

"And the heat!" she quietly replied as she brought the beam of light to rest on some stacks of cardboard boxes leaning against the wall to our left. "What's this?"

I reached down, pulling a brick of cheddar cheese out of an open box. "It's cold storage. Doc must use this as a kind of refrigerator for our food supplies."

"So, that's where the mac and cheese comes from. What else has he got in here?" she quietly asked, her steaming breath made visible by the beam of light from her flashlight.

"There's some packaged meats, and here's a big box of eggs." I walked further along the wall, shivering as I studied the contents of other open boxes where I found familiar foods I'd been eating since arriving here. "Looks like we're stocked well enough to last us a while."

"Yeah, well, it's too bad we won't be staying." Pepper moved the light further up the walls, illuminating a windowless space where an ornate spiral staircase of wrought iron followed along the walls, almost encircling us as it wound its way upward to another space above us. The stairs headed some thirty feet into the air before finally disappearing through an opening in the ceiling.

"That's our way up!" I whispered, quickly stepping to the base of the stairs. "Hey, and look where the stairs go down here, too." In the dim light, I pointed to an opening in the floor where the stairs spiraled down into darkness.

Pepper lowered the beam of light, shining it into the hole in the floor. "Looks like a generator down there, and a shovel and some other tools, too." She moved the light slightly, trying to reveal more of the room. "But I don't see a door."

"So, we can check that out later if we need to, but come on now!" I stepped onto the iron grating at the base of the upward spiral.

"But what are those?" Pepper brought the light back up to the space under the stairs, walking closer to what looked like propane tanks for a backyard barbeque. There were four of them, each one white with a large black cap and spigot on top.

I gripped the freezing iron railing on the staircase. "Doc must use these to heat the place, or maybe keep the light going." I took a couple of steps up the stairs. "Let's go before somebody hears us... or before we freeze to death!"

"Just a sec," she insisted, holding the flashlight down close to one canister so she could see the black lettering on its side. "14–17 week holding time," she quietly read aloud.

"Gas doesn't keep? That's weird." Letting go of the icy railing, I rubbed my hands together. "I'm really cold here, so come on – We can't get caught!" Rubbing my sock-covered feet against the iron steps, I tried to keep my toes from freezing.

"Here. Use these." Pepper reached down next to the tanks and picked up two oversized pair of thick, blue gloves with extended wrists, tossing one pair to me.

Quickly pulling them on, I was pleased to find them insulated. "They're warm, thanks." They went up my arm, covering the tubing still taped to my skin as they nearly reached my elbow. "I wonder what Doc uses these for?"

Turning one of the tanks, Pepper read from its side, "Willington Abel Cryogenics... Hmm. That's what I thought."

"What?"

"Embryos," she whispered. "They're in those tanks."

"You're kidding!"

"Wish I was." Quickly pulling on the other pair of blue gloves, Pepper left the tanks and headed for the stairs. "Doc must use these gloves when he works with those tanks."

I didn't wait around for any further explanations, turning forward and quickly ascending the steps. Pepper came up right behind me as we both made our way up the stairs encircling the darkened tower, finally making our way through the opening to the next floor.

I stepped off the stairs, looking around the interior of the room. "No boxes up here – not a surprise. Looks like this might be... what do they call it? A lookout, or a widow's walk?"

"It's the watch room," Pepper corrected me as she came up from behind, pointing her flashlight at a large grouping of oversized iron wheels protruding from the center of the ceiling above us. "And that's the clockworks."

"Clockworks? But there's no clock."

"Yeah, but there *is* a lens up there, and it's got to turn – same idea, same system." Pepper waved the light at the gears. "We've got to get above all that, up to the lantern." She turned and walked right over to a ladder angling up to the ceiling along another wall.

"It doesn't look like those go anywhere," I quietly told her, staring above the ladder at what appeared to be solid planks of wood fitted tightly together to form the ceiling.

Pepper continued to climb, shining the light around the ceiling surface. "No, there's a trap door up here. See?" She directed the beam tightly on the weathered panels of wood.

A glint of light suddenly winked at me from a spot at the top of the ladder where the space between two planks seemed wider than others. "Is that a latch?"

"Yeah, with a lock," she answered, her breath visibly rising as she climbed toward the unusually high ceiling until she could finally reach it. "And it takes a key," she added, pulling off one glove so she could reach in her pocket. "You'll have to hold the light." She dropped the flashlight down to me.

Catching it, I turned it back toward the panels while rubbing my arm and rocking in place, trying to keep warm.

"Hold it steady!" she whispered as she fiddled with the lock. "And try to keep it out of my eyes."

"Please work!" I murmured to myself through chattering teeth, holding the light as steadily as I could.

"Come on!" she muttered. "Don't – quit – on – me – now… Damn it!"

"It's got to work!" I whispered to her in desperation.

"No, it doesn't… and it won't." Pepper whispered back as she climbed back down the ladder. "But we're not giving up now." Grabbing the flashlight from me, she went for the stairs, heading through the opening and back down to the floor below.

"Hey, wait for me!" I stepped toward the stairs.

"No, just wait there a minute while I check something."

"But you've got the flashlight! I won't be able to… see." I paused, noticing that despite Pepper's descent, I *could* see.

I'd been so focused on the ceiling that I hadn't noticed that this room had four very tall windows, each one reaching nearly from floor to ceiling. All four were the same in shape and size, straight at the lower sill and arched at the top. Each was centered on its own wall, positioned directly across the octagon-shaped room from one another so that all four windows were spaced apart by a windowless wall between them.

Now surrounded by windows, I could constantly see the lighthouse beacon as it continued its unending spin from above the watch room. Although the lantern emanated most of its light outward, it still managed to cast a bit of its golden glow back in on us, spilling light onto the lower portion of the watch room. It was almost mesmerizing to watch my shadow as it swirled in a circle around me.

"Yeah, there's some kind of electrical control box down here," Pepper quietly announced from below.

"What are you up to?" I asked, looking down the stairs to where she'd stopped to have a better look at the space below.

"I thought we might be able to cut the power source, but it's all locked up down here, so we can't get at it – at least, not right now." She started back up the steps. "The wires I can see coming from it are all encased, and looks like they run up here."

"So, we can cut the wires," I caught on. "Good idea."

"We'll see." Climbing back up to the watch room, she directed her light toward a place by one window where a thick, plastic tube extended from the floor toward the ceiling. "That must be it."

"Shoot! We can't get at those."

"No, but we can get at that!" she whispered, pointing the light at the ceiling where the tubing met with a large metal box that was positioned right next to the iron gears. "That must turn the beacon."

"But we can't get at that box way up there. It's too far over from the ladder. We can't reach it."

"Don't worry – you'll reach far enough."

"Me?" I stared at the distance between the box and the top of the ladder. "No, I can't reach that far, and even if I could, how could I cut the power? We should go back, find something sharp and…" I shivered, rubbing my arms with my insulated gloves. "… we should warm up before we come back."

"No, all we need is…" Pepper bit her lip, then her eyes widened as she spotted something under the ladder. "I think I've got it!" she said softly as she reached under the stairs, pulled out a broom, and then handed it to me. "We can use this!"

"To cut wires?"

"No, jam the gears!"

"What?"

"Someone's sure to notice if that light stops spinning!"

Finally catching on, I took the broom from her. "Great idea!" I whispered.

"You've got longer arms, so you should do this." Pepper pulled me toward the ladder.

I went along willingly, grabbing the side of the ladder with one hand and holding the broom in the other as I quickly scaled my way about halfway up the steps.

Pepper pointed at the clockworks as they slowly turned. "Stick the handle in between the teeth on that closest wheel, and then just hold it there until it jams up against the next gear."

Holding the broom by the bristles, I tried to maneuver the handle into the gears. "Hey, this is harder than it looks," I grunted.

"Just keep trying!"

I swatted at the gears, missing my mark a couple of times before finally catching between a couple of teeth.

"Got it!" I quietly exclaimed, but my optimism proved premature. As the gears turned, the broom was yanked from my hands, dropping from its slot and falling to the floor.

"Try again!" Pepper insisted, retrieving the broom and handing it back up to me. "And hurry it up before somebody notices we're missing!"

With the bristles back in hand, I jabbed the handle at the gears again, finally catching between two teeth once more.

"Now hold it there!" Pepper encouraged me.

"I'm trying," I answered, wobbling as I extended my arm as far as I could.

"Whoa!" Pepper grabbed at my thighs, trying to steady me as I kept the broom in place.

"I've got it! I've got it!" I whispered, keeping my eyes on my task.

Still holding the broom in place, the teeth clicked one into another, finally making their way to the wooden stick I'd wedged in their path. Then with the next click and a quick snap, the end of the broomstick shattered, splinters of wood dropping to the floor when the metal gears continued to turn as if nothing had been in their way.

"Shoot!" I whispered, dropping the broom to the floor. "We need something stronger. We'll have to go back."

"No, there must be something else!"

"What?" I looked about the room, spotting nothing else that might help us. "We'll go back and get what we need, and then we can sneak back before —"

"I know!" Pepper grabbed the flashlight and dashed to the steps, descending too quickly for me to keep up.

"Hey, I need some light, too!"

Left in the silence of the spinning shadows, I realized that she either didn't hear me or chose to ignore me; whichever it was, I was left to negotiate my way down the steep iron stairs with very little light to guide me.

"I'm coming, too," I whispered into the darkness below as I took the first couple of steps. "Now we've got to go back — got to find something else to hold those gears." I rubbed my arms with my insulated gloves, waiting for an answer from Pepper, but one didn't come. "I said it's too cold," I repeated, shivering as I carefully stepped further down the stairs.

"Wait!" Pepper's urgent whisper echoed up to me.

I froze in place, looking down to see the glow of the flashlight bouncing off the walls until it dimmed, descending further down into the hole far below that lead to the first floor. I wanted to yell down to Pepper, asking her where she was going and what she was trying to do now, but I didn't dare. I also didn't dare follow her now that the thirty-some feet of space between us had fallen into total darkness. Fearing that I might slip and fall, I just stood still, feeling my heart continue its frantic race in my chest.

Suddenly I heard a loud bang like something heavy had hit the floor. As the sound echoed upward, I held my breath, listening for what would follow. I looked down through the iron grated steps, watching the faintest bit of light far below as it flickered about like the flame of a candle does when someone tries to blow it out.

"What's going on?" I futilely whispered into the empty room below. "Is someone else down there?"

The faint light continued flickering as I listened to what sounded like a scuffle. Then I heard a clank, the sound of metal hitting metal.

"Who's down there?" I muttered as I carefully reached with my toes down to another step. "Are you okay?"

I noticed that the flicker of light was regaining strength, dancing about the space below until it abruptly turned bright white and glared directly into my eyes, making it impossible for me to see what was beyond it.

"Pepper?" I whispered downward, but she didn't answer, so I spoke up. "Pepper? Is that you?"

"Sh!" a voice scolded from behind the light.

Uncertain of who was coming at me, I used the growing light to see my way back up the steps into the watch room and take what little cover I could find in the shadow of the ladder. I watched as the light quickly made its way up the steps and turned immediately to me.

"I've already made enough noise down there," Pepper whispered to me, lowering the light as she stepped toward me. "What are you doing, talking so loud?"

"Oh, thank God, it's you!" I whispered back, letting out a heavy sigh of relief as I stepped out from under the ladder.

"Of course, it is, and look what I dug out down there!" She held out a long, iron pipe with a solid brick of iron about the size of my hand soldered at the bottom end of it. "Let's see if those gears can break *this* sucker!" With a jerk, she hoisted up the tool's heavy head, revealing three blunt prongs that had been forged into the end of the solid block of iron.

"What is it?" I asked.

"It's an ice spud, for breaking ice." She lowered the iron head and jabbed its three fingers downward to demonstrate; she made sure, though, that she never struck the floor. "That's how they use it, for making holes for ice fishing or whatever, but we're going to use it to break the clockworks instead!" She stepped to the ladder, whispering, "So, hop back up here!"

As directed, I quickly scrambled back up the steps and then reached down, lifting the spud from her grasp and using both arms to heave the head upward, pointing it at the gears.

"Oh, my gosh! This thing is heavy!" Using both hands and all of my strength to reach as far as I could with the spud, I swayed a bit, finding the tool even harder than the broom to maneuver.

"Just jab at it!" Pepper dictated. "With those flat prongs at the end, it should jam right in there."

"Easier – said – than – done!" I grunted at her, jabbing at the gears with each word until I finally managed to hit dead center, right between the teeth on one wheel as it turned upward into another. With the next click, the gears screeched loudly as they ground to an immediate halt.

"Way to go!" Pepper exclaimed.

"I think that'll hold." I released my grip and the heavy pipe handle turned slightly upward, the gear teeth pressing down so hard on the spud's iron wedge that it pushed it slightly out of its place.

"Shit! It's going to pop!" Pepper muttered as she ducked for cover, expecting it to fall. "I bet we're going to have to hold it there."

We both watched in silence, anticipating the worse. But as the seconds passed and it didn't fall, we eventually let out a collective sigh of relief.

I stepped down the ladder. "That should do it!" I quietly told Pepper as I looked to the floor for my shadow. Finding it to my right, I went quickly to the far left window, looking out at the glow cast from the lantern above us. Like the ice illuminated by the brilliant beam from the lantern, the beacon was now frozen both in time and place.

Pepper came to my side, rubbing my shoulder with her gloved hand. "Way to go, girl!" she quietly exclaimed, the steam of her breath visible in the stationary glow of the beacon.

Rubbing my own gloved hands together, I turned back for one final glance at the heavy spud still suspended in space. At that very moment, as I pondered how amazing it was for this heavy object to almost float in air, the pressure became too great for even the mighty spud to handle. With the split-second sound of metal scraping metal, the spud popped from its spot, hurdling at the nearest window.

"Look out!" Pepper yelled, ducking.

The airborne spud's momentum was more than enough to shatter the entire window. While most of the glass shot outward, some shards were blown back in by the howling wind, dropping to the interior floor along with the heavy spud as it fell to the inside with a mighty thud.

"Oh, no!" I ducked, the sound of breaking glass echoing around me.

Then holding my hand to my eyes, I tried to look up at the damage, finding it difficult as the wind blew chips of glass and snow toward us. Looking back downward, I saw that the floor was littered with shards of sparkling glass, all twinkling as the glow from the beacon twirled around the room. I then spotted my shadow, realizing it was spinning around me once more.

"We've got to stop it again!" I brushed aside the smaller sparkles of glass with my stocking feet, carefully making my way around the larger shards as I reached for the spud.

"No, we've got to get out of here!" Pepper yelled.

"Ouch!" Smaller pieces of glass poked at my feet as I hiked up the spud with my gloved hands and hauled it back to the ladder. "We can't give up now or we're done for good!"

"No!" Pepper headed for the stairs. "If we leave it and go now, they won't know it was us! I'll put the spud back and we'll come back later, but we have got to go *now*!" She waved with her flashlight for me to come with her.

Starting up the ladder, I told her, "Just a second." I was shaking with fear as well as from the frigid wind that was now gusting into the room. "I'll get this quick, and then I'll come."

"Oh, too late!" Pepper came back up the steps, directing her flashlight at the floor as she quickly tiptoed around broken glass to make her way to my side.

Missing my next swing at the turning wheels, I noticed the spud casting a shadow on the gears. Suddenly the wheels were illuminated by a broad, erratic glow that was coming from the stairs. The light quickly intensified on the gears, tightening to form a definite circle that grew smaller and brighter as its source quickly crept upward.

Pepper reached up the ladder, taking hold of the hem of my robe to tug me toward her. "Better bring that thing down here," she whispered. "We've got company."

Chapter 46

THE SOUNDS IN SILENCE

DETERMINED NOT TO SURRRENDER, I recklessly persisted with jabbing the spud at the gears even as the light from below emerged into the watch room.

"What the hell are you doing!" Annahede yelled as she pointed her flashlight at us. "Look at the window! And you're going to break the lantern!"

"That's the idea," Pepper confessed.

"Well, stop it!" Her light came closer, blinding us from seeing her. "I don't know how you got up here, but you need to get back to your rooms now!"

"Not yet," I answered, catching the spud between two teeth on a wheel but unable to hold it there as it slid from its place. "Shoot! Almost got it!"

"Get down now!" Annahede demanded, lowering her light as she grabbed Pepper by her robe and yanked her forward, away from my side.

"Ow! Ow!" Pepper yelped, stepping through broken glass before pulling away from Annahede and carefully stepping back around the glass to the foot of the ladder. "She said she's not done!"

"She's done!" With boots on her feet, Annahede walked right up to the ladder, glass crunching under her steps as she again reached for Pepper. "You get going before I have to –"

"What!" Pepper slapped her hand away. "Go get Doc?"

"Why, you little…" Annahede's jaw tightened as she lowered her head, glaring at Pepper.

"Is Doc coming?" I asked, lowering the spud.

"Yeah, he's on his way right now."

"No he's not!" Pepper confidently snapped as she stared down Annahede. "He'd be here by now if he'd heard us. Keep trying, Carly. It's just her we have to deal with."

Annahede's dark eyes darted back and forth between us. "Don't even think about it, Carly! Doc'll be here any second!" Although her expression clearly conveyed her rage, I thought I could detect a glimmer of uncertainty. "If he finds you messing with that lantern, he'll strap you down for good, so you better —"

"Then I better keep trying!" I lifted the heavy spud and tried again to jam the wheels. "If we're — already — caught, then — I've got — nothing — to — lose." I grunted between words while swinging the spud at the gears.

"Okay, you're coming down right now!" Annahede said as she tried to reach past Pepper for my leg.

"No, she's not!" Pepper stopped her, grabbing her arm and shoving her aside.

Catching her balance, Annahede came at us again, but Pepper would not let her near me. She stepped around the glass and over to Annahede, grabbing her by both arms to wrestle her further away from me.

Annahede stumbled, falling to the floor. "What is your problem!"

"You!" Pepper brushed off her gloved hands. "You're going to stay back until she gets that lantern stopped, and then we'll go!" Turning back to me, she asked "Have you got it yet?"

I lowered the spud. "Maybe you should try. I'm getting tired of lifting this thing."

With Pepper's back turned, Annahede took advantage of her blindside, taking up the splintered broom handle from the floor and dashing at us with it held high.

"Look out!" I yelled, but not in time.

With a quick swing, Annahede wacked Pepper along the side of her head. Reeling from the blow, Pepper whirled slightly to one side before stumbling to the floor, falling onto scattered bits of broken glass.

"Oowww!" she screamed. Lifting her gloved hand to her head, she pressed against her ear where Annahede had struck her. "What the…?" Then lowering her hand, she looked at the dark stain of blood soaked into the palm of the glove.

Annahede didn't wait for further reaction from her first victim, quickly dropping the broom handle and grabbing me by the ankles, pulling my feet out from underneath me.

With the spud held in both of my hands, I had no grip on the ladder, and so I easily slid down the steps.

"Ow! Ah! Ouch!" I yelped in pain as my limbs and side banged against each step all the way down the ladder. Losing my grip on the spud, it dropped freely with me as I fell with a thud against the glass covered floor.

"I told you to stop, but you wouldn't listen!" Annahede scolded us.

I huffed in short breaths, pain surging through my body as I lifted my eyes just soon enough to see Pepper crawl up off the floor and head back at Annahede.

"No!" Annahede held up her hands at her. "I told you to stop it!" She then reached for the floor, picking up the spud from where it had fallen.

"You bitch!" Pepper yelled, stepping heedlessly through broken glass. "You hit me!" She lunged at Annahede, grabbing a fist full of her hair as they both tumbled to the floor.

"Aahhh!" Annahede screamed before managing to strike Pepper's chest with the spud's pipe handle.

Pepper dropped back, gasping and coughing as if the wind had been knocked out of her.

"You pulled out my hair, you idiot!" Annahede panted as she rubbed her head. "I can't believe you did that!"

"What!" I struggled to get up. "*You* can't believe *that*! You hit her with – Aaahhhh!" I screamed, excruciating pain shooting from my ankle as I tried to stand but couldn't. "Oh! I think you broke my foot!"

"Yeah? Too bad!" Using the spud for support, Annahede stood back up. "All right, I've had about enough of all this," she muttered as she gimped her way to the broken window. "Time to call for back up." Standing to one side, away from the wind blowing inward, Annahede ran her hand along the wall in search of something.

"Yow!" I exclaimed as I failed again to stand. "What are you doing?"

"Sending a signal," she answered as she found her spot and, with a flip of her hand, threw a switch that triggered a low, thunderous bellow from the foghorn.

Startled, I reached for my ears as the tower seemed to shudder from the blaring sound. Then just as abruptly, silence fell over the room. In the sudden quiet, I looked over just in time to see Pepper return to her feet, the spinning light revealing patches of blood from all of her cuts that had soaked into her robe. Holding her chest with her left arm, I watched helplessly as Pepper fiercely charged at Annahede.

At that same moment, Annahede turned to see Pepper starting at her. Quickly sidestepping to the broken window, Annahede tried to avoid her onslaught, but Pepper altered her path as well, charging right at her as the wind whipped wildly through their hair. In the last instant, Annahede raised the spud, pointing the sharp end of the solid iron wedge at Pepper. Unable to stop, Pepper rolled to her left to try to avoid striking the spud, but it was too late to turn away. She plowed forward, burying the end of the spud like a spear into her right side.

The force jarred Annahede backward toward the broken window, the momentum pushing her backward toward the vast openness behind her. Releasing the spud, she reached out for the side of the wide window frame, but she only grasped hold of the shards left behind that sliced her hands before they, too, gave way. With nothing left to hold her up, and nothing left for her to hold onto, her knees bent as she toppled backward over the low sill and fell into nothingness, dropping from the watch room into the darkness as the foghorn blared again, obscuring the sound of my screams.

My heart raced as I gulped in a breath of air, quickly lowering my wide eyes to Pepper. She had taken the brunt of the collision, folding over the spud before collapsing with it to the floor.

"*No!*" I screamed again, half crawling and half limping my way to Pepper where she had fallen and rolled to her side. "Pepper! Are you all right!" I dropped to my knees beside her.

"Can't – breeh!" She grunted as she tightened into a ball, her body heaving with each quick, short gasp for air.

"Just relax! Blow out!" I frantically suggested as I tried to carefully roll her toward me so I could look at her injuries. Leaning over her bleeding head, I gingerly insisted, "Let me see – you've got to let me see."

As if willing herself to comply, Pepper's gasping ceased and her body went limp.

The foghorn blaring, I noticed blood smeared across the gloves on my hands.

"You're okay, you're okay," I tried to reassure her as I rolled her to her back.

In the light shed from the two abandoned flashlights and the lantern spinning overhead, I could see where the spud had struck. It pierced her right lower ribs, a spot made evident by the dark, circular stain now forming as Pepper's blood soaked into her white cotton robe.

"Oh, dear God, no," I muttered, taking the blood-tipped spud from the wound and casting it aside. The spud clanked as it hit the floor, followed by another blast from the foghorn.

"Who's up here?" Doc's voice echoed upward as his rubber-soled shoes squeaked against the iron steps. "What the hell's going on?"

"Help us, Doc! You've got to help her!" Pressing my gloved hands to her wound in an attempt to stop the bleeding, I leaned closer to Pepper and repeated the reassurance, "You're okay. You're okay. You're going to be okay." I prayed that repeating it would make it true.

"What the...?" Doc rushed up the stairs and, with a light in his hand, came over to us. "What happened!" he yelled at me, barely wincing as he knelt on broken glass. He brushed Pepper's bloodied hair away from the gouge on the side of her head. "What did you do!"

"I didn't!" I yelled over the next blast from the foghorn. "It was Annahede!"

"Annahede?" Pulling the glove off Pepper's hand, Doc grabbed her wrist. "No pulse." He pumped on her chest then lowered his ear to her face. "Damn it! She's not breathing!" Tilting her head back and plugging her nose, he blew air into her lungs, then returned to compressions. "How'd this happen? How long ago?"

"Just... just now... they were fighting and —" The foghorn blared, interrupting me.

"Up here?" Doc blew into her mouth again. "So, what were you — Oh, crap!" Doc pulled back Pepper's blood-soaked robe and nightshirt, revealing her wound. "She's bleeding out!"

"Well, stop it!" I frantically begged.

"Shit!" Doc threw up his arms, glaring at me as the foghorn sounded again. "Do you have any idea what you have done here!"

"Is she going to make it?"

"No, she's not!" He stopped working on her. "I can't do anything with this!"

"*What?*" My chest heaved in spasms. "No, you... you've got to save her, Doc. You can —"

"No, I can't!" he yelled at me "She's *gone!*"

Trembling, I couldn't catch my breath. "No...no..."

The foghorn bellowed.

"What in the hell's been going on here!" Doc demanded to know, his eyes glinting like steel in the lantern's light.

"We tried — to stop the... lighthouse, but..." I sputtered as tears fell from my eyes. "You have to save her, please!" I reached down, pressing against Pepper's wound with my gloved hands as if I could somehow stop the bleeding.

"She's gone, Carly!" Doc shook his head. "Just thinking about yourselves again, weren't you!"

I didn't answer, the foghorn filling the momentary gap of silence. I kept pressing against Pepper, the thick insulation of my gloves soaking up her blood like a sponge. The lining was now warm and moist as it pressed against my palms. My body shuddered.

"You said *Annahede* did this?" He stood up. "But that doesn't make sense."

"She..." I gasped. "...speared her..." Lifting my blood soaked gloves from Pepper's side, I pointed at the spud. "...with that."

"She what?" Doc picked up the bloody spud from where I had tossed it. "Why would she... Where is she?"

As the foghorn blared, I waved my blood-soaked glove at the broken window.

"*What!*" Dropping the ice spud, he stepped frantically through the pieces of broken glass scattered about the floor, carefully negotiating around large shards still in the window frame to look out on the grounds below. "No-no-noo!" he yelled into the wind, his voice echoing out into the frigid night air.

I didn't need for him to tell me what he saw. I already knew that, just like Pepper, Annahede was now dead, too.

"Did you do this!" He pointed out the window to where Annahede had fallen, glass crunching under his shoes as he stepped back toward me. "Is this how you try to stop me?"

The foghorn blasted its signal, but I found no silence afterward, the pounding of my heart now throbbing in my ears. I looked down at my friend, her blonde, blood-encrusted hair blowing across her closed eyes as the rotating beacon dispersed moving shadows across her motionless body.

"You just couldn't cooperate, could you!" Doc ranted as he stepped one foot across Pepper's limp, bloodied body. "Got yourself all worked up into some holier-than-thou ethical frenzy and then came up here and tried to wreck everything I've tried to accomplish!"

Reaching down, he grabbed Pepper from under her arms and heaved her upper torso toward him. With her body propped upright, her head drooped forward, her hair blowing about her ashen face as her chin fell to her chest.

"I've had more formidable foes than you, Carly!" Doc yelled over the next blast from the foghorn. "My colleagues tried to rob me of my work but couldn't... and neither will you!" He knelt down, awkwardly lifting Pepper's body further upward and toward him until her lifeless frame flopped like a ragdoll over his shoulder. "I'm trying to save people here... and you do this!" The foghorn sounded again as he struggled to his feet. "This is on *your* head, you know... not my fault, but *yours*!" He then turned from me, lugging Pepper toward the staircase.

With his cutting words, I gulped a deep breath before crawling up on my knees, trying to get up. Numb with grief and from the cold, I no longer took notice of the glass cutting my shins or the injury to my foot. It hurt, but so did everything else, and I just didn't care.

"I'm going down to see if I can still salvage anything from this," Doc told me as he started down the stairs. "I'll trust you won't try to do any other stupid things up –" The foghorn blared, cutting him off. "Damn that noise! Well, at least it'll bring help. In the meantime... can't have you get hurt, too... go back... don't say anything... the others will... it'll upset them... can you just go back to your room on your own?"

I heard words coming from him, but they were gibberish to me. I no longer paid any attention to him, or the foghorn, or any other sounds. Instead, I listened only to my heart as it rapidly pounded away in my head. Its fierce rhythm now took precedence over everything else happening around me. Even the whirling glow of the rotating lantern no longer mattered; it played tricks with the shadows, weaving flashes of light through darkness, but I was now staring past it with indifference, gazing instead at the specs of twinkling glass on the floor.

I thought I heard a voice, muffled and slow... maybe it was Pepper's that was asking me, "Are you... all right?"

Looking up, I found the twinkles went beyond the floor as stars flickered in the air. The cold washing over me was not from the wind; it descended through me as if all the blood in my body was being drained. The pounding faded, the stars flashed, and I gave in.

"No," I whispered to the shadows, just before collapsing to the floor.

Chapter 47

THE WILL TO FIGHT

TRY AS I MIGHT, I COULDN'T REMEMBER HOW Doc had managed to get me back to my room, let alone into my bed. I dozed on and off throughout the night, the pain from my legs waking me occasionally to find myself so confused – wondering where I was and what was happening to me, but unable to piece it together. So, I'd drift back off into a restless, drug-induced sleep, only to wake with a start again a short time later.

It wasn't until dawn that whatever I'd been injected with wore off, allowing me to gather my wits enough to recollect all that had happened. But as it all came flooding back, I found myself wishing I could forget it all once again.

From behind me, I heard the deadbolt turning, so I shot up in bed and turned quickly to see who was coming. But I must have moved too quickly as I found the room beginning to spin, the after-effects of both the sedative and the trauma taking their toll. As a wave of nausea rose up in me, I quickly dropped back to my mattress, listening intently as the door opened and the visitor approached.

"Now look at what you've done!" Doc scolded me as he came to my side. "That foghorn signaled Eino to come over, and he says you've made too much trouble for him and he wants you out – but he's got another thing coming if he thinks he's taking you away now!" He took my arm and wrapped a blood-pressure cuff around it.

Still numb from the events of the night before, I took no refuge in this news. "Why?" I half-heartedly asked.

"Why!" Doc glared at me. "Because your little stunt with the beacon caught the attention of the powers that be, that's why!" He pressed the stethoscope to my arm and pumped up the cuff. "And now, after all the trouble you've caused me, you sound like you don't even care!"

"I don't." Tears pooled at the sides of my eyes.

"Really?" Doc paused, releasing the air from the cuff as he watched the gage and listened through his stethoscope. "So, those girls – supposedly your friends, as I hear it – they both died over nothing? Is that it?"

"They died…" I choked. "…because of this."

"This?" He waved about the room. "No, this didn't do it. They died because *you* were too busy thinking about yourself, about what *you* wanted, and you lost sight of the bigger picture – of how all of *this* could help others." He ripped the cuff from my arm. "They died because *you* were selfish."

"No." I shut my eyes, tears dropping to my pillow. "This wasn't my fault."

"Oh, you don't think so? Well, it sure wasn't my fault, because I wasn't even there!" He brushed a strand of gray hair from his broad forehead. "No, I was downstairs trying to get just a little bit of sleep before I had to get back to work, trying to show a bunch of know-it-all scientists that they *don't* know it all… and then I hear the foghorn blast for Eino, and I jump out of bed thinking, *What the hell?* – Come to find out that while I'm just trying to get a little rest before getting back to saving lives, you're up in the tower *taking* them!"

"But I didn't –"

"And your antics cost me more than just two lives," Doc went on. "Now I've lost another volunteer, which translates to a severe setback in my research, and sick people dying while they're waiting for a cure."

I sniffled, barely able to speak. "What did you do… with them?"

"What, you mean their bodies?" Doc gruffly answered, his fists pressed to his sides. "They're stored in the procedure room for now, until Eino can deal with them. They're not my problem anymore – I've got bigger problems to deal with now."

My body shuddered with his callous words.

"So, we'll need at least one more recruit, and of course if Eino gets his way and you get to leave, then that'll be another setback and we'll need two... or more."

"Eino's way?" I muttered in confusion, choking back my tears. "He brought me here," I sniffled. "Why does he want me back on the island?"

Doc crossed his arms, staring down at me. "First of all, you're not going back to the island."

I gasped, my body going cold. "But I thought you said —"

"I said you might be leaving; I didn't say for where."

"Well, where else would —"

"Probably St. Maarten, okay!" he snapped. "Just worried about where you can go hang out, aren't you, instead of being concerned about all the death and destruction you've left in your wake!" He walked to the window, looking out through the wind-driven snow. "So, you can go far from here – some place tropical that Eino's arranged for all the women to retire to once they're finished here. But I guess you don't have to wait if you don't want to. You don't have to *earn* it like the others have to, because all the *important* people on the island miss you... and that's making them ask too many questions." He paused, seeming to calm down a bit. "I still need your help, Carly, but your abrupt disappearance has gotten D'Arcy agitated again."

Gathering myself, I tried to slowly lift myself from the mattress. "D'Arcy?"

"Of course." Doc turned from the window back to me. "He's one of your connections, isn't he? Yes, he came right out here the day after you went missing. And that wasn't the first time he'd come around asking a bunch of questions, insisting that I shut down my work."

"He knew you were up to something out here," I vaguely remembered, putting my head back down on my pillow.

"Well, it's none of his business!" he snapped. "But he kept on threatening to tell the Coast Guard that we were up to something – claimed the only thing stopping him was his respect for Vincent. What a joke!" he scoffed. "He feels no loyalty to the Hanikas, no compassion for them – not if he can't just leave it alone!"

"He does care," I quietly disagreed.

"Oh, of course you think so," Doc snapped. "Well, he's been such a problem, I had to make him believe I'd shut things down just to get him off my back! And then, when you disappeared, he *really* got on my case, and Vincent's, too."

"Vincent?" I muttered.

"But, of course, it was easy to convince Vincent that this was *your* choice. I just told him that the deal with the checks led to you figuring all this out, and that once you knew about our work, you wanted to help – wouldn't take no for an answer. Of course he was all worried and very protective of you, but I told him you knew Libby was in good hands with Maeve Kavanaugh and that you felt you could be of much more help here, so he *reluctantly* went along with your wishes."

"*My* wishes," I grumbled.

"Yes, I assumed it was still your wish to do whatever was in *their* best interest," Doc answered. "But D'Arcy, he is a different story. He won't let this go, even with reassurances from Vincent that you chose to leave Windemere. So, he keeps poking around here trying to get some answers, and then when you and Pepper went and jammed up the beacon, it was just my luck that he would be the one to take notice."

"He saw it?" I half-smiled, a painful sense of satisfaction washing over me as I realized our attempts to signal for help had worked.

"Of course, he did! That guy doesn't miss much," Doc replied as he fiddled with the tubing to the saline bottle hanging at my bedside. "So, when he decided to go to the island cops and ask them to take a look around out here, fortunately it was Eino he talked to, giving us the heads up that he's on our case again."

"So, D'Arcy's coming," I sighed. "And he knows I'm here, so he can –"

"No, he *thinks* you *might* be here, but that's a far cry from knowing." Doc reached down to the tubing on my arm and removed the stopper from my IV port.

"What are you doing!" I asked with a start.

Doc leaned back, looking down his nose at me with a look of surprise. "Why, I'm doing what I've always done: taking care of you." He pocketed the IV port cap.

"Usually what you do is knock me out!" I snapped.

He shook his head. "You've been through a lot, and I'm just trying to give you some fluids. That's all."

I took a deep breath and blew it out before hesitantly allowing him to insert the saline tubing into my IV port. "Well, no more drugs. I've had enough sleep, and I want to be awake when D'Arcy comes looking for me."

"Yes, well, I want to talk to you about that." Doc said in a gentler tone as he checked the flow on the saline. "You know, I have no doubt he'll come by soon, and when he does, I first want him to help me out with another patient – one who needs to leave here much worse than you do."

"You mean Leila, don't you?" I remembered.

He paused. "Yes. She's still sick, so I've been trying to talk Eino into taking her to a hospital where I know a doc who can quietly care for her, but he won't do it. He's too afraid that someone might figure out our project here, and no matter how much I try to assure him that I'd never let that happen – that I *know* this doctor and he'll be discrete – he still won't take her."

"Well, you've still got to get her some help, don't you?" I lifted my head, the sound of my raised voice reverberating painfully between my temples. "You can't let anyone else die here, Doc!" Unable to bear the dizzying pain, I lowered my head back to my pillow.

"I knew you'd understand. So, when D'Arcy gets here, I'm going to have Leila ready to go and insist that he take her first – before I even consider letting him in this place. Knowing him, as I know you do, I'm sure he'll see the urgency and he'll agree to take her. And then... that'll buy us some more time."

"More time? For what?"

"Well... for you to reconsider."

"Reconsider!" Pain seared through my head again, but my voice remained raised. "You mean about leaving? Are you kidding!"

Doc scowled. "No. I'm not."

"You think I would stay here, after all that's happened!"

"I thought you might stay here if you knew it could save Gretchen's life! And what about Libby, and countless others, all waiting for me to save them with this research. I thought you'd care enough about *them* to stay, at least just a little bit longer."

"And do what? Be your guinea pig?"

Doc grasped my hand as he pleaded, "It's not like that! It's much more, and I know it'll work if –"

"I *know* what you're doing!" I jerked my hand from his, struggling through the pain and nausea to sit up.

"No, you really have no idea what –"

"Yes, I do! Pepper told me!"

"What!" His eyes were wide as the color drained from his already pallid face. "She told you about... what happened?"

I pressed my hand to my throbbing head as the sensation of nausea overwhelmed me. Chocking back my gag reflex, I fell back to the mattress, grabbing my knees and pulling them to my stomach.

"I told her it wasn't how it seemed," Doc continued. "It was just what I had to check before –"

"We found the tanks... in the tower," I interjected as I let go of my knees and lowered my legs. "Those frozen embryos – they're what you implanted in her... aren't they?"

Doc's jaw dropped and his shoulders slouched, his veil of secrecy falling before him. After a long pause, he answered. "Yes."

"And that's what you want *me* to stay for?" I muttered, raising my hands to press once more against my aching head. "You aren't doing research – you're just running a... a baby farm!"

"Oh, no! No!" He waved his hands at me. "That's not it at all! This *is* for research. You see, I'm doing trial experiments with embryonic tissue I get from –"

"You're using the *babies* for experiments?" I rolled to my side, no longer able to bear either the physical or emotional pain.

"No! It *never* gets that far!" He wiped his stringy hair from his forehead. "I take them early – before they even reach a fetal state, after just a few weeks. That's when the brain's still forming, early enough to extract brain stem tissue we can use."

"You're killing them?"

"No! Just hold on and let me explain." Doc slipped off his glasses, rubbing the bridge of his nose before placing them back on his face and looking me in the eyes. "I'm just working with tissue – undeveloped, but extremely miraculous tissue that otherwise would be discarded. All I'm doing is extracting this tissue and then transferring it to a colleague who will use it to repair adult brain tissue destroyed by neurological diseases, like Parkinson's… and Huntington's, which I know you've heard of before." His face tightened as he turned from me. "And I know it'll work – I just *know* it! All I need is enough tissue to try."

I shut my eyes, rolling my head slightly from side to side in total disbelief. "You brought all those embryos here… to destroy them?"

"You don't understand," Doc insisted "They're as good as dead anyway."

"But that can't be – not if you're implanting them, and they're actually able to grow!"

"But you miss the point! That's not going to happen for these embryos, because they've already been abandoned. They were left to be thrown away, or to just rot away in this kind of medical purgatory that they've been stuck in for years."

"No," I shook my head in total disbelief. "That wouldn't happen. They wouldn't let that –"

"Oh, yes – they would." Doc nodded. "Their parents have already gotten their children, and so these are extras."

I pushed against my head, trying to stop the pain so I could think this all through. "I'm sure their extras go to other people who want to have kids but can't."

"Well, of course a *few* go to women considered qualified to have them, and then those infertile people try to bring them to term, but you have to realize that there are *so* many fertilized eggs and *way* too few parents to adopt them. Some women just *can't* carry to term, and many parents would prefer to adopt a child that's already been born. That way, they're guaranteed a child and not taking the financial gamble of losing the baby – and they can check out their child ahead of time to make sure it doesn't have any problems. Adopting an embryo can be risky business, and then there are a lot of people who just can't afford the implanting process."

"So, this happens because of the risk, and the money?" I surmised.

"No, it's because of the numbers," he argued, pushing his glasses back up his nose. "All of the embryos in those tanks were leftovers from parents who no longer could or no longer wanted to implant them. Most come from couples who simply wanted to have a child... and that's *one* child, maybe two, but not *thirty*!"

"Thirty!" I glared at him.

"...or more!" he added. "Fertility clinics are notorious for creating way more embryos than most couples will ever use, and that's because they want to have plenty left for a second try... and a third and a fourth. For these clinics, it's all about efficiency, and keeping down the costs."

"The money," I repeated.

"And with each try, a doctor will usually implant more embryos than a woman would ever be able to carry to term, and they do that intentionally because they figure some won't take but they'll still succeed if at least one does."

I was surprised to hear this. "But what if they all make it?"

"That sometimes happens," Doc rubbed his chin. "And when it does, they don't want to risk miscarrying all of them, so the doctor will do a selective reduction – which is what I do, except I don't leave any of the embryos."

"Selective reductions? Is *that* what you call it?" I took a deep breath, stunned by the cavalier tone of his remark. "So, you implant them – bring them to life – just to kill them!"

"You know, I just *don't* understand it when you and all these high and mighty ethicists have a problem with this." He scowled at me, shaking his head. "I mean, if you don't think life begins until birth, then this shouldn't be an issue for you; you'd be pro-choice, and you'd see this as a *matter* of choice. And if you think life begins at conception, as you apparently do, then you'd have to realize that I'm not the bad guy here – that the bad guys are the ones who created way too many eggs in the first place! *They're* the ones who gave life to all of these eggs, and really, if you want to get technical, they didn't even do that! They gave rise to *thousands* of souls that *can't* live… and they *can't* die. They're just *stuck*, waiting for… for something – for anything!"

"This is *not* anything. This is…"

"This is what? What!" Doc yelled. "*This* is the *only* chance they get to at least… to at least matter!" He turned his eyes away from me, almost as if he couldn't bear it himself. "At least in death they get to make a difference for somebody else. At least *something* good comes out of their paltry, momentary existence."

I rolled onto my back, facing the ceiling. "But it's still wrong to implant them when you know you're just going to turn around and destroy them."

He turned back to me, leaning in close my face. "So, it's okay to just throw them in the trash, but it's not okay to use their cells to save people who are already alive – is that what you're saying?"

"I didn't say that! I didn't know any of this, and it all sounds so terrible!" I squeezed my forehead between my palms, wishing it would all go away. "My head hurts – it's making me sick. And I just don't want to be involved in this – in any of it!"

Turning away, Doc walked to the cupboards and turned on the small sink's faucet, pouring a bit of water into a paper cup. "And isn't it convenient that you can say that and then just walk away, when there are others dying right now who can't." I heard him shake what sounded like a bottle of pills.

"But all of this implanting and *selective reduction* stuff – those kinds of procedure…" I squirmed, aching all over just at the thought of it. "They must hurt you – do a lot of damage – and I don't want –"

"No, it doesn't," he stepped back to me, suddenly trying to sound reassuring. "If a woman trying to conceive can have some of her implants removed while others are left, and she's able to carry one or two of the remaining one's to term, then surely you can see that it does no harm." He handed me a couple of pills and a cup of water. "It's just Motrin – nothing narcotic."

After briefly studying the pills, I popped them in my mouth and chased them down with a swig of icy water.

"So, can't you see why I *have* to do this work?" Doc continued, taking the cup back from me. "I have to show all the nay-sayers of the world that they're wrong – that something good can come from their... their lack of vision?"

I held my stomach as it turned. "But not this way – there has to be another way to do this."

"No, there's not." Doc stood stoic. "Someday there may be, and that's only *if* I can ever get some federal funding to make that happen. It'll take some big bucks to figure that one out, but for now, this is the only way."

"Vincent," I muttered. "This is why he went off to DC, isn't it?"

"Yes, but don't hold your breath on that one!" Doc stepped to the waste basket. "All of those politicians with their black-and-white way of looking at things; they think this business is too controversial to touch. So, in the meantime, more people keep dying while all of those embryos keep dying, too. And for what? For the sake of somebody's re-election campaign?" He tossed my cup in the garbage. "No, I can't wait around while a bunch of politicians fail to grow a backbone."

"So, instead of waiting for a better way – for an ethical way – you just go ahead and implant all of these women with embryos. And on top of that, you do it without them even knowing what it is you're doing to them!"

"Well... I thought it would be easier." He stepped back to the head of my bed, looking up at my saline bag. "Then no one would have to get all emotional about it."

"Wouldn't get emotional!" I scoffed. "You have all of this secrecy – this kidnapping and knocking people out, and you think we wouldn't –"

"But it wasn't supposed to be like that!" he snapped. "I can't help it if Eino's a lunatic! Why, he was *just* supposed to protect the place and keep things covered up – not scare people with threatening notes and fires, bodies in dumpsters and –"

I shot up. "Did you say *fires?*"

"Yes, well, and he did do some other things, too," he replied uneasily. "He put that note on that poor girl just to make the locals think —"

"Did Eino start the fire at Me-Wanna-Go-Home?" Despite my head throbbing, I had to know.

"What? Of course not!" Doc fiddled with the saline bottle. "He just tried to make it look like the girls had left for good or —"

"He did, didn't he!"

"I said *no*!" Doc repeated.

"All of this!" I yelled, now more than just my headache making me feel sick. "That Eino's a kidnapper and an arsonist, and he's a killer!" I screamed.

"It was an accident!"

"The fire? If he started it, then he killed Abel!"

Doc grabbed me by the arms, trying to lower me to the bed. "It wasn't like that at all, and you need to calm down."

"Really!" I shook him off. "And Pepper — he dragged her here, so it's his fault that she —"

"Her loss is a terrible tragedy!" Doc interjected. "I wish something good could have come of it, but she was never able to help us."

"What did you say?" I glared at him in disbelief.

"Her death, and the loss of all her implants — it was all so senseless," He stared back at me, his eyes magnified by his thick lenses. "She hadn't carried long enough for me to harvest those embryos, so we lost everything, and nothing good ever came of it." He shook his head. "It's a great loss, not just to them but to all of those who're still waiting to be saved. So, that's why I need you, Carly, now more than ever."

"You *are* crazy!" I insisted as I tried to rub the pain from my temples. "After all of this, you still expect me to stay here and let you implant me with a dozen or more embryos!"

"After all of this, I'd expect you to see why the people you claim to care so much about desperately need your help!" he answered. "It's for such an important cause — one *I'm* willing to fight for, and *you*, of all people, should be, too!"

"You *really* think I'd willingly let you do this to me?"

"I assure you, I've been doing this for a while now and with no lasting effects," Doc excitedly insisted. "I know we're right on the edge of a breakthrough, and that can save —"

"You are *not* going to impregnate me, and you are *definitely* not going to put me through an abortion!" I closed my eyes, trying to shut him, along with everything else, out of my mind.

"Well…" he sighed. "We, ah… we still have some more time." He fiddled with my IV tube, making it occasionally tap against the side of my arm. "I want you to still think about it, at least while D'Arcy takes Leila to the mainland."

Unable to shut out this nightmare, I listened to him turn from me and walk to the cupboards, his shoes squeaking against the floor. As drawers rolled open and cupboard doors slammed, I quickly grew suspicions about what he was up to. With little time to react, I did what Pepper had done before; I slid the saline tube out of my port and tucked it under my pillow, leaving it to soak into the mattress under me. Then I quickly adjusted my arm and covers, making it appear that I was still connected. Finishing just in time, I resumed my docile posture as Doc returned to my side.

"So, do you think you can behave yourself at least long enough for me to get Leila shipped out?" he asked.

I looked at him. "Yes, for Leila's sake I will, but don't think that means I've changed my mind."

"Well, I hope you still will but honestly, after that stunt you pulled last night, I guess I won't count on it." He took the tubing into his hands again and moved it to behind the head of the bed where I could no longer see it.

I didn't try to look, turning away from him instead. "So, does D'Arcy know…" I swallowed hard. "…about Pepper, and Annahede?"

"Of course not," he answered. "And he's not going to know, either — at least, not for now."

"But he'll know when —"

"I'm not telling him," Doc said matter-of-factly, now finished with his fiddling and leaning over to my side. "And you won't tell him either."

"Oh, yes, I will!" I argued defiantly, but then suddenly realized that maybe I shouldn't – that if Doc was trying to knock me out, as I suspected he was, then I'd better act like it was working. "I'll tell him... when he's here," I added in an intentionally groggy tone, closing my eyes and going limp.

"But it won't help anything, Carly. Those girls are gone, and his knowing won't bring them back," he replied, pulling up the covers around me. "I wish it would," he added in a soft voice, now sounding like he was talking to himself. "I needed a harvest from Pepper, and now I really need to get one from you, too." With those last words, he stepped to the doorway and, shutting off the light, left the room.

As I heard the deadbolt click, I opened my eyes to make sure he was gone. Then I slowly sat up, my head still aching some despite the medicine but I was determined not to let that stop me. I reached over to the regulator on the saline tube, turning it off so that the saline would no longer flow out onto my bedding. Then slowly turning my legs to the side of the bed, I carefully tried to stand up.

My ankle throbbed from where I'd twisted it, but I found that at least I now could put pressure on it. Taking a couple of slow steps, I grimaced through the pain as I made my way to the window.

Looking out across the lake, I could see where the snow bridge curved off from the side of the lighthouse and headed out into the distance. Relieved to see the path looking solid and complete, I could finally envision my imminent rescue, but I found no solace in this. It didn't seem right that I would make it when others didn't. Survivor's guilt set in, especially in regards to Pepper. She had been such a good friend, bringing me hope so many times when I needed it most, and I wondered what she would do if she were here with me now.

I knew the answer: she would bring me hope again. She would urge me to fight on and not give up, just as she never did.

Biting my quivering lip, I was absolutely determined that I would no longer cry. If I wanted to be rescued, I would have to be tough and resolute to make it happen. After Doc's stunt with my IV, I had no doubt that he was determined to keep me here if he could. And since Eino was the one who kidnapped me in the first place, I wasn't so eager to trust him with getting me out of here, even if he was offering me a place in the Caribbean. So, I knew I had to be prepared to get D'Arcy's attention once he arrived. I still wasn't sure how I'd do it, but I was determined to do it somehow.

The will to fight had returned to me, stronger than ever, and I wasn't about to let go.

Chapter 48

A NEW PATH

I MOVED QUIETLY SO DOC WOULDN'T HEAR me limping about the room in search of some way to get D'Arcy's attention when he arrived. Making my way to the countertop, I looked through the cupboards and drawers for something I could use to at least let him know I was here. But try as I might, I couldn't find anything that would help.

I had heard Doc lock the deadbolt when he left, yet I still tested the door and found it was locked as I'd thought. Searching for ideas, I thought back to last night, recalling our attempt to signal for help. I remembered the key, wishing now that I'd taken it when Pepper... No, I couldn't think about all that had happened and wonder *what if;* not now, when I had so little time to act.

I limped back to my bed, looking over my bedding and figuring that the sheets and blanket remained my only chance to get a signal to D'Arcy. Pulling the corner of the fitted sheet off the head of the mattress, I matched it to the corner of my top sheet so I could tie them together to make a long, draping flag that would hopefully get noticed – or better yet, that I might even be able to use to climb down if I had to. With my injured foot, it would be difficult, but I remained determined to do whatever it took this time to finally get out of this place.

Suddenly, I heard a thud come from the other side of the door. Freezing in place, I waited, assuming I was about to be caught trying to escape once again. But after a moment passed, nothing came of it. Although relieved, I suddenly realized an important point: if I were caught again, Doc would somehow subdue me, and then I'd have no chance at getting out of here. So, untying the knot I had started, I carefully tucked my bedding back in place, deciding that I would wait until I knew D'Arcy had arrived to put my plan in motion.

Still hurting from my fall the night before, I felt like resting but couldn't. I felt too anxious and wanted to keep alert for any sign of help arriving. So instead, I moved a chair over to the window and took up post, gazing out at the open, frozen plane where the gusting winds were lifting up the recent dusting of snow and hurling it in tornadic twists around the icy surface.

In spite of the early hour, someone was already out on the ice, driving his snowmobile with a sled on a path leading away from the lighthouse area. The machine then turned and sped away from the rising sun until it met with one of the Christmas trees left to mark the path of the snow bridge. The driver then slowed, circling the tree before coming to a stop.

I couldn't help but hope it was D'Arcy out there working on the bridge, probably doing a last minute task before coming over to the lighthouse. Squinting, I tried to make out who it was as the person dismounted and walked to the back of the sled he was hauling, but it was hard to tell as I could only see the man's bulky parka and snow pants at this distance. I watched as he grabbed the tree lying on the ice and, with a bit of a struggle, dragged it a short distance to a different location where he apparently wanted it positioned. Then turning back, he stopped only a moment to pull up his parka, reaching under it to hike up his snow pants before sauntering over to his snowmobile.

"Eino," I sighed, recognizing his trademark pant-hike.

Figuring he was only making some final adjustments to the path before the holes were augered and the trees stuck into the ice, I returned to my bed to make sure all was in order for my signal. With little else to do now but wait, I found my thoughts drifting back to the tragedy of last night. Still in a state of disbelief, I kept replaying the scene over and over in my mind, wondering if there had been something I could have done to stop it all from happening. Of course, if we hadn't been up in the tower to begin with, if we had just stayed put and accepted all of this then it wouldn't have happened. I thought about how desperately

I'd wanted to stop that light and that maybe if I hadn't been so determined to not give up that at least Pepper would still be alive.

My regrets were growing, multiplying – beginning to consume me as they so often did. It was my tendency to do so – to regret, to wonder what I could have done differently, and then, ultimately, to blame myself for all that had happened. But I had to stop this incapacitating reaction and find a constructive way to react, instead. I needed to realize that sometimes bad things happened and they weren't my fault – that maybe I was just as much the victim, and that the best thing I could do was to fight back and not let myself be victimized.

I hobbled to the window, checking to make sure I'd be able to slide it open when the time came for my signal. Turning the lock open, I tugged up on the lower frame and felt it give. Not wanting to give away my plan, I slid it just about and inch before shutting it and turning the lock back into place. All seemed in order, so I now felt prepared to act.

A sudden gust of wind rattled the glass on the window, calling my attention again to what was happening outside. The wind seemed to be picking up, further blowing and whirling the loose snow around the open lake surface. With the sky turning a dull gray, I looked about the horizon for any signs of movement but found none. It was not an inviting day to be out on this vast, unprotected plane.

Looking out across the ice, I watched Eino continue his work on foot. He'd moved the second and third trees away from their original spots, placing them a bit further from the trail at approximately fifty-yard intervals, and now he was positioning the fourth another fifty-yards away from the third – even further than the others from the original path.

"Hmm." With bewildered fascination, I leaned in closer to the window, feeling the cold emanate from the frozen panes of glass.

Hiking his pants again, he went back to his snowmobile and drove out to rejoin the old trail, stopping every fifty yards or so to retrieve another tree and load it onto his sled. Once he'd gathered about a half-dozen trees, he circled back to deposit a fifth and sixth along the new route, seeming to form a curve that directed the path away from the original.

"What's he doing now?" I questioned aloud as he sped another fifty yards to a position noticeably distant from the other path, stopping only long enough to tug off the seventh tree.

I wondered if he thought the trees had been blown from their original placement – what seemed a wrong assumption from my perspective. Certain that he was making a mistake by moving the trees, I strained my eyes to see the pines that remained much further out on the old path. There were a number of them that curved off into the distance, heading at what appeared to be solid ice all the way to the mainland. Then looking to where Eino was placing the next tree, I noticed that the new arch he was forming still veered off toward the mainland but only by way of open water.

The whirlwind of snow was surely making it difficult for anyone on the ice to see off into the distance, but from my higher vantage point, I could see Eino heading for trouble. From his perspective, he probably hadn't realized how far he'd veered the trail off track, something he'd soon find out when he took a tree too far out on fragile ice and plunged into the frozen water.

Watching him work, I felt this gnawing, vengeful desire well up inside of me; I *wanted* to see him fall through the ice, left to struggle like a helpless dog before finally sinking into the unforgiving water, never to resurface. That was the hatred now seething within me, its cold grip of malice enveloping me with a powerful yearning for revenge. It took my breath away.

But this prospect was quickly snatched from me as Eino moved trees eight and nine with more caution, testing the ice with a long-handled object as he moved about to position them. Apparently well aware of the looming danger, he took a few steps beyond the last tree, poking at the ice as he went. Then seeming to find the ice too thin to go further, he turned and cautiously made his way back to where he had been parked.

"Oh, no!" I whispered to myself, the nausea returning with the realization that something was terribly wrong.

My heart raced, now clearly visualizing Eino's heinous plan to thwart any possibility of disclosure by setting a trap for our would-be rescuer D'Arcy, and for Leila or me, or any one of us who might attempt escape. As I played out the likely scenario in my mind, the ending was always the same: I could envision D'Arcy and Leila breaking through the ice, falling helplessly into the biting waters, quickly succumbing to the frigid lake.

Shaking all over, I ignored my ankle and stormed toward the door to bang on it as I yelled for help. But once I got there, I wasn't so sure I should. I wanted to believe Doc wasn't aware of Eino's lethal plans, but if he was, I had no doubt Doc would sedate me and then I'd have no chance of warning D'Arcy. Deciding to wait for the moment, I hobbled back to the window to keep watch.

Eino was back on his snowmobile, leaving the scene of his treacherous work and heading toward the lighthouse tower. Circling off to its far side, he waved in my general direction before driving out of my range of vision, leaving me to wonder if he knew I'd been watching and was stopping here to check.

In a panic, I reached for the tubing on the saline bottle and pressed the end to the side of the mattress before turning on the regulator to release the saline. Washing any remnants of the sedative out of the tube and into my mattress, I then reattached the tubing to my port. Now if Doc and Eino paid me a visit, I could still make them believe I'd been unconscious, unaware of Eino's perilous deed.

I stayed close to my bed and listened for the slightest hint of someone coming, ready to climb quietly back into bed and fake a loss of consciousness if I heard the deadbolt turn. But it didn't, and so I kept watch at the window, waiting for what seemed an eternity for something to happen.

As I watched a couple of seagulls struggle in their flight against the swirling winds, I remembered Pepper – how she despised those white crows. She despised Annahede, as well, but not enough to want to kill her. Surely Pepper only intended to subdue Annahede, not to knock her out of the window. And I was equally certain that Annahede never meant to kill Pepper, as well. They were just trying to defend themselves – trying to survive – but sadly, neither one did.

Tiny chips of stone and ice tapped against the glass as the wind pelted the window with bits of debris it picked up in its long journey across the open terrain. I tried to listen beyond the tapping and whir of the wind – even beyond my anxious anticipation of footsteps and the click of the door. I kept listening for the rev of a full-throttle engine accelerating closer and closer, coming to our rescue. But the last time I'd heard that sound was when Eino last approached the lighthouse, just before he vanished behind the backside of the lighthouse. Since then, I hadn't heard it again.

Suddenly, though, I heard sounds made familiar on my occasional visits to the Kavanaughs' home – the sounds of dogs yelping and howling as if playing in their kennel.

"He's here!" Pressing my face to the glass, I strained to spot the team of dogs out the window, but could only see the flurry of snow now descending, swirling in a frenzy against the somber, overcast sky.

I leapt to the window, turning the lock and throwing it wide open. "D'Arcy! I'm up here!" Hopping back to the bed just long enough to pull off the sheets, I returned to the window to frantically add, "Don't go! It's a trap!"

Quickly tying the sheets together, I pulled the IV tubing from my port and wrapped the corner of a sheet tightly around my hand. Then thrusting my head and shoulders through the open window, I released the sheets into the wind.

"Aaahhh!" I screamed at the cold as the winds thrashed against me. "Help! I'm over here!" I screamed before pulling myself back into the room, leaving the sheets still draped out the window, flailing in the air.

With what little strength I still had, I grabbed the side of my bed and, ignoring the pain searing through my foot and leg, pushed the frame over to the window. Then taking my blanket in one hand, I tied the end of it to the sheet corner I unfurled from my other hand, making it possible to lower my signal even further out the window.

"Don't leave!" I yelled. "You've got to get me first!" I tied the blanket tightly to the metal frame of the bed, giving it a firm tug to make sure it was secure before releasing it. Then leaning back out the window, I looked to see how far it reached. It draped down to the first floor window, its end now just a short drop from the cement platform where I'd have to land.

"I'm up here! Don't leave! You've got to come now!" I yelled before coming back into the room. Spotting my robe hanging on the back of the room door, I hobbled over to grab it and to throw on a pair of socks. "A lot of good these'll do," I mumbled to myself as I quickly yanked them over my feet. Then I gave the door a few swift kicks. "Don't leave me! You've got to come get me *now*!" I insisted, pounding against the door with my fists. I heard no reply, and so I quickly slipped on my robe as I hobbled back to the window, prepared as best I could be to execute my last option.

"You can't leave! It's a trap!" I yelled again, my voice quickly dissipating into the wind. Climbing up on the window ledge, I gritted my teeth in pain as I tried to lower my legs out the window. I screamed, "Help me! I'm here!"

"Yes, I did!" a male voice spoke from inside, sounding somewhat muffled by its distance as it seemed to come from the other side of the door.

Thinking it might be Eino or Doc, I didn't really care at this point. "You have to stop them!" I yelled as I grabbed the sheets, preparing to jump for it. "They're going to die!"

"It coming from down here," the voice returned.

That's when I realized who it was.

"Deke!" I screamed, climbing back into the room. "I'm in here!" I yelled out in pain as I fell to the floor. "Don't go or you'll die! Come here first! You've got to get me!"

"...all for the best, so you can't!" Doc yelled from the other side as the deadbolt clicked.

Then the door opened, "Carly?" Deke said as he stepped into the room. "So you *are* here!" He rushed to my side. "Are you all right?"

"I told you, she wanted to help!" Doc insisted as he also came over and knelt beside me, reaching for my arm. "When did you... how'd you end up on the floor?"

"Stay away from me!" I screamed, slapping his hand aside. "You're crazy!"

Doc drew back, his eyes wide as he pushed up his glasses. "It must be the medicine. She's still a little groggy."

"No, I'm not drugged!" I snapped, pointing at my arm. "I pulled the plug before you could knock me out this time."

"This time," Deke repeated as he helped me up. "What's been going on? Why did you come here?"

I pointed at Doc. "They kidnapped me for their – ouch!" I stumbled on my bad foot.

Deke caught me before I fell, helping me hobble over to sit on the edge of the bed. "Kidnapped! So that's why you just –"

"She wasn't kidnapped!" Doc insisted. "She volunteered to help, just like the others! She's just reluctant now –"

"Now?" I yelled at him. "You mean, now that people are *dying*!"

Deke shook his head. "Who's dying?"

"Pepper! She's dead!" Tears streamed down my cheeks.

"What!" Deke grabbed me by the shoulders. "But she went to visit her family. How could that –"

"And Annahede..."

"It was an accident!" Doc interjected.

Deke scowled in disbelief. "Annahede?"

"...and Helena? Another accident?" I shot back at Doc and then lowered my head, sobbing.

"Okay, okay," Deke tried to comfort me, wrapping his arms around my shoulders and rubbing my back. "We're going to get you out of here just as soon as –"

"But it was all inadvertent!" Doc asserted. "Their deaths had *nothing* to do with the work we're doing here! They just –"

Deke turned on him. "I don't know *what* you're trying to do here, but it's been nothing but trouble since it started, and it's got to stop now!"

"You know what I'm trying to do!" Doc snapped back at Deke. "Your whole family knows that I've been trying to help the Hanikas ever since I came here!"

"What?" I retracted back from Deke's embrace, looking him squarely in the face. "You knew about this!"

"No!" He shook his head. "We knew he was doing some research, but I had no idea *this* was what he was doing." He turned back to Doc. "What, are you nuts! You've been *making* these girls stay here?"

"They volunteered!" Doc insisted.

"Well, I sure didn't!" Standing up on my good foot, I leaned against Deke's arm for balance. "And I'm getting out of here, right now!"

Deke helped me toward the door. "I'll take you now and then get some help to come back for the others."

Doc stretched his arms across the door, blocking it. "No! You can't do that! The others chose to be here – they *want* to stay!"

"We'll see about that," Deke said firmly as he reached past Doc for the doorknob. "We're leaving now, so get out of the way."

Frowning, Doc lowered his arms and stepped aside. "I can't believe you're doing this to me, just when I was on the verge of a breakthrough."

"I can't believe *you're* doing this!" Deke retorted as he opened the door. "When my Dad comes back from the mainland, you tell him to wait here and I'll –"

"What!" I sudden rush of fear surged through me. "Did you say your Dad was here?"

"Yeah, Leila's here, too, and she's really –"

"No!" Releasing Deke's arm, I quickly hobbled through the doorway and headed for the hall. "We've got to stop him!"

"Hold up! He's gone by now." Deke dashed up behind me, helping me through the next doorway.

"We have to go help him!" I gimped down the hallway, my foot screaming with pain. "He'll go through the ice!"

"No, he'll be okay out there," Deke argued as he tried to help me along. "He helped set the bridge – he knows where –"

"Eino moved the trail!" I stopped long enough to yell at him. "He set it so it's headed toward thin ice!"

"Macke?" Deke scowled, shaking his head. "But what's he got to do with —"

"He's in on this, too!"

"That damn fool!" Doc yelled as he followed up behind us. "He didn't want us discovered — wouldn't take Leila for help because someone might find out about us, so he must have done this to stop —"

"He didn't!" Deke dashed past me toward the tower.

Doc chased after him. "Take my snowmobile. It'll be faster!"

I hobbled after them, reaching the tower in time to see them descending the stairs to the lower floor.

"Here's the key," Doc yelled as he pulled it from his pocket and tossed it to Deke.

Holding the cold railing, I hopped down the stairs. "I'll come with you!"

"You wait here!" Deke insisted as he climbed on to the snowmobile and turned the key. "What the...?" he muttered as the engine failed to turn over.

"Give it just a little pump," Doc told him as he reached over to the wall and grabbed a wound-up tow rope that was hanging there. "You might need this." He handed it to Deke.

Deke took the rope and then, giving the machine a little gas, he turned the key again and the snowmobile roared to life. "All right — let's go!"

Doc turned the deadbolt on the double doors that stood just to the side of the snowmobile. "This wasn't my doing!" he insisted as he pushed open the doors. "Eino's a lunatic! He keeps doing crazy things like —"

"Like you!" Deke concluded with a rev of the engine. Then steering toward the open doors, he squeezed down on the accelerator and the snowmobile lurched, shooting out of the open doors and promptly fading into the flurry of snow now descending in swirls from the sky.

Chapter 49

A JOURNEY INTO NOTHINGNESS

"WE CAN'T LET HIM GO OUT THERE ALONE!" I yelled at Doc. "We have to go help him!"

"He said to wait here."

"I don't care! He might need our help!" I limped toward the double doors.

Doc grabbed at my robe. "You can't go like that! You'll freeze to –"

"Let go of me!" I jerked from his reach, continuing out the doors where the freezing winds whipped my hair in my face. "I'll take the dogs – just need to – whoa!" Wet snow soaked into my socks, burning both of my feet. "Ow-ow-ow!" Hopping on my good foot, I returned to the shelter of the lighthouse.

"You can't even walk!" Doc stayed back, seeming to know better than to try to help me.

I dropped to the floor so I could pull off my socks. "Get me some boots I can wear – and a coat."

"You should just let him go on his –"

"I said to get me some boots!" I demanded. "If you don't help me, and they die, then it's going to be your fault!"

Gritting his teeth, Doc tapped his toes against the floor as he considered my words for a moment. "Well… all right, then!" He turned from me and headed through another door that led to the first floor of the attached house, yelling back, "But you know this *isn't* my fault. I never meant –"

"Just get me the boots!" I yelled as I rubbed my freezing feet. "Hurry up!"

Waiting in the frigid room, I heard a muffled female voice yell from behind a door down the hallway. "Hey, what's going on out there, Doc?"

"Just getting some things," Doc yelled back. "Nothing to worry about – I'll be by in a bit." Then he dashed back with two parkas and a pair of Sorrels. "These'll be too big for you."

I took the boots, quickly pulling them on despite the pain surging from my injured foot. "They'll be fine." Gritting my teeth, I rolled to my side and stood up. "Let's go!" Grabbing a parka from Doc, I pulled it on as I hobbled back out the doors.

Doc followed, pulling on his parka as he stepped with me out onto the cement platform that surrounded the building. "Here… let me help you," he cautiously offered.

Glancing at the large, snow-covered boulders I'd have to climb over to get down to the lake, I reluctantly agreed to Doc's assistance. Leaning on his arm, he helped me quickly negotiate my way down the rocks and then around to the other side of the lighthouse. There we came upon a sled anchored to the ice with a team of four yelping dogs harnessed to it. At the sight of us, the pack barked even louder, leaping in place as they eagerly anticipated their chance to pull.

"There's a blanket in the basket," Doc yelled over the howl of the wind. "You sit on it, and I'll mush."

The dogs jumped playfully at us as we made our way past them to the sled. With Doc's help, I managed to climb into the front bed of the sled, easing myself around to sit upright and face the leaping dogs.

"Hold on," Doc yelled as he stepped on a lever behind me, pressing the brake of the ice.

"Hurry up!" I yelled back.

Doc reached behind him and pulled the snow hook from the ice and then tucked it into a pocket hanging behind my head.

I yelled again, "We don't have time for –"

"Hike!" Lifting his foot, Doc released the brake and the dogs leapt at the command. "Hike dogs! Hike!"

With an abrupt tug, I slammed back in the basket, the snow now pelting me in the face. "We've got to hurry!" I yelled as I squinted, trying to see through the flurries. "Do you know what you're doing?"

"Of course, I do!" he answered from where he stood on the sled runners behind me. "I had to make sure the snow hook didn't drop off the back of the sled; if it did, it'd lock us up and send us flying."

"I mean, do you know where we're going?"

"We'll pick up the trail here," he answered.

Pushing my hand to my forehead, I blocked snow and hair from whipping into my eyes long enough to discern the pine tree directly ahead. Turning my head one way and then the other, I managed to spot trees running off into the distance in both directions.

Doc yelled to the dogs, "Haw! Haw!"

With this simple command, the lead dogs veered left and the wheel dogs followed, all four pulling us in the direction of the most distant of the visible trees. Never slowing as they made their turn, they seemed to sense the urgency of our mission with all four dashing full speed toward the trail where more trees were now coming into view. Then as they closed in on their target, they veered slightly again, this time without command. It was as if the dogs knew where to go, continuing onward along what appeared to be the new path.

"On by, dogs!" Doc directed them past the trees. "Haw! Let's move it!"

"Are we almost there?" I yelled back to him.

"Almost," he answered. "Hike! Hike!" Doc pressed the dogs onward. "Come on, dogs! Mush!"

"But I don't see them!" I'd counted half-a-dozen pines from the one we'd first approached, and looking ahead to those I could see, I began to worry about where we'd picked up the trail. "Do you know where we are? How far do we go before the ice starts to —"

"Be quiet!" he yelled, silencing me.

I listened, at first hearing nothing more than the runners skidding over the snow-covered ice and the wind as it raced past my frozen ears. But then I heard other sounds, faint at first but quickly growing louder. It was a mixture of yelling and yelping that echoed across the lake.

"Whoa! Whoa!" Doc commanded the dogs as he pressed down on the brake, dragging us to a stop. "That must be them."

"So, why are you stopping! We've got to get to them!"

With his foot still on the brake, Doc tossed the snow hook off the back of the sled. "Not on the sled," he yelled back. "The ice'll get thin up ahead – too risky." He released the brake and the dogs lunged, lodging the hook in place. "I'll leave the dogs here. Catch up when you can." Awkwardly jogging in his boots, he took off past the leaping dogs, leaving me still in the basket.

"Hey, wait!" I yelled after him, but he didn't stop.

I rolled out of the sled basket and onto the snow-covered ice, the wet snow burning my legs and the palms of my hands as I struggled to get up. The dogs continued to bark and leap high in the air, begging me for another chance to run. But I ignored their pleas, hobbling past them to follow Doc in the direction of the remaining trees.

"Watch your step," Doc yelled back, well aware that I was trailing along behind him. "Can't be losing you out here."

Ignoring his warning, I charged ahead as quickly as my bad leg would take me. Passing another tree, it became easier to distinguish the yelps of the frenzied dogs from the terrified cries exchanged between men.

"...onto the rope, Dad!" one voice echoed.

I gained on Doc who had slowed down, checking the ice before he moved forward. Beyond him, I could make out the image of a dark figure lying flat to the ice, and beyond that, a larger patch of dark in motion. Sounds of whining and splashing came from the distant spot.

"We're here, Deke!" Doc yelled. "We can –"

"Stay back, Carly!" Deke's voice was high and frantic. "It's right by you, Dad! Grab it!"

Dodging Doc, I continued cautiously toward Deke.

"Stop, Carly!" Doc yelled at me, but I ignored him.

"Can't... reach... it..." D'Arcy gasped with each word.

As I made my way closer, I could see D'Arcy struggling to grab the rope. Reaching up with one arm, the ice would break off under him, sending him sliding back into the dark waters.

One dog was next to him, whining as he, too, tried to climb onto the fragile ice only to have it break out from under him. With one last whimper, the dog slid underwater and never resurfaced.

"Hold on!" Deke yelled at his father. "I can get the rope closer to you."

"No," D'Arcy muttered, spitting water. "I'll... try..." He reached out again with the same result, the ice cracking beneath his reach.

Deke pulled in the rope, looping it around his hand and elbow before crawling further out toward his dad.

"Don't... son..." D'Arcy insisted, dunking then under the surface just a moment before coming back up with a gasp.

"Hold on!" Deke crawled faster.

"No, Deke!" I feared the worst. "Just toss it from there!"

He did stop and, winding up with his arm, tossed the rope just short of his father. Quickly winding it back up, he tried again, this time hitting his mark as the end of the line dropped into the open water. There was a mighty splash, but it didn't come from the rope; when throwing the rope, Deke's toes had struck the ice, his boots breaking through the surface and plunging him now into the deadly waters, as well.

"Noooo!" I yelled, hobbling for him.

"Stop, Carly!" Doc headed for me. "You'll go in, too!"

Deke resurfaced with a gasp. "Don't!" He shook water from his face. "Stay – back!"

With a rush of adrenaline, I dropped to the ice, ignoring the burn of snow and ice against my bare skin. Carefully sliding toward the rope between them, I yelled, "I can get you both!" It took only a second, though, to realize I couldn't. "Doc!" I yelled back. "Get out here! I need your help to pull them!"

"No, Carly!" Deke insisted and then yelled to D'Arcy, "Pull with – me – Dad."

With the rope ends held by father and son, the two tugged against each other, trying to climb out of their holes. But the thin ice broke around them both as the pressure of the rope chipped away at the edges. In short time, D'Arcy released his end, the rope snapping back up onto the ice and sending Deke splashing back into the water.

"Deke!" I screamed, crawling closer.

Deke resurfaced with only one concern. "Dad! – I'll toss – again!"

"We can get you both!" I insisted. "Doc, come on!"

"I'm almost there!" he yelled as he crawled his way up behind me.

D'Arcy tilted his chin up so his mouth was just above water. "Deke… first…"

"No!" Deke pulled at the rope, his teeth chattering as he struggled to bring it in for another throw.

"Leave it!" I yelled at him. "I'm almost to it!"

Then there was a sudden crack that came from beneath me. I froze in place, certain I'd plunge in at any moment.

Deke must have heard it, too. "You wait – there!" he chattered. Then managing to wrap up the rope, he tossed the whole bundle to me without keeping an end to hold on to. "Dad – first!" he demanded.

Moving ever so slowly, I slid away from where I'd heard the crack, reaching over until I could grab the line and pulling it to me. Then readying to toss it, I looked to my target; there I found only a circular ripple on the surface of the water… and no sign of D'Arcy.

"Dad!" Deke yelled. "*Dad!*"

There was no answer.

Grimacing with grief, I turned back to make the only rescue I thought was still possible. Tossing the rope at Deke, I managed to hit the open water on my first try. "Grab it!"

But he ignored the rope, instead grabbing at the edges of the hole like a crazed lunatic trapped in a cage. "*Dad! Dad!*" he wailed, his thrashing about getting him nowhere as he broke away more of the ice surrounding him.

"*Grab the rope!*" I screamed. "If you want to help him, you've got to help yourself *first!*"

My words seemed to snap him out of his rage, and with what little strength he had left, he grabbed onto the line. At the same moment, Doc finally crawled up along side of me, his parka pressing against the side of my numbing leg as he grabbed onto the rope.

"Pull if you can!" Doc yelled at Deke as the two of us pulled from our end.

Using all the strength I could muster, I pulled hand over hand at the rope. Doc tugged at our end, as well, providing the extra leverage we needed to finally extract Deke from the hole. Then with Deke continuing to pull along, Doc and I gave one final heave to get him safely away from the breaking ice.

"Keep a hold and back up," I yelled at Doc. "We've got to pull him further before we stand up."

"No," Deke muttered through his chattering teeth as he pulled against us, scooting himself sideways toward the other hole. "I've – got to get – Dad." Steam rose from his purple lips as he reached for his pallid face, wiping wet hair from his eyes.

"It's too late, Deke!" Doc gave a hard yank on the rope, pulling him back toward us. "He's gone."

"We – can still – save – him!" Deke argued, his whole body shuddering in his wet clothes as he tried again to pull the rope from us.

"We've got to get you first!" I yelled, trying to coax him into letting us pull him in. "Then we'll do what we can."

With these words, Deke surrendered, no longer pulling against us as we scooted backwards with him in tow. Cautiously tugging him far enough onto thicker ice, Doc and I were finally able to stand before dragging him the rest of the way.

"Get those wet things off from him," I said to Doc as I dropped the rope, hastily brushing the burning snow from my frozen shins and knees with my wet, frostbitten palms.

"You do that," he countered while backing away. "I'll go get that blanket for him." Heading off toward the sound of barking dogs, Doc's silhouette quickly disappeared in the midst of the mounting assault of an oncoming snow squall.

"Take your coat off," I yelled over the howling wind as I hobbled to Deke. "You can have mine."

"Dad…" Deke muttered as he slowly pulled in the rope, reeling it into a circle on the ice in front of him.

Pulling my arms out of my parka, I dropped it on the ice beside him and knelt down to his side, reaching across him to help take off his wet coat. "Get this stuff off before you freeze. Doc'll bring me a blanket," I added with grave concern for both of us, the frigid wind now cutting me like a thousand knives.

Ignoring me, he didn't move. He just lain there shaking all over, still holding the rope as he moaned, "Dad?"

I pushed at his side, trying to roll him as he put up little resistance. "You'll freeze to death if we – don't get you – out of this!" Ignoring the tears falling to my cheeks as well as Deke's pleas for me to help his father, I knew this was not the time for either. "Come – on – Deke! Help me – here!"

Whether it was his overwhelming grief or the merciless cold, something had taken its hold on him and wouldn't let go. As his shaking slowed, I could tell he was slipping away. But at the moment, he just didn't seem to care.

Unzipping his coat, I pulled out his arm. "Don't you – give up – Deke!" I yelled, rolling him to his other side. "Don't – you dare!" Tugging his other arm out of the coat, I tossed aside the wet garment and rubbed his shoulders, futilely attempting to warm him. "Come – on! Stay – with me – here!" Pulling my coat out from under me, I draped it over him. "Put – this – on!" I chattered.

Closing his eyes, he barely shook.

"No!" I yelled, struggling to roll him into the coat. "You – can't – do – this!" With the coat between him and the ice, I climbed on top of him, trying to pull the coat around him while warming him with my own body. "Hang – on!" I chattered. "Do – you – hear – me?"

He didn't answer.

"Doc!" I called out, my voice rapidly swept away by the wind. Listening for a reply, I thought I could still hear the dogs yelping in the distance. "Hurry – up – Doc!" I listened again, this time thinking I'd heard the distant revving of a snowmobile; whatever it was, though, it didn't last long as it swiftly dissipated back into the roar of wind. "*Doc!*" I cried out again. "*Come – on!*"

No answer.

In the flurry of snow, I gazed at Deke's face. He looked like a ghost of himself.

"*Deke!*" I yelled at him, but his emerald eyes remained unwillingly to open.

The relentless wind blew through my hospital gown and whipped my robe into the air, burning my skin as snow squalls ripped across my unprotected back. In desperation, I reached to my side and grabbed Deke's wet coat, pulling it over me for protection. But in short time, I realized the error of my choice; the water from his coat soaked into my clothing, making me colder than I'd been before – as if that were even possible.

"Doc," I tried to yell but couldn't, my body trembling uncontrollably. With the wind blowing my hair about my face, I squinted to look around the ice for something else to help us, but couldn't find a thing. There was nothing left to protect us... no one left to protect us.

I pressed my icy cheek to Deke's, whispering in his ear, "Don't... give up... on... me..."

But I was beginning to give up myself, allowing the vast nothingness surrounding us to take over. Doc had gone, leaving his last loose ends to be tied up behind him so he could continue his research... and Pepper was gone, and Leila and D'Arcy were too, and now Deke and I... We would be next. I felt my mind and body going numb, a welcomed reprieve from all of the physical and emotional pain I'd endured. I closed my eyes to rest a moment...

The cawing startled me. I looked up into the whirlwind of snow where I thought I spotted a seagull hovering near us. He didn't land, slightly shuttling back and forth to hold his position overhead. On his mission of survival, he came to us in search of food but found none. But as he lingered over us, he seemed more like a vulture than a crow, as if he had seen the signs of death approaching and was waiting for it to arrive. But he tired of waiting, flying off in search of better prospects.

I tired of waiting, too, closing my eyes to rest and fading off...

"It's a shame, by golly," a voice said in the distance.

Yes, it was... my mind drifted... so many lives lost... such a horrible tragedy... and I didn't want to think about it anymore.

All I wanted to do was rest just a little bit longer, and then maybe all of the pain would finally go away...

"Ya just couldn't go along wid helpin', could ya, eh?" the distant voice spoke again.

Despite the overwhelming urge to sleep, the voice willed me back to consciousness. Turning my face slightly upward, I squinted to see who it was through the blowing snow. There, standing just a few feet from us, was Officer Macke.

"Well, looky dare!" Macke stepped closer to us, kneeling down just a few feet away. "So, Carly, yer still wid us, are ya, eh?"

I willed myself to speak. "Help..."

"Oh, now I can't do dat 'cuz den ya'd go back tellin' da whole caboodle about ar research, don't ya know."

"Help......him..." I managed to mutter, my cheek still pressed against Deke's frigid face.

"No, I can't do dat eider, dat's fer sure."

"He'll......free-ze!" My whole body shuddered.

"Yeah, dat's da plan." Scooping up snow in his leather-gloved hands, he tossed it across us as if he were burying us in a sandbox. "Wouldn't want blood on my hands, don't ya know."

"Stop," I murmured as snow hit me in the face.

"All righty den." He clapped his gloves together, dusting the snow off from them as he stood up. "Just tryin' te get it over wid lickity-split fer ya, but if ya don't want ta, I'll let ya linger."

Closing my eyes, I looked inward to summon up enough strength to call out once more. "Doc!" I cried out.

"No, he won't be comin'," Macke told me. "Yeah, I sent him back to da lighthouse on my snow machine. Alls I had te do was tell him some girl's sick back dare and he went flyin' on outta here – a'course, wid da promise I'd get yous two back, but I guess dat's not gonna work out now, eh."

I moaned, realizing our fate was sealed.

"Dat Doc really wanted ya back dare in a bad way, Carly – wants te use ya like he does all da girls. But I just can't trust ya anymore – not after da shenanigans ya pulled. So, yer gonna have te stay here while nature takes care of yas, and den dat way I can in good consciences say I didn't kill yas – just a bad ting dat happened – no one te blame – just like wid da oddars."

Pepper… Annahede… Helena… Abel… The images of those lost before passed through my mind.

Macke's voice sounded more distant now as he told me, "…won't be so bad fer ya, Carly… ain't such a bad ways te go, don't ya… pretty painless once yer frozen… and it's better dan drownin'…"

I was drowning, in my own way. The wet and the cold took my breath from me as the image of floundering about in the frigid waters played in my mind. "D – Ar – cy," I mumbled.

"Yeah… real doosey… and dat Leila girl too…" Macke whistled. "…D'Arcy didn't watch da trail… kinda careless… if he didn't butt in… my business… his own fault."

Macke's words sounded garbled as my thoughts drifted past D'Arcy… and past Leila… and then to Deke. I could no longer feel his lifeless body under me, my own body now falling into lifelessness, as well. There was no fight left in me – nothing left of me with which to fight – and so I let myself fall, fully surrendering to the elements.

"What de…" Macke's words were the last I heard from him in the dimming recesses of my mind.

The hum of the wind no longer lulled me, its rhythm broken with the sounds of a thump, and a scuffle, and then another heavy thump against the ice beside me. But it didn't matter to me; I could no longer feel the burn, or the cold, or the wind as it whipped across my body.

And then there was a voice. It called to me, summoning me to come – and I wanted to go, but I wanted to stay, and I wasn't sure which way to turn. The voice was insistent, never giving up, and I thought it might be Deke calling out for me to escape from the fire.

"You get Deke!" the voice commanded, but I knew I couldn't. I just needed to rest…

"Carly!" he yelled to me, his voice somewhat irritating when I just wanted to sleep. "Wake up!" he insisted.

I felt the burning again, but there was no fire — only the wind as it hummed in my ears again. And there was a tremor, something that rattled and shook my very core, my very existence. I could no longer lay there in silence, my body now shaking, rolling, jostling… and I could hear my name, repeated over and over again.

"Carly… Carly!"

I opened my eyes to a vivid hallucination. It was Rafae, his face so close to mine, framed in a halo of wintry white fur. He was lifting me up from the ice, carrying me as I flew through the air. He seemed to be running, panting, and for a instant, I thought I felt the sensation of his warm breath blowing against my face.

"An – angel," I mumbled as I gazed at his frightened face encircled with white fur, sure he'd come to whisk me off to heaven.

"I'm getting you out of here." His voice was garbled and distant as he lowered me to earth, placing me in a sled where he frantically wrapped me in a blanket. "You hang on!"

Finished with my flight, I closed my eyes to rest once more.

Chapter 50

FOR SOMEONE WE LOVE

LIKE FROZEN HANDS SOAKED IN TEPID WATER, my skin felt as if it were burning beneath this strange object – something similar to a thin air mattress that had been stationed over me like a hovercraft. Continuously pumped full of warm air, the blanket-like object blasted tiny bursts of heat through pinhole openings on the blanket's underside, prickling as they struck all over my body.

"Ohh," I moaned at the uncomfortable sensation. "That's burning me." Rolling back and forth, I tried to escape the awful sensation but couldn't.

"Whoa- whoa!" an unfamiliar, older woman dressed in purple hospital scrubs came to my side, pressing her hands down on my shoulders to steady me. "We're just trying to warm you up, Carly," the nurse gently told me. "You're coming along nicely. Just hang in there."

Looking around the unfamiliar space, I spotted monitors and an array of medical equipment. Blinds covered the room's one window where slices of sunlight peeked in between the slats. The walls were stark white, reminding me of the room where I'd stayed at the lighthouse...

"No!" I tried to sit up. "I've – got to – get away from –"

"Calm down. It's all okay now, so just try to relax," the white-haired nurse insisted with a soothing tone as she rubbed my shoulder. "You're in the hospital, and you're safe now." She helped me to lie back down, repositioning the hovering blanket. "We've been warming up your body – getting your temp back to normal." She added as she stroked my forehead, brushing my hair from my eyes. "Dr. Tsai says you should be okay."

Despite my apprehension, I lacked the strength to fight, and so I relented to the reassuring, grandmotherly nurse. Closing my eyes, I must have drifted back to sleep.

Waking again some time later, I found myself in the same room where nighttime had fallen, a lamp on a nearby table dimly lighting the space around me. The hovering object was gone, replaced by normal sheets and blankets that were snugly tucked in around me. Loosening them, I tried to roll onto my right side but thought twice when I felt the tug of sticky tape stretched taut under my right wrist. Lifting my blanket just enough to see underneath it, I found my IV port still in place but now held snugly to my arm with medical tape. Saline flowed from a bedside machine, its digital thermostat reading 98.6 degrees as it dispensed warm fluid through my arm to the rest of my body.

"You're awake," a perky, petite nurse said as she entered my room carrying a bag of saline, chomping away on gum. "I'm Janey, your night nurse," she added with a hint of southern drawl. "I'm just going to change your bag real quick. Ya think ya need anything for pain before ya try to go back to sleep?"

I wasn't sure as I rolled onto my back, my skin no longer prickling under the warmth of the blankets covering me. But I did notice some patches of skin that felt tight and a little numb even though they were still burning; spots were on my face, some fingers, and along my knees and calves. I reached for one place on my cheek that felt particularly annoying, but Nurse Janey took careful hold of my wrist before I could touch it, gently guiding my hand back down to my side.

"You'll feel some weird sensations in spots where your skin mottled," Janey stopped chewing long enough to explain, pausing to look at an object shaped like a broad clothes pin that was clipped to the end of my finger. "Lack of oxygen will do that to ya, but don't worry about it — no signs of permanent damage and ya seem to be reestablishing your circulation nicely. That's a real good sign."

I looked around the room, bewildered by my unfamiliar surroundings. "I'm in... the...?"

"Mercy Hospital, honey," she answered as she worked at replacing my nearly empty saline bag. "And your friend, he's right here with ya, still sleeping." Janey nodded across me in the direction of the opposite corner just beyond the head of my bed. "He's been keeping vigil since my shift started – hasn't left your side since."

Rolling my head, I craned my neck until I could see that there was a person slouched in the chair beside me, his mop of disheveled black hair pressed against the white wall behind him.

"Rafae?" I barely uttered with my scratchy voice.

"Ya want me to wake him for ya?" Janey asked as she finished switching the bags. "Hey, Rafae honey," she spoke up, her jaw still working her gum. "Your friend Carly's awake now – she wants to talk with ya."

Rafae's eyes slowly opened as he took in a deep breath, sitting up quickly before releasing it. "Carly," he said, stretching as he reached over to lean against the side of my bed. "So, you finally decided to wake up, did you?"

"Now don't bother her too much there, mister," Nurse Janey insisted as she walked to the door. "Ya'll can chat for a minute or two, but then she needs more shut-eye. I'll be back to check on ya soon." She winked, still chewing her gum as she left the room.

My voice was raspy as I asked, "How did I... did you get...?"

"I found you out on the lake, nearly freezing to death, so I put you in my sled and –"

"The ice..." I muttered as the memories came flooding back. "And Deke – Where is he? Is he okay?" I started to sit up.

"He's fine, just like you, so you don't need to worry." Rafae gently pressed me back to the mattress. "He's in the next room – came around earlier, and he's been asking the same questions about you, too, so he's okay."

I put my head back down to the pillow, now trying to recall what had happened. "D'Arcy, and Leila..." I remembered. "They're dead... aren't they?"

"You know, you need to concentrate on getting better right now and stop worrying about everyone else." Rafae patted at my pillow, fluffing it up. "So, you close your eyes and I'll –"

"It was… *so* awful," I sniffled, tears welling up in my eyes.

"Hey-hey-hey," Rafae whispered as he wrapped his arms around me. "No crying now. There'll be time for that, but right now you've got to save your strength and get better."

"It was just… *so* bad," I sobbed. "Words just can't…"

"Sh-sh," he tried to quiet me.

"But I couldn't – save him! I just – pulled in Deke and –"

"You did all you could." Taking hold of the edge of my sheet, he pulled it to my face and carefully dabbed at my tears. "Try to stop crying – your skin's so dried out, it'll probably sting."

"Poor Deke – he must be *so* upset," I sniffled. "I need to go see him."

"Well, not now," Rafae insisted. "I'm sure he's sleeping, just like you should be."

"Yeah… but I still should be there –"

"It's okay, Carly," Rafae insisted. "He's got family with him, and they'll help him through this."

"Oh…" Reclining back against my pillow, I envisioned the scene of Deke surrounded by his loved ones, all of them despondent over their horrendous loss. There would be many who would mourn the death of D'Arcy… and then I thought of others who would be missed, as well. "Pepper…" I muttered to Rafae. "She's…"

"I know – I know," Rafae whispered as he rubbed my arms. "We know what happened to Pepper, and Annahede, and we know that Leila and Helena had been there, too. We got quite a bit of info out of Doc Arlington when we –"

"Doc – He's the one that – kept us there! He's the –"

"Yes, don't worry – Sinclaire knows *all* about him now," Rafae answered with a tone of indignation. "No need to worry about him anymore; they'll be putting him away for a long time."

"But – there were – other girls…"

"And they've all been accounted for, Carly," Rafae assured me. "Chief's seeing to them, making sure they're all out of there safe and that they get someplace where they can get medical attention."

"They'll need that," I told Deke, choking up as I recalled what Doc had been doing for all this time. "Doc did – bad things –"

"We know, Carly." He sighed, rubbing the scruff on his face. "Doc's admitted to trying to... do some pretty sick things out there. He kept ranting on with some crazy ideas about how he's not taking lives but he's saving lives – probably'd still be blathering on with his nonsense if his lawyer hadn't shut him up." Rafae then looked at me with sadness in his dark eyes. "You've been through hell, Carly, and there's no good reason for you to keep on reliving it. So, try not to worry. Everyone's being taken care of – I promise."

But I couldn't stop mulling it over. "Yeah, but what about Macke? You know – he's the one that –"

"We *do* know about him, too, Carly. He's the one who led us to you, so –"

"What?" I was dumbfounded. "So... so, why didn't you come sooner? Couldn't you... do something?"

"Well, I didn't know anything about what he was up to at first – not right away, anyway," Rafae explained. "He tried to convince us that you'd gone off to do some urgent work for Vincent, and then I couldn't reach Vincent to ask him about it because I no longer had his number. And Macke kept saying he'd talked to Vincent and you, and that it was all 'okey-dokey' as he'd say."

"And you... you believed him?"

"Not really, especially since he wouldn't share with me how to get a hold of you. Yeah, I had my suspicions, what with all the stupid charges he kept dropping on me. And so I talked it over with Chief Sinclaire, and I guess he'd also been thinking that Eino knew something – but we just couldn't figure out what was going on." Cautiously reaching toward my forehead, he brushed a strand of hair from my eyes. "All we could do was just kind of keep an eye on him to see what he was up to, but we could never manage to catch him at anything... that is, until today."

Although exhausted, I couldn't rest as survivor's guilt gnawed away at me. "So, when he was moving the trail, why didn't you stop him then?"

"Carly, we didn't even know he was out there until he came back from his first trip... the one when he must've moved the trees," he replied, his tone sounding equally regretful. "But when he went out the second time, that's when Sinclaire and I snuck out after him — followed at a distance so he wouldn't know we were onto him. We even parked at a distance away so he wouldn't spot us, and then walked through all that snow to try and find where he was going – and we lost track for a while, the snow was blowing so badly." His voice was rising, sounding a bit defensive. "But we still tracked him down, and then... when I saw what he'd done, and what he was doing..." He bit his lip, shaking his head.

"How did you stop him?" I tried to recall that moment, but couldn't remember anything. "What did you do with him?"

Rafae gazed longingly at me, "I don't own a gun, Carly — just a Louisville Slugger." Pausing, he looked down. "Before the Chief could stop me, I cracked him up the side of the head."Taking a hold of my covers, he pulled them snuggly over my shoulders. "So, you don't ever need to worry about him anymore, Carly. He's never going to hurt anyone again."

"My God... you killed him?" I asked with astonishment. "I mean, well... won't you – get in trouble for that?"

"With all he'd done, and all he was trying to do... why, he was trying to..." Swallowing hard, he heaved a sigh. "No, I don't think I'll be in trouble after this is all sorted out. But if I am, I don't really care, because I did what I had to do." He cocked his head at me. "And now you know everything that you need to know for now, so I want you to stop thinking about this and focus in on getting better." He smiled. "Then, when you're up to it, maybe I can bring you a visitor or two.You know, Rosie's been asking about you, and of course, there's a little girl who'll want to visit."

"Libby..." I whispered. "Is she doing okay? Does she know about —"

"She knows very little, and we'll keep it that way – at least for now."

"Are ya'll *still* talking?" Nurse Janey popped her head into my room, incessantly snapping her gum. "I told ya just one minute, so it's time to give it a rest."

"Yeah, it is," Rafae agreed, standing up at my side. "Since you're doing so well, I'll sneak away and get a coffee so you can get back to sleep while I'm gone."

"Good idea," Janey said as she ducked back out of the room. "I'll be right back to make sure you're sleeping," she added from the hallway.

"And I'll be back, too," Rafae assured me as he stepped to the doorway.

"But where's Libby?" I asked, stopping him from leaving. "Is she still with the Kavanaughs."

"She's with my dad – just for now, while the family's here with Deke," he answered as he looked back at me. "She's missed you, but she's been doing fine."

"So her mom, and Vincent… they're not back yet?"

Rafae looked down at the floor, gritting his teeth. "No… and I don't know when they'll come." He ground his heel against the linoleum floor. "I don't think it'd be such a good idea right now – not with all that's happened, you know… on Vincent's watch."

I rolled to my side, facing toward Rafae. "But I don't think Vince knew… all that was going on."

Rafae looked up, staring at me with disbelief. "What?" His eyes were scowling.

"He couldn't know everything," I contended. "He wouldn't let Doc continue – if he knew."

Rafae walked back to my bedside. "And what makes you think that?"

"Because, I heard him – well, overheard him, when he told Doc… to be ethical… or he'd have – no part in it." I swallowed hard, tiring of talking as my mind kept spinning.

"Ethical?" He sat back down on the edge of the chair, bringing his face close to mine. "Do you know, Carly, exactly what it was that Doc was trying to do out there?"

I looked away. "Yes."

He paused, his expression turning to one of grave concern. "And are you okay with it?"

"Of course not!" I snapped. "We were kidnapped – held against our will – drugged so we –"

"I know, I know," Rafae shook his head. "It's just… beyond comprehension, what he did."

As I grew more exhausted, so grew my outrage. "And he wanted me to – stay there… and help him!"

Rafae paused, and then he looked me squarely in the eyes. "And I guess that's what I'm asking: If you hadn't been kidnapped – if Vincent, or anyone, had just asked you to help with this… well then, would you've considered it?"

"What?" I gasped. "No! I mean, don't you know? I was trying – to get away – and so was – Pepper!" I panted, feeling a bit lightheaded.

"Okay-okay-okay! Stupid question!" he realized. "I was just seeing if we were on the same page about this, that's all. So, don't –"

"What Doc was doing, with those embryos…" I cleared my throat, growing more winded. "That's just wrong. But that doesn't mean… Vince knew – what Doc was doing."

"Hey, now you're just getting yourself all worked up about this," Rafae noticed. "I was stupid – I didn't mean to –"

"But Doc told me," I continued. "He told Vincent… we volunteered… including me…"

"Okay, I hear you," Rafae stroked my hair back from my forehead, trying to soothe me. "They'll be plenty of time to sort this out later, but now you need to close your eyes and get some rest."

"It's not his fault," I interjected my last point before taking a slow, cleansing breath. "So don't be… hard on him… when he's back." I closed my eyes. "I'm sure… he didn't know…"

Rafae didn't reply, still stroking my head as I heard my nurse return.

"I thought I still heard ya'll talking," she whispered, no longer chomping on gum. "Where's your coffee, honey?"

"I don't need it now," Rafae answered her.

"Don't need it?" Stepping to my bedside, she flicked a switch and the blood pressure cuff around my arm quickly inflated. "Caffeine? Or Nicotine? I can't get by without mine," she confessed as air escaped the cuff, gradually releasing its tight grip until the machine at my bedside emitted a protracted beep. "Ninety-three over sixty-eight – that's great!" She stepped around my bed, checking this and that. "Okay, so ya set to sleep a while, sweetie?" she whispered, not waiting for my answer. "Don't keep her awake, big guy, or I'll kick ya out of here," she added for Rafae's sake as she shuffled from the room.

Except for beeping sounds coming from the hallway, all was now silent. I opened one eye to see if I was alone. "Rafae?"

"Right here," he answered from where he sat ever so quietly at my side.

"You're still here?"

"Never left," he kindly replied.

I closed both eyes. "Rafae?"

"Yes."

"I'm so sure... Vincent couldn't have known..."

"I won't argue with you, Carly... Now rest."

I paused, mulling it over. "I think he's desperate... to save Gretchen..."

"I know."

"...and Libby..."

"I understand."

"He'd do anything... to save them..."

"I know, Carly."

"...because you'd do anything... for someone... you love... Wouldn't you?"

"Yes... I would..."

"Yes... I think... I would, too," I agreed as I faded back to sleep.

Chapter 51

EXPRESSIONS OF REMORSE

"CAN YOU COMMENT ON THE EMBRYO FARM?" a lanky, bearded news reporter begged from my doorway as he pointed his microphone in my direction. "What did they do to you there? Were you —"

"What are you doing! Get out of here!" Officer Sinclaire ranted at the man as he pushed him from my room, still yelling as they scuffled in the hallway. "You know you're not supposed to be up here! You need to go back to the PR room and just wait there with the rest of the vultures. You'll all get your dirt soon enough."

"I'm so sorry about that," I overheard my sweet, stocky, daytime nurse Laurie apologizing to Chief Sinclaire as they walked back into my room. "We've been trying to keep them away, but sometimes they —"

"Yeah, I know, they're tough to catch. Guess that's why somebody's got to keep hanging around here." Sinclaire replied with a wink to me. "Sorry about the commotion," he apologized to me.

"It's not your fault," I replied. "You, and the others — you've been great about hanging around, running interference for me these past few days."

"Well, we figure that's best, at least until this story has a chance to settle down." Walking to the chair, Sinclaire took a seat. "Guess we could spring you from this joint, but you'd just have the same problems at the Landings, or anywhere else we'd move you, for that matter, so it's probably best to keep you here for now."

"I suppose, but it is getting old staying here — sorry to complain," I told him as I sat on the edge of my bed, dressed in the comfort of my own robe that Rafae had brought me the day before. "You know, I was pent up so long at the lighthouse, I'm kind of eager to get back outside."

"I imagine so." He reclined, folding his hands across his oversized stomach. "Guess we can talk to your doctor when he comes by – see what he thinks."

"Well, I must be getting better – no more IV today!" I held up my arm to show him my bandage, feeling so relieved to finally have the IV port out of my arm after it had been in me for so long. "I really need to get out of here, especially with my finances as they are. I don't even begin to know how I'll pay for this, but they keep telling me not to worry about it – that it's all being taken care of."

"It is," Sinclaire smirked. "So don't."

I studied him. "It's Vincent, isn't it? He said he'd pay for this, didn't he."

Sinclaire nodded. "And he should."

"So, do you blame him for this, too – just like everyone else does?"

"No, I didn't say that," Sinclaire shook his head. "Yeah, he had a hand in it, but I can see where he might've not known everything that was going on. I mean, for God sakes, there was the longest time when *I* didn't even know Macke was up to his eyeballs in this." Slapping his hand against his thigh, he brushed lint from his pants. "We're still sorting the whole thing out, but I figure if I was fooled, then there's reason to believe Vince was fooled, too."

I smiled at him, glad he saw it the same as me.

"I'm bock! I'm bock!" Rosie boisterously announced as she burst into my room. "Beddar late den nevar!" She sounded a bit winded as she strutted over to my bedside dressed in her usual brightly colored moo-moo.

"Well, it's about time," Sinclaire remarked as he stood up. "I thought you said you'd be here by nine."

"I said *o-bout* nine." Her fists went to her hips as she shook her head. "Don't you liston? I'm beginon' te tink dot you might need a hearon' aid, Beauregard!"

"Yeah, I'll get right on that!" he laughed. "And now I'm late for work on the island, so I got to go." Quickly stepping to the door, he told Rosie, "Carly's already had unwanted company this morning, so keep an eye out."

She lowered herself down in the chair. "You know you don't hov to tell me dot. I hov it all takon' care of."

"I'm sure you do," Sinclaire replied with a quick wink. "Ladies." He tipped his hat toward us. "Carly, you just keep on getting better and we'll try to get you out of here soon." With that, he hustled out the door.

"Silly mon, tellon' me my businoss," Rosie scoffed.

"But Rosie, didn't I just see him wink at you?" I asked with total surprise.

"Oh, dot mon, he tinks he con woo me ovar wid all his flirton' and bowon' his hot ot me." Pulling yarn and two needles from a bag she'd been carrying, Rosie set about knitting, unable to hide the smile that played at the corners of her mouth. "If he tinks I'm still a poosh-over, den he hos onoddar ting comon'."

I smiled. "So, what's he late for?"

"Well, for de memoriol, of course. He hos to do..." She suddenly stopped knitting. "Oh my... I wosn't sopose to —"

"It's okay, Rosie," I assured her as I realized she was divulging what others had tried to keep from me. "I suppose it's for D'Arcy... isn't it?"

She hesitated. "Well... yos, it is."

"Oh... So, must be that they... found his body."

"Ah no, dey hovn't – con't imogion dot'll hoppon until ot least sprin'time..." In a low tone, she added, "...if it hoppons ot all." She shook her head. "I shouldn't of said ennatin' obout dis. Me ond my fot mouth!"

"Don't worry, Rosie – It's okay, really,".I tried to assure her. "I knew there'd be some kind of service for him, and after yesterday's little visit from Deke and his mom, I figured I'd be asked to stay away from any kind of ceremony anyway."

She frowned. "Whot littal visot?"

"Why, didn't Rafae tell you?" I asked, surprised that he hadn't. "When Deke was released, once he got checked out, he and his mom came in my room. That's when Mrs. Kavanaugh decided to give me a piece of her mind – told me all of this was my doing, and that I'm the reason why Deke got hurt, and why D'Arcy..."

"Whot! Why, dot mean old –"

"Oh, don't worry about it – Rafae shooed them off." I waved my hand at Rosie, encouraging her to let it go, just like I had.

"I bet he gave har a piece a' his mind!" She scowled. "But I jost don't undarstond dot woman, or dot boy Deke for dot mottar. Why didn't he stop his moddar from sayon' all dot?"

"I'm sure he knows that's just how she is," I reached for my stomach, pressing against it as I felt a twinge of queasiness. "And besides, I think Deke may feel the same way… at least a little bit."

"Whot! You hov got to be kiddon' me!" she exclaimed indignantly. "Doesn't dot boy hov enna idea whot you've been go-on' troo!"

"Yeah, I think he does, and I think I can understand what *he's* going through, too." I nodded, biting my lower lip. "This is just his way, I've learned. He tries to make his peace by putting the blame on others, just like his mom does – just like so many people do."

"Well, jost because you know why dare do-on' dis, dot doesn't make it right!"

"I suppose not," I agreed. "But there's no sense in confronting them about it. They'll still think whatever they're going to think, and I guess I figure what's most important is for me to be right with all of it myself." I pressed my fist to my lips, trying to will away my latest onset of nausea.

Rosie noticed. "Are you feelon' sick aggon?"

"No, I'm fine," I fibbed, determined to persuade the doctor to finally release me.

"Well, let me know if you need de narse, ond don't you be blamon' yourself obout all dis, 'cause you know none of it was your fault," Rosie insisted as she continued her knitting. "So, I bet Rofae didn't take too kindly to all her carryon' on."

"No, he didn't," I smirked. "He all but pushed the Mrs. right out the door, and then he turned on Deke… which I really hated to see."

"Boys!" Rosie scoffed. "Dare like Peacocks – got to be flaunton' all dose feddars to let evra-one tink dare da boss."

"Maybe."

"Sounds like dot Deke hod it comon'."

"Another time, maybe, but not right now," I disagreed. "All the Kavanaughs must be really hurting right now, and I know all too well how that can feel."

"Well, we're all hurton' right now! Dot's all de more reason why dey shouldn't be takon' it out on you!" She pulled more yarn from her bag. "Bot dot's enough talk obout dem. Hov you hod enna oddar visitors? I mean, besides de ones dot brin' dare microphones ond cameros?"

I leaned back against the raised end of the mattress. "Yeah, Callahan stopped by for a short time yesterday – just after you'd been here."

"Dot's good. Whot's up wid him? Lookon' te hirer you bock once your outta here?"

"Yeah, he seems to always be short on help, and I don't understand that. He's such a great guy to work for."

"Well, dis time a' year's especially tough; whot wid most of de Saints gone, it's got to be hard for him to find enna help."

"And he's lost some good people – first when Collette left, and then when Pepper and I both moved to the Landings…" I paused, patting at my pillow before tucking it behind my back. "But I guess I always hoped it wouldn't be for good – that someday, we'd all… be back."

"Dey'll be beddar times again," Rosie assured me. "Bot it won't do us enna good to wollow in misary, so let's talk obout someton' else – someton' hoppiar." She held up the span of yellow and red wool she'd been knitting. "I *wos* makon' dis scarf for Beauregard, bot since he's been tinkon' he con jost flirt oway wid me do-on' all his winkon' ond soch, den I'm dinkon' dot maybe I should give dis to dot sweet friend a' yours, Rofae."

"Maybe," I answered, unsure of what she'd asked. My mind was still back at Biminis, remembering the friends I'd made there – the friends I'd lost. "So…" I hesitated to ask, but wanted to know.

"When will they have the others... you know, the memorials... for Leila and Pepper ... and, for Annahede?"

Rosie lowered her scarf, looking solemnly at me. "Dose garls... dey'll hov servosses at dare own homes, wid dare own fomilies... dare's notton' plonned for dem ot Windemere."

"Oh..." Although this took me by surprise, I supposed it shouldn't have; after all, none of them were natives to the island – not even Pepper. "Well, I guess I'd just thought they'd do... *something.*"

Rosie stopped knitting, still looking down. "Your friend, Collohon, did – he hod a remembaronce ot his bar, ond it wos vera nice."

"He... did?" Surprised to hear this, I felt sad in realizing I hadn't been able to attend – and that I hadn't been told about it. "Callahan – he didn't mention it."

"Didn't want te upset you, I'm shar," Rosie explained. "Ond I probably shouldn't a' told you."

"No, I'm glad you did."

She gazed up at me from her seat. "Well, den you should know dot a lot a' people showed up, ond dey said some real nice tin's obout..." Rosie lowered her head, her body trembling as tears fell onto her knitting.

I slid off the bed and knelt at her side. "I'm sorry. I didn't mean to upset you, Rosie."

"It's all right – it's all right," she waved her beefy arm at me.

"I just wanted to know what's been done, but nobody's been willing to tell me anything... so, thank you." Tears were welling in my eyes, too, but I was determined not to shed them. I'd already cried so much during the past few days and I was trying to get past that, plus now I'd upset Rosie and I really didn't want to hurt her anymore.

Rosie brought up her head, sniffling as she tried to compose herself. "Now look ot whot you made me do!" she grumbled. "I said I wos done wid cryon', evon dough I still miss dem. Bot it won't do enna good – doesn't brin' dem bock – so were jost go-on' te dink obout hoppiar times, okay?"

"Okay." I smiled, rubbing her shoulder.

"Now, you get bock up on dot bed!" she ordered me as she tried once more to continue her knitting. "You may dink you're all beddar, bot you still hov te take it easy while you're on my watch!"

"Okay." I climbed back up on my perch, sitting with my legs hanging off the side of the bed. "So, about those colors…" I pointed at the yellow and red yarn. "I do think those would look nice on Rafae."

"Do you?" Holding up her work again to study it herself, she was still sniffling, trying to take back the remnants of her good cry. "I dink dey'd look pretty good on him, too, now I gotta odmit." She rubbed at the darker patches where her tears had fallen. "You don't dink he'll mind dot it's bon used, do ya?" She asked, continuing her work.

"It might be better to give it to the chief now, if you don't think *he'll* mind."

She looked at me and then at the scarf as she chuckled. "Oh, yos! We'll jost hov to see how moch Beauregard still wants te flirt wid me oftar I give him dis tear-soaked scarf!" She laughed harder.

Despite my queasy stomach, I giggled, realizing that this was the first time I'd laughed in almost a month. At first, I held back somewhat, feeling a bit guilty for it. But then I looked at Rosie and considered all she was doing to try to cheer me up – to look out for me. I felt so grateful for her kindness, and for everyone's – and for the second chance I'd been given at life.

"There's someone here to see you, Carly," my nurse said as she brought me a Styrofoam cup of 7-up on ice. "He's not with the press, but I'm still not sure if you want to see him."

"Really," I said. "Well, who is it."

"It's a Mr. Hanika."

Dropping her knitting, Rosie leapt from her seat. "No! He shouldn't come here – she doesn't need dot kinda trauma when –"

"It's all right, Rosie," I insisted. "I want to talk to him."

"No, dot's not a good idea," she argued with me. "It'll jost opset you when you're still not beddar."

"I'm fine, Rosie – just a little tired still, but I'm okay to talk with him."

"I'm not so sure either," Nurse Laurie added with a tone of concern. "Maybe you should just rest and –"

"I'll rest afterward, but I want to see him," I insisted. "Send him in."

Laurie squinted, twisting the corner of her mouth, but she gave in. "A *short* visit, and then everybody's out for a while so you can get some rest." Quickly turning on her heels, she headed off to retrieve Vincent.

"Dis is a bod idea," Rosie complained, waving her finger in my face. "He's jost go-on' te opset you, ond whot good will dot do!"

"Sooner or later, I need to talk to him, Rosie," I argued. no better time than now."

She shook her head. "No, dare *are* beddar times den dis, ond you should –"

An ever so quiet knock on my open door halted Rosie's rant. She stood upright, throwing out her chest as she struck a stern posture.

With his hat in his hands, Vincent cautiously entered; his tall, slender physique hunched over as he scanned the floor, carefully watching where he stepped. He moved in silence, the gray shadows under his bloodshot eyes set in stark contrast to his pasty complexion. Looking more haggard than ever, I could still discern the Vincent I'd once known, but his face was wrought with the pain and grief that had always been there. I just hadn't noticed, until now.

"De garl is *very* tired, Mr. Honiko," Rosie announced, breaking the silence. "She really shouldn't evon be hovon' enna guests right now."

Vincent stopped, finally looking up at me. "Oh, I'm... sorry," he stammered. "Maybe I should... come at a different... time, then."

Rosie nodded. "Yos, dot would –"

"No, this is fine," I insisted. "Rosie was just going to go get me something to drink."

She pointed at my Styrofoam cup. "Bot Laurie jost gav you some 7-up, ond you hovn't evon –"

"But I'd prefer some Coke, if you don't mind."

Rosie scowled at me, but I met her gaze.

"Okay, som Coke den," she snapped as she grabbed the 7-up from my tray. "I'll be right bock, ond den you're go-on' te get some rest." With that, she left the room.

"You should sit down there," I suggested, motioning toward the chair as I studied Vincent's fragile state. "Just move Rosie's knitting – she'll get over it."

"Oh… yes." He glanced around, almost as if checking to see if anyone was watching. Then he slid the bundle of yarn and needles to one side, sitting down on the other edge of the chair. "I thought I'd… just stop by for a minute, to see if you were… okay."

"Just tired, but otherwise, I'm doing all right, I guess."

"I see…" He paused, his eyes darting about before returning to me. "And so, I also came to tell you… how very sorry… I am." Jerking slightly, he looked to the door and then back to me.

"No one's coming here, Vincent," I tried to assure him, assuming that was his concern. "And Rosie'll be gone at least a few minutes."

"Of course," he answered, nervously twirling his hat in his hands, seeming to be no more at ease. "I talked to… Chief Sinclaire."

"You did," I replied, somewhat surprised.

"I… need to explain… to tell him what we… what *I* was trying to do…" He looked to the floor, seeming distant.

"Well… and what did you tell him?" I asked.

His eyes returned to mine. "I am *so* sorry, Carly." Tears pooled at the edges of his eyes. "This wasn't what was supposed to… I didn't know that…" his voice trailed off as he lowered his head.

I wasn't sure what to say. "So, you did know I was there, then, didn't you?"

"Well, yes. Doc said you…" He jerked upward, staring at me with an expression of fear. "He didn't hurt you, did he?"

I bit my lip, unsure of how to explain all of the ways I'd suffered from the experience. "No, I'm okay, I guess."

"…because, I thought you… he said you volunteered."

I scoffed. "Yeah, I think he said that about all of the girls there."

"So, they didn't… choose to be there?"

"Well, I guess some did, as crazy as that seems to me. But there were others that Macke kidnapped, like me."

He shook his head, staring off with a look of disbelief. "And Macke…" he murmured. "Sinclaire told me… I didn't know he was Doc's –" He stopped abruptly, his eyes darting to the door.

"Are you okay?" I asked, puzzled by his behavior.

" – I didn't know he was helping Doc," he finished his previous thought. "And I didn't know… about Annahede, too."

"Yes, she was –"

"And Helena?" he interrupted, sounding a bit agitated. "I thought it was… an accident. It was all an accident!" Lowering his head again, he studied the floor. "And then D'Arcy… and your two friends… I didn't mean for this…"

Feeling the tears come again, I tried to blink them away. "I suppose you didn't know people would…" I swallowed hard. "…would die. But I've got to wonder, Vince, what *did* you know? What *did* you mean… to do?" I asked awkwardly. "I mean, you *did* know about the embryos, didn't you?"

His answer was almost a whisper. "Yes."

"Well, of course, you did. But did you know… what he was doing with them?"

Again his voice was barely audible. "Yes."

I gasped. "You *did?*"

He clasped his hands to his face. "Yes."

"But I… I didn't think you knew! The whole time, I just figured you thought the volunteers were like… lab workers, not guinea pigs!"

"Is everything all right in here?" Laurie poked her head into the room to ask.

I quickly composed myself to answer, giving her a calm smile. "Yeah, it's okay."

"Well buzz if you need me," she said as she left.

Gulping a short breath, Vincent looked at me. "I thought the girls knew what they'd be doing when they… volunteered. That was the deal with Doc – that they'd know everything."

"So, you *knew* Doc would have to... implant them, and grow the embryos, and then turn around and... abort them!"

He shut his eyes. "I knew, no matter what, those beings were all going to die. And I knew that, if I didn't do something soon..." Opening his eyes, he looked sorrowfully at me. "...my daughter was going to die soon, too."

Taking a deep breath, I bit my lip, somehow managing to understand the desperation that had driven Vincent to resort to such drastic measures. I envisioned Gretchen, wondering how it might be possible to save her. And then I thought of the others – of Pepper and Annahede, Leila and Helena, D'Arcy... and Abel... and even my family – and I wondered to what lengths I would have gone to save them.

Vincent jerked suddenly, turning his gaze up toward the ceiling. "I just wanted to help Gretchen, and people... like her – that's what I've been trying to do all my life," he began to rock slightly in his seat. "With my fertility clinic, I brought new life into the world... I just wanted to help... people to keep living... prolong their lives... end all this suffering..." He rocked a bit harder. "...but now, it seems... I've only caused more." Bowing his head, he heaved with each short breath he gasped, tears now falling to his lap.

Climbing off my bed, I pulled two tissues from the box on my nightstand and offered them to Vincent. "I don't think..." I bit my lip. "You know, this wasn't your fault," I told him as I knelt down at his side. "I don't know about this experimenting business, but I do know your heart, Vincent, and I know you didn't mean for anyone to get hurt."

"If I'd known what was... going on, I never..." His body shook as he wept.

"Okay, okay," I said, trying to calm him down. "It's over now, so we'll just have to find a better way to help Gretch." I patted him reassuringly on the back. "Maybe the people you went to see had some ideas. Did they?"

Catching his breath with a gasp, Vincent wiped his eyes with the tissues. "No, they didn't." His eyes quickly glanced at the door and then darted about the room. "They told her... the disease has progressed too far for trial therapy. There's nothing more… they can do."

I took a deep breath. "Well, we still can't give up hope," I tried to encourage him. "There's always new research, and I'm sure with time some new prospects will –"

"Gretchen always said she didn't want to suffer." He sniffled, his voice rising as he added, "I didn't want her too, either."

"And you won't let her suffer," I assured him. "I know you'll make sure she's… kept comfortable."

He looked to the ceiling. "She knew I'd never be able to end it, and she was losing control – what little she still had."

I paused, unsure of what he was saying. "Vincent… what happened?"

"The dementia, the depression… makes people lose their will to live…" Choking on the pain of his words, he found it difficult to speak. "…then after the fire, when Abel…" His face tightened with grief. "…that's when she made me promise… no resuscitation, no life support… so, when I found her like that…" He wept, unable to finish.

"Found her, like what?" I grasped his arm. "Vincent, what are you saying?"

He took in a deep breath. "I'd left her meds by her bed, like I always did – and she knew it." His eyes were pleading for me to understand. "I wasn't gone that long! I don't know how she… she choked them down. I must've… left the bottle open. It's all my fault!" His body heaving, he wept again.

"What! Did she overdose?"

"What is going on in here?" Laurie rushed in, obviously concerned by the scene she found.

Vincent held his hand to his mouth, barely able to reply. "I thought… I had a pulse… but she…" Collapsing to one side of the chair, his body heaved as he cried inconsolably.

"I think he needs some help," I told Laurie as I held firmly to Vincent's arm, trying to keep him upright.

She hustled to the other side of Vincent, helping me to right him. "Mr. Hanika?"

His body lurched again as he sobbed incessantly, and I wondered as I gazed upon his seizing body, his tortured soul, how this man could survive the relentless agony of losing those he loved most in such horrific ways.

"I couldn't – save her!" he sputtered. "She's gone!"

Chapter 52

SPREADING THE BLAME

"I'M REAL SORRY I GOT TO DRAW THIS AGAIN, Carly, but the doc wants to run a full battery," the lab technician Marcus apologized as he tapped at my veins with his stubby fingers. "At least you got good veins – makes my job a whole lot easier," he grimaced, jabbing the needle into my arm.

"Glad to help out," I replied without flinching, growing all too used to the needles. "Just make sure my test results say *Let her go*, will you?"

"I'll see what I can do." His eyes remaining trained on his task as he switched vials, beginning to fill another one. "You got Doc Tsai stumped on this."

"That's what I hear," Rafae said as he strolled into my room, tossing his parka onto the foot of my bed. "Still tired, and an upset stomach – what's the deal with you?"

"About time you came back," I scolded him. "So, how's Vincent doing? What'd you find out?"

"He's fine," he answered flatly, then turned to Marcus. "So, what's going on with her? Have you figured this out yet?"

"Still working it," Marcus replied, filling another vial.

"What about Vincent?" I insisted. "He's *not* fine – I saw that with my own eyes."

"And you shouldn't have." Plopping down in the chair at my bedside, Rafae leaned toward me. "He shouldn't have come in here and unloaded more grief on you – not now, when you're already trying to get through this, and get better."

"Oh, I'm fine," I insisted as my stomach rumbled.

"We'll be the judge of that," Marcus interjected, pulling the needle from my arm as he applied pressure with a cotton ball.

"Fold up your arm on that, and I'll be on my way." Grabbing his plastic tray by its handle, Marcus headed for my bathroom. "Left a cup in the john, didn't you?"

"It's on the back of the toilet."

"Got it." His voice echoed in the tiny, tiled room. "The nurse can run this while I do rounds," he added as he reemerged, then headed out the door with a wave. "See ya."

"I hope not," I quietly replied, certain he was long gone.

"What? Don't you like having your blood drawn?" Rafae asked sarcastically.

"No, and what I *really* don't like is being stuck here!" I pushed the button on the side of my bed, cranking the back up until I was upright. "But I suppose if I've got to be here then at least I can go down and see Vince for a bit, just to let him know I'm thinking of him."

"You don't need to go down there," Rafae insisted. "I told you he's fine."

"I know, but I can still go and... you know, maybe try to comfort him."

"You should just rest, and maybe try to eat dinner."

My stomach turned at the thought. "No, I'm not hungry. I'll just have some 7-up." Picking up my cup, I took a drink.

"You can't live on that."

"I know." I set the cup down. "I'll have something later, after I go to see Vince."

"No, I don't want you going down there!" Rafae's eyes flashed and his jaw tightened.

I paused, considering Rafae's resolve. "He's *not* okay, is he?"

"He's just agitated, that's all... and he should be."

"Well, that's a pretty harsh thing to say about someone whose daughter just... just killed herself."

"But he didn't need to come in here and tell you that – at least not right now, not after everything else you've just been through," he snapped back.

Turning my legs, I sat up on the side of the bed. "But he also came to apologize – he wanted me to know that he didn't mean for all this to happen."

"Didn't mean – !" He stopped himself, shaking his head. "Look, I know we don't see eye to eye on this blaming business, so I'm not going to get in an argument with you over this…" He bit his lip, gathering his thoughts before continuing. "…because that'll just upset you, too, and then I'll be no better than anyone else if I do that."

"So… we'll just agree to disagree?" I suggested.

"Guess so." He slouched back in his chair. "But you're *not* going to go down there to visit him, at least not today," he persisted. "They have him pretty heavily sedated, and I don't think it'll do either of you any good right now."

I sighed. "He just wasn't himself when he was in here. I've never seen him like that before – all anxious with his eyes darting around. He seemed kind of paranoid, like someone was after him, or like he was expecting something bad was about to happen."

"Hm. Sounds kind of post-traumatic, or something like that," Rafae speculated. "But it's kind of weird that he'd have that because… well, I know losing Gretchen's a terrible thing, but it's not like he hasn't been through this before – with his wife, and Abel."

I frowned, remembering. "Yes, but both of them… their passing away must've been… expected. I know it took a long time for Vince to accept that Abel was already gone, and maybe it was that way with his wife, too. But it wasn't with Gretchen."

"But it's not like he didn't know Gretchen was dying."

"I know, but I don't think he was ready to give up. He was still fighting, with the trip, and the research."

"Well, and now with everything else that's happened…" he paused, carefully choosing his words. "I guess it doesn't matter whether we blame him or not – he probably still blames himself for what happened."

"Maybe." I yawned as I pulled up my legs, reclining against the upright portion of my bed. "We can get caught up in that sometimes – blaming ourselves."

"Well, *you'd* better not, because it's pretty obvious that none of this was *your* fault."

"I suppose," I replied, wishing I could be so sure. "It's just all… so sad."

"Yes, it is, but you've been a real trooper through all of this," he feigned a punch to my shoulder. "It's good to see you hanging in here with a good attitude, not letting this get to you."

"Well, I guess I've seen so much… tragedy – enough for a lifetime. Maybe I'm just getting used to it, growing numb… and I guess that's not such a good thing."

"I don't think you're numb," Rafae argued. "You care, but you're just not dwelling on it, and that's a good thing."

"Well, maybe I am getting used to losing people, but I don't care to lose any more, thank you very much."

"Fair enough." He smiled, picking up the remote control from my nightstand. "So, want to watch something?"

"Nope. It's the news hour, and for now, no news is good news."

"Right on that." He tossed the remote aside.

Feeling a wave of nausea coupled with exhaustion, I rolled to my side. "I'm so tired of being stuck between these four walls. Tell me something good that's going on out there in the big world."

"Really not much." He slouched back again, looking up to the ceiling. "Same old stuff mostly."

"Have you been by Biminis?"

"Nope. Too busy hanging out here with you."

"Well, but you've been back to the island, haven't you?"

"Not for long," he answered.

"Well, you must've gone… to D'Arcy's memorial."

He looked at me with a start. "Oh, that…"

"Don't be mad – Rosie let it slip."

"I see." He nodded. "No surprise there."

"You *can* tell me these things, you know. I mean, it's not like I don't know what happened. I've already been through the worst of it, so you might as well just help me… make peace with it."

He rubbed at his five o'clock shadow. "I suppose."

"So, since I couldn't be there, tell me about it."

"Well, it was all very nice, very formal with some nice music. Pastor gave the sermon and DK gave a good eulogy."

"Really? So, did he do all right with that?" I wondered, imaging that would be difficult for Deke to do.

"Yeah, the boy did his pop proud." Rafae smiled. "Sure, he choked up a bit a couple of times, but all in all, he did okay – just kept it light, remembering better times."

"Good. I'm glad it went well." I smiled. "I just wish I could've gone – could've heard what he had to say."

"Well, I can tell you one story Deke told, about this time back when we were just boys." He nodded with a quick laugh. "He was remembering how his mom wouldn't get us any of that pre-sweetened Kool-Aid stuff, because she thought we'd get all wired up on the sugar – and of course she was right about that!"

"I bet!" I smirked at the thought of the two young boys in a happier time.

"Well, D'Arcy got us some anyway, and he had *my* dad stash it in the pantry, to keep it until he could surprise us with a pitcher of it sometime. But Deke and I, we managed to find the packs right away, and so one time when Abel was over…" He paused, acting as if he'd just said the wrong thing.

"It's okay," I assured him. "I want to hear. So, what did you do?"

"Well, we took all the packs to our new, double-secret hideout, a spot we'd taken up in the attic crawl space."

"And whose bright idea was that one?" I asked, figuring I knew the answer.

"Hey, I may have come up with the hideout, but it was all Geek's great idea to take off with the Kool-Aid!" he insisted. "And Abel, he was right in there with us when we ripped open those Kool-Aid packs, licked our fingers, and dipped them in for a taste."

"You were *eating* Kool-Aid."

"Oh, definitely – licking it off our fingers!" he answered. "Why water down a good thing when you can have it straight!"

The thought turned my stomach. "That's disgusting."

"Not to a nine-year-old!" he argued. "So, there we were, sucking back powdered Kool-Aid, when Deke decides he's not comfortable sitting on the plywood flooring, and so he slides over to sit in the space between the rafters and *Bam!* – he drops right through the drywall to the next floor."

"Oh, my gosh, you're kidding!"

"Nope," he replied, shaking his head. "Dust everywhere, me and Abel looking down through this big hole in the ceiling at him sprawled out there on the floor."

"Was he all right?"

"Got the wind knocked out of him, but that's it. And so, here comes D'Arcy, first one on the scene to see what the racket was all about, and what does he do when he sees his son lying there? He just shakes his head and says, 'Better clean this up, and hide all those Kool-Aid packs before your mom finds out what you were up to...' And with that, he calmly turns and just walks away."

"Really – no lecture?" I asked.

"Nope. I guess he figured the lesson learned – he didn't need to say any more. Just clean up after your own messes, and move on... or at least, that's what I got out of it, anyway."

"Hmm," I replied as I closed my eyes to rest them for just a moment. "So, all the people at the memorial – how'd they react to his story?"

"Oh, they smiled, and there were a few laughs – except for Connie Kavanaugh, of course. She was too busy being all solemn and proper, and I'm sure she expected others to be that way, too. So, she looked almost mad when Deke was telling that story – maybe because he was being funny, but I think it's more likely that she never knew about the Kool-Aid."

"Maybe it's just because... that's how she's coping."

Rafae looked confused. "By being angry?"

I opened one eye to peek at Rafae. "People grieve in different ways. Maybe she's mad at D'Arcy – for dying."

"Like he chose to!"

Opening my other eye, I lifted my head. "No, but she might be angry that he left her behind. I know I kind of felt that way, when my family died."

"Did you... Well, I guess you could –"

"I'm telling you, we did check it before!" my evening nurse Wanda said as she scurried into my room.

Marcus was right on her heels, nipping at her. "You guys can run a simple urine check up here. We just assumed you'd take care of something that –"

"I told you, we did, and it was negative before,"Wanda strapped the blood pressure cuff around my arm.

"What's going on?" I asked.

Rafae stood up. "Yeah, what are you talking about?"

Pumping up the cuff, Wanda's stern look quickly turned to a gentle smile as she gazed at me. "Oh, it'll be okay, I'm sure. I just need to get your vitals now before the doctor gets here." Releasing the cuff, she studied the dial on its side.

I was sure something was wrong. "The doctor's coming in *now?*"

Marcus headed back for the door. "Well, you better get it straight before Tsai gets here, Wanda, because he's not going to be happy about this."With that, he quickly left.

"Happy about what?" Rafae snapped. "What'd you do?"

Listening through her stethoscope, Wanda finished her count and then ripped the Velcro cuff from my arm, setting it aside. "It's Mr. Battiste, right?"

"Yes," Rafae answered.

"And that means you're not family," she continued. "So, I think maybe you should go down to the waiting room until the doctor's done talking with –"

"He's staying here," I insisted. "What's going on?"

"Oh, well..." She paused just long enough to remove an instrument from her lab coat pocket and insert it in my ear. "It's probably best to wait..." Pushing the trigger, she removed the thermometer and read it aloud. "98.7. Good." She pocketed the instrument, reaching then for my wrist to take my pulse. "When Dr. Tsai gets here, he'll explain what we're going to need to do, and then we'll –"

"No, I don't want to wait!" I snapped at her. "You know what's wrong here, and I want to know what it is, and what you're going to do about it."

She lowered my wrist, holding off on her count. "Carly, I really shouldn't say anything until –"

"Look, you've obviously already upset her with the way you two came in here!" Rafae scolded her. "You don't need to upset her anymore, so out with it!"

Lowering her eyes to her watch, Wanda held my wrist and paused long enough to check my pulse. Then she looked at me. "We checked your urine sample again and got a positive reading – for pregnancy."

"What!" The rush of adrenaline made me feel faint.

"You what!" Rafae chimed in. "Well, what does... does that mean?"

"Well, we're thinking that it means..." Looking me in the eyes, she lowered her voice. "...well, unless you have some other reason to believe this could have happened..."

I was shaking. "No. No, there's not."

"So..." Wanda took a deep breath. "I guess we're going to assume that somehow you were... well, that the doctor at the lighthouse must've implanted you at some point when you were unconscious." She reached down the bedside, lowering the back of my bed.

"Oh, my God!" I murmured, tears welling in my eyes. "I don't remember when... how could this happen?"

Rafae took my hand and stroked my forehead. "It's all going to be okay now. You're going to get through this, and I'm going to be with you, so just hang in there."

I closed my eyes, wishing this would all go away. "So... what are you... what am I... going to do?"

"Well, that's why Dr. Tsai's coming in – to talk about your options and make sure you're stable for the transfer."

"Transfer? To another room?"

"To another hospital," she answered.

"What?" I sat upright. "Where am I going!"

"Oh, it's okay." She gently took me by the arm and tried to coax me to lie back down. "I'm supposed to get you ready so we can move you to University Hospital downstate, but don't you worry about it – you'll like it there. The people are really –"

"Why am I..." I felt the room spinning as I gagged. "Oh, I think I'm – going to be sick."

"Wait! Here you go!" She quickly grabbed the kidney-shaped plastic dish from my bedside tray and held it to my chin.

Heaving, I spit up the bit of clear 7-up I'd been drinking, then gulped for air.

"Why does she need to go there?" Rafae asked for me as he rubbed my back. "Can't they just, well, deal with it here?"

"We're just a small town hospital," Wanda answered, taking the dish from my sight. "We're not prepared to handle someone expecting that many... you know, multiples like that."

I took another deep breath, trying to keep from passing out as I broke out in a cold sweat. "So, you're going to send me down there to... and then what am I... am I going to –"

"Okay, here's the deal," Wanda said as she stepped into my bathroom and turned on the faucet. "You don't have to be deciding anything right this minute." She turned off the water. "You'll have time while we transport you, and also when you get down there."

"And how's she getting there?" Rafae yelled to her. "Do I need to take her?"

"No, the ambulance is on its way. Of course, they'll want to run some tests – do an ultrasound." She stepped back out of the bathroom. "Then they'll talk to you about your choices – once they know more."

"More?" I wondered what she meant.

"Yeah, they've got the best equipment to figure out what you're dealing with here – you know, so they can tell you what you really need to know for making any kind of decision." Then she headed out the door, telling me, "So, you hold on here and I'll be *right* back."

"What else does she need to know?" Rafae yelled after her, but she was gone, so he looked at me. "Sorry. I don't know what she meant, but we'll find out. You just hold on there and I promise everything will be –"

"I know," I muttered.

"Yeah, you'll be okay."

"No, I mean, I know what she meant." I shut my eyes.

"What?" he asked. "What else is there to know?"

"How many," I answered solemnly. "I need to know how many are in me, so I can decide what to do – with each one of them."

Chapter 53

LEFT TO WAIT

IT DIDN'T TAKE LONG TO DEDUCE MY CHOICES but the specialists at University Hospital insisted on reviewing them with me anyway. They proved to be well versed on all the potential risk factors – information that I preferred not to know, but they insisted on telling me anyway. Besides, as a patient in a teaching hospital, I couldn't help but overhear my prognosis every time the interns made their rounds with their instructor.

"And this is another victim from that botched stem cell project," the teaching doctor announced to her three attentive students as they all stood at the foot of my bed. "She's just back from ultrasound with the technician's report indicating detection of at least twelve embryos, all of them measuring about 8mm in length… so they're how far along?"

One overly eager student who looked like he was still in his teens answered before the others could. "That's the fourth week of development." He smiled proudly, swiping his blond bangs from his eyes.

"Yes, it is, Tom," the teacher nodded. "And so, with this set of circumstances, we're going to offer the patient what options, Naomi?" she asked the one female student before Tom could enthusiastically interject his own response.

"Well, of course the safest option would be a vacuum aspiration. I'd recommend that as the easiest on the patient," she answered confidently.

"Yes, that is one option." The teacher then turned to the shortest of the three. "What's your recommendation, Kemper?"

"Well, I'm not sure." His tone sounded less confident, but he followed up with the best response I'd heard from any group so far. "I don't know yet how the patient feels about this. I think we have to ask her."

While the other two students sneered, the teacher smiled, saying, "Excellent point, Kemper. So, go ahead – ask."

"Oh, okay." He raised his eyebrows, then turned to look at me for the first time. "So, you understand your situation here, don't you…" He paused, shuffling through his notes for my name. "… Carly?"

"Yes, I've heard about it a few times today," I answered.

"Okay, well, how do you feel about it?"

"It sucks," I told him matter-of-factly.

"Yeah, I suppose it does." He had to laugh. "But we've got to deal with it, so what are you thinking you'd prefer to do?"

"I'd prefer to do nothing."

"Well, unfortunately, that's *not* an option. You couldn't carry that many babies to term, and if you tried, they'd choke each other out until you aborted them all anyway – and that would be very dangerous. You'd become septic as the fetuses died, and then you'd possibly bleed to death, as well."

I nodded. "That's what they tell me."

"So, did they talk to you about a selective aspiration?" Tom asked. "That's where they abort some of the embryos but leave some to be carried to term."

"Yes, they explained all that."

"So, would you rather do that? Do you think you want to try to carry at least some of these babies to term?"

I looked down, shaking my head. I *had* thought about it, wondering about the eventual outcome of such a choice. Would the babies then be returned to their biological parents, or would they all be mine? And if they were mine, what would I do?

"So, you don't want to have these babies?" the instructor asked, trying to interpret my silence.

"No, it's not that," I replied, still searching for my answer." Of course, I'd always wanted to have children, but not like this – and not when I had no job, no husband, no home… I knew that even one child would be tough in my circumstances, but multiple babies? How could I ever care for them when I was all by myself?

I looked at the teacher. "It's just that... I guess I don't know yet," I answered honestly.

"Well, when making your decision, you should consider the fact that this procedure is fairly new with no guarantees of success," the teaching doctor explained. "Some of the embryos might not survive the process, especially since they're crowded and they're —"

"I've already heard this disclaimer," I snapped.

"Oh. Well, then it sounds like you've been educated on the matter," she replied, speaking not just to me but also for her students. "Information is empowering — it helps the patient make the healthiest decision on his or her own behalf."

"But it's not just about me. I'm deciding for others, too." I looked down, rubbing my stomach as the burden of my need to decide intensified. "I'm pro-life, you know, and so it's like an instinct for me to want to save them all."

"But you can't," the blond abruptly stated.

"Yeah, that's what everyone keeps telling me," I replied. "So, does that mean I have to decide how many of them live and how many die? And then when they're born, do they stay with me or do they go to their biological parents? And what if the parents don't want them — I mean, if I have, say, six or seven babies, then how can I even begin to take care of them?"

"Oh, I wouldn't try any more than five," the blond told his instructor, ignoring me and my concerns as he continued to work at impressing his superior. "To date, we've never had any more than that survive."

"But that's not for him to decide," the student named Kemper told his teacher before he turned back to address me. "I understand your dilemma, Carly. You *could* go with five, but then if a couple of them abort on their own, you might feel badly that you didn't try more. Then again, if you *did* try more — say like six or seven — and they all thrived, then they'd most likely be born too soon to save."

My mouth felt dry as I replied, "Really?" I rubbed my bare arms, my skin feeling cold.

Kemper scratched the top of his head. "Why, even five might prove to be too many, causing premature births that could result in defects for some, death for others —"

"Some important points to consider, Kemper, but let's not dwell on too much detail here," the teacher remarked as she wrote something in her notes. "We don't need to be making this decision any tougher on the patient than it already is."

"Oh, sorry, Carly," Kemper apologized. "Just trying to help you realize that no matter which way you go with this, there's no getting around that you're going to lose at least some of those babies. But at least with the selective procedure, you'll probably save some; whereas if you do nothing, you'll definitely lose them all — and they may take you with them."

"Maybe," I admitted. "But I just don't feel like I'm supposed to play God. I mean, these aren't even my children, you know? So, how do I decide for other people which of their babies are going to live, and how many of their babies are going to die?"

The four of them looked puzzled as they turned to their notes for an answer I knew wasn't there.

"Have you got company *again*!" Rafae exclaimed as he entered my room, returning from his quick trip out for lunch.

"Yes, and it's time for us to move on," the teacher announced. "Thanks for allowing us to look in on your case."

"Yes, good luck with your decision," the female student added, looking to her instructor to see if she'd receive good marks on her bedside manners.

"I'm sure you'll do fine," the youthful Tom contributed, determined not to be outdone.

I was grateful to the short one for saying nothing. His smile, coupled with his apparent understanding of my dilemma, meant more to me than any of their contrived comments as they all exited my room.

"What did I miss? The latest freak show?" Rafae joked as he sat down on the unoccupied bed in my double suite. "They just keep coming, don't they?"

"Yes, and they all keep on bringing me the same bleak prognosis: abort or die."

"Wow! They're not saying *that*, are they?"

I looked to the ceiling. "No, but they might as well."

"I see," he said, reclining back on his bed. "So, are you any closer to deciding?"

"You know, every time I think this through, I just keep coming back to the same decision – the one everybody keeps telling me I can't make." I sighed at the thought. "I guess I'm thinking I should let this ride itself out."

"Hmm." Rafae crossed his arms across his chest. "So, you've decided to abort them all, huh?"

"No, that's not what I said."

"Yes, it is." He rolled to his side, looking over at me. "If you don't do anything, you *know* you'll lose them all."

I looked back at him. "Well, I don't think that has to be the case. Yeah, I'll lose some, but maybe some will make it, and that way I don't have to decide how many or which ones. And then maybe their birth parents will want them and I won't have to decide how I'm going to care for them or how –"

"Carly, you *know* that's not going to happen. The doctor told you this morning that you'll go into labor way too soon, and if that happens –"

"Then they'll have to figure that out then, won't they!" I snapped. "*They'll* have to decide, not me."

"And you might die!" He sat up, raising his voice. "Are you trying to kill yourself over this?"

"No! I just don't want to have to be the one... to decide. That's all!"

"Well, then I'll decide for you! When your doc comes by tomorrow, I'm telling him you've decided to abort them all, and then you can always blame it on me."

I shook my head. "And if I let you do that – decide for me – that still makes it my decision."

"No, it's not."

"Yes it is!" I sat up, yelling back at him. "And besides, I'm definitely *not* aborting them all. I either do a selective or let nature take its course."

"Nature? Hey, there's nothing natural about this! You've got to do something before *something* happens to *you*," he said fretfully. "Even if you don't remember, we almost lost you once, and I don't want to just sit around here and wait for…" He shook his head, unwilling to finish his thought.

"Yeah, I remember," I replied, understanding his reasons for concern. "But that was different. I've got people here taking good care of me. Out there on the ice I just had one guy who was standing around waiting for me to die."

"Because he thought if he just stood there, letting nature take its course, then it wouldn't be on his conscience."

I paused, glaring at him as I mulled over his point. "That's not the same thing, and you know it!" I scolded him. "He *wanted* us to die, and you *know* that's not the case here!"

"I suppose so." He bit his lip, looking down. "But it just seems like you're going to feel even guiltier in the long run if you just let this happen, and I don't want to just stand by and let something bad happen… to you."

I sighed. "Yeah, well, I appreciate your concern." I felt tears coming to my eyes so I looked away, making sure he wouldn't notice. "I just need some more time to think about it – and about how I'd care for them all by myself."

"Now, you know you won't be alone," he insisted. "I'm not going anywhere, so I'll help you, and I know you'll get all sorts of help from –" he stopped at the sudden ringing of my room phone.

"Just a sec," I told him, reaching toward the phone.

"No, you just relax," Rafae insisted as he leapt to answer it. "Hello?…Yeah?…Yeah, I'm still here… I told you I don't have to be back for at least a couple more days…What, you left already?…" He looked at me, smiling. "Yeah, she's doing okay right now… No, that's great! That's great! Are they doing okay so far?… Good. Well tell them thanks for me…Yeah, you take your time and we'll look for you by six… Okay, see you then." Pushing the off button on the receiver, he hung up the phone.

"Who was that?" I asked.

"Oh, I can't tell you." He smiled again.

"No, really, who was it," I demanded to know. "They're on their way here?"

"Yes, surprise visitors." Reaching down to me, he gently tucked a strand of my hair behind my ear.

I sat upright. "Coming to the hospital… to see me?"

"Maybe."

I couldn't imagine who that might be. "Someone from Windemere?"

"Now if I told you that, then I'd have to kill you."

"Oh, come on!" I slapped his arm, wondering who might make the trip here – and whether or not it was someone I'd even care to see, given my circumstances. "Just give me a hint."

"Okay," he said with a smirk. "Bigger than a breadbox."

"What! No, a *real* hint."

"Okay! Okay!" He laughed. "There are… more than one of them."

"Really. Now you've *really* got me stumped."

"Good." Leaning to me, he kissed my forehead. "That should keep you guessing while I get you to eat something. How about munching on some more soda crackers?"

"Oh, I don't think so," I moaned at the thought. "I just had some –"

"Well, I'll have them bring you their bland tray and you can pick out whatever sounds good to you at the moment."

"But I don't think I can –"

"Of course, you can!" he insisted. "I'll be right back," he said as he ducked out the door.

And so I sat there, propped up in my bed, dreading the smell of whatever food would soon be coming. At least now I had a distraction. The thought of visitors gave me something to look forward to – that is, until I started worrying about who it might be. I really didn't want to have to explain my dilemma to any more people, and so my excitement soon turned to dread.

I couldn't help but wonder if these visitors would be people I'd be glad to see or if they'd just be more of the same gawkers who'd come to see the freak show, taking their gossip about my circumstances back with them to Biminis where they'd embellish it, telling tall tales of my situation – of how it happened and why I deserved it. *That* was something I *definitely* didn't want to have happen.

Catching myself fretting, I realized I had much bigger concerns than who might gossip or who might come for dinner. Besides, I trusted Rafae, and if he was pleased that these people were coming, then I figured they must be visitors I'd welcome, too.

For the moment, all I could do... was wait.

Chapter 54

THE WISDOM OF EXPERIENCE

THE OVERCAST SKIES OF GROUNDHOG DAY had left me and the residents of southern Michigan with the hope that winter would be ending soon. For that reason, I didn't mind missing out on the day's sunset, the dreary sky continuing to darken as my dinner tray arrived.

"Thought I'd get this up here early so you'd have more time to pick at it," my freckled student nurse Stephanie said as she placed the tray on the wheeled side table. "I noticed on your chart that you've been eating better today."

"Yeah, your hospital chef makes a mean orange Jell-O," I told her with a laugh.

She wheeled the tray up to me. "Well, looks like you've got a different flavor this evening – maybe it's a strawberry or a raspberry flavor."

I looked at the red cubes jiggling in the bowl. "Or maybe cherry – the red's always a surprise."

Swinging her long, braided ponytail of frizzy, black hair back behind her, Stephanie smiled as she lifted the plastic cover from my hot entrée. "Ooo! Looks like the chicken noodle soup is homemade!"

"I doubt that." I studied the chunks of soft carrots and dark green peas: tell-tale signs of soup from a can. "I don't think I can eat that – maybe I'll just have the crackers."

"Well, you might change your mind in a little bit," she replied, setting the plastic cover aside.

"Maybe, thanks."

Stephanie exited just as Rafae came in with my guests.

"Soup's on!" he said. "And now your company's here." He extended his arm, ushering in Nana Maeve and Deke.

"Oh, my!" In my surprise to see them, I knocked my tray, nearly spilling my soup.

"Hello, dear," Nana Maeve said as she shuffled with small steps over to my bedside. "It's good to see you." She rubbed my arm.

"Wow! What are *you* doing here?" I asked.

"What, sorry to see us, are you?"

"Oh, no! Not at all," I replied with a quick glance at Deke. "I'm just… surprised, that's all. You're a long way from home!"

"Well, this young whipper-snapper friend of yours here thought it might be a good idea," she said, lifting her cane to point at Rafae. "And for once, I agreed." She slowly lowered herself into the chair next to me. "Then my darling grandson here agreed to drive us down, and so here we are!"

"Well, that was really nice of you," I pushed away my tray on wheels.

"Yes, we thought it might be good for us to get away from things." She shook her head. "It's all been so terrible, what happened and all."

There was an awkward pause when I wasn't sure what I should say, feeling afraid that I'd say the wrong thing. I looked at Deke who looked away from me, shifting his weight from one foot to the other.

"Well, the memorial was very nice," Rafae offered.

"It was, wasn't it?" Nana Maeve agreed. "And Deke… he did a nice job."

Rafae patted his back. "Yeah, you did good, DK."

"Thanks," he muttered.

"I am *so* sorry for… for your loss," I managed to say to both Deke and his grandmother.

"Thank you, dear," Nana Maeve replied.

"I wish I could've come to the memorial," I told her.

"No need," she assured me. "We understood."

"Glad you didn't," Deke mumbled.

"What did you say, child?" Nana Maeve asked, scowling at her grandson.

Deke looked back at her. "I said it was probably best that she didn't – you know, with the way Mom feels about this."

"Deke, your mother's crazy!" she snapped. "Carly had every right to be there, and I wish she could've come."

"I'm sorry," I told her. "I didn't even know about it until that morning and –"

"Don't you worry about it, dear," she insisted. "I knew where you were, and why you couldn't make it."

"Well, it probably was for the best. I didn't want to upset you or your mom," I said to Deke. "I mean, I can see why she thinks I'm somewhat to blame for what happened."

"Nonsense!" Nana Maeve exclaimed.

"I've tried to tell her that." Rafae shook his head at Maeve. "It's pretty obvious that Carly was a victim, too, and I keep on telling her it wasn't her fault."

"Of course, it wasn't!" Nana Maeve agreed, then turned to her grandson. "Isn't that right, Deke?"

"Right, right," Deke chimed in, none too convincingly.

"So, you see, I want you to know you're not to blame *at all* for this," Nana Maeve emphasized her point. "My D'Arcy was a very strong-willed man – been like that since childhood – and he'd always had this driving desire to do what was right. He *chose* to go out on that ice, and he *chose* to help that girl, so it wasn't…" For a brief moment, she faltered, but then she regained her composure. "It's a shame – a terrible, terrible shame – but I couldn't be prouder of my son, and no one is ever going to take that away from me."

"He *was* a great man, your dad," Rafae added, patting Deke's back. "…a lot like *his* dad."

"What! And am I chopped liver?" Nana Maeve objected.

"Oh, no," Rafae back-peddled. "I didn't mean to –"

"Yes you did, you little hooligan!" She replied jokingly.

"Well, speaking of Grandpa, I should go see if he found his coffee." Deke headed for the door.

"What! Is your husband… did he come, too?" I asked Nana Maeve, feeling my jaw drop.

"Yeah, I'll go see what's keeping him," Deke answered and then left.

"Yes, I insisted that he come, too." Nana Maeve scooted to the front edge of her chair. "We're both so sorry to hear about your situation."

Still shocked by the appearance of the Kavanaugh clan, I looked to Rafae, wondering what he had told them.

Rafae stepped closer to me. "Yeah, I told them that the doctor shipped you here because Doc Arlington managed to... well, put you in a touchy situation, so to speak... like he did all those other women."

"Oh." I felt a bit sheepish about others knowing.

"That crazy little man!" Nana Maeve referred to Doc. "I always told Vince I didn't trust that fruitcake, but he wouldn't listen to me."

Rafae stepped backward, away from my bed. "Maybe I should just leave you ladies to talk."

"Where are *you* going?" I asked him.

"Uh, I'm just going to see if DK found the Captain." He pointed toward the door as he headed toward it. "I won't be long – be right back." And with that, he left.

"So, Rafae told you about my... situation." I looked at Nana Maeve, unsure of what details Rafae had shared with her.

"Yes, but he didn't tell me how many he put in you, if you don't mind my asking."

"Oh, no, I suppose not," I replied, realizing he'd told her enough. "They've counted twelve, but they suspect there might be more."

"Good gracious, girl!" she exclaimed. "What an *awful* situation that deranged lunatic has put you into!"

"Yeah, it's pretty bad."

"Well, that's why I brought Nolan here – to talk to you about it, if you don't mind, and try to help you out."

I squirmed. "No, I don't mind." Despite my curiousity about the mysterious captain, I felt uncomfortable with the idea of discussing my circumstances with him. "That's thoughtful of you, but I'm afraid I'm kind of on my own on this one."

"Nonsense!" She waved her hand at me. "With the help and wisdom of friends, you're never alone. Now, I hope you don't mind my prying some more, but what did the doctor say?"

"Ah, well, actually I've seen a bunch of doctors and they all agree that I've either got to abort some of them if I want to carry any, or else they want me to abort them all."

"Oh my! They didn't have such options in my day — that is, unless you wanted to go risk your life in some back alley."

"Well, I suppose no one was pregnant with twelve-plus in your day, either."

"That's probably true, but if by some small chance that did happen, then I guess the unfortunate soul would miscarry them all, wouldn't she?"

"Or maybe just some," I argued.

"Oh, did they tell you that could happen?"

"Not really, but I think it could."

"Hmm." She sat back. "Is that just wishful thinking on your part?"

I paused. "Yeah, I guess it is. I just don't like feeling like I have to... decide. I mean, I wonder if I just wait, then maybe a better option will come along that I'll know is the right thing to do."

"Honey, I can barely imagine what you're going through with this," Nana Maeve sympathized. "I don't see how anyone with any compassion could find this a simple decision to make, right Nolan?"

Turning my eyes to the doorway, I was a bit startled to find the elderly Captain quietly hovering there.

His lips barely parted to answer. "Right," he answered softly.

"Oh, and you brought me coffee, too! Bring it in, bring it in." She waved her hand, motioning for Captain Kavanaugh to bring her one of the two Styrofoam cups in his hands.

Making his way past the foot of my bed, he cautiously walked to his wife. Handing her a steaming cup, his voice was raspy as he quietly told her, "Extra sugar, just how you like it."

"Yes, it is – how nice of you to bring me a cup." Smiling at him, she took the cup and stirred its contents as she turned to me. "You don't mind it if we have our drinks in here, do you, Carly?"

"Not at all." My stomach churned as I took in the strong aroma.

Nolan stepped back from his wife, looking around and then leaning back against the wall beside her, his head lowered and eyes looking down.

"Maybe we could get another chair for you, dear," Nana Maeve suggested to her husband, her tone unusually gentle.

"I'm fine, Maeve." His eyes glanced to her then back to study the coffee cup he held with both of his frail, pallid hands.

I reached for my bedside call button. "I can check with the nurse and see if she'll bring one, Mr. Kavanaugh."

Taking one hand from his cup, he pressed it against the wall to one side of his black slacks that hung loosely from his fragile frame. "No, thank you," he faintly spoke to his cup.

"What's this *mister* nonsense you're calling him?" Nana Maeve questioned. "You call him Nolan, dear. Didn't you two meet before at the house?"

"Well, not formally – just in passing." Gazing again at Nolan, I smiled. "Nice to make it official."

He lifted his chin, pressing his head firmly against the wall as he quickly glanced my way. "Yes, it is." He nodded once, a smile playing on his lips only a moment before lowering his head again, his subdued green eyes returning to his coffee.

There was an awkward pause I chose to fill. "…and as I told your wife, it's such a nice surprise that you all made the long trip just to see me here, especially realizing…" My throat caught, the whole realization hitting me once again. "…well, when you think about all *you've* been going through. I am *so* sorry, Nolan… about D'Arcy."

"Thank you." The captain's gaze remained downward as he bit his lip.

Nana Maeve reached over to where the captain stood beside her and gave his arm a gentle pat. "It always hurts to lose someone, but it seems you know a thing or two about that yourself, Carly, with all the losses Deke tells us you've suffered in your family, too." Nana Maeve took a sip from the cup.

I was surprised to hear Deke had told them about this. "Yeah, it can be hard to get over – guess you *never* really do."

"That's very true." Nana Maeve leaned her cane against the wall beside her, folding her hands in her lap. "Rafae had suggested, and I agreed, that it'd be a good idea for Nolan to talk to you – that is, since he also knows a thing or two about how you're feeling."

"Oh, my, that's right." I felt my eyes widen as I looked at Nolan in a new light. "You lost *your* dad, and your brother, on that… that ship," I tried to remember. "What was its name?"

"The *Perseverance*," he answered heavily with a sigh.

"So, you've heard the stories, have you?" Nana Maeve nodded. "It's mostly gossip – people saying that the captain was so wise and how his one son was obedient while the other one was crazy."

Nolan looked to his wife, rolling his eyes with another sigh. "That… would be me."

"Oh," I replied, recalling the story yet not knowing what to say. "Well, I guess I *have* heard that story, but not that you were crazy or anything like that."

"Then you *haven't* heard the story," Nana Maeve argued. "*Nobody* tells it without making Nolan sound like a lunatic!"

Burying himself deeper into the wall, Nolan winced.

Nana Maeve took notice. "But I guess there's no sense in getting worked up about it," she added in an unusually level tone. "We've lived with those stories for a very long time, and I refuse to let a bunch of whisperers get the better of us."

I had no doubt she wouldn't, but didn't understand what this had to do with me.

"So… you came all this way just to tell me not to worry about the gossip?" I wondered. "…because, you didn't have to tell me that – I've gotten pretty much used to ignoring it, too. So, whatever they're saying about me, I don't –"

"Oh, no dear," Nana Maeve interrupted. "Of course, we do think you should ignore the gossip, but we didn't come to tell you the obvious."

"Okay." Now I was really stumped.

"Rafae and I thought Nolan could… well, just let him tell you his side of the story – about what *really* happened. Then I think you might understand."

"Well, all right," I said, failing to see the point, but intrigued to hear the story, nonetheless.

"Go ahead, Nolan. Tell her about it – it'll do *you* some good, too."

Stepping to a side table, Nolan set his coffee down and then twisted his hands into his pockets, fiddling with his loose change. "Well, I'll tell it as best as my memory can recall." He looked off for a moment and then rubbed his chin. "Let's see now." Turning his gaze back to the floor, he took a couple of steps, seeming a little hesitant to begin. "I guess… well, it all happened so fast, when we got caught off guard by that storm."

"Off guard, my foot!" Nana Maeve firmly crossed her arms with total indignation. "Hell, your father knew better than to launch in such conditions, especially that late in the shipping season!"

Nolan looked to his wife, wincing again. "And you still defend me, don't you, Maeve?" He took a step back. "It's probably best if you tell it, dear…"

"No, it's not, but I just want you to be fair to yourself, that's all," she insisted. "It's best if Carly hears it from you, and I promise I won't say another word." She put her hand over her mouth.

Nolan sighed, still seeming hesitant. "Well, all right, then I guess I'll try." Looking down to his feet again, he took two steps forward before gazing up at me. "So, you probably heard about how the storm caused our ship to crash up against another one." Drawing his hands from his pockets, he crossed his arms and then uncrossed them again. "Well, it was a big whaleback freighter, and it caused a lot of damage – destroyed the larger one of our two dinghies."

"Yeah, I remember that," I told him as I recalled the tale from when Pepper and I had gone to the old museum – a time that now seemed so long ago.

"So, our ship was taking on water, about to sink, and we only had the smaller dinghy – too small to hold the entire crew."

"So didn't the captain – your dad – didn't he command everybody to try to get in that dinghy anyway?"

"That's right!" Nana Maeve interjected.

Nolan glanced at his wife and then looked down again, pacing along the side of the vacant bed. "My brother – D'Arcy was his name, too," he added with a quick glance at me. "He agreed that ten was the most that dinghy could hold, especially in bad weather." He shook his head. "But Dad wouldn't hear of it – said to save every one, or no one."

"But, if you don't mind my saying so – about your dad – that seems too extreme, don't you think?"

"I'll say!" Nana Maeve couldn't help herself, agreeing and then quickly covering her mouth again before her husband could look her way.

"Well, my dad was kind of a military guy even though he never enlisted." Nolan tapped his toe against the linoleum floor. "Guess he held duty and loyalty above all else."

I nodded. "I see."

"So, I was raised to always obey the person in charge, no matter what, no questions asked." Nolan turned his eyes, gazing out my window at the snow beginning to fall in the darkness. "And I suppose, if we'd had a shipload of grown men, then I would've done whatever Dad told me to do; I'd have boarded that dinghy and willingly gone to my death with the others." He looked at me, but he appeared to be seeing right through me, staring at something far beyond. "But as I stood there, in that driving rain, loading those poor, soaked little boys into that dinghy – staring into each one of their frightened faces…" He looked down, tapping his toe again. "I saw the fear in their eyes, and I could imagine each one in his last, frantic moments, quickly drowning in that cold, unforgiving lake."

Looking down myself, I tried to hide the tears I felt forming in my eyes. "That's so awful," I muttered.

Nolan turned, now pacing in the other direction. "Those brave little souls – each one worth fighting for… I figured those boys still had a lot of living to do, and I couldn't just stand by while we lost all of them." He stopped, staring at the floor. "So, I committed the ultimate sin in my family: I disobeyed a direct order. Once D'Arcy was in the dinghy and I'd counted about ten in with him, then I cut the thing loose, dropping them down to the water."

Biting his lip, he shook his head. "I knew I had to do it – to at least give them a fighting chance to live."

Nana Maeve lowered her hand from her mouth. "You did what you had to," she said softly.

Nolan studied where he had walked across the room and back again, getting nowhere. "Just like everyone says when they tell this story, I *did* disobey my father – my captain – and I *did* cut that dinghy loose before all the boys were on board." With a wipe at his nose, he then scratched the white stubble on his face. "Then I stood there, holding onto the rail as I tried to keep my balance, staring into the eyes of those remaining, fearful souls who were holding on, too – all of us about to face our deaths."

I could no longer hold back my tears, sniffling as I took a tissue from the box on my nightstand. "I am so sorry, Nolan. No one should ever have to face that."

He looked my way again, shaking his head as he seemed to notice me for the first time since he'd started his story. "Oh, I didn't mean to upset you." Looking down, he sheepishly took a step backward. "Maybe I shouldn't keep –"

"Yes, you should." Nana Maeve broke her silence. "I'm sure she wants to know how things turned out, dear – about the boys who survived."

"Yes, I do, and really, I'm fine." Wiping my eyes, I tried to assure him. "Sometimes I just get emotional in my state, but they tell me that's normal."

"Of course it is," Nana Maeve agreed. "Now finish the story where you left off, Nolan… on the deck, looking at the rest of the boys, still trying to help them, too…"

"Well, yes, we had to try," Nolan told his wife. "As the ship was going down, I yelled for them to jump before it sucked us down – to give it a fighting chance – but they were so scared, I only got one to jump with me… and sadly I lost him." Closing his eyes, he turned away. "The rest stayed on board – every one of them probably cursing my name as they went down with the ship."

I thought back to my experiences with the frigid lake – the time when Libby had fallen in, and also D'Arcy. "But the water… it had to be horribly cold, so how did you survive?"

"By fighting!" Nana Maeve chimed in. "He was bobbing around out there, nearly frozen to death, when by some miracle he came close enough to the boys' dinghy that they were able to pull him in."

"Amazing they didn't tip over," Nolan added. "I was so lucky, but my brother, he wasn't." Pausing, he tucked his hands back in his pockets and began to pace again. "When I came to in the dinghy, the boys told me my brother had fallen out while trying to grab a boy who'd been thrown out in the giant swells."

"Your brother was trying to save those boys, just like you were," I noted, trying to comfort him. "Sounds like that runs in the family."

For the first time, he smiled at me. "I've always wished I could've saved more, but at least I know I tried."

"But you saved some, and that's what matters." I was beginning to see the connection between our situations.

"Yes, I suppose that *is* what matters." Nodding, he gazed at me, his eyes suddenly sparkling.

"Of course, there were others who didn't feel that way," Nana Maeve noted. "There've been many people who've judged you harshly, Nolan, like that Talbott man. He's a real vindictive son-of-a-"

"Now, now, Maeve..." Nolan patted his wife's shoulder. "I understand his bitterness, especially over losing his boys."

"Talbott," I repeated, the name suddenly coming back to me. "Weren't they the twin boys on board?"

"Yes, and their father blamed Nolan for all of this when it wasn't even his fault!" Nana Maeve's face had tightened into an expression of more anger than I'd ever seen in her before – even when it came to her daughter-in-law.

"They both died, didn't they," I seemed to remember.

"One boy made it in the dinghy but fell overboard, and the other one fell off the ship trying to get in the dinghy in the first place," Nolan recollected as he stared off into space. "But I never told the father that."

"Why not?" I wondered.

Nolan tapped one shoe against the other, knocking some dirt from the sole that fell to the floor. "Because he's just one of those people who needs someone to blame, and I figured if that helped him make his peace, then I wasn't about to take that away from him." Cocking his head, he looked me in the eyes. "But you don't seem like one of those people, Carly. You seem like the type that makes her peace the same way I do – in knowing you didn't leave things to fate, and that you at least *tried* to do something."

"So, that's what you're here for – to tell me that's what I should do?"

"No." He shook his head. "I'd never presume to tell you what to do."

"But we did think his experience might help you sort it out for yourself," Nana Maeve added. "You know, we didn't come to sugar-coat this for you. It certainly hasn't been easy for Nolan to live with the choice he made, but it seems like every time he relives what happened, he always comes back to the same conclusion: that he made the best of a bad situation."

"So, you don't think that it's a good decision to just… do nothing."

"Well, Rafae told us that's too risky for you, and really it's the same decision you'd be making if you aborted them all anyway."

"I suppose," I nodded, knowing she was right.

"Sounds like you know that's what will happen, even if you wish it wouldn't," Nolan said as he backed up to the wall, leaning against it. "But you have to realize, Carly, that doing nothing is, in itself, a choice… and if you already know what the consequences will be if you do nothing, then I suppose *that's* what you're going to have to live with."

I looked away, mulling over his words.

Nolan rubbed the back of his neck. "You know, there've been plenty of times I've wished that accident never happened, but it did, and that's just the way it is."

"I can understand that," I told him, thinking about all the things *I* wished hadn't happened, as well.

Nana Maeve took hold of her husband's hand as she looked at me, speaking to us both. "Sometimes these bad things just happen, and all we can do is make the best out of the worst there could be."

Looking at his wife's hand in his, Nolan shook his head. "Unfortunately, though, that often means you've got to make a choice, and sometimes that's a really tough thing to do... but you still have to do it."

Studying the devoted couple, I told them both, "I think I see your point, and I'll take it to heart."

"I'm sure you will, dear." Nana Maeve released her husband's hand and reached for her cane. "We just thought it might help for you to know you're not alone – that we understand how tough this decision must be."

"Thanks, and I appreciate your coming all this way just for me."

Using her cane for support, Nana Maeve slowly stood up. "It's our pleasure, dear, but now we should probably get going – go find those two boys before they get into another one of their silly little fights." She moved stiffly toward the door.

Standing upright and tucking his hands in his pockets, Nolan glanced at me as he, too, headed for the door. "Glad we had the chance to talk, Carly."

"I am, too." I smiled. "And again, I'm really sorry about D'Arcy."

He nodded. "So are we, but at least we know he lived a full life without regrets." Pulling one hand from his pocket, he raised it and pointed at me. "You live that way, too – a full life without regrets, never needing to wonder *'what if'* when you look back."

"I'll try, sir."

Nana Maeve stopped at the door. "I know you'll make a good decision, Carly. Just promise that no matter what comes of it, you won't second guess yourself."

I paused, considering her request with total sincerity. "Okay... I won't."

"Good for you. We'll be off to our hotel then, as soon as we find our driver. Come on, Nolan."

"Yes, dear," he replied, extending his arm to his wife.

Nana Maeve took hold. "We'll send that rascal Rafae back up to your room as soon as we find him – bet he's a good sounding board for trying to figure this out."

"Yeah, he's given me a lot of support," I agreed.

Turning to leave, Nana Maeve spoke over her shoulder. "So, we'll stop by in the morning before we leave town, if you don't mind another visit."

"That would be great."

"...see if you've decided anything yet," she added.

Nolan escorted his wife out of the door, never looking back as he added, "Then you can tell us *your* story about the choice you finally made."

Part IV

BEYOND PERCEPTION

Chapter 55

STARTING OVER AGAIN

EVENTUALLY TWINS INSTINCTIVELY WONDER who was born first and who came last. At some point in their young lives they discover that a matter of minutes determined who was older, a revelation that in turn leads them to question whether this brief time-span also decided who was wiser, and stronger, and faster, and somehow superior to the other.

That time finally came on the last day of August, the day when Hope and Chance turned five.

"Who's older – me or Hope?" Chance asked first from his seat at the breakfast table.

Hope swallowed her last bite of pancakes. "I must be, 'cause I'm bigger." She was showing signs of carrying a chip on her shoulder, always the more competitive of the two. "Did I come out of your tummy first?"

"Actually Chance came out first," I told her, but then realized that wasn't the total truth – that there had been one who was born before both of them, and then there was one who came after them all as well. "Yeah, Chance was born before you were, Hope," I corrected myself.

Hope scowled, turning to her brother just in time to see him sticking his tongue out at her.

"Mom!" she complained.

"Oh, now we won't have that," I told Chance.

Quickly retracting his tongue, he argued, "Well, I bet *I'll* be bigger *some* day."

"Could be," I replied, wondering that myself.

"Not if I hov te keep beaton' on you, child," Rosie said to him as she entered the kitchen, pulling a clean towel off the countertop to whip it at him. "Now, you two need te get outside ond play before it gets too hot out dare ond you gotta come bock in." She snapped the towel at Hope, as well. "You hear me, garl? Now scoot or dare won't be enna cake for you latar!"

Hope scrambled from her chair and dashed for the door, leaving her brother behind, as she so often did.

"Hope, I've told you before, you should try to help your brother," I yelled after her.

Chance grabbed the short, metal crutches that leaned against the wall beside him, adeptly sliding his arms into the c-shaped rings and grabbing the handles. "I can do it by myself, Mom," he informed me – and he certainly could.

"Come on!" Hope waved for her brother to hurry up and follow her.

"I'm coming!" Swaying his crooked legs forward with each reach of his crutches, he moved with surprising agility out of the kitchen and out of the door.

"I'm starting to wonder if Hope's competitiveness is rubbing off on Chance," I said to Rosie, lifting my coffee cup for a sip.

"Well, dot wouldn't be soch a bod ding, would it?" She poured herself a cupful from the pot in the coffeemaker.

"For him, it might," I replied. "With his condition, he'll always struggle to keep up."

"Yoss, but you need te give de boy more credot. He con see he's got a disobilloty, bot dot doesn't mean he won't find oddar ways to excel." Carrying her steaming cup, she came to the table and took a seat next to me. "Dot littal mon, he's a brave one."

I could see them out the window, playing in the sand that had piled up a distance from the beach. "I suppose he is." I smiled, taking another sip.

"So, I heard your littal slip-up on de birt ordar," she said, scooping sugar into her cup.

"I'm just trying to keep it simple for now," I replied. "I don't think they're ready to hear the whole sordid story."

"Dot's for shar," she nodded and took a long drink from her cup. "Bot you *are* go-on' te tell dem som day, aren't you?"

"Eventually." I watched the two of them shovel sand into the same pale, glad for this time when they didn't need to know – when they still could keep their innocence.

"Do you hov some idea when you dink you'll tell dem?"

"No, but I know it'll probably have to be soon." I looked down at my coffee cup, rubbing my thumb along its rim. "Of course, I don't have to tell them everything now. It'd be too much for them to take in all at once."

"Yoss, dot would be on undarstatemont!" Rosie said and then took another long drink. "Where con you evon begin wid dot story?"

"Well, first of all I've got to explain how I can be their birth mother without being their biological one."

"Ond dot one'll be tricky onough!" She shook her head.

I gazed back at the two playing in the sand, noting once more the stark difference between Hope's Asian features and Chance's light chocolate complexion. "But all too soon, they're going to want to know why they don't look like each other, and why they don't look like me."

"Wid dem starton' school next week, you know soonar or latar some kids go-on' te notice ond say someton'," Rosie pointed out. "I'm surprised Libby hosn't said someton'."

"She won't, but you're right about school – some kid might say something." I nodded, worrying how the two would react. "You think I should tell them now, before that happens?"

"Oh, I don't know!" Rosie half-chuckled. "I'm jost here helpon' wid de chores. You don't pay me de big bocks to make de big decisions!" She laughed a bit harder.

"Are you asking for a raise, Rosie?" I smiled.

"No, ond I wouldn't osk *you* if I wonted one, ennaway. I know it's Mr. Honiko who'd make dot decision, ennaway."

"Not anymore," I reminded her. "Speaking of Vincent, have you checked on him yet this morning?"

"Looked in on him before I came out here," she replied. "He's still sleepon', ond so is Libby."

"That girl will sleep until noon if I let her – guess she's getting an early start on teenage behavior."

"Moust be," Rosie agreed, sliding out her chair. "I con go get har op if you wont me to."

"Oh, no. Not yet." I waved for Rosie to stay put. "She worries so much about her granddad now that he's deteriorated so much. It's probably best that she gets plenty of rest."

"Well, I know you're use-on' all de money Vince turned ovar to you to pay de bills here – whot, wid takon' care 'a Libby *and* him wid it – bot hov you considard ogain de possobiloty of putton' Vince in dot home ovar ond de oddar side of de islond?"

"No, I just can't do that, Rosie." Closing my eyes for only a moment, I shook my head at the thought. "He spent so much of his life caring for those he loved, and so I feel the need to do the same for him. It's not right if I don't."

"Bot I've seen de home, ond it's verra nice!"

"I'm sure it is, but it's too far from here, and I know it means so much for him to be near Libby. She's all he has left."

"It's not *dot* far away," she argued.

"On St. Maarten's back roads, yes it is," I argued as I waved my hand toward the inland. That one road we took just yesterday that heads in that direction was so torn up that it's *really* dangerous. I don't need to risk our lives driving on that when Vincent's just fine staying here… that is, unless it's getting to be too much for *you*," I added.

"No, no! You con't get rid a' me dot easoly!" she replied as she waved both her hands at me. "I jost dink dot sometimes it con be a bit hard on you."

I smiled at her, appreciating her concern. "We have this lovely cottage right in the middle of the Caribbean, and I've got my good friends and the children… How can that be so hard?"

Cocking her head, she scowled a bit at me. "You may hov sometin's givon to you, dot's true, bot it's still hard for you to get… a new start on life, you know, when you're surrounded by all de old stuff – me ond Mr. Honiko included."

"Rosie, you are *so* far from old stuff, and you've been so good, coming here with me when… well, when I needed to get away. I mean, you left everything behind, too, and I really –"

"I didn't leave ennaton' behind ot Windemere," Rosie insisted. "When Mr. Honiko sold de hotel, ond undarstondably oftar his daughtar possed oway, dot wos de second time I'd lost a place te live in de time since de fire." She looked away, a look of sadness coming over her. "Ond oftar looson so mony garls – so mony of our Saints – ond nobody seemon' to moch care, too busy gossopon' obout de whole sorted offair… well, you know I needed te get oway, too." Then she smiled. "Ond besides, *dis* wos always my real home, ond I'm glod to be bock."

"But you still left your life behind," I argued. "And you left Sinclaire –"

"Whot!" She tossed her arms into the air. "How mony times hov I got to tell you, garl… I'm so ovar dot mon!"

I had never believed that. "But I saw when you two were together, how you –"

"Now dot's enough of dot!" She leaned back, shaking her head as she crossed her arms firmly over her chest. "I don't wont to hear anoddar word obout dot mon, or Windemere, or none of it – or else I'll be bringon' op dot littal proposal *you* left behind yourself!"

"Oh, now that's not fair," I scolded her.

"Dot's *totolly* far!" she insisted. "You left a mon behind, too, don't forget!"

"That was *so* different. You know he was just asking out of some crazed notion of male chivalry, wanting to give my kids a father."

"It wos so toughtful, dough, bot den you went ond shot him down. Tsk-tsk on you!" She smiled broadly, reveling in her verbal payback.

"He's happier now for my saying 'no,' and so are we," I added as I looked at my children just in time to see Hope whack her brother on his arm with a small, plastic shovel. "Hey! Hey!" I yelled as I rapped on the glass.

Both of them scowled back with expressions of confusion, seeming to wonder why I'd interrupted normal sandbox behavior. Glancing at one another, they shook their heads before turning their gaze to the sand, resuming their work.

Rosie reached over and picked up Hope's plate, using her fork to scrape her leftover syrup onto Chance's dirty plate. "Well, I'm shar his moddar wos hoppy when you tarned him down." Sliding Hope's plate under Chance's, she placed all the dirty silverware on top. "I know dot Constance would a' hod a conniption fit if you'd married har son."

"It never would have happened," I assured her. "Deke just asked because he thought his dad would've wanted him to, but I convinced him otherwise."

"You dink dot's why, huh?" she wondered as she got up from the table and took the dirty dishes to the sink. "'A course, I always tought he wos tryon' te beat Rafae to de punch."

"Whot? Why would you think that?"

She came back to the table. "Well, he wos olways competotov, like he wos wid Abel, you know."

I remembered. "Well, I doubt he'd propose marriage just to beat someone to the punch, but even if that was his reason, that just proves my point – he never would've seen it through."

"Maybe – maybe not." Picking up her cup, Rosie headed toward the coffeepot for a refill. "Who knows?"

"We sure don't," I shook my head. "I can't understand men – just hope I can figure them out just enough so I can raise Chance up right."

"'A course you will." She filled her cup. "You've been a good moddar."

"Yeah, and hopefully I'll get to keep on being a mother," I sighed. "I hope none of the other parents decide to change their minds."

Rosie walked to my side and considerately rubbed my back. "I know dis con be a tough day for you, too, 'cause I know you're tinkon' obout de one dey took from you."

I lowered my head, remembering. "I always thought that when the parents said they didn't want her back when she was born, that it'd always be that way."

"I know, honey." She gave my shoulder a squeeze and then returned to her seat, sliding her chair over closer to me. "I nevar understood why de judge let dem take dot littal garl from you, especially oftar you'd brought har into de world ond you'd been raison' har for, whot... wosn't it ovar a year?"

"Yeah, but in their defense, they did change their minds after just a couple of months, so I should have known. But I just couldn't..." I took a deep breath. "It was just so much easier to give up Baby D, you know... not because I didn't care about her, but I knew when we contacted all the parents involved that she was the only one who was wanted – no doubt about it. So, that's why they took her right away during my C-section. I never bonded with her, never took her home, never even gave her a name. But with Faith... well, they renamed her Essa."

"Yoss, it's Greek for *gift from God*."

"It is? Where'd you get that?"

"Looked it op ot de librory – you're not de only one dot reads, you know."

"Well, anyway, I found it surprising that they didn't like the name Faith, because that's really what brought her into the world in the first place, isn't it?" I swallowed hard. "Now I look back and wonder why I fought the parents for her to begin with. Maybe it wouldn't have been so hard to let her go if I just hadn't kept her for so long."

"Maybe, bot now you're forgetton' whot you told me de Kavanaugh's made you promise: no second guessos."

Raising my chin, I nodded at her. "Yeah, that's right. I did what I thought I should do at the time, and that's just how it ended up. It's just hard sometimes when I think about those people coming all the way here to St. Maarten and taking her... Sometimes I just can't help but wonder if it'll happen again."

"You know it won't," Rosie insisted. "Dot lady wos so mod obout you birthon' Hope from one of har eggs."

"Yeah, she *was* ticked, wasn't she," I recalled the angry mother who had wanted her embryos destroyed once the clinic admitted to accidentally fertilizing them with sperm from the wrong father. "I really felt badly for upsetting her like that."

"It's not like it wos *your* fault." Rosie scooped sugar into her second cup of coffee. "Ond besides, when you look ot dot littal garl…" She nodded toward Hope whose satiny black hair was blowing about in the tropical breeze. "Dot's when you know you did de right ting."

I smiled. "And with Chance's condition…" my smile left me as I bit my lip, turning my gaze to my son. "…well, that's left me to believe his parents probably won't try to take him back, at least if the father has his way."

"Dare crazy not te wont dot lovely boy!" Rosie angrily denounced them.

"Oh, but the mom did want him. She's the reason why I worry," I remembered as I leaned my elbows on the table with my warm cup still in my hands. "If she ever develops a backbone and stands up to her jock-husband… well, after he said he didn't want a son who couldn't play ball, you'd think she'd leave the jerk."

"Bot she won't," Rosie speculated. "Ond she won't try te take Chonce bock."

"Well, I wish I had your confidence. I just –" I paused, noticing someone approaching the children from the beach.

"Ah, we've got compony," Rosie announced. "Look's like Uncle Rofae made de long trip to de islond for on early visot."

"It *is* him," I said, surprised he'd managed to get away from Windemere at the onset of the Labor Day weekend. "I wonder why he's here – if something's wrong."

"I'll tell you whot's wrong!" Rosie scolded me as she reached for my cup. "Jost onoddar heart you keep on breakon'."

"No, he's just another sailor who can't decide where he belongs," I disagreed, holding back my cup to drink down the last bit of lukewarm coffee as I watched Rafae approach my kids. "Guess he spends too much time on the water to figure out which place is home."

"He knows whar his home is," Rosie argued, snatching my empty cup from me. "It's jost dot evra time he show's op ot de door, he keeps findon' it locked, you know." Staring at me, she raised her eyebrows as she added. "Stop baracadon' de door on him, Carly."

"I'm not," I replied, knowing that I was.

"Ond look ot him wid does littal childron," Rosie said sweetly, waving her hand at the window.

For just a moment, the two of us watched in silence as Rafae summoned the kids down closer to the water. Chance was struggling in the sand to get up, and so Rafae went to his aid – the only person Chance was happy to let help him. As Hope gathered up the plastic buckets and shovels, Rafae picked up the crutches and lifted Chance to his shoulder. Then he walked both of the children down to the shoreline.

"You go down dare ond see him while I clean dis op."

"Oh, I don't need to." I slid out of my chair. "He'll be up here soon enough, and I need to help clean –"

"Nonsense!" Rosie scowled. "I con clean all dis op in no time. Dot's why I get paid de big bocks, remembar?"

"But I can help."

"Dot mon didn't come all dis way *jost* for dose kids!" she insisted. "Now, you go out dare ond enjoy your childron on dare birthday. I'm shar dey want te play in de sond wid dare moddar, too – de only one dey've evar known, ond de one dey'll olways love."

I smiled at Rosie and, taking her up on her offer, left the table to head out the door.

Chapter 56

THE CHOICES MADE CLEAR

IT TOOK US A WHILE TO BUILD OUR CASTLE on the beach, the kids packing wet sand into their buckets as Rafae and I worked together to construct a large, elaborate fortress. When it was finally completed to the children's satisfaction, Rafae convinced them to move back closer to the cottage where we could sit in the shade, protected from the heat bearing down on us from the sun as it approached high noon.

"Oooo… and the sand feels so much cooler here. See?" he showed Chance, setting him next to a cluster of palm trees and guiding his hands through the soft, white sand.

"It *is* cool!" Chance exclaimed as he held up a fistful and let it sift between his fingers, blowing off in the breeze.

"Hey, you're getting it in my eyes!" Hope complained as she plopped down in a spot downwind from her brother. "Stop it!" she demanded, rubbing her eye with one hand while picking up a fistful with the other in preparation to throw it back.

"Oh, no, don't do that, princess," Rafae told her before I could say a word, gently taking hold of her fist filled with sand. "Can you feel it, too?" he asked her with unabashed enthusiasm. "It does feel really cool, doesn't it?"

"Yeah," she admitted, letting the sand sift through her fingers, as well. "But it still hurts in my eye."

"Well, don't rub it or you'll make it worse," he warned her. "Let me look at it."

Without argument, Hope surrendered herself to Rafae's care, cautiously opening her eyes as he held her tanned cheeks between his weathered hands.

"I don't see any – oh, wait!" His eyes widened as if he'd just found a prize. "It's right at the corner. Hold still." Ever so carefully, he used the hem of his T-shirt to wipe something from her tear duct. "That should do it."

"Did you get it?" I asked from my spot in the shade of a nearby tree. I wondered if he'd really found something or if he was just trying to soothe the beast by using mind over matter.

"Of course, I did!" he insisted, still speaking to Hope. "It'll probably still itch for a while but don't rub it or it'll keep itching. Just try to leave it alone, okay?"

"Okay." She smiled, still squinting but willing to return to digging with her brother without incident.

"Uncle Rafae wins them over again." I grinned at him as he left the kids and came toward me.

"Stop calling me that!" Brushing sand from his knees, he took a seat in the cool sand beside me. "They shouldn't think I'm they're uncle."

"But it's sweet and enduring," I told him. "I don't know why you don't like it."

"Well, it'd just be… confusing, that's all – you know, if I ever got to be something more to them."

I laughed. "Still pulling me along on that fantasy, huh?"

"Oh, it's a fantasy!" He smiled broadly. "*That's* good to hear!"

"You know what I mean," I pushed him playfully. "I've told you before, I don't think that works for us. I mean, I can't ever sort out if you're here for me or the kids or –"

"And why can't it be both?" he argued. "I love you all, and you know that."

I pushed the sand around with my bare feet, feeling it ooze up between my toes. "Yeah, but I've got so much else here that I'm responsible for, and you shouldn't have to deal with… I'm sure you don't *want* to have to deal with it – like Vincent, for instance."

"But don't you remember? I told you a while back that I wouldn't fight you on that anymore – that I finally understand why you wanted to help him, and I said I'd even help take care of him, too."

"Yeah, but I've got Rosie here to help me take care of him and the kids, and that's why I told you it wasn't necessary," I reminded him. "Besides, I could tell you still blamed Vincent for what happened, and that's why his... just being here would always come between us."

"No." Rafae shook his head. "I've learned a lot from you, Carly, and the biggest thing is how to forgive. I really *don't* think it was his fault anymore... because you don't, and that's helped me to finally stop blaming him."

I looked at him, seeing in his face that he really meant it. "Well, that's good... that's nice to know."

Rafae wrapped his arms around his knees, pulling them toward his chest; he looked off toward the rising tide of the ocean. "So, one more obstacle conquered. What else have you got to throw at me?"

"Is that what you think I'm doing?"

"Sometimes," he answered with a grin. "But I'm not so easily discouraged when you keep on telling me about all the responsibilities you have that stand in our –"

"But I *do* have a lot of responsibilities!" I snapped back, a bit miffed that he didn't seem to appreciate the gravity of all I had to deal with. "I mean, along with Vincent, I've got my kids to take care of, and then there's Libby and Rosie –"

"Hey, I believe you!" he interrupted me, nodding. "You *do* have a lot of responsibilities, but all I'm saying is that I don't think it's fair for you to decide for me whether or not I'm willing to share them with you." Picking up a small shell, he tossed it aimlessly away from us. "You've found room for all of them in *your* life, so I'm just asking why I can't be allowed to find room for them in *mine*."

"Well, I suppose you can, but it's just... well, you know it can't work with you still working in Windemere."

"I told you, I quit."

I laughed. "Yeah, of course you did..."

"I don't know why you don't believe me."

"I don't believe you because you've told me that whole story before."

Releasing his knees, Rafae stretched out and rolled to his side, looking me closely in the eyes. "I told you last winter that I quit because I *did* quit, and I only went back there last spring because... well, because you kept telling me there was no room for me here in your life." He looked down, picking through the sand in search of something else. "I guess I should consider myself lucky that the boss took me back that last time, but I don't. In a way, I kind of wished he'd turned me down so I'd have been forced to stay here."

Feeling a bit uncomfortable, I turned my gaze toward the shoreline, studying the large waves that were rolling in from the wake of a distant, passing ship. "Well, you couldn't leave your dad there with the Kavanaughs. He'd miss you too much."

"I have his blessing," Rafae quickly countered. "Why, I think he may even retire here soon himself – about time for him to break the chains and finally get away from Constance."

"I don't know how he's stayed this long," I contended. "And I still don't know how you talked all your captain buddies into covering your shifts while you came down here for the kids' birthday, because I know it's the busiest time there and –"

"Carly, I quit," he insisted, his dark eyes begging me to believe him.

I paused, thinking it through. "You really *did* quit again, didn't you?"

"I joke about a lot of things, Carly, but you know I'm not joking about this."

I nodded, letting him know that I did finally believe him. "So, is Crocker going to let you start up work here this early?" I asked him as I pushed my fingers into the sand, digging through the tiny pebbles and shards of shell for something I could grab onto. "I don't think he gets enough tourist traffic down here during this time of year since it's still so warm in the States and nobody's flying here to snorkel or scuba dive right –"

"I bought Crocker's boat, Carly."

I could feel my mouth gaping open. "You what?"

"Crocker's been wanting to retire, and I've been saving everything I could," Rafae told me as he dug his fingers into the sand, his hand coming up under mine and taking hold. "That's why I haven't been down to visit, and why I agreed to go back – so I could make enough to make this work, on *my* terms. I could never live off Vincent's money. It wouldn't be right." He looked at my hand in his as I felt the sand sifting away from between our palms, what little that still stood in our way. "I'll have my own business here now, year 'round, and a decent place to stay once I fix up the back of Crocker's old ticket office – that one dumpy room where I stayed before." He squeezed my hand. "I just wanted you to be the first to know that you've got a new neighbor just down the beach."

"I... I don't know what to say," I muttered. "It's such a surprise and it's... it's so nice to have you here."

"...for good," he added, reaching for my shoulders and embracing me. "From now on..." he said softly in my ear. "... I'm going to always be here for you, however you'll have me." Releasing me, he kept his hold on my shoulders, grinning as he leaned in to press his nose to mine.

With this all happening so suddenly, I found myself at a loss for words. All I could do was smile back, for I knew at least one thing to be true: I was happy.

"When do we get our presents?" Hope interrupted us, walking toward us with her shovel held high.

"After we have your cake," I answered.

"Well, when do we get that?"

"After lunch."

"And when's –"

"Lunch is when I'm done fixing it," Rafae interjected, standing up and brushing the sand off from his shorts.

"No, Rosie's got it," I told Rafae, standing up myself.

"What, you don't think I can fix lunch?" he asked.

"Of course, you can, but Rosie wants to fix her version of macaroni and cheese – it's Chance's favorite."

Chance's ears perked up. "Yea!" he cheered from his perch by the palm trees.

"But what about me?" Hope whined.

I looked down at her. "Don't worry. I'm fixing your favorite this –"

"Hey, Carly," Libby interrupted, yelling to me from the doorway to the cottage. "The phone's for you — Hey, Rafae!" she added, dashing out the door toward him, her long, bleached-blonde ponytail swaying behind her. "What're you doing here?"

"Just stopping by to visit for a while," he replied as the blossoming twelve-year-old charged into his arms for a big bear hug.

"Nice to see you're up by lunch time," I said to her. "So, where's the phone?"

"I left it in there," she answered, waving her slender arm back at the cottage, her attention now focused on Rafae. "How long are you here for?"

"I'll let you explain that one," I said as I began to walk toward the cottage. "Could you just keep an eye on the tribe while I take this?" I asked.

"My pleasure," he grinned his charming smile. "Thanks for letting me help out."

"And could you bring them in pretty soon," I added as I opened the screen door. "It's getting pretty intense out here — time to turn on the air-conditioning."

"Not a problem."

Stepping through the doorway, I shut both the screen and glass doors behind me before quickly flicking on the air-conditioner. Then spotting the phone where Libby had carelessly tossed it, I grabbed it and quickly pressed it to my ear.

"Hi. This is Carly. Sorry to keep you waiting."

The woman on the other end sounded undisturbed by the wait, her tone even as she said, "Please hold the line for Senator Hamilton." Then she put me on hold before I could respond.

"Oh, no," I sputtered as classical music played in my ear.

"Hello, Carly Malloy?"

"Yes, that's me."

"Senator Frank Hamilton here. Good to finally get to talk with ya'll directly there. How ya doin'?"

"I'm fine, Senator Hamilton," I replied. "And you?"

"Oh, busy as a horsefly in a pig sty! That's how it is here in DC – just crazy!"

"I'm sure," I replied, waiting for him to get around to his request.

"Well, I won't keep ya, 'cause your time's valuable."

"I appreciate that," I said, knowing full well that it was really only his own time that concerned him.

"Okay, so we've got this senate hearing coming up that my gal Friday spoke with ya'll about before – the one on that stem cell research business, remember?"

"How could I forget?"

"Yeah!" he laughed. "Suppose that's true! So, anyway, I'd still like to have ya come testify for us, being that you've had so much experience with all that can go wrong with this kind of craziness and all."

"Really," I feigned surprise. "And how would that be?"

"Well! Ya know, we read up on how ya were victimized by that crazy scientist, a… uh… Dr. Arlington, as you recall," he added, obviously reading it from the file like all the others did when they really didn't know what they were talking about.

"Of course, I recall… I was there," I answered, keeping my voice even.

"Uh… well, yes. So, anyway, we thought we'd fly ya on up here to DC on the thirteenth and put ya up over at the Hotel Monaco on F Street. I'm told it's very posh."

"Is it?" I interjected.

"Yeah, that's what they tell me."

"And will my kids like it?"

"Uh… well, we were hoping you could wrastle up some kinda child care for the little ones while ya came here, because we'll have ya *very* busy meeting with other senators and key supporters before the big hearing."

"I see. And so, what is it I'd be hearing?" I asked with a smirk on my face.

"Oh, ya won't be here to listen, ma'am. You'll be here to talk," he explained.

"Really? About what?"

"Well, about your experiences, of course – that's what!"

"Oh, but you won't want to hear that," I told him matter-of-factly.

"Beg your pardon, ma'am, but yes we will."

"No, you won't... You won't want to hear *anything* I'd have to say."

"Beg your pardon?" he repeated. "I guess I... don't quite understand."

"Let me ask you something, Senator Hamilton: tell me what it is you *think* I'd have to say if I spoke at your hearing."

"Well, we were hoping you'd enlighten us about the awful experience ya must've had at that lighthouse while you were held there all that time."

"I might... and what else?"

"Well, ya'd tell us how this... this Dr. Arlington fella implanted you with so many of those poor embryos, and all for his own selfish purposes."

"Something like that, and..."

"And then you'd tell us about the horrible conclusion – about how ya had to kill some of those poor babies just to save the little darlings you still have today."

"Did I..."

"Yes, that's what it says in the articles I've got here."

"From a newspaper, I suppose... and they always print the truth, don't they?"

"Well, except when it's just some bad gossip about me!" he said with a laugh, the only one amused by his joke.

"Hmm," I nodded, the phone rubbing annoyingly against my ear. "And is that all you'd expect me to say?"

"Oh, not at all. Then you'd finally tell the committee the most important point – that your story illustrates all the abuses that can come from this stem cell research business, and that's why we still shouldn't fund it."

"Now, there's the problem," I told him, my voice finally rising. "You see, that's *not* what I'd tell your committee."

There was a very long pause. "It's not?"

"No, Senator Hamilton," I replied. "I would tell you and the people on that committee that my experience shows exactly why we *should* fund stem cell research – so desperate people don't keep resorting to such desperate measures."

"Beg your pardon, ma'am, but I think ya may be a bit mixed up on this," he said somewhat condescendingly. "Maybe they didn't explain this to ya'll very well before, so let me tell ya what happens: they have to kill those babies to extract those cells. Do ya understand that, Carly?"

"Yes, I know that's the current process, Senator. In the years that've passed since this whole episode happened to me, though, researchers have refined the process. You must be aware that they no longer have to extract from the brain stem of a developing fetus – that they now can get stem cells from a days-old blastocyst, when the egg is still just a ball of cells."

"Oh, yes, but that 'ball-a-cells' is still a life, and they still have to destroy it to get what they want, don't they?"

"Currently they do, but at least they're never implanted. Researchers can place a fertilized egg in a petri dish and coax it into multiplying for a few days until they –"

"Miss Malloy!" the senator interrupted. "We obviously have some kinda misunderstanding here. It seems that ya fail to realize that those coaxed eggs in a dish, as ya so freely refer to them… they're living beings that are still being destroyed for the sake of all these pie-in-the-sky notions."

"Senator, there's no misunderstanding. I *do* realize that's how it's being done right now, but I've also had the chance to talk with a researcher who believes he'll eventually be able to extract cells from the blastocyst and *not* destroy the egg. He just needs the funding and the opportunity to work with fertilized eggs that've already been abandoned and marked for disposal."

"Sounds like ya've been talking with some more crazy scientists, if ya asked me," he sarcastically responded. "These guys are just lookin' to make a name for themselves with their nutty experiments, and all at the expense of these human lives. But I've got to tell ya, Carly, that ya surprise me. I mean, I just can't imagine how, after all ya've been through –"

"First of all, Senator, let me tell you that you have *no* idea what I've been through, and quite frankly, I plan to keep it that way."

I paused and, hearing nothing from the other end of the line, I continued. "Secondly, what *you* fail to consider is that I'm not talking about Snowflakes here – you know, the frozen embryos that belong to parents who've agreed to donate them to others who want to implant them and try to –"

"Yes, yes, of course I know all about the Snowflake children that've been brought to term – and that's exactly what we'd like to see happen with *all* of these frozen embryos."

"And ideally, that'd be great, but you know that's not what's going to happen, sir, because there are way too many eggs and not nearly enough willing people who have both the physical and financial ability to make that happen."

"Well, our office is working on ways to –"

"And that's just the abandoned eggs that *might* still have a chance," I interjected. "Then there are the ones that belong to parents who *aren't* willing to put them up for adoption because they just can't imagine surrendering their children to be raised by strangers. These people signed paperwork requiring their clinic to either discard their eggs or else send them home in a zip-lock bag to be buried in the garden – a choice that results not only in loss of life, but also in nothing good ever coming of their loss."

"You know, we have a saying around these parts, Carly, that two wrongs don't make a right. So, I gotta tell ya that I just don't see how the unseemly destruction of those poor, innocent children for the purposes of research can be justified by the fact that people are already destroying them anyway."

"But it's no more justified for these eggs to be destroyed for *no* reason, Senator, or worse yet, to leave the abandoned ones frozen for years upon years while they just rot away, never getting the chance to live or die or make any kind of difference," I argued passionately. "You see, I think the *real* wrong here, Senator, is that too many eggs are being fertilized in the first place. That practice puts vulnerable people who are so desperate to have a child in the terrible situation of having to decide what to do with all of those... those souls that are still there, waiting."

"Well, Miss Malloy, it seems I might've made a bit of an error in contacting ya'll on this."

"Maybe not," I suggested. "I do consider myself pro-life, Senator Hamilton, and so maybe I do bring something to your table. I've had way too much time to think this through, sir, and I've come to some different conclusions in the process."

"I hear ya on that! So, we should probably –"

"I *do* believe each of those fertilized eggs bears a soul," I continued. "So, I'm not okay with losing them, but I'm also not okay with losing people that are sick or injured, especially if there might be some way to save them."

"But there's no proof that this procedure will –"

"And I guess I'm a believer in trying, Senator," I added. "But I've also had to learn the hard way that sometimes people die and there's nothing we can do about it – except maybe try to make something good come from the tragedy of their deaths."

"My goodness! You *have* been thinking on this, haven't ya, Carly," the senator recognized. "Well, there certainly are a lot of moral lessons ya'll can learn from losing the terminally ill, of course, but that's not really the topic we're going to be trying to hog-tie at this session. So, we might as well just forget about having ya'll come, at least for now."

Suddenly I heard the door open behind me and turned to find Rafae bringing the three children into the house. I held up my index finger to him, indicating I'd be just a minute finishing my call. Nodding in reply, he herded the kids past me and over toward the kitchen.

"Just let me make this one last point with you, and then I'll let you go," I assured Senator Hamilton, the tables now seeming to have turned. "Do you and your colleagues… do you all support organ donations?"

"Well, as long as the sanctity of life is respected and people aren't needlessly left out to pasture to die, then of course we do," he blustered.

"So do I, and so that brings me to the most important point: isn't extracting stem cells from an embryo that'll never come to term – that'll never experience any quality of life and is soon to die – isn't that the same as extracting an organ from a person with the same prognosis? Don't you think it's the same, Senator Hamilton?"

"Well... it's really not for me to say," he side-stepped. "I'm just doing the people's bidding here, ya know, so I best just pass on that thought. But I do thank ya for chatting with me, Miss Malloy, and if we should still need your input, I'll be sure to give ya another holler. In the meantime, ya'll take care down there in St. Maarten, ya hear."

"I do hear, Senator, and we'll do that. Good-bye," I said and then hung up the phone.

"Who's bugging you now?" Rafae asked from the kitchen as I walked toward him.

"Just more bureaucrats that think they're mind readers — always assuming they know what I'm thinking."

Rafae smiled. "Well, and you know what they say about people who assume..."

Chapter 57

A SEARCH FOR HIGHER GROUND

FOLLOWING THE WAFT OF DELICIOUS AROMA, I walked with Rafae into the kitchen where we found Rosie at work while the children watched.

She looked up, smiling at Rafae. "So, did you come all dis way jost for some of my special mocoroni, Uncle Rofae."

"Yeah, of course… but please don't call me that, Rosie."

"Whot! Bot why?" she scowled at him. "Don't ya wont te be —"

"We've already been over this," I told Rosie. "Rafae just wants the kids to think of him as a friend, because that's what he is… for the time being, anyway."

Rafae winked at me.

"I see," Rosie said in a bit of a huff. "Well, den I'll jost hov te retink wheddar or not I'm go-on' te let you hov enna of dot mocoroni!"

"Oh, come on!" he pleaded.

"But it's really *my* macaroni, isn't it Rosie?" Chance asked her.

"Why, yos it is, littal mon!"

"Well, I want to share it with Uncle – I mean, Rafae. Is that okay?"

She smiled at him, her stern ways always dissipated when Chance asked something of her. "Of course he con, littal mon. Now you come on ovar here ond take a look in de ovon te see whot's cookon'."

"I want to look, too!" Hope dashed to the oven window, waiting for Rosie to click on the light.

"Wait! Me first," Chance insisted, clunking his crutches as he ably made his way to his sister's side.

"Let me know when it's ready," Libby told Rosie. "I'm going to go pick up my room so I can show Rafae how I fixed it up. Can you come down in a few minutes?" she asked.

"Whot, is dot all it takes te get you te pick up dot mess you got go-on' in dare, garl?"

"I'll be down in a few," Rafae assured her. "Just want to talk with Carly for a few more minutes first."

"Okay," she smiled. "I'll come get you when it's picked up." And with that, she dashed off for her room.

"How about we go sit in the den while we're waiting," I suggested to Rafae.

"Shar, leave Rosie te do de cookon' ond cleanon' *ond* deal wid de wild ones," Rosie said, waving her towel to fan her face.

"Oh, I'm sorry, Rosie." I stepped toward the stove. "It just looked like you had everything under –"

"A' course, it's ondar control!" she said, finishing my thought. "Ond it's jost fine – I'm jost kiddon' you now, so go! I'll let you know, too, whon it's all ready. Now shoo!" With a turn of her hand, she playfully waved the towel at the two of us, chasing us from the room.

Walking toward the den, we passed the hallway to the bedrooms where Vincent was now emerging, looking frail as he wandered toward us.

"Hey, Vincent, good morning," I greeted him. "And look who's come to pay us a visit."

"Oh, hello," Vincent said to Rafae, almost looking as if he didn't recognize or remember him.

"Good to see you, Vince." Rafae extended his hand.

"And you," Vincent feebly gripped Rafae's hand, barely shaking it. "So, what brings you here?"

"Oh, birthdays and work, and whatever else I can find to keep me out of trouble."

"Yes, well, you do that," Vincent said to him. "We want to keep you out of trouble, you know."

Rafae nodded. "Yes, sir."

"So…" Vincent paused. "How are things… back at the island, you know?"

"Pretty much the same as always, except that you all aren't there," he added, motioning toward the two of us. "Just isn't the same without you running the Landings, sir. Those new people that bought it – they're just not… well, as nice as you always were, Vincent."

"Yes, well… that's nice of you to say," he replied, still seeming a bit confused. "Well, I guess I better clean myself up now." Turning from us, he headed toward the bathroom. "Good to see you, Rafae. Be sure and tell your dad 'hi' for me, and give my best to D'Arcy and the captain. I miss those fellows." Then he opened the bathroom door and shuffled in, closing it behind him.

"Wow," Rafae said to me as we continued into the den. "Well, at least he got my name, and the others… but D'Arcy? Doesn't he remember anymore?"

"Sometimes he does, but I don't think it ever really sank in with him," I replied, taking a seat in a wicker chair where I could look out at the ocean. "There's so much that happened all at once, and he wasn't there to experience it because of all that happened with Gretchen, and then his long hospitalization after that. I just don't think it sank into his memory that well before it all started… slipping away."

Rafae sighed, sitting down in the matching chair beside me. "Well, at least he still seems to be able to get around on his own most of the time. Must still be the early stages of the Alzheimer's."

"That's what they tell us, but it's more than that. He's never been the same, you know – always sad and reflective, but even that's beginning to slip away. So, he spends a lot of time in this room, just looking out there." I turned my eyes toward the ocean. "I find him in here just staring out over the water… and that's when he reminds me of Nolan."

Rafae nodded. "Yeah, I guess that's how they've dealt with their losses – searching for the answers, hoping they might find them somewhere out there."

I turned my eyes back to Rafae. "I've looked, but they're not there." I pressed the palm of my hand to my chest. "You've got to start here – in your heart."

Reaching over, Rafae took my hand from my chest and held it in his, the warmth from his palm reminding me that I wasn't alone. We sat there, comfortable in a lingering moment of silence as we gazed out at the gorgeous sun-filled day, simply glad to be in one another's company once again.

"Libby's grown so much – really starting to look like… well, a grown woman."

"Yeah, she is," I agreed. "She's getting a bit boy crazy, too. It's starting to be a bit of a challenge."

"Well, don't worry about it. I've got a spear-gun down at the shop that'll take care of that problem."

I laughed. "She'll be so pleased to hear that."

"And otherwise, how's she doing?" Rafae asked, leaning forward with his elbows on his knees.

"Pretty well," I answered. "Sure, she has times when she misses her mom, but she's getting on with her life pretty well."

"But I was wondering about her… prognosis. Have you thought anymore about that genetic testing?"

Pulling my bare feet up from the floor, I tucked them under me. "Yeah, but I'm going to wait. She doesn't need to know that now. It wouldn't do her any good, anyway, and I'd just as soon wait for her to decide when she's an adult whether or not she wants to have that done. Besides, maybe by then there'll be an answer – you know, some kind of treatment she can get if she has it." I looked at Rafae's eyes, wondering if he'd agree. "I just want her to at least have some hope."

Rafae gazed back, nodding with agreement. "Yeah, we could always use that." He waved back toward the kitchen. "So, I take it the bureaucrats weren't peddling hope today in that phone call."

"They never are," I sighed. "They're always on one side or the other."

"Well, I heard a little of your speech there. Hope you don't mind." He smirked.

"Nope."

"Just wanted to tell you that you sold me."

"Yeah, well then I wish *you* were in charge," I told him. "I just keep on getting all these calls, mostly from the political right, but occasionally from the left, and I just can't please *any* of them."

"That's because they're not calling to hear what you've got to say – they're calling to have you say what they want to hear."

"Well! That's pretty profound, Rafae!"

He cocked his head. "I thought so."

"Well, all I can do is keep trying, and in the meantime, just do the best I can right here."

"And I can tell you're doing that," he smiled. "The kids all seem happy and content."

"Well, we'll see if that continues once they start school next week."

"It's okay to be cautious, but don't turn pessimistic on us here, Carly. I mean, you've done so well with making the best of your situation, and so you should pass that gift on to your kids."

"You think so?" I asked, truly unsure.

"You bet," he answered. "That's what makes you such a great mom."

"Well, thank you," I patted his knee. "So, do you charge for ego boosts?"

"Oh, yes!" He bounced his eyebrows, giving his most mischievous grin. "I'll be collecting later."

"Hmm." I sat back, staring back at the ocean as I thought about how we'd come to this point. "This sure wasn't how I'd imagined my life turning out, but it's a good life just the same – one I can live without too much regret."

"Not *too* much?" Rafae questioned. "Hey, I thought your motto was *no* regrets. So, what's got you wondering if you did the wrong thing?"

I looked back to him. "You."

"Oh, I see…" He paused, grinning. "You know, what's done is done, Carly, and if everything that's happened so far has brought me back here right now, right this minute… then I have no regrets, and I hope you don't either."

"It's ready!" I heard Chance cheer from the other room.

"Finally!" Rafae yelled back, jumping up and, with my hand in his, pulling me out of my seat and toward the kitchen.

Rosie was complaining as we approached. "Whot do you mean by sayon' *finolly?*" She scolded Rafae. "I been out here slavon' oway to put dis hot meal on for you, you ingrate! Why, I don't evon know why my littal mon here's go-on' te let you hov enna of his special lonch if dot's de way you're go-on' te be, so I don't know…"

And so it went on like this all afternoon – the bantering and laughter, meals and cake and gifts, and all that made life worth living. Then when the sun finally made its descent in the evening sky, Rafae and I took the five-year-olds back down to the shoreline where the tide had come in.

From his perch on Rafae's shoulder, Chance was the first to notice. "Our castle! It's gone!"

"It is?" Hope dashed ahead to where the foaming waves had washed away all but just a slight remaining outline of where the fortress had once stood. "Oh, no!"

"Well, that's too bad," I sympathized.

"It's your fault!" Chance yelled at Hope. "You started it too close to the water!"

"No, I put it where *you* told me," she argued back. "It's all your fault, Chance!"

"Wait a minute, kids," Rafae interjected as he lowered Chance to his hip and knelt by Hope to talk with them at their eye level. "Your mom and I are the ones that put that thing where it was, and I thought it was far enough back, but I guess I was wrong. So, I'm sorry. Hope you'll forgive me."

"No need to forgive," I told them all, kneeling down beside them. "You know, sometimes bad things just happen and there's no sense in blaming." I pointed to the waves. "Looks to me like Mother Nature was just doing her job, and so we'll just have to build another one."

"Well, okay!" Hope eagerly agreed. "I'll get the shovels and buckets."

"So, where'll we put it this time?" Chance asked with concern. "'Cause I don't want it to wash away again."

"Well, I'm not sure," Rafae answered, lifting him back up and over his shoulders. "Let's look over the sand and see where you think high tide will hit, and then we'll go in just a bit further."

"Okay," Chance agreed, and the two of them began searching about for a new foundation.

"Just make the best choice you can, boys, and then we'll go with it," I yelled to them over the sound of the breaking waves.

So we stayed there until the sun had nearly set, building our new castle in the sand – enjoying one another's company as we lived in that moment. And when we were all satisfied with our newest fortress, we picked up our pails and shovels and then returned home.

But later that night – long after Rafae had left and we'd all gone to bed – a powerful storm rolled in with the waves crashing much higher and stronger against the shoreline than I had ever seen before. Within a short time, both children had taken refuge in my bed, bringing with them their concerns over the likely consequences for our latest sand castle.

As we huddled under the covers, I assured them that we would make things right once the storm had passed – that I'd ask Rafae to help us build a new castle, and that it would be even better than the one we'd had before. Seemingly comforted by my words, their eyes grew heavy as I described in detail how grand our castle would be. Even I was nearly dozing when I told them the most important detail; that I'd find us a better place this time, and that I'd make sure it was far enough from the waves before we started building our castle once more.

ACKNOWLEDGEMENTS

WERE IT NOT FOR THE KINDNESS OF SO MANY, my dream of writing and publishing this novel would never have come to fruition.

Of course, I must begin where I began – by thanking my parents, Phyllis and John Heidenreich, whose dedication to their children's lives gave us every chance to dream big and to pursue every opportunity.

I'm also most grateful to my supportive husband, Kelly, and my incredible kids, Raleigh and Cameron, who've given me just what I've needed – some quiet space when I needed to work, and much love and laughter when I needed it most.

I wish to posthumously thank the Very Reverend Father David Amo for ministering to me when I first began deliberating the ethical issues that now lie at the heart of this story. I'm also grateful to Pastor Budd and Kathy Wagner for their guidance and reassurance as I struggled through the dilemmas addressed within these pages.

For all medical references, I'm indebted to Dr. Boogs Burandt and Nurse Janna Heidenreich whose detailed explanations of procedures and suggestions for terminology gave authenticity to the story.

I'm so grateful to Ken and Wendy Pletcher for their detailed descriptions of ice, including the idea for the most lethal of weapons: the ice spud. Wendy also helped by connecting me with lighthouses authorities Lisa Craig-Brisson, Steve Brisson, and Bruce Lynn, who all contributed ideas toward the creation of a realistic lighthouse for Beacon Point.

I appreciate the helpful information gleaned from Mark Dombroski and Cheryl Heiny in regards to work horses.

A big thank you goes to Randy Scott for lending his photographic talents to early drafts of cover art, and to Cameron Cavitt for patiently posing as Abel for the photo shoot.

Thanks to the great people at BookSurge, especially my publishing consultant Lee Sanderlin, my cover copy editor Lindsay Parker, and my design coordinator Laura Bonam, all of whom patiently and professionally guided me through the process of bringing this book to press.

To all of my fellow Bohemians of the Gildner Gallery, especially Ann Gildner and Molly Jo Noland, I thank you for opening your creative hearts and home to include writers.

As for my first and second round readers – Michele Ackerman, Marlene Alexander, Mickey Castagne, Chelsi Utsler, Janna Heidenreich, Heidi Heidenreich, Kelly Cooper, Flora Balog, Boogs Burandt, Ali Burandt, Nancy Burandt, Clem Pletcher, Sue Bronson, and John Sherwood – my thanks to all of you for the invaluable feedback you gave me on how to improve my work and, more importantly, for the encouragement you gave me to press forward with this project.

For my insightful and gifted editor, Maggie Catchick, I reserve the grandest thank you of all. Her passionate efforts and tireless devotion were instrumental in resurrecting this project from its previous, lifeless form. Without her, this work would only be a shell of its potential, but with her, it has become something from which I derive great pride and pleasure – and so to Maggie, my greatest teacher, I remain forever indebted.

There are so many people who contributed to this novel with the simplest of gestures. To those whose actions triggered my imagination and those who encouraged me to persevere, please know you're a part of what's made this book whole. You traveled the journey with me, but it doesn't end here; it continues each time you read from these pages, and so I thank you for continuing the journey, and for taking me along at your side...

Jeanene Cooper

IF I SHOULD NEVER WAKE

Jeanene Cooper has taught writing and public speaking for more than twenty years since earning her degree in English and Communication from the University of Michigan. A number of her essays and short stories have been showcased at the Gildner Gallery of Northern Michigan, including "Limbo" which received first place distinction in the 2005 A-SEED juried theme exhibition, "Through the Window." In 2009, her first novel was selected by Independent Publishers to receive the Bronze IPPY Medal for Best Regional Fiction. A Michigan native, Jeanene currently resides at the Tip of the Mitt with her husband and two sons.

Look for other novels by Jeanene Cooper coming soon to bookstores, www.CreateSpace.com3582977, and at www.amazon.com

Made in the USA
Columbia, SC
12 August 2018